The Wanderers
Bloodbrothers
Ladies' Man
The Breaks

Clockers
Richard Price

[signature]

Bloomsbury Modern Library

First published in Great Britain 1992
This edition published 1994

Copyright © 1992 by Richard Price

The moral right of the author has been asserted

Bloomsbury Publishing Plc, 2 Soho Square, London W1V 5DE

A CIP catalogue record for this book is available
from the British Library

ISBN 0 7475 1230 2

10 9 8 7 6 5 4 3 2 1

Typeset by Hewer Text Composition Services, Edinburgh
Printed by Mackays of Chatham

WITH DEEPEST LOVE FOR MY WIFE,
JUDY HUDSON,
AND MY DAUGHTERS,
ANNIE AND GEN

ACKNOWLEDGMENTS

This book could not have been written without the guidance and generosity of many people

Foremost, Larry Mullane, who was helpful beyond calculation

My editor, the brilliant and relentless John Sterling

Geoff Sanford, whose friendship often kept me afloat

And Gene Canfield, who opened the first door

And they brought up an evil report of the land which they had searched unto the children of Israel, saying, The land, through which we have gone to search it, is a land that eateth up the inhabitants thereof; and all the people that we saw in it are men of a great stature.

And there we saw the giants, the sons of Anak, which come of the giants; and we were in our own sight as grasshoppers, and so we were in their sight.

– Numbers 13:32–33

Part One

A DEATH IN THE LAND OF THE TWO-MINUTE CLOCK

1

Strike spotted her: baby fat, baby face, Shanelle or Shanette, fourteen years old maybe, standing there with that queasy smile, trying to work up the nerve. He looked away, seeing her two months from now, no more baby fat, stinky, just another pipehead. Her undisguised hunger turned his stomach, but it was a bad day on his stomach all around, starting with the dream about his mother last night, with her standing in the window looking at him, pulling the shades up and down, trying to signal him about something, then on to this morning, being made to wait for an hour in the municipal building before anyone bothered to tell him his probation officer was out sick, then Peanut this afternoon not respecting two-for-one hour, and now, right here, some skinny white motherfucker coming on to The Word, trying to buy bottles, The Word looking to Strike like, 'What do I do?' Strike turned away, thinking, 'You on you own, I told you that,' his stomach glowing like a coal, making him want to go into a crouch to ease the burn.

Strike was seated on the top slat of his bench, his customary perch, looming over a cluster of screaming kids, pregnant women and too many girls, drinking vanilla Yoo-Hoo to calm his gut, watching The Word try to think on his feet. The white guy, a scrawny redhead wearing plaster-caked dungarees and a black Anthrax T-shirt, looked too twitchy and scared to be a knocko, but you never knew. Knockos making street buys usually came in colors, or at least Italian trying to be Puerto Rican, but not piney-woods white, and they usually acted cool or sneaky, not jumpy. The guy was probably a customer for real, but it was The Word's call – on-the-job training.

The guy took out a twenty for two bottles. Strike watched The Word thinking, thinking, finally saying, 'Go change it for singles.' Strike shook his head: Marked bills, Jesus, they ain't gonna go to the trouble of using marked bills to make a case on a two-bottle buy from a fifteen-year-old boy. A kid getting busted for that would probably get revolved at Juvenile and be back at the benches before the dinner-hour lull was over, right on time for the heavy night traffic when he was really needed.

The white guy nodded and loped away, looking for a mini-mart, the twenty-dollar bill sticking up out of his fist like a flower. Nobody would take him off with Strike here on the bench rolling the Yoo-Hoo bottle between his palms, but Strike knew that if he was to go take a leak, the guy would be lying in the grass with a crease in his hat. Rodney had said it: most niggers out here want all the money now. They kill the golden goose, the return customer, because they never see past the next two minutes. A bunch of sneaker dealers: get ten dollars, run out and buy a ten-dollar ring.

Like Peanut earlier in the day, trying to make a little extra selling bottles one for ten instead of two for ten during Happy Hour. On each clip he had been pulling in a hundred instead of fifty, then turning over forty and pocketing sixty, until some pipehead came up to Strike and said, 'I thought it be *Happy* Hour.' Strike looked at Peanut now, sulking on the corner, demoted to raising up – looking out for the Fury – a flat twenty-dollar gig, no bottles, no commission. Watching Peanut probe the raw bump on his cheek-bone, Strike swung into his usual recitation: Sneaker dealers, pipeheads, juveniles. Stickup artists, girls, the Fury. You can't trust nobody, so keep your back to the wall and your eyes open – 24,7,365

Strike scanned the canyon walls of the Roosevelt Houses. There were thirteen high rises, twelve hundred families over two square blocks, and the housing office gave the Fury access to any vacant apartment for surveillance, so Strike never knew when or where they might be scoping him out. The best he could do was to get somebody to spot them sneaking into a building from the rear, yell out 'Five-oh' so nobody did anything stupid and then just wait for them to get bored and leave.

The Fury consisted of only a handful of cops, and they had half a dozen housing projects to cover so they couldn't hole up for more than an hour. But it was no secret that Andre the Giant had a surveillance apartment too: 3A in 14 Dumont, the apartment Housing couldn't rent out because six children and their grandmother had died in a fire there a year before. Andre was obsessed with the dope crew that worked the Dumont side of the projects, unlike the Fury, who liked hitting the Weehawken side, Strike's side. But Andre was a free-range knocko; he could show up anywhere, anytime, and he could see the benches just fine from Dumont.

Strike's clockers got jumpy if they thought they were being watched. They'd start singing too loud, get into idiotic arguments, let go of the pent-up tension in a hundred dumb ways, becoming a danger both to themselves and to Strike. And then there were the girlfriends to worry about. They were the worst – flirting with other guys in front of their boyfriends, gassing up their heads, starting fights. To Strike, the girls were good for one thing only. The Fury were all male, so if a girl kept her mouth shut, acted like a lady, she could carry two clips down in her panties, another two up top, and the Fury couldn't do anything unless they pulled her into the precinct for a strip search. And it was a lot quicker to serve up bottles out of a bra than to have everybody running in and out of the stash apartment for every ten-dollar sale.

But girls could steal too, just disappear around a corner with the product. They could have a lovers' quarrel, give the dope to a new boyfriend not in the crew, sell it themselves, smoke it themselves. So Strike wasn't up on using girlfriends; he'd rather go slow and steady, get the boys to make the trip up to the apartment, at least for the Fury hours, four to ten. He moved the apartment around every day: knockos can't go through a door without having paper, and by the time they got the paper signed by a judge, the apartment wasn't there anymore.

Girls. Strike always told his crew: 'Don't let the girls wrap you around their little fingers. It's just pussy, and if you play your cards right, pussy always be there, and you play your cards right by making the money, then saving it.' Strike would say it word for word, just like Rodney said it to him almost a year ago.

Strike watched the baby-fat girl – Sharelle, Sharette, something like that – finally get up for it, walk over to him, a smile pasted on her face like she was happy or something.

'Hi, Strike.'

'No.'

'I didn't – '

'No. Go on outa here.'

Futon came out of 6 Weehawken scanning the street, eating Cheetos and holding a big jar of Gummi Bears, bobbing his head in time to whatever was coming in over his aqua-blue headphones. He nodded to Strike and walked back to the benches.

'Re-up, re-up,' he announced, blaring out the words over the music in his head.

Strike pursed his lips to respond and was startled to feel the sudden seizing up that hit somewhere between his mind and his mouth. 'Woo-what you got?'

He hadn't had a stammer attack in weeks: What a goddamn day.

"Bout forty, forty-five.' Futon seemed to ignore Strike's flustered speech.

Strike thought about the night to come, calculating the traffic. It was the twelfth of the month. People still had some money from the mailbox. On the other hand it was Wednesday, five days from the last payday. Strike thought about the weather too: Rain coming, maybe. Two hundred bottles should do it.

Getting up off the bench, legs stiff, Strike limped to the pay phone and rang up Rodney's pager, punching in the code for the day and then a two-zero on the end. The bottles would be coming by bicycle in about fifteen or twenty minutes, the delivery boy just another twelve-year-old zooming by, a kid going into 6 Weehawken with his schoolbooks under his arm and a lunch box. Strike hated beepers, kept his in his pocket, out of sight. It was too obvious, like wearing gold. Besides, everybody had a beeper these days. Strike preferred talking on the phone, mouth to ear – one thing about dope corners, nobody ever vandalized the phones. But Rodney said, Wear your beeper.

Back at the bench, Futon offered him the Gummi Bear jar. Strike waved it away, Futon saying 'Lookit,' unscrewing the false bottom and revealing a nest of four bottles, his voice a slick murmur: 'They sell it on JFK at that *smoke* shop.'

Strike scowled at him. 'That's stupid. I-I-If they sell it, the knockos be knowing about it. Soon they see anybody with that, they go right for the bottom, buh-bust your ass.' The stammer was coming on strong now, Strike's consternation only making it worse.

Futon got sulky.

'Besides, what you got the Cheetos for too? Tha-that don't look right, two kinds of junk you holdin'.'

Futon shrugged. 'I don't *like* Gummi Bears. And they ain't coming back for a month anyhow, right?'

The day before, Futon had raced one of the Fury, a knocko named Thumper, and beat him by twenty feet. The Fury had said that if Futon won the race they'd lay off for thirty days – just a joke, but now Futon was acting like it was bonded and true. And Futon was Strike's second in command.

The baby-fat girl started talking to The Word, saying something Strike couldn't hear but knew was flirty because The Word started to dance around and grin like a fool. The girl was trying to mooch a bottle, and The Word would have given it up in a minute if Strike wasn't here. Always had to be here, always. He thought of telling Futon to go over and tell that girl he was going to tell her mother, but then decided he wasn't Jesus on a stick. Girl wants to pipe up, it's a free country. As long as she got ten dollars. And if The Word gives up the bottle, then The Word better have ten dollars.

Strike drank some more Yoo-Hoo and massaged his gut. Sweetness coated the pain, lukewarm sweetness now that he'd been holding the bottle between his palms for an hour.

The red-headed white boy came loping back into the semicircle and Strike had a bad feeling. He looked to Peanut, who was watching the street to see if the Fury was playing peekaboo around a corner. Peanut looked to Strike and touched his cheek again. Strike had whacked him good with a full bottle of Yoo-Hoo, and Peanut had fallen down so fast his hat stayed in place right over where his head had been, like in a cartoon. People stealing from him turned Strike's brain red: If somebody pulled something like Peanut did, you had to kick their ass, then put them back on the street. And if they did it again, then you had to really fuck them up bad. And you never, never let that shit slide, because if you did they'd be all over you, them and everybody else, and then the game would be over.

Strike knew he'd done the right thing; Peanut knew it too. But then Strike began to wonder if Peanut would try a little payback now, let the Fury come by without raising up. Can't trust nobody: everybody was dense one minute, devious the next, always talking about being brothers, watching each other's back, but when it came down to it Strike preferred enemies to friends. At least with enemies, you knew what they were right up front. Either way, this business could chew you up, and Strike would do anything to get off the street and just deal weight like Rodney.

The white guy fanned out the singles to The Word as if he wanted The Word to pick a card, any card. The Word swept the bills into his hand, said 'Two-oh' to Horace, and Horace vanished into 6 Weehawken.

The Word walked away and the white guy said, 'Hey . . .' For a minute he stood there alone, blinking and confused, but then Horace came back out of the building holding a crumpled-up paper bag. He dropped it in a garbage can, hissed 'Yo' to get the customer's attention, then walked away too. It took a few seconds for the guy to figure it out, but then he snatched up the bag and hustled off toward the street.

It was Strike's idea to move the store to the benches at the edge of the projects. Whites were too scared of walking all the way in and copping their bottles while being surrounded by the towers, too scared that they wouldn't make it back out. Working from the benches also made it a lot easier to spot the Fury when it rolled, especially when the knockos pulled a pincers move, trying to sneak attack from both sides at once.

Strike had suggested it to Rodney, Rodney saying, 'Hey, you're the man,' letting him run his own show as long as he moved half a kilo a week. And in six months on top out here, Strike had never failed to hit that figure, partly through his vigilant fretfulness, partly through marketing novelties like two-for-one Happy Hours, Jumbos, Redi Rocks and Starter Kits, but mainly because he understood that good product rules. People always knew who had it; all Strike had to do was not get greedy and step on Rodney's bottles when they came in. That way he'd always have the best, because all the other lieutenants stretched out their re-ups by diluting the product. Strike counted on the greed, knowing it would drive all the pipe-heads right to him.

'Five-oh!' Peanut hissed, whirling, spinning on one foot.

Shit. Strike looked past Peanut to the street, saw the knockos still in the car and heard one of them, Crunch, calling to the white guy, 'Hey, you!'

Strike looked to Horace and The Word, both of them flying back into the building. Strike sat tight, just watched as Crunch stepped out and escorted his grab to the rear of the Fury.

Blasting from the open door was some Rolling Stones garbage, one of the tapes the knockos played in order to get pumped up when they were hunting bounty.

Strike saw Spook and Ahmed walk away as if they had something to hide – wannabes, the only idiots who walked. He heard Big Chief still in the shotgun seat whisper into the hand radio: 'Batman Hat guilty, Red Hat guilty.' Then Strike saw Smurf and Thumper sneaking up on foot from the Dumont side, closing the pincers, grabbing Spook and Ahmed and throwing them up against the chain fence.

The white guy was pleading with Crunch, yammering, 'Oh Jesus, oh Jesus, look listen I'm, look listen,' then babbling on about how he was a caulker, how he just got the job this week.

Crunch began cutting a deal right on the street, and Strike heard him say something about 'just a desk appearance if you ID the kid who served you.' The white guy was barely able to talk, wanting to say so much so fast. He called The Word 'stocky' instead of fat: 'Stocky kid in a St Louis Cardinals cap, Officer.' Officer, like he was in the army.

Strike, hunched over on his perch, watched Thumper press a splayed palm on Ahmed's chest, saying, 'What's up, Yo? Where you going?,' saying it with that honking street lisp he liked to use. Trembling and pop-eyed as if he was really holding, Ahmed squeaked back, 'I ain't going nowhere, Thumper!'

'Whatta you so nervous about, Home?' Thumper was already in his pockets, shaking out the snotrag, scrabbling through his vinyl wallet.

'I ain't nervous!' Ahmed sounded like a fire alarm at noon.

'Ya ain't nervous? Feel ya heart!' Thumper squawked, moving his hand on Ahmed's chest, *whump whump*, as if it was pulsing. He pulled out Ahmed's money – two dollars, a real big-time gangster – then put the bills back in Ahmed's pocket and pulled off his Batman hat, checking inside before flipping it over the fence, into the grass.

Big Chief was giving Peanut the same drill, while Smurf sniffed around the benches, picking up paper bags and looking for bottles, rooting around in the garbage cans like a bum. They all looked like bums, except they were healthy bums, six-foot, two-hundred-pound white bums with lead saps and Glock Nineteens on their hips.

Strike had no idea why, but the Fury definitely had a thing for the Weehawken benches. Knockos, whether Housing, City or County, were just *like* that, getting fixated on one corner, one building, one dealer, even though their arrest turf took in entire cities. It was known as the Knocko's Prerogative.

'Pea-nut, Pea-nut, gimme some bottles, Pea-nut.' Big Chief towered over him, crowding him against the fence. 'You ain't no raiser, Pea-nut. Where them bottles?' Then he saw the bang on Peanut's cheek. 'You do something bad, Peanut?'

Big Chief turned slowly, looking over to Strike.

Strike stared at his own sneakers, taking a breath, recalling the exercise the speech therapist had taught him back in school: envision a scene that relaxes you, she'd said, and now Strike conjured up a picture of palm trees and ocean, literally a picture, since he had never seen a real palm tree.

'Strike,' Big Chief said, 'Peanut do something bad?'

Strike took a swig of Yoo-Hoo, shrugged, said nothing. Futon ignored it all, bobbing his head to his Walkman, his fingers orange from Cheetos dust as he scraped the bottom of the bag.

Peanut did his gooney-bird dance: arms raised, elbows cocked, wrists curled. 'C'mon, Big Chief, you know I ain't *do* nothin', 'cause how come I ain't *runnin'* nowhere?'

Big Chief pulled at the front of Peanut's pants, looked down into his crotch, growling, 'Pea-nut, Pea-nut, lemme see ya pea-nuts.'

'Watch out it don't bite you.' Peanut laughed. Big Chief laughed right back.

Strike heard the white guy going on to Crunch about how he just got engaged, how he did A.A., a hundred meetings in a hundred days, how his father was a fireman in Jersey City. Strike could see Crunch's eyes going dull.

White people. Strike thought the Fury was OK but most of the others, in his experience, were for shit. Whenever they got grabbed, they got so scared they babbled; at least most of the boys around here knew to get stony stupid when the police came down. No matter what the knockos did to you, whatever they called you, all you had to do was weather it out, because the knockos couldn't do shit if they couldn't find nothing, so anybody who understood survival out here just hung tight and took the abuse until the knockos went away.

But if Big Chief or Thumper caught one of the boys dirty, someone like Peanut, then got him alone . . . well, everybody was out for himself. Peanut was being cool and funny with Strike sitting there, but Peanut went to Catholic pay school, his mother was a working woman and he was scared of her. If Peanut ever got caught, he might turn.

Big Chief had finished with Peanut, and now both of them were looking over at Strike. Big Chief knew Strike was clean, but here it came anyhow, just like always. Strike took a swig of Yoo-Hoo to brace himself.

Big Chief clomped over, six foot five, reddish-gray hair, bounce-lurching on the toes of his sneakers like a playground Frankenstein, wearing his Fury T-shirt – six wolves hanging out of a police car – growling, 'Strike, Strike, Strike.' Thumper shoved Ahmed away and chimed in, 'No, Big Chief, it be S-S-S-Strike S-S-S-Strike.'

Strike eased off the bench top, raising his arms, looking deadpan, solemn, enduring.

'You got bottles there, Strike?' Big Chief began finger-walking his front pockets, pulling out Strike's money – ten dollars, never more – his house keys and the house keys for three other people who held his dope, his money.

'What are you, a janitor?' Big Chief jingled the keys, giving them to a baby in a stroller, and lazily scanned the curious and growing crowd around the benches.

Strike's eyes went straight to Big Chief's throat, then shifted over his shoulder, across the projects to where his mother lived with his brother, Victor. Strike imagined them looking out now, seeing this, drawing down the shade.

Thumper barked to a few eight-year-olds, 'What's up, yo, you got bottles?'

'I ain't got no bottles,' said one little kid, rearing back in disdain.

'Who's Mister Big?' Thumper leaned down, growling like Big Chief.

'*This* Mister Big,' the kid said, grabbing his own crotch, then running away.

'Open your mouth there, Strike.' Big Chief checked his teeth as if he was a horse, or a slave.

Strike, yawning wide, saw Rodney roll by in the beat-up rustcolored Cadillac that he'd bought from a pipehead for two hundred dollars cash and another hundred in bottles, kicking the guy in the ass on his way out the door. Rodney in his Jheri curls, his gold wraparound sunglasses and his Cadillac: an old-timer, thirty-five, maybe older.

Strike saw Rodney smirk in disgust, shake his head and raise a lazy hand off the seat back. But he kept moving; he never even slowed down.

'OK.' Big Chief looked right, left, then moved close. 'Drop your drawers there, Strike. Dicky check.'

Strike hesitated as always, holding it in, weighing his options, finally unzipping and pulling down, some of the tenants in the crowd looking away and talking under their breath, some cursing out the Fury, some cursing out Strike.

'Drop your drawers, bend over, say ah-h-h,' Thumper said, getting in on it now.

Strike held his underwear band out so Big Chief could look in.

'Short and sweet there, Strike.' Big Chief frowned. 'Let's see under your balls, there. See what you got taped under your balls.'

'Strike's balls,' Thumper drawled. 'Strikes and balls, three and two, full count.'

Strike pulled up his scrotum, caught Peanut grinning on the sidewalk and then looking away quick when he saw Strike watching him, Strike thinking, Peanut's a dead man.

Thumper peeked in. 'Jesus, Strike, you got some bacon strips in there, brother. Where's your hygiene?'

Strike bugged out: it was a damn lie. Nothing sickened Strike more than filth, *any* kind of filth. He was *clean*, cleaner than any of them. Losing it, Strike looked right into Thumper's eyes, totally blowing his own play.

'W-w-w-what's a m-m-m-matter, S-S-Strike? Y-y-you OK?'

Strike looked away, pulled up his pants, took his keys back from the baby. It was all Thumper's show now, Big Chief moving off to look under the bench for bottles.

'How come you never smile, Strike? You're clean, man. Crack a smile.'

Strike looked off sourly, although he was smiling a little on the inside as he caught sight of the twelve-year-old mule with his two-hundred-bottle lunch box zooming right by Big Chief – Big Chief even stepping out of the way, the kid going into 6 Weehawken to make his delivery.

'Look at Futon.' Thumper used his chin as a pointer. 'We bust Futon every month, right, Futon?'

Futon smiled, holding the bottles in the Gummi Bear jar.

'See? Futon smiles all the time. What's your problem, man?'

Strike stayed mute, glancing over at Futon doing the gooney bird.

'It takes six muscles to smile, two hundred forty-eight to frown, you know that?'

'C'mon there, Thumper.' Big Chief rummaged in the garbage can now like a hungry bear. 'Strike's got rights.'

'I never said that,' Strike protested, flinching as soon as he opened his mouth. Shit.

'Hey, you didn't stutter, that was very good.' Thumper put out his hand, forcing Strike to shake it. 'Now say, "She sells seashells by the seashore."'

Strike's stomach turned red, pulsing. Thumper held his hand, waiting.

Big Chief yawned, going up on tiptoe, then grabbed a bunch of Gummi Bears from Futon's jar, chewing them open-mouthed and then lazily sticking his big paws in Futon's pockets, feeling around in his socks, up his legs.

'*Cold*, Big Chief, cold, cold . . . *warm*, getting warm now,' Futon said. He offered the Gummi Bears to Thumper. A dumb play, to Strike's eye, but at least Thumper let go of Strike's hand to take some candy.

'Yo, Big Chief,' Futon said, feigning anger. 'What you doin' back here *any*how? You said if I won Thumper, you leave off on us for a *month*.'

'You know not to trust the po-lice,' Big Chief grunted. 'What's wrong with you?'

'Gah-damn, ain't *that* right? Man, I dint even get out of first gear. I was like *lopin*'.' Futon was talking to Strike now, as if Strike hadn't been there. 'Thumper was like, huh huh huh. Man, he was huffin' so bad I thought he was gonna drown me in wheeze snot. You alls *drink* too much, *eat* too much, *smoke* too much.' Futon counted off their habits on his fingers, making a face.

'See, the problem is, I don't like to run.' Thumper flashed teeth. 'So how 'bout next time we get into an elevator, push fourteen, and have us a one-on-one?' Strike could almost smell the rage coming off Thumper now, behind the grin. ''Cause I hate to run.'

'Yeah? I put my whooping crane style on you?' Oblivious to Thumper's heat, Futon went up on one leg, wrists high over his head like the Karate Kid, lashing out a kick, switching feet, trying to come off delicate and lethal. 'You be *beggin'* to get off by three, bawh.'

The Word came out of 6 Weehawken too soon. Big Chief saw the St Louis Cardinals hat and went after him with a little hobble-skip, snatching him up against the fence, a big hand on his heart. 'What's up, yo?' Big Chief plucked a fat roll of singles, fives and tens out of The Word's pocket.

The Word started to whine. 'I dint serve no one, Big Chief! It's for mah mother's birthday, I *swear.*'

All the knockos bellowed in chorus, 'Mother's Day! Mother's Day!,' everybody having a good laugh as Big Chief escorted The Word to the car.

'Please, Big Chief . . . My mother, I *swear.*'

Strike forgot about Thumper for a second, thinking, What's that nigger doing still holding all the money? Was he stealing? Will he set me up? Rodney just met guys in diners, made payoffs over coffee like a gentleman. Strike swore to himself: If I don't step up, I'm stepping out. I can't take it no more.

The bounty run over for now, two of the knockos walked back through the projects toward the second hidden car.

Thumper came back in his face. 'Strike, why you always look depressed? Are you depressed? Are you angry at me?' Thumper looked concerned, waiting for an answer.

'You gotta do what you gotta do.' Strike controlled himself, the words coming out low and lazy.

'Yeah? Let me ask you something else. Do you think I'm an effective deterrent in the war on drugs?' He stared Strike in the eye, mouth open, innocent and earnest. Strike turned his head away, but Thumper moved his own head to keep up the eye contact. 'Or do you think I'm just a big asshole?'

Strike caught Peanut looking at him again: Peanut definitely out of work. The Word out too.

'Oh shit.' Thumper snapped his fingers. 'Did we do socks and shoes?'

Strike breathed through his nose and hunched over to unlace. Thumper said, 'Allow me,' then dropped to one knee as if they were in a shoe store, undoing Strike's sneakers and then slipping off his socks.

'Let's go, there, Thumper,' Big Chief yelled from the car. Thumper sighed, rising, shaking out the socks for hidden dope.

'OK. I gotta go, hon.' Thumper swiveled on his hips like a discus thrower. Strike tensed, bracing himself for the goodbye. Thumper uncorked it, slapping Strike between the shoulder blades, a heavy, bone-rattling *pock*, sending a shock wave of pain through Strike's 125-pound frame. 'Catch you later.'

Thumper walked over to a group of little kids who were watching the show, dropped his hand on a six-year-old shoulder: 'Walk me, Big Time.' He strolled to the car with the kid as security against a toaster thrown out a window, Strike's socks dangling from his back pocket.

Strike pulled on his sneakers over bare feet, clenching his teeth so the porcelain squeak was a hundred times magnified in his head, thinking: Lose *all* the idiots around me. Clowns, thieves, juveniles . . .

Strike walked to the curb and looked into the Fury: The Word sat in the back. Strike tried to catch his eye, throw some fear, but The Word was sitting on the street side and wouldn't look his way. Crunch sat on the curb side, elbow out the window, waiting to roll. Little kids hung all over the car, wide-eyed; Big Chief nodded to one kid and growled, 'What's up, yo? Dempsy burnin'?'

Strike turned and noticed a boy of eleven or twelve standing there staring at Crunch, stick legs in wide-cut shorts, arms crossed high on his chest like an old-time comic-book weightlifter. The kid was giving Crunch the thousand-yard stare, testing himself, putting on his I-ain't-afraid-a-no-knocko face. Crunch, feeling the eyes, the attitude, stared right back. 'What's *your* problem?'

The skinny boy didn't answer, just kept staring, and Crunch went with it, playing, staring back.

But Crunch couldn't hold it. He started laughing, and what happened next threw Strike completely. Strike expected the kid to go on staring or walk away triumphant, but when Crunch started laughing, the kid laughed too. The kid had play in him. The kid had *flex*, and flex was rare. Flex was intelligent, special, a good sign, like big paws on a puppy. For a minute Strike lost his anger, entranced by this kid, by possibilities.

As the Fury rolled off, Big Chief said goodbye to Strike by making a gun with his fingers and winking. As soon as they were gone, the baby-fat girl came up to him again.

'Can I ask you something?' she said. Her smile was tense, jittery, begging.

Strike ignored her, then asked a question of his own. 'Who's that kid there?'

'Where?'

'Him.'

'That Tyrone Jeeter.'

'He live here?'

'He just moved into Eight Weehawken from over on the other side. You know his mother? That woman Iris? Strike, can I borrow a bottle?'

Strike started to walk away, thinking about flex, when the rust-colored Caddy came rolling up again, Rodney at the wheel with his arm flung out along the back of the shotgun seat. Rodney ducked his head down to see over the gold frames of his sunglasses, then curled a finger for Strike.

Strike looked right and left, frowning, not liking to be seen talking to Rodney out in the open, even though any kid in the street could draw a diagram: Champ on top, then down to Rodney, then down to Strike and finally down to whomever Strike was trusting this week.

Strike walked to the car, stuck his head in the passenger-side window and got hit with a heavy cherry smell coming from the deodorizers Rodney had in front and back. Six Garfield cats were suction-cupped and spread-eagled on all the rear and side windows, staring bug-eyed out at the traffic.

Rodney sat with a hand on his crotch. Zodiac and *Apollo XII* patches sprouted from the thighs of his dry-cleaned jeans, and a button was missing from the belly of his white ruffle-paneled shirt. But he was handsome, smooth-skinned and in pretty good shape from all the prison time and from being an ex-boxer.

'Who'd they take?' Rodney thumbed his glasses up the bridge of his nose.

'The Woo-Word.' Strike was annoyed to hear the stutter come back on him. 'He ain't holding or nothing.'

'You gonna go tell his aunt to get him?' Rodney spoke in sing-song, like a schoolteacher.

'I'll take care of it.' Maybe Rodney should take care of some things too, Strike thought, like losing the Garfields. And lose the Caddy while he was at it – the only monied nigger left in creation to drive a big-body Cadillac.

'What you want?' Strike sniffed, picking up a vague fried-food smell underneath the cherry scent.

'You go to that *doc*tor yet?' Another singsong nag.

'I ain't had time.'

'That shit'll kill you quicker than anything out here.' Rodney tilted his chin at the Yoo-Hoo.

'What you want, Rodney?' Strike tried to come off patient, but barely, wanting to get back to the bench and reorganize the post-attack situation.

'Come by the store.'

Rodney's long fingernails were shiny and gray with food grease. Strike's gut rippled reflexively. 'When?'

'Later.'

'It gonna be busy.'

Rodney shrugged. 'Let Futon run it.'

'Futon's a idiot.' Strike looked away, scowling, not wanting to see those fingernails anymore.

Rodney sighed, shook his head. 'You got to get off that bench every now and then, my man. You gonna get all crabbed up.'

Strike couldn't respond, the stammer hitting strong, right up from his feet. And he didn't even know the words yet.

'Just come by, OK?'

'I-i-if I can.'

The baby-fat girl worked her way up to Rodney's window in a shy slide. She peeked in, smiling. 'I like them *Garfields*.'

Rodney gave her a slow eye, fanning his knees. 'What *you* want?'

Strike pushed away from the car, headed back to the bench. Turn my stomach.

'Yo yo, check it out.' Horace shoved a Childcraft catalogue under Strike's nose and pointed to a brightly colored set of 250 blocks standing at twice the height of a blank-faced, five-year-old redhead. 'That's some bad shit for a kid, them blocks.'

They were sitting on the top bench slat, thigh to thigh.

'What the hell you want with blocks for? You a *infant*?' Strike had a Hold Everything catalogue open on his knees.

'Not for *me*, motherfucker. I'm just *sayin*' . . .' Horace got all red and choke-faced.

'Yo yo, Horace want *play* blocks.' Peanut haw-hawed, spinning out in a tight circle, his own catalogue rolled up into a baton.

'Hey, *fuck* you, nigger!' Horace flew off the bench and Peanut danced away, his laugh exaggerated, pushing it.

Strike thought Horace did want the blocks. He wanted the blocks, the deluxe colored pencil sets, the construct-a-castle, the miniature rescue vehicles and maybe even the plastic microbots. Strike knew Horace had been taking his money and buying toys on the sly since the beginning, but he never said anything about it because Horace never had anything before in his life, and he was only thirteen.

Ever since Peanut fished a dozen catalogues out of a garbage can, everybody was in a state of mild disorder, passing around the thin glossies as if they were sex books. Strike would have cracked a whip if it was anything else, but he was the worst. He'd meant to go over to Rodney's store an hour before, during the dinner lull, but had remained glued to the bench, a half-dozen catalogues on his lap, running his fingers down page after page of camisoles, hand-carved Christmas-tree angels, computerized jogging machines, golf putting sets for den and office, personalized stationery, lawn furniture – anything and everything for man, woman or child. The catalogues made him weak in the knees, fascinated him to the point of helplessness, the idea of all these *things* to be had, organized in a book that he could hold in one hand. Not that he would ever order anything – possessions drew attention, made you a target. None of the boys would order out of a catalogue either, not necessarily because they were paranoid like Strike, but because the ordering process – telephones, mailings, deliveries – required too much contact with the world outside the street. It was easier to go to a store on JFK Boulevard, flash your roll and say 'Gimme that.'

Strike didn't have a watch, but he knew it was seven o'clock because Popeye came out of 4 Weehawken. Popeye was forty-five but looked sixty, a hobbled-up twist-backed pipehead with a bulging left eye. He shuffled over to the bench licking his lips, probably broke but liking to be near the bottles anyhow, hoping he'd find one in the grass or something. Strike had given Popeye a bottle out of pity a few weeks back, but that had turned out to be a bad mistake, because the only thing worse than a pipehead with no bottle to smoke was a pipehead with one bottle, and Popeye had spent the rest of that night in a frantic scuttle, hassling the crew for hours until Strike had to slap his face. Strike still remembered the slick bristles of Popeye's cheek and something wet – spit, blood – left on his own hand. Strike had rubbed it off against his pant leg in disgust, and all that night he dreamed about that wetness on his palm and fingers.

Popeye came hobbling past the bench now, not looking at Strike but pacing back and forth like a sentry, mumbling, 'Strike the *man* . . . Strike the *man*.'

Seven o'clock: the Fury last rolled on them at four-thirty, and processing The Word at Juvie, if it went that far, would take them out of action for about ninety minutes. Then they'd probably hit O'Brien, then Sullivan,

which meant they'd probably roll on Strike again about eight, eight-fifteen
– unless they scored at those other two projects, in which case they
wouldn't come back tonight, because a second booking would bring
them to about ten o'clock and the Fury always knocked off at ten to
drink away the last two hours of the four-to-midnight shift. They didn't
like to snatch clockers later than ten and risk getting stuck until two A.M.
with paperwork and all the requisite stops along the way to the county
bullpen. So they were either coming in an hour or not at all. Strike couldn't
take another dicky check tonight, decided to be out of there before eight,
come back at ten when all was clear one way or the other.

He went back to the pictures on his lap, flipping past a gold-plated
razor, bocce balls, thick merino wool undersheets and a child-size police
cruiser, four feet high like a bright blue cartoon car, a blond three-year-old
grinning behind the wheel like he'd just shit his pants.

Strike had no real love of things for themselves, but he loved the idea of
things, the concept of possession. Sometimes he was crazed with wanting,
blind with visions of things he was too cagey to buy, and at moments like
this he felt tortured, tantalized, sensing in some joyless way that he was
outsmarting someone, but he wasn't sure who.

Finally revolted with the catalogues, with himself, he slid off the bench
top, walked over to Futon and took away Futon's catalogue, a sexy
Victoria's Secret, Futon going, 'Hey hey,' his fingers snapping like fish
after the pages. Strike had to hold the catalogue behind his back to get
Futon's attention.

'I'm going out. Watch the bench.'

'Where you goin'?'

'If I wanted you to know, I would've said to you.'

'You goin' to Rodney's store?'

Strike stared at him.

'Gimme back the book, OK?'

Strike continued to stare, as if his silence carried some kind of lesson
he wanted Futon to learn.

'I got it covered. Gimme back the motherfuckin' book.' Futon faked left
around Strike, then snatched the catalogue from the right side, laughing.
Strike guessed he liked Futon as much as he liked anyone: not much.

On his way out of the projects, Strike spotted the boy who had stared
down Crunch – Tyrone. He was standing by the fence, watching Horace
and Peanut huff and puff, looking disgusted. Strike noticed that Tyrone
had a half-assed Mercedes symbol shaved into his hair, mostly grown in
now, looking more like some kind of indentation than a design. Strike

walked up closer to the boy, checked him out a little, got the smell of him, the boy so aware of Strike coming near that he locked his head at an angle to be looking away, Strike taking that as a sign that the kid was alert. Tyrone . . . the kid needed a street name. Strike would think about it.

Walking the three blocks to his car, Strike performed casual 360-degree turns every minute or two to see if anybody was walking behind him. He had no money on him, no dope, but he was known.

He kept his car in an old lady's driveway, paid her a hundred a month to keep it off the street. The lady was seventy-five, half blind, liked to listen to gospel radio and sit in her window, watching the two-year-old Accord as if it might drive away by itself. Strike liked old people. They were more sensible, less likely to be greedy, had no taste or inclination for getting high. He had six of them on his payroll: this one for the car; three others to keep Sears-bought safes in their houses, for his money; another to keep a safe for his surplus bottles; and another to do his laundry. Old people were his biggest expense, $2,000 a month. But he was making between $1,500 and $2,000 a week now, his cut for selling anywhere from fifteen hundred to two thousand bottles, depending on what kind of shorts he encountered – thefts, breakage, police. He was afraid to do anything with the money, didn't want to flaunt it or acquire anything that could be taken away from him, so all he had to show for his hard work was cash, more cash than he could count. His car was used and leased; the cops couldn't confiscate a leased car, and a used car didn't draw that much attention anyway. His apartment was rented in someone else's name, in a bad but quiet neighborhood, a whore strip, but there weren't any clockers and a bank of pay phones stood right across the street.

His apartment was spotless and spare. No great sound machine or television setup, no phone, nothing hanging on the walls, just a three-piece bedroom set and a four-piece living room ensemble, all bought in a half hour at the House of Bamboo in a shopping center over in Queens where no one knew him. He had moved in six months before, after a showdown with his mother over his dealing. Even though he was only nineteen, he had enough money to buy himself a house somewhere, but if he got arrested the house would be confiscated; even if he bought it in someone else's name, jail time would mean no cash flow, no payments to the bank, and the place would be repossessed. But at least Strike had considered the idea: most of the dealers he knew never even thought about houses. Like Horace, they spent all their money on toys – man-toys maybe, but lightweight vanity buys – living in dumps and wearing too much gold. They couldn't get out of that minute-to-minute survival head long enough to take the money and buy something substantial. 'They don't *have* no future because they don't be*lieve* in no future' was the way Rodney put it, although in Strike's mind Rodney wasn't really anybody to talk.

Every time Strike stopped on JFK for a red light on his way over to Rodney's store, his hand dropped to the .25 automatic he'd stashed under a homemade flip-up lid on the step well. There was a stickup crew from Newark that was hitting on Dempsy dealers, following them home or getting them at the lights. And they were shooting too: one guy in the Sullivan crew was on a respirator, and some clocker from Cleary Avenue was dead. Of course some people said it was Erroll Barnes, but every time some no-witness mayhem went down, Erroll's name came up. Erroll Barnes was a Dempsy bad man, had served seven years for killing a TV reporter who was accompanying the cops during a raid in Elizabeth. He didn't get life because his lawyer convinced the jury that Erroll thought it was other dealers coming to kill him, that he'd never knowingly shoot at cops. That's how it went sometimes. But if Erroll Barnes *was* behind all this, that could be the best insurance for Strike, because Erroll and Rodney grew up together, used to pull stickups together, did time together, and now Erroll was Rodney's troubleshooter and dope mule, and Strike couldn't see Erroll shooting up Rodney's people. Still, it wasn't unheard-of once you understood that after all the We Are Family bullshit went down, everybody was really just out for themselves.

Strike hated having a gun, only got it because Rodney had told him he was too little and skinny to get anybody to toe the line just on say-so, that he had to have a piece to do the job. But the truth of it was, he was scared of the gun once he got it – not scared of shooting somebody, but scared of his own anger and what trouble he could get into for shooting somebody. His fear of having to use it probably served him just as well, sometimes even made him creative. One evening three months before, he had found out that some kid working for him was going over to Rydell and selling his bottles for fifteen instead of ten, then pocketing the extra five for himself. Not wanting to use the gun, Strike went over to a pet store, bought a dog chain and whipped this greedy little motherfucker to the ground in front of an entire Saturday night's playground crowd, standing over him like some heave-chested slave master. It was just business, but Strike didn't like to think about how good it felt, didn't like to imagine where that might have ended for him if he'd had that gun in his hand.

Strike took a vanilla Yoo-Hoo out of the glove compartment and sipped it as he trolled the boulevard. About every two blocks some JFK clocker would wave in recognition or yell out his name, or some pipehead girl from the projects would get all happy-faced seeing him, tiptoe out into traffic and try to wheedle a bottle out of him before the light changed. Despite his wariness, there was a part of him that loved the charge he generated in others: the lit-up look the pipeheads got on seeing him, the salute of the clockers. Someday it would be the end of him, this recognition, this power, but other than the lifelong tug of war between him and his mother, it was the closest thing to love he had ever experienced.

At the light before the turn to Rodney's store, two plainclothes cops pulled up alongside the Accord. Strike made a point of casually looking into their window, then looking away. It was only natural to look at a cop car; nothing gave a clocker away to a profiling cop like that stony straight-ahead stare at a red light.

The cop in the shotgun seat, a pink-skinned albino with a wild white Santa Claus beard, rolled down his window and tilted his chin at Strike. Panicking a little, Strike forgot about the gun in the step well and worried instead about the open Yoo-Hoo.

'Yo, Strike.'

Strike rolled down his window.

'Tell Rodney to give me a call.'

Strike nodded, relieved, but freaked too. The guy must be on Rodney's payroll, but how did the cop know who he was? Strike had never seen him before. The light turned green and Strike let him roll off first.

Give me a call . . . like Rodney would know which cop this was. The guy probably thought he was the only eyes and ears Rodney had. Strike hissed out his disgust: everybody was full of shit in this game. The cops bullshitted each other, the dealers bullshitted each other, the cops bullshitted the dealers, the dealers bullshitted the cops, the cops took bribes, the dealers ratted each other out. Nobody knew for sure which side anybody was on; no one really knew how much or how little money anybody else was making. Everything was smoke. Everything was pay phones in the middle of the night. Being in this business was like walking blindfolded through a minefield. It was hard to know what to do or what not to do, but in order to survive Strike went by three unbreakable rules: trust no one, don't get greedy, and never do product. Most people who lasted out here lived by the same rules as Strike did, plus rule number four, which was kind of a balancing act with rule number one: you got to have someone watch your back. You got to have a main somebody to cover your ass. You didn't have to trust him completely, but alone is tough. There's always something you'll need help with. Bail, jail, collections, muscle, the impossibility of being in two places at one time. That's why Rodney had Erroll. Strike didn't have anybody like that in his life yet, but he was thinking hard on it.

The store was called Rodney's Place, a little hole in the wall on a side street off JFK Boulevard. Rodney had hand lettered the name on the painted sky-blue cinder blocks under the window, following it with a partial list: 'candy, sofe drinks, milk, games.' No one, if they noticed, had the guts to tell Rodney that he'd misspelled 'soft.' Rodney had learned to read and write in prison when he was twenty-one, had earned his high school equivalency degree there and had been reading- and writing-crazy ever since. He was obsessed with tests, taking every possible written exam just to show he could pass and get some payback for all those humiliating classroom years. He now held six licenses: barber, beautician, real estate, travel agent, driving instructor and Xerox repair. Strike knew Rodney was deeply proud of his mail-order education, even though he had little to show for it outside of a bunch of framed diplomas hanging on the walls of the candy store. He never used any of the skills that came with all that paper, save for giving the occasional free haircut when he couldn't stand looking at some kid's scruffed-up head anymore.

Rodney wasn't there when Strike walked in. Six young teenagers played pool under the harsh fluorescent overheads, another two banged away on the Super Mario video game, all of them silently taking in Strike with dopey frowns. The kids weren't clockers: Rodney didn't allow any hustling in the store, and working for Rodney meant *working*.

Strike knew about that up front. He had spent a full year in here making five dollars an hour under the table, straight, no-nonsense, mule-team shopkeeping – inventory, cash register, mopping the floor, sometimes putting in fifteen-hour days, sleeping in back, then putting in another twelve. He had loved every minute of it and thought he was rolling in dough until Rodney sat him down one day and offered him a different kind of job. Now Rodney carried Strike on the books as the night manager of Rodney's Place; if Strike ever got stopped with a few thousand on him, he could account for the roll by saying he was on his way to the bank to make a night deposit for the store. Rodney was smart that way, and he charged Strike only five hundred dollars for the honorary title. Sometimes Strike missed working here; his stomach hurt him less back then, and he used to savor the charge he felt whenever Rodney would roll in and make some noise about how shipshape the place looked.

The first time they met, Rodney had startled Strike by telling him that he 'admired' his speech defect because Strike didn't let it stop him from wanting to make something of himself, didn't let it turn him into one of those people who would drown in a rain puddle. Rodney said he could see that Strike knew that the only place a man can be truly handicapped is in his mind, and that a man who can conquer his own mind has got the world at his feet.

Strike didn't know he knew all this until Rodney said he did, but once he heard it, Strike began believing it. Rodney was always doing that to him: teaching him things in a way that made him feel as if he knew it all along, making Strike recognize himself. And sometimes Rodney introduced Strike to people as 'my son.' He was smart that way too.

The only other guy who had worked as hard as Strike in here, and who Rodney liked as much as Strike, was a kid named Darryl Adams. Darryl was a lot like Strike's older brother, Victor: heads down, brick-by-brick, never shooting off his mouth but never smiling either. He was quiet, neat and dependable, the sort of person Strike's mother would like. These days Darryl held down an assistant manager's job at Ahab's, a fast-food shithole a few blocks from Rodney's store, the same kind of job Strike's brother had over at a competing grease pit called Hambone's.

Strike wandered the cramped store in a lazy circle, scowling, resisting the impulse to clean up: the place looked like shit.

Rodney's chubby teenage daughter sat behind the counter, staring into space and chewing air. Across the room and under a Budweiser Kings of Africa poster, Rodney's father sat propped up on a bar stool behind his thick glasses and his cigarette smoke, watching the game of pool and jabbering away, mostly to himself. An eighteen-month-old boy chewing a Pay Day bar sat in a stroller in front of the candy counter, dressed in a denim jumpsuit. His hair had two neat slices running front to back like stripes on a football helmet, and he wore high-top baby Nikes on his feet. He was Rodney's son, one of three Strike knew about, this one by the woman who lived a few houses up from where Rodney lived with his wife and two teenage daughters.

The kids around the pool table and video game were mostly here by default, half of them living on the street or with mothers on the pipe. Rodney kept the store open twenty-four hours, and a lot of them never went home. They wore linty sweat suits and cheap sneakers, baseball hats and no jewelry. Two of them were still sucking their thumbs.

Strike watched the game for a minute. None of the kids could sink more than one ball at a time or had the patience to line up a shot right, and with him standing there, they all got worse, knowing he wasn't just a clocker but Rodney's lieutenant. Some of them, and some of the other kids Rodney was constantly collecting, would be getting a tryout on the street in the coming months. Most would fall off into the product right away, but a few would wear Nike Airs and gold for at least a little while before they went down too. A good run on the street was six months, and you had to have a clear head and a lot of self-confidence to make it even that long. Strike had been out there almost nine months now, and he knew that almost nobody made it out of the game in one piece, and almost everybody thought they would be the exception.

Strike turned away so the players could relax. Everything for sale in the store was behind the counter; that way no one could walk out with anything. Strike scanned the shelves: diapers, Similac, light bulbs, Tampax, dry cereal, kitty litter, coffee, kitchen matches, lighters, plus the trinity of base coke preparation: Arm and Hammer baking soda, Chore Boy scouring pads and McKesson rubbing alcohol. A pinch of baking soda mixed with a ten-dollar bottle of powder, sprinkled with water, heated, then cooled, left you with a pure nugget of smoking cocaine. And a pinch of Chore Boy wedged into your pipe would trap some of the cocaine vapors as they fled the burning nugget. Once the fumes hit the Chore Boy they reverted to an oily substance that hung in the strands; you could fire up the Chore Boy itself for a second hit, not as strong as the first but still included in the price. And the rubbing alcohol was just a poor man's butane, although some people preferred 151 proof rum.

Every small grocery and candy store on every poor street in Dempsy always carried the trinity, no matter how skimpy and random the stock behind the counter. Not only did they carry it but they charged double what it would cost in a wealthier neighborhood – supply and demand being what they were. Rodney was a full-service ghetto capitalist: he'd sell you the bottles on the street and the paraphernalia in the store.

Strike walked over to the glass counter and stood in front of Rodney's daughter. She stared right through his chest, her jaw rolling, her hands palm up in her lap.

'Where's he at?'

She shrugged and gave him a barely raised eyebrow.

Strike went over to the refrigerator where Rodney stocked milk and drinks. It was a regular kitchen refrigerator but nothing in it came free. It always caught Strike up short, taking a Yoo-Hoo out of the refrigerator and then having to pay for it. And you *had* to pay for it, no matter who you were. One of Rodney's favorite quotes was from some billionaire: 'A dime's a dime.' Twisting the cap and leaving two quarters on the counter, Strike wandered the small room feeling restless. He hated waiting for people, became vaguely jumpy when there was nothing to react to, nothing to be in motion for, and too much time to think random thoughts.

The overhead fluorescents were cold and ugly, their light bouncing harshly off the chipboard walls. Rodney had this store plus a craps house, both of them lined with salami-textured composition board. The man cleared twenty to forty thousand dollars on the two-plus kilos sold every week by Strike and his two other lieutenants, but he couldn't put up decent wood or even a coat of paint. It was like buying a ten-year-old fat-ass Cadillac instead of something that didn't cough blood every time you put the key in. Strike understood Quiet Storm, but to him this seemed like a sickness.

Strike turned to Rodney's diplomas, correspondence degrees for the most part, all hanging in Woolworth frames on pushpins jammed into the chipboard. Strike thought all this was some silly shit on Rodney's part – who went to school to cut hair? Anyway, he knew that Rodney really learned barbering in jail.

But Strike felt a little tug when his eye fell on the New Jersey State high school equivalency diploma. He had never finished school himself. It took too much time away from making money, first in here and then out on the street. Anybody could get a high school diploma if they hung in, but it didn't lead to anything except more school, or some hour-pay job.

Besides, his stammer had made each school day hell. Nobody ever made fun of him directly, but they always watched him talk, and usually the teachers wouldn't call on him if the answer required more than one word. One time in English, after a particularly bad attack complete with head-whip and eye-flutter, the teacher had said, 'Well, we have a Claudius among us.' After class Strike had gone in his face for an explanation, and the guy had danced out of it by telling Strike it was a compliment, that Claudius was an emperor of Rome, but the teacher's jittery grin betrayed him. School had made him sick to his stomach with anger, and the speech therapy class he had taken two afternoons a week was more like a punishment than a help, the other two kids in it almost retarded. Strike remembered that the therapist smelled like a cafeteria, like a big vat of boiling hot dogs. Somehow it didn't surprise him that his stammer had started lifting from the moment he had dropped out of school, so that now, except for the bad days, like today, his tongue rarely seized on him.

Still, he hadn't been a bad student. He was bright and he had worried over his work the way he worried over everything. Once in tenth grade, one of his teachers called in his mother and told her about a boarding school up in Maine that was giving out scholarships to inner-city kids. A few weeks later he took a three-hour test in English and math, and then spent another three hours being interviewed by a white-haired white man and then by a black lady with an Afro and glasses on a bead chain. He didn't get accepted: he was smart but there were other kids who were smarter, and that was that.

He felt bad about being rejected only because it meant his mother had lost a day of work for nothing. Work had always been a kind of religion with her, and Strike couldn't remember a time growing up when his mother didn't have two jobs, sometimes three – everything from geriatric care to waitressing to supermarket cashiering. He must have gotten his work drive from her – that and his bad stomach. He remembered their kitchen in the Roosevelt Houses: all those bottles with the chalky stuff for her to drink, and sometimes the caked residue of the medicine around her mouth. At least he didn't inherit her asthma.

When Rodney finally walked in, waddling with the weight of three cartons of Coca-Cola, it was like an underwater surge: everybody felt pulled toward his presence. Even the baby kicked his heels and yelled, 'Yahh!' The kids around the pool table and the video machine forgot about their games and began sputtering out his name as he dropped the cases by the refrigerator with a sharp whack.

'Yo yo, Rodney, this nigger say Chuckie could kill Freddy, man,' said a skinny snaggle-toothed kid holding a cue stick with no tip.

'Freddie *who*?' Rodney bent over and began filling the shelves with cans, both hands moving from crate to shelf to crate as if working a speed bag.

'Freddy *Kruger*, man, who you think?' They all watched Rodney work, as if his hands and body might speak to them.

'Yeah, and who's Chuckie?' Strike noticed that Rodney always sounded slightly pissed off and threatening when talking to kids, as if he'd just about had it with them, although none of them ever seemed to care.

'*Chuckie*, man, you know, the doll from *Child Play*.'

'I don't know none of that horror shit,' Rodney said, 'But I do know y'alls wasting time on it. I know *that*.'

Strike seconded that with a nod. A movie was ninety minutes of sitting there.

'Who-alls minding the bench?' Rodney asked Strike without looking up.

'Futon's on it.' Strike watched Rodney hunched over the soda in a spread-legged stoop, wearing high-top boxing shoes and a broad leather weightlifter's belt. His hands were a blur and there was a constellation of sweat breaking out on his forehead and through the back of his shiny gold acetate T-shirt.

Strike grunted in amazement: the man was making almost a million a year on the street, yet here he was unloading sodas. Well, a hustler hustles; that's what he does.

'Feels *good* to stretch your legs, don't it?' Rodney was puffing a little, working with his head lower than his chest. 'Walk around, take a ride, see the sights.'

Strike found himself going glassy staring at Rodney, struck with a hazy memory of who he looked like, someone from Strike's past, the face and the name just out of reach. Strike only knew that part of his fascination with Rodney had always been connected to this vague memory of another man from somewhere, his childhood or something. Not Strike's real father, dead eleven years now, but maybe a friend of his father's. He couldn't remember who.

'So I'm here now. So what's up?' Strike sounded pissy even to himself, a man with a watch.

'We get there, we get there,' Rodney said, his voice going high and singsong. 'Y'all gotta *relax*, learn how to *relax*.'

Strike rolled his eyes. Nothing made him more tense than relaxing.

'Yo, Rodney, Rodney, you know what?' said a kid whose sweat suit was so thin and cheap it looked as if he was wearing pajamas. 'Jason the baddest, 'cause Jason be dead already, so you can't kill him.'

'Freddy dead too!' bellowed another kid. 'Freddy dead too!'

'Gah-damn Jason fuck Freddy up, man, he'd just fuck him up.'

Rodney straightened, arching his back and pushing out his stomach. 'Yeah, well, I tell you who the baddest. The baddest is *me* 'cause I'm for *real*, so why don't you all go out to the van and get the rest a them sodas before I drop some heavy violence on your ass.' Watching three of the kids mill out the door, Rodney unbuckled the weightlifter's belt and dropped it between the wall and the refrigerator.

Strike took his measure – the sweat-blotched, gaudy T-shirt, the dark blue polyester warm-up pants with white piping down the leg, a loud gold ID bracelet on one wrist, six rubber bands on the other – Strike thinking, Goddamn, where do all the money go?

Rodney frowned down at his son in the stroller, clucking his tongue in disgust, snatching the Pay Day sucker away from him and moving to the shelves behind the counter.

'What you let him have this shit for?' Rodney crabbed at his daughter as he pulled down a Frosted Flakes box, ripped it open and dropped it in the baby's lap. 'Where's his ma at?' But Strike could see that Rodney wasn't really interested in getting an answer. Rodney considered himself the only responsible adult in the world, a notion that he cherished, like his diplomas.

The Yoo-Hoo quarters were still on the glass counter. Rodney absently swept them into his pocket and nodded to Strike. 'Let's go.'

He took two steps to the door, then wheeled back, snapping his fingers and sliding past his blank-faced daughter again, squatting down behind the counter and coming up with a Toys R Us shopping bag folded over and Scotch-taped into the size and shape of a double bread loaf. From the bulk, Strike figured the bag held about twenty-odd thousand, probably in twenties and smaller bills, the money explaining the rubber bands on Rodney's wrist.

But before Rodney could make it out to the street, his beeper went off and he stopped in the doorway, squinting down at the numbers coming up on his hip.

Strike stole a peek: just two zeros. Rodney scratched his neck, made a face and returned the Toys R Us bag under the counter. He walked Strike out of the store with a palm on the small of his back, stood out in the night with him, humming something tuneless.

Rodney started to shadowbox. 'Futon's a little immature yet, so why don't you go back to the benches before he fucks everything up, you know what I'm sayin'?'

Inexplicably disappointed, Strike shrugged. For a moment they watched the traffic on the boulevard, Strike musing on the fact that Rodney was about the only guy in town who could leave a kilo's worth of cash with a mopey teenage girl and not have to worry about it.

'C'mon by tomorrow night.' Rodney cocked his head, giving Strike a smile as if he could read his mind. 'Give them legs another stretch-out.'

Strike drove back to the projects, thinking, Shopping for kilos. How come and why with me?

2

Bored and bloated, Rocco Klein and Larry Mazilli drove slowly back to the Dempsy County prosecutor's office after a long and too rich dinner in a Portuguese restaurant way out in Newark. It was nine o'clock on a hot June night of a fairly busy year by Dempsy standards: forty-one murders so far in the county, almost all of them, as usual, in the city itself, a city of three hundred thousand mostly angry blue-collar and welfare families. Still, forty one jobs in close to six months was not exactly a tidal wave of blood, and tonight's biggest problem was how to look like they were actually earning their pay.

Rocco was slowing down on green, stopping on yellow, thinking back on some graffiti he had seen on an apartment door earlier in the tour, when he and Mazilli were trying to locate a possible witness on some three-week-old stabbing. The witness, who wasn't home, lived in O'Brien, a major public-housing tiger pit, and walking down the piss-reeking hallway to the apartment, Rocco had seen a bumper sticker someone had plastered on someone else's door: I WORK FOR A NON-UNION SCAB EMPLOYER. And under that, presumably written by the tenant himself, was a fierce Magic Marker response: LEEST I GOT A JOB, MOTHERFUCKER. Now, four hours later, Rocco was still marveling at the ferocity of the gesture, somebody scrawling that profanity on their own goddamn door.

Rocco stopped for a red light and found himself profiling three black kids sitting on a tenement stoop. The kids made Rocco and Mazilli instantly but toughed it out, swallowing their startlement, their faces going heavy-lidded, deadpan and unhappy, looking everywhere but straight ahead at the sky-blue Aries ten feet in front of their noses.

Mazilli leaned forward slightly to glance across Rocco's chest. 'Guilty, guilty, guilty,' he exhaled in a trailing drawl, then dropped back in the shotgun seat and waited for the light to change, his pinkie ring rapping a spacey tune on the roof of the car.

Rocco figured the kids saw all the gray hair and made them as Homicides; otherwise they might have taken off like track stars. The light turned green but Rocco stayed put, vaguely insulted, trying to draw one of the kids into eye contact.

'Hey you.' Rocco picked out the tallest of the three, a kid sporting red acid-washed dungarees, L.A. Gear sneakers with the price tag still attached and a Chicago Bulls cap jerked sideways. 'C'mere for a minute.'

The kid groaned to his feet – definitely holding, Rocco decided – and limped to the car.

'Let me ask you something.' Rocco squinted up. 'Where do you get those hats with the bills over the *ear* like that? Alls I can find are the ones with the bills in front. I looked all over . . .'

The kid shrugged, scowled down the street. 'All you got to do is turn them around sideways.' The answer was so straightforward that Rocco couldn't tell if the kid was stupid or just throwing it right back at him.

'Yeah? Let me ask you. We're looking for a guy, he wears two hats, one on top of each other, like this.' Rocco mimed holding a cap bill over each ear. 'You know anybody who does that? It's real important.'

'I knew a guy with two *heads* once.' The kid fought down a smile, still looking off.

'Oh yeah?'

'He was in my homeroom.'

'Did he graduate?'

'Yeah, but he only wore one hat.'

The kid looked Rocco in the eye, Rocco reading it clear: Fuck you too. Despite the challenge, Rocco let it slide, rolling off with a little wave.

The kid's play was pretty subtle considering he was living in a city that had always valued lungs and legs over brains, and Rocco was never one for coming down on a good mind out here just because a kid refused to kiss his ass. Besides, he was tiring of the streets and no longer had much stomach for the million little attitude contests every tour, to say nothing of the occasional roll-around or footrace.

In the beginning, the Job had seemed more of a privilege than anything else – getting paid to walk through walls and witness the wildest and most riveting details of human struggle – but after a few years you could drown in it, and what had once made you step back in awe could begin to slide past your eyes, as unseen as the air you breathed.

You had to be like Mazilli to keep it up out here after a certain number of years. Mazilli was so deep into the streets that he regularly hired his own informants and their girlfriends to do the shit work around his house and his war-zone liquor store, even babysit his kids. He paid them five dollars an hour too.

Mazilli and Rocco were an odd-looking team. Rocco was heavyset and ruddy, his usual expression one of sly expectation, as if listening to a long-winded but funny joke, and Mazilli was dead white and painfully thin, all blaze and bones with a teenager's waistline, a forward-thrusting blond-turning-gray duck's ass haircut and a humorless, thin-lipped pucker of a mouth. And while Rocco usually got by on the street with a laid-back talk-show affability, Mazilli counted on his naturally choleric aura to survive, although in the eight years they had been partners, Rocco had never seen Mazilli ever truly lose control.

Cruising up JFK Boulevard, Rocco spotted some unscheduled activity alongside the Eisenhower Houses: three plainclothes Housing cops stood on the street side of a primer-splotched Plymouth Fury, nervously stepping in place and trying to ignore a growing crowd of hotted-up tenants. As Rocco rolled up, one of the cops, Big Chief Scanlon, stepped up to the driver's window, his face melting a little in relief.

'Rocco, Rocco, how you doin' there,' Big Chief said. 'The fuckin' war wagon died.' He had one hand around the neck of a Latino kid in cuffs, and when Big Chief stooped to speak with Rocco, the kid was forced to bow too. 'The herd's getting restless there. Give us a lift?'

The other two cops, Thumper and Crunch, both wearing high-top sneakers and cut-off sweatshirts, started walking backwards to the Aries, the crowd getting louder, bold now that Housing was making its getaway.

The three of them slid into the back, big, quick, the suddenness of their bulk making the car buck and tilt. The last cop in, Thumper, grabbed the kid in cuffs and passed him over thighs until he came to rest on Big Chief's lap like a wild girlfriend. Despite the warm weather, the prisoner wore a varsity-style Troop jacket, wool with leather sleeves, DOG AROUND BOYS CLUB in chenille lettering across the back, the jacket dropped down around his shoulders like a shawl.

'Yo Big Chief, we watch the Fury for you,' some kid yelled out, making everybody around him laugh. Rocco, feeling the car lurch again, turned to see Thumper fly out onto the street, reach into the crowd, pluck the kid loose and hold him up by his T-shirt.

'Yeah? Let me tell you something, you E.T.-looking mother-fucker.' Thumper was talking close enough for a kiss. 'You *best* watch that fucking car. We come back to get it? It better be in mint condition or I'm takin' you for a ride, you understand?'

The crowd pulsed around the new confrontation, opening and closing in little waves, Big Chief bellowing, 'Yo Thumper; c'mon there,' the kid squealing, 'Yo Thumper, man, I was goofin', I was goofin'.'

Thumper flicked the kid free and backpedaled to the Aries again. 'That's *your* fucking car, E.T. Remember that.' Slamming his door, Thumper hung out the window for a last stare.

'Take us to the office there, fellas?' Big Chief cleared his throat, the noise sounding like a thunderclap, making the kid in cuffs flinch.

Rocco had known Big Chief since high school, had known him when he played semipro football, when he had spent six months in the hospital with a broken back, when he was a stockbroker and when at thirty-six he had become the oldest rookie in the history of the Dempsy P.D., and in all that time his name had been Artie. He had become Big Chief only in the last two years, since he had organized the Fury. All the cops in Big Chief's squad were given their street names by the kids they policed, and by now they had heard the names so often, they had started using them among themselves. Even their wives and children used them after a while.

Rocco finally rolled off, his rear view completely blocked by the kid on Big Chief's lap. 'You guys radio for repair?'

'We get back there tonight?' Thumper said, pausing to light a cigarette. 'We'll be lucky if the thing's only on fire.'

'Yeahp, yeahp,' Rocco said, thinking about how many cops, lawyers, social workers and politicians in this town he had known since high school – easily more than a hundred.

'What's your name?' Big Chief asked the kid on his lap.

'Stan.' The compressed space forced the kid's chin into his chest and his voice came out somewhat strangled.

'What's your name. Stan?'

'The Man. They call me the Man.'

'Oh yeah? You weren't acting like no man out there on the street. What you cry for?'

''Cause I knew you were gonna grab me and I was clean, so . . .'

'What you think, you're gonna get everybody all worked up, get a little riot going, get us all distracted so you could like, sneak out the back door? We'll arrest all your friends too. You want that?'

'No, you know I was *clean* so like, I got up*set*, you know?'

'You clean? OK, fine, we'll take you to the office, give you a strip search. If you're clean, we'll only charge you with the clips in the bag, OK?'

'That bag ain't mine.'

'Yeah OK.' Big Chief sighed.

'Stan the Man,' Thumper snorted.

'Who these guys?' The kid tilted his chin to Rocco and Mazilli. 'They knocko too?'

Rocco held his prosecutor's ID behind his head. 'Vatican Secret Service.'

'What? What's that?'

Rocco saw Mazilli smile out the window.

'They be Homicide, Stan.' Thumper delicately removed a shred of tobacco from the tip of his tongue. 'You kill anybody?'

'Homicide?' The kid caught Rocco's eyes in the rearview mirror and Rocco saw something working in his face.

'They're probably jacking off on the steering wheel right now,' Big Chief muttered.

'I got the tapes out at least.' Crunch held up two Rolling Stones cassettes, a Megadeth, Willie Nelson.

'Hey Big Chief, can Stan the Man sit on *my* lap for a while?' Thumper goosed the kid, made him bump his head.

'Awright, awright.' The kid sighed theatrically. 'I'm gonna save you a strip search. I got a clip in my drawers.'

'There you go.' Big Chief patted his head.

'I never did that before,' the kid said, his tone mournful.

'What?' Thumper and Crunch said simultaneously.

'I never did that before.' Rocco thought the kid sounded a little shaky this time.

'Never did *what* before?' Thumper scowled in concentration.

'Sell. I never – '

'Ex*cuse* me?' Thumper hunched up, mouth hanging open. 'You never – I'm sorry, say that again?'

'I only been doing it a month.' The kid's voice was down to a small mutter.

'A month.' Thumper bobbed his head in mock enlightenment.

'I quit, I tell you that.'

'Fuckin' A skippy you did,' Thumper sputtered with delight. 'Five clips? I'd say you just quit for at least ninety days, wouldn't you?'

The kid gave Rocco another look in the rearview, and Rocco saw that Stan the Man was thinking hard about a trade, maybe something for the gray-hairs in the front seat.

In the heart of the Sullivan projects, across town from the Eisenhower development, where he had been arrested, Stan sat handcuffed to his chair at the far end of the converted storage room that served as the citywide office for the Housing police. Protocol required that Rocco and Mazilli be in isolation with the kid, but the room was so long – seven unused desks between them and the Housing cops, all of whom were now clustered around the TV, sofa and refrigerator – that for all intents and purposes they were alone, except for a parrot that Big Chief kept in a cage right over their heads, the thing squawking periodically like a smoke detector, making Rocco feel as if he was conducting the interview in a pet shop.

Rocco watched the kid try desperately to come off like he was in control. Sitting back in his wooden swivel chair, his legs crossed, the Troop jacket still down around his biceps, the kid affected a hiked-eyebrow smirk, as if this whole situation was nothing more than an amusing inconvenience, the handcuffs an annoying but obligatory part of his wardrobe.

'So OK. Nelson Maldonado – where's he at?' Rocco absently swung side to side in his swivel chair, picked at a stain on his tie. Mazilli remained standing, sucking his teeth and squinting long-distance at the TV.

'Well, what kind of *deal* I got here?' The kid said, then flinched as the parrot squawked.

'Well, what do you want?' As usual, Rocco did all the talking. Mazilli was better at other things.

'I want to walk.' The kid smiled as if he'd been asked a stupid question.

'Well, I tell you what. You give me Nelson Maldonado right now, you can walk. I'll pick up this phone' – Rocco placed his hand on the receiver – 'call the prosecutor and work it out right in front of your face.'

'Sounds good.' The kid shrugged, but there was a pearl-size tic pulsing in the corner of his eye.

'What kind of history you got?'

'This my first arrest.'

'What?'

'As a adult.'

'Good.' Rocco nodded approvingly. 'Beautiful.'

Rocco walked to the other end of the office, sat next to Big Chief on the sofa, cracked a beer.

'Kid giving you anything good?' Big Chief spoke directly to the television.

'Yeah, well, he *says* he can serve up one of the do-ers on the Henderson job.'

A month earlier, a local landlord named Frank Henderson was speeding through a Puerto Rican block when he struck a child. He was pulled from his car by enraged neighbors and within five minutes of the accident, he was dead with a bullet in his brain.

Big Chief yawned. 'I thought you had the do-ers on that. The Gonzalez brothers, no?'

'Yeah, but this kid here says he knows the guy who gave them the gun and hid it afterwards – some fuck we've been looking for named Nelson Maldonado.' Rocco bent over to retie his shoe; when he straightened up, his face was red and his temples were throbbing. 'I want that gun, so . . . How many vials you catch him with?'

'Ten on his person, forty in a bag by his feet.' Big Chief got up from the sofa, adjusted the color on the TV; the two other cops, sneakers up, sipped beers and made wisecracks about the characters in 'Cheers.' Rocco felt a twinge of envy for the clubhouse atmosphere here. The Fury was a tight unit, all handpicked from the Dempsy P.D. – city cops working for the city. The Homicide squad in the prosecutor's office, on the other hand, was composed of a dozen investigators, and most of them – including Rocco and Mazilli – were detectives on loan from the City of Dempsy or the three other police departments in Dempsy County. There was also a handful of county appointees, test takers who had never even gone to the police academy, and the result was a cold and paranoid squad, everybody mainly out for themselves and those who came with them from whatever township, city or political tit that had been their point of origin.

'The kid wants to walk.'

'Hey, if he gives you Maldonado? We'll eat the forty, how's that?'

'Good.' Rocco stood up, took a long last pull on his beer and walked back to the gloomy end of the room. Mazilli had already paged the nighttime assistant prosecutor on call.

'So Stan, you and Maldonado, you guys good friends?'

The phone rang before the kid could answer.

'Rocco!' Down by the sofa, Big Chief held the receiver high and Rocco picked up his extension to hear 'Cheers' playing on the prosecutor's TV too.

'Hey, who's this? Hey Gene, how you doin'? I got a kid here says he can serve up Nelson Maldonado on the Henderson job. Housing snatched him with ten bottles on his person, forty in a bag. He's looking for a noncustodial; can I offer him a deal to walk if he pleas out on the ten? If he doesn't give me Maldonado, the deal's off.'

The assistant prosecutor was chewing something, the sound of which drove Rocco nuts. Rocco waited for the guy to swallow, take another bite of whatever it was he was eating and say, 'Sure, no problem.'

Rocco hung up and slid close to Stan the Man, talking soft and to his eyes.

'Stan, what I want from you is to know exactly where Nelson Maldonado is, right now.'

The kid opened his mouth but Rocco put up his hand. 'Before you answer, let me tell you what I *don't* want to hear. I don't want to hear, "He's in town." I don't want to hear, "He's on the boulevard." I don't want to hear, "He's on the hill." Right now, *exactly*. Where is Nelson Maldonado?'

'Where? Well, right now I'd have to say he's at this club.'

'*What* club.'

'In like Paterson.'

'What's its name.'

'I don't know the name. I would, like, have to take you.'

'Fuck you.' Rocco stood up, faked a yawn.

'Yo *wait*, wait. You said right this second. That's all I know for right this *sec*ond. I mean I'll tell you where's he's living.'

'Where?' Rocco stayed on his feet for the heat of it.

'With his father, but he don't like come home until like two, three in the morning 'cause of the police looking for him.'

Rocco turned toward Mazilli, who had been sniffing around the father's bodega on and off since the kid had vanished.

'Where's the father live?' It was the first thing Mazilli said since they got out of the car.

'On Ramsey, like Twelve Hundred Ramsey.'

Mazilli and Rocco exchanged a glance: the address was right. The kid could be telling the truth, and Rocco felt a surge of old-time adrenaline, although he'd be goddamned if he'd hang around until three-thirty, four in the morning to grab some piece-of-shit number-three man on a homicide – the little prick didn't even pull the trigger. After all, Rocco had a wife and child now; it wasn't like the old days when he had nothing better to do.

'So what do you want to do?' Rocco asked Mazilli, not hiding his unhappiness.

Mazilli put on his coat and uncuffed the kid from his chair, taking his time.

'Why don't you go home,' he finally said. 'I'm gonna be up all night anyhow on shit. I'll grab some guys off the midnight tour, stake out the house. We'll take care of it.'

'No hey, I'll do it.' But Rocco was just saying it now that he was off the hook.

'No big thing.' Mazilli gave Rocco his back as he returned Stan the Man to Big Chief's crew.

'I owe you one,' Rocco called after him, tossing off a small salute as Mazilli disappeared out the door. Thumper and Crunch followed him, escorting Stan the Man to the car. The kid wouldn't be eligible for his noncustodial until Maldonado was arrested, so he had to be taken over to County.

Rocco intended to go straight home, but then he remembered his half-drunk beer down by the recreation end of the room and thought: First a word from our sponsor. And two hours later, well past midnight, Rocco sat spread-legged and shiny-eyed on the Housing police sofa, watching David Letterman with Big Chief. All the lights were out and both of them were bathed in the shifting silvery cast of the TV screen. At eleven o'clock, the unofficial end of the tour, the beers had turned to vodkas, and for the last thirty minutes Rocco had been eyeing the Mr Coffee machine. But the coffee didn't pour itself, so nothing had come of it.

'Rocco, yesterday?' Big Chief whacked his chest to force a belch. 'Thumper raced with this kid in Roosevelt, some fucking idiot named Futon.'

'What do you mean, a chase?'

'A race. We did a pincers on the benches there, came up empty, so we're just sniffing around, bullshitting with the yoms, this kid Futon says to me, "Yo Big Chief, you-all can't catch me. I'm the black Jesse Owens."'

'The black Jesse Owens.' Rocco squinted at a plastic milk crate filled with harshly graphic porno magazines under the TV stand.

'Yeah, so him and Thumper raced. Right through the projects, Weehawken to Dumont. I told the kid, Thumper beats you, you gots to give up the stash apartment. You beat Thumper, we lay off the benches for a month.'

'So?' Rocco looked at the time again, the clock starting to feel like his enemy.

'What, are you kidding me?' Big Chief poured himself a little tonic. 'The kid's sixteen.'

'So now you're laying off Roosevelt, right?'

'Yeah, I was hoping those humpheads would think that. We grabbed some kid there tonight, killed an hour at Juvie, released him to his aunt.' Big Chief cracked an ice tray. 'War on drugs.'

'Dempsy burnin',' Rocco said halfheartedly. He hadn't broken into a dead run in five years, maybe eight.

An ad for the new *Batman* film came on the television, and it reminded Rocco of the sunny afternoon last month when he had taken his two-year-old daughter to her very first movie, just the two of them, some endless Disney thing with seagulls and mice. Erin had spaced out after five minutes and Rocco sat there filled with an anxious boredom, letting her toddle up and down the center aisle of the empty theater, yelling 'Lights! Lights!' and putting a finger on every tiny bulb screwed into both sides of the carpet from the front row to the exit sign, each and every one, 'Lights! Lights!' He had stared at the screen and fanned his knees like an insect until it was time to go home.

'You see *Batman* yet there, Rocco?'

'Nah, I'm . . . you know.' Rocco felt his voice go small, smaller.

'Last week I took Jeannie over to the Triplex? We go to see *Parenthood*, and *Parenthood*'s like in the middle theater. *Batman*'s on the left, *Nightmare on Elm Street, Part Sixty-two*'s on the right, right? All three movies break at the same time, it's like an Oreo cookie coming into the lobby. All of a sudden we're fuckin' surrounded, every goddamn kid I ever strip searched, busted, smacked upside the head, coming out of the other two theaters, we're in the middle with the white people? Like a wagon train. I'm thinking, Holy shit *I'm* dead, my *wife's* dead, but they're all around us, looking at me like . . .' Big Chief cocked his head and shot Rocco a goofy smile in the TV light. 'You remember when you were a kid, when you would see some teacher outside of school, it was like this amazing thing? That's how they took it, seeing me. They're all, "Yo Big Chief, Big Chief, you go to movies? How you like your movie?" This one kid from Roosevelt, Peanut? I must've busted him three times, Johnson-checked him a million times, I know his underpants better than my own by now, he comes up to Jeannie, he says, "An' you must be the lovely *Misses* Big Chief."'

Rocco threw him a glassy smile. Big Chief's wife wasn't even five feet tall, but whenever they were together Big Chief was all over her like the weather. He seemed so flustered with love when he was around her that he appeared to be standing slightly tilted in her direction, like a comic miming a drunk.

'The kid's leaving the movie, he says, "Yo Big Chief, you take care a her now, I see you on Monday, OK?"'

'I love it,' Rocco said faintly. He caught the time off the wall clock and experienced a stuporous surge of anxiety: Go home.

*   *   *

Rocco finally walked in at two A.M., knotted, loaded, hallucinating the smell of a scene on him, that sweet, husky, close smell of an indoor homicide, like watered-down Old Spice or a sweating fat lady – not altogether unpleasant, kind of intimate, the smell of a whole life opened up to him with all its embarrassments and little drawers. Of course it would have to be a relatively fresh one: last summer he had one job that had lain there over a three-day Fourth of July 95-degree weekend with the windows closed, and halfway down the hallway Rocco had to stop and strip down to his T-shirt and shorts so he wouldn't have to burn his suit after he came out of the apartment, the body so bloated with gas that he couldn't tell if it was male or female, white or black. He was bombed at the time, but he had saved a nice two-hundred-dollar pinstripe seer-sucker.

Patty was still awake. Rocco could hear the murmur of television conversation, and a bar of light beamed onto the hallway carpet from beneath the closed bedroom door. His stomach jumped with dismay: Go to sleep already, Jesus Christ. Tiptoeing into the vast living room/kitchen, he stood at the windows eleven stories over Manhattan and looked west and south across the river and into the Job. The loft had been a wedding present from his in-laws, their former New York pied-à-terre; apparently a garden apartment in Dempsy was some kind of punishment in their eyes. Rocco headed for the freezer to take a Breyer's Pledge, aware of every creaky board, tensing for when Patty would open the bedroom door and give him hell, although technically speaking he couldn't imagine what for.

Gazing into the freezer, he heard the baby whispering from her crib behind the sliding rice-paper partition. He exhaled through puffed cheeks, closed the freezer, eyes bulging in exasperation: What the hell *is* this, an all-night house party?

Rocco found himself thinking again about that movie outing with his daughter, how badly he had wanted to run out of there, but also how he had returned to the same theater a week later by himself to see *Predator*. He'd sat there with his popcorn, taken one look at the carpet lights and felt stabbed through the heart with longing for her, wounded by the memory of their spacey outing together seven days before.

Father and child: the image had never found an easy home in Rocco's mind. At his wedding, his father-in-law, only four years older than Rocco, put his arm around his new son-in-law, pointed to his pregnant daughter and said, 'Rocco? Until you're the father, you're nothing but the son.' At the time it sounded reasonable, almost memorable, but thinking on it later, Rocco had realized that although he had a hard time seeing himself as a father, he had *ever* thought of himself as anyone's son. His parents had divorced when he was eight, and nobody wanted to take him. His mother ran off somewhere with a tire salesman, and his father moved back in with his own parents. For an entire year Rocco was passed around to various relatives until his maternal grandparents took him for keeps. Even now, as a middle-aged cop, he still considered himself less an authority figure than some kind of pissed-off orphan with a gun.

Sliding back the partition, he saw Erin sitting in a corner of her crib, holding a zebra in her lap, patting its head gently and muttering, 'Oh, you make me so happy.'

Rocco looked down at her, outlined in silver, her hand moving steady and gentle, her voice sensual in its rhythmic reassurance – casually alert, self-contained, not even looking up at him. Two years old, two A.M.

'Oh, zebra.'

'Lay down, baby,' Rocco said softly, on tiptoes, rubbing his gut.

'You make me so happy.' Her voice was a groany growl.

'I'll be right back, baby.' Rocco moved to the freezer for reinforcements. Desperate both to be there and be gone, he took out a cold quart of Stoli and positioned the ice cream so he could read the Breyer's Pledge on the side of the carton. Raising the bottle to his mouth, he held up his left hand, palm out, as if taking an oath. He let down a thin steady stream of vodka for as long as it took to read the Declaration of Purity, all the bullshit about fresh milk and vanilla beans, from beginning to end.

A few months before, he had caught a hamster run, a black three-year-old boy hanging by his neck from a doorknob in the O'Brien projects, the face turned away from Rocco as if ashamed. The kid looked like a forgotten laundry bag, and Rocco took it home with him *that* night, going right for the freezer, not worrying about creaking boards. But then he'd overheard Erin behind the rice paper, chanting, 'Poor David . . . It's OK, it's OK, it's OK,' and Rocco, drifting to the crib, floating on fear, had said, 'Who's David, baby?' and Erin had looked up at him, her demeanor solemn, and said, 'Black David . . . He hurt he neck.'

That small exchange had been the closest he had ever come to experiencing the supernatural, and thinking about that night again, Rocco took a fast, unofficial non-Pledge nip, hissing against the bite and slowly recapping the bottle.

He stood above Erin, watching her scratch the side of her nose, a jarringly adult gesture. Even though he was hovering over her, face to face, somehow her eyes still casually avoided his, as if she was pointedly ignoring him.

'You want Daddy to sing "Michael, Row the Boat"?' Rocco felt warm with the Pledge, strong.

'No, donk you.' Her voice was low and smoky.

'"This Old Man"?'

'No, donk you.'

Rocco was gripped with the panic he often experienced around her, around himself. He seemed to be both here now and simultaneously five years in the future looking back at this moment, at the loss of this moment. He was always sliding past the nowness of being with her, throwing himself at her like a cranked-up insincere clown for an exhausting fifteen minutes a day or getting cozy with booze in order to achieve the proper mood, and from the time she was born he had felt that he was on his deathbed, remembering with regret how skittish and slippery his time with her had been. *Had* been, as if she were a hard thirty-seven and divorced instead of a two-year-old baby, as if he were eighty-six and senile instead of forty-three and slightly overweight.

'Rocco! Get in here, hurry!' Patty put a whipcrack in it from behind the door, and Rocco automatically started running down an inventory of excuses and defenses.

Patty lay in the old four-poster bed, her hair sea-fanned out on the pillow, her face all horn-rims and pearlescent skin, young immortal skin. She pointed the remote control at the TV, which was framed by the tiger maple newels at the foot of the bed.

'Lookit – that's him, right?'

'Oh yeah,' Rocco said mildly.

Some tabloid-style newcaster was interviewing Sean Touhey, a blond, thirtyish stage actor coming off a revival of *Sweet Bird of Youth* that had drowned him in movie offers.

'I'm not really interested in entertainment per se.' Touhey paused, neck hunched, mouth slightly open, the camera quick-cutting to the middle-aged gossip journalist, the old bird nodding narrow-eyed, hamming up her fascination. 'I'm interested in *info*tainment, *edu*tainment. I want both to agitate . . . and to heal.'

'Jesus Christ, was that what he was like?' Patty looked up to Rocco.

'He was OK.' Sean Touhey had spent three days hanging around the prosecutor's office the week before, waiting for someone to get murdered. He was researching the role of Homicide investigator for one of the movies he'd been offered. 'You know what he drove? A Volvo station wagon.'

'Wow.' Patty smirked.

'No really. You know, you might say that people are people, but that isn't always the case.' Rocco was surprised to find himself defending the actor; he had actually found him to be a little too verbal, too fragile for his taste. But Touhey's glamour had gotten under his skin, and for reasons he didn't yet understand Rocco had become eager to please and even entrance the guy. In fact, he had gone borderline doggy, and when the guy disappeared without so much as a thank-you, Rocco had taken it personally. What the hell was he supposed to do, go out and cap somebody himself just to keep the guy infotained?

Rocco stared at the TV for a minute, then turned to his wife. 'You knew I came in?'

'Yeah, I heard you.' Patty finger-combed out her hair, yawning.

'Well, how come you didn't say hello?'

'How come *I* didn't say hello?'

Rocco took in her incredulous smile: everything was so funny to her. 'No, I'm just saying, you know, the baby's up and all. You didn't hear her?'

'No.' Patty shrugged.

'But you say you heard *me*, and like, I was *with* her, so . . .' Rocco began to regret starting this, but he hung in. 'I don't understand. How could you hear *me* and not hear her?'

For a second Patty looked confused. Then she curled both wrists toward him so he could clap on some cuffs. She was fighting down a smile.

'What, I'm saying something funny?' He was unable to meet her eyes now, fighting down a smile himself, feeling a sudden flush of happiness at being home. 'This is not funny,' he said, clenching his teeth in order not to grin.

Rocco and Patty lay in bed, the cable box on his belly, Rocco flipping the dial, *Mighty Joe Young*, a variety show from Taiwan, Joe Franklin, Hair Club of America. Patty wasn't wearing the right stuff for sex, any of the silky options, just an old Brooks Brothers shirt, her father's no less.

On the nights they went to bed at the same time, Rocco would lie there and watch her go to the closet, watch her choose either silky slips or mannish shirts, like running up sex flags from across the room. Whatever the signal, Rocco would accept it: he could go from spaced-out to hard by the time she made it under the covers, or he could reach for the cable box. Either way was fine as long as she didn't think *he* wasn't willing, too tired or too out of shape for it.

Rocco ran his finger along the cable channels as if riding a riff on piano keys, stopping on an astrology phone-in show. He was thinking about the actor again, stuck on how burned he felt when the guy just vanished. But what had he expected, a farewell banquet? A tip? Touhey had walked around the Homicide office with a huge buttery-soft leather shoulder bag and a four-inch-thick calfskin date book – accessories from another planet, both beautiful and ridiculous.

Rocco had had a few brushes with celebrity himself – if you could call a dozen or so mentions in the *Dempsy Advocate* for various homicide arrests celebrity – and once about three years ago when he was still living alone in Dempsy, a local journalist had come to his apartment to interview him for an article, 'The Manhunters.' After two hours of talking, they had finished up with a fast fuck in the living room, and Rocco had been pretty pleased and excited by that. But afterwards, when she was putting her clothes back on, the journalist had burst into tears and said, 'Why do I always do this to myself?' and he had wound up alone, sitting on his couch in his underwear, staring at the wall.

In those days he was working the midnight tour, and he had fallen into the habit of wearing a sleep mask. He couldn't drop off without one, in fact, but after the journalist had left he had envisioned dying alone in his sleep, pictured the local cops, all of whom he knew, coming upon his body in boxer shorts and the mask. It would be the most humiliating scene imaginable, like coming upon an auto-erotic asphyxiation or something, and two weeks later, after having forced his way into a house, responding to a report of a woman possibly murdering a child, he had met Patty and decided for the first time in his life that it was time to fall in love.

'It's like three o'clock, Patty.' Rocco eyed his .38, which now lay behind a box of maxipads on the top shelf of her open shoe closet.

'I know,' she mumbled, not taking her eyes from her reading, something about myths and origins.

In the beginning – not now, thank God – Patty was always sharing the important books of her life with him, like *Black Elk Speaks*, *The Golden Bough* and *Hero with a Thousand Faces*. The books always vaguely hippie-ish to him, although 'hippie' was a word from *his* life, not hers, since she had been Erin's age when Woodstock went down.

'It's like three-oh-five, in fact.'

'What – you're going to tell me the time every minute?'

'Hey, fine, I'm just saying, whatever, but . . .' He tilted his head to the door, to Erin.

'I'll get up with her. Don't worry, OK? I do it all the time.'

'You're gonna walk around all day on four hours?'

'I do it all the time.'

'No problem then.' Feeling sulky, Rocco thought about marriage, how it should be an island of comfort. He liked that, an island of comfort. Rocco wondered what his marriage would be like in six months when he planned to retire. He had no idea what the future would hold for him except that he would be going out at half pay, about twenty thousand dollars a year. But Patty had a trust fund that reduced his full salary to mad money, so maybe he could just live off her, be a dapper drunk private investigator like the Thin Man. The Fat Man.

'I'm gonna grab something,' he said. 'You want tea or anything?'

'No thanks.' Patty gave him a quick look, as if she knew what snack he had in mind but didn't want to take him on at this hour. Still, her silence didn't make him feel any less accused.

Rocco got up, took another Pledge and then stood over Erin again. If he died at sixty, Patty would only be a hot forty, the baby a teenager. He had to stop drinking, get back into fighting trim.

Erin looked up, but not at him. She made a clicking noise with her tongue, over and over.

Rocco reached in, picked her up, held her high against his chest. The baby was wide awake, calm, but far away. Here I am, Rocco thought, I'm picking her up in the middle of the night, a good father.

He carried Erin over to one of the big kitchen windows and began counting irons in the fire: going in on Mazilli's liquor store, employment and security polygraphs, private investigator. But tonight those prospects all seemed like bullshit, the usual clichés, no hedge against oblivion in any of them. At times like this, with his days on the streets coming to an end, his nights behind a Homicide desk flat and without edge, Rocco often felt as if he was standing in an airport surrounded by his luggage and holding a blank ticket.

Rocco stood cheek-to-cheek with his baby and looked down at the city.

'Say, "Good night, taxis."'

'Good night, taxis.' Her voice was dutiful.

'Good night, bridges.'

'Good night, bridges.'

'Good night, crackheads.'

'Good night, crackheads.'

'Good night, werewolves.'

'Good night, werewolves,' Erin chanted, imitating his voice, beat for beat. Then, raising her eyes, she pointed up and said in an eerily precise singsong, 'There's the moo-on.'

'Yeah, baby . . . there's the moon.'

Rocco imagined looking back from his deathbed and remembering this moment of holding her, validating the moon in the middle of the night, being calm, tender and strong: a good father.

3

'Do you know that more young mens get killed on Thursday nights than any other time of the week?' Rodney drove with a long Vienna Finger sticking out of his mouth. 'This *cop* told me that.'

'Yeah, huh?' Strike watched the cookie shrink under Rodney's mustache.

'Yeah, 'cause it's like the longest time away from the last paycheck, so everybody's all strung out and it's kind of like the beginning of the *week*end, so . . .'

'Huh.' Strike wasn't really listening. He sat in the shotgun seat with ten dollars on his hip and twenty-odd thousand on his lap, the Toys R Us shopping bag like a lump of radiation as Rodney rolled through the red lights as if they were stop signs.

'So you got Futon running it again?'

'Yeah well, he's the least worst.'

Rodney had left the Cadillac in front of the candy store and taken his van, a hollow rusty hulk with two naked S-frame seats in front, nothing in back except a few loose orange soda cans rolling around on the carpetless floor, the lazy rattling driving Strike crazy.

Strike thought cash and dope exchanges were Erroll Barnes's department. He had wondered and worried about it nonstop since the night before, but now he didn't want to bring it up, preferring to be in the dark than be told to stop and sniff the motherfuckin' roses again. He assumed they were headed over to the O'Brien projects, where Champ held court. Rodney was Champ's lieutenant like Strike was Rodney's lieutenant, and Champ controlled the bottles in Dempsy, buying three kilos a week from New York, stepping on it to make six and distributing the six kis to Rodney and five other lieutenants. The kis cost Champ eighteen grand each for the three, but he sold the stepped-on six for twenty-five grand each to his lieutenants, making a profit of a hundred thousand dollars a week for a few hours' work. Champ had it knocked – no fuss, no muss, no sweating out a million ten-dollar bottle transactions. Champ even had four baby Rottweilers, each one named after a cop in the Fury. That's why he was Champ. Strike just hoped that when they got to O'Brien Rodney would leave him in the car, because he didn't want to know where Champ's dope apartment was. He could live without that information.

Two blocks into JFK Boulevard Rodney got waved over by a pipehead with two shopping bags. Rodney pulled over and peered down, his chin on his arm, the pipehead shiny-eyed, stinking, holding a taped-up box for Rodney's consideration.

'A waterator.' His voice dropped to the lockjaw bass growl that came from hitting the pipe.

Rodney stared at the picture of the water-purifying siphon on the box, clucked his tongue, reached into his pocket and pulled out a fat wad, lots of hundreds. He counted out ten singles, then tossed the box in the back of the van. The basehead mumbled something in the neighborhood of thanks and loped away.

Rodney drove on, saluting his street crews on the boulevard like a general, the clockers dancing in place, absently swinging their arms, smacking fists into open palms, yelling out his name, every once in a while dashing up to the van to ask him something, including one of his other lieutenants, who told Rodney to stop daydreaming and answer his damn beeper, they were down to next to nothing.

Strike didn't really know these clockers. They worked the boulevard, lived on the side streets and didn't do nearly as much business as the clockers in the projects – but they also didn't get hassled by the Fury, which only worked public housing. It cost Rodney four to five thousand a week in envelopes to keep the flow going out here. Strike knew that Rodney had worked out something with enough police in various squads and shifts so that as long as the JFK crews were discreet, no one would bust them. But the Fury wouldn't take a dime. Not that they did much more than harass when it came down to it – any night they grabbed as much as two clips was a good night for them. But they were still a pain.

A girl moved along the sidewalk in a mincing half jog, pacing the van, waving for Rodney to stop. The dragging of her high-heeled sandals on the pavement sounded like someone shoveling snow. She was dressed in a red bolero jacket with padded shoulders and a brocade pillbox hat, but Strike saw that she had that sickening gloopy smile of some bitch that'll do anything for a bottle.

Rodney pulled over, and she started in by making small talk and flirting. Then she got down to it.

'Rodney, I got to get this nice sweater I want. This girl sewed it for me, but she says she wants her money tonight.'

Rodney, heavy-eyed, grunted, 'Uh-huh.' The girl worked a gold ring off her finger, its diamond chip a pinhole of light.

'She wants twenty dollar, so you hold this here.' She gave him the ring, pointing out the diamond. 'You know me, you know it's real, see that? I'll come back get it from you tomorrow night, OK?'

Rodney exhaled through his nose, dug out a twenty, held it out between his fingertips, then snatched it away at the last second. 'You don't come back with my twenty tomorrow night, don't bother coming back at all, now. The ring be mine then, you understand?'

The girl looked at her ring, hesitating. 'What if you hold it till Saturday? I'll get you the twenty back Saturday.'

Rodney shook his head and gave her back the ring, the twenty vanishing into his fist. She didn't like that at all, chattering 'OK, OK, OK,' and coaxing the crumpled twenty out of his hand. 'I'll see you tomorrow.'

Rodney drove away from her, studying the ring for a half block, then stuffing it into his pocket.

He made three more stops, once to buy two factory-wrapped horror videotapes from another pipehead with a shopping bag, ten bucks, once to take a leak against the side of a building, some other girl coming up to him as he was pissing, saying, 'Can I talk to you private?' and finally pulling up on a side street in front of a shabby and dark wood-frame house, getting out on the sidewalk and whistling as if for a dog. A scruffed-up pipehead with a ragged beard and a dirty plaid shirt came out of the house onto the porch, a shard of wood sticking out the side of his hair like a chopstick.

'What's up?' Rodney rocked on his heels.

'I almos' finish, man. I tol' you I get it done tonight, right? I got almos' all the downstairs all cleaned up, *boxed* shit, *bagged* shit. You want to see?'

Rodney shook his head. 'You don't leave till you finish, right?'

Seeing no light on inside, Strike wondered how this guy cleaned up in the dark.

Then he saw Rodney take a rubber-band-bound clip of ten purple-stoppered bottles out of his pocket, pluck out five and pass them up to the raggedy guy on the porch. The guy bowed his head and retreated into the house with his bottles. Watching Rodney pass out the dope on the street as if they were cigarettes made Strike sink into his seat with panic: Rodney might as well wear a damn 'Bust Me' sign while he was at it.

Rodney climbed back into the van, pissing and moaning about the house. 'I can get five, six families in there we get it fixed up right, you know? But I can't get a goddamn home improvement loan. 'Cause I do it up front with cash, the IRS is gonna say, Whoa, how you pay for this? Then it's theirs, you know?'

Strike was silent, shaking his head, thinking of the other five bottles still riding in Rodney's pocket.

'You got to have houses,' Rodney said as he pulled into the road. 'I tell you niggers that all the time. This shit's gonna be over someday. Put it in houses, you can get off the street and still make some serious bread. 'Cause I'm getting too old for this shit and I got to make my break, you know? I got me the candy store, the crap house, and I got me four properties now like for rentals. Soon's I get the motherfuckin' improvement loans, I'm off the *street*, I'm in *houses*.' He nodded, tight-lipped. 'Give me houses, bawh . . .'

Strike didn't want to hear it: 'What the fuck's *wrong* with you, man, paying that nigger in *bottles*, drivin' aroun' with *bottles*. Let me know up front about that, OK?' Strike rubbed his gut, his face swelling with agitation. 'I mean god*damn*, Rodney . . . I mean Jesus Christ.'

Rodney smiled. 'I say to the nigger, I give you fifty dollars clean out the ground floor. So it's like this, do I give him five ten-dollar bottles cost me a dollar fifty each? Or do I give him fifty dollars cold cash? What do I do?'

'What you *do*,' Strike said, 'is you don't take a chance on getting caught holding. You pay the nigger his fifty dollars so *this* mother-fucker' – he stabbed a finger at the Toys R Us bag – 'don't wind up in a goddamn police locker and *this* motherfucker' – he grabbed his own crotch – 'don't wind up in no county bullpen. Goddamn, how you get to be *you* anyhow?'

Rodney was still smiling, off somewhere. 'I tell you what happened last week? I got pulled over by this new knocko team. You know that new flyin' squad they got? They got me with a clip. I'm thinking, I don't even *know* these motherfuckers, ho shit, what do I do now, 'cause I got so much violence on my goddamn jacket, they pull me in even with this itty bitty clip, I'm going away three years if a *day*, an' like this flyin' squad supposed to be the goddamn Texas Rangers or the Green Berets, you know? I don't even know what to say, they got me hands up on the car, this little old pink-eyed Santa Claus-looking motherfucker patting me up my legs. He gets up around my chest, you know like *hold*ing me from behind? Starts whisperin' in my ear, "I want a Cadillac." Just like that.' Rodney drove on, smiling. '"I want a Cadillac."'

Strike stared at him, waiting for more.

'I had to give him five thousand dollars and I'm supposed to get up another five for him tonight. After that, me and him'll work something out but goddamn, that little ol' clip cost me a thousand a bottle, ain't that some shit?'

'So why you carrying again tonight for?' Strike's voice dropped to a sullen mutter. He was thinking about the cop who had the message for Rodney, the cop working on getting a Caddy for himself.

Rodney just shrugged. 'I'm getting outa this life.'

'Houses.' Strike said it to mock him.

'Houses. You learnin'.'

Strike knew why Rodney was carrying the bottles. He was a damn addict as sure as any other bug-eyed dope fiend out here, hooked on being the *man*. The man? Rodney was more like God because of those bottles. He couldn't drive twenty feet without causing someone to bubble over with hope and joy. He couldn't walk into a room without every lost child in there jerking his way like he was some kind of magnet. All that from bottles: the bottles were the beginning and the end of it. It wasn't the money itself, because no one ever felt that way about a holdup man or some other kind of thief no matter how much they took in.

And Rodney was talking about houses. Strike could just see Rodney giving up his bad-man bottle-king glamour, giving up all that love, to be some landlord chasing down pipeheads for back rent they'd already spent on bottles, giving it to whatever new king had taken over Rodney's throne.

All the kilo men and ounce men around town talked about real estate, about getting out, but Strike knew they were all full of shit. They were all stone junkies like Rodney, hooked on a lifetime of hustling, of making it the outlaw way, hooked on their status as street stars. It was just like Strike's mother said when they'd had their big fight: 'How much is enough? How much money do you have to make to retire? Who do you think you're hustling with that nonsense, me or yourself?'

As Rodney trolled JFK, Strike conjured up his mother's face when she spoke those words, saw again the set of her mouth, the unblinking conviction in her eyes. She had been so sure of her knowledge that she hadn't even raised her voice. Well, now he knew that she was right, knew that he was probably no different from Rodney by now, hooked on the dope of recognition, of adoration. And Strike was just getting started.

They drove along a miracle mile strip of Highway I-9, one side of the road lined with carpet outlets, waterbed showrooms and Chinese restaurants, the other by a dark park bordered by a low stone wall. Strike saw the towers of the O'Brien projects about a mile ahead, but long before they got there Rodney slowed down, coming to a full stop on the park side of I-9 behind a Ford Taurus with New York rental plates. There was no one in the car, but Strike saw three Latinos sitting in the shadows on top of the stone wall and listening to a Spanish radio station on a boom box.

'Leave the money in the car.' Rodney grunted, getting out of the van. Strike did as he was told, then slipped onto the sidewalk, feeling jittery and exposed. He didn't know what was happening but would have felt better about it if everybody was indoors.

The Latinos slid off the wall, and the biggest one clasped hands with Rodney, Rodney drawling, 'Papi, my man Papi.' No one looked at Strike, not Papi or the other two, both of them wearing jackets in the warm weather to cover their guns.

'Where you been, brother? I beeped you like three times.' Papi giggled and danced nervously from foot to foot as if he had to pee. He was huge – six three, 230 pounds – wearing an orange Milwaukee Brewers T-shirt over baggy khaki pants. He had calico eyes, a mustardy cat color, the exact tone of his skin. 'I figure my man Rodney's takin' care of some heavy business. Your beeper fucked up, man? I figure maybe you dint recognize the number 'cause I was calling from a *pay* phone.'

'Yeah, I knew it was you.' Rodney's voice was a high singsong. 'Anytime I don't know a number coming in, I know it be Papi.'

Papi exploded into giggles again, tossing his head like a horse. 'Rodney, fuckin' Rodney, man.'

Strike saw tombstones and granite angels in the shadows over the park wall. He looked back at the Latinos' car, and the New York plates made him sick to his stomach: Rodney was getting into something here that might be way out of bounds.

''Cause we waitin' like an *hour* here,' Papi said, pushing it. 'I got fuckin' people stacked up like airplanes, you know? So what was it, like you didn't hear it when the number came in? You like looked down at it later?' Papi smiled, waiting for an explanation.

Strike noticed one of the Latinos studying him. He was a slender, baby-faced teenager, smaller than Strike. A black watch cap pulled down over his hair made his black eyes enormous. The boy looked away, spit a pearl of saliva over the wall into the cemetery.

Rodney gave Papi a backhanded wave. 'Naw, man, I heard it. I heard it every time. It's what you said, I was takin' care of business.'

Papi looked dreamily at Rodney for a beat, as if wondering where to take it. He abruptly reached behind him, elbow high, and Strike's stomach shot a red stream: gun.

But Papi only came up with a beeper that had been clipped to his belt. He pushed a button and it began to vibrate. Papi held it out in his palm to Rodney.

Rodney took it, turning it this way and that. 'Gah-damn, man, what the fuck?'

Strike saw the black-eyed gun boy disappear around the street side of the van.

'Sometime you don't want the beeper noise, that beep-beep, you know?' Papi beamed.

'Gah-damn, I stick this up some bitch's pussy? She can take a message and get off at the same time, ain't that something?'

The boy rejoined the group holding something between his ribs and his elbow but out of sight under his jacket. Papi was howling at Rodney's comment, staggering as if he was gut shot. The others seemed not to understand English. Rodney handed the vibrating beeper to Strike. Strike made a fast pass at looking intrigued but then didn't know who to give it to. The thing had a powerful, insistent pulse that made it seem alive.

Suddenly the two gun boys became casually alert, turning at the same time and leaning back to look down the dark sidewalk at a lone figure emerging from the shadows, walking toward the group, about a hundred yards off. Papi noticed him too, and his wet laughter subsided into sighs, then just a dewy smile. Rodney winked at Strike, Strike thinking: Ho shit, now what? But as the figure came closer – average height, shoulders hunched as if he was cold, taking small unhurried steps – Strike saw who it was: Erroll Barnes. Everybody made him out at the same time, became relaxed again, but Papi's jokey hysteria was replaced by a sober calm. Strike watched Erroll draw near. He was thirty-five but looked fifty, frail with close-cropped gray hair and beard. His face was deeply furrowed, like a thumb had plowed lines though clay across his forehead and down his cheeks. His mouth was a flat line and his eyes were both furtive and blank. He looked as if he had never uttered a full sentence of conversation in his life.

When Erroll was still a few yards from the group, Rodney raised both hands overhead as if someone had said 'Stick 'em up.'

'Papi,' Rodney barked, hands high, backpedaling to the van. 'Vaya con Dios.'

'Mi amor.' Papi saluted, then turned to Strike. 'My friend . . .' He smiled expectantly, an open sentence.

Strike nodded goodbye but didn't think that was what the guy was driving at. It took a moment before he realized that Papi was asking for his beeper back.

Strike and Rodney pulled away from the curb just as Erroll reached the group. Reading faces, Strike could tell that Papi had a completely different manner with Rodney gone and Erroll there.

'What you into here?' Strike asked. 'What was that?'

'What was what?' Rodney said, his mouth puckered with secret amusements.

'I didn't *like* that.' Strike pointedly looked out his side window.

'Didn't like what?' Rodney laughed. 'You just said you dint know what that was, so how you know you dint like it?'

The gloomy towers of the O'Brien projects were coming up at the next light and Strike braced himself for the turn. 'Just get the business over with and take me back to the benches.'

But Rodney flew right by the projects, then drawled out of the side of his mouth, 'Business *is* over with.'

Startled, Strike sat up, automatically feeling under the seat for the money. The Toys R Us bag was gone.

'See now usually I let Erroll do it *all*, you know? Carry the cash and take the dope, but tonight I figured I do the cash half so's I could show you the people. Let everybody get a look at everybody for future reference, just in case I got to ever ask you for some *help*. See what I'm sayin'?'

Strike was sitting in Rodney's living room on a plastic-slipcovered turquoise couch, keeping his mouth shut, thinking that as long as he held his peace he wasn't involved.

He had never been invited to Rodney's house before, never had the security status of 'house-comfortable,' and he felt both dizzy and alert: What the fuck was going on? He couldn't stay quiet any longer.

'But y'alls buying from New York people. Champ is gonna *kill* you man. You can't do that.'

Rodney, nude to the waist, stood by the refrigerator eating a chicken leg. 'Champ is cool.' He licked his fingers. 'Champ's getting his money. He got no complaints.'

'You can't *do* that,' Strike said weakly, too freaked to expend a lot of heat in argument.

Rodney's apartment looked like every other seventy-five-year-old shotgun flat in Dempsy: a small living room going straight back to a same-size bedroom, continuing back to a kitchen behind which, in a small T, were a bathroom to one side and a tiny bedroom to the other. There were no doors to separate the front rooms, just the barest bit of indented molding to define one area from the next, so that sitting in the living room, Strike found himself staring directly at a pink satin-covered queen-size brass bed twenty feet away and at the kitchen sink fifteen feet beyond that. Rodney had moved in here twenty-two years ago, Strike thinking, Big real estate man.

'You want some?' Rodney extended a Tupperware bowl full of chicken. Strike reflexively touched his stomach as if he was full. Rodney shrugged. 'You go on like this, you ain't gonna have no ass on you at all.'

'I eat.'

'Yeah, you a real pig.' Rodney sighed, then got into it. 'Look, let me tell you about Champ. Champ is on the street, but Papi's about *weight*. It ain't got nothing to do with Champ. What I buy from Papi goes out in ounces and it never see the light of day. I got people coming up from south Jersey, from Pennsylvania – shit, I even got me a customer from Vermont. I don't even know where Vermont *is*. Alls I know is I get me a ki from Papi so good I step on it three times and I can still sell a ounce for nine hundred dollars. And the goddamn ki is cheaper up front than the stepped-on shit I buy from Champ.' Rodney belched, hunched over, squinted into the refrigerator. 'Champ is bottles, so don't you worry about Champ.'

Strike dropped his forehead to his palms. 'You can't bring in no dope to Dempsy and sell it. Champ's gonna fuck you up.'

'Who said I sell it here?'

'Well, where you sell it then?'

'Out of town.'

'Where at?'

'I got me a partner.'

Strike gave up. Nobody told nobody nothing save for what they wanted them to know, and even then they were full of shit, just out of habit.

Rodney took a long chef's apron off a hook on the kitchen wall, draped it over his naked chest, fished around the kitchen, reaching into the cabinets, under the sink, then came into the living room holding a big stainless steel wok, a brown jar of lactose, an eggbeater and a fold of cheesecloth.

He sat down across from Strike, placing the paraphernalia on a heavily varnished driftwood coffee table. He rubbed his face with both hands and leaned back, his arms spanning the length of the couch. The matching couches were too big for the tiny front room, but to Strike it seemed that the room itself was too big for the room. Thick blue shag rugs, heavy tan drapes, cutesy statuettes of dentists and drunks and milkmaids everywhere you turned, a fake antique white telephone, three televisions stacked one atop the other, at least two of them looking broken, figurine lamps with suedelike pleated shades sheathed in plastic, graduation pictures, wedding pictures and more diplomas mounted or propped on every flat surface, vivid sunsets painted onto sections of driftwood to match the coffee table, a laminated Jesus holding out his heart from some more driftwood over Rodney's head, a four-foot-high stuffed pink panther like a prize from a carnival standing in a corner of the room – for some reason even that was in a clear plastic bag – and finally a small mini-bar refrigerator, which Strike guessed held dope, booze, money or guns. The whole room made Strike feel like smashing his head through a window just to get some air.

Rodney leaned forward suddenly, looking at his watch. 'You hear what happened to one of my boys on the boulevard?'

Strike was silent, thinking about Newark stickup men, Erroll Barnes, Champ, retribution. Maybe Rodney's new dealings were cool if he kept them out of town. But they seemed dangerously shortsighted, and Strike felt his stutter coming back even though he had nothing to say.

'This old boy like fourteen? He got dumped by a girl so he put some Comet in a glass of milk for hisself, they take him to the hospital and who do he call for, his mother? Hell no, he call for *me*. Ain't that somethin'? Called me first. I got up there like to tear him a new asshole, almost killin' hisself over a thirteen-year-old girl. I tol' him I ain't havin' no business with a fool like that, he better *learn* some things if he wants to continue on with me. Called me first . . .' Rodney palmed his mouth to mask a satisfied smirk.

'Woo-what you got me up here for, Rodney?' Strike felt as if he was breathing through a pinched straw. 'What's up, like juh-just . . .' His lips fluttered, then clamped shut, and Strike just let it go. Too much trouble.

There was a soft rap at the door and Rodney lunged to his feet. The apron, untied at the waist, flapped in front of him like a fivefoot bib.

Rodney opened the door for Erroll Barnes, who floated into the living room as if he didn't own footsteps. His furrowed face seemed as big as a balloon, and Strike sat frozen, never having been so close or even indoors with him before. Erroll looked at Strike for only a second, then glanced to Rodney for verification that everything was OK. Rodney shrugged and Erroll took a quart-size Ziploc bag filled with coke out of his jacket, laid it on the coffee table, glanced at Strike one more time and left the house, Rodney saying a soft 'Awright' at the door.

Strike felt as if Erroll was still in the room. He was amazed at how frail the man seemed – more shadow than flesh. And then Strike realized what he'd seen when Erroll was actually standing before him: stuck in Erroll's waistband, right over his belly, was a .38.

Coming back to the table, Rodney stood over the coke, chin on his chest, as he tied the apron strings behind his back. 'Ol' Erroll ain't gonna be aroun' much longer.' He said it softly, as if Erroll had an ear to the wall.

'He goin' up for sentencing?'

Rodney made a quick face. 'He got the Virus.'

'Virus?' Strike's voice fell away. The Virus, for Strike, was something out of the monster closet that struck at the heart of his lifelong dread of others, a ghastly reminder for him to stay true to his instinct for distance. The Virus wasn't a disease; it was a personal message from God or the Devil, and in Strike's imagination the messenger would look something like Erroll Barnes. Erroll's having the Virus was like death squared.

'Yeah, ol' Erroll . . .' Rodney sat down again. 'The nigger mostly smoke and bluff now, you know, but everybody so scared a him on legend alone, man, that people are gonna be walking tippy-toe two years after he's dead.'

Strike scrambled to remember if he had touched Erroll at all. He imagined he felt something scuttle up his thigh. He slapped at it, then scratched his chest and ran a thumb down his temples. He was sweating.

'Yeah, dint you see that white shit up in his mouth? That the Virus, man. Las' week I had to carry him up a flight of stairs like a baby.' Rodney shook his head sadly as he dumped the contents of the plastic bag into the wok. Then, measuring by eye, he added about two ounces of lactose, draped the cheesecloth over the bowl, slipped the eggbeater through a slit in the cloth and stepped on a quarter kilo as if making whipped cream.

'Erroll give up the needle a little too late, you know? All *proud* a hisself for going on the methadone. Tch-tch. That's why I don't sell that heroin shit anymore. Too disgusting.'

Strike hugged himself, his hands up under his armpits, as he watched Rodney make product. He tilted his chin at the wok. 'That Papi's?'

'Naw, man, this for Champ, this for *bottles*,' Rodney said with contempt. 'Erroll dropped off Papi's shit somewheres else. This for tonight's re-up. You all's gonna help me bottle this, then I'm gonna drop you back by your car.'

Strike didn't know much about Rodney's dealings on the kilo level, mainly the logistics and a little of his marketing strategy. He knew that when Rodney bought his weekly ki from Champ, Erroll picked it up, divided it into quarters and delivered three of the quarters to three old people who held the dope in exchange for having their rent paid, and maybe a little walkaround cash if Rodney had known them from his childhood. Erroll delivered the fourth quarter to Rodney for bottling. Rodney liked to do it himself, converting a loose quarter ki into anywhere from eight hundred to a thousand ten-dollar bottles. Every other day or so, as the bottles started drying up on the street, Erroll brought over another quarter. As a rule, Rodney stepped on alternating re-ups, sending the first bunch of bottles out on the street uncut, getting the pipeheads all excited by the quality, so that by the time the word had gone out and the first batch was sold, the second quarter was out on the street – not as good, but with a built-in market ready to snatch it up. And by the time *that* was all sold and they started complaining that it was weaker, up came the third batch all strong and pure again, the word going out and the ensuing rush to buy spilling over into the last quarter's bottles, which Rodney stepped on again.

All the pipeheads knew Rodney's game, and each day they tried to guess which quarter ki was out there. But even if they wound up with a weaker bottle, they still hung around because tomorrow's bottles would probably be better. Rodney made more money faster than any of the other lieutenants who put a heavier cut on their packages, because half the time his product was the best in town and because, as Rodney had told Strike more than once, 'everybody likes to find out what's behind door number three.'

Finding himself once again lost in a drifting list of all that Rodney had taught him over the last year or so, Strike suddenly remembered who Rodney reminded him of, the long-ago resemblance that had been nibbling at the edges of his consciousness: Wilson Pickett. Strike's father had had an album of Wilson Pickett songs in the house when Strike was a kid, and the singing face of the sky-blue cover was a dead ringer for Rodney's. Now, sitting on Rodney's couch, Strike recalled that when he was little, when he was five or six and his father was still alive, his father would sometimes throw back a few beers and call his boys into the living room. He would plant them on the green couch opposite the record player and sing for them, accompanying Wilson Pickett on 'International Playboy,' or the Impressions on 'It's All Right.' Strike's father had never been a heavy drinker, and whenever he did get a little messed up he'd never do anything mean or violent. He'd just want to talk about things, like how he could have been a professional singer, how he'd grown up in Jersey City with Kool of Kool and the Gang, and how Kool had wanted him to join the group, but he said no because he didn't want to leave 'you boys' mother' all alone while he went out on tour. He would explain all this to Strike and Victor as they sat on that couch all solemn and quiet, legs swinging, only slightly scared as their father would abruptly kick in on 'Ninety-nine and a Half Just Won't Do' or 'I Found a Love' with a powerful tenor that turned the living room into a church of regret.

Now Rodney removed the cheesecloth, carefully shaking some coke off the folds back into the wok and gently tapping the eggbeater against the side. He pulled out several gray cardboard boxes from under the couch, passed a box to Strike and opened one for himself. Each box contained a gross of glass bottles about two inches high and a half inch in diameter. Next came two plastic bags, each filled with hundreds of tiny purple stoppers. Purple stoppers were Rodney's street brand. If anybody was caught selling any other color in Rodney's territory, whether they worked for Champ or not, Rodney had the right to take away their dope and put them in the hospital – something he had only needed to do once, to some green-stoppered clocker about six months before, in order for everybody in town to get the message.

Strike looked down at all the piecework to come, thinking about how he was the only guy he knew his age who had no interest in or reaction to music, going back in his memory again to hear his father singing in the living room, with the nubby rub of that green couch on the backs of his legs, then snapping out of it as Rodney took a pocketknife out of an end table drawer, dipped the blade into the bowl and silently offered Strike a chunky hit. Strike just stared at him, not in the mood for jokes. Neither of them so much as drank beer, although Rodney had been a heroin addict all through the 1970s.

'Yeah, I got me a partner on the Papi thing,' Rodney drawled as he tilted the coke off the blade back into the wok, took two glass bottles, one in each hand, and dipped them daintily into the mix. Then he tapped them against each other, letting the coke settle, measuring roughly a tenth of a gram by eye. 'He's a real fuck-up, though. I just found out the nigger stealing me blind since the gitty-up.'

'Oh yeah?' Strike hesitated before joining in the bottling operation. It had been his very first job around dope for Rodney and he always hated it, but once he started, his fingers fell to it automatically, and soon he was lost in thought, starting to put the night together a little, figuring that if this other guy was on the way out, Rodney was probably asking him in.

'Greedy, greedy, greedy,' Rodney clucked, eyes on his work. They labored in silence for a few minutes, building up a nice scoop-and-tap rhythm, seesaw style, each one hesitating for a beat as the other one dipped, like two lumberjacks manning a double-handled saw. Between the two of them they were filling two dozen bottles a minute.

'Stealing from you how?' Strike asked flatly.

The door handle rattled. Gently, swiftly, Rodney put the wok between his feet, the cardboard boxes on the floor. The filled bottles vanished into his hands, then under the couch.

The front door opened and Rodney's wife, Clover, came in. She was light-skinned, a bit chunky with a flattened-down face, her hair straight and short, shiny and stiff, curling up on one side like a frozen wave.

Strike stood up awkwardly and bobbed his head. She ignored him, her hands filled with plastic shopping bags, yarn spilling out of one.

'You find something in the kitchen?' she asked Rodney.

'Yeah. I'm good, how're you?'

'The Lord's seein' me through.'

Rodney winked at Strike, and they both watched her move straight through the shotgun flat: first to the bedroom, dumping her bags and her coat on the bed, then into the kitchen, where she ducked into the refrigerator and pulled out a pink bowl covered with plastic wrap, and finally into the back bedroom, the only room that had a door, which she shut behind her.

Rodney pulled out the dope and the bottles again and got back to work. Strike knew that Rodney had been some kind of dope dealer since high school, but he insisted that his wife thought he just ran the candy store. He also insisted that she didn't know anything about the eighteen-month-old boy who was in the store every time she came in to talk to him, or about the constantly changing cast of teenage girls who hung around, including one or two who looked slightly pregnant. His wife was a cashier supervisor for New Jersey Transit, a notary public and an ordained Pentecostal minister. In their own way they got along fine, Rodney and Clover: they'd been tolerating the hell out of each other for more than twenty years.

Strike's back started to knot up from the bottle work. His thoughts returned to Rodney's greedy partner. 'Stealing from you how?'

'Stealing from me hand over fist, that's how.' Rodney turned his head away from the coke and sneezed. 'You know, Erroll won't hurt nobody no more? The nigger killed a TV reporter once – four, no maybe five, six other motherfuckers that *I* know of. I say to him, Yo, Erroll, this boy done stole my money, is *stealing* my money.'

Rodney hissed in disgust and shook his head, his hands a blur of bottles and stoppers. 'But Erroll's all worried about dyin' now, you know, he's feeling *bad*'n shit about his life, like he's gonna make amends and not do nothing bad no more.' Rodney laughed. 'The motherfucker startin' to sound like my goddamn *wife*.'

Strike nodded. 'Lot of people think heaven is in this bo-bowl, here. That's all the heaven they want.'

'I tell you one thing, bawh.' Rodney passed a finger alongside his nose. 'If God invented anything better'n drugs, he kept it for hisself. That's the *damn* truth.'

Strike rolled his eyes: this was Rodney's second-favorite saying, right behind 'A dime's a dime.'

They went back to working in silence for a while, about two hundred bottles ready to sell, maybe six, seven hundred more still in the bowl.

'Yeah, ol' Erroll . . . Right about now I just pay him to walk around scare the piss out the people with that damn *face* of his.'

Strike held his peace, waiting Rodney out.

'See, people get killed around here 'cause they can't see two minutes in front of they nose. Somethin' feels good *now*, that's all they want to know about. But you know, if you fuck that girl her boyfriend gonna *kill* you. If you get high off that product you supposed to be sellin', if you get greedy, go into business for yourself when you supposed to be out there for the man, well, the *man* gonna kill you.'

Yeah, Strike thought, and that's exactly what Rodney's pulling on Champ. Fucking Rodney should be talking into a mirror right now.

Suddenly Rodney put down the bottles, lifted his hands and let them drop on his kneecaps, as if he was too upset to go on. 'Goddamn greedy motherfucker.'

Strike worked faster as a way of keeping still, sensing that Rodney was finally about to spell it out.

'That boy do nothin' but lay back, pass some baggies, rake in the dough. We clearing two hundred a ounce each, me an him, *sell*in' maybe seventy ounces a week. Nice indoors work, clean, safe, all the dope heading out of town, out of state, Jersey City, New Hampshire. Shit, it almos' legitimate the way we got it set up.'

Allowing for the lying-dope-dealer factor, Strike figured thirty-five ounces at about a hundred each. Strike found himself starting to fume: Are you telling me something or are you asking me something? He didn't know what he would say if it was *ask*.

'We got no hassles with the knockos, no ten dollars here, ten dollars there, no pipeheads all licky-lipped with their greezy little eyes. I tell you, man, it's sweet.'

Strike dreamed his dream: no more bench, no more retail, no more Fury. But right behind it came a newspaper photograph of a maverick dealer who set himself up in Dempsy last year and was found by the police with the brass peephole of his apartment door embedded in his face, courtesy of a shotgun blast from the hallway. Fucking with Champ: Strike was torn between visions of paradise and survival.

'Least it *was* sweet, but the nigger a thief, so like, you know.' Rodney stared at Strike as if looking at someone through blasted black earth. Strike stared back at him, as still as a cat.

Rodney cocked his head and spoke with a terrible softness. 'He got to be got.'

And there it was. Strike had been thinking all along that Rodney was about to offer him something for free, had been debating with himself whether to pass it up, but now Rodney was telling him that it would cost to get in on this partnership and that the cost was high to the point of stupidity. And despite his passion for prudence, Strike suddenly couldn't imagine saying no.

Got to be got. No one had ever challenged him with something like this, but he couldn't think clearly now, couldn't mount any arguments and instead was reduced to blindly searching for something he knew was inside him, an impulse that as yet had no name.

'Yeah, ol' Erroll want to go to heaven, ain't that a bitch? Useless Virus-ass motherfucker – after all I done for him.'

Strike stumbled for a second: maybe Rodney was talking about taking out Erroll all this time. But that didn't make sense. Rodney was just underlining the problem. Well, who was this partner he was talking about? But it didn't make a difference yet. It was a secondary consideration right now.

Strike tried to examine the pros and cons, the Fury versus Champ, the relative jail time for selling bottles versus ounces. But pounding up from under the practical concerns, his heart was quick with colors, brilliant colors that had nothing to do with business, with judgment. He was a virgin in some areas of experience, and somewhere inside his head, inarticulate but powerful, was the understanding that all his life he had it building in him – the stammer, the burning in his gut, the crazed cautiousness, the dicky checks, the minute-to-minute rage and disgust, all begging for an outlet just like the one being offered him right now.

'And you gonna fall *out* when I tell you who I'm talking about too.'

Strike knew that Rodney was trying to tantalize him, draw him in. But there was no need for that now. Strike was so unmanned, so filled with a primitive recognition, that his hands were shaking. 'You sellin' this shit out of town, right?' They were just words.

'Just about,' Rodney said pleasantly. 'Just about.'

'Yeah . . . huh.'

'Say, what the fuck you doin'!' Rodney's voice climbed to a raw squawk.

'What . . .' Strike jerked as if an alarm had gone off.

'Lookit.' Rodney pointed at the last one hundred bottles Strike had stoppered. He had forgotten to put in the coke.

Strike stared at the empty vials and shook his head. He wondered if this was what it felt like to get high.

After Rodney dropped him off by his car, Strike drove back to the benches, forgetting to perk up at the red lights, forgetting the Newark stickup artists, even flooring it a little on the boulevard.

Strike had been so overwhelmed with his decision to get wet and do this that at first he hadn't given the target more than a passing thought. But when Rodney dropped Darryl Adams's name Strike had almost fallen down, stumbling backwards against the coffee table, and flopped into the easy chair.

Darryl Adams: the hardest-working and least-smiling kid in the history of the grocery business. Strike had worked with him six, seven days a week for an entire year in Rodney's Place, and he had been the only guy who had ever made Strike feel like a frivolous fuck-up.

Darryl Adams. Goddamn Darryl Adams. Strike thought of his mother, spoke to her out loud – 'What you think of him *now*?' – even though she didn't know Darryl from the mayor of Dempsy.

Darryl had been selling ounces for Rodney out of Ahab's, the fast-food hole three blocks from Rodney's store. Trying to figure out why the ounces were selling so slowly, Rodney had found out that Darryl had picked up a second supplier, a white guy in Bayonne who had offered him a forty percent commission to Rodney's thirty-five. For the last two months Darryl had been alternating ounces, half the time selling Bayonne weight to Rodney's customers, telling Rodney business was slow and risking his life for an extra five percent cut.

Steamed up, breathing through his nose, Strike drove blind toward the benches. Fucking Rodney, calls me 'my son,' then puts me on the street like some ice cream man, and Darryl's indoors selling ounces like a human being. Well, you get what you sow. Strike conjured up snapshot memories of Darryl: sorting candy bars, stacking Chore Boys, hauling out trash bags.

He spoke to his mother again, to Rodney: 'Yeah? Well, what do you think about him *now*?'

My son. Shoot Rodney too.

Not bothering to stash his car in the old lady's driveway, Strike pulled up to the curb hard by the semicircle of benches that cupped the entrance to the central walkway of the Roosevelt projects like a yawning mouth. It was ten-thirty and the place was rocking now that the Fury were downing various heart medicines at the Pavonia Tavern. The clockers had their bottles in bags under benches and in the grass, using tonight's apartment only to re-up whole clips or more, giving the mule eighty dollars out of the hundred sold to go upstairs and bring down another ten bottles.

They were selling Redi Rocks this evening, precooked nuggets ready to smoke, purer than crack and no mystery ingredients like Raid or formaldehyde. But having the rocks in hand, ready to burn, made some customers itchy to be high right *now*, and people were piping up on the street, on the corner, up against a building breeze-way, crouched down between parked cars, their faces flaring up yellow as they fired up the cocaine.

Futon saw Strike fuming in his car and reluctantly came up to the window. 'I just sent out for another twenty clips. It feel like somebody won the *numbers* out here, the way it going.'

Strike counted three pipeheads lighting up in plain sight. 'Look at that.'

'What?'

'What's wrong with you? Get them motherfuckers out of here.'

Futon stood up straight, curling his hands under the belly of his shirt, taking in the pipeheads and making a face, clucking his tongue, doing nothing.

'Get them the fuck out of here.' Strike flicked his hand.

'They ain't doin' nothin'.'

'We got families up and down here. This look like shit, stupid.' To Strike, selling bottles was clean, no more than a handshake, but piping up was dangerous to the crew – they might as well put up neon signs. Plus, he found it disgusting to look at.

'I go look for Hammer.' Futon backed away from the car, glancing around for the nighttime muscle and security man.

Livid now, Strike jumped out of his car and sprinted toward a pipehead lighting up while leaning against 8 Weehawken. Strike picked up speed as he moved, breaking into a dead run the last ten feet, the pipehead holding a lungful of coke as Strike rammed him in the chest with both hands. The dope expelled in a white cloud of shock, and the doper went down, Strike kicking him under the armpit, the guy gasping, 'Yo wait, wait.'

Strike hissed, 'Next time I see you, I will *kill* you.' He marched back past two other startled dopers, one backing away, the other running, and Strike lunged two steps off his march to take a swinging slap at the doper who didn't run, missing him, but the guy got the message and took off. Strike came back to the curb and found Futon and Hammer standing there, blinking, mouths open. Hammer, big but stupid, said, 'What you want me to do?' Strike didn't answer, just got back into his car and drove off, thinking, If I do take care of this other thing about Darryl, Futon'll run this corner into the ground, but then thinking, So what – it won't be my problem if he does.

Strike was pumped up from the beating and didn't want to work the bench tonight, didn't want to see Futon's face. He drove in square circles around the neighborhood for a while before deciding to get out of town altogether, go across the river to the Bronx, see Crystal.

Strike hated going through the tunnels to New York. Port Authority cops were sometimes parked by the toll booths, profiling the drivers and stopping whoever looked like they might be transporting. Recently he had heard two guys talking about a secret radar-TV scanner the cops had that could somehow videotape what was going on inside the car once you were actually in the tunnel, so that if you were getting high or just being three niggers laughing a lot, you could get pulled over when you came out the other side. Nothing had ever happened to Strike, but he always rolled into the Manhattan streets or out to Jersey City with a backache from trying so hard to come across blank.

Driving up the Henry Hudson Parkway, with Dempsy across the neon-black river now, he transferred his gun from the step well to his belt – this being New York, an exception to any rule you had for conducting yourself. The streets that took him from the Cross Bronx Expressway exit to the garage near Crystal's house were unrelieved stretches of blasted moonscape. They always filled him with awe: every broken block was spoken for, every dead building a different nation, a different drug. Colombian, Dominican, Jamaican; pot, heroin, coke; weight, bottles, nickel bags. He never stopped for a red light here, just treated it as a slow-down signal. He had New Jersey plates and that made him a customer, a mark, and the streets were crawling with crackheads emerging from the shadows, silent and purposeful, pop-eyed, pushing shopping carts for scavenged booty, rinsing out soda cans, beer bottles, even washing off stolen car tires in open hydrants, which flooded the gutters with billowing arcs of water.

Most of the streetlamps were out and the disembodied glow of flaring pipes sent up jerky constellations between buildings, in vacant lots and under the odd tree. Here the clockers worked mostly indoors, set up security gauntlets with guys hanging out in front of the buildings, on up the stairs and straight into the apartments. The ownership of the streets was not in question, and even with his gun Strike felt like an outraged citizen, a potential victim. He never considered himself a criminal: clocking was just what he did, what he considered his best shot at having a life, like going into the army or working for UPS. But this place was out of control, these people should be punished, and he wished the New York knockos would do something about it.

Crystal's apartment house was on a bad block, but not so bad that there wasn't more than one kind of life on it. There were some dope houses in the dirty blond brick apartment buildings and so a lot of robberies, three or four killings a year, a rivalry or turf battle sometimes spilling over into the street. But there were no dope crews on the sidewalk and no abandoned buildings. Most of the people here worked for a living, and kids played outside all day and late into the night. And after the dinner hour, the adults would drag out fold-up aluminum beach chairs, drink beer and make small talk around the stoops and courtyard entrances.

Crystal was like a lot of the others: she saw this address as a stop on the way to somewhere else. She was twenty-eight, had a six-year-old son and an ex-husband in jail. She worked as a waitress and two nights a week went to a business training institute over on Fordham Road, the school a big loft room on the second floor above a shoe store. Crystal studied basic computer skills and bookkeeping; she planned to hit the employment agencies with her double degree any week now.

Strike liked her because she was clean, not bummy, a working woman with a kid, holding down the world. She didn't drink, didn't smoke, didn't get high except for a little reefer now and then. Strike also liked the fact that she lived far away from his business, didn't know any of his associates. She knew what he did – not that he ever told her in words, but he had a gun, never talked about his work and always had money for her. So what else could she think? Besides, she had seen him in action the day they met. She had come to the Roosevelt projects to visit a girlfriend and seen Strike sitting on the top slat of the bench, apparently doing nothing but watching all this clocker action around him. She had gone into her friend's apartment, had left to go home six hours later, and there he was, still perched on the bench as if he hadn't moved. Crystal stood in front of him, smiling with that space between her teeth, light green eyes in a heart-shaped face, a sexy cat, saying, 'Don't your butt hurt?' He said no, coming off a little sulky, maybe shy, but she didn't miss a beat: 'Then how come you look so sad?'

That's what got Strike, her saying he looked sad. He couldn't say why but it got him good.

Strike had once asked her what she liked about him and she had said she just liked the way he seemed so together: clean, neat, not loud with gold, sitting there so alert, all serious and composed. She'd also said he was too skinny and his head was kind of small but then quickly added he had a maturity that put weight and age on him, so he could get away with it. For two days after she told him all this, he walked around palming and probing his skull, eyeing other people's heads, and came to the conclusion that Peanut's head was even smaller – that's why they called him Peanut.

Once Strike and Crystal started in, he made her cut off her friendship with the girl from the projects. He didn't like seeing Crystal when he wasn't expecting to, and he didn't want this girlfriend gossiping about his business to her. Strike would usually come by Crystal's apartment one or two times a week, unannounced, late at night. He would watch some TV, maybe eat a little. They would have sex, although not every time. He rarely fell asleep in her bed, but sometimes he stayed overnight and he always left her money. Sometimes he'd come over earlier, like on a slow Sunday evening, and he'd take her and her son for dinner on City Island and then to a movie on Fordham Road. He didn't like movies or restaurants – they made him impatient – but he figured that this, along with leaving them some money, was what he was supposed to do when he was with someone. In fact, he had no clear idea why he was involved in this relationship except that he kept waiting for Crystal to say something like 'You look sad' again to him – not those exact words, but something that would make him feel the way he did when she said it to him that first day.

Sometimes he got sulky thinking that maybe Crystal liked him more for what he wasn't than for what he was: he wasn't fucked-up on drugs, he wasn't about beating her, he wasn't about taking her money, and he wasn't going to give her the Virus. He wondered sometimes if her reason for going out with him was that he filled a gap without causing her pain.

Strike parked the Accord in an all-night garage, slipped his gun behind his belt buckle and walked two blocks, past corner groceries, past rows of older men leaning on building walls, past teenage girls sitting on car fenders and teenage boys doing loud and jumpy things to get the girls' attention. Her block was an ethnic stew – Puerto Rican, black, African black, even some Vietnamese – and Strike thought this was probably a good thing, since most people were not inclined to mess with anyone outside their own blood. He spotted dope traffic coming in and out of one building's deep front courtyard, but they were coming off sneaky, slipping into shadows, so it could have been worse.

It felt strange walking around with the gun right after talking about actually shooting somebody. The small .25 had always seemed unreal to him, somewhere between a toy and a symbol, but right now, passing all these people, the piece seemed to be breathing up against his belly, growing teeth. Strike found himself wondering for the first time since he had left Rodney's house if he really had it in him, either the coldness or the heat, to point the damn thing at someone's head and pull the trigger.

Strike walked up to Crystal's building, a beat-up 1920s beauty, white brick with rounded edges, also with a deep front courtyard, angular aluminum molding on the front door and half-moon door handles. He stepped into the wide lobby, with its spare Navaho floor design and its curdled green stucco walls under naked fluorescent bar lights, and headed for the elevator but then saw a white guy talking to a young Latino smeared head to toe with dried plaster. Reading 'cop,' Strike veered toward the stairs, but the white guy called out, 'Hey, you, wait a minute, wait a minute,' and stopped him dead in his tracks.

Strike had never seen this guy before, but he had a vague recollection of Crystal once telling him that the super here was a moonlighting cop, Ralphie or Malphie, and this had to be him. The guy was forty or so, sandy-haired, cowboy lean, wearing dungarees, construction boots and a plaid shirt with rolled-up sleeves, revealing on one forearm a tattoo of a scroll with a crossed-out name.

Once he had Strike nailed in place, the cop turned his back on him, put a hand on the elevator door and returned to his conversation with the Latino.

'So, wait, you didn't know you were gonna have triplets?' His voice was languidly dense, as if he was a little slow on the uptake, but Strike knew that tone came from the man's feeling of complete control. He had heard cops speak that way before.

The Latino kid was tall and thin. A corrugated-paper dust mask hung around his neck. He was too shy or embarrassed to answer, as if he had screwed up in some way.

'Didn't she have that thing when she was pregnant? That test, you know, what's it . . .'

'Yeah,' he murmured.

'So didn't you hear three heartbeats?' The cop sounded casual and interrogatory at the same time.

The kid shrugged, blushing, dying to go back to work.

'Jesus,' the cop drawled, 'what did the doctor say?'

'He thought it was a boy, a strong boy,' the kid said in a quick burst.

The lobby was silent. The cop chewed over this last comment while both the Latino and Strike fidgeted on either side of him. The cop stared at the kid, shaking his head. 'Jesus. Fucking doctors, hah?'

Then, his back still to Strike, the cop slowly turned his head until his chin was almost touching his shoulder. He peered behind him at Strike now with an arched eyebrow, giving him the up-and-down.

'You hear this?'

Strike shrugged, said nothing.

'Unbelievable, right?'

The Latino took the opportunity to back away. 'I talk to you later.' He started down the basement stairs.

'OK, Benny. Leave the garbage for tomorrow,' the cop said, then turned around to examine Strike. 'Where you going?' he said, tilting his chin.

Strike hesitated, thinking how to answer that without giving him any information. 'Six.'

'Six what?'

'Six C.'

'Six C? You going to see Crystal?'

'Yeah.'

'Yeah? What's your name?'

'Dunham.'

'Dunham?' The cop had gray eyes, flashlight eyes. Strike tried to keep his hands away from his waistband.

'Yeah.'

'She's a good lady, Crystal, right?'

Strike said nothing.

'I'm Malfie. I'm the super here.' His slow, chewy way of speaking was like torture.

Strike nodded, hoping to come off shy.

'You made me for a *cop* when you came in here, right?' His tight smile showed perfect teeth, meat teeth.

Strike mumbled something like no.

'Yeah,' Malfie growled through his grin, 'that's why you went for those stairs, right?'

'No.' Strike was running out of evasions, his gun glued to his gut with a band of sweat.

'No, hah? What are you, a health nut? You always walk up six flights with an elevator right here?'

'Elevator too slow,' Strike said, his voice small.

'Yeahhh.' Malfie almost groaned with satisfaction, showing those teeth again, square like wood. 'You Crystal's boyfriend?'

'I don't know.'

'You don't know.'

Silence. And then Strike felt a blow of redness in his gut. He was desperate to touch it but resisted, the gun like a hot iron right over the pain.

'What's a matter?' The chin pointed again, the gray eyes narrowed.

'Nothin'.'

'You look like you got an ulcer attack.'

'Naw.'

'You have an ulcer?'

'Naw.' Strike waited a respectful beat, then asked, 'Can I go?' He was vaguely furious at having to get permission from this moonlighting motherfucker for next to no reason. This wasn't even Strike's goddamn *state*, but the cop just assumed he had the natural authority. But Strike assumed the cop had it too.

'Can I go?' He put a little more juice into it this time.

The cop ignored the question. 'I want to ask you something. Can I ask you something?'

'What?' Strike tried to stand up straight, the anger cutting down on the pain a little.

'I had this job out in Brooklyn last night? I get there with my partner, we got a guy in a basement, he was dead maybe five days. You'd think somebody would have smelled it, right?'

The cop waited for Strike's answer just like Thumper would, aping Strike's head movements, tracking him with his eyes. Strike murmured, 'Yeah.'

'Yeah, I would too. Anyways, we get there. The guy was laying there, we thought he was still moving a little like maybe he was alive, right?

Nah, it was the maggots under his clothes. It looked like he was crawling, you know? Anyways . . . oh, Jesus. Maggots. Blowflies. You ever see blowflies around a dead body? Those black flies?'

Strike quickly said no to get him going to the end.

'Anyways, we're there to make a determination, right? Homicide, suicide, accident, but the needle's still hanging out his arm, so, you know, it's an overdose. But anyways, we're there and all of a sudden, *zing*, I get bit' – Malfie slapped the side of his neck – 'by a fuckin' blowfly, see?' He tilted his head to expose his jugular. 'I slapped it, right? The thing popped and it was full of blood. So I'm thinking, I got bit by this fucking blowfly filled up with this dead junkie's blood, so . . .' He studied Strike eye-to-eye. 'What do you think, should I get an AIDS test?'

'I don't know.' Strike stared at Malfie's chapped construction boots, the anger totally replacing the gut ache. Yeah, he could kill Darryl Adams. Easy.

'You don't know? What kind of answer is that?'

'I don't know.' He forced himself to look Malfie in the eye. 'I got to go, OK?'

Malfie shrugged. 'So you're Crystal's boyfriend?'

'Yeah,' Strike muttered, almost losing it, unable to keep the heat from his voice.

'She's a good lady, Crystal.'

'Yeah. She a nice person.' He curbed the rage into a neutral tone again. 'Can I see her now?'

Malfie sighed, then yawned, bringing clasped hands high over his head in a one-eyed stretch. 'Tell her Malfie says hello.'

He opened the elevator door for Strike to enter, but when Strike stepped forward he closed it in his face.

'Sorry, I forgot.' The cop nodded toward the stairs. 'The elevator's too slow for you, right?'

Using his key, Strike opened the door and looked through the arched entranceway to the sunken living room. Crystal sat curled up on the couch, hugging herself in a cheap-looking pink bathrobe. She was watching David Letterman on the big TV: James Brown was slip-sliding across the stage in front of the interview chairs and screeching like a cat. The TV was on so loud that she didn't even know Strike was there. Already in a twisted head, Strike hissed in distaste at the pile of light blue plastic dishes sitting unwashed in the sink. A piece of dirty masking tape ran across a tear in one of the vinyl-covered kitchen chairs, and Strike saw that the ironing board still stood out in the living room, as if she had decided to consider it furniture after all these weeks.

Crystal's chubby six-year-old son, José, came running down the hallway. Behind him Strike could make out a Yogi Bear video on a smaller TV in his bedroom. The kid stopped short on seeing him, looking a little tense – he didn't like Strike, but the feeling was mutual and so not Strike's problem. Then he veered sharply into the living room and fell onto his mother's midriff, and Crystal jerked up into a jackknife. The boy held her face in his hands and whispered into her eyes.

Strike was angry at this too: twelve-thirty at night, the damn kid up watching TV. Plus, where'd the TV come from? There was no damn TV in his room last time, not a VCR either.

Crystal turned her head in surprise, her narrow harlequin glasses accentuating her broad cheekbones. 'Jesus, *knock* or something. How long you been here?' She smoothed out the couch on either side of her, and José jumped up, barreled out of the living room past Strike and back down the hallway to his bedroom.

'You should tell me sometime, you know, 'cause all I got in the house is dry cereal and coffee now.' She spoke to him in a softly reproachful tone. Strike saw a roach on the wall space between the dish rack and the bottom of the cabinet and quickly looked away. Sighing, he moved to the refrigerator and took out a vanilla Yoo-Hoo, one he had stashed way in back, rolling it between his palms to take out the chill.

Crystal shuffled into the kitchen, her hand closing her robe over her legs. She looked at him through narrowed eyes. 'You OK?'

The concern in her voice caught him up short: he thought he had put a cork in his anger on his way up the stairs. Actually, since coming in here, the TV, the dirty dishes and the wide-awake kid had all become problems that were more real to him than the run-in downstairs. Sometimes he found it impossible to keep straight what exactly it was that was pissing him off from day to day, hour to hour.

'That cop – you know, the super?' Strike coughed, twisted off the top of the Yoo-Hoo, took a long swig. 'Yeah, I never met him.'

'Malfie? Yeah, Malfie can be a teaser sometime.' Crystal's voice sounded a little too light to Strike's ear.

Strike blew air out his mouth, felt the sweetness creep like a sheet down his guts. 'A teaser,' Strike repeated. Teasing: is that what it was? He took out his gun, and for a second Crystal's face went statue-blank. But Strike just walked over to the Formica hutch in a corner of the living room, its shelves holding mainly junk – painted dishes, bobble-head dolls – and laid the gun behind a loving cup on the top shelf.

'Malfie, he's a good guy, you know?' Crystal rubbed her nose, her eyes wide as if she was afraid to blink. 'I didn't pay my rent for three months because the landlord didn't paint the apartment like he promised last year? But like, when he did I had to come up with thirteen hundred and fifty-five dollars back rent and I was freaking out on that, and Malfie came up to put the child guards on the windows? I told him about it and he just said I should forget it. He said the landlord never looks at the books, he's got like six other buildings in better neighborhoods so I shouldn't worry about it. He even gave me a phony rent receipt in case, you know . . .' She began braiding her fingers.

Strike stood in front of the wall unit, looking at all her crap. There was a white ceramic dinner bell with a gondola painted on it, a large scalloped bowl filled with matchbooks. How come she was talking so fast?

Strike was about to say, 'Oh yeah? And what did you do for him?' when José bellowed 'Mommy' from his bedroom and Crystal flew out of the living room, leaving Strike glaring at her trinkets, feeling the sweat cool behind his belt where his gun had been.

Strike wandered down the hall after her and stood in the bedroom doorway as she and José began arguing about bedtime, she clicking off the TV, he clicking it back on, back and forth like a comedy, the kid bellowing, 'You promised,' Crystal yelling, 'I said one more, *one*!' Then the kid did a back flip of despair onto his bunk bed and whacked his head on the side of the top bunk by accident, probably not hurting that much but fresh fuel for more sobs. The kid slept alone in this room, but Crystal got the bunk bed in there because it was free, offered to her by a neighbor.

As José thrashed on his back, both hands to his temples, inconsolably aggrieved, chanting, 'You promised, you promised,' Strike scanned the array of photographs on José's dresser and desk: José in a kindergarten cap and gown, with his grandparents in Ponce, on Santa's lap, with his jailbird father in front of the apartment house.

Crystal stood over José, letting the storm pass. She turned to Strike: 'It's almost one o'clock and he got school tomorrow. Am I wrong?'

The kid sat up, his little barrel chest rising high against his collarbone. Wringing his hands, he looked like a tormented dwarf. 'What does a promise mean, Mommy, what does a promise mean?'

'Turn out the lights,' Crystal said. 'I'll bring you a Coca-Cola.'

She brushed past Strike on her way to the kitchen. Strike thought she smelled like lamb chops. It was a close and heavy smell that made it hard for him to breathe.

Alone with the kid now, Strike avoided his eyes. He took in the bedroom window, gridlocked with bars and rails to keep José in and the crackheads out, stared up at a plate-size paint flake hanging from the ceiling – *real* hard to breathe.

The kid looked a little frightened by Strike's presence, his wails subsiding into deep shudders and sighs as he stripped to his underwear and crawled wearily under his Ghostbusters blanket.

Strike didn't know if he was supposed to say something, but felt that he should give it a shot.

'Y'all goin' to sleep like a *man*, now.' Strike backstepped out of the room. The kid didn't say anything. He seemed to hold his breath until Strike was gone.

Strike lay on Crystal's bed in his undershorts, hands behind his head, staring at a yellow butterfly revolving on the end of the sweep-second hand inside a big diorama clock filled with plastic flowers. A Japanese beetle was at the tip of the minute hand and a snail on the hour hand. The clock's business and clutter filled him with fascinated disgust.

The butterfly clock read one-fifteen. Outside the window behind Strike's head, a car stereo boomed up brassy from the street. Strike lay there thinking about how ever since he had left Rodney's house everything had been going wrong: first Futon, sloppy by the benches, then that cop downstairs, then Crystal, yakety-yak ninety miles an hour like she was hiding something. But the worst was Rodney himself: Rodney picking the wrong man to count on, then coming to Strike to rectify the situation. So much betrayal in the air, and Strike tried to think it through and concentrate on the rewards – being off the street, how much money he could be pocketing. Think it through, lay out the potential consequences, the advantages, envision the future.

Crystal came into the room, her quilted robe gone. She wore a bell-shaped shorty nightgown and Strike, studying her silhouette in the darkness, tried to guess the color. She crawled up on the bed next to him on all fours and looked out the window, clucking her tongue.

'I hate this. Every night they down there with those goddamn radios, like all night long.'

Strike turned over and peered out. The rear of the building was built into the side of a hill, and a junk-littered slope ran from the basement windows down to the street. On the other side of the sidewalk was another trash-strewn vacant lot in between two abandoned buildings, the cement-filled windows covered with red and gray life-size decals of windowpanes complete with potted plants, kittens and louvered shutters. Two clusters of people stood out on the street, one crowd hanging around an Isuzu Trooper, the other at the end of the block under a bodega's red and yellow awning. Loud music shook the Isuzu, and the heaviness of the bass line suggested to Strike that the rear seat had been ripped out to make space for the speakers. The crowd around the car seemed relaxed, but the people by the corner were silent and disconnected, as if strangers to each other. Strike looked from one group to the other, thinking, Crew here, customers there. He mused on the difference between walking out the front of Crystal's building and looking out the back window at this other world, this other reality.

'Yeah, here they come,' Crystal drawled with irritation. Strike saw a small bony guy with an affected street limp detach himself from the Isuzu crowd, walk halfway to the corner and gesture to the group gathered at the bodega. The entire bunch began to racewalk down the block and line up in front of one of the abandoned buildings, maybe twenty people all told. The guy with the rolling limp and another, bigger guy from the Isuzu gang came over to shape up the line, pulling elbows, pushing chests, getting everybody nice and compact and quiet. A third guy from the car crowd moved out to the street side of the Isuzu and, after making a big show of putting a gun over the rear tire, just stood there, arms crossed, staring down everybody on the line.

Fascinated, Strike watched as a Nissan Pathfinder complete with overhead stun lights suddenly came flying down the street, rocking to an abrupt stop. Someone jumped out and everybody in line held out money, the guy snatching up the cash, jumping back into the Pathfinder and rolling out of sight. Thirty seconds later another car rolled up, a Hyundai with blackout windows, and another guy hopped out and passed around either heroin bundles or crack bottles, wham wham wham, before getting back into the Hyundai and tearing off. By the time the Hyundai was two blocks away the entire line had evaporated, every doper into the wind, across the lots, around the corner, down the street, inside the deserted buildings – all vanished.

Strike said, 'Huh.' He watched the muscle take his gun off the top of the tire and go back to the other side of the car to bullshit with his buddies, the limpy guy and the other line-tender joining them as if nothing had happened.

'Huh.' Strike nodded, feeling that what he'd seen was as fast and efficient as a tire change in a racing pit.

'Last week?' Crystal whispered as if the Isuzu crowd downstairs could hear her. 'The police did a sweep, right? They busted so many guys, they had to put them on a city bus. It was on the news. It was funny because the bus had a big poster on the side for *Les Misérables*, this play?'

Strike blinked at her, not getting it.

'There's like ten bus windows with busted dope dealers in them over a big sign that says *Les Misérables*,' she said, pronouncing the French words as if they were English.

Strike was silent. Crystal hesitated, looking like she might be worried that she had offended him. 'They all back the next night anyhow,' she added.

Strike said 'Huh' again, thinking about betrayal, about how everything and everybody were just so much smoke.

'Anyways, they're down there all night with those radios? And you know, if you complain? You know, like yell out for them to turn it down? They shoot at you. My girlfriend almost got killed because someone the floor below said something out the window and this guy down there just shot blind at the building.'

Strike looked down, thinking about the dopers winging shots at the windows. He scanned the street and the corners, seeing one guy at either end of the block, lookouts he hadn't noticed before. Suddenly he got a pounding, a rush, an impulse that he didn't want to think about right now.

Crystal was still on all fours, staring out the window. Strike flipped over on his back and slipped a hand up along her thigh, up and into her, doing it slow, thinking, Like a gentleman. Crystal grunted softly, her eyes still out the window. She absently reached over and grabbed his dick, giving it a slow yank before coming away from the show downstairs to sit on him, closing her eyes now, lolling her head from shoulder to shoulder and making husky moans.

Strike was skeptical of the moans: she seemed to be lolling her head and making those noises in an effort to roll out some waitressing kinks in her neck and back. Maybe to Crystal it was either this or a hot bath. She might even be thinking about her kid right now up there, thinking about replacing his Coca-Cola with Tab because of the sugar. He never understood how women could do one thing with their thing, another with their head, all at the same time.

Strike glared at her, watching her ride him without making eye contact.

Or maybe she was thinking about Malfie. Yeah, she's got to be thinking about that cop right now. Strike pictured Malfie's teeth – 'Tell her Malfie says hello' – the cop going right up in his face, like saying, What you gonna do about it? But Strike didn't want to think about that anymore. His mind slid off to Rodney, to Darryl, to the dope crew downstairs.

Crystal snapped him out of it by putting her hands on the caps of his shoulders, making a deeper sound and lowering her head toward his face, her hair tickling his eyes. When she was about to kiss him, Strike got tight with self-consciousness. Kissing made him feel awkward, and he never knew what was expected of him – tongue? just lips? for how long? He wasn't good at it, didn't like it.

But then Crystal jerked her head back and straightened up, and even though he had been unhappy about the prospect of messing up yet another kiss, he felt disappointed when he realized that the kiss was a false alarm, that she had probably lowered her head just to work out the knots in her neck. And then he came, thinking, Smoke, everybody's just smoke. Crystal slid off him sideways and fell on her back, stroking her own belly and making a distracted humming sound. Strike lay there, blank with rage, enveloped in the insistent thumping bass coming up from downstairs like a monstrous heart: arrogant, invading, filling his head, drowning out the hiss of his own clenched exhalations.

'That was nice,' Crystal whispered hoarsely, and suddenly Strike was up, striding naked through the apartment, his wet and chilling hard-on leading the way. He reached for his gun behind the loving cup and brought it back to bed with him. Crystal panicked again on seeing it, but Strike ignored her. Tingling with the unrealness of it all, he stuck his gun hand out the window, turned his head away to the butterfly clock and fired down into the music below, the grip snapping back in his palm like an angry dog. He pulled the gun back in, dropped it on the rug, then flopped on his back, giddy and amazed. It was the first time he had ever fired the .25, and his mind was stuck on a single thought: That sucker was *loud*.

Chest pumping, he looked over at Crystal, regarded her frozen on the bed, heard her say in that sad voice of hers, as if in a trance at the speed of things: 'I don't think we should see each other that much for a while.'

Strike ignored that too, listening, the radio still down there but moving now, driving away, Strike waiting another minute before peeking out the window. The street was deserted – no cars, no crew, no bodies, no blood.

Strike drifted down. This shit was easy.

★   ★   ★

Strike had a nightmare: he was on the PATH train from Dempsy to New York, dressed all in white like a bride. White dungarees, white hooded sweatshirt, white high-top Nike Airs – everything spotless, crisp, dazzlingly clean. But then some bummy pipehead, red-eyed, stinky, pulled a big knife from the pocket of his ripped-up overcoat and started cutting people right and left, black and white, drops of blood spraying every which way, people screaming and crying, begging for mercy. Strike was up like a shot, dancing out of the way of the drops, trying to keep them off his clothes, people dying now, yelling for help. Strike couldn't stay clear, drops of blood all over him, yelling at the pipehead, cut it out, cut it out, the guy working his knife arm like a buzz saw, mowing everybody down, Strike's clothes a bloody bunch of rags, everything ruined, blood on his sneakers, blood in his goddamn *hair* . . .

4

Driving in for the start of Thursday's four-to-twelve tour, Rocco negotiated a road that was more pothole than asphalt, weaving his way down a lane of truck stops and Highway Department equipment sheds before pulling into the Dempsy County prosecutor's office parking lot. The lot lay in the shadow of the rusted and hulking Majeski Skyway, which spanned a flame-belching marsh that separated Rocco's office from a long-defunct coke smelting plant one town over in Rydell. The office building itself suited the neighborhood: an asbestos-lined snuffbox with a cracked flagstone and concrete façade, it was fronted by a dedication plaque honoring six freeholders, four of whom were either acquitted, convicted or suicides.

Rocco strolled into the Homicide office, jiggling the change in his pocket. He nodded to Vy at the reception desk.

Wearing headphones, her lips moving silently, Vy momentarily ignored him as she transcribed a confession off a tape recorder. 'Rocco.' Vy spoke directly to her typewriter. 'Is "them all" one word or two?'

'One.' Rocco checked his mailbox: nothing. 'Like "whatnot."'

Vy finally looked up, slipped the headphones onto the back of her neck and hiked her eyebrows to draw him close for a confidence.

'He's back.' She tilted her chin to the corridor that led to the squad room.

'Why, what happened?' Rocco sank back on his heels, thinking tripleheader, assassination, something volatile enough to yank the captain of the squad back to the office only three days into his two-week vacation.

Vy read his face. 'Not him,' she said. 'The actor. Touhey.'

'Yeah? I thought he almost died of boredom.'

Vy shrugged. 'He's back.'

'No shit.' Rocco straightened up, experiencing a small rush of excitement. He headed back to the squad room feeling light on his feet, hoping something would come in tonight.

He saw Sean Touhey sitting alone in the darkness right outside the interrogation room. Head down, elbows on knees, fingertips to temples, he sat as if in prayer, the buttery orange shoulder bag lying between his shoes.

Rocco walked up to the actor but Touhey didn't acknowledge him, apparently lost in concentration. Not wanting to disturb him or say something stupid like 'Hello,' Rocco studied the actor's perfect hair for a second, then leaned over his huddled form and peeked through the interrogation room window.

Mazilli was working on Nelson Maldonado. Both of them were chain-smoking, and the kid kept kissing his own fingertips, then shaking his hand in the air, the gesture a new one for Rocco. Suddenly the kid broke into tears and Mazilli waved him off in disgust.

Rocco recognized Maldonado from a year-old mug shot he had been carrying in his jacket for the last two weeks. The kid must have just been picked up in the last few hours; when Rocco had phoned in at noon, he was still at large.

Rocco could barely hear through the door, but he could tell from the pantomime that the interview with Mazilli had already deteriorated into no-win bullshit. He turned back to look down at Touhey. The actor had been eavesdropping, picking up interrogation techniques: he sat with his chin in his hand, shaking his head sadly, wisely, as if he knew something. A real hambone, thought Rocco, but he was worried that Touhey might be getting a crush on Mazilli, might wind up basing his character on him.

Rocco dropped into a squat in front of the actor and spoke to him in a confidential murmur. 'You know the back story on this?' Back story: Jesus Christ, listen to me.

Touhey made a wavering gesture, looking up to Rocco open-mouthed, waiting.

'About a month ago this guy, Frank Henderson? He owned a building on Dover Street? He just came from collecting rent from his super, and driving out of there he hit a four-year-old Puerto Rican kid running after a ball.' Rocco looked into Touhey's face, tickled that it was so close to his, this giant movie screen face in this seedy hallway. 'The people on the street went fucking nuts. They stopped his car, dragged him out, these two shitheads, they came up, one grabbed him, the other . . .' Rocco gently pressed his fingertip to Touhey's yellow hair, whispered 'Bang' and watched him flinch. 'Community action.'

'Jesus.' Touhey winced, entranced.

'The shooters we got, but everybody says this is the guy who supplied the gun, took it back after and hid it.'

'What do you call that?'

Rocco hesitated, not understanding the question.

'Is he an accomplice?'

'It's his gun, he supplied it, he's a fucking murderer.'

'Did the guy try to drive away after he hit the kid?'

'So they say – he was probably scared shit. White people drive too fast in colored neighborhoods. They want to get out, you know?'

'If he tried to drive away, then he got what he deserved.'

Rocco felt his heart break with disappointment: Another fucking asshole. But he just shrugged and kept his voice amiable. 'Yeah, well, the kid only had a broken leg.'

Rising, Rocco heard a loud pop in his knee. 'Another thing just to mention. The guy had a money belt on, and when we got there it was empty. You know what I mean?'

'No, what do you mean?' The actor was suddenly pissy, challenging, and Rocco sank with dismay. The guy probably thought he was a Nazi now.

'You want to see the case file? We got some good pictures.'

'Pictures?' The actor cocked his head, a hot curiosity coming into his eyes.

Rocco walked down the hall to the twelve-desk office, empty save for Rockets Cronin, one of the detectives on the four-to-twelve, and a middle-aged, silver-haired Latino sitting against a wall, wearing shorts, black socks and white loafer-style sneakers. He had a decent-size gut under a red tank top, and Rocco thought he detected a whiff of scotch.

Rocco ignored Cronin, who sat at his corner desk working his way through the five newspapers he read from cover to cover every eight-hour shift. Turning to the Latino, Rocco smiled. 'How you doing?'

The man nodded solemnly, pointing to the hallway. 'My son.'

'Oh yeah?'

'I take him down here. Dect' Mazilli, he come to me in my store. "Where's the kid?" OK, no problem. OK? No problem.' He swept the vision of his son away with both hands.

'Good, good. The best thing you could do for him,' Rocco said, thinking, Next to helping him escape. Rocco guessed that the guy probably had some bolida action, the Puerto Rican numbers, and Mazilli most likely had sat in his bodega all day, shutting down the game until the guy coughed up his son.

Mazilli wasn't especially good indoors, but he was superb on the streets in a way that never interested Rocco. Mazilli owned a combination deli and liquor store on the worst block in the Heights. He got tight with the populace, found out who had open warrants, played middleman between his customers and the sheriff's office, kept people out of jail and built up accounts in the information bank, the whisper bank.

'The best thing,' Rocco repeated. 'Right, Rockets?'

'What?' Cronin blinked up at him, a total deadbeat as far as Rocco was concerned, but with enough political connections to get away with calling himself a homicide investigator and wear a gun around his ankle.

Rocco pulled the file on the Henderson job from a row of green metal cabinets and started back toward the actor, but as he passed the bathroom he impulsively ducked inside, flushing all the toilets and scooping up all the *New York Posts* and *Dempsy Advocates* lying on the floor or jammed behind the pipes, hoping Touhey hadn't had the urge yet.

Following the same impulse, he walked into the evidence room right next door and opened a few windows. Thirty-odd stapled paper bags sat on deep steel shelves, each bag containing the clothes and personal effects of some of the forty-one Dempsy homicides so far this year. Every once in a while you had to let some air in; otherwise the collective aroma of blood, guts and b.o. coming off the shelves could make it a little close and disagreeable. Rocco straightened up the room, wondering why the hell he was doing this, feeling vaguely humiliated but undeniably high.

Out in the hallway, Rocco hunkered down in front of the actor again, studying his face, watching him absorb the crime-scene glossies.

Touhey sat hunched over in disbelief. 'I didn't think eyeballs were that long. That's real, right?' He held up a photograph.

Rocco duckwalked around Touhey's chair so he could study the picture too. Henderson had been photographed sprawled on the hood of his car, his gaping profile soaking in a puddle of blood. He had been shot in the back of the head, and the gases released by the bullet inside the skull had thrust his eyeballs two inches out of the sockets. The gleaming white elongated cylinders were capped by pupils, the end result an expression of cartoon astonishment on the dead man's face.

Touhey's eyes bulged a little in empathy – or maybe, Rocco thought, he was just *doing* the guy, an acting thing.

Suddenly a hopeless cry came from the interrogation room, followed by a rhythmic banging. Rocco and Touhey jumped up, Rocco praying Mazilli wasn't beating on the kid, but it was only Maldonado smashing his own forehead against the desk in grief.

Mazilli saw them looking in the window, crossed his eyes, stuck his tongue out sideways and pumped his fist near his crotch.

'Jesus, I think this kid is clean,' Touhey murmured.

Rocco nodded as if considering it, but he was just being polite. He noticed that he and Touhey were the exact same height: Hey hey.

Maldonado's voice, muffled through the door, rose to a high, raw wail: 'I don' *know* these guy. I don't know these *gon*.'

Driving over to County Jail, Rocco put Maldonado, who was handcuffed, in back with the actor, figuring he'd give each of them a thrill. Maldonado, tilted slightly forward, his hands behind his back, kept squinting at Touhey as if thinking, Where'd I see this blond bitch before, maybe thinking he was a pay lawyer, because he was well groomed and looked like long money.

But Touhey looked tortured. Rocco saw his mouth working, as if he wanted to say something to Maldonado, but *what, what* . . .

After an hour of watching Mazilli threaten Maldonado with every cliché in the book, from thirty years of darkness to unspeakable sexual bondage, and after an hour of watching the kid respond with a heart-rending performance of baffled and quivering innocence, Rocco had gotten bored and decided to cut short the whole damn passion play. He returned to the squad room for a one-on-one with Maldonado's father and simply told him that unless his son gave up the gun in the next five minutes, the old man could kiss his bolida action goodbye. And in the time it took for Mazilli to smoke a cigarette out on the front steps, Rocco and Touhey sitting alongside him watching the sun go down behind the steel spider of the Majeski Skyway, Nelson Maldonado had changed his tune, deciding to come clean and cough up the murder weapon. Rocco had no idea what the father used to threaten the kid that was actually worse than County, but in the end he really didn't give a shit.

Rocco watched Touhey in the rearview mirror, amazed that sitting next to a little three-legged rat like Maldonado could be so involving to the actor, that a job that dealt with an endless parade of shitskin losers – hunting them down, befriending them in order to get their confessions, then tossing them into County – could possibly be of interest to anybody who didn't get paid to do it. And his wife's friends were the same way: all he had to do was clear his throat at a restaurant table and conversation trailed off, everybody waiting for him to say something terrible and gripping about his workday. Rocco recalled the office toilets with their newspapers on the floor, the evidence room with its dozens of sad-sack lives reduced to shopping bags reeking of b.o. and poverty: about as shabby and grim a gig as you could ask for.

On the other hand, Touhey and the rest weren't completely off the mark: the Job used to be enough to take his breath away. And now only six months to go. Then what? Maybe this thing with Touhey would lead somewhere. Maybe he could be an actor if he was offered a role in a movie or something. Well, not an actor, he didn't know shit about that, but something like that, something with Bigness in it, something that would halve his years, put him on par with Patty and Erin. Rocco glanced at Touhey in the rearview again, feeling a vague anxiety, wanting a drink.

The County Jail looked like a tall, forbidding elementary school. Seven stories of dirty brown brick, one hundred years old and now operating at 330 percent of capacity.

Mazilli pulled up to the gate of the drive-down ramp and honked the horn. On the sidewalk, a half-dozen women were shouting conversation up to faceless male voices, stick arms protruding from the bars that vertically striped the length of the building.

With an electronic blare the gate rolled up and Mazilli shifted to drive.

'We're going in?' Touhey asked.

'Usually we just drop them off on the sidewalk,' Mazilli said, 'tell them to go in on their own from there – you know, like an honor system?'

'I meant, am I going in?' Touhey's voice was even and good-natured. He seemed determined to be a sport.

'Whatever you want, Sean.' Rocco tried to sound indifferent so Mazilli wouldn't start in on him too.

Once down in the courtyard by the entrance to the receiving unit, they were surrounded on four sides by the exterior walls of the jail, like being in the pit of an open-air elevator shaft. The only other car waiting to unload was a housing project Fury, looking like a rusted alligator skull. Rocco watched Big Chief and Thumper pull a handcuffed black kid from the rear, maneuvering him out over the folded-down front seat of the two-door junker.

Someone up near the top floor yelled, 'Yo, Thumper, you white, Pee Wee-looking motherfucker!' A dixie cup drifted down, hitting the ground empty, but followed by a light mist – piss, most likely. Rocco reached over and hit the wipers and the washer spray.

'Who do dat?' Thumper bellowed up, half laughing.

'*Ah* do dat!'

'Who *ah* is dat?'

'Dat *mah* ah!' Everybody laughed – convicts, Fury, Rocco, Mazilli – everybody but the two prisoners and Touhey.

Rocco's crew followed Big Chief's through the steel door, handing over their guns. Touhey moved quickly, involuntarily ducking his head every few seconds as if another yellow rain was about to come down.

Rocco was always startled by the sharp rise in noise inside the receiving unit. Everything was covered in glazed tile; nothing absorbed the disembodied shouts and barks that ricocheted off the walls like bullets fired inside a steel drum. The unit was small, a thirty-by-thirty lobby ringed by doors, three of steel leading to other parts of the prison and two barred, fronting the bullpens – the holding cells that faced each other catercorner across the floor.

At the center of the room stood a raised desk that stretched across an entire wall. The receiving sergeant who presided over all intakes was flanked by two cigars propped upright on invoice stakes on either side of his sign-in book, the wafting smoke eating into the deeper and more outrageous smells that always hung in the air here. Rocco stood against a wall between Touhey and Maldonado, out of the milling confusion of uniforms, plainclothes and unprocessed prisoners as Mazilli attempted to wade over to the desk and hand in Maldonado's paperwork, his progress checked every time he shook hands or smacked backs with the correction officers and street cops in his path. Sometimes the crush in the room, combined with the post-arrest highs, made Rocco feel as if he was at a church-basement police smoker; all that was missing was an open bar.

Despite the din, Rocco could hear Touhey breathe through his mouth. The actor looked awestruck and ready to cry. But Maldonado was completely transformed now, cold-eyed, bored, trying to look problematic for the dozen or so trusties who had the run of the place and were walking around in T-shirts, drawstring gym pants and rubber flip-flops. These prisoners leaned against the walls or sat on ancient metal-and-wood public school chairs, tilting them back on the rear legs, rocking idly, sizing up the bullpen meat. A lot of them held half pints of milk, and a few had apples. The snacks, the school chairs and the glazed tile walls made the room seem to Rocco like recess time in hell.

'Thumper.' Rocco pushed off the wall and backhanded him on the arm. 'What's up, Cheech?'

Rocco had known Thumper since Thumper was fourteen, when Rocco had grabbed him for dropping full soda cans onto traffic from a highway overpass, then let him slide with an open-handed smack-around because

Thumper's older sister turned out to have been one of Rocco's girlfriends back in high school.

'Check it out, Roc.' Thumper jerked a thumb at his prisoner. The kid was six three, dressed in blood-red gym pants, a red Nike warm-up jacket and a white T-shirt. He had snow-white high-top British Knights on his feet with no laces, the tongues hanging out and almost curling over the toes of the shoes. He also had his hair molded into a sloped-back six-inch-high fade, with the words 'Street' and 'Smart' shaved in over his temples.

Rocco read the kid's head and laughed. 'Not too.'

'It gets better,' Big Chief said. 'You know how we popped him? On a shoplifting beef. He boosted a sixty-nine-cent Chap Stick. We go through his pockets? He's got the Chap Stick in the same pocket with two bundles of heroin and six bottles of powder.'

Rocco squinted at the kid, who had adopted the standard defensive mode of averted eye and tightly closed mouth.

'Maybe he should shave his head,' Rocco said.

'Yeah, grow something new up there.' Thumper made a frame with his hands. '"Humphead,"' he said, rapping the kid on his unprotected abdomen. 'What do you think of "Humphead"?'

Rocco looked around the room, then down at the kid's sneakers. 'You ready to fight tonight?'

The kid blinked open-mouthed now, uncomprehending. Rocco gestured toward a 250-pound trustie across the room who was pumpkin-headed, bald and wearing a nylon stocking over his scalp. Tilting his chair back against the wall, a milk carton in his lap, the convict pointed at the BKs and then tapped his own chest.

Rocco guffawed at him. 'Two small for *your* fat fuckin' boats.'

'I'll stretch them.' He shrugged, then took in Touhey, locking eyes with him across the room. 'I can fit into *any*thing if I stretch it out first.'

Touhey became so disoriented that he started to turn in circles, blinking, his elbow pressing his shoulder bag into his ribs. Rocco watched him turning on a spit, soft white underbelly head to toe, thinking once again, Why the hell would anybody dip themselves in shit like this voluntarily?

Mazilli came back to them from the processing desk accompanied by a correction officer, who ushered Maldonado into a living room-size cement-floor bullpen to await the next morning's arraignment. He was issued a pallet to sleep on and locked up with twenty other all-nighters. The bullpen's walls were covered with graffiti, a thousand predictable messages, all seeming to center around the words 'fuck' and 'AIDS.'

As they turned to leave the jail, Touhey almost took Rocco's arm, trying to avoid looking at everything and everybody, stumbling along like a half-blind old man crossing a rush-hour highway on foot. Rocco felt bad for him, wondered if he overestimated what the actor could handle. He decided to give him something to make up for it, a little treat. 'Sean, I want to show you something.'

'What?' The actor answered too quickly.

'Come here.' Rocco guided him over to the bars of the bullpen, Maldonado already receding into the anonymity of the room, already out of Rocco's mind. 'Look where I'm pointing.'

Touhey seemed to have a hard time focusing past the blank stares of that night's haul. Most of the prisoners were right up in his face, gripping the bars.

Rocco nudged the actor. 'There on the wall.'

The naked overhead light bleached out a lot of the detailing, but Rocco could still make out the rainbow someone had drawn. At least six bands of color arched through clouds and birds and valleys, a loving and lush pulp-art vision completely devoid of sexual challenge.

'That fucking thing has been on that wall for as long as I can remember,' Rocco said, 'and nobody's ever drawn over it. You think of all the animals and mutants thrown in here over the years, day in, day out, everybody writing Fuck You, Kiss My Ass, floor to ceiling, and yet nobody ever drew over that. So what does that mean? What does that say to you?'

Touhey was looking at his shoes, trying to become invisible. 'I don't know.'

Rocco was about to hold forth about the human spirit but decided to let it go; either you got it or you didn't. 'Well, think about it there, Sean.'

'I will, I will,' the actor said, blurting it out with a tense and clammy abruptness that made Rocco realize that he might be torturing the guy in a way that would never be forgiven.

'Good.' Rocco found himself scanning walls and faces, searching for something else to give the actor, some gift, some glue that would make him stay.

Rocco sat with Mazilli and Touhey in the Camelot, a gaudy Italian restaurant with a lobster tank, white tablecloths and six-page tablet menus, but also with blinding overheads, drinks that came in short skinny glasses with straws and a loud TV behind the bar. The Camelot was on the DMZ between the Heights and the last vestiges of old-time German-Irish Dempsy, and cops were always welcome. If you were Dempsy P.D., no matter how much you ate or drank the bill would never climb over twenty-four dollars a table. A few cops even took turns moonlighting here, picking up and driving home the elderly white Catholic regulars, chauffeuring them in a fifteen-year-old limo that the owner kept parked right out front by a fire hydrant night and day.

Rocco took a sip of his vodka and cranberry juice; it was too sweet, like Hawaiian Punch. He felt a thickness in his blood, anxious for something to happen, for somebody to kill somebody, for the beeper on his hip to go off before Touhey faded on them again and started thinking about hanging out with Narcotics, Emergency Services or, God forbid, firemen. Well shit, they weren't New York with its two thousand homicides a year. They pulled in sixty, seventy, most of them grounders, somebody doing his wife or his best friend, the occasional fag stabbing, although the solve rate was slipping a little, the violence getting more random and impersonal given all the crack and base coke out there these days. In Dempsy, the Homicide four-to-twelve was mainly this: drinks, staring at an over-size menu wondering what to eat, watching videos or news on TV back in the office, waiting for the phones to ring or the pagers to beep.

Touhey sat with his elbows on the table, a hand over his mouth, looking pensive. His club soda with lime was untouched. Next to Rocco, Mazilli hunched over his scotch, sucking it through a straw, his hands buried under his arms.

Touhey's eyes found Rocco's. 'I think I finally see what you mean about the rainbow.'

'Yeah? Good.'

'What rainbow?' Mazilli sounded as if he was gargling, trolling the bottom of his glass with the straw.

'You ever see that rainbow in the bullpen?'

'No.'

Rocco smiled at Touhey. 'If you can't eat it, fuck it or sell it something, Mazilli goes south.'

'What do you think will happen to Maldonado tonight?' Touhey looked worried.

'What'll happen?' Mazilli waved for another scotch. 'That big fucking b.o.-smelling shit-on-his-dick gorilla you saw? He's gonna put his arm around him like this' – Mazilli grabbed Rocco in a light open-ended headlock – 'and then he's gonna take them big licorice lips and plant one right on the side of his face like this' – Mazilli put his hand like a starfish on Rocco's head from temple to chin and made a loud sucking noise ending in a pop – 'suck out his fucking eyeball and say, "You *mine*, Nelthun." *That's* what's gonna happen to Maldonado tonight.'

Touhey stared at Mazilli.

'Can you believe this guy's acting head of Homicide for the next two weeks?' Rocco chucked a thumb at Mazilli, trying to lighten the moment.

'How come you don't ask about Henderson?' Mazilli squinted at the actor. 'You see the photos of Henderson with the eyeballs? How come you don't ask about *him*? Or his *kids*? Or his *wife*?'

'Maz, ease up,' Rocco said.

'No, hey, alls I'm saying is, this guy, you . . .' He pointed at Touhey. 'I mean, you're probably a good soul and all, you want to help people, you care, like "Here I am, what hurts?" Right? Right?' He waited until Touhey shrugged in tentative agreement. 'Yeah? Well this is what I have to say to you. You don't know shit. The lines are drawn. Whites and blacks? For the most part? They were never meant to be together. You know why Henderson got killed? He showed *fear*.'

'Well, OK, but . . .' Touhey sounded rattled. 'He hit a four-year-old kid, no?'

'*He . . . showed . . . fear.*' Mazilli blared it out. 'White people show *fear*, white people *smile*, white people say *please* and *thank* you. To the whites, all that's decency, OK? It's just being human. But to the blacks? The Spanish? You know, not *all* of them but the ones on the bottom? They're all signs of weakness. It's like throwing chum in the water and that's the way it is.'

The waitress slid a scotch in front of Mazilli. He grabbed her hand. 'Am I right or am I right?'

The waitress, a thirty-year veteran of the Camelot, shrugged. 'Last time I voted? It was for John Kennedy.'

Rocco was hesitant to look at Touhey, but when he did he was surprised to see that the actor looked entranced, as if he had just discovered something amazing.

'"What's gonna happen to Maldonado . . ."' Mazilli muttered. 'You interested in the downtrodden? Their plight? Let me tell you something. Before you get *down* with them, you better start thinking like them and acting like them, because they're *never* gonna think and act like *you*, and you're gonna wind up like Henderson there, with your eyeballs buggin' out.'

The waitress stood over them, ruffling her pad. 'You boys ready to order?'

'Hey, I'm not signing up to do social work, I was just asking.' Touhey seemed calmer now, almost laughing.

'Yeah, well, I was just answering.' Mazilli went nose down into his menu, his upper body knotted with anger.

Rocco tried to draw Touhey off, give him a signal to take his partner with a grain of salt, but the actor only had eyes for Mazilli.

Suddenly Mazilli unclenched his shoulders and sighed into his menu. 'Look, I'm not saying the whites are all that great, but it's like, if we're maybe only five steps *out* of the jungle, they're still five steps *in*.' Twisting his head and looking up to the waitress, he said, 'I'll have the veal parmigian' and a house salad.'

She nodded at Touhey as if she disapproved of him for getting Mazilli upset. 'You?'

'I feel like having something light.'

'How 'bout a bowl of feathers,' Mazilli drawled.

Touhey horse-laughed, and Rocco couldn't tell if it was tension or a growing affection for Mazilli. Either way, Rocco wanted to come up with a good one, something to show the actor he could hold his own here.

Touhey asked for a double order of house salad, dressing on the side. When the waitress turned to Rocco, he was so distracted he just raised his half-full drink to signal for a refill. He turned to the actor and smiled. 'So, Sean, what's the story of this movie – you know, the plot?'

'Huh?' Touhey grunted blankly. 'We're working on it.'

'So what do you have, like a concept?' Concept: Rocco felt as if he was on a bad blind date trying to make some conversation.

Touhey didn't bother to answer. He turned back to Mazilli, hunching down, drawing a bead. 'I'm going to give you a concept, you give me a reaction, OK?'

Mazilli shrugged and lit a cigarette.

'Rehabilitation,' Touhey said.

'What is this, "Password"?' Mazilli tossed his match on the tablecloth. 'You want to know what *I* believe in? I believe in punishment, I believe in fear, and I believe in *revenge*.'

Lips moving silently, Touhey cocked his head and peered at Mazilli as if trying to memorize him.

Rocco sighed, announcing to himself, My turn. 'Yeah, well. You say rehabilitation. You know, we're human, I mean most of us, and nobody starts out hard. I come on the job twenty years ago? I wanted to be a cop. Why, to beat up the minorities? No. I wanted to help people. Somebody yells "Police," that's me. I hit the ground running – white, black, yellow, whatever.'

Rocco sneaked a glance at Mazilli and was surprised to see that he wasn't rolling his eyes.

'OK? But rehabilitation . . .' Rocco paused, drawing breath for the tale. 'It's like when I was in uniform. My first week I had a partner, Frog Phelan. Maz, you remember Frog?'

Mazilli shrugged.

'Frog Phelan, he came on the job when Truman was President. I'm like twenty-one, twenty-two, and we get a call. Lafayette Houses, there's a kid screaming in an apartment, door's locked. The elevator's broke so Frog sends me up alone, he ain't gonna jog up six stories, he's blotto anyhow. I get up there, Housing's just popped the lock. We go in, there's a three-year-old kid handcuffed to a burning hot radiator, nobody else in the house. The handcuff's metal, right? Metal conducts heat? I don't know how long the kid was hooked up like that, but he had a ring of cooked flesh around his wrist, OK?'

Touhey looked as if he had turned to glass.

'We call the ambulance, cut the cuff, they take the kid to Christ the King. Housing leaves, but I just stay in the room by the radiator. Sit there on the windowsill. Sitting there forty fucking minutes, and finally in comes the mother. That's forty more minutes the kid would have cooked if we didn't get in, OK? She walks in, she's fuckin' got them half-mast heroin eyes, right? Went out to cop? She walks in, no kid there. She looks at me. I look at her. There's like this moment, you know? All of a sudden she tears ass. I chase that fucking bitch down six flights of stairs. She makes it to the lobby, runs right into Phelan, he grabs her but here *I'm* coming like the avenging angel, ninety miles an hour. Frog throws his shoulder into me. Boom, I go right into the mailboxes. I'm looking at him like, What the fuck? He takes her out, gives her over to another cruiser, they take her in. He comes, gets me. We're sitting in the car, he says to me, "Rocco, that lady you were gonna brain? Twenty years ago when she was a little girl I arrested her father for beating her baby brother to death. The father was a real piece of shit. Now that she's all grown up? *She's* a real piece of shit. That kid you saved tonight. If he lives that long, if he grows up? *He's* gonna be a real piece of shit. Rocco," Frog says to me, "it's the cycle of shit and you can't do nothing about it. So take it easy and just do your job."'

Touhey, all Rocco's again, shook his head. 'Wow . . . wow.'

'You have the same experiences over and over in this job,' Rocco said, feeling on solid ground now, 'so when you say rehabilitation, Sean, what you find over the years is that it takes all your strength just to maintain the status quo out there.'

'The cycle of shit,' Mazilli announced, but Rocco couldn't read his tone.

'So what happened to the kid?' Touhey asked.

Rocco had no idea what happened to the kid and was debating making something up when Mazilli chimed in: 'He's the fucking mayor of Dempsy, and last week he instituted across-the-board pay cuts for all city detectives.'

Touhey didn't hear Mazilli, just narrowed his eyes at Rocco, nodding to himself, tapping his lips with a thumbnail. After a long moment, he rose from the table. 'I'll be right back,' he said.

Rocco watched him go, then smiled down at his fork, slightly embarrassed. Mazilli sat sideways, hunched over, elbows propped on the chair arms, fingers laced over his lap. He nodded to a white Dempsy councilman at another table who was dining with a black fire chief who had run for mayor a few years back and lost a close one. The councilman was a known coke addict and the fire chief was weathering an investigation by the IRS.

Gazing around the room, Mazilli suddenly imitated Rocco doing Frog Phelan. '"Rocco? It's the cycle of shit and you can't do nothing about it."'

Rocco smiled and began beating his fists rhythmically on the table, distant jungle drums. '"I believe in fear. I believe in punishment. I believe in revenge."'

Mazilli said, 'Fuck you, it's true.'

'I believe that each man,' Rocco said, raising his voice, 'whether black, white, yellow or brown, is entitled to have his ass kicked free of charge, regardless of race, creed or color.'

'Cycle of shit,' Mazilli shot back.

Rocco stopped the drums, not wanting to push it too far. But Mazilli was steaming, and for a minute or two he looked around the room, avoiding Rocco's eyes. When he had calmed down, Mazilli nodded in the direction that Touhey had gone. 'Fuckin' jamoke,' he said.

Rocco snorted in agreement. The tension between them evaporated.

The waitress came back with the salads and another vodka cranberry juice. As soon as she put the food down Rocco's beeper went off.

Mazilli was stone-still, staring heavy-lidded at the pager as Rocco reared back to catch the number coming in on his hip.

Rocco couldn't read in the glare, pulled the pager off his belt for a closer look.

'It's your wife, right?' Mazilli's voice was dull and low.

'It's the office.'

'Don't fucking tell me.' Mazilli dropped his fork in disgust.

Rocco tried to sound casual, but he prayed it was a job. 'It's probably bullshit,' he said, sucking down half his Cape Codder through the straw and rising from the table.

'It's probably a fuckin' tripleheader.' Mazilli signaled the waitress, raising his glass, pinging it with a flick of his fingernail, 'Outdoors, in the rain, in a fucking mud puddle, sixty fucking shells laying around and a big herd of niggers stepping all over everything. Tell me I'm wrong.'

Rocco headed across the room to the pay phone. Ten feet from the phone alcove, he stopped in his tracks as he heard his own voice coming at him loud and clear from around the corner.

'"The father was a real piece of shit. Now that she's all grown up? *She's* a real piece of shit. That kid you saved tonight . . ."'

Touhey was impersonating him on the phone to someone. The performance was pitch-perfect: the Dempsy accent, the tongue clicks and pauses, all his verbal fingerprints. Both thrilled and disoriented, Rocco debated hanging back, just out of sight, then decided he couldn't listen and he couldn't walk away. He turned the corner so that Touhey would see him and change the subject.

But Touhey's back was to Rocco and he continued, leaning into the glass partition, hunched over the mouthpiece, his fat calfskin date book open on the steel shelf below the phone.

'"Rocco, it's the cycle of shit, so just sit back and do your job." The cycle of shit — is that perfect or what? I was thinking the other guy, but he's too one way, too hard, too . . . I dunno. But "cycle of shit," it's like, you take innocence and cynicism, put them in a blender for twenty years and that's what comes out, you know what I mean? This guy's the key on a silver platter. I want to *kiss* this poor fucking guy.'

Rocco cleared his throat so loud it actually sounded like 'Ahhem.'

Touhey didn't straighten his posture, didn't stiffen, just hung up the phone in midsentence and turned around.

'How you doing?' he said, as if they hadn't seen each other in days. There wasn't the slightest bit of embarrassment in his face. He was playing it straight and innocent; Rocco had to marvel at how good he was.

Rocco held up his beeper and smiled. 'Might have a job coming in.'

Touhey almost clapped his hands. 'Yeah? Great. I mean, you know, finally.' He turned for the tables, his date book under his arm.

Rocco dug for a quarter. 'The key on a silver platter.' He liked that. But why 'poor fucking guy'?

On his way back to the table, Rocco saw Touhey and Mazilli staring at him like Comedy and Tragedy, each rooting for separate verdicts.

'Don't tell me,' said Mazilli. 'Dempsy burnin', right?'

'Nah, it's bullshit. Patty just left some message for me.'

Rocco saw Touhey's face collapse in petulant disappointment.

'Thank God.' Mazilli dug into his salad.

'It's a funny job.' Rocco forced himself to sound hearty as he took his seat. 'The pager goes off, it could be a double homicide or it could be your wife reminding you to bring home bananas.'

Touhey did not look amused, and Rocco felt queasy and a little desperate, as if he had just had his key-on-a-silver-platter status revoked.

'You know, Sean . . .' Rocco hesitated, sensing he was about to get himself in trouble, then forged ahead. 'I actually met my wife off this thing here.' Rocco patted his pager as if he felt great affection for it.

Mazilli's head rose from his plate. He fixed Rocco with a narrow-eyed gaze.

'Maz, did I ever tell you how I met Patty?' Rocco hated the false chirpiness in his own voice.

Mazilli continued to stare and Rocco looked away. Rocco had never told anyone, not even his partner, how he had met his wife, and the fact that he felt compelled to tell the tale now, in front of the actor, made him feel sick with shame, although he had no intention of shutting up: he was too hungry for Touhey's attention.

'About three years ago? I'm in the office on a Sunday morning and I get this call. The radio station in town, 'QRS, they have this phone-in show for mothers to talk to some pediatrician? Apparently this lady called in, asks him over the air, "Dr Wiley, I have a nine-month-old son, but the problem is, I know he's really Satan, and I was wondering, if I throw him out the window, will he just be reincarnated into another body? Or will I have truly done away with the lord of all evil in this world?"'

Rocco winked at Touhey, gauging his interest: he seemed absorbed now. 'So they have this lady's home number coming up on their board and they're freaking out. The poor doctor's talking to her on the air, trying to get her not to do anything. Meanwhile, the producer calls nine-one-one and for some reason they pass it on to Homicide. I take the number, get the

phone company to get me the address, it's in Guttenberg, which is Hudson
County. But I'm bored, fuck it, I call the Guttenberg police, give them the
address, I say, "Wait for me by the door." I go over, it's a nice high rise,
expensive, I'm up there with two uniforms, I bang on the door. I hear
this lady inside: "Who is it?" "It's Rocco." She opens the door – pretty,
young – "Rocco who?" "Rocco *police*." My foot's wedged in now, and
I can see it in her eyes, home run, she's the one. She says, "What's the
problem?" – not "Can I help you?" I say, "I don't know, but we have
to come in." She says, "What about my rights?" and I start pushing a
little on the door. I say, "Call your lawyer, but we have to come in."
She's looking from me to the Guttenberg cops, I'm ready to knock her
down if I have to, but then she says, "Just you." And the way she said it?
Well . . .' Rocco paused, weighed down a little with emotional memory,
suppressing the desire to get up from the table right then and go home
to be with Patty. 'I was hoping it would be a false alarm, everything
would be OK. So I say, "Fellas, thanks, resume patrol." I walk in, nice
place, plants, Levolor blinds, Turkish rug. I see she can't be more than
twenty-two, -three. I go in, I look out the windows first, nothing down
there, no bundles, so I just start opening closets, the refrigerator, toilet
tanks, anywhere you could hide a dead baby, taking out suitcases – and
she's not saying anything, just standing there twisting her hands. I can't
find nothing. I say, "Why am I here?" She says, "Why," but guilty, you
know? I see she's got a big stereo system set up next to the TV. I just
go over and turn it on, don't touch the dial, and of course it's set to the
station and we hear the phone-in pediatrician on the speakers. I just look
at her. She says, "There's no baby," and I believe her.

'I'm looking at her now, her hair's a mess, her face is all puffy from
crying. She says, "Am I under arrest?" I say, "Why'd you do it?" She
says, "You ever *listen* to that creep? He's so . . . 'Well, Mother, first
I'd like to thank you for having the courage to call in with a question
like that. It's a *hard* question but a *good* question.' He's a phony." I'm
just looking at her still, I ask again, "Why'd you do it? You look like a
nice kid." And she bursts into tears, says, "I'm so lonely." After a minute
she calms down, tells me that the day before? She had an abortion, and
the guy who knocked her up? Didn't show up at the clinic, didn't call,
just vanished. She went herself, paid for it herself, came back home to
an empty apartment, she's all cramped up, in pain, miserable, she wakes
up Sunday morning *still* with the cramps, the guy *still* didn't call. She
turns on the radio, starts hearing all these mothers calling in with these
problems about babies, like, "Is it OK if they sleep in bed with me?

Is three too early to teach them the alphabet? When I take them to the petting zoo, is there any animal they could catch something from?" And she got a little wiggy, thought she'd rattle the guy's cage, so . . . I figure what the hell, this poor kid, so I go into her kitchen, make us some tea. We talked for like four hours and, because I was kind of in rocky shape myself at that time . . . So, I don't know, we found each other. The funny thing is, when she gets pregnant by *me*? I start freaking out, remembering the circumstances of how we met. I'm thinking, Holy Christ, what if what if . . . Anyhow, it turns out she's a fan*ta*stic mother, meanwhile *I'm* the one now who feels like, "Dear Doctor Scuss, my kid is driving me around the bend," you know? But she's a fan*ta*stic mother, fan*ta*stic. Just fan*ta*stic . . .'

Rocco trailed off, furious at himself for telling the story that both he and Patty swore to keep to themselves, furious at himself for betraying Mazilli's primacy as a confidant. It was just that the actor made him feel so off balance, so desperate to say, 'This is me, this is what I know, this is who I am.' Maybe all movie stars had that power to effortlessly strip a person down, but Rocco was perfectly willing to serve up every shadow and angle of his heart if he could only get back a little of that recognition he had won earlier in the meal, re-experience the momentary sensation that his life was somehow of consequence.

'That's wild.' Touhey was smiling, nodding, blatantly intrigued again. But Rocco couldn't tell if it was the story or the desperation behind the telling of it that had captured the actor's fancy.

Rocco briefly caught Mazilli's eye and sensed that if they'd been alone now, Mazilli would have lunged over and punched him out. Rocco smiled sheepishly at his empty drink, thinking: Be my guest.

5

Hood up, Strike entered Ahab's, the air dense with a burnt closeness, as if a fire had been put out just hours before. It was seven-thirty on a Friday night but the restaurant was nearly empty, no one seated at the handful of littered tables, one raggedy man at the stand-up counter running along the window, the guy breaking up a fistful of begged change into pennies, nickels and dimes, lips moving as he tried to tally up some kind of meal. In the kitchen – a long glinting stainless steel confusion sealed off from the customers by streaked and dull glass – the food handlers appeared in silhouette, moving around the fryers and heat lamps like shifting shapes inside a steam room.

Three people stood on line along the kitchen glass, and Strike watched them shuffle restlessly from foot to foot. They were silently fuming at the languid counter girl, who was wearing a blue tricot service smock and chewing gum so open-mouthed that her tongue flapped out like a third lip.

Strike held the .25 in his pocket. But what was he supposed to do, get on line, ask for Darryl and then shoot him through the service window, hoping no one would give a shit? The insanity of the situation made him feel as if he was sleepwalking, inhabiting strange skin.

A fat, balding white guy with long sideburns and a Fu Manchu mustache came out of the bathroom and got on the food line. He was wearing a fatigue jacket and ripped-up tennis sneakers. The guy rapped on the kitchen glass with a key as if signaling someone inside, and a moment later the counter girl was replaced by a tall, rail-thin kid with a flat nose. He wore a red nylon running suit, and a Lion of Judah medallion hung from his neck.

Strike stepped back, sliding out of the kid's line of vision. It was Darryl, and the sight of him, the *real*ness of him, made Strike want to fall down.

How to play this? What to do? Got to be got: maybe that meant something else, like a warning. Or a wounding.

The white guy asked for a Golden Mobie, a Coke, fries, and an eight-piece. Darryl served him up quicker than the girl would have, and the guy moved off to the stand-up counter with his grease platter, dropping a spray of loose change on the beggar's army of coins and looking out into the parking lot as he tore into the glistening fishburger.

The girl came back on counter duty right after the guy was served, and then Darryl emerged from the kitchen and quickly slipped into the bathroom. Strike saw the white guy furtively catch the reflection of Darryl's movements in the window.

Eight-piece: there wasn't any 'eight-piece' on the menu. Eighth of a kilo was probably what he meant. Had to be, Strike reasoned, because an eight ball – just three and a half grams – wouldn't be worth the risk of selling in such a public place. Strike also guessed they were using the bathroom for dope and money exchanges, given that Darryl was in and out in ten seconds, too fast to piss. Strike studied him, entranced with the vitality of his every gesture, the absoluteness of his existence. Tracking his silhouette behind the kitchen glass, Strike tried to believe that Darryl's beating heart was a throw-down challenge to his own welfare and future and manhood. Strike tried to muster fury but only summoned a lightness in his guts: Darryl was so *real*.

The white guy returned to the bathroom for another ten-second trip, in and out, snagged his french fries on the way to the parking lot, got into a LeMans with Pennsylvania plates and disappeared out onto JFK.

What to do?

'Hey, Strike.'

Strike flinched, wheeling to face that fourteen-year-old girl Shanette, Sharette, that baby-fat girl, the one who was just dying to throw it all away on the pipe. She was still trying the same play, giving him the hungry happy face, that licky-lipped gleam.

'What *you* doin' here?' the girl said, eyeing his clothes. Her gaze traveled up and down from hood to sneakers. 'You gonna get yourself all dirty.'

Strike gave her his back and practically ran to the Accord. He drove with the windows open, as if the Ahab's air had followed him into the car like a hellish breath.

But once he was clear of that sizzling choke of grease and fear, clear of Darryl Adams, he found himself coming into some kind of resolve again. He must have been dreaming to think he could do something right in the restaurant. It would only draw attention to Darryl's job, make the cops think, What's here? Still, how to play it?

Darryl lived in a shabby, mostly welfare-subsidized motel over in

Tunnely that always had lots of business going on because of its proximity to the Lincoln Tunnel. Day and night, cars drove around back of the Royal Motel for dope or sex. It was a place of whispers, quick reflexes, and shadow play. Anything could happen to anybody out in back of the Royal; everybody there was either guilty or just about to be. Shootings, stabbings, robberies – the Tunnely cops spent so much time at the Royal that the management had once joked about giving squad cars a designated parking section.

Strike drove up I–9 toward Tunnely, wondering why Darryl would choose to live there, then remembering that Darryl didn't get along with his mother too well either. He probably moved out in a huff one night, and where are you going to go to live after a fight? A motel. Darryl likely checked in on impulse and wound up staying. When you were on your own, it was easier to have just one room than a whole apartment, and sometimes Strike felt like giving his own place up, get a nice furnished room somewhere.

Strike drove up the ramp to the rear of the Royal, pulling in under the long second-story catwalk. A crowd of regulars hunched over the railing and watched the New York cars entering and leaving with the jerky frequency of customers in a 7-Eleven parking lot.

Strike turned off the ignition and sat there waiting for Darryl's night to end. But what if he went out after work? What if he came home with a girl? What if . . . Strike thought of Rodney waiting on the news, waiting to judge his heart: This is my son.

Then Strike remembered he had heard somewhere that Darryl's mother had moved back down to Georgia. Somebody told him that; who would have told him? Strike started thinking about his own mother, about how ever since he moved out of the house he never ran into her, even though he was working the benches in the same projects where she lived. He never saw his brother either. Maybe they were going out of their way to avoid him, always coming and going from the other end of the projects, Strike thinking, Is that good or bad? But did he really want his mother to see him overseeing business on the bench? Maybe she was just showing him consideration. He had said to her that his dealing was short term and that he'd end it quick, coming back to her rich and on the level, but now look what he was up to, sitting here outside this sinkhole with a .25 on his lap. How would *this* lead to *that*? Rodney once said about Kennedy, the President who the boulevard was named after, that his family made its first real money smuggling booze, but Strike couldn't imagine an American President starting out on the road to respect and real money by sitting in back of the Royal Motel with a gun, waiting to ambush a dope dealer so he could take his place dealing ounces. Rodney had gone on about the hypocrisy of whites, how they were dirtier, in a bigger and more subtle way, than any black kid trying to hustle and survive on the street, but Strike always had a hard time seeing that. White-trash pipeheads and corrupt knockos were right in front of him every day, he had no trouble reading them, but anybody with a tie and a briefcase had him buffaloed.

Strike drifted off, thinking about making it in this life, how hard it would be to draw a picture of himself that could be entitled 'Making It.' He couldn't imagine what he would be doing in that picture, what he would be holding, wearing, even what the expression on his face would be.

But his father had almost made it, or so he was told. Strike used to believe that his father's stories about being asked to join Kool and the Gang had been beer bragging, talking trash. But a year or so after the funeral, Strike had finally asked his mother about Kool and the Gang, and his mother had said it was the God's own truth, your daddy was asked and he really did turn it down. But just because his mother had said it was the God's own truth didn't necessarily make it so. Maybe his father was bullshitting her too.

Strike reluctantly scanned the parking lot again. Ambush: Who the fuck was he kidding? There were twenty, thirty people around, people hanging right over his car on the catwalk. Ambush: right. He didn't have the heart, he didn't have the plan. What if he just wounded Darryl, put him in the hospital. Or maybe he could tell him that Rodney wanted him dead, that he should split and save himself.

Think it through. Think it through. Strike felt himself sinking: no heart, no plan. He thought again of his mother, his promise to come back rich and legitimate, and he began working up a little rage, hating Darryl for putting him through these changes, for making himself *see* himself right now. Strike gripped the .25, praying that Darryl would come right up in his face and –

Whomp. It sounded as if someone had dropped a cinder block on the roof of his car from the second-story catwalk, the explosion so sudden that Strike yipped like a dog.

Whomp. A husky white guy in dungarees and a New York Jets T-shirt pounded his fist on the roof of the Accord again, then bent down, pressed his face against the driver's side window. 'Hi there.' Wiggling his fingers in greeting, he grinned at Strike with the casual proprietariness of a cop.

Strike dropped the gun between his shoes, kicked it under the seat. The cop moved off to hoist himself up on Strike's front fender, not even looking at him, just planting himself, hunched over and smiling at the action. He whistled and rocked, enjoying the ripple he was causing in the lot: cars pulling in, hesitating, then throwing it in reverse and pulling out quick, driving back onto I-9, people coming out of their rooms and seeing him squatting like King Toad, then retreating behind shut doors.

Strike sat stone-faced, pinned in his car. He watched a chunky middle-aged Latino emerge from one of the ground-floor rooms and heard the cop whistle him over. The guy paused for a second, as if weighing options, then walked over in a bent-knee waddle. He was dressed in a white shirt, white slacks, white shoes, white Panama hat. He was high as a kite.

The cop tilted his head and beamed at the guy as if he was proud of him. 'Let me ask you,' the cop said, jingling an ID bracelet on his wrist. 'What do you want to be when you grow up?'

The guy mumbled something with the word 'student' in it.

'You want to be a student?' The cop nodded reasonably. 'What do you like to eat?'

'I am working, sir.'

'Yeah? How long you working on the pipe?'

The guy hesitated. 'Two days.'

'Two days? Do you know if you lie to a police officer your dick falls off?'

The guy nodded solemnly. 'I don't speak English, sir.'

'Oh yeah? Do you like spaghetti? Where'd you buy that hat?'

'I speak Spanish.'

'Spanish? Donde de yomo doo-doo.'

'Como?'

'You don't speak Spanish. You're full of shit.' He took the guy's hat off his head, the guy's hand coming up five seconds too late. The cop took out a lighter.

'You ever try to smoke a Panama hat?'

'It's my hat.' The man in white remained flat-faced, not even daring to frown.

The cop sighed, playing with the lighter, then took the hat and screwed it down on the guy's head all the way to his eyebrows.

'Thank you for coming to the Royal. Please don't ever fucking come back again.' He waved the guy off.

Strike slunk down low in his seat, the cop beating a paradiddle on his fender, throwing him the same beckoning head tilt through the windshield. Strike made sure the .25 was kicked deep under the seat, then slowly emerged from the car.

'How you doing?' The cop gave him that same pleased-to-meet-you beam.

'OK.' Strike knew to keep his answers to one or two words, not give the guy a chance to goof on him. The cop wore three gold chains and a gold ID bracelet, which made Strike wonder if he was really a cop after all.

'You here for dope or pussy?' The cop looked up at the catwalk, waving, some of the people waving back.

'Neither.' Strike cleared his throat, said it stronger. 'Neither.' He felt OK now, not too shaky – in fact, somehow relieved.

'So what are you here for?'

'Nothing,' Strike answered, hearing the stupidness in it.

'Nothing. You just like to drive up the rear of the Royal, sit in your car and like, what . . . think?'

Strike shrugged, tried not to smile.

'What do you think about? The environment? 'Cause this is some fucking environment, let me tell you.'

'A friend . . .' Strike felt as if he was on TV.

'A friend. Who?'

'Donald.' He'd almost said, 'I don't know his name.'

'Donald. Donald. Yeah, well, you know what happened? Donald moved to Orlando.'

'Oh yeah?'

The cop shrugged apologetically. 'Yeah, he's down there with Mickey and Goofy so . . .'

'Uh-huh.' Strike started to backpedal to the car door.

The cop was momentarily distracted by another kid, who was walking briskly through the lot. 'Whoa, whoa.' He flagged him down.

The new kid, clam-colored, pockmarked, came up fast, charging right into the cop's face as if he had nothing to hide, even though his eyes were bugging out of his head.

Both Strike and the cop stared, the cop turning to Strike and saying, 'Do you see what I see?'

The kid shook his head, laughing a little too heartily. 'No sir, please.' He sounded foreign but not Latino. He touched a surgical scar across his throat and said, 'Thyroid.'

'Thyroid,' the cop repeated.

The kid reached into his pocket and pulled out three colored disks on a key ring; 'A.A.' was stamped in gold on each one. 'Thirty, sixty, ninety days.' He gave a froggy smile, but Strike saw a little tremble in his fingers.

The cop extended his hand for a shake. 'Congratulations. Really, really, I swear, congratulations. Now why don't you take your fucking tags and get the fuck out of here.'

The kid nodded animatedly as if it was a great idea.

'But first, I want you to meet . . .' The cop looked over at Strike.

'Charles.' Strike looked away.

'Charles.' The cop brought their hands together, the other guy's palm a swamp, the kid actually saying 'Hi.'

'Charles is a dope dealer. Why he's coming around here I don't know, but now that both of you know each other, why don't you both get off my fucking beat, out of my fucking domain, and do some business on the other side of the highway, OK? Hey Charles, is that reasonable of me or what?'

Back in the Ahab's lot, Strike paced under the trembling shadow of a huge plaster statue of a whale hunter that rotated on top of the restaurant. The gun was back in the Accord where it belonged.

What to do. Darryl was killing him, kicking his ass. *Talk* to the guy. *Explain* the situation. Then if he doesn't . . . Then if . . .

Strike continued pacing, hissing to himself, scowling up at the revolving Ahab, his hands whirling before him in pantomimed debate, the restaurant's exhaust fan sending out a cloud of reek that came over him like an emotion – the smell of panic. Strike felt as if *he* was the victim, and he imagined Darryl in there laughing his ass off, tormenting Strike with his status as Rodney's number-one man, Rodney's choice-boy. Strike tried to get puffed up with anger one more time, but it was like willing himself to sprout wings and fly. The cop had seen him, that baby-fat girl had seen him; it was hopeless. He imagined explaining all this to Rodney – I *would* have gone through with it but I ain't *stupid* – and his stomach bellowed for something cool and soothing. Scanning the street across from the Ahab's lot, Strike looked for some kind of sanctuary, some shadow place to sit down for a minute so he could regroup.

The music coming out of the speakers in Rudy's Lounge was so loud that it went all the way around into a kind of silence. Strike walked in under the blare, hand on his stomach, instantly regretting his choice. The room was illuminated by a few bare red-tinted light bulbs. Under the dull, hellish glare, a half-dozen customers hunched over their drinks at the bar.

Sniffing the yeasty odor of slopped beer, Strike turned to leave, but before he could complete his about-face, the bartender slapped a cardboard coaster in front of him as if staking a claim. 'How's it goin'?'

Strike squinted at the hand-drawn announcements of dinner specials and charity events wedged into the frame of the bar mirror, then turned and eyed the revolving plaster Ahab directly across the street. He turned back to the bartender.

'You don't have, like, Yoo-Hoo here?'

The bartender struggled to keep a straight face. 'Yoo-Hoo?'

'Well, you got something like . . . I don't drink ah-*al*cohol. Muh-milk, you got milk?' The stammer caught Strike by surprise, but it wasn't anything he couldn't control right now.

'We got dairy creamer.' The bartender hunched forward as if fascinated by Strike and his strange tastes. 'You want a glass of dairy creamer?'

Strike bared his teeth, miming disgust.

'How about Coco Lopez mix?'

'What's that?'

'Piña colada mix, it's sweet.'

'Yeah, that, but not too cold.'

The bartender straightened up, snapped his fingers. 'I got to go get it.' He whirled in place, patting himself as if he'd lost something. Abruptly sinking from sight, he descended into his storeroom through a trapdoor under the duckboards. Strike was left staring at the empty spot behind the bar where the bartender had been standing.

'Hey.' The voice came from his right – now what? – and Strike turned as one of the hunched-over shadows unfolded and extended a hand. Strike hissed in exasperation, thinking, Not my night, then shaking hands with his brother, Victor, a dry awkward clasp as if they were going to arm wrestle in midair.

'Yeah, I was just thinking about you.' Strike said it flat and quick, moving away from the bar and then pacing behind his brother's back, too jumpy to take a stool.

'I'm OK.' Victor spoke to his drink, a tight smile on his face. He seemed liquor-loose, although Strike hadn't ever been around him in a bar before.

'You still with that girl?'

Eyeing the room, Strike didn't even hear his own question. A drunken security guard sat three stools down, looking at him through droopy lids, his cap on the bar, soaking up a splash of wetness.

'Yeah, we still together.'

'She have that baby yet?'

'Which one?'

'The other one,' Strike said, pacing, fighting down the urge to shake the security guard and tell him to drain his damn hat.

'Yeah, we got two. Ivan and Mark, Ivan and Mark.'

'Uh-huh. How's Ma?' Everything coming out of his mouth was automatic.

'She hangin' in.'

That one caught Strike's attention. Victor's tone was tentative and a little mournful, suggesting that in fact their mother was having her problems. But then Strike thought about Rodney, Darryl, himself, all of it – well, she wasn't the only one. 'Oh yeah?' Strike said. 'I'm hangin' in too.'

Victor turned to him, reared back to assess his face, and Strike saw concern in the gesture. Strike felt so moved by Victor's reaction that for the first time in years he wished that Victor was his brother again, his older brother.

'You know that Ahab's there?' Strike blindly jerked his hand in the general direction of the front door.

'Hell, yeah, that's the competition.' Victor sounded sarcastic as he hunkered back down over his drink.

Strike spied a bloom of orange polyester peeking out of a gym bag at Victor's feet. His Hambone's uniform, probably: How come Darryl didn't have to wear no goddamn uniform at Ahab's? 'You-all know the manager?'

'Muhammad? The Indian guy?' Victor began writing something on his napkin.

'Naw, the submanager, the *under* guy, Darryl. Tall guy, skinny.'

'Naw, well yeah. But I only know him from being tall, you know, not like for conversation.'

'That guy is real nasty. He's some bad people.'

'Nasty how?' Victor was talking down to his napkin, still writing.

Strike didn't answer. Why the hell was he saying all this? And what was Victor writing?

'Nasty how?' Victor repeated flatly.

'He beat up this young girl.' Strike flashed on the baby-fat girl, wanting to say rape, but rape was too distasteful. 'Yeah, he beat her up. She was like thirteen, fourteen, some such.'

'Where?' Victor wouldn't look up from the napkin. Was he writing down what Strike was saying?

'Where what?' Strike tried to see over his brother's shoulder to the napkin.

'Where'd he beat her?'

Strike was momentarily distracted by a heavyset elderly woman looking at him in the bar mirror. She wore huge glasses that made each eye-blink seem as if it took place in slow motion.

'Where'd he beat her?' Victor sounded patient, persistent.

The lady locked eyes with Strike in the mirror, then grudgingly turned away.

'You don't know?' Victor's tone was gentle, but his words came out almost in a blurt, as if the liquor, more than any natural curiosity, was urging him on.

'Nah, I don't know.' Strike finally managed to get a look at Victor's napkin, reading WASHINGTON WARRIORS and DALLAS DEVASTATORS in small block letters.

Strike shook his head: Goddamn, he's still fucking around with that dumb-ass Aroundball. Two years earlier, when they had shared a bedroom, Victor jumped out of bed one night and started to write down the rules of a game he had just dreamed about. He called it Aroundball but Strike never really understood how it was played – it seemed to him like a cross between dodgeball and soccer. The game had become an obsession of Victor's; for months he was writing up new bylaws or trying out new names for the franchises. But Strike had almost forgotten about it since leaving home.

The security guard started coughing, a sharp, wet, painful sound, and when Strike turned to the noise he caught the guy staring at him. The bar was starting to resemble a mental hospital now. Where the hell did the bartender go? Strike wanted to leave, took a step to the door, looked out at Ahab's across the street. He backstepped to stand behind his brother again.

'This girl, her muh-mother's all gassed up, you know, like to kuh-kill him too. Sh-she don't have no brothers or no father but her old lady is buggin'. I mean, she wants this guy *dead.*' Strike was making all this up on the fly, desperate for his brother's commiseration, insisting on Darryl's condemnation.

'Yeah, huh?'

Strike had seen Victor wince at his stammer, and now he thought about Darryl, so slick and quiet. It bothered him that Darryl didn't have to wear

a uniform like Victor or that dreamy counter girl in the blue smock at
Ahab's. He didn't even have a name tag on his chest. He was above it all
in his expensive red running suit, his gold medallion. Darryl had never
worn stuff like that back when he was working in Rodney's store.

Strike was fuming now: That dope-dealing piece of shit. 'He deserve it
too, you know? I mean, it was like, sh-she come into the store. He gets her
to go in the back office or something, like for a *job* interview, he says "Give
it up," but she's like a nuh-nice girl, clean and all, you know, innocent? So
he just wound up *beatin'* on her, muh-messed up her face, and then he goes
right out to the front, starts servin' up food again like nothin' happened.'
Strike stopped abruptly, overwhelmed with shame, revolted by the sound
of his own sputtering speech and the lies that dressed his cowardice.

'Are you in trouble with him?'

'I ain't afraid a him.' Strike reared back, then realized he hadn't answered
the question and quickly added, 'I ain't even *seen* him in like *months*.'

'You know why I ask, right?' Victor gave Strike a sloppy knowing
look.

Unnerved by Victor's question, Strike turned away. An old man in a
blue skipper's hat walked in behind him, made a face at him in the mirror.
Crazy house. Strike felt a pang of sadness for his brother. What the hell
was he doing in here with these people?

Again he wanted to leave, but the bartender emerged from the trapdoor
holding a can of Coco Lopez mix. Strike noticed the film of grit on the
can. The bartender shook it up and punched it open with a can opener
without wiping it clean first, just pushing the dust and rust right inside.

'So how's Ma?'

'She's good. You know, she's working.' Victor wrote CLEVELAND
CATASTROPHES on the napkin. Peering over his shoulder, Strike picked
up the smoky sweet scotch fumes coming from his brother.

'Yeah, I hear that. I was gonna come by, you know, say hello.'

The bartender poured the mix into a beer glass, slid it toward Strike.
No way on earth he was drinking that.

Not wanting to dwell on the subject of their mother, Strike returned
to his Darryl and baby-fat girl story. 'Yeah, Darryl got to be got. He
de-deserve it. That girl was really nice, clean, all the time clean. Huh-*hair*
brushed . . .' Strike decided that it was too much trouble to complain
about how dirty the can was – the Coco Lopez, Victor and Darryl, all
conspiring to muddle his head.

'Yeah, he sellin' dope, too,' Victor said mildly.

Strike went still as a deer. 'I don't know nothin' about that.'

'Yeah, he *got* to be *got*,' Victor said in a mock-dramatic tone, as if toying with Strike and his transparent tale. 'Dope-dealin' Mobie-sellin' *rape* artist '

'Yeah, well, I don't know nothing about that.' Strike put down two dollars for his untouched drink. Victor knew about Ahab's – shit, everybody probably knew.

'*Got* to be *got*,' Victor said again, lightly pounding the bar with his fist.

Strike heard an edge of anger underneath the mockery in Victor's voice, and he couldn't tell if it was directed toward himself or Darryl. Without thinking about it, Strike took a sip of the filth-and-rust cocktail, then wiped his lips with the back of his hand.

'I know somebody who'd do it, too,' Victor said softly as he returned to his inkings, his shoulders hunched in concentration, the cocktail napkin more black than white now.

'What you say?' Strike stared at Victor in the mirror.

'I said I know somebody who'd do it, too.' He fixed Strike's eye with a fast, sober look.

'Who?' Strike heard the hopefulness in his question.

'My man.' As if that explained it all, Victor's eyes dropped to his writing again.

'My man *who*?'

'This guy.'

'You *know* him?'

Victor fixed him with that cold, sober stare in the mirror again. 'I said he was my man, didn't I?'

Strike suddenly knew what to do: Pass it on. Shit, that's what Rodney did. Pass it on.

'What would he do it for?' He took a gulp of Coco Lopez, forcing himself to sound casual.

Victor shrugged. 'For nothin' . . . For me.'

The bartender poured Victor another shot, and Strike instinctively turned his back so it would look as if they weren't even talking.

'Where's he from?'

'Here.'

'Here where?'

'Town, the houses . . .'

''Cause this lady is *serious*.'

Victor threw back his drink. 'My man's serious too.'

'Do I know this guy?'

'I don't know. I don't know *who* you know anymore. But you might, yeah, you might.'

Strike decided not to ask any more questions – what you don't know can't incriminate you. ''Cause this lady will pay. Money's no expense to her.'

They fell into silence. Strike thinking, This is great, this is perfect, pass it on. Pass it on. He felt flushed with relief. He was using his head, as always, thinking on where to take this now, how to play it out, when Victor abruptly announced: 'If you can't do the *time*, don't do the *crime*.' He said it like a deep-voiced TV announcer and then started in on a new napkin, the first one an ink-stained crazy quilt. Strike watched him doodle for a moment and found himself sinking like a rock.

'If you *play*, you *pay*.' Victor's voice was still theatrical and officious, and now Strike saw that his brother was very drunk.

Strike scanned the bar – all the inmates, the old people, the yellow-eyed winos – his eyes coming to rest on Victor's hunched shoulders. Probably the screwiest drunk in the room, talking trash just like their father. Strike was heartsick with disappointment. He'd been so desperate for help that he'd been blind to Victor's condition and fallen right into his bullshit. And then disappointment became rage, and Strike was furious at himself, sorry he even opened his mouth. He'd dropped even deeper into the hole: now his brother was nothing more than another witness to his whereabouts. Badmouthing Darryl too – shit, shit.

'I got to go.' Strike looked toward the door, the street. He'd tell Rodney it would have to wait.

'Anything you want me to tell my man?' Victor raised a hand for another shot, his nose still down over his napkin.

'I'll ask that girl's mother about it.' Strike paused, wanting to leave on a different subject. 'You still living at home?'

'When I'm there.'

Strike hesitated for a second, thinking about what else to say, when Victor added: 'I miss my kids.'

Strike heard real sadness and remorse in that and resisted an impulse to tell his brother to go home. 'Yeah, well . . .' He started backing to the door, then stopped when Victor spoke again:

'Davishing.'

'What?'

'You ever hear of a word "Davishing"?'

'Unh-uh.' Strike was restless to go.

'I was doing security work today in this clothing store in New York?

I got this *other* job too, now. So I was like, standing there, and this lady came up to me, she just tried on this shorty kimono. She came up to me, she says, "How do I look?" You know what I said? "Davishing." I got all flustered, so I said, "Davishing."' Victor hissed and reared back as if someone had shoved smelling salts under his nose, talking to Strike casually as if they were still sharing a bedroom, saw each other every day. 'Davishing. God*damn*.' He shook his head, laughing at himself.

Strike continued backing away. 'Yeah, I was just thinking about you. Say hi to Ma.'

Victor raised his hand in a farewell gesture without turning around, his shoulders bunched higher than his head, still writing out his list of dream teams on a wet cocktail napkin.

'*Da*vishing.' The word was a final disgusted hiss that followed Strike right out into the street.

6

On Friday night, exactly one week after their last job, and just as Mazilli was pulling into the parking lot of the Lemon Tree Family Restaurant, Rocco's beeper went off. This time, everybody including the actor knew that this was no call from home.

Mazilli rocked to a disgusted stop in the middle of the parking lot and made Rocco walk to the phones indoors. When Rocco came back out, Mazilli was still sitting there, an obstinate fifty yards away from the restaurant entrance, as if boycotting the inevitable.

'Dempsy burnin'.' Rocco slid into the front seat, throwing Touhey a fast wink: showtime.

'Likely to die? Maybe we can have a little nourishment here?' Mazilli pressed his palms together, praying to the steering wheel. If the heart was still beating, no matter how imminent the death, the Homicide squad was officially on hold.

'Sorry.' Rocco couldn't help smiling. 'Out of the picture.'

'In the hospital?' Mazilli begged.

'Body on the scene.'

Rocco saw that Touhey understood *that* at least, the actor getting happy eyes that he couldn't mask.

'Indoors?' Mazilli chewed his thumb. 'No, fucking outdoors, right? Outdoors in the jungle, right?'

Rocco dragged out the guessing game. 'Well, it's kind of indoors and outdoors.'

'What, doubleheader?'

'No, but the guy's laying in the doorway of a restaurant, half in, half out.'

'Beautiful.' Mazilli sighed, turning on the ignition again. 'What are you calling a restaurant? McDonald's? Hambone's? Kentucky Fried Chicken?'

'Close. Ahab's on De Groot.'

'Ahab's.' Mazilli muttered something inarticulate, then tilted his head toward the back seat. 'You have an Ahab's where you live?'

Touhey blinked and shrugged.

'Deep-fried *fish* assholes. You should try one.'

Riding across town to his first murder, Touhey acted like a kid, bobbing up and down on the rear seat, elbows between the front headrests.

'It's amazing,' he chattered, 'if you think about it. That pager, it's a pipeline to the belly of the beast. Every time that thing beeps, it means the beast chewed up another one. It's like having your finger on the rage pulse of an entire city, you know what I mean? You can actually monitor the homicidal rage of a city on your hip. It's a *rage* meter, that beeper.'

Rocco, relieved that the actor was in a good mood, smiled at him. 'I never thought of it that way.'

'De *rage* meter,' Mazilli said dryly, an announcement to no one, then started to sing, '"Beep-beep, beep-beep, the horn went beep-beep-beep." You remember that song? "While riding in my Ca-di-*lac*, much to my sur-*prise* . . ." You ever meet them? The guys who sang that?' Mazilli looked in the rearview mirror.

'I never heard it before,' Touhey said.

'You never heard it? How about, "Who Hit Annie in the Fannie with a Flounder"? You ever hear that?'

The Lemon Tree Restaurant was in the town of Rydell, twenty minutes from the scene, and the drive took them from white working-class aluminum siding to black housing projects to JFK Boulevard. JFK was two miles of funk: storefront churches, deserted lots, hair salons and private day-care centers. Most of the store signs were hand drawn – lots of reds and light blues, crudely rendered heads and faces painted on cinder block or plywood, long-winded church names, blinking yellow chase lights over the combination smoke shop/video rental/candy stores, cameras mounted on every other telephone pole to monitor drug transactions. There were enough people on the streets just standing around to make Rocco feel as if a parade would turn the corner any minute.

'This looks like Central America,' Touhey said happily.

'When I was a kid?' Rocco arched up, shifted his gun slightly off his hipbone. 'This was Frawley Avenue. You could walk down the street naked, middle of the night. It was a pleasure.'

'How come you guys are stopping for all the red lights?' Touhey started bouncing on the edge of his seat again.

'Well, how do *you* drive?' Mazilli looked in the rearview again.

'Yeah, but there's a murder, right?'

'The guy's *dead.*'

Mazilli pulled the car over about two blocks from the scene. From here Rocco could see the municipal block party shaping up: a half-dozen green and yellow cruisers slant-parked in the Ahab's lot, along with another half-dozen unmarked tan Plymouths and an ambulance, its beacon swinging out shafts of red in a lazy whirl. The herd was jumping, people running to and from the outer edge of the growing crowd, lots of yelling and laughing, and on the restaurant roof the plaster Ahab – complete with pegleg, Amish beard and harpoon – revolved thirty feet in the sky, one arm outstretched as if inviting one and all to view the body.

Mazilli threw the car in park, ran a hand over his mouth and sighed through his nose. Then he left the car and sauntered into Shaft Deli-Liquors, which was flanked by Keisha's Hair Salon and the Thunderball Lounge.

'What's he doing?' Touhey tried to keep the impatience out of his voice, but Rocco knew he was jumping out of his skin.

'Getting a few of those airplane bottles – you know, a little shnortsky before we get into the shit.' Rocco hoped Mazilli wouldn't be a cheap bastard and grab a Smirnoff, with the Stoli sitting right next to it. 'You didn't want anything, did you? I didn't even think to ask. You know, I saw you nursing that club soda there.'

'No.' Touhey drew his mouth down and nodded.

They both stared in silence at a life-size cardboard cutout of a black woman in a sequined dress slit up the side, fondling the tip of an ebony cue stick placed six inches above a pair of eight balls on a pool table. There was something orange and foamy in a brandy snifter held in her free hand.

'Well, what if someone in there sees him buying booze down the street from a murder? He's the investigator of record, right?'

'Well yeah.' Rocco shifted his gun off his hip again. 'But he owns the store.'

When Mazilli came out a few minutes later, they left the car where it was and walked to the Scene. Rocco liked to come up on homicide crowds from the rear, weave his way up to the tape so he could overhear snatches of street speculation.

It was hard to drink straight out of the small-mouthed bottles but they managed, tossing the empties while they were still a block away. Rocco let Touhey carry the steel forensic case. He nudged the actor, tilting his chin to the sky.

'Anytime the moon's full like that? Any cop with half a brain goes around with his safety off.'

'Get out.'

'Mazilli, am I lying?'

'Nope.' Mazilli was already working, noting people on high stoops, in lit windows and open stores, any hangout spot with a good view.

'Jails, mental wards, kennels, they all put out No Vacancy signs,' Rocco said.

'Come on,' Touhey burbled, a little trot in his step.

'The full moon is for real. It's got enough magnetic power to affect the tides of the Atlantic and Pacific oceans, two of the biggest we have, OK? Meanwhile, the human *brain* is eighty percent fluid, you follow me?' Rocco mimed pouring from a pitcher into his ear, feeling more drunk than he wanted to be.

Touhey laughed. 'So the full moon comes out, people walk around all night sloshing?' He tilted his head from shoulder to shoulder. 'Low tide, high tide, low tide?'

'Hey, I'm no scientist. I just . . .' Rocco sidled into the rear of the herd, standing on tiptoes, craning his neck, going to work.

'What the fuck happened?' he said out loud to no one.

'That ol' boy got shot *up*,' drawled a teenager without turning around.

'Yeah? Who shot him?'

The kid turned and gave Rocco the once-over, smirking.

Rocco decided to push it a little. 'He was a nice guy, right? Who the hell would want to shoot *him*?'

'I wouldn't know.' The kid was watching the local detectives take down the license plate numbers on the few cars still parked in the lot.

'Got any ideas?'

'Yeah, well, I don't want to cast out no false criticisms per *se*, you know?'

Rocco laughed. 'Hey, I wouldn't want you to.' He slipped the kid his card, down low at hip level, then moved on through, Touhey almost stepping on his heels.

The crowd was held at bay by a thirty-foot-long crime scene tape. Rocco duckwalked under the fluttering yellow strip, then held it high for the actor. He caught a quick glimpse of Mazilli walking away from the action, heading off with one of his street connections, the two of them trudging uphill, carefully avoiding the glaring cones of streetlights that marked their path. From experience, Rocco knew that in roughly a half hour Mazilli would return with either everything or nothing.

Entering the DMZ that was the Ahab's parking lot was like walking on stage, both Rocco and Touhey getting what was known as the Dempsy Stare from some of the young bloods: a furrow-browed, open-mouthed, swivel-headed look of defiance that followed every cop who worked JFK Boulevard or the housing projects or in any poor section of the city.

Rocco turned to size up the crowd across the tape, feeling as if he was inside a movie screen, looking out at the audience. He grinned at the actor. 'You want to throw 'em some *Sweet Bird of Youth*?'

'What?' Touhey blinked, starting to look shaky now.

'My public,' Rocco said, enjoying his own quip. He was content to hang back near the crowd for a few minutes more, soaking up fragments of conversation, scanning faces beyond the tape, but then he found himself in an eyelock with one kid who stared back from under a Rock of Gibraltar sculpted fade with an orange tint. Rocco's gaze went from the kid's eyes to his hair and back to his stare; the kid was not so much defiant as unintimidated.

Hands in pockets, Rocco absently belly-bumped the tape as he nodded to the kid. 'What's up, Money?'

The kid shrugged, curling his hands under his perforated blue-and-orange Mets jersey, exposing his flat belly. The blue hem of his boxer shorts was two inches higher than the waist of his gray acid-washed jeans. 'Nah, you know, nothin'.' The kid smiled, apparently enjoying the idea of bullshitting with a Homicide.

'Nothin'?'

'What, they kill the manager in there?' The kid tilted his head toward the building.

'Who's "they"?'

The kid shrugged again, an arm disappearing up to the elbow inside his shirt, caressing his chest. 'Nah, you know.'

'*You* do it?'

'Me? Nah, man. I go to school.'

'Oh yeah?' Rocco grinned with delight: Dempsy logic.

'I don't even *like* that place.'

'You don't like the crab legs? I thought you guys lived off crab legs.'

'Crab legs cost *money*.'

Two of the kid's friends rolled by, hanging all over him, staring at Rocco, intrigued.

'How 'bout you guys, you like crab legs?'

They continued to stare without speaking.

'How about Golden Mobies?'

Ignoring Rocco, one of the new kids zeroed in on Touhey, who was standing ten feet back, the steel case between his ankles, trying hard to look casual. 'That ain't no cop. That nigger look *scared*.'

Rocco waggled a finger at the kid, a laid-back warning, and then, as much to remove Touhey from the curious and vaguely hostile stares as to actually get down to work, he finally turned to the darkened restaurant.

The body lay in the side entrance, surrounded by yet another ring of ribbon, the spotlit plaster Ahab revolving over the corpse like an amusement-park angel of death, the grinding of its motor audible in the stillness of the inner circle.

Rocco held up the second tape for Touhey. The body lay at their feet now, covered except for a pair of snow-white Filas sticking out from under a white sheet, heels down, the ankles crossed as if death was just another way of taking it easy. An arm peeked out from the sheet, the wrist cocked back languidly so that the hand, palm up, was slightly raised off the ground, resting on its knuckles. Blotches of red still bloomed at the head, blood seeping out from the top border of the sheet, carrying along bits of brain matter like a floating scatter of baby teeth and encircling a purple and white University of Maryland cap.

The sheet annoyed Rocco: it was a contaminant. He could understand if the local squad had been worried about crowd control, the herd getting all jacked up by the sight of blood, but they should have just parked a car nearby to block the view. Now, if he got some of the shooter's hairs off the victim, any semiconscious defense lawyer would claim they came from the sheet, not the body. Rocco started brooding about the possible trial: reasonable doubt can be a real ass-kicker sometimes.

'Hey Rocco.'

Rocco turned to the wheezing voice. 'Heyyy . . .' He shook hands with Vince Kelso, a precinct detective who'd married Thumper's older sister, Rocco's ex-high school sweetheart. Kelso weighed three hundred pounds and owned a local scrap-metal yard, buying scavenged scrap from junkies. The yard stayed open around the clock to accommodate their hours.

'What you got there, Vince?' Rocco decided not to say anything about the sheet. He didn't want Kelso to get all sniffy and defensive. If the guy had lived, this would've been Kelso's catch, an aggravated assault. But given that the guy had gone out of the picture, any work Kelso was doing now had to be considered a favor.

Kelso wheezed, gave the actor a cool glance and flipped open his notebook. 'Darryl Adams, twenty-one, -two, assistant manager. The kid was out here by the door getting ready to close up, nobody else in the restaurant. Talking to a black male in a hooded sweatshirt, pop pop poppity pop, Adams goes down, the black male's in the wind, running south in the direction of the mini-mall. You got four nine-millimeter casings by the body and that's, more or less, all she wrote.'

Rocco nodded to the body. 'Was he a scumbag?'

Kelso shrugged. '*I* never heard of him.'

'A robbery?'

'Too fast.'

'So what do you think? Drugs? Nine millimeter, right?'

Kelso shrugged again.

'Got some witnesses?'

Kelso took Rocco by the elbow and walked him around to the back of the restaurant, past the dumpsters, out of everybody's view. At the far end of the rear wall, a black woman, anywhere from thirty to fifty years old, sat on the ground with her chin in her chest, her back against the brick. Someone had penned her in with crime scene tape in a loose, three-garbage-can triangle.

Rocco shook his head as if to clear his vision. 'What's with the fucking corral?'

'I told her it's electronically treated tape. If she walks off she'll trigger an alarm.'

'She's a fucking witness, Vince! What the hell are you doing?'

'Roc, listen, it's OK, believe me. She's totally fucking zotzed. This way nobody bothers her.'

'Ah Christ, Vince.'

'You want to talk to her?'

As if to answer the question herself, the woman rolled on her side and fell asleep on the ground. Again Rocco thought ahead to the possible trial, the defense bombing out his only witness for being soaked on the night of the murder. Great.

'Awright, look,' Rocco said, 'can you do me a favor? If you got a free car, maybe somebody could take her to the prosecutor's office.' He turned away from Kelso to hide his disgust at how the scene had been mishandled. 'Let her sleep it off on the couch. Somebody'll come back, talk to her later.'

'No problem.' Kelso seemed oblivious to Rocco's mood.

'Just give me her name and shit, in case she gets lost in the shuffle.' Rocco frisked himself, realizing he'd left his notebook in the car. He went to his wallet, rummaged around looking for a blank surface to write on, settling on the back of a two-by-three photograph of Erin. He took down the woman's name and address, then walked away from Vince and held the picture of Erin high over his head, showing it the corpse, the cops, the herd, talking to it: 'See what Daddy does for a living, honey? See all the nice people?'

Crouching down to unsnap the forensic case, Rocco reached in and took out a few rubber bands, popped them in his mouth and began chewing, something he always did when processing a body. He took out a loaded Nikon and stole a glance at Touhey, who was gaping at the bloody sheet.

'First thing, Sean, always tuck in your tie.' Rocco talked through the rubbery crunch, sucking up saliva.

'What?' Touhey sounded hypnotized, eyes pulled down, mouth open.

'Bend over a body, you get your tie in the chest.' Rocco made a face and handed up a six-cell flashlight. Touhey moved slowly, looking at the light before extending his hand, staring at Rocco as if from a dream. Rocco smiled at him. 'I don't know where the fuck Mazilli went. You mind helping me out?'

'Really?'

Rocco smiled again, thinking, You asked for it.

Down in a squat now, Rocco gingerly removed the sheet. Detectives and uniforms, stone-faced but curious, sauntered over for the show.

'Hello dere.' Rocco looked into the kid's slack eyes, which came alive with the reflected beam of the flashlight.

The body, dressed in a red nylon running suit and sporting a heavy gold Lion of Judah medallion, was stretched out on its back: legs crossed, arms crooked at identical V-shaped angles of surrender, the head turned in profile so that the cheek was resting on a grimy Ahab's take-out bag adorned with a cartoon version of the plaster whale hunter waving goodbye, the legend FARE THEE WELL, MATEY! streaked with blood.

Rising, Rocco turned to the gathered cops. 'Fellas, you want to step back or you want to smile for the birdy.' The detectives strolled off, and as Rocco focused his camera, Touhey's hand wavered, the beam of light wandering from Darryl Adams's face.

'Hang in there, chief.' Rocco made a clicking sound that was supposed to be reassuring, then started to photograph the murder, snapping the body from all points of the compass, both in close-up and from a distance. Then he photographed the streaked and greasy side door. According to what Rocco had been told over the phone, the door had been propped open by the body, and the fact that it was closed made him fret that the scene had been tampered with even more than he knew. Next, Rocco snapped off photos of four 9 mm shell casings that lay near the upturned sneakers, and then he shot everything else, all the random and mundane objects: garbage cans, soda bottle empties, a coat hanger – anything that because of its proximity to the corpse could be reasonably, or even wildly, considered part of the crime scene.

When he was certain there was nothing left to shoot except the full moon, he went back to the suitcase, left the camera in its shadow on the ground and took out a fat leather-encased roll of measuring tape. He fixed the location of the body and the casings by triangulation, getting the actor to read off the distances from the corner of the building and from a telephone pole. Touhey called out the measurements as if he was reciting names off the Vietnam War Memorial.

After bagging the casings, Rocco went back to the suitcase, this time coming up with a pair of yellow Rubbermaid gloves. He winked at Touhey as he worked them onto his hands. The other cops strolled back in for more.

Bouncing on his hams over the body, Rocco gently rocked the head back and forth by the chin, then lifted the dented Lion of Judah medallion, which lay up by the kid's ear and was still on its chain around the neck.

'Sean, give me some light here. Look.'

Rocco pointed at the medallion, then traced a path with his pinkie. A bullet had skidded off the lion's head right up into the underside of the gullet and straight through the skull, ending in a pinkish floret of brains peeking out the top of the head.

'Some fucking shot, huh?' Rocco smiled blind into the corolla of light.

'Good thing he was wearing that medallion,' someone said.

'Kid's got brains.'

'I still think it's the food here.'

'What the fuck are you eating, Rocco, *dog* biscuits?'

The voices coming at him had no faces. Then he heard Touhey's: 'I'm OK, I'm OK.' The voice sounded hoarse, and Rocco did a double take at that, the ridiculous self-centeredness of it. He shrugged it off and got back to work, spotting a bullet hole a few inches below where the medallion would have hung when the kid was standing. He pulled up the kid's jacket to take a quick peek at a neat, almost bloodless entry wound, like a small purple welt in the apex of the kid's solar plexus. 'That's two,' Rocco announced. Examining the kid's hands, he saw another entry wound

Victor came out of the bathroom, his damp hands curled to his chest, a spray of tap water spotting the front of his gray slacks. He looked directly at Rocco as if waiting for instruction.

Rocco reached for a fistful of tissues on an unoccupied desk and gestured to the kid's pants. '*I* don't care, but . . .'

Victor took the tissues and tried to blot himself dry.

Rocco leaned against the desk, regarding his prisoner and feeling a vague ripple of curiosity. Facing a possible thirty in, the kid washes his hands after taking a leak.

'All set?' Rocco lurched upright off the desk and gently gripped the kid's elbow. Washing his hands – like making his bed with the house on fire.

Part Three

MAKE YOU PAY

dead center in the right palm. 'That's three.' The bullet was trapped, bulging out of the back of the hand below the knuckles but not breaking the skin. Rocco held up the bloody palm to the crowd. 'Padre Pio, you remember him?'

'That's the mystic eye.'

'Who the fuck's the shooter here, Annie Oakley?'

Rocco looked up, squinting past the light, surprised to see Rockets Cronin, groggy and cranky. In his trench coat and holding his own steel suitcase, he looked like a Fuller Brush man on a losing streak. Rocco thought he must have been bored out of his mind to make the scene.

'Rockets, my man, we need blood and we need prints off this door here.' Rocco indicated an already browning comet-tail of splatter on the lower pane of the side door.

Rockets looked at the door with horror. 'What are you, shitting me? I'll get every nigger in town off there.'

Rocco quickly looked around to see if there were any black cops within earshot. Relieved to see none, he looked down at the body again, blocking out Rockets, thinking, Four casings, fourth bullet, where's it at? He grabbed Darryl Adams's head, giving him a rude, penetrating scalp massage with all ten fingers. He looked for a hole, avoiding the bud of brains, and found nothing, his gloved hands coming away bloody. He began undressing the body, unzipping the red nylon sweat suit, pulling up the white Duke University T-shirt, pulling down the red sweatpants, the red Jockey shorts, probing into the kid's groin, performing the same vigorous dig around the genitals, nothing, his fingertips imprinting the kid's skin with bloody coins. He flopped the kid over, face down in his own blood now, noting the jagged hole in his back, the exit wound from the solar plexus shot, saying 'Exit' out loud, moving on, stroking the kid's back, the ash-gray buttocks, then spreading the thighs. Rocco bobbed on the balls of his feet, his calves starting to cramp, and wiped sweat from his hairline with a curled wrist, the rolled rubber cuff of the glove catching some hair, pinching. 'C'mon, mother-fucker, where you at.' The smell of the rubber bands in his mouth started to get to him, and then he noticed tiny white fragments clinging to the kid's shoulder blades: What the hell? Thinking bone, lung, then getting some on his fingertips, playing with it, looking into Touhey's flashlight and holding up his finger. 'Rice. Came right out the exit wound. He must've just ate.'

Touhey whispered something with 'God' in it. Most of the detectives hanging around started to wander off.

'But where the fuck,' Rocco said, probing, squinting, 'is the fourth

entry? Shit.' He flipped the kid on his back again, his face and hair matted
and spooled with the blood he had rolled in, his penis lying high up on
his belly.

Rocco looked up again, and for a woozy second the shadows made
Touhey, stiff as a statue behind his beam of light, seem ten feet tall. Now
on his knees, Rocco felt like a high priest at an altar, preparing the corpse
as an offering.

Finally Rocco groaned himself upright, standing with his elbows cocked
to keep his bloody Rubbermaids from his clothes. He watched a Mister
Softee truck trolling the crowd, its gentle theme song jingling, before it
stopped directly across the parking lot from the body and drew off some
of the people who had money.

'You finished?' A short bearded paramedic stood next to Rocco,
smoking. A bright orange body bag reeking of fresh vinyl was draped
over his shoulder like a serape. He offered Rocco a cigarette.

Rocco held up a bloody glove. 'No thanks.'

'You not finished?'

'Not yet.' Rocco turned to Touhey. 'Hangin' in?'

Touhey nodded without saying anything.

Rocco spied Mazilli in the semidarkness under some shot-out streetlights across the street from the far end of Ahab's parking lot. He was
talking to a ragged bunch of people squatting against the whitewashed
side wall of a Chinese restaurant; the wall was a known hangout for a
crew of harmless junkies who ate, slept and got high there twenty-four
hours a day. If Mazilli was down to canvassing this crowd, none of his
blue-chip informants had come through.

Rocco moved close to Touhey, stared down at the body with him,
thinking, Chinese restaurant, white rice, white rice, the food in Ahab's so
bad the assistant manager, who's probably getting paid next to nothing,
still goes out to eat.

'Sean, you know what frustrates the fuckin' hell out of me?'

'What . . .' The actor's voice was flat, his hand still training a beam on
the blood-frosted face, fifteen minutes past the time that Rocco had last
needed the light.

'I watch what I eat, I race-walk, I read all this stuff about health and
nutrition, and here I am, a middle-aged two-hundred-pound tub of shit.
This son of a bitch, he works in a fast-food place, probably eats greasy,
soggy fried shit two, three times a day, goes out after, has three, four
forty-ounce malt liquors, Ring Dings, grape soda, all kinds of crap,
probably never did a sit-up in his life. And look . . .' His hand on

Touhey's, Rocco tilted the flashlight down to the body's midriff. 'See that? A washboard gut. I have yet to observe the black male victim in this town with more than a thirty-inch waist.'

'That's 'cause they all get killed when they're twenty-one.' Mazilli walked up out of the darkness.

'Hey, there you are,' Rocco said. 'So?'

Mazilli looked back up to the junkie wall. 'We keeps our ear to the grindstone.' He nodded to the body. 'Was he a scumbag?'

'Well, it's nine millimeter.'

'You go through his pockets?' Mazilli straddled the kid's hips, working his fingers into the clothes, finding nothing. He put a foot under the kid's ass and rolled him over again, grimacing, blowing air and waving a hand in front of his face as some of the gas settling in the body silently escaped. Mazilli pulled up the waist of the kid's running suit, stuck two fingers into the hip pocket and daintily extracted a folded wad of money.

'Here you go,' said Mazilli, counting as he walked back to Rocco. 'A thousand, fifteen, two, twenty – twenty-five hundred in hundred-dollar bills. The guy was a scumbag.' He flapped the money against his thumbnail, reached into the suitcase and came up with two brown sandwich bags, a roll of tape and a pair of Rubbermaids.

'What do you think?' Mazilli held up the bags to Rocco.

Rocco shrugged. 'Why not?'

They each took a bag, slipped them over the kid's hands and taped them shut around the wrists.

Rocco looked to Touhey again. 'Death mittens, in case something's under the nails. You know, like hair, skin, from a struggle.'

'Keeps the freshness in, not the flavor out.' Mazilli was down on one knee, writing the body's name and the Homicide run number on each bagged hand.

Rocco walked over to the stone-faced actor. 'Hey, Sean, these are the jokes. You got to laugh to keep from crying, you know what I mean?'

'Hey, Roc.' Mazilli stooped spread-legged over the body, opening the kid's mouth by squeezing together the hollows of his cheeks. 'Check it out.'

Rocco guided Touhey's hand so that the flashlight was trained on the face again as Mazilli brushed the blood away from the teeth with a rubber fingertip. Something metallic gleamed through the blood into the beam.

'Ho!' Rocco squawked.

'Marvello the Magician. Catch a bullet with his teeth.'

'Hey, Sean. C'mere, check this out.'

Touhey didn't move.

'Hey, Sean.' Rocco squinted past the light, into the face. 'You OK?'

'He's *grieving*,' Mazilli muttered, then, digging at the metallic shine in the kid's mouth, extracted a gold tooth cap. 'False alarm.'

He peeled off his gloves and dropped them on the body before going to check out the dumpsters around the bend.

Rocco walked up to the actor, looked into his face. Grieving: Mazilli was right. Rocco was stunned.

'You finished here?' the paramedic asked again.

'Yeah.' Rocco spit out his chewed rubber bands. 'Watch the bags on the hands.' He peeled his gloves off, tossing them between the legs of the body, his eyes on the actor. Grieving.

The paramedic whistled for his partner to pull the ambulance up, then snapped out the body bag like a picnic blanket.

'Rocco!' Mazilli called to him from around the back of the restaurant.

Rocco moved hesitantly away from Touhey. 'You OK? You want to go back to the car?'

Touhey shook his head vigorously, his eyes glittering with held-back tears. 'This is what it's all about, no?'

'You should see the autopsy,' Rocco said.

Mazilli was hunkered down near the restaurant's service door, his flashlight playing on the graffiti scrawled on the side of a full-up dumpster. Rocco scanned the messages: DO RON KORVETTE SUMO TAKWAN ONE LOVE PIGIN SHAKIRA.

'One Love,' Mazilli said.

'What about it?'

'Touch it.'

Rocco pressed a fingertip into the silvery spray paint. His hand came away with shiny patches on his skin. The paint was not exactly wet, more like tacky, about two hours old.

'What's One Love, a name?' Rocco asked.

'Are you kidding me? That's nothing,' Mazilli said. 'There's some kid in O'Brien named Buddha Hat.'

'So what are you thinking? The shooter did the guy, stopped, sprayed his name and ran off?'

'Maybe he sprayed his name before – you know, like to kill time waiting for his guy to come out. We're not talking masterminds here.'

'One Love,' Rocco said. 'How do you know it's not a soul group?'

'There's this other kid, from Booker T.? His name's Say the Truth.'

'So what do you want to do? Go down, check the moniker file?'

'It wouldn't hurt,' said Mazilli. 'Hey, maybe it's a witness.'

Rocco took the picture of Erin out of his pocket, wrote 'One Love' on the back. 'Lemme get Rockets back here, do a scraping, take a picture.' Rising, Rocco surveyed the grounds: coffee cups, candy wrappers, cigarette butts, a coke vial. 'We should bag all this shit up, right?'

They exchanged reluctant looks.

'What else? Canvass . . .' Rocco twirled his finger to signify all places within sight and hearing. 'Get the fucking employees back down here, the family, I got that fucking blotto witness. What else, what else?' Rocco sighed, assessed the turf. 'We're talking breakfast here – who's coming in on the midnight tour?'

'Brown and Honey.'

'Better than nothing.'

'Hey, Roc.' Mazilli was still down on one knee, his elbow resting on his thigh.

'What?' Rocco waited, not liking the tone of Mazilli's voice.

Mazilli's eyes went from ONE LOVE to the ground and back to Rocco. 'Get that asshole out of here.'

'Which one?'

Mazilli blew out a stream of air, his humorless eyes now fixed on Rocco's face.

Rocco cracked a smile. 'Hey, Maz. You're fucking with my meal ticket there.' Rocco flushed the minute he said it. It came out too fast, and he didn't even know what he meant by it.

Mazilli stared at him, spitting out a shred of dinner between his thin lips. 'Your fucking *meal* ticket? You want a meal ticket, you come in with me. I told you that.'

'What, the liquor store? Are you kidding me? I just spent twenty years of my life up to my tits in this shit, you think I want to spend the next twenty swapping welfare checks for half pints of Knotty Head?' Rocco laughed. 'Give me a break.' Then, worrying he had stepped over the line, he put a little pleading into it. 'C'mon, Maz.'

Mazilli continued staring, giving him the eye. Rocco forced himself to keep his mouth shut, wait out Mazilli's silence.

'Just get him out of here.'

Coming around the corner, Rocco saw Touhey leaning against the wall, hugging himself. The body had gone into the back of the ambulance; only a few small squiggles of blood and Rocco's scuffed suitcase were left to mark its ever having been there.

As Rocco walked Touhey back across the parking lot, there seemed to
be a whole parade coming the other way: an Emergency Services truck
with a bank of searchlights, the two homicide investigators coming in on
the midnight tour and Vince Kelso escorting the restaurant manager, who
was carrying an attaché case and looking extremely pissed off to Rocco's
eyes, the cuffs of his pajamas peeking out from beneath his pant legs.

As Rocco approached the sidewalk tape again, he spied the kid with
the high orange fade still hanging in with his two buddies. 'I was gonna
bring you guys out some Golden Mobies but they shut down the fryers
in there.'

The kid with the fade waved Rocco off. 'I don't eat none of that fried
shit. My body is the *temple*.'

Rocco had a fleeting pang of envy for the kid's youth, his lightness.
He wondered what it would feel like to give one of his Rubbermaid scalp
massages through all that strange hair.

An older pipehead wearing a Runnin' Rebels T-shirt loped over, almost
barging into the three kids, taking in Rocco with bugged-out eyes.

'What kind gun you got?' His voice was a head-over-heels gobble, his
tongue flicking across his lips, his head jerking like a turkey, right, left,
right. Rocco tried to estimate how long the guy had been on the street.
He still had some good prison muscles on him, so he must've just got
out; the pipe melted weightlifters down to nothing but a cobblestone gut
in only a few weeks.

'Two-inch snub-nosed thirty-eight,' Rocco said amiably.

The guy spun around in disdain, guffawing. 'Thirty-*eight*! Ho, *shit*!
Ho, *shit*!'

'Yeah? How 'bout you?' Rocco was distracted by the restaurant's
lights, which had just blinked on. He saw Mazilli inside, talking with
the manager.

'I got me a *Uzi*, bawh.' The guy thrust out his hips on the brand
name.

All the kids danced away, laughing. 'Nigger got a Uzi.'

Insulted, the pipehead got a look in his eye that Rocco knew could lead
to some show-and-tell retribution. Shit happened that easy all the time
these days.

'You guys know anybody with a nine millimeter?'

Three of them were half gone in laughter, one in rage, everybody losing
interest in him.

Rocco repeated himself: 'You know anybody packs a nine millimeter?'

'Nine millimeter?' The original kid, the orange fade, came back to him.

Rocco reached for a card, thinking: Not a bad kid, half a brain at least. But how do I say it now? Do I say, Where's One Love at?

'Yeah, they be *lots* of people I know with that.'

Or: Hey, are you One Love? Real casual, then hope the kid would say something like, Me? Naw, man, One Love's over *there*.

Clearing his throat, putting on his mildly curious face, Rocco gave it a shot. 'Hey, you're not One Love, are you?'

Before the kid could answer, a young, wild-eyed black woman burst through the tape and ran right into Touhey. He staggered back with an explosive 'God!' The woman bounced off his chest, shifted to the left and hobbled forward. A uniform flew up to meet her, grabbed her by the arms and said, 'Whoa, whoa' and danced her back to the sidewalk, her hobble becoming more pronounced the slower she moved.

The woman was cocaine skinny but stylishly dressed in a bolero jacket with padded shoulders and a brocade pillbox hat. As she tried to sidestep the cop's momentum and work her way up to the blood puddles, she seemed oblivious to the fact that she had lost a high-heeled sandal.

'I want to see my brother. I just want to see my brother.'

'You can't.' The uniform was young, and Rocco could see that he was anxious, not sure how to handle this.

'I just want to see him for a second.' She sounded both reasonable and crazed.

'No you don't.'

'Yes I do.' She tried to break free, and the cop shifted his grip up to her biceps.

'No you don't.'

'He's my brother. Why can't I see my brother?'

'Lady, please.'

'I'm OK, I'm OK, I just – ' Suddenly she erupted vomit, showering the cop, who tried to hop away but too late. Then he went up on tiptoes and stared down at himself. 'Cock *sucker!*'

The woman dropped to her knees, crossed her arms over her gut and, dry-eyed, bellowed, 'Dar-*ryl!*' as if the kid was still in earshot. Mildly surprised at the grief, Rocco moved to where she was crouched and put a hand on her shoulder. He scanned the uniforms, then called over a black female officer. 'Take this lady wherever she wants to go. Wash her up, stay with her. She's sister to the body.' He gave the officer his card. 'And call me at my office in about ninety minutes.'

'Yeah, well, I get off in forty-five.'

Rocco didn't answer, just glared. Unintimidated, the woman officer called over another uniform, gave him Rocco's card, Rocco's instructions, and walked off.

'Fucking bitch!' The vomit-sprayed cop lurched across the parking lot, shouting, 'Hoo-wah fucking *bitch*!' He stopped and hunched over, trying to delicately shake out his shirt with his fingertips. Someone drawled, 'Lookin' good there, Home!' and the entire herd broke up in laughter.

Rocco looked around for the kid with the orange fade: gone. Then he turned to Touhey. 'Had enough?'

As two of the Homicides, one chunky and gray-haired, the other blond and handsome, began to carve their way back out through the crowd to the sidewalk, Strike, clutching a Yoo-Hoo, found himself unable to resist sliding right into their path, so that the gray-haired one had to gently backhand him to the side, saying 'Beep-beep' as he did it. Strike horrified himself with his impulse to go right in their faces, as if begging to have his eyes read. As they plowed past him, Strike picked up a scent coming off the blond one – a piney soap smell, the smell of cleanliness, cut with a more curdled odor, one of exhaustion or desperation, like the stink of a pipehead with no money and too many hours left to his night. The cop worried him: he was like no other Strike had ever seen before, maybe some kind of expert or commissioner, somebody they brought out only for heavy investigations.

Strike had watched the cops and detectives mill around Darryl's body and decided that most of them were just taking up space. They seemed to be playing with themselves, making wisecracks, one guy in uniform even saying to one of the sport jackets, 'Mud person down,' as if a dead black man was some kind of joke. And when that pipehead woman from JFK, the one who hocked her ring to Rodney, had burst out of the crowd and knocked right into that blond Homicide before puking all over the cop in uniform, a lot of the other cops were laughing along with everybody else. The fact that no one seemed to care that much about the murder made Strike feel safe, but what did safe mean now?

Strike hung near the perimeter of the crime scene. With the body gone, along with most of the police, Strike noticed that a good part of the crowd around him had wandered off too, the only show left being Darryl's sobbing sister. Strike was riveted by the skinny woman's grief, but as a cop tried to bring her back to her feet, she locked eyes with Strike across the tape, recognition in her face, and a thrill of horror flashed up from his groin to his chest, sending him out of the parking lot. He walked blindly up the De Groot Street hill above Ahab's, keeping to the shadows.

Strike tried to think about how things would be better now, but he couldn't even remember why Darryl was supposed to get shot, couldn't get a grip on what had gone down. He listened to his body tell him about trouble coming, felt his stomach act up even against the sweet white coolness of the Yoo-Hoo, the bottle heavy in his hand now, his kneecaps flaming from the exertion of the climb, his scattered mind periodically returning to the one truth he felt capable of comprehending: everything had changed.

Strike rested in the doorway of an abandoned tenement building high above the Ahab's lot. He climbed the stoop and looked down on some Emergency Services cops strolling the grounds with heavy-duty flashlights, searching for bullets or something. As he watched, a little kid worked his way up the stoop. He climbed like a cub, using hands and feet, then grabbed the half-empty Yoo-Hoo at Strike's side and took a drink.

Glancing down at the kid, Strike felt a rush of inspiration coming on, a high in his chest: buy a car seat, one of those baby seats, strap it up in the back of the Accord, make it look like a family car, maybe even throw some toys in, mess things up like kids were back there all the time. Nobody looks twice at a car with a baby seat – knockos, pipeheads, nobody. Strike clapped his hands once, laughing. Some people walking by turned to look at him, then quickly turned away.

Strike watched the kid drink. There was a snotty crust on the boy's nose, and Strike's stomach rippled in disgust. He looked down at the parking lot again and imagined that Darryl was still there in the doorway under that sheet, the blood blooming through the whiteness. He imagined that he heard Darryl's sister's shell-shocked cawing again. He shut his eyes against the vision of her puking up her misery, but the image stuck and just wouldn't leave him. Her splattered vomit hadn't had any chunks in it because she was on the pipe, and wasn't putting anything in her stomach except for maybe orange juice and soda, maybe some potato chips for the salt. Strike feverishly fixated on all this, and then he felt his own stomach rise. Wheeling around toward the hallway of the abandoned building, he roared vomit, a wave of Yoo-Hoo splashing on the broken tiles.

There was a full moon out, so even without lights in the hallway Strike could see that what came up was shot through with streaks of red. He crouched over the mess, stunned, hearing again the heartbroken callings of Darryl's sister, for real this time, coming from somewhere down the hill.

Strike's trembling hand hovered over the thin, snaky swirls of his own blood. He tried to concentrate on exactly what he had said to Victor in that bar earlier tonight. 'I'll get back to you.' It wasn't anything more than that. Just some empty words to ease out of the whole crazy conversation about Darryl beating up some girl, about Victor knowing some killer named My Man, both of their stories equally full of shit, or so Strike had thought. But now Darryl was dead, and Strike had no idea who did it.

Strike palmed the wetness from his mouth, thinking, Who the fuck is My Man? Where did Victor get to know anybody like that? What the fuck did Victor do?

Thinking: *Everything* changed.

Part Two

CLOSED BY ARREST

Rocco sat with Sean Touhey in the back of the Pavonia Tavern. The waiter, a moonlighting cop from Jersey City, stood over them, and the Fury, two hours into a shitface, sat three tables away.

Rocco had decided to allow himself one quick drink before getting back to work. They'd be going all night on Darryl Adams, plus he felt a little bad for Touhey; his last two visits had ended in some kind of trauma, so a brief decompression round seemed like the decent thing to do.

'What's your poison, there, Sean?' Rocco asked over the horse-laughing din for the third time.

The actor blinked. 'My poison?'

The guy's putting it on a little heavy here, Rocco thought. It was just a homicide, not a thermonuclear blast. The waiter lost interest and was now watching the TV behind the bar.

Rocco tilted back in his chair. 'Two vodka cranberries.' He winked at Touhey: Trust me.

Both Rocco and Touhey turned as the Fury table exploded. Thumper jumped up, knocking over his chair. 'Thumpa! Thumpa!' he squawked in a honking bass sputter, doing the floppy fish, acting like a hyperventilating pipehead. 'I'm rocketin'! I'm rocketin'!'

'Rocketin'!' Crunch hooted between cupped palms. '*He'p* me, Thumpa!'

Touhey turned back to Rocco. 'I should have coffee,' he said tentatively.

'Are you kidding me? After tonight?'

Touhey was silent for a moment, then said, 'I saw it, didn't I?'

'What's that?' Rocco smiled in confusion.

'I looked right into his eyes.'

'Who, Adams? The kid? Yup, right in there.' Rocco felt as if he was in a play, a big haunted speech coming up. He stole a peek at Touhey's watch, a gold, black-faced antique Hamilton electric: midnight. Rocco gave himself a half hour here, knowing that at least three other investigators would be working the job by now.

The drinks came and Touhey stared at his as if it was a test tube foaming with forbidden knowledge.

'I looked right into his eyes . . .' The actor held up his drink. 'So what's *this*,' swirling the cubes, 'compared to *that*?'

Rocco smiled, thinking maybe a half hour was too long.

'Where'd he go?' Touhey's eye followed him from the side of his uptilted glass.

'The kid?'

'Where'd he go?'

'They took him to Newark.'

'Newark.' He gazed at Rocco with loopy affection, his drink half gone. 'You're amazing. Newark.'

Rocco turned red, insulted. 'Well, what do you mean, where'd he go? Heaven or hell?'

'Newark. Fucking perfect.' Touhey gave him the one-eyed whale again as he drained his drink.

Rocco stared back at him, thinking, Fuck you too. Everybody in New York, all of Patty's friends, assumed that just because he was a cop he was incapable of any but literal thoughts.

'I would *kill* to be you,' Touhey hissed across the table. Rocco, startled out of his irritation, downed his glass to keep pace, laughing self-consciously as he wiped his lips with a fist. 'You mean, to be me all the time or in a movie?'

Touhey signaled for another round. 'In a movie.'

The actor's words were almost drowned out by another explosion from the Fury table. 'It juth be power-phenalia, Big Chief,' Thumper lisped in a high frightened voice, standing again, leaning forward as if his hands were cuffed behind his back. 'Tha's awl you find here be power-phenalia, I swear it.'

The Fury, in chorus, said, 'Power-phenalia!' like a toast. Crunch waved for another round even before his glass made it back down to the table.

Touhey cocked his head, fixing Rocco with a challenging squint. 'Do *you* think I could be you?'

Rocco shrugged. 'Hey.'

'Why could *I* be you. Why me?'

Rocco was stumped for a good answer. Why? Because he wanted him to – but could he just say that? Big Chief belched sharp enough to crack glass. Rocco was grateful for the distraction and saluted across the room. 'Nice.'

Big Chief raised his drink in acknowledgment.

The actor touched his forearm. '*Why*, Rocco?'

Before Rocco could respond, Touhey answered his own question, abruptly becoming Rocco, talking about the time he had first met Patty, leaning across the table, reciting the story in a way that Rocco found riveting, as if he had never heard this tale before, his own story, the actor somehow capturing in the rushes and hesitations all the mixed feelings Rocco had about his marriage, even his fatherhood. When Touhey leaned back in his chair, all Rocco could say was, 'You weren't even there.'

Rocco took a deep breath, seeing his life in the hands of this man, seeing himself vindicated and elevated on a gigantic movie screen. He suppressed a desire to call Patty, tell her this vague good news. Touhey watched Rocco's face as if he knew just what he was thinking, and before Rocco could say anything else, Touhey reached across the table and hugged him.

'Whoa there, big fella.' Rocco gently pried himself free and Touhey laughed, still pleased with Rocco's stunned reaction.

Both their drinks were gone again. Rocco glanced at his watch – time to go – but Touhey motioned to the waiter again, and Rocco didn't protest.

The actor tapped the back of Rocco's hand with a fist. 'There's only one thing. If I do this, if I do Rocco Klein, you have to be with me.'

'With you?' Rocco cocked an ear. 'Like . . . your friend?'

'You got to keep me honest.'

'You mean like technical shit? Like an advisor?'

'Anything you want. What do you want?'

'Whoa, whoa.' Suddenly Rocco didn't trust Touhey, became deeply wary of his impulsive, liquor-fueled buoyancy. Rocco decided not to finish his drink, a first.

'I'll make you a producer.'

'What's *he* do?'

'Anything I want.' Touhey laughed. 'Can you get off next October? I want to do this next October. I figure three weeks in Dempsy, for exteriors, two months in Toronto. They'll want to do the Dempsy stuff in Toronto too, but that's why they're just a bunch of suits, a bunch of sweaty fucking suits. We don't do Dempsy, we don't do it at all.'

'So you're not gonna do it?' Rocco shook his head in confusion. 'Hold on.'

'Hey, hey.' Touhey drained his third or fourth drink. 'You know why it's going to happen?'

'Why?'

'Because I go like this' – he wiggled five fingers – 'and five people die in Oklahoma.'

'Great.' What the fuck was he talking about?

'So we're talking October, three weeks Dempsy, then two, three months Toronto. Can you swing it?'

'October, I'm retired. I can do anything I goddamn want.' Rocco was growing angry, but he wasn't sure if he was angry with the actor or something else, something bigger.

'Well good, you can do this.' Touhey dug a business card from inside his jacket, found a pen and haltingly recited as he wrote: 'Rocco. We are happening. Bank on it. Sean Touhey.'

Handing the card to Rocco, he winked knowingly. 'Being a cop, a detective, you'd probably want something in writing, something in your hand, no?'

Rocco tapped the card against the rim of his glass and managed a twisted smile. Meal ticket, he had said to Mazilli, you're fucking with my meal ticket. Rocco felt his face go red again.

'You know what's gonna be great about this, Rocco?'

'Hit me,' Rocco said, but his head was back into the Job, thinking, Interview the witness first. He hoped she was in his office by now, waiting for him.

'I'm directing. There's all this mystique and hype about directors and it's all a bunch of shit. It's the easiest job in the world. I, I am directing this picture.' He leaned back as if waiting for Rocco to clap or throw his hat in the air.

'Great.' Rocco rose and gestured for the actor to follow. 'OK there, Sean, let me earn my money.'

Rocco had to half carry Touhey into the prosecutor's office – the actor was a delayed-reaction drunk, and the twenty minutes of unconsciousness in the car during the drive to the office had completely bombed him out.

Rocco pushed open the door with his hip. One hand was around Touhey's waist, and the other hand gripped his arm, which was slung around Rocco's neck. As they staggered through the brightly lit reception area, Rocco saw the witness curled up on the tattered couch next to Vy's unoccupied desk, snoring away. Someone had pinned a note on her hip: 'Do Not Disturb. Darryl Adams Hom. Witness.'

The actor began trying to walk down the hallway on his own, his shoulder sliding against the wall. 'You got a drink around here?' he said.

'Coffee. That's all we got.'

Rocco steered him into an alcove where a small refrigerator and a coffee machine lined one wall. Facing them was a holding cell that was being used as a storage room.

Anxious for Touhey to be gone, Rocco made a pot of coffee as fast as he could. 'I'm gonna have somebody come in, drive you home, OK? I'll take care of your car, get it back to you tomorrow morning.'

'I want to sleep *there*.' Touhey raised a limp arm toward the cell and sat on the coffee machine table, knocking over a box of sugar packets.

Rocco poured the water into the machine, laughing. 'What do you think this is, Mayberry?'

'I can't play a policeman if I don't see him through the eyes of the *policed*.'

'Sean, that's a fucking hole. The toilet doesn't even have any water in it.'

'I approach all my people through the reverse angle. That's my secret.'

'C'mon there, Sean . . .'

'The secret of my success.'

Losing patience, Rocco decided to settle for allowing Touhey to pass out again as quickly as possible. In order to make the cell at least marginally habitable, Rocco had to move out a dozen cartons filled with old homicide files, a collapsible wheelchair in which an old woman had been clubbed to death and a tagged shotgun used in a homicide-suicide two years back.

Finally Touhey lay down on the sleep rack fastened to the wall. Rocco leaned against the open bars, his stomach suddenly in knots, somehow unable to resist asking for a brief recap.

'Hey, Sean, maybe you told me this already and I was too bozo to hear it, but, ah, what's the story of this movie again?'

'Rocco,' Touhey declared, eyes closed, hands clasped across his midsection, one shoe up on the rim of the lidless toilet, 'you're asking the wrong question. It's not what's the *story*' – he pointed blindly in Rocco's general direction with a wavering finger – 'it's who's the *guy*. We're home free.'

Rocco walked into the main squad room, pulling a yellow legal pad and a half-full bottle of Seagram's gin from a supply closet. He thought Seagram's tasted like nail polish, but for some reason that's what most of them seemed to ask for when they were getting ready to talk about what they had seen.

Balancing the gin, the yellow pad and a full cup of black coffee with four sugars, Rocco walked back down the hallway to the reception area. He put the gin and the black coffee on an end table at the head of the couch, not knowing which one the witness would go for, then rolled Vy's chair up alongside the sleeping woman and dropped the yellow pad on his crossed knee.

For a moment Rocco sat quietly, watching her ribs rise and fall. Lying there in a tight ball, bony and frail, both knees sporting scabs, she looked to Rocco like a wizened child. She smelled more like wine than gin, but the office was all out of wine. His eyes fell to the blank pad and he began doodling, filling the top of the page with trapezoids, not really pumped up for this one, drifting off, pulling out the business card with Touhey's declaration and for the first time reading the words on the printed side – PRESSURE POINT PRODUCTIONS – daydreaming about being an actor, imagining cops all over America watching TV, watching him play – what else? – a cop. He was slightly embarrassed by his own fantasy, reminding himself that by the end he had been talking to a walking vodka bottle. Spooking himself sober, Rocco realized he had never rung up Patty to say he wouldn't be home until morning, but he also felt that he didn't have it in him to pick up the phone right now. The actor had put him through so many changes that he had no idea what to say to Patty, as if a simple call home suddenly required a declaration of self.

The witness snored like a clogged drain. Rocco took out his wallet, extracted Erin's picture and flipped it over. 'Carmela Wilson,' he read out loud, then pulled the taped Do Not Disturb sign off her meatless flank and crushed it into a ball.

Rocco wrote her name on the top line of a fresh page, then lightly smacked her hip with the pad. 'Carmela. Carmela. Wake up, wake up.'

Carmela shifted, croaked 'Damn' and then, hugging herself, went nose down into the upholstery, trying to burrow in.

'C'mon there, Carmela. Wake up, Mommy.' Rocco kept after her halfheartedly until at last she rose to a sitting position, blinking and groaning, elbows on thighs, her knotted hands cupping her neck, caressing the pain at the base of her skull, her jaw slowly twisting toward one shoulder, then the other.

'How you feeling, Carmela?' Rocco tried to sound chipper.

She squinted at him. 'This a hospital?'

'It's the prosecutor's office. You remember what happened tonight? You remember that shooting thing?'

She grunted, grimaced against the fluorescents. 'It's too hard, that light.'

'No problem.' Rocco turned off the overheads. The hallway light coming through the glass doors cast just enough light for Rocco to write notes and read her face.

'Better?' He debated whether to ask her if she wanted to use the bathroom, deciding not to because she might fall asleep on the toilet.

'Would you like some coffee?' He gestured with his pad to the end table.

'Yeah, OK.' She reached out and brought the cup to her lips with a surprisingly languid grace, draining off the whole shot in one steady swallow, her eyes popping for a second, muttering 'hot,' then reaching out for the gin bottle, filling the cup half full and throwing that back too. She slowly passed a hand across her mouth. 'Yeah, OK.'

Rocco took a breath, then started in. 'Listen, ah, just be patient with me. I'm gonna have to ask you the same questions you probably just got asked by Detective Kelso a few hours ago.'

'Fats?'

'Fats? Is that what you call him?'

'Yeah. He OK, Fats. He told me last week I had a warrant out on me, 'cause I didn't show up at court that time? He took care of it. He made a phone call for me.' She snapped her fingers. 'Bam, it's over. Fats awright, he got me on this twenty-one-day methadone program? Yeah . . .' She nodded in appreciation.

'So what did you see tonight, Carmela?'

'Yeah, well, I was across the street.'

'What street?'

'You know, De Groot.'

'De Groot where?'

'You know, in front of Rudy's.'

'Rudy's.'

'You know, the bar?'

'Were you in the bar?'

'Well, I was before, but mostly to use the bathroom and buy potato chips. I ain't got no money for cocktails, just like once in a while like to celebrate something. Mostly I buy a pint at the package store and hang out in front of Rudy's.'

Rocco began writing. 'What time we talking?'

'Late.'

'How late?'

'Well, I don't know 'cause I don't have a watch.'

'Take a guess.'

'Well, it got to be around ten-thirty because I was hungry, so I walked over to the Ahab's to get some food, 'cause Rudy close his kitchen at nine, and after that they got nothin' left but them pickled sausages and eggs in them *jars*, and I got a stomach situation, I got my stomach operated on so I can't eat that garbage, but I see the lights go off inside the Ahab's like they closing up? So but they close up like ten, ten-thirty, yeah.'

'Where were you when the lights went off?'

'I was in the parking lot at the end.'

'What do you mean, the end?'

'You know, like right by the street. You know, like far away from the building? I see the lights go off and I say, "*Damn*, I just missed."'

'What you do then?'

'I see the manager or someone come out. You know, like to lock up on the side, and I keep walking to him because I figure maybe I can get him to give me something, and I saw this other man leaning against a car near the door like waiting for him, and when the guy locked up, the other guy came off the car and he just . . . *boom boom*. You know, three, four times, and then he ran. It was fast, the whole thing was *fast*.'

'Whoa, whoa, back up. This car – do you think the car was his?'

'I don't know. He was leanin' on it.'

'Did you see him get out of the car?'

'Nope. Didn't get back in either.'

'What kind of car?'

'Red, like, *red*. I saw the po-lice taking down the plates, you know, the numbers? They got on that car when they did that, yeah.'

'Where was he leaning?'

'On the car.'

'Where? Front, back?'

'In the middle on the door.'

'Driver's door or passenger's door?'

'The side door in front.'

'You don't know what kind of car?'

'It looked nice, new.'

'Big? Compact?'

'I don't know.'

Rocco stopped the interview to go over to Vy's desk and call the Bureau of Criminal Identification, to get a print man over to the scene and find the car, dust the doors. A million to one, but what the hell. He watched Carmela refill her coffee cup with gin.

Sighing, Rocco returned to his chair. 'OK, so Carmela, where were you when the shooting happened?'

'About halfway to the Ahab's.'

'Did you recognize the guy who did the shooting?'

'Nope.'

'Can you describe him?'

'Nope. He was wearing a hood.'

'What do you mean, a hood?'

'Like a sweatshirt hood.'

'What color?'

'Dark.'

'Dark. What else he have on?'

'Pants, I guess.'

'Dungarees, gym sweats, dress pants?'

'I didn't look.'

'Sneakers or shoes?'

'I didn't look.'

'Did he have any decorations on his clothes – words, designs, stripes?'

'Maybe.'

'Maybe what?'

'I don't know. I heard that *boom boom* or, you know, *pop pop*, and I just turned and walked back. I ain't gettin' in *that* mess.'

'Did he say anything? Did they talk?'

'Naw, it was like he just went up in his face and started shooting, you know? And like, the manager, he was backing away and shaking his head like, No, no.'

'He said "No, no"?'

'No, just like, shaking his head.'

'You see the gun?'

'Not really.'

'Would you know if it was automatic or a revolver? Do you know the difference between an automatic and a revolver?'

'Yeah. An automatic you put the bullets in the bottom.'

'Right.'

She shrugged. 'I didn't see.'

'OK, so nobody said nothing. Where'd the guy run to?'

'Like towards the mini-mall, just runnin' runnin' runnin'.'

'Did he say anything when he was running? Did he yell out anything?'

'Nope. Shit, I was runnin' too.'

'Was the guy white or black?'

'The manager was black, I know that.'

'The shooter.'

'I don't know . . . I couldn't see.'

'What color were his hands?'

'I didn't see.'

Rocco flipped his pen onto his pad: Horseshit on a platter.

'Listen to me, Carmela. I know you're probably afraid, but I want you to know you're covered, you're protected. I'm personally gonna protect you.' Rocco hated saying that. The fact was she was on her own, they all were, but if they weren't sold on protection, they would never testify. 'In fact, you're not even here. I'm writing this up like an anonymous citizen gave me this. You're a confidential informant. It's just me and you.'

'I ain't afraid.' She made a face.

'Look, a lot of people are. I'm just telling you, you got nothing to worry about. Your name's not gonna be in the papers, nothing. In fact, there might even be some money in it for you, like a cash reward from the Ahab's company.'

'Hey.' Carmela tilted her head forward, scratched the bulging bone below her ear with an amber thumbnail. 'You say cash, shit, I'll *make* things up, I *like* cash.'

Rocco heard a dull thud and excused himself to check on Touhey. He was still passed out inside the cell, mouth open, forearm across his eyes. It must have been the refrigerator kicking over. That, or somebody landing on the roof. He ducked into the stillness of the Homicide office, the silent sea of clutter, the phones, thinking: Call Patty. Maybe she could help him figure out this actor thing. But he still didn't feel up to it.

Rocco walked back into the reception room. It was one-thirty in the morning. 'OK, Carmela. What did you do after the shooting. Where'd you go?'

'I ran into Rudy's. I go to the bartender, I say call the police and he called, and, you know.'

'What's the bartender's name?'

'Rudy? I don't know. Rudy the bartender, I guess. He's nice, though. I can go to the bathroom six times a night, not buy a beer, he don't say nothin'.'

'Did you go back out to the lot?'

'Well, yeah, but like the police was there by then. Shit, I wasn't gonna say nothin' to nobody except when I saw Fats, because Fats helped me with this warrant thing I had last week?'

'Did anybody else see the shooting?'

'Well, you know, you had some people by the wall, but I don't run with them, and I can't say because I wasn't looking over there, except they most always there.'

Rocco remembered Mazilli's canvass coming up empty. 'Did you know the guy that got shot?'

'Yeah, but just from eating.'

'Did he have any problems with anybody? Any enemies? Anybody didn't like him?'

'I mind my own business. I go in there, I want food, not stories, you know?' She took a little more gin.

Rocco paused, looked at his notes and tried to put a few of the pieces together. It seemed more like an execution than a random assault or a botched robbery. No struggle, cash still on the body – a living-large dope roll, most likely. Somebody waiting around to do what was done and then splitting. Not much to go on, but it was better than nothing.

'Anything else you can think of telling me?' He sat with legs crossed and pen poised, waiting ten seconds, twenty, thirty . . .

'Carmela?'

She had fallen asleep with her eyes at half mast. A frozen stillness came over her, and Rocco watched the eyelids, like space ship doors, smoothly dropping shut, cutting off contact with the known world.

Rocco fretted momentarily about not getting her social security number, her date of birth. 'Carmela, baby . . .' He stretched and yawned, then took out the photo of Erin again and wrote down Carmela's address at the top of his first sheet. He would have to bag the taped formal interview until tomorrow.

Rocco slid his chair over to Vy's phone, gliding on the casters, and dialed home. He turned back to look at Carmela: eyebrows high, lids shut, she slowly rocked forward, jerked back, then tilted forward again, threatening to pitch face first off the couch.

Now that he was finally making the call, he felt desperate to hear Patty's voice. But just after the first ring, an echoey racket came from the hallway and Rocco had to hang up before she could answer.

A uniformed cop escorted the victim's sister into the darkened reception area.

'Where the fuck *is* everybody?' the cop crabbed. He hit the overhead lights and almost reached for his gun when Rocco materialized by the desk.

'Easy, easy.' Rocco held his palms up and slid in his chair to the center of the room.

'You wanted her, right?' The cop nodded to the woman he had just brought in, who stood slightly hunched over, her hands jammed into her armpits.

'Absolutely.' Rocco stood up and gently cupped one of her bony elbows. He steered her down the hall to the squad room, then stopped and looked back at the cop. 'Jesus. Can I ask you a favor?' He pointed toward Carmela. She was still asleep, perched on the edge of the couch and undulating like a cobra. 'You can drop her off anywhere down there.' Rocco gestured vaguely to the city beyond the office and turned away before the cop could object.

Rocco and Darryl Adams's sister sat facing each other in oversize black naugahyde desk chairs back in the squad room, both of them absently rolling back and forth on kidney-shaped plastic rug protectors.

'Harmony – that's a nice name. Where you live, Harmony?' Rocco held the legal pad on his knee-desk again, Carmela Wilson folded underneath now.

'I live at Four Forty Allerton Avenue, third floor rear, and my social security number is 182–40–3947,' she sang out, her bolero jacket draped backwards across her chest, arms hidden underneath. Her chin had sunk below the high collar, and she peered out brighteyed and shaking. '182–40–3947 – I never forget that.'

There was something burbly and loose in her voice, a slightly hysterical chattiness, as if she was freezing. Rocco looked at her bare feet and remembered that earlier in the evening she had been hobbling around on one high-heeled sandal. He gazed at her legs a moment too long, and she leaned sideways and pulled them under her bottom.

Rocco took a deep breath and made a kind face. 'Would you like something to drink? Some coffee? Something else?'

'Do you have something to eat?' Her voice was nervous, coy.

'We got doughnuts, Entenmann's, we got a candy machine . . .'

'Doughnuts is fine. I like doughnuts.'

Rocco got up and went past the holding cell to the coffee machine. He found a paper plate and took two stale dunkers from a grease-saturated cardboard box. Turning back toward the squad room, he saw the actor whimper in his sleep, pumping his legs on the cot like a dreaming dog.

Rocco shook Touhey's shoulder. 'Sean, Sean.'

The actor whooped and whimpered, weakly battling the air.

'Sean, you want to learn something? C'mon out with me. I'll tell her you're my partner.'

Touhey bolted upright, stared around with bulging eyes, then crashed back into tortured sleep. Rocco waved him off, castigating himself: Just do your fucking job.

Rocco let the sister get a few bites down, watching her delicately scrape away a blotch of powdered sugar with a broken pinkie nail.

'I haven't eaten all day, then I threw up. My stomach's so empty I'm getting a headache.'

'Hey, please.' Rocco reared back, palms up. 'Knock yourself out.'

Her eyes caught the Homicide blackboard flanked by two Marine recruiting posters over the rear wall filing cabinets, and Rocco studied her face as she read the latest news:

6/11 Homicide #41–89-Cesar Cerrano-28-Floater-Dempsy Bay near 48th Street-Possible

6/14 Homicide #42–89-Darryl Adams-23?-Gunshot DOA 747 De Groot (Ahabs)

Homicide Picnic – Liberty State Park 6/30. Ten dollars/head to Petey Brennan by Friday 6/24 or you're shit out of luck and that means *you* and *you*

Her lips moved as she read, and when she finally looked away her shoulders rippled involuntarily in a shivery spasm that dropped her jacket to her lap.

Rocco lowered his voice. 'Listen, ah, let me extend my sorrow to you. I understand your brother was a good guy.'

She nodded in acknowledgment, but her eyes were focused somewhere over his left shoulder. 'I had a cousin in the Marines. He's at Drew University now, cumma sum laude.' It took Rocco a minute to make the connection with the recruiting posters, or maybe it was the red-and-gold-trimmed Marine desk blotters that covered about two thirds of the desks in the room.

'When was the last time you saw your brother?'

'To the dot I can't say. I see him all the time you know, in the street? But he doesn't talk to me because I'm a cocaine addict. He hasn't spoke to me in like three months.' Her tone was matter-of-fact, and she stared blankly at Rocco's pad, nodding in agreement with herself.

'So he didn't like drugs?' Rocco flashed on the twenty-five hundred dollars Mazilli had plucked from the body.

'I don't know *what* he didn't like.' She shrugged, brought her eyes up to Rocco's again, snapping back into focus. 'I just want to tell you

something. I'm not just a cocaine addict. I *work*. I'm on sick leave right
now? But I got a job at New Jersey Transit as a cashier, so I don't want
you getting the wrong impression of me. I have cancer of the pancreas
but I'm gonna beat that. I'm going back to work on Tuesday, in fact.
I'm gonna stop this cocaine thing this week-end. Get my kids back on
Monday from my mother? This time next week? I'll be walking down
the street? You won't even *know* me.'

'Great.' Rocco nodded in approval, then squinted at her, earnest now.
'Harmony, do you know anybody who'd want to hurt Darryl?'

She chewed her doughnut and stared at Rocco's knee. 'Yeah, *me*. I'd
like to smack him in the head for not talking to me. I used to change his
damn diapers for him. Who the hell does he think he is?'

She sounded a little too hearty now, as if she was enjoying answering
his questions. Rocco smiled patiently, hoping she wasn't about to freak.
'Anybody else?'

'I don't get into his mess. I don't even know where he is.'

'Who were his friends?'

'I see him with this boy name Lovejoy.'

'Lovejoy? Is that a first name or last name?'

'Lovejoy, that's all I know.'

'You know where he lives?'

'Nope. I see him on JFK a lot.'

'Who else?'

'There's this boy Chickadee. They're friends.'

'Chickadee what?'

She shrugged. 'Chickadee. When Darryl was working at Rodney's
Place? Chickadee used to hang out there and they got to be friends.
That was like in the fall, or like Christmas, before Darryl went over to
Ahab's, but he still hangs out with Chickadee sometimes.'

'Rodney's Place?'

'You know, that grocery on Blossom? You know, Rodney Little? He
drives around all the time in that Garfield car?'

'Rodney Little, yeah, OK,' he said mildly, red flags going up all over,
like she'd said John Dillinger. Rocco wasn't up to speed on Rodney's
action these days but remembered him just fine from the seventies,
when they were both on the street, Rocco in anticrime and Rodney in
holdups.

'Yeah, I see him and Chickadee sometimes but, you know, Darryl,
most times he's a loner, he doesn't hang out.'

'How about Rodney Little? Does he ever hang out with Rodney Little?'

Another fishtail ripple ran through her upper body. 'I don't know. See, like I said, he doesn't talk to me. But I *am* gonna stop. People say, Oh, you can't ever stop. People, nobody, can't ever stop except maybe in jail. But I stopped lots of times. It's no big thing. You know the newspapers pump it up, but you can stop if you put your mind to it, if you got the maturity.'

'Harmony, do you think your brother was into any kind of . . .' Rocco shrugged slightly. 'You know, funny stuff?' He made it sound like pranks.

'You have to ask him that yourself.' Rocco gave it a moment of silence, then went for the home run. 'Harmony, listen to me. I want you to do something. I want you to close your eyes.' He paused. 'Don't think. Just say . . . who did this.'

The phone started to ring out in the reception area. Rocco let it go, waiting on Harmony, who now looked as if she was at a seance.

'You,' she said in a low mutter.

'Me?' Rocco reached for the phone on the nearest desk, staring at Harmony, her eyes still closed as he punched in the transfer. 'Homicide, Klein,' he said in a distracted monotone.

'Somebody get killed or is it something I should worry about?' Patty's voice touched him like a cupped palm to the side of his face.

'Hey.' He grinned into the phone. 'I'm working.' Rocco felt instantly grounded. What was the big deal about calling home?

'No time to drop a dime, right?'

'Sort of.'

Harmony's eyes were still shut, the lateral movement of her eyeballs visible under the thin skin.

'I'm just asking, because it's like two A.M.'

'I was at a scene.'

'You just got into the office, right? This call just caught you as you walked in the door.'

Rocco swiveled around so his back was to the victim's sister. 'Can I call you back? I'm with somebody.'

'A murderer?'

'Yeah,' Rocco said, thinking that sounded more dramatic than a relative.

'Break 'em *down*, baby.' She said it with a mild street spin.

'I always do.'

'Call me.' Patty hung up and Rocco turned back to Harmony. Her eyes were open now, her cheeks slick with tears.

Rocco felt his concentration slip. He gave himself a moment to get it back.

'Why'd you say "me" for, Harmony?' He guessed she would say something about racism, the pigs, or society in general, but she just tilted her chin to Rocco's hip, the gun there.

Rocco touched his .38. In twenty years on the job it had never entered his head that the sight of his piece might ever upset any of the family or friends of a gunshot victim. Learn something new every day.

'Try again. Who did this?'

Harmony took a deep breath, her thin fingers trembling at her cheekbone. 'You say who did things. You know, people *do* things but . . . I mean, it's not like anybody's *proud* of themselves. It's just situations, you know? It's where they *find* themselves.' The tears were running free but the voice was still chatty and light. 'I mean, I don't know anybody who's proud of themselves. Nobody. You know, it's like a race, and sometimes people don't have the conditioning. You know what I'm saying?'

Rocco nodded, staring at the smudge-faced Marine in the recruiting poster, who stared back at him with righteous eyes.

The door to the reception area rattled, then opened and closed. Rocco heard Mazilli's working whistle, a tuneless tea-kettle hiss through his teeth. Rocco smiled at Harmony, putting all questions on hold, and a moment later Mazilli waltzed into the squad room, came up behind Rocco and lifted his interview notes. Still whistling, he ran a finger down the border of the page as he read.

'Lovejoy, Robert Lovejoy. He moved down to Florida two weeks ago.' Mazilli's eyes trailed the page. 'Chickadee, Chickadee Willis. He sells bottles for Rodney Little. Yeah, there he is. Rodney, Hot Rod.'

Mazilli dropped the legal pad on Rocco's desk. 'Your brother sell dope, Harmony?'

'My brother *hates* dope.' She ran her hands across her face, then pressed a palm into her forehead, comforting herself. She rose with her bag. 'Do you have a bathroom?'

Rocco pointed the way and they watched her pad across the room.

Mazilli flicked an invisible object off Rocco's notes. 'I bet he sold weight. That twenty-five hundred? He must've just sold an eighth of a ki.'

Rocco stood up and yawned, stretching for the ceiling.

'I searched the restaurant,' Mazilli said. 'The manager says nothing's going on there, but I think he's a lying dothead geek.' Mazilli chewed his upper lip with his bared lower teeth. 'I'm gonna go scare up this kid Chickadee. You want to do the house?'

'Sure,' Rocco said.

'He lived at the Royal.'

'Aw, get the fuck out of here, the Royal,' Rocco moaned. The prospect of tossing a room in one of Tunnely's worst sex-and-dope motels made him suddenly ache with the hour. 'The fucking Royal.'

'Also, she's gotta ID the body. The family's all down south.' Mazilli nodded to the john. 'She gonna make it?'

'She can do it tomorrow.' Rocco wasn't in the mood to top off the night with a drive to the morgue in Newark.

Mazilli nodded back toward the cell. 'Your friend in there – what you do, arrest him for driving you nuts?'

Rocco sat back down. 'He got a little bozoed.'

'We should get one of them big pumpkin-headed brothers out of County, throw him in there, lock the door. See how fast he sobers up.' Mazilli leaned over Rocco from behind, pinching his nipples. 'Honey, you awake?'

Rocco laughed as Mazilli loped out of the office and disappeared into the night.

Rocco wandered over to the bathroom door, hunching his neck, trying to unknot the hour. 'How you doing in there?'

The bathroom was dark and she took a few seconds to answer, her voice coming out in a strangled monotone, as if she was trying to speak while holding her breath. 'In a minute.'

At first Rocco thought she was in trouble, but then a whiff of butane drifted through the door, followed by a steady low exhalation.

Rocco hissed, too tired to be the law just now. 'C'mon out. I'll drive you home.'

As they left the office, Rocco remembered Touhey, passed out in the cell, then shrugged it off. The guy would keep.

He drove through the three A.M. streets with Harmony in the shotgun seat. She was sinking before his eyes; he could smell the crash coming off her like musk. And as they turned onto JFK, Rocco realized it had been six months since he'd been on this street at this hour. He drove slowly, taking in all the activity like a tourist, even waving like a homecoming queen to a street crew that was trying to blow out his tires with their eyes, one of the knuckleheads shouting out, '*Fuck* you!,' Rocco shouting back, 'Fuck your *mother*!' then instantly feeling juvenile about it.

He turned to Harmony. 'You're on Allerton, right?'

'Uh-huh.' She was pointedly not looking out the window at the crews and customers.

'You know anybody named One Love?'

'One Love?' She squinted as if racking her memory. 'I know a song . . .'

'Yeah?'

'One lo-ove,' she sang faintly, off key, trailing away. Rocco turned off JFK onto Allerton and she touched his hand. 'I can get out here, walk a little.'

'No, I'll take you to your door.'

'I like walking.' She collapsed onto the seat, hugged herself with impatience.

'That's OK, it's late. Somebody's gonna come by, take you to the coroner's tomorrow. You better get your sleep.'

Rocco dropped her off in front of her building and sat there until she went indoors. He drove down half a block and parked. Within five minutes she was back out of the house, wearing shoes now, heading for the boulevard.

Rocco debated whether to roll up on her, read her the riot act, but instead he drove off toward Tunnely and the Royal, feeling like enough of a prick for not dropping her on JFK to begin with.

The Royal Motel: the last time he was there, two years before, he had been an observer with a basic life support ambulance crew as part of a statewide police refresher course in emergency medical treatment. The ambulance had gotten a call about a white female having a seizure, most likely drug-induced, in the parking lot in the rear of the motel. When they rolled up the front drive they came upon a Hispanic prostitute sprawled in the grass by the office, bleeding heavily from a gunshot wound in the chest.

Rocco and the crew figured the dispatcher had screwed up the run description, but when they delivered the half-dead hooker to the hospital, their supervisor lost it, yelling that the white junkie was still lying in the parking lot. The woman they had brought in was someone else, a customer without a number.

Rocco flew down I–9 now, the moon riding with him, silvering up refineries and housing projects. He felt juiced, wondering what he would run into at the motel, thinking that it really wasn't the worst thing to work through the night. Besides, all he'd be doing instead is tromping around a silent house, maybe even sleeping himself, sleeping right through the Dempsy wee hours, when even the shooters started to freak.

9

As Strike drove down JFK, away from the cops and the crowds, he ran his tongue over his lips, trying to lick off the red he knew was there, the red of his own vomit, the red that had bloomed through the white sheet covering Darryl Adams. Strike was headed for Rodney's Place, wanting Rodney to work his magic teachings on him, wanting Rodney to explain tonight in a way that would make him strong with self-recognition and understanding.

He turned down Blossom and pulled up across from the store – except the store wasn't there. Strike jumped out of the car and trotted back to the intersection to check the street sign. Hand on his gut, he floated back down to where Rodney's Place should be, but plywood covered the windows, the recessed doorway and the sky-blue cinder block, fragments of script peeking out from around the boards.

Strike looked up and down the street, tasting bile at the back of his throat. Rodney's Place had been the only lighted building on that stretch of Blossom; now, with the store boarded up, the street had vanished, surrendering to moonlight and desolation, a tiny wilderness of empty lots and broken buildings.

Strike grabbed a sheet of plywood and made a halfhearted effort to yank it loose. Maybe Rodney was hiding inside, he thought. Or maybe Rodney was dead, laid out behind the boarded-up storefront – Champ's doing – or maybe Rodney had skipped town now that the dirty work was done, closed up shop and split until Strike was either dead or in jail.

'But I didn't *do* nothing!' Strike squawked to the empty street.

After marching up and down Blossom in helpless agitation, Strike returned to his car, deciding to hit Rodney's hangouts, continue his search. He headed first for a craps house on Begonia Avenue, Rodney's newest operation. The game was three blocks from JFK Boulevard, on a beaten down but peaceful side street, and Strike drove up the weedy curved driveway to the garage, hidden from the sidewalk by a clapboard house. He parked on the back-yard grass between a disemboweled Chevy Nova and a gleaming cherry-red Audi, hoping to see Rodney's rust-eaten battleship. But it wasn't there.

Strike entered the soot-and-shadow garage and saw a hunched figure sitting on a small stepladder next to a wood-burning furnace that was throwing off so much heat that Strike felt his face redden from halfway across the room. A small grate was open at the base of the furnace, and a milk crate of broken wooden venetian-blind slats lay at the figure's feet. Wearing a leather car coat, arms crossed over his chest, the man stared straight ahead into the shadows, looking like the doorman for hell.

Strike moved closer; the man on the ladder was Erroll Barnes. It must have been 70 degrees outside, but Rodney once told him that Erroll always felt cold, the way old men do. And if Erroll Barnes decided to build himself a raging fire in the middle of June, who would tell him to put it out?

Strike nodded, catching Erroll's eye, but he got no acknowledgment. Erroll would know where Rodney was, he might even know who killed Darryl Adams, but Strike couldn't even imagine asking him for the correct time, so he said nothing. Passing Erroll, he picked his way through car parts and open buckets of motor oil and moved to a rear corner of the garage. Four older men were playing poker on a netless Ping-Pong table under a suspended worklight.

It was still early, and Strike knew that by one-thirty or two in the morning, when the Dempsy weight men and their lieutenants started knocking off for the night, the game would shift to craps, and by sunrise a lot of the players would have blown off all of the night's street profits, some even losing their re-up kitty too. In fact, some guys lost so bad in this garage that they went out of business. And when that happened, people sometimes got a little desperate, which was why Rodney paid Erroll Barnes to sit and feed the furnace, keeping the garage nice and warm and peaceful.

The garage belonged to Rodney, in partnership with someone Strike knew only as Curtis, who also owned the clapboard house out front. At the house cut of a dollar a throw on the craps table alone, Rodney and Curtis made at least fifteen hundred a night hustling the hustlers. In the last three months, Curtis had made so much money off the Ping-Pong table that he was negotiating to buy two more houses on either side of his first house, which was a joke, given that he bought the house and garage for a hundred dollars at a government auction. They even gave him a no–interest home improvement loan as part of the deal.

Strike watched the poker game for a few minutes while standing back in the shadows. Curtis wasn't around, and the four men were playing just to keep the table warm, stud games for a nickel and a dime. Behind them, a tall skinny girl with blazing pipehead eyes danced in a corner as if she had to pee. Her hooded sweatshirt was filthy, and Strike saw her size him up with a sidelong glance. He knew that the minute she could get him alone she would hit on him for five dollars or two dollars or one dollar. Strike furtively watched her dance in and out of the cone of light, thinking, This is no place to be right now. He wheeled and headed out, hands in pockets, head sunk into his collarbone as if expecting a punch.

'Hey.'

Strike wasn't sure he heard it; if he did, it came from Erroll, but Erroll was still looking at the shadows on the far wall.

'Give me fifty dollar.'

It was like a voice in his head. Strike turned back. Erroll sat as still as death, composed, distant, not even giving Strike the courtesy of eye contact. He didn't repeat himself.

Strike stared at Erroll, weighing responses, concluding there was nothing to weigh. Erroll was like New York City: he broke all the rules of do and don't.

Strike walked back to the furnace, digging in his pocket. He held out two bills. 'Alls I got is forty.'

Still without looking at him, Erroll forked the two twenties with his fingertips and refolded his arms.

Strike walked out of the garage, thinking, I just got held up, I just got fucking held up, I'm a goddamn victim my *damn* self.

Standing by his car in the moonlit back yard with his keys in his hand, Strike jumped when the girl from the garage came up fast alongside him.

'You looking for Rodney, right?'

Strike stepped back from her: she smelled bad. 'I ain't looking for Rodney.'

'Rodney's in his new store.' Her eyes were on his car keys.

'What new store?'

'It's on like Jury and Krumm.'

He stood in confused silence for a second, then said, 'I ain't looking for Rodney.'

She moved closer, inches away now. 'Give me some money.' She said it low and fast, thrusting her upturned palm at Strike's belly.

Strike gripped her by the shoulders and pushed her back a couple of feet so he could open his car door, get inside and away.

'I'll tell Erroll on you,' she said with childish menace as he floored it in reverse out onto the street.

Jury Street was two blocks over from Blossom, but there was little difference between the two: both gave off the same ash-gray air of decrepitude, the same haunted stillness. After parking his car, Strike stood on JFK and looked down the length of Jury. He saw a single ray of yellow falling on the sidewalk, maybe a hundred yards into the gloom, like a flashlight at the bottom of a pond.

Rodney's new hole in the wall had no name out front. Standing in the doorway, Strike saw that the new store was three quarters the size of the old one. But in every other way it was identical – the same pool table, video game, refrigerator, cracked vinyl bar stool, diplomas, glass counters; the same linty crew of teenagers and relatives strung out through the tiny room as if they'd been there for years.

Rodney stood in front of the counter, his back to Strike, wearing a neon-yellow tank top and a skin-tight pair of bicycle shorts. He was yelling at his daughter for stacking the Goody Cakes under the pork rinds in the display rack, asking her if she thought the cakes were some kind of goddamn secret, tearing into her in a climbing sarcastic drawl.

When Rodney was in this kind of mood, Strike usually kept walking, but he was so eager to talk that he charged across the store as if to leap on Rodney's back. One of the teenagers playing pool saw Strike and yelled, 'Yo Rodney! Rodney!'

Rodney turned just as Strike stopped short and said, 'Hey.'

The kid relaxed, hand on chest. 'I see him coming in all crazy, I thought he a hit man. I was gonna *hook* him. I was knotted, bawh.'

'He ain't no *hit* man.' Rodney gave Strike a fast, knowing wink that made Strike feel almost sleepy with relief. Sometimes just seeing Rodney, hearing his voice, worked on him like hypnosis. Rodney had that power.

'What the hell you do, what's this, what you move for?' Strike's voice came out high and squeaky.

'What for? This morning the motherfucker tried to up the goddamn rent on me from like four hundred to *six*. He figured like I did all that *work* in there, the wallboards, the bathroom, the light fixtures – like I'm stuck, you know? The hell with him, man. I got me some of the kids, we took everything out this mornin'. Everything that *could* go, went.' Rodney leaned over the counter and rearranged the popcorn and Fritos bags. 'The man a opportunist.'

'Y'all should give out a warning, you know?' The words came out faster than Strike intended.

'A warning for what?' Rodney looked at him flat and hard.

Strike looked away.

'You ain't gotta know all my business.' Rodney's voice went high with righteousness. 'I don't ask after all y'*all* business, do I?'

Strike turned back to him and spoke with exaggerated courtesy. 'Can I talk to you?'

'Shit, you be tellin' people all your moves before you make 'em, next thing you know they got their hand in your pocket more'n *you* do.'

'Can I talk to you, Rodney?'

'Shit, that's just common sense, that's just business.'

Strike turned for the door – he just couldn't take it – but before he made it past the pool table, Rodney let loose with a dramatic sigh and said wearily, 'Hang on.' Then he reached over the candy counter and brought up a sledgehammer, and its sudden appearance, its oversize power and bulk, was so startling to Strike that he thought of a clown prop at a circus.

'Take us a *walk*.' Rodney jerked the sledgehammer up to his shoulder and brushed past Strike. On his way to the door, Rodney pushed the *Penthouse* his father was reading into the old man's chest, almost knocking him off his bar stool. On the street, he strolled with the sledgehammer on his shoulder as if coming home from work at the rock pile.

'What's that?' Strike nodded to the sledgehammer, but Rodney didn't seem to hear the question.

'You want to hear some shit?' Rodney sucked on his teeth. 'That old fool wants to get married. You believe that? My father been going into the O'Brien Houses for this little thing about six months now? He-all wants to *marry* her, I'm fit to block his hat for him. Saying to me, "I loves her, you don't understand."' Rodney shook his head. 'Jesus Christ, the stupidness.'

They walked in silence for a moment, Strike having no idea where they were headed. He licked at the imagined blood on his mouth again, hungry for both absolution and praise. And when he finally spoke his voice came out both high and low.

'So you hear about it, right?'

'Hear about what?' Rodney asked. They got to the corner of JFK and passed a knot of people marking time in front of the boarded-up storefronts.

'What you think?'

Rodney's eyes went bright with recognition, then flat again. 'I ain't heard nothin'.'

'Wait – ' Strike began to sputter.

'I ain't heard nothin', I don't *wanna* hear nothin'. I told you, I don't ask about all y'all business, do I?'

Off balance, feeling helpless, Strike ignored Rodney's message. 'I don't know who did it.'

'Did what?' Rodney stopped in front of his old store. 'I don't even know what you're talkin' about.' Rodney went face-to-face with Strike, eyebrows high – a last warning. 'Don't *care* neither.'

Strike took a step back, searching for some way to deal with this.

Rodney turned away from him, put the sledgehammer on the sidewalk and addressed the sheets of plywood, working them loose with violent two-handed tugs, throwing his crouched weight into it, growling with the effort, looking more like an animal trying to get out than a man trying to get in.

When the plywood came free, he climbed inside, unlocked the front door and waved Strike in.

Rodney stood in the center of the empty room, the sledgehammer back on his shoulder, a hand on his hip. He looked down at Strike. 'You don't know nothin', or you don't know all?'

Strike was suddenly afraid that he had walked into a trap. Being close to one death made it seem easy to die, as if it was a flu going around.

'I don't know all. I know like half. Or like *maybe* I know half.'

'Front half or back half?'

'Front half. Alls I did was hold conversation, you know, like, I was in this bar, and – '

'Six hundred dollars.' Rodney cut him off, walking in a slow distracted circle with the sledgehammer. 'Unh, unh, unh.'

Strike backed away to the door, reached behind him for the knob, but Rodney, ignoring him, disappeared behind a half wall, and in a moment Strike heard a steady bubbling splash.

Rodney came back out to Strike while zipping his fly with his free hand. 'Y'all got to take a leak?'

Strike shook his head no.

Rodney adjusted the sledgehammer on his shoulder, spread and set his feet. 'Last chance.'

'What you gonna do?' Strike wanted to run, but he was torn between not wanting to look foolish and not wanting to die. Then Rodney turned his back on him again and went to the half-wall bathroom. Strike heard the toilet flush. Rodney said, 'I took out everything I put in 'cept one thing, and now *it* got to go too.'

It sounded like a series of explosions, and water raced through the store even before Rodney was finished smashing the porcelain. He sloshed back out into the main room, clucking his tongue at the damage. 'It a damn shame, ain't it?' He looked around, spied a framed diploma on one of the walls and tucked it under his arm before wading out to the sidewalk.

'How much did it cost you?' Rodney drove in circles around Dempsy Heights, a presence on the streets, keeping up the morale of his troops.

'Did *what* cost me?' Strike sat in the shotgun seat, knowing they could circle like this for hours.

'Tonight.'

Strike needed a second for the question to sink in, remembering Victor saying his man would do it 'for nothin' . . . for me.' Avoiding Rodney's eyes, Strike said, 'That's my business, just like you said.'

'Uh-huh. Did you bring up my name?'

'*Hell* no.'

'Do I know this guy?'

'He's like from New York.' Instinctively, Strike wanted to protect Victor from that tone in Rodney's voice.

'So then he don't know me.'

'Unh-uh. Shit, I just met him my damn self, and it got passed on from *there* so . . .' Strike looked out the side window, feeling heavy with disappointment. Rodney had said, 'Don't tell me,' but obviously what he really meant was, 'Tell me I'm in the clear.' His self-interest was so naked that Strike wondered why he had ever imagined that he could come to Rodney for help. Probably, he thought, because at the moment Rodney was the closest thing he had to day-by-day family.

Strike shifted gears, still looking for a little sympathy. 'Yeah, so, I just got myself *robbed* by Erroll Barnes. About two hours ago. Ain't that some shit?'

Rodney seemed amused. 'How much he get from you?'

'Forty, right in the damn garage.'

'Big bad Erroll.' Rodney laughed. 'What he do, just ask for it, right? Dint even look you in the face, right?'

Strike didn't answer.

'You know why he do it that way? He *shy*.' Rodney waved lazily to a crew in front of a bar called Shut Up. 'Yeah, when we were growin'

up he was the shyest boy. He never had no dealin' with girls. I got him
every girl he ever had until he was like eighteen.'

'Huh.'

'Yeah, you could say Erroll always had a problem dealing with the
public, you know, at parties, on the street an' shit.'

As they rolled past the Dumont side of the Roosevelt projects, Strike
sneaked a peek up at Victor's bedroom window. The lights were off and
he couldn't decide if that was good or bad. He felt a surge of remorse for
having cast his lot with Rodney over his own true blood.

'Can I tell you something?' Rodney's voice was soft and solicitous. 'I
think you fucked up tonight.'

'How?' Strike asked distantly, not wanting to know.

'You should've done it yourself. Shit, *I* would've.'

'I ain't you.'

'I hear that.'

'*You* would've? Then why didn't you?'

''Cause I thought you needed to get a little bloody, you know? Have
like a personal in*vest*ment in things.'

'Bloody.' Strike shook his head, thinking about what his life would be
like without Rodney in it.

'Yeah, see, I could've got any pipehead out there to cap Darryl for a
handful of bottles, but I needed me a hit man with some in*tell*igence, you
know? Somebody who I don't have to keep an eye on their *mouth* every
time my back is turned. You get what I'm saying?'

'Uh-huh.'

'Somebody who knows me and what I'm *about*.'

'I hear that.'

'So now I just hope whoever you got on this knows *you*, because right
now their head is on your head. See what I'm sayin'?'

Strike didn't answer.

'Because I'm out of this. If the police or anybody else ever ask me, I
just don't know and that's the truth.'

Strike fought down the feeling that he did fuck up by not doing it
himself, that if he had murdered Darryl personally, everything would
be perfect right now. But he had a hard time holding on to that with
any conviction.

'Anyways, I hear Ahab's lookin' for a new assistant manager.'

'What?' It shouldn't have come as a surprise to Strike but it did,
because he had never thought about how things would play out after
Darryl was gone.

'Yeah, they got a opening.'

'Whoa, wait up.' Strike smelled grease in the air.

'Naw, it's a good deal. You put five hundred in the manager's desk every Monday night, he looks the other way, let you use his office, anything you want. He's never there anyhow. It's perfect because this is a lot of traffic you gonna be drawing, and you got to work it so it blends in and don't draw attention to itself. You got out-of-state plates, white people – and coming in an' out of an apartment in the Heights or like comin' in an' out of my store, me, with *my* goddamn jacket? It's kind of obvious, you know? Anybody standing across the street for a half hour is gonna know, specially if they see customers comin' out with nothin' in their hands. So I got to be free of this, I got to have someone in *front*. And this is perfect. My man comes in, goes to the bathroom, comes out, orders food or something, he already put the money behind the toilet tank for you, you all go get it, count it, the guy sits down with his Golden Mobie and a orange soda while you get his ounce, put it right up where you got the money. He goes in gets it himself, nobody knows nothin'.'

Strike recalled the play in Ahab's with the white guy, thinking, Bullshit, I ain't handling no dope. He thought about a mule, a buffer between him and the consequences, just like Rodney was doing to him. He thought about business, the murder fading a little in the face of details, in the face of the future. 'Do I have to be in the damn kitchen all day?'

'Y'all could be out front with a *mop* if you want.'

Rodney suddenly slammed on the brakes and flew out of the car, across JFK to a double-parked Chevy. He hunched over and yelled at the driver, a gray-haired man with a mustache, a Tyrolean hat and heavy-framed glasses. 'Where's my damn money!' The guy extended a placating hand, saying something soft, Rodney saying, 'Naw, naw, naw,' reaching in and taking the guy's keys out of the ignition. 'Get out my damn car. This car *mine* now, so get on out.' Rodney, keys in his fist, backed into the middle of JFK so the guy could get out on the driver's side, the guy rising shakily, going for his wallet, Rodney quickly looking to Strike, winking, then exchanging keys for money, saying to the guy, 'Y'all got to live up to your word. That's the most important thing a man owns, his *word*.'

The guy got back into his car, said, 'Yeah, I hear that,' then peeled out. Disregarding the traffic, Rodney made his way back to the Cadillac, counting the money.

'The houses you use, you got a room anywheres or you just keep a safe?'

Rodney drove with his knees doing the steering, his hands busy refolding his cash roll.

'For what?'

'For answering me. You got somewheres you can close the door, put a lock on it?'

Strike shrugged noncommittally.

''Cause when Erroll gets the ki, he's gonna bring it to *you* now.'

'Erroll just robbed me.'

'Yeah, but this ain't yours to rob – this shit is *mine*. You take the ki, split it up in quarters, take three of the quarters and stash 'em with three of your houses. You take the last quarter to the house with your locked room. That's gonna be your working quarter. I'm gonna tell you who's coming by to cop the next day, so you have everbody's stuff all bagged with you when you go into the restaurant. Somebody comes by Ahab's I dint tell you for, you don't even look at them twice, you don't even serve up no *food* to them, OK? But here's the thing: everybody getting ounces but different. If somebody coming in from Jersey City, you give 'em a straight-up ounce 'cause they can get pretty good stuff right in town. Somebody coming from like Fairlawn? You put a half on it 'cause it's a little harder for them to get better closer. But, like if somebody's coming up from Virginia? You put a one, one and a half on it 'cause stuff is so shitty down there you can step all over the ounce and they still bringing home the best stuff around. So like I'll tell you who's coming in for what, and you cut it up, throw a different color tape on the bag so's Virginia don't go crazy with happiness and Jersey City not come back at all. Some people we making a lot more off than others but it's all profit, and it's all easy.'

Strike thought about teaching someone to cut and bag: No way on earth I'm gonna be up to my goddamn elbows in that. Spend half my life breathing in grease, the other half walking around with felony time in my pockets. Goddamn Rodney – heads I win, tails you lose.

'Yeah,' Strike said. 'Real easy. I'm taking delivery, cuttin', baggin', sellin', takin' money. What the hell *you* doin'? What the hell I need *you* for? Damn.'

'What the hell you need me for?' Something hard and icy came into Rodney's voice. ''Cause Erroll Barnes ask you for forty dollars and you rip open your hand on your zipper you tryin' to get the money out your pocket so fast.'

Strike exhaled in a clammy huff. 'I fuh-feel bad for him, you know.'

Rodney laughed. 'Who you talking to?'

The laugh made Strike tense with dread, something starting here that he was helpless to stop.

'Shit, I nail me a hundred-dollar bill to a tree on JFK and Weehawken in front of a crowd? I'll go around the world, get me some Chinese pussy, come back, that goddamn money still gonna be up on that tree 'cause everybody know it's *mine*. What you think happens *you* put a hundred-dollar bill up like that?' He stared hard at Strike, then talked straight ahead out the window. 'What you need me for? Goddamn, you just a fuckin' front for my jacket.'

Strike glanced over and saw Rodney's lips, tight and bloodless.

'Rodney, faw-forget it, man.'

'Shit, get you in prison, see what you need *me* for.' Rodney was practically barking now.

'Rodney, man. I was just crackin'.'

'Crackin'.' Rodney's eyes got whiter, bigger. He seemed to balloon with rage, transforming himself from an elder-statesman dope dealer back to the psycho stickup man from the seventies, the oldtime Rodney who once drove five hours from Dempsy to New Haven to beat a guy half to death with an aluminum bat for paying for a bundle of heroin with five counterfeit twenties.

'You ain't nothin'.' Rodney spit out the words. 'You too scared to steal from me. That's all your value to me, right there. I finally got me a front too scared to steal from me, and that's all I want. Shit, Darryl had him some balls, that was *his* problem.'

They drove in a tight three-block circle for the better part of an hour, past gaudy flagstone façades and riot gates, past caved-in brownstones and gardens of glass, past the same people in front of Macho Man Social Club and Who Is That Lady beauty parlor, everybody always looking as if they were headed somewhere but never going more than fifty feet all night. Rodney kept muttering about prison and nailing up money on trees and Erroll Barnes, ignoring all his people hailing him, while Strike sat rigid in the shotgun seat, hardly breathing, his whole world going upside down.

Strike was used to seeing Rodney drive by the benches in a bug-eyed funk about once a week, usually because someone just dissed him or cheated him or in some way underestimated his essence, and it often ended in violence, the news coming back through the grapevine a few hours later. But now Strike was on the inside of that rolling nightmare; he'd gotten sucked out of his movie seat and onto the screen. He took a deep breath and tried to derail this thing.

'Yo Rodney, man, c'mon man, it's me, it's me, I luh-love you, man.'
He tried to make it sound hearty and offhand.

'You *love* me?' Rodney cupped his crotch, staring straight ahead.

Strike blew air through his cheeks. 'Rodney, man – '

Suddenly Rodney screeched up short, jumped out of the car before
Strike even had a chance to flinch, ran over to a man and a woman
standing in front of an all-night video store. The man was about Strike's
age, but tall and muscled, with a close-cropped beard.

Strike prayed that Rodney was going to do some mayhem on this
guy instead, but then the two men started talking, Rodney relaxed and
smiling, laughing even, doubling over and making that hissing sound
of his. That was surprising enough, but when the conversation ended
and Rodney kissed the bearded guy full on the mouth, Strike just about
levitated with shock.

Rodney got back in the car, himself again, grinning and juiced. 'You
know him?'

'Naw, who's that?' Strike kept his tone mild, feeling as if he was sticking
his head out of a foxhole.

'Yeah, you wouldn't know him, he's in college.'

Strike felt slightly insulted but didn't show it.

'Yeah, he my son.' Rodney continued driving, waving to the clockers
now. He turned to Strike. 'You know what he just said to me? He said,
"Hey Pop, I just got paid. You have dinner yet?"' Rodney looked as if
he was going to cry with pride. 'Goddamn, that old boy, he can take a
computer apart and put it back together in the dark. He working over
at First Federal paying his own damn tuition. Did I have dinner yet . . .
goddamn.'

'Not bad,' Strike said distantly, wondering why, despite everything,
he felt jealous.

'You know he had a chance to go to Nevada to college? Yeah, they
wanted him to play basketball out there but he got hung up on that ugly
thing he was with? You see her?' Rodney shivered. 'So now he's stuck
in town going to school like ten blocks from where he grew up 'cause
she don't wanna go out west. Goddamn, between him and my father? I
swear, pussy make you stupid.'

'I hear that,' Strike said, starting to calm down.

'So,' Rodney said. He looked in the rearview, made a face and pulled
over, allowing the car that was right behind him for the last five minutes,
taking all his turns, to pass and vanish. 'You got any other comments for
me to hear?'

Rodney reared back like a cobra, tight-lipped, big-eyed, waiting . . .

Strike shrugged, his head almost bowed. 'You tell me what I need to know, I luh leave it at that.' The night had finally broken his back, the murder a dull fact now, all of it dull but overwhelming.

'*Now* you acting like you got the knowledge,' Rodney said approvingly. 'Now you . . . Aw, shit.' He groaned and Strike became alert again. 'Look at this motherfucker here.' Rodney raised a limp hand to indicate a tall overweight kid trudging across the street from in front of a boarded-up Dairy Queen. The kid lurched up to the car and leaned heavily on Rodney's window, looking like a woeful basset hound wearing glasses, nodding to Strike, saying 'Wha's up' and looking at Rodney over the tops of his glasses, doing Old Man River before he even opened his mouth. Strike vaguely remembered him as one of his brother's friends from back in junior high school.

'Wha's up, Bernard?' Rodney put a smirk in his voice, but Strike saw him fight down a smile as Bernard slid his hot-dog-size fingers under his glasses to rub the fatigue out of his face.

'Yo Rodney, man, you hear about Darryl?' He shook his head, his lips hanging loose.

Strike reeled with adrenaline, flashing on Darryl's sister screaming out Darryl's name. Bernard's knowing tone made it seem to Strike like the connections were so obvious that nobody on the street needed to think about who did it, or at least who was probably involved, and suddenly the entire city felt cramped and airless, like a gigantic fist from where there was no escape.

Rodney shrugged, made a sad sound. 'Yeah, I hear it was like a stickup.'

Bernard exhaled into the car. 'That's cold, man.'

'I hear that.'

'I *liked* Darryl, man,' Bernard said. 'He was a funny guy. He always had jokes on him.' Jokes. Strike didn't want to hear about any humanness. But then he thought, What jokes? Darryl never told no jokes.

'Yeah, well, life goes on.' Rodney looked straight out the window.

'Yeah?' Bernard cocked his head, as if Rodney's words had another meaning. 'Well, where at?'

Rodney looked off.

''Cause I need to talk to you about something.'

'Like what?'

Bernard hesitated, ducking down to eye Strike. Rodney nodded, letting Bernard know that Strike had security clearance. 'Oh Rodney, man, I'm fucked up, man.'

Strike seemed to remember Bernard lugging around a French horn case in his schooldays. He was bright, but fucked up then too.

'I'm desperate, man. She snatched my goddamn package, man.'

'Yeah?' Rodney said. 'She told me you snatched it from her. Says you walked out the house with six clips and you came back with no money.'

Bernard shook his head. 'Yeah, you go on believing her. But I'm *tellin'* you, man. I swear. I need a favor, man. I need a favor *bad*. I need like half an ounce on consignment, man.'

Rodney nodded. 'You need a half ounce?'

'I'm desperate, man.'

'You need a half ounce.' Rodney's face became stern. 'How long you coming to me?'

'Three months, man.' Bernard tucked in his ass as a car whizzed by.

'Three months. Now you broke, right? Y'all should be working with some serious weight by now, but you broke.' Serious weight. Strike had assumed that Bernard was on one of Rodney's other crews, but a bottle clocker had no business talking about serious weight.

'Rodney, man.' Bernard held out his palms for understanding.

'What I say to you in the beginning?'

Bernard sulked for a minute before reluctantly answering. 'Sell a ounce, buy two.'

'Then what?'

'Sell two, buy four.'

'Then what?'

'Buy four, bleed in a ounce of cut, make it five.'

'And the cut is what?'

'Your profit.'

'You take the profit from that first cut and do what?'

'Put it aside for bail.'

'*Then* what you do?'

'Buy another four, do it again, keep the profit.'

'You put in more than a ounce cut in four, what do you do?'

'Lose business to better stuff.'

'You keep that steady four-to-one ratio, you got what?'

'Consistent product and steady customers.' Bernard spoke grudgingly, as if reading from a manual.

'And where you at?'

'Sitting pretty.'

'Yeah, uh-huh. So Bernard, you sitting pretty or you on your ass?'

Bernard looked out to the street.

'How come you never come to me for more than a ounce?'

'Rodney, man, you don't know . . .'

Turning to Strike, Rodney kept Bernard hanging on the window. 'I meet this nigger in jail when they got me on that ten-day traffic thing? I like him, right? Pay his bail, get him out, give him a ounce, right Bernard?'

Bernard stared at his hands.

'I say to him, here, you gonna *pay* me for this ounce, seven hundred dollars, but first you gonna break it into bottles, sell the bottles for fourteen hundred, give me my seven, buy another ounce with the other seven, get it rolling, right? Now he supposed to make another fourteen hundred in bottles, buy *two* ounces from me. Does he do that? Hell no. He takes seven hundred, buys one ounce, takes the other seven hundred and parties. Comes back next week after that, buys a ounce for seven, parties for seven, every goddamn week. Seven-and-seven Bernard. He ain't got *no* money for bail, can't *ever* get up enough of a package to put any kind of cut on it. Week in, week out, hand-to-mouth Bernard.'

Strike felt numb with revelation: Fucking Rodney, never showing his whole hand, never telling the whole truth.

'I got expenses,' Bernard muttered weakly.

'Party-to-party Bernard.'

'See, Rodney, man, you don't know.'

'The man should be looking for *real* estate by now, but instead he's hangin' over my window beggin' for half ounces to get back on his feet. He depress the hell out of me.'

Bernard hung his head.

'Put out your hand,' Rodney snapped. Bernard did as he was told, his palm up but jerking back and forth nervously as if Rodney was going to cause it pain.

Rodney peered down like a fortune-teller. 'What color you see?'

Bernard looked at his own hand. 'Light brown,' he said, sounding confused, then, second-guessing Rodney's game, correcting himself and trying to sound proud: '*Black.*'

'Yeah, well you *should* be seeing green.'

Bernard straightened up, sighing.

Rodney eased off a little. 'I give you a half ounce, you best come back in two days, buy a ounce off me. Next time after that you best buy two then four, or I ain't gonna have no truck with you 'cause I don't like doin' business with wastrels. My man Strike here, I throw *him* a half ounce, in six months he own the building you *live* in, throw your ass out on the street.'

'Yeah, I hear that,' Bernard said.

'I doubt it,' Rodney drawled, enjoying himself immensely. 'Come on by the store around two, two-thirty.'

'Yo thanks, Rodney, man. You saving my life, man.'

'Yeah, yeah,' Rodney clucked as he drove off. 'Yeah, ol' Bernard. I like that boy.'

'He sellin' buh-bottles for you, right? And he's sellin' them in town, right?'

'He sellin' for hisself. I sell him a ounce, I don't know what he do with that. That's his business.' Rodney sounded blissful in his artificial ignorance.

'You told me *weight*, man. Goddamn, you into bottles. You on the *street*, Rodney.' Strike suddenly wanted to sleep, his words coming out drugged and petulant.

'It ain't better than Champ, you know, when I put my cut on it? It about the same, so it don't draw off Champ's business or anything. Besides, pretty soon now? Champ is gonna be havin' him some *problems*, an' he ain't gonna be that involved in what I'm doing.'

'What you mean, problems?'

'I can't say right now. It's on confidence. You'll find out later. All I'm sayin' is, don't you be worried about no Champ.'

Strike covered his mouth, slowly shook his head.

'Besides, Bernard the only one.'

Overwhelmed with fatigue, Strike was unable to keep the disgust from his voice. 'Yeah, *right*.'

Rodney slammed on the brakes so hard that Strike flew forward, his head banging on the dashboard.

'Look. You in or you out on the business end, 'cause I already got me a goddamn naggy wife on the *ass* end.'

Strike, holding his forehead, was reduced to begging. 'Just be *straight* with me, man. You say you ain't suh-sellin' in town but Ahab's right in the middle. You say all the customers from outside, Bernard right in the middle. You-you say – '

Strike slammed back into the seat as Rodney floored it, doing sixty on the side streets, Dempsy flying past, Strike silent, his stomach wriggling to break free, Rodney skull-faced, blasting through lights, whipping corners, screeching up to a halt ten minutes later in front of the crescent of benches

at the Roosevelt Houses, Futon and everybody staring at the car. Rodney
leaned across Strike and pushed open his door.

'Get your ass back to work.'

Strike looked at the crew looking at him. The benches seemed smaller
somehow, the ten–dollar–bottle men like children. Strike didn't move.

'Get on out, motherfucker. I'll pick me up Bernard. Let *him* make the
goddamn money. Take *him* off the goddamn street.'

Strike sat there, ear almost touching his shoulder. A Virginia-bound
ounce stepped on one and a half times would be six hundred dollars in
his pocket, free and clear. Sixty ten-dollar-bottle transactions done in one
minute flat.

'Yo Rodney. Look, alls I'm saying . . .'

But Rodney cut him off, jumping out of the car and blocking the path of
a skinny young woman pushing a stroller toward the projects. He started
in on her, jerking a hand toward the stroller. 'What you takin' him out
for now?'

'He sleepin',' she said.

'You know how late it is? What the hell's wrong with you?' Rodney
ducked down and lifted the baby into his arms.

'I *said* he's sleepin'.'

'You goin' to the store?'

She didn't answer.

'I'll meet you at the store, you take him upstairs. An' don't you make
me wait.'

She walked off with the empty stroller, her face puckered into a pout.

'Goddamn, don't I even get a kiss?' Rodney shouted after her. He
ducked back into the car, cradled his son in his lap, turned on the ignition
with his free hand and then looked up at Strike, eye-brows high in mock
surprise. 'You still here?'

10

Rocco stood in the littered motel room, hands in his pockets, watching Duck Gathers chew out a part-time dope dealer who lay spread-eagled in his boxer shorts on the unmade bed, one half-mast eye on Duck, the other on 'The Joe Franklin Show,' playing behind Duck's left shoulder on the wall-mounted television.

'You listening to me? You go down to your caseworker tomorrow. You say, The Duck says I got to move out of the Royal or I'm gonna get violated. You hear that?'

The room stank of unwashed laundry and imitation grape candy. Short strips of tinfoil lay on the dresser top, crumbs of crack nestled in the folds and dimples. The guy on the bed was smashed on crack and gin, and Rocco was surprised he was acting so stupefied; Rocco thought crack made you fly backwards like an untied balloon. But Rocco had rarely seen crack, since Dempsy was primarily cook-it-yourself powder-coke country.

'What I say, Orlando? Tell me what I just said.'

'My caseworker on vacation.' Orlando had both eyes on the TV now, one hand over his crotch, the other across his chest, cupping his nipple.

'So you go to whoever's covering her files. Because I swear, I come by tomorrow and you're not packed up? Or if you don't at least have a letter for me saying you went in and they're working on it? I come in here tomorrow and you're laying there playin' with your peenie, I swear I'm gonna fuckin' tune you up so fuckin' bad you gonna wish you were fuckin' dead, you hear me?'

Orlando didn't answer, now totally absorbed by the TV show. Duck looked to Rocco with helpless dismay, walked over to the bed and yanked up the mattress, spilling Orlando onto the floor. When Orlando struggled to his feet, he looked annoyed.

Duck stood in front of a dresser mirror, sighed, adjusted his three gold chains and patted his perfect hair. Rocco knew that Duck was trying to calm himself down with a little preening. Duck was obsessive about his appearance, and he was the only non-Jewish, non-Italian white man that Rocco ever met who favored gold.

'Get in the shower, Orlando. You stink.' Duck shook his wrist, frowning down at his ID bracelet until it lay initials up.

'Can I wait for the commercial?'

'You go in now, you get to mix the hot and cold yourself. You wait, I do it for you.'

Orlando hesitated a few seconds more before heading off.

'And wash your armpits,' Duck yelled after him. He turned to Rocco. 'You remember getting laid here?'

'Are you kidding me?' Rocco yawned, feeling in need of a shower himself. 'This place was like my entire sex life.'

Back in the sixties, everybody used to bring their girlfriends to the Royal because it had the cheapest rates. Now it was Duck Gathers's fiefdom, and having the Duck as escort would make Rocco's life easier tonight. If he had tried to toss Darryl Adams's room on his own, he might have gotten the shit kicked out of him, since he was sport jacket and wing tips – one-time police not likely to return – whereas Duck was high-top Ponys and jeans, daily life and endless payback. The problem was, when you were Duck's guest, you had to go at Duck's pace.

'I don't hear no water running,' Duck blared in a distracted singsong as if talking to children upstairs. He swept all the tinfoil and crack and crumpled it up into a golf ball, batting it back and forth between his palms. He looked at Rocco and shrugged. 'Darryl Adams was a good kid. That's too bad.'

'Yeah, so, can we go over now?'

'Hang on.' Duck spied a loose ceiling tile, got a chair to stand on and poked the tile free. He felt around inside, then hopped off and smacked his hands clean. 'Take a picture of this room in your head, and when we get there, compare it to Darryl's. You'll see what I mean.'

The shower kicked in. They headed for the door and bumped into a petite black whore tripping into the room with a twenty-dollar bill in her hand.

'Oop, it Sergeant Duck.'

She turned to leave but Duck snatched the money. 'What's this?'

'I owe it to Orlando.' She turned to Rocco. 'You motel squad too?'

'Vatican Secret Service,' Rocco said.

Duck draped an arm around her shoulders. 'Who you scoring bottles for, Tina?' In Tunnely, crack came in tinfoil because it was easier to hide and cheaper to package, but out of habit everybody still called it bottles.

'I ain't for nobody. I just owe.'

'Let's go back to your room.' Duck held her hand, their fingers clasped like lovers, the ball of dope in his free fist. 'Rocco, you mind?'

'Hey, no problem.' Rocco said, thinking, Here we go again. He had already been following Duck for an hour like this.

Duck Gathers patrolled a dozen motels from eight P.M. to four A.M. He and the others in his squad were roving zookeepers, kicking in doors at will and on whim, half the time walking in on some illegal tableau, from professional cocksucking to crack smoking. Duck was on a first-name basis with two hundred hookers and small-time bad guys, and he rarely arrested anybody if he could help it – the jails were full up already. He mainly tried to harass, hound and torment the lowlifes on his turf into picking up and moving on, out of the town of Tunnely and back into Dempsy, where most of them originated.

Cruising with the Duck was like being trapped in some hellish cartoon of endless two-bit crime and punishment, a time-chewing symphony of banging doors and uh-oh eyes. A cop had to be suicidal to patrol the Royal solo, but the Duck was a special case: more than anybody else on the motel squad, he considered the Royal his personal mission, regarded himself as the town marshal and spiritual maintenance man for all souls contained in its eighty rooms.

When Duck clocked out and went home, all he had in his studio apartment was a bed, a TV and a rowing machine, and he rowed for two or three hours a day to unwind, and sometimes to rewind. He had no wife, no kids, no hobbies – just motel patrol, gold jewelry and that rowing machine, which gave him the upper body of a home run king and the wrists of a strangler. As the longtime Royal tenants told the newcomers: Pay your rent, lock your door, and don't fuck with the Duck.

Rocco followed Duck and Tina out of Orlando's room and onto the exterior walkway that ran the length of the building and connected all the second-floor rooms. The three of them strolled like two sweethearts and a chaperone, with Rocco slightly behind and eyeing Duck's trademark waddle. They headed past clusters of people who listlessly hung on the railings and peered over the side to watch the now dwindling number of New York cars rolling up for some predawn business. To Rocco, everyone here looked irreparably damaged: they were too thin, too skittish, too aimless. It seemed to him that the Royal was less a motel than a kind of hospital ship, a quarantine ward of the soul, and that the highways separating the motel from the New York skyline might as well be rivers, and the Hudson River itself an uncrossable ocean.

A skinny, crook-backed Dominican kid with a scratchy goatee walked toward them. As Duck came abreast of the kid, he finger-hooked him by the shirt with his crack-ball hand, announcing, 'Reynard, Reynard,' and making him stagger backwards, taking him along for the ride to Tina's room, number 47, the four of them barging in on a tall blonde hooker sitting with her legs crossed, arms folded, eyes puffy with anxiety.

Duck stamped his foot when he saw the blonde. 'Jesus Christ! You again! What the hell is wrong with you?' He pushed Tina aside, planted Reynard flat against the wall and hunched over the blonde whore.

'Nothing,' she said in a hoarse and tiny voice. At first Rocco thought she was a transvestite, then decided she was just big-boned. Her face seemed to belong to two separate women, as if a see-through hag mask had been superimposed on the features of a Nordic milkmaid.

'What, you gave her twenty dollars for a bottle, you thought she was gonna come back with something good?'

'No, I'm just visiting.' Her eyes were blank.

Duck raised his hands in exasperation. 'What do you think she's gonna do for you? She's gonna get a razor, a bar of soap, shave off some flakes, fold it in foil and take your money. You walk off, go somewheres and blow bubbles. What the hell's the matter with you?' He held out the twenty to her.

'I just came by to visit,' she said, deadpan, as she took the money.

'You ain't too street-smart, sister, you're gonna get killed. Don't you ever want to play the violin again?'

Rocco laughed out loud. He didn't think Duck had the wit to come up with such an offbeat line.

'Roc, no shit, six months ago she was playing violin in the orchestra pit.' He turned to the hooker. 'What was the show? *Nicholas Nickleby*?'

'*Phantom of the Opera*.' She followed the ball of tinfoil with her eyes as if she could smell what was inside.

'Can you believe that? She hooks up with this scumbag boyfriend, gets a taste of the pipe? Now she's playin' nighttime skin flute in the Toys R Us parking lot. Is that a fuckin' waste or what?'

'*Phantom*, huh? I tried to get seats to that. It's fucking impossible.' Rocco turned to the hooker. 'Do you have any connections still or are you all the way out of it now?'

She looked at him from the corner of her eye, not knowing if he was kidding, and Rocco felt bad for being a smartass.

'You just gotta get them bottles, huh? Just got to get them bottles.' Duck shook his head in disgust, then pointed his finger at her. 'You want to throw your life away, don't do it in front of me. I don't ever want to see you here again.'

The whore nodded, gathered her bag and rose. She was the tallest person in the room.

'*Shit*!' the tiny black hooker exploded and everybody jumped, Rocco thinking maybe she had seen something scurrying along the floor. But Tina charged across the room, almost belly-bumping Duck in her rage. 'Goddamn motherfuckin' Duck, you a motherfuckin' *racist*, you know that? Every time you snatch some white bitch or some white boy you come on like they you goddamn relative. You always like chew 'em out, sayin' how they wastin' they lives an' shit, but you grab a nigger an' it's like, it's like . . . ho shit, more garbage, like someone left out the garbage. You just like, *fuck* with us, you know, call us names, smack us around, make insults, take away the dope. But you never get upset. It's like niggers are niggers, they're sup*posed* to be doin' this shit, they can't help it. So you a motherfuckin' racist, Duck.'

'I'm a *racist*? How many times I catch you with dope, with johns, with a gun that time? I always let you go, *al*ways.'

'You know why? 'Cause you could care less about *me*. It's like what I do, that's not a *waste*, right? It's OK 'cause I'm just a black ho'. But she's doin' the same shit? Whoa! Watch out, here comes the Duck. Don't throw your life away. So you can *kiss* my ass.'

'Hey! Hey!' Duck pointed back at the blonde. 'She's a professional violinist.'

'Yeah? Well I'm a goddamn high school graduate. Where I come from, you think that's no small thing? I know Spanish, I know French.'

'I'll bet you do,' Rocco said, impatient to toss Darryl Adams's room and get the hell out.

Tina turned her rage on Rocco like a spotlight. 'Who the fuck *you* crackin' off to?' She gave him the up-and-down. 'You don't even belong here.'

'Thank God for that.' Rocco kept his hands in his pockets, bouncing on the balls of his feet, showing his teeth but feeling exhausted and a little down.

'See, all you motherfuckin' cops – motel, knocko – you all alike. Goddamn. I'm gonna take me some goddamn violin lessons, see what happens next. Shit . . .' Tina trailed off, finally spent.

Duck smiled, looking slightly abashed; Rocco thought he might even have been blushing. But Duck suddenly turned to the blonde whore and went dark-faced. 'Did I tell you to get lost?'

Whispering 'Excuse me,' the blonde brushed past Rocco, eyes disconnected to everyone and everything but the craving. She slipped out the door.

'Hey, Tina,' Duck said gently.

'Fuck you, Duck. Get the fuck out of my room.' Tina's eyes wandered from the bed to the TV to the dresser as she pretended to look for something.

'Tina, tell you what. You're under arrest, OK? You feel better?'

'Just get the fuck out of my room.'

Duck looked to Rocco sheepishly and nodded to the door. 'I'm gonna be watching you, Tina.' Duck pulled Reynard off the wall as if he was an overcoat on a hook. Rocco followed them back out onto the balcony.

Tina stood in the doorway. She looked at Duck one last time, all the anger in her face drained into a sad disgust. 'You even gave her back the goddamn twenty, you know what I mean?'

She softly closed the door. Duck looked down at his scuffed high tops for a moment, then smiled up at Rocco. 'I like her.' He turned to Reynard at the end of his fist. '*You* on the other hand . . .' Duck yanked Reynard into an open-air corridor and slammed him against a cinder block wall. 'You're goin' in, because you're a lyin' no-good, spic motherfucker snake. I told you I want a ounce by midnight. It's after four – where the hell were you?'

'I was lookin' for you.'

'Right. Last chance, my man. Give me an ounce.'

Reynard breathed through his nose. 'I was in the hospital.' His voice was a distant murmur, as if he had no interest in his own alibi.

'You were in the hospital. For what?'

'I got stabbed.' Reynard half turned to show Duck a bloody crust on his triceps. To Rocco's eyes it looked more like a burst cyst than a puncture wound.

'Yeah? Who stabbed you?' Duck didn't look convinced either.

'This guy, I was just walking – '

'That's a heart-rendering story. You see this?' Duck held up the foil ball of crack that he had taken from Orlando's room. 'You got like until I count to ten to give me an ounce or this is yours.' Duck stuffed the dope behind Reynard's fly and left his hand there.

'One . . . two . . .'

'I tell you who's got *some* shit in their room but I don't think it's a whole ounce. Maybe. I don't know.'

'An *ounce*, Reynard.' Duck jerked on Reynard's pants. 'Three . . .
four . . .'

'Well then, like you better arrest me, I guess.'

Rocco rolled his eyes in frustration.

'An eight ball,' Duck said. 'Give me an eight ball. Five . . . six . . .'

'You know that guy Orlando?' Reynard said. 'He's got *some* shit in
there. I saw it on his dresser.' He scratched his chin. 'That's all I know
for now, but maybe I do better for you tomorrow, you know, 'cause I
know I owe you, so . . .'

Duck looked at Rocco and sagged. Then he kicked Reynard in the ass,
a little punt that sent him stumbling down the stairs. He flung Orlando's
ball of dope off the walkway into some weedy bushes on the far side of
the parking lot.

The New York skyline had begun to bruise purple with the dawn.
Rocco glanced at Duck, who suddenly resembled a terror-stricken
vampire miles from his coffin, an expression that Rocco imagined
was pretty common around the Royal at this time of night. It was
an occupational hazard: work your people long enough and you got
addicted to their rhythms of soar and plunge.

Rocco pressed his splayed hands together in supplication. 'Hey Duck,
I gotta get in there.'

'See what I mean?' Duck stood just inside Darryl Adams's room, arm
extended as if he was trying to rent it out. 'This kid had pride, no?'

Rocco hallucinated the sweetish smell of indoor death even though the
kid had died one town over. It was probably that grape candy scent he
had been smelling all night, which he now realized was deodorizer coming
through all the vents.

The room was pristine. The bed sheets had hospital corners and the
bedspread was perfectly folded under and then over the pillows. A bottle
of holding spray, an Afro Pic and three brushes lay on a paper napkin on
the dresser, along with loose change in an Ahab's plastic soda cup and
three gold-tooth jackets in a Styrofoam cole slaw cup. Pots and pans
were stacked underneath the hot-plate counter in a cubbyhole over which
a plaid cloth had been thumbtacked as a curtain.

'This kid was OK, hah?' Rocco said, taking a thirty-gallon trash bag
out of the side pocket of his sport jacket and flapping it open.

Duck shrugged. 'Never gave me grief, never ran with any of the
scumbags, always looked presentable, hello goodbye, how you doin'.
He even complained about the noise once or twice.'

'We found twenty-five hundred bucks on him.'

'Twenty-five?' Duck said. 'So I guess he was a scumbag after all, hah? Had *me* fuckin' fooled. Quiet Storm scumbag. Live and learn . . . I'm very disappointed.'

'He ever bring anybody home?'

'Not that I know of.'

Rocco looked over the open surfaces in the room for possible booty. 'Who's the girl?' He picked up a color photograph of a black teenager with spray-stiffened bangs. She was smiling, her head frozen at that chin-cocked graduation-picture angle.

'That's his sister,' Duck said. 'She lives in Dempsy.'

Rocco stared hard. It was Harmony, the woman he had dropped off at Allerton less than two hours before. But she looked thirty pounds heavier in the photo.

'She ever come by?'

'Once, about six months ago. She came over to borrow money or something. They had some argument out in the parking lot. Looked like she was hitting the pipe.'

'He have a girlfriend?' Rocco was absently opening drawers, noting that the kid had folded his underpants and pinned pairs of socks with hair clips.

'Down south, I think. He sent money down south. I think he might of had a kid down there, North Carolina, South Carolina. Listen, are you gonna do the bed? I wanna flop.'

Rocco pulled out the bed cover and felt under the pillows. 'It's all yours.'

Duck lay down on the dead kid's bed and threw a forearm across his eyes. 'There's a bag of hypos in the bathroom, but the kid had diabetes so don't sweat it.'

'Fucking Duck. You know your people.'

'I didn't know about no twenty-five hundred dollars.'

'So who did this kid?' Rocco came across a stack of crossword puzzle paperbacks in the shirt drawer. It wasn't exactly literature, but at least the kid had some books. 'Who did it, Duck?'

'Well, if he was laying there still with the money, it must've been an execution, right? Who was he selling for? Champ? Or maybe he wasn't selling for Champ. Maybe *that* was the problem. Or maybe it was just a fucked-up robbery. Who knows? I be *motel* squad.'

Rocco searched the medicine chest and came across the hypos, vials of insulin, some blood pressure pills and asthma spray. 'Kid's in great shape.'

He picked up a tube of Ghostbusters toothpaste and felt a fleeting pang of sadness.

Working the closet, Rocco found a stuffed animal in a cardboard box addressed to someone named Isaac Adams in Valdosta, Georgia. Probably the victim's son. He bagged it, then looked under a stack of empty sneaker boxes in the rear corner and found a small safe with the door open. Inside were three rolls of tape – red, blue and black – a packet of unused envelopes, a sheet of twenty-five-cent stamps and a scattering of rubber bands.

By the time Rocco was done, Duck was snoring. He shook Duck awake and they walked out to the balcony together and leaned on the railing.

'Anything else, Roc?'

Rocco thought for a moment. 'No phone, huh?'

Duck shook his head.

'You ever see Rodney Little around here?'

'The dope dealer?' Duck spit into the parking lot below. 'I know who he is, but I never seen him here.'

'You ever hear of someone named One Love?'

'One Love? I heard of Unlove. You know, UNLV, the college? A lot of the kids are into that school 'cause of the basketball team. Why?'

So much for One Love, Rocco thought. Probably some idiot who couldn't spell or even listen right.

'Duck, be well.'

Rocco pushed off the railing, gave Duck a light slap on the back and trudged down the metal steps to the parking lot. Crossing over to his car, he heard a faint rapping from above and then Duck's voice: 'Tina, it's Duck. Open up, I want to talk to you.'

Rocco sat in his car, spasming with fatigue. The sky was a mustard-mauve now, giving no clear sign of the weather for the coming day. He shivered, threw the car into reverse, thinking about the actor, who was probably still asleep in the prosecutor's office. He decided to go back and drive Touhey home.

Half an hour later Rocco stood inside the cell, feeling as if there had been a legitimate jailbreak. Sean Touhey was gone. Rocco looked around the cell for a note: nothing. He searched his desk, checked the reception area, Vy's desk. The guy must have just staggered out. Rocco told himself he was worried that the actor might have an accident driving home, but it was more than that: he couldn't help feeling that Touhey had simply dumped him again. Rocco tried to remember if he had said anything about coming back for the following four-to-twelve tour, then took Touhey's business card out of his pocket, read the scrawled promise on the back: 'Bank on it.'

Bank on it. What a self-approving jerk. But still . . .

Finally ready to go home, Rocco drove through Dempsy toward the Holland Tunnel. The sky was still undecided, a flat, washed-out white, and the JFK war zone, stripped of the night and its suggestions, looked shrunken and tamed, a street of forlorn and battered doll houses under artificial light. The few remaining people, mainly the odd skull-faced whore tromping home or the occasional clocker still on his corner, stamping his feet in boredom or fatigue, seemed miniaturized too – dope dealer dolls. Rocco drove by, taking in the last dregs of his clientele, feeling up to his eyeballs in the nothingness of people's lives, the objects and odors, the petty game plans and deceptions, underwear and tinfoil, dope and booze, all the shitty little secrets, the hiding places, everything adding up to a stain on a sidewalk, the only evidence that these people had ever existed.

Soar and plunge. Rocco thought about Duck roaming the catwalk of the Royal, just another haggard and restless wee-hour wanderer, so completely digested by the job that he had become almost indistinguishable from all the others.

Rocco shot under the river, heading into New York, thinking, But I'm more than that – I just have to be.

11

Saturday was a sweet and sunny day, the kind that made people think about getting it together once and for all – health, kids, jobs, personal appearance, doing things *right* this time. Mothers stood around smoking and laughing, their kids shouting and running as if their hair was on fire. The shards of bottle glass that studded the chained-in grass island behind the benches caught the sun and turned an eyesore into a field of diamonds.

Strike sat locked in a crouch on his perch, red-eyed and stiff, feeling as if the benign weather and buoyant voices that surrounded him were some kind of setup. He had been waiting for the hammer to drop since ten o'clock the night before, waiting for the news of Darryl's death to fan out into a plague of misery and chaos, yet here it was, the day after, a Saturday so luminous and joyful that he hadn't sold a single bottle all morning.

Futon, The Word, Peanut and the others were hopping around, flicking make-believe jump shots, lashing out roundhouse karate kicks, celebrating the first full day of summer vacation. Tuning them out, Strike squinted across the projects, trying to see into his old bedroom, Victor's room, but the window was a gleaming shield of light, and Strike forced himself to look away, to forget about it, deal with the bottle flow: What you don't know can't hurt you.

Strike could care less about the selling slump. He was just marking time now, keeping up appearances. The night before, Rodney had said no sudden moves, can't have people saying, Hey, what happened to Strike? Rodney wanted to run ounces out of his store for a while, risk the traffic for a few days, a week, let Strike hang out a little, see customers' faces. In another week or so, when the murder died down, crowded out by fresher jobs, Rodney would slide the whole thing over to Ahab's again.

But Champ – he was still out there, even if they got away with the Darryl Adams end of it. Rodney had said something about Champ having

his own problems soon, but he didn't say what. And there was Victor
to deal with too, and My Man . . . Strike hugged himself, knowing that
too much hung in the air, that this could never have a happy ending, that
right now, for all his talk about how important it was to think about the
future, he had acted like a sneaker dealer, just another bonehead living by
the two-minute clock.

A waddling baby dropped a bottle of red juice, the spillage billowing out
right under Strike's perch. The baby let out such a penetrating yowl that
Strike jumped off the bench and began walking toward 41 Dumont, his old
apartment house, not knowing what he would do when he got there.

Halfway to the building, he saw Victor's wife, ShaRon, in the playground, playing a kind of handball with herself against a graffiti-covered
wall, her infant son in a stroller parked on the sidelines. Overweight and
mope-faced, she was flinging the ball with a girl's cocked-elbow toss,
then missing it on the bounce-back when she tried to hit it with an open
palm. After every missed contact, she trudged to the fence to retrieve the
pink high-bounce, then threw it up again, missed it again, walked after
it again, her gait like a bored camel's.

Strike leaned against the mesh, watching her, knowing she knew he
was there by the way she didn't notice him.

ShaRon had moved into his old bedroom about two years before,
bumping him to the sofa, and Strike remembered the day he first learned
about her. He found a letter she had composed lying on Victor's night
table, a torn-out page of a spiral notebook on which she had written a
formal greeting to the child in her belly, telling it that she hoped it was
handsome or beautiful, asking the child if it was scared, reassuring it that
she loved it and so did its father. The letter ended in a dozen possible
names, most of them champagne-toned, right out of a soap opera.

Strike didn't think ShaRon and Victor even liked each other that much.
Victor had gotten her pregnant, and he'd always had this iron-bound
notion about being responsible and cleaning up his own mess, which
was a lot more than Strike could say for most of the guys he knew. And
his guess about ShaRon was that she had simply wanted to get out of her
mother's apartment any way she could.

Strike had met ShaRon's mother once. She was a skinny, scooped-
out, chain-smoking woman with a face like a fist and a startlingly
deep and sharp voice. But moving away didn't seem to solve anything for ShaRon, and the girl looked as unhappy playing handball
with herself today as she did the first time Strike had laid eyes on
her.

The ball rolled to where Strike was standing, and ShaRon had no choice but to meet his eyes.

'How you doin'?' Strike squinted at her through the mesh.

'I'm OK.' Her brow was furrowed like a prisoner's or a child's.

'Where my brother at?'

'Workin'.'

'At Hambone's?'

'At the other job. I don't know.'

'He OK?' Strike's mouth went dry with the question.

'I don't know. Yeah, I guess.'

'Everything OK?'

'Yeah.'

'When you see him last?'

'I don't know. Last night, this mornin'.'

'Everything was OK, huh?'

'I guess so. I don't know.'

Caught between irritation at her deadness and a sudden gust of anxiety, Strike wanted to push it, to ask her straight out if she knew who killed Darryl Adams, but he had a feeling that she wasn't enough a part of Victor's world to know, even by a guess.

Giving up, he stared at the tiny thing lying flat in the stroller. Ivan, his nephew – he had never seen him before. No, this was Mark – Ivan was the older one.

'My brother,' Strike said. 'Tell him to come see me.'

'OK.' Her face was blank.

'If he wants to. You know, if he needs to.'

ShaRon stared at him, waiting for him to leave.

'Yeah OK.' Strike walked away, wondering why Victor was killing himself for a girl like that. He recalled all the evenings his mother had come home from one of her two jobs and had to zip through the kitchen, cleaning the dishes still in the sink from the morning. ShaRon sat goggle-eyed and mute at the kitchen table, holding her baby in her lap, Strike's mother moving around her like water running around a rock. The minute any of them got home from work – Strike, Victor, their mother – they'd instantly start to tidy up, keeping the apartment spotless and proud – everybody except ShaRon, a sullen nineteen-year-old with no appreciation for all Victor was doing for her. Strike allowed his outrage to overwhelm him now, his righteous anger almost a relief. At least it got his mind off Darryl.

Back at the benches Peanut was still yammering, tossing off put-downs,

The Word and Futon listening, eyes shining, waiting for the next cut. 'Yo yo, I went up to Horace this morning? I go up there, knock on the door, this big motherfucker *rat* come to the door 'bout six feet high.'

'Ho shit.' Futon jackknifed with pleasure.

'Yeah,' Peanut said. 'He come open the door. He say, "What you want?" I say, "Yo, is Horace home?" He say, "He still sleepin'." Wham! Slam the door in my face.'

Everybody bent over with laughter, watching for Horace, hoping he somehow heard that and would come running, jump on Peanut's head.

'Leave the motherfucker alone,' Strike said. 'I see *your* house. Goddamn, the couch so motherfuckin' buggy it up and walked across the goddamn room, turned on the TV.'

The kids got pop-eyed with delight, mouths perfect *o*'s. They pointed to Peanut and barked, 'Oh! Oh! Oh!'

Peanut went dark but was afraid to start trading digs with Strike. 'Yeah, but we gettin' new furniture this week,' he said in a lame mumble.

'Yeah, how?' Strike said. 'The roaches chipping in?' The woof chorus went through the roof, everybody high-fiving, hopping in glee.

Strike didn't like to crack on anybody, but he wanted to shut Peanut down because Peanut always goofed on Horace, and something bad was going on with Horace these days. His mother had a new boyfriend, and whatever was happening in his house was making Horace choke-faced crazy. He had gotten into two bad fistfights over the last two weeks, and more recently he started carrying a steak knife in his pocket. He'd already had the knife out once. The day before, a fight had broken out around the corner that was unrelated to any crew business, and when people started running from everywhere to watch, Horace ran toward the fight too. But he ran with the steak knife in his hand, and Strike had imagined him blindly plunging the knife into somebody's chest or back, for no reason other than that violence was already in the air.

Pinch-faced and mumbling, Peanut stalked off, everybody else fanning out to the corners to see if they could draw some car business. Alone now, beginning to brood about Darryl again, Strike was hungry for a distraction and found himself locking eyes with that kid Tyrone from 8 Weehawken, who was perched on the low chain surrounding the glass-littered patch of lawn. Figuring that the kid had overheard all the banter, Strike checked first in the direction that Peanut had gone, then back to Tyrone, shaking his head with disgust. Tyrone glanced away, fighting down a smile, rocking the chain like a cradle.

One of the new clockers, Stitch, a tall gangly kid with tiny folded-down ears, appeared from the rear of 6 Weehawken, race-walking toward Strike, his face cemented with furious determination. Strike groaned, Now what?

Stitch marched up to the bench, glaring at Strike. 'I just got *beat*. Nigger in a Nissan want a clip, I go get it, come down, the motherfucker put a gun in my face and drive off, so what I'm sayin' to *you* is, I got to go home and get my gun, because I know who the nigger is and I got to get it straight. So like, I'll be back.'

Strike put his hand out, holding him in place, thinking fast, knowing Stitch was full of shit. He probably smoked it himself or sold it for more in some other neighborhood. 'Hang in, hang in,' Strike said. He looked into Stitch's eyes, not seeing the dope there as he expected. But the body language was all wrong. Stitch's ear was almost kissing his shoulder and he kept rubbing a spot on his shirt with his fingertips.

'What's the guy's name?' Strike said.

Stitch jerked his head back. 'Who?'

'Who *stole* from you, stupid.' Strike watched him think, as if it was a physical activity. Strike had taken Stitch into the crew because he was Futon's half-brother, but brains didn't run in the family. He'd had 348 stitches up and down his chest and arms from when he stole money from another dealer about six months before. Proud of getting cut up like that, he had given himself his own street name – as if walking around looking like a human baseball was some kind of mannish accomplishment. Some people would hang on to anything to hold their head up.

'Reebok,' Stitch finally said.

'Reebok?' Strike ducked his head and stared up and into Stitch's face. 'The motherfucker a stickup man or a sneaker?'

'Reebok, that's all I know.'

Strike followed a kite-tail curve of suture marks that climbed out of the kid's shirt and up to his jawline, thinking, What to do? The kid just stole ten bottles, and the bottles should come out of his commission. He'd have to sell five clips with no two-bottle cut to make it up, but if he already stole ten bottles, why give him more?

Strike had to split the bottle profits with Rodney, sixty percent for Rodney, forty percent for Strike and his crew, but any kind of shorts – theft, usage, breakage, police – came out of Strike's end. Rodney always got his sixty percent, and Strike took his losses out on the people responsible, insisting that everyone account for what he held, one way or the other.

But right now all Strike wanted to do was ease out of this job without any undue grief; it wasn't a time for coming down on people.

'Get your ass on out,' Strike muttered.

'I'm gonna get mah gun.'

'You ain't *got* no gun. Just get the fuck out of my face before I give you a taste of something you ain't gonna like.'

Stitch backed away, looking even more gangly and awkward. 'Damn,' he whined, trying to come off bruised.

'Yeah, right, *damn*. Just get the fuck on out.'

Stitch walked off, mumbling his story to himself as if he actually believed it. Strike gave him about another six months before he was either locked up or killed.

Tyrone, still rocking on the chain, looked at Strike again, and this time the kid was the one to initiate an expression of eyes-to-heaven disgust.

Strike nodded, thinking, Spy boy, ounce mule, brightful and young, too young to be noticed. Strike stretched his legs, slid off the top bench slat like a lazy meat eater, walked up slow and distracted toward Tyrone, stopping in front of him, looking down at the top of his head, the kid going blank, but too blank. Strike towered over him, then lightly plucked the hair around the nappy Mercedes Benz symbol. 'What the fuck is this?'

The kid stared off, shrugging as if Strike's voice was in some daydream.

'You look like motherfuckin' *Buck*wheat.'

The kid jerked erect with embarrassed dismay but still didn't get up and face Strike. Feigning a fed-up weariness, Strike slipped a half-inch roll of cash from his pocket and put on a show of counting all the tens and twenties, pretending to check whether he had enough to spring for a haircut. A lot of the young boys around the projects liked to tear and fold paper until they had a stack of blank pretend money and could play dope dealer, whipping out their roll, hiking one foot up on a bench and counting out loud like it was a good night. Strike thought such behavior in real-life clockers was embarrassing, and in little kids it was just sadder than shit. But sometimes you had to play games in order to get things going: this morning he had broken his ten-dollar-limit rule and taken a roll of money with him, thinking that maybe he'd run into this kid today, begin working on him, though he couldn't say exactly what he had in mind.

'Yeah . . .' Strike palmed the cash, slid it into his front pants pocket and scanned the street. 'C'mon, get in the damn car.' He walked off without a backward glance, glad for the excuse to get the hell away from here, away from Rodney, Victor, Champ, that bloody sheet, all of it.

Tyrone rose off the chain, rubbing the backs of his thighs and self-consciously hobbling like an old man. He followed Strike for three blocks, to the old lady's driveway. Strike liked the way he understood how to lag behind without having to be told. It was intelligence or shyness or maybe both, but it was a good sign. He had done it right, and nobody watching from the bench would have thought they were going off together.

Sitting in the car now, with Tyrone in the shotgun seat staring straight ahead, Strike massaged his temple, wondering how he would play this thing. Finally he turned and broke the ice.

'What's wrong with your leg?' Strike sounded peevish, like Rodney talking to his kids.

'Nothin'.' Tyrone shrugged, eyes still facing forward.

'Then how come you limping?'

'Foot fell asleep.'

'You see something in front of the car I don't see?'

'Uh-uh.'

'Then why don't y'all look to who you're answering?'

Tyrone turned and stared at Strike's throat. 'Foot fell asleep.'

Strike jerked back, eyelids fluttering. The kid's breath was bad enough to make him forget the lesson in manners.

Strike drove the two blocks to Shaft Deli-Liquors. He was three steps inside before he saw the tall, skinny, gray-haired Homicide behind the cash register; by then he had been noticed, so he had no choice but to go ahead and do his business. Otherwise, the man would win without a fight.

The Homicide owned the store but rarely worked there, and nine times out of ten Strike dealt with the two blacks or the Puerto Rican who worked for him. They treated Strike with respect, but the Homicide was a hawk-eyed motherfucker, and anytime they were under the same roof it was a goddamn pissing match.

Strike walked to the back of the store and stopped in front of the glass-doored refrigerator, the Homicide making a big show of following him with a half-amused smirk. Dope dealers came in and out of Shaft around the clock, buying everything from cigarettes to lottery tickets to hero sandwiches, but Strike had never heard of the Homicide breaking anybody else's balls, only his. As far as Strike could figure, the cop despised him because he didn't *act* like a dope dealer, he didn't *act* like a street nigger. Apparently the cop took it as a personal and professional insult that Strike could walk into his store and think he could come off like some bona fide human being.

Strike took a small bottle of club soda and a vanilla Yoo-Hoo from the glass case. Everything else he needed was behind the counter and he had to ask for it, but just as he was about to open his mouth, it dawned on him that he was probably face-to-face with one of the cops charged with investigating Darryl's death. Strike took a second to compose himself, catch his breath.

'Give me that small Colgate,' he said, sounding slightly winded, pointing behind the Homicide's head. The man reached for it, repeating '*Colgate*' like a homeboy, challenging Strike with his eyes.

'Yeah,' said Strike, 'and that toothbrush.'

The cop took down two plastic-wrapped toothbrushes and held them up to Strike. 'Dis *tooth*brush? O' *dis* toothbrush?' He threw Strike a leering smile.

'The green one.'

'De *green* one.'

'Naw, *the* green one,' Strike said, surrendering to his anger, going eye-to-eye despite the danger.

'That's what I said.' The Homicide was pleasant now that he had succeeded in yanking Strike's chain. 'De green one. Anything else?'

Strike paid and walked back to the car. He had the kid sit sideways in the front passenger seat, with his feet planted on the street and his head hunched over his knees as if he was puking. Strike gave Tyrone the toothpaste and toothbrush, then hugged the open car door to his ribs to block the show. 'Get the inside teeth too.'

The kid did as he was told, and a moment later spit out a bright plug of toothpaste that splattered between his beat-up sneakers.

'Now do it all over again. Make them circles with your elbow.'

His movements wooden and slow, Tyrone brushed his teeth again, too embarrassed to look anywhere but straight down.

'Spit.' Strike shifted his stance and wedged the car door even closer to his body.

An old man had stopped nearby, frowning at Tyrone. 'That boy sick?'

'He OK.' Strike waved the guy on, then cracked the top of the club soda and gave it to the kid.

'Don't swallow, just pump your cheeks and don't splash on your sneakers.'

The kid stretched his neck and let out the club soda in a thin, careful stream.

'Put the brush in the bottle and get it clean like you mixing up chocolate milk.'

After Tyrone finished, Strike took the bottle away, trying not to look at the whitish foam, and slipped it down a sewer grate.

Inside the car again, Strike took the toothbrush and the small tube of toothpaste and slipped them both into the kid's sweatshirt muff. 'What's your name?'

'Tyrone.' The kid shied from Strike's eyes.

'Over here.' Strike snapped his fingers, and the kid forced himself to face Strike.

'Ty*rone*,' he said again.

Strike made a show of sniffing the air between them. He leaned back, took a slug of Yoo-Hoo, burped up some bile and fought down a glower of redness in his belly.

'Y'all got to brush them teeth twice a day, my man,' Strike said, starting the car. 'You got to fight the dragon.'

The trip to New York took only thirty minutes, and as they flew around the glazed fluorescent curves of the Holland Tunnel, a false promise of daylight around each bend, Tyrone sat stiffly next to Strike, immobile and mute, the lights running across his face in staggered bars. Strike couldn't tell whether he was shy, bored or terror-stricken, but he would bet that the kid had never been to New York before in his life, or at least not without his mother.

Strike had done some casual asking around since he had first laid eyes on Tyrone and found out that although his father and two of his uncles were in prison, that woman Iris was one of those grizzly bear mothers, the type who walked her kids to school every day, waited for them outside at three o'clock and monitored their health, education and welfare from dawn to midnight.

One of the girls who hung around the crew said she once saw Iris walking her three kids through the projects, giving them a Just Say No tour, pointing out the odd pipehead and saying things like, 'You remember her? You remember how clean she used to be? How nice she used to dress?' And one of the clockers on the Dumont side had told Strike that when Tyrone's family had lived on that side of Roosevelt, Iris would get into shouting matches with that crew, right on the street, and one time had even gotten into a fistfight with a kid for selling bottles in front of her building, as if she had never heard of payback. Or maybe she didn't have to worry about payback: one of the hazier rumors going around was that her secret boyfriend was Andre the Giant. But even if that was true, the woman had to be crazy, since *any*body could catch a bullet.

'We're under the water now.' With both hands on the wheel, Strike twisted his head up to grimace at the arched dome overhead. 'One of them ceiling tiles come out? Like from the pressure? Shit, that's all she wrote.' Strike made a clucking noise, putting it on a little, trying to get the kid to say something, anything. Maybe his mother made him leave his tongue in the house, keep him out of trouble.

On the New York side, Strike made a show of taking the .25 out of the step well, checking the clip, announcing in a grim singsong, 'New York, New York, city of dreams, sometimes it ain't *all* what it seems.' Tyrone continued to sit straight ahead, ignoring what Strike was doing. The kid's stone face was starting to get on Strike's nerves. Maybe still waters didn't run so deep after all. Maybe the kid was quiet because he had nothing on his mind.

Strike retreated into his own moody silence, thinking again about Tyrone's mother, imagining himself in an argument with her, knocking her speechless by saying, 'Yeah, maybe I sell dope, but at least *my* mother taught me how to brush my damn teeth.' But maybe the kid just had halitosis or a stomach problem, Strike softening a little as he considered that possibility, believing that you can't criticize someone's heart for the failings of their body.

Strike drove across 116th Street into East Harlem and pulled up to a barbershop on the ground floor of a high-rise apartment house. The place had wood-grain vinyl wallpaper and smelled of scented hair oil, the type that lathered up white in the barber's palms before he slicked it onto your crop if you let him. The shop was run by an eighty-year-old straight-haired Puerto Rican and his three straight-haired grandsons, but they cut Afro hair just fine. Strike came here for his own haircuts because he once saw an old photograph of an Italian gangster shot dead in a barber chair, and he didn't like the idea of getting his head cut in a place where people knew him from business.

The four barbers were occupied, and Strike motioned Tyrone to a salmon-pink plastic chair, then sat down next to him. Across from them was a huge man with a prison physique who wore a Jesus head with ruby eyes on a gold chain.

In the barber chair closest to the door sat a kid who looked to be eleven – about Tyrone's age. The kid was flanked by two older friends, skinny boys in baggy pegged dungarees who were loudly commenting on each snip of the scissors. Swathed in a tricot sheet, the kid was scowling into the mirror as his two friends poked his skull and argued about what kind of slice to put in. The barber, the old man who owned the place, stepped back to let them work it out, winking at Strike in recognition.

'You see anything you like?' Strike asked Tyrone, nodding to a style display pinned to the far wall over the ex-convict's chair – fifty unsmiling Polaroid head shots of customers, taken over the last year. Tyrone shrugged, refusing to walk over and get a better look, and again Strike felt annoyed at his indifference.

'Excuse me, brothers!'

They both jumped at the abrupt bellow. A young tieless black man in a suit and clean white shirt stood in the doorway. Bespectacled and goateed, he looked like the ghost of Malcolm X.

'Ex*cuse* me!'

The whole place got quiet, everyone turning toward the door.

'Excuse me. I just want to *say*, I just want to re*mind* the young mens in here of the *time*. What time is that? The time for you to start respecting yourselves, the time for you to start taking care of yourselves, the time for you to stop victimizing each other, the time for you to pass on the easy dope money, the blood money, the time for *this* brother' – he nodded to the weightlifter – 'to realize that chain gold is *fool's* gold.' Strike winced, expecting some kind of explosion, but the ex-con was placidly nodding in agreement.

The man in the suit went on: 'The time for you to *give* something to the community instead of *take*, to stop disrespecting our mothers, our sisters, our women, and to rethink the word *power*, the time for you to realize true power ain't about muscle, revenge, payback, pain or sexual ability, but that true power means education – spiritual, economic, political – that true power means *love*, of family, community and of race, and it is the time, the time, the time to realize that you got to understand that no one's gonna help us 'cause no one wants to see a black man with true power, so we got to love ourselves, do it ourselves, *spread* it ourselves . . . Thank you and I love you all.'

The barbers had all retreated politely from the heads in the chairs during the man's rap. But the minute he said thank you, they stepped up and went back to work without expression.

The customers were impassive too, the kids around their little friend in the chair exchanging blank glances. Only the ex-con across from Strike seemed to react, nodding in approval, raising a huge fist and making a yanking gesture as if pulling on a train whistle.

'Thank you,' the man in the suit repeated. Hesitating in the doorway, he looked to Tyrone, to Strike, and then he gestured with a leather-bound book that could have been the Bible, the Koran or a dictionary. He pointed to Tyrone but spoke directly to Strike, his voice intimate and conversational now: 'The children today, they *wiser*, but they *weaker* than ever before too.'

Strike nodded noncommittally. Tyrone twisted in his chair, slinking down and making a screwy face in his embarrassment at being singled out.

The guy in the suit marched out into the sunlight. Strike thought about everything he'd said, agreeing with most of it, then shrugging it off. A moment later the little kid hopped out of his chair, handed each of his older friends a dollar and led them out of the shop.

'Next,' the old man announced, nodding to Strike. Strike nudged Tyrone to rise and stood behind him as he took a seat. Tyrone sat in the porcelain-framed barber chair and stared at Strike and the barber in the mirror. The old man had secured the paper neck cuff too tight and Tyrone's eyeballs bulged slightly. He coughed but said nothing.

'What you want?' The barber, holding his scissors to his chest, spoke to Tyrone's reflection.

Strike followed Tyrone's eyes to the cluttered work shelf and saw assorted clipper heads, brushes, a jar filled with homemade hair gel, a garden spray bottle filled with hair oil and a tiny stand-up calendar with Jesus holding out his crowned heart, just like the picture in Rodney's house. Pinned alongside the mirror was a color photo of a woman's midsection, from thighs to lower rib cage, glowing with oil and barely girdled with a G-string.

'What you want, young sir?' The barber sighed, clacking his scissors.

Tyrone looked to Strike in the mirror and the barber made a half turn, speaking to Strike now. 'What you want?'

'Close and clean. Get all this' – Strike plucked at the unruly head – 'out of here.'

The barber started in with his scissors, and clumps began tumbling into Tyrone's lap and catching in his eyelashes. When the hair was close enough to the scalp, the barber switched to electric clippers and began racing over the temples and around the ears. Tyrone's eyes dropped and Strike sensed that the kid was fighting down a smile, afraid of laughing or in some way getting childish.

'You about five pounds lighter now,' Strike said, not expecting a comment in return and not getting one.

The barber slapped witch hazel into his palms, then caressed Tyrone's

scalp, his fingers sliding back along the sides of Tyrone's skull, the scent
making Strike think of blue ice, jumping into blue ice, and he watched the
kid involuntarily turtle his head into his shoulders, goofy with sensation,
teeth clamping onto his lower lip to keep up the wide-eyed poker face.

'You too?' The barber tilted his chin to Strike.

'I'm cool.' Strike took a pic from the work shelf and fluffed out his hair
in the mirror.

The barber hunched over Tyrone and trimmed the edges of his hairline
with squinting two-handed precision, then went for the hair oil in the
spray bottle. Strike put out a staying hand and the barber asked Tyrone,
'You want a slice?'

Tyrone said nothing, just looked to Strike in the mirror.

'You want a slice?' The barber bowed down to Tyrone's ear to make
sure he heard the question.

Eyes still on Strike, Tyrone mumbled something inaudible.

'Give him here.' Strike ran a pinkie nail from Tyrone's hairline back
three inches, tracing the arc of a clean part. The old man switched clipper
heads, stood on tiptoe, elbow high, and cleared a thin, exact path down
to the scalp like the tail of a whippet. It seemed to Strike that the kid was
so flushed with pleasure that he could barely look at himself.

The barber shook some scented talc on a silver whisk brush, dusted
Tyrone's neck and ears, then held a red plastic mirror up to the back of
his head for his approval. But Tyrone's eyes were closed.

'Yeah, OK.' Strike nodded, and when Tyrone finally opened his eyes,
the old man was standing in front of him, frowning critically, pursing his
lips, putting a hand to his chest.

'Don't move,' the barber said.

Tyrone, open-faced in his anxiety now, looked to Strike as the barber
retrieved a Polaroid camera from a cabinet below his work shelf, leaned
back and took a shot of Tyrone, profile on the slice side, the photo sliding
out like a tongue.

When the old man released Tyrone from the tricot smock and the tight
neck cuff, Strike had to help the kid from the chair, as if removing a
passenger from a roller coaster at the end of a ride. And as Strike waited
for his change, he saw Tyrone steal a peek at the developing picture,
watching himself emerge – star-eyed, solemn, handsome, new.

'How's that?' Strike spoke with an edge in his voice, talking across the
roof of the Accord.

'Good,' Tyrone mumbled, patting his head.

'You look clean.'

Strike waited for a response. Nothing. He jerked open the door and slid in, leaving Tyrone standing on the locked passenger side, annoyed that the damn kid couldn't even say thank you.

They drove down the Henry Hudson Parkway in silence, and for half the ride Strike was stormed up with the kid's ingratitude, until he saw Tyrone steal a look at himself in the exterior side mirror, cocking his head slightly to study his new crop, then return his gaze to a straight-ahead stare, fighting down another smile, trying hard not to blink. He reminded Strike of a dope dealer playing it all wrong when he's rolled up next to a police car, his saucer-eyed profile screaming out 'guilty' to the cops. Strike relented a little in his anger, seeing that the kid needed to conceal his pleasure, hide it like it was felony-weight cocaine.

After they had passed through midtown, Strike cut over to Seventh Avenue, and as they approached Greenwich Village they drove by sporadic clumps of people with shopping bags standing on the edge of the curb, competing with each other to flag down a taxi.

Tyrone took in their stiff-armed saluting and their pinched faces, then started chanting, 'Sieg heil, sieg heil, sieg heil,' in a high soft voice. It was the first thing he had said since Harlem.

'What's that?' Strike said.

'Hitler. They look like they going sieg heil, sieg heil.'

'Hitler, how you know about Hitler?'

'From school,' he answered, turning away from Strike. 'And from my mother.'

Strike pulled over to a hot dog stand on a crowded stretch of Broadway above SoHo.

'Y'all hungry?' He passed the kid a five-dollar bill. 'Get me a Yoo-Hoo.'

Tyrone returned to the car with a vanilla Yoo-Hoo – not a chocolate one, like most people would have. He carried a hot dog with ketchup and a can of orange soda for himself, but the smell of hot dogs made Strike sick, so he had Tyrone eat the same way he'd had him brush his teeth, hunched sideways over the street, shielded from people by the open car door. Once again the kid didn't say thank you, but after he finished his meal, wiped his face and took the garbage – including Strike's empty Yoo-Hoo – to a trash can, he returned the two fifty change without being asked for it. Fastidious, observant, honest, secretive, obedient – Strike wondered what he might do with this boy, feeling a flash of pleasure himself now, masking it behind a scowl while looking down at the kid's ratty sneakers.

'What the hell you got on your feet?'

Tyrone looked down.

'Goddamn, they feet or *hoofs*?'

Strike took him to the Foot Locker, where the new sneakers were mounted like model ship hulls on individual transparent shelves. Strike scanned the room and got a rush of greedy arousal – collect the whole set.

He turned to Tyrone. 'What you like?'

Tyrone took it all in, then talked to the air. 'BKs, high-top white with light gray trim.'

As the salesman slipped Tyrone's foot onto the metal measuring brace, the kid put up the hood of his sweatshirt, pulled hard on the drawstrings and disappeared.

Next to him, Strike fought off his irritation once again. He had never run up against this combination of paralyzed shyness and oblivious ingratitude. The sneakers were $69.95 but the kid didn't even blink, as if he believed he had it coming to him. Strike glared at Tyrone hiding inside his hood, but then spied the toothpaste peeking out of his sweatshirt muff and retreated from his anger, thinking maybe nobody ever said 'What you want?' to him before. Maybe he was inexperienced with having things. Maybe he never had the occasion to say thank you before.

As they stepped out of the shoe store, the sidewalk sunlight lit up the thick snow-white high tops as if they were a pair of giant fluorescent marshmallows.

'Now you clean at both ends,' Strike said in a dry drawl, cocking an eyebrow.

The kid didn't answer, but his mouth jerked as if he was hiding a frog in there.

The weather had turned without warning, and when they emerged from the tunnel the sky was a yellow-gray luminescence, charged with the promise of a downpour. Driving past the oppressively familiar scenery of gas stations and highways and housing projects, all tinted by the threatening weather, Strike felt the weight of the past two days come down on him with such force that he gave out an involuntary hiss of pain.

He stopped the car two blocks from the projects and threw it into park, then tilted his chin to the sidewalk. 'Go on out.'

He watched Tyrone walk off toward Roosevelt, a flinching self-consciousness in his gait, as if there was a gun aimed at his back.

Every few feet the kid half turned his head, trying to catch the car in the corner of his eye.

Strike returned the Accord to the old lady's driveway and sat for a few minutes to collect himself. He resisted getting out of the car, sensing that to return to the benches would be like walking into his grave.

He tried to imagine going straight back to New York, starting a fresh life in a fresh head in a fresh place, but he couldn't even get the pictures up on the wall. He heard the man in the suit back at the barbershop booming, 'It is the time, the time, the time,' but he didn't believe that it would ever be his time, that he would ever be free of his life.

Back at the benches, Tyrone was perched on the garden chair exactly where Strike had found him that morning. For some reason, the kid had changed into his old sneakers again, the new ones back in the box and wedged between his ankles. When he saw Strike coming, Tyrone hoarsely whispered 'Hi' as if they hadn't seen each other all day. But Strike wouldn't look at him, just walked on past and cut him dead as if the day had never happened.

The benches were busy now despite the threat of a downpour — or maybe because of it. Strike took his perch, feeling stiff and old and hopeless. He watched The Word palm a bottle out of his mouth and pass it to a customer in a long handshake, watched Horace take a bottle from his sock, jerking his knee high to snag it. Saturdays were always sloppy because the Fury never rolled on weekends and any other knocko squad going for overtime preferred nights to weekend days because of the ten percent pay differential.

Tyrone's little brother came up to him crying about something, and Strike saw a flash of irritation register in Tyrone's face, watched him gently backhand the eight-year-old on the hip, sliding him out of his line of vision to the benches, to Strike.

The clouds cracked like a staggered round of musket fire and the rain came down all at once, long drops that seemed to leap up intact from the pavement. Everybody ran for the two buildings on either side of the benches, 8 and 6 Weehawken, the clockers mainly breaking for 8, since it was closer. Tyrone was perhaps twenty feet from 6, a hundred feet from 8, but as Strike ran toward 8, he saw Tyrone stand up, hesitate for a second, then slip the sneaker box under his sweatshirt and follow.

Strike stood under the breezeway overhang with Futon and some others, the scene a wet and funky surprise party. With them was a forty-year-old pipehead who got caught in midpurchase, a tall, scratch-bearded mess of a man who hadn't copped yet and stood hovering over everybody,

grinning tentatively, half wolf, half beggar, trying to figure out if there
was something in this situation that he could turn to his advantage.

Strike leaned against the wall, staring at a toothpaste tube lying out
by the benches. The kid must have dropped it when he ran for the
breezeway.

Patting his haircut, Tyrone followed Strike's gaze, then hissed 'Damn'
and bolted out into the rain to retrieve the toothpaste. Strike watched
him splash out there, noticing that the kid hadn't even thought to put
up his sweatshirt hood, asking himself what the hell he had in mind for
this boy.

Strike's beeper went off and Rodney's number came up. He looked
out to the pay phones, saw the rain dancing on the aluminum shelves.
Just as he decided to call from the bottle apartment and began turning
toward the stairs, his eye caught a flash of brown and orange, a figure
with a gym bag loping through the rain all the way down by Dumont,
and suddenly Strike found himself sprinting right past Tyrone, kicking
up raindrops all the way across the projects, finally skidding to a stop in
front of Victor just as he was bending down to unlock his car.

Victor reared up, hugged the gym bag to his chest and blurted,
'Jesus!'

Strike thought his brother looked half crazy in his drenched uniform:
brown cinch-waisted slacks, orange short-sleeved shirt, brown baseball
cap with 'Hambone's' scripted on the crown. Everything was soaked dark,
and Victor's eyes were big with fear and exhaustion.

Strike blocked his path, not knowing exactly what to say now, how
to say it, both of them standing in the rain as if unable to move.

'How come you don't have no umbrella?' Strike asked.

'Car's right here.' Victor lifted his chin, shivering.

'What happened last night?'

'I don't know.' Victor tried to move around Strike.

'Well, who'd you talk to?'

'Nobody. I don't know. Somebody else. I got to go. It's wet, man. It's
late.' A ripple ran through his shoulders. 'I'm late, I'm late.'

'Are you OK with them?' Them: Strike was unable even to say 'him,'
let alone 'My Man.' His beeper went off again. 'How'd you leave it?'

'Don't worry about it.' Victor slid around Strike to the street and
fumbled with his keys by the driver's door. 'It's not your play, that's
all you got to know.'

'How'd you leave it? Just tell me that.' Strike scrambled for the right
words.

'Not your play,' Victor muttered again, head down, unlocking his door now.

'Take me back over to Weehawken,' Strike shivered, pulled on the locked passenger door, trying to buy himself a few more minutes.

Victor gave Strike a brief blank stare over the roof of the car, then slid in behind the wheel. Ignoring Strike's hand on the locked door, Victor peeled out down Dumont, disappearing in a screeching turn onto JFK. Strike stood there shaking, dripping, achy, certain he was about to get sick. He knew all the signs.

12

On Saturday afternoon under a lowering sky, Rocco pulled into the prosecutor's office lot and parked next to a mud-splattered three-year-old black Corvette, all hood and looking like a long-barreled handgun. For a moment he wondered if the car belonged to the actor, but it was too dirty. County Narcotics, he decided with a small twist of disappointment.

Rocco felt enervated and down, in need of some kind of pick-me-up. The previous night's marathon was bad enough, but then earlier this morning, before he had finally crashed, he had driven Erin and her babysitter to the kid's play group, and no matter how much he begged and wheedled and pouted, he had been unable to get his daughter even to wave goodbye to him. She had just stepped out of the car as if he was a chauffeur, taken the babysitter's hand and disappeared inside the lobby. Later, Rocco had drifted into a fractured sleep, feeling anxious and emotionally hungry, and his mood hadn't improved since waking.

When he entered the office, Vy was talking low on the phone and sucking a lipstick-stained Merit.

'Is he here?'

Vy put a hand over the mouthpiece and made a squinty face.

'You know, what's his name.' Rocco couldn't bring himself to say Sean Touhey.

'*Talk*, Rocco.'

'The actor.'

'Nope.'

'Where's Mazilli?'

'Out in the field.'

Rocco knew that could mean anything from working an old homicide to playing rummy in a Mafia-run social club. He might not be back for hours.

Rocco walked toward the squad room and saw that the chair the actor had used while eavesdropping on the interrogation the day before had never been removed from the hallway. The empty chair prompted an eerie feeling that Touhey was still somewhere in the building, but Rocco shook that off and took a seat at his desk.

He turned on the TV over the filing cabinets, caught a few minutes of a 'Hawaii Five-O' rerun, then turned it off. Pulling the actor's business card out of his sport jacket, Rocco reached for the phone.

'Pressure Point Productions,' said a young male voice.

'Yeah. Is Sean in? This is Rocco Klein.'

'One minute.'

Rocco cradled the phone along his jawline, held the business card in both hands, flipping it over, reading once again the scrawled promissory note on the back.

'Hi.' The new voice was female – husky and intimate.

'Hi. Who's this?' Rocco leaned forward, his elbows propped on the desk blotter.

'This is Jackie. Can I help you?'

'Jackie, hi, this is Rocco Klein. Is Sean in?'

'Sorry, he's not in right now. Can I help you with something?'

'Do you know who I am?'

'Sure do.'

'Great. I wasn't sure, is ah . . . is Sean coming over to my office tonight? We left it kind of up in the air.'

'I, I don't think so. I think he might have gone upstate.'

'Upstate?' Rocco was momentarily confused: upstate was a local euphemism for jail. 'What, he's on vacation?'

'No, he just . . . he should be back tomorrow.'

'Back where?'

'Hard to say. Do you want me to tell him anything?'

Rocco was tongue-tied for a moment. 'Tell him I called, and to call me, OK?'

'What's your number, Rocky?'

'Rocco, not Rocky.'

'Did I say Rocky?' She laughed, Rocco thinking, Real funny.

Just as he hung up, Vy's voice came crackling over the desk intercom, telling him he had a visitor. Rocco hopped to it, a rush of blood making his temples pulse. It had to be him – Vy had that teasing note in her voice.

Rocco strode down the hallway making up tonight's real-life research menu, so pumped about seeing the actor standing there that he looked right at the tiny, hollow-faced, pale woman slouched on the couch and shrugged to Vy.

'Where'd he go?'

'Where'd *who* go?' Vy squawked, giving Rocco a bug-eyed look.

It took a few moments before he understood that the woman was his visitor. 'How are you?' he said tightly, stepping in front of her. The woman's reddish-brown, broom-textured hair was gathered into a foot-long ponytail that sprouted out over her ear. She wore a tight pair of dungarees, neon pink socks and laceless tennis shoes. Underneath her denim jacket she wore a white T-shirt that bragged 'Here's the Beef,' but she couldn't have weighed more than ninety pounds.

'I know who shot that guy.' Her voice was raw and gravelly, her eyes sullen and steady.

'Good,' Rocco said mildly and extended his arm toward the interrogation room, bowing slightly.

She walked down the hallway swaybacked, leading with her pelvis like someone who was suffering from borderline starvation. Junkie, Rocco decided, or maybe an ex-junkie, since she seemed to be clean and her clothes were more or less color-coordinated.

In the interrogation room she sat with her elbows touching the insides of her thighs, already on her second cigarette before Rocco could even get her name spelled right.

Rocco sat at right angles to her, his legal pad on his crossed knee. He glanced at her name: Susan Phelan. 'So Susan – '

'Suky, Suky.'

'So Suky, what can I do for you?'

'I told you.' She took a drag on a Newport, her fingertips reddish and nibbled. 'I know who did that – who shot that guy.'

'What guy is that?'

'The Ahab's.' She had smallish blue-gray teeth, and when she coughed into her fist Rocco quickly turned his head, pretending he heard someone knocking at a door.

'Ahab's? Give me a name.'

'Almighty.' Her eyes shifted to the floor as she said it.

'Almighty . . .' Rocco cocked his head. 'You mean *the* Almighty?'

'No, that's his name.' Her eyes found Rocco's face. 'His real name is Gary White.'

Rocco wrote down the name, listening to her wet cough, gritting his teeth. 'Almighty, Gary. You know where he lives?'

'Yeah. With me.'

Rocco was instantly skeptical. 'And where's that?'

'The Buckingham on Warton?'

'Uh-huh.' Rocco nodded mildly. The Buckingham was a ten-story flophouse across from the Dempsy Greyhound station.

'And how old would you say Almighty is, roughly?'

'Shit, I'll tell you exactly. He's twenty-eight.'

Rocco regarded her through narrowed eyes. 'I'll be back in a minute. You sure I can't get you anything?'

She shrugged and Rocco returned to his desk. He called the Bureau of Criminal Identification and got Bobby Bones on the line.

'What can I do you for, Roc?'

'I need a look-up on a Gary White.'

There was silence on the line for a few seconds. 'We got three – a twenty-eight, a fifty-one and a deceased.'

Rocco hesitated, bracing himself as if preparing to race. It was a point of pride for Bobby Bones to cut off an inquiry as soon as he got a name, then begin to spit back entire criminal histories before you could reach for a pad of paper. Bobby Bones had a photographic memory and was obsessed with the rap sheets of every criminal in Dempsy. He was able to retain thousands of numbers: addresses, social security, FBI, SBI, dockets, dates, dispositions, warrants – everything down to age, height and weight for roughly five thousand bad guys going back twenty-five years. The year before, when the computers had gone down, all the calls to BCI were rerouted to Bobby Bones's mother's house for thirty-six hours, to keep the wheels of justice rolling.

'I'll take the twenty-eight. He got a moniker?'

'Almighty. Mostly small-time junkie shit these days – he likes to boost aspirin and steak, mainly. Got about a dozen trespass and petty-theft charges going back five years, some heavier shit before that. A real gnat.'

'Where's he live?'

'Forty-four Monticello, Four F.'

'Yeah? I got the Buckingham.'

'Oh yeah?' Bones sounded insulted. 'I think someone's jerking your bird over there.'

'Maybe. Can you cut me a picture, send it over?'

'You got it.'

'Bones, what's this guy, white or black?'

'Yomo. But he's got a white girlfriend, Susan Phelan, Suky. Another fucking gnat. You want her sheet too?'

'Not now, maybe later.'

'Hey Roc, you know whose daughter she is? You remember Frog Phelan?'

'You're shitting me.' Rocco felt depressed. 'Jesus Christ. Poor Frog
– another cop with a fucked-up kid. If they're not shooting smack,
they're marrying Martians. She's a junkie too, right? Ex-junkie? Why
do they *do* that, these kids – Frog Phelan, hah? He was a good guy, a
real nice guy.'

'He was a prick.' Bobby Bones put a shrug in his voice.

'Listen, this Susan, Suky, she got any outstanding warrants?'

'Petty shit. A two-year-old possession, like that.'

'Frog Phelan, hah? OK Bobby, be well.'

Rocco settled back down into his wooden chair in the interrogation
room. There were four Newport butts in the tin dish in front of Suky
now, and the room was adrift in smoke.

'Suky, how do you know Almighty did it?'

She looked away. 'He told me.'

'When did he tell you?'

'You know, before. He showed me the gun and he said he was gonna
kill that guy. Next thing somebody did it, right?'

She looked at the ashtray as she spoke, avoiding his eyes, Rocco
thinking, This really stinks.

'Why'd he do it for?'

'Why?' she said, chewing on the word for a while. 'He was in
there buying a fish sandwich and he was paying in small change –
you know, nickels and pennies? And the manager was getting pissed
because he was slowing down the line, giving him shit like, Let's
go, let's go, let's go. Then Almighty came up three cents short and
the manager made some crack, so like everybody was laughing at
him and then the manager wouldn't let him slide for the three cents
and you know he just made him feel bad, made him feel like *two*
cents.'

Rocco couldn't tell if the story was true. It seemed heartfelt despite her
monotone delivery.

'And when was this?'

'The day before he showed me the gun. Like Wednesday? Yeah.' She
nodded. 'Wednesday.'

'Were you there when this happened?'

'Unh-uh. He just told me about it.'

'Can we talk to him? I'd really like to talk to him.'

'Hell yeah. You find him, you can talk to him.' She paused. 'You *better*
talk to him.'

'You know where he is now?'

'Minute to minute I can't say, because I haven't like seen him since when he showed me that gun.'

'What kind of gun was it? Do you remember?'

'What kind?' She shrugged. 'I don't know nothin' about guns.'

Bullshit, Rocco told himself. Her old man was a cop. 'OK, you think he's home now?'

'Nah. I would try that field behind the methadone clinic. He might be there.'

'Off Cooper?'

'Yeah, he's probably there.'

'Where's he work?'

'He ain't working now. He's kind of sick.'

'Oh yeah?' Rocco assumed that sick meant the Virus.

'But when he's well? When he can get hired? He works *hard*.'

Rocco was taken aback. Here she was trying to put her boyfriend away for thirty years, but she said it like Rocco shouldn't think Almighty was a bum.

'Suky, how come you waited twenty hours to come in on this? I'm just curious.'

She looked at the ashtray again. 'I just heard about it this afternoon.'

Another lie. 'Did you know the guy that got shot?'

'Just from eating there sometimes.'

'How long you and Almighty been together?'

'Six, six and a half years.'

'Married or just . . .'

'He's my husband – and my father.'

'Your father?'

'Of my baby.' Her face got far away and pained-looking.

'How many kids you got?'

'One, a girl.'

Rocco drifted off for a moment, thinking about Erin, thinking of her married to an Almighty, shooting smack. Erin's father was a cop too.

'Is he a good daddy, Almighty?'

She didn't answer. Rocco drifted again: it wasn't too late to become a good father. He just needed a little time to get his bearings, a little luck, and then it would be all downhill, he'd start taking Erin on long walks somewhere, pony rides, you name it.

'So he doesn't do shit with the kid, right?'

She snapped back into focus, looked directly at Rocco, annoyed but calm. 'Why are you asking all this?'

Momentarily flustered by her bluntness, Rocco changed his tack. 'Suky, let me think out loud here for a second. I'm thinking, you live with the guy six years, he's the father of your child, you only know the victim from eating, yet you're coming in here on your own, you're voluntarily putting this guy in the shit – and I'm talking an automatic thirty in, no parole if we get a conviction – and so *I* think, is there anything else going on here? Is this a personal beef? You know, like a lovers' quarrel that's a little out of hand? I know you got a warrant out on you. I mean, are you trying to work that off here maybe? Do some swapping? What's up?'

Rocco stared at her, and she met his eyes with an unflinching steadiness. 'I ain't looking for nothin',' she said, her voice low and flat. 'You do to me whatever you want.'

Rocco leaned back. Shit, now he'd have to go hunt down a goddamn scavenge rat junkie. He knew something else was going on here but he just couldn't crack it, and he hated feeling that he was being used to settle a private score.

Vy stood outside the interrogation room wiggling her long nails, catching Rocco's eye and then slipping a manila folder under the door.

Rocco scanned Almighty's rap sheet, sent over from BCI. He could see the Virus come on him: armed robbery six years ago, car theft and burglary three years ago, then down to selling drugs, then to the crimes that didn't take much energy or carry much risk of jail time – shoplifting and criminal trespass.

'Is this him?' Rocco put the mug shot on the table, next to the ashtray. Suky looked away as if not on speaking terms with the photo. 'Yeah, that's him.'

The field was a full acre of wasteland bordered by a low-slung housing project, an orange-shingled trailer that housed a methadone clinic, the salvage yard owned by Vince Kelso, the cop, and curving around at the farthest end, a soaring, abandoned hospital complex.

Following a local squad car, Rocco drove a Chevy Nova down a paved but cratered cul-de-sac that was littered with mangled shopping carts and fire-blackened oil drums. At least a dozen men were toiling quietly, burning the rubber off stolen phone cables, piling up battered hubcaps or filling shopping carts with soda cans, refrigerator ribbing, liberated plumbing fixtures and other, less identifiable metal salvage. A hundred feet into the field stood the club-house, a rickety lean-to under a tree accompanied by two legless couches which faced the hospital. None of the junkies looked up at the cop caravan, everybody focused on the task at hand, preparing scrap for sale to Kelso's yard across the way, all moving in an unhurried yet purposeful glide like insects programmed for a life task and knowing of nothing else.

Rocco got out of the Chevy and stretched. The air stank of burning insulation. The oily smoke, the charred metal carcasses, the ashy mounds of old rubber-stripping fires and the zombie lope of the scavengers made him feel as if he was visiting a major battle site three days after the troops had buried their dead and moved on.

He didn't know too much about the life out here anymore, but he did know that these people were at the bottom of the junkie chain, too weak to support themselves with violence or fast reflexes and too sick to survive prison. Most had the Virus, although Rocco guessed that not a one had been tested. Nobody wanted to know for a fact, but they all walked around as if they had already died, as if there was nothing left to fear, as if the news in their bones had finally liberated them, allowing them to embrace without excuse or pretense the only thing that had ever given them comfort, even though it was the same thing that had killed them: intravenous drugs.

Rocco leaned against the door of the Nova and watched the two uniforms emerge from their squad car, both of them older guys with ballooning guts, humped necks, cigarettes and shades. They walked back to Rocco with a casual lumbering roll. He knew them pretty well; they had been cruising this section for years, and one, Eddie Dolan, had once spent six months in Homicide. Bored to death, he had begged to be returned to the street.

Rocco wrinkled his nose. 'It's like fuckin' Bhopal.'

'Dempsy burnin',' the two cops chimed in chorus.

They all stood together by the Nova and watched a tall, string-muscled black man tie the end of a roll of phone cable around a tree stump, cut an incision down to the copper strands with a bowie knife, drape the cable around his waist and yank back violently, each jerk stripping back the thick rubber and exposing more of the precious metal.

Eddie Dolan stepped up to the guy. 'What's up, my man.'

The junkie stopped wrestling with the cable, straightened and gave Dolan a look of patient annoyance.

'How you be?' Dolan eyeballed the bowie knife.

The guy said nothing, waiting for a real question.

'Where's Almighty at?'

'For what?'

'For telling me.' Dolan took the cable from the guy's hands, coiled it around his own hammy fists and gave it a yank. It wouldn't budge and Dolan offered it to Rocco.

Rocco took off his sport jacket, exchanged it for the cable and dug in his heels, throwing everything he had into a long jerk and wrenching his back. The junkie stared at him, unamused.

Rocco winced and handed him back the cable. 'Thank God for guns, right?'

'You just don't have the *need* to strip that bad boy,' the other cop, Willy Harris, drawled. 'You gots to have the *need.*'

'So where's he at?' Dolan gave Rocco back his sport jacket.

'Ask the desk.' The junkie gestured to the lean-to under the tree. 'He's around, I know that.'

Under the tree but hidden from the road by the lean-to sat an old-fashioned teacher's desk and chair that someone had boosted from a high school basement. The furniture was never meant to be used outdoors but the heavy oak was indestructible, its surface marred only by bird droppings. The desk drawers, once filled with school supplies and attendance records, were now used to store community-shared sets of works, and the chair and desk sat tilted at opposing angles on the rocky ground.

The thin, bare-chested guy at the desk was otherwise engaged, and Rocco and the uniforms stood two polite steps back, Rocco wincing as the guy shot some dope between the knuckles of his left fist and then carefully placed the needle in a water-filled jelly jar on top of the desk. Running a hand over his mouth and staring toward the hospital, he looked passively amazed, as if he had been teaching a class and the school, the classroom, all the students, had suddenly been atomized, leaving him shirtless but intact at his desk in the middle of nowhere.

He tilted back in the chair, twisting his head up to the cops standing behind him. 'You ever hear of privacy?'

'I can't help it. I watch that needle going in, it gets my dick hard.' Dolan pulled on his crotch.

'Well, then you a pervert, Dolan,' the junkie said.

'Hey.' Rocco squinted at him. 'Hey, I know you.'

The guy sat motionless, heavy-lidded.

'Robert Johnson, right?'

The guy batted his eyes, sniffed.

Rocco smiled. 'Didn't you die?'

'Somebody's here,' the junkie said, smirking.

'Yeah, Robert Johnson. I arrested you in 1978 coming out of Dinardo

Liquors. You had that shotgun down your leg. Don't you remember me?'

'Nope.'

'Yeah, so how you been?' Rocco asked without sarcasm.

Johnson stared out into the field. 'Working on my tan.'

'Yeah, I could've sworn you died two, three years ago, no?'

'Where's Almighty at?' asked Dolan.

Johnson jerked his chin to the gigantic hospital complex across the field, its Gothic arches so expansive in the twilight that the building seemed to be floating.

Rocco and the two uniforms made their way through the field toward the hospital. 'You ever see *War of the Worlds*?' Rocco asked Dolan. 'No one can stop the Martians and they're blasting the shit out of everybody? You remember what finally killed them?'

'The Virus?' Dolan asked.

'Sort of, yeah, some microbe they couldn't handle. And that's what this is like. Robert Johnson? You remember him, Willie? All the badass motherfuckers from like ten years ago? They're all dead, dying. They killed themselves. You think of all the old names – Robert Joy, Johnson there, Chuckie Grover, the Carter brothers, all of them.' Rocco shot an imaginary needle.

'I hear Erroll Barnes got it.' Willie Harris pulled up the waist of his pants.

'Good. Fuck him.' Rocco said.

'So what are you saying there, Rocco?' Dolan skipped over an unidentifiable object covered with flies.

'Hey, I'm not saying the Virus is a good thing, but . . .' Rocco faltered, suddenly feeling defensive. 'Don't put fuckin' words in my mouth.'

The hospital loomed before them. Built in the 1930s, the Anne Donovan Pediatric Center, known to everybody in Dempsy as the baby hospital, was a spectacular ruin, a thirteen-story Depression-era monolith abandoned in the 1970s for a variety of reasons – too expensive to heat, structural fissures, not enough babies. From a distance the gray granite building appeared to be functional; it was only by standing in the necklace of knee high weeds and debris that ringed the grounds that you could see the blackened and shattered windows and the graffiti-tattooed plywood boarding up the entrances.

The cops picked their way through the booby-trapped vegetation and came to a boarded-up side door. Dolan threw his shoulder into a loosened corner, allowing them to squeeze inside, into the clammy darkness of a

stairwell. Following flashlights, they entered the circular main lobby, the
heart-stopping base of a thirteen-story atrium that was ringed with interior
balconies connected by skeletal staircases, all spiraling up to the skylight
like the icing on a multitiered wedding cake.

Surrounded by a herd of shopping carts, they stood on marble tiles
that had been scattered and smashed over the years by scavenged booty
tossed from above. Once their eyes adjusted to the anemic light filtering
through the opaque ceiling, they could pick out three or four junkies at
various heights on the stairs, shadowmen mining the carcass, the sounds
of their hammering and dragging ricocheting up and down the hollow
heart of the hospital.

Rocco was seized by a combination of nostalgia and anxiety. He had
come to this place many times as a kid – for vaccinations, stitches, a
broken arm, a tonsillectomy – and the visits were always accompanied
by pain and panic. Even now, amid the choking must and filth, he could
swear he still smelled the fear-inducing pungency of antiseptic alcohol.

Wary of getting winged by flying brass, they all backed up under an
overhang.

'I was *born* here,' Dolan grunted, as if the thought made him angry.

'You and every other fucking cop.' Harris caught a junkie three flights
up in the watery beam of his flashlight.

'About six years ago?' Rocco stooped to pick up a loose tile, put it in
his pocket as a keepsake. 'Me and Frank Delgado, we'd hit a dry spell?
You know, it's cold, no one's killing anybody, we'd park out back here
and wait for them to throw shit out the windows. You know, you smash
up a toilet on the twelfth floor, who the fuck wants to lug the pipes down
all those stairs, right? Shit would come down, ka-*boom*, we'd run out there,
grab up the brass, the copper, the whatever, throw it in the trunk and
take it over to the yard ourself. Sometimes there'd be six other cops out
there waiting for the same thing. We'd *race* for the shit, bend down at the
same time, bang heads.' He shrugged. 'Paid for a few beers . . . Guys still
doing that?'

Neither of them answered, although Rocco caught Dolan throwing
Harris an amused look.

Seeing no sign of Almighty, Rocco motioned for Dolan to lead the way
to the stairs. As they climbed, Rocco thought about stealing the salvage
from the junkies, imagining telling that story to Patty, the look she'd give
him, telling her his half-serious theory of the Virus as a weapon against
crime, the look *that* would get, and suddenly Rocco was overwhelmed
with a ferocious sense of pride at being born in this ruin just like Dolan,

pride at being a local boy, a son of Dempsy, a street kid, a regular guy. He thought of Erin: she had never been in Dempsy in her life. That had to be rectified; she had to know.

As they reached the fourth floor all three of them began breathing through their mouths, and at the fifth, Dolan called for a cigarette break. At every landing Rocco noticed that the fire hoses, racked like compressed intestines on the wall alongside the exit doors, had had their brass nozzles neatly razored off. Compact, heavy, valuable, they must have been the first things to go.

On the sixth floor they ran into a guy sitting on the stairs drinking an Olde English and smoking cocaine.

'Randy, my man.' Dolan put a hand on his own sweating chest. 'Where's Almighty at?'

'He up there.' On the wall alongside Randy's head was a starburst of rust-brown dots where someone had booted the blood from their hypo.

'How many floors?' Dolan sounded as if he was begging.

'Just one.' Randy pinched his nose, turned his glass pipe around and took a hit from the other end. 'You can make it if you try.'

Rocco picked his way down a chalky, rubble-strewn hospital corridor illuminated by the dying sun descending over New York harbor, the slanting rays coming through the windows of a lane of doorless recovery rooms, the Statue of Liberty tracking his progress so closely that he could count the spokes on her crown.

'Dr Almighty, paging Dr Almighty,' Rocco droned through cupped palms. 'Paging Dr Good God Almighty.'

Harris and Dolan laughed, high-stepping over chunks of fallen ceiling. The three came to the corner room, the one with the best view, ducked in and saw a man who had to be Almighty, sitting slightly hunched over on the wrecked rusty springs of a hospital bed. The man started and clutched his chest, the arm of the Statue of Liberty sticking straight up out of his head like a prosthetic device.

'Dr Almighty, you're wanted in surgery.' Rocco leaned in past the doorframe, pointed his finger like a gun, then pulled the trigger. 'Gotcha.' He tried not to laugh; the poor guy looked so seized up that maybe he thought the hospital had come back to life for real.

'Almighty. How you doing?' Rocco walked into the room, hand out like a salesman. Almighty tentatively extended a junkie's swollen mitt, and Rocco forced himself to keep smiling as he shook his hand. Almighty was wearing a dirty plaid shirt open over a dark blue T-shirt from a place called the Good Girl Lounge, red gym pants and an Orlando Magic cap.

Something about his lanky frame, his sleepy yet precise movements, suggested a former athleticism.

'I'm Detective Klein from the prosecutor's office. How you been?'

'I'm OK,' he said in a frail drawl. 'I ain't bothering nobody.'

Rocco ducked down, took in the Statue of Liberty. 'Jesus, nice view.' Harris and Dolan joined Rocco at the window.

'You could charge money for this.' Rocco straightened up. 'You wanna take a ride with me?' A huge but odorless human shit lay in the far corner of the room, most likely the grand finale of a week's worth of some junkie's constipation.

'You locking me up?' Almighty had swollen almond-shaped eyes that perpetually quivered with a promise of tears.

'Hell no.' Rocco waved the question away. 'If I was locking you up, I'd be putting cuffs on you.' He extended his arm for Almighty to rise. 'C'mon.'

Shuffling out of the room, Almighty stopped next to a parked shopping cart in the hallway. He had scored two faucets, a stainless steel tray, a bundle of traverse rods and a metal drawer from a filing cabinet. He looked to Rocco. Rocco looked to Harris and Dolan, the uniforms shrugging in assent.

Almighty led the way, pushing the cart, walking on his toes with a slightly forward lurch. In his unhurried gait, in the slow bob of his head, Rocco saw that the guy probably loved working this place, thirteen floors to stroll with his cart, nice view of the lady of the harbor, run into friends, always something to score, some wiring to rip out of a dropped ceiling, a radiator everybody missed, a shower head. It was like a garden, or a dream, the smashed toilets and gutted ceilings an outside to match Almighty's inside – shattered, sick, still, peaceful.

Rocco shook himself out of his ruminations, shouted 'Ho!' just to hear the echo. On the way down the corridor to the stairs, he stopped at a twenty-foot-long rectangular window that looked in on a barren and lightless room. A glass-walled cubicle stood off to one corner, and a red–on–yellow sign was still taped to the back wall: 'Please Do Not Tap on Glass.'

'What the hell was this?' Rocco peered through the filthy window.

'The baby room,' Dolan said. 'You know, the observation room, where guys made horses' asses out of themselves waving to their new sons?'

'No . . .' Rocco took in the chalky desolation through the long window. He couldn't imagine the room looking any way other than it did right now, and it made him think of unloved, unclaimed infants. 'That's a shame,' he said, clucking his tongue.

'What is?' Harris helped Almighty maneuver the cart over a pothole.

Dolan and Harris stood over the balcony and helped Almighty toss his booty down to the lobby. Elbows on the railing, observing the swoop and glide of the falling objects, Rocco couldn't shake the image of the ghostly observation room. He began to imagine that the entire atrium was some kind of celestial flue or baby aviary and that the air was filled with the nightgowned spirits of long-gone infants.

'Do you know something?' Rocco squinted into the hollow gloom. 'If you shoot a pregnant woman and they deliver the baby before she dies? If that baby is delivered dead, even if it was killed by the bullet, it's still a single homicide. In order for it to be a homicide, a baby's lungs have got to be fully aerated before it's killed. Does that suck or what?'

Almighty seemed to be the only one listening.

Dolan stepped up beside him. 'Double or nothing I get it right in a shopping cart.' Dolan dropped a faucet, which hit the handle of a cart and shot out of the lobby like a rocket.

'*Kill* my ass!' someone yelled from below. 'Walk it *down*, motherfucker! Walk it *down*! Jesus!'

They threw Almighty's scrap into the trunk of the Chevy Nova. Dolan rode in back with Almighty to make it two against one, and Harris brought up the rear in the cruiser.

'So, Gary, still living with Suky?' Rocco sought out his eyes in the rearview mirror.

'Yeah, uh-huh . . . kind of.' Almighty slouched down, hand over his mouth, watching the world slip past.

'You ever meet your father-in-law?'

'The cop? Unh-uh.' He laughed as if he knew what would have happened.

'I bet not,' Rocco said. 'So what are you doing with yourself? You working?'

'Yeah, I was helping on the trucks? But I'm sick now.'

'How much is that shit in the trunk worth? Kelso still giving good prices?'

'He OK.'

They drove past the precinct house. Almighty was probably used to being booked here, and he sat up straight, frowning. 'Where we going?'

'*My* office,' Rocco said.

'What's that?'

'Homicide.' Rocco watched the rearview for his reaction.

'Homicide?' Almighty slouched back down, barely interested. 'Huh, you think I did somebody?' he asked, sounding almost amused.

'I dunno.' Rocco laughed. 'Did you?'

'There are those who would,' Almighty drawled. 'I can tell you that.'

Rocco was silent for the rest of the ride. Almighty remained indifferent, dreamy, and only when he first sat down at the desk in the interrogation room did he become momentarily alert, frowning, jerking his chin into his neck as if he could smell his wife's scent from three hours before. But then he seemed to let it go. He slid down into his chair and popped open a bag of potato chips from the vending machine in the hallway.

Rocco settled in across the desk, absently smoothing out the top page of his legal pad and clearing his throat. 'Almighty, can I call you Gary? I just can't get my mouth around the other.'

'You can call me what you want. We in *your* house now.' He rubbed a tattoo on the meat below his left thumb; Rocco saw 'King of Kings' in blue and a crude three-cornered crown like a child's drawing.

'Gary, what do you know about Ahab's? What happened there?'

'What happened there?' He dipped his long fingers into the bag. 'You mean the guy that got killed? I don't know nothin'. Guy got killed.' His eyes were unfocused, drifting. 'That's what I know.'

The room smelled of grease and salt. Rocco rubbed his face. 'C'mon, you're a sharp guy, you're always in the street, nothing gets past you. What do you hear?'

Almighty hunched his shoulders, staring silently at a spot on the wall behind Rocco's right ear.

Rocco sighed. 'How many warrants you got out on you now?'

Almighty snapped to attention, sitting up and trying to find Rocco's eyes. 'Only but one. But that time I was supposed to be in court? I was in jail on some other thing. I was in *jail*, so how could I be in court too. That's not right.'

'So Gary, come on, what do you hear?'

'Yeah, I hear it was something . . . something with drugs.' Almighty leaned forward now, anxious to please.

'Who's saying that?'

'You know, people.'

'What people?'

'People. You know, people talk. It just words.'

'What, he had drugs, he was selling drugs, buying drugs?'

'It just words, I don't know.'

'You own a gun?'

'Me? Hell no.'

'You ever find a gun?'

'Me? No, but if I did? I'd sell it.' He nodded. 'I'd sell the *shit* out of that bad boy. A gun cost money.'

Rocco tapped his pencil on the desk. 'When was the last time you were in Ahab's?'

'Ahab's?' Almighty went blank again. 'Week, two weeks. I don't like that food they got in there. It hurts my stomach.'

'Anything happen that last time?'

'Bought some food, I guess.'

'You have any problems?'

Almighty touched his stomach. 'With the food?'

'Anything.'

'Nope.'

'You sure? You have the right change on you?'

'The right change? I guess.'

Rocco stared at the ceiling, took a deep breath. 'You weren't short a couple of cents?'

Almighty jerked upright in confusion.

'You didn't have any problems with anyone?'

'Unh-uh.'

'And the last time you were there was a week or two ago.'

'Somethin' like that. I'm mostly day-to-day in my lifestyle right now.'

'Where were you last night?'

Almighty shrugged. 'I was where I always am. All over.'

'Who were you with?'

'Shakwan, Dave and them all.'

'They'll back you up on that?'

'I guess.'

Rocco wasn't even bothering to take notes anymore. The guy was innocent.

'Well, then let me ask you this. What would you say if I told you I got someone who says you showed them a gun, you told them you were gonna cap that guy and' – Rocco threw this in for the hell of it – 'saw you do it.'

'Who say *wha*?' Almighty's voice went faint and high, his damp eyes staring. He leaned closer to Rocco. '*Who* . . .'

Rocco smelled true confusion, almost hurt, coming off him, but he simply stared back for a few seconds, letting Almighty sit on his own question.

'Who said that?' The words came out gently, more wounded than outraged.

'Well, let me put it another way. Why would somebody, out of the blue, come to us, seek us out, tell us all this stuff about you, try to get you –'

'Oh my Lord. That motherfuckin' woman. That . . . Jesus Lord.' He put a hand out to touch Rocco's arm. 'Look at me. Look at me.'

Rocco tilted back slightly.

'I got the Virus, man. I'm a *ghost*. Who'm I gonna mess with now? That woman, it's like . . . she says I *killed* her, you know? But I love her, man, I *love* her. I didn't, I wouldn't touch a hair on her head. I didn't know, I didn't . . . "You killed me," she says, "you . . . killed me."' Almighty was shaking his head, crying now. 'Goddamn, how's I supposed to know.'

Rocco ducked his head in mock astonishment. 'How are you supposed to *know*? Are you not of this *planet*? You show me one fucking junkie out there who don't know how you catch the Virus, I'll buy you a whole deck of heroin, how's that.'

'Yeah, but see, she had some problems when the baby was born? They tied up her tubes for her so she can't have no more babies? And she says to me, "I can't get nothing now, you know, no sexual diseases, because my tubes is tied." She tells me some doctor told her she was immune now.'

'*What* fucking doctor.'

'Well, maybe she misheard. Alls I know is, she tells me she's immune 'cause her tubes are tied.' His eyes went inward. 'She says to me, "You made the baby a *o*rphan. You took me from my baby." But it's my baby too, you know? She got my hair. And she's got this skin, it's like, it ain't a black person's skin like mine and it ain't a white person's skin like her mother. It's like, it's like, when you stripping cable? It's like copper, it's like that soft red gold? And she's gonna be tall, like me. She's got them long legs for a kid, like a runner. She's gonna be like a eight–eighty runner when she gets big. That was *my* event, the eight–eighty. Yeah, she's gonna be something else.'

Rocco looked at the tattoo again, thinking, What a fucking goose chase this turned out to be. He mulled over pressing charges against Suky Phelan for hindering the prosecution.

'So you're a proud daddy, hah?' Rocco asked, the frustration of his day seeping into the question.

'Yeah,' he said, slow, nodding. 'You could say that. But, you know this last year I'm sick? Shit, I don't *want* to be around her. 'Cause when I see her, you know like in the park? All I can think on is I ain't gonna see her for too much longer now. You know, like maybe a year from now she's gonna be playin' an' fall down hurt herself, start cryin' an' needin' help or whatnot? Where am I gonna be? I'm gonna be in the *ground*, so I don't wanna see her because it makes me think on that, an' I can't take it, man. I just can't take it.'

Wanting Almighty out of his office, Rocco went for the standard closer. 'Would you be willing to take a polygraph?'

'A what?' Almighty squinted. 'For what? About the Ahab's thing? Fuck yeah, I take that and I tell you what else you can do. You can give one to her, man. Ask her what's up, 'cause she just tryin' to get me booked for murder, one way or the other. But I swear I'm murdered every day I got left out here. Alls I got to do is lay down, close my eyes, think on shit? It's like a execution. A goddamn execution. "You killed me," she says. Well goddamn, I'm killed too, you know? I'm killed too.' He looked to Rocco for understanding, but Rocco retreated to his notes, avoiding Almighty's moist gaze.

'Yeah,' Almighty said to his swollen hands. 'I never wanted to hurt nobody my whole damn life, but look at this shit now.'

Rocco stared deep into the yellow pad, recalling his half-cocked comments about the Virus being a crime fighter, thinking about the haunted baby hospital, about Erin.

'Look. I got enough reason to lock you up right now, but I'm gonna give you a play.'

'You do that.'

Rocco ignored the sarcasm and put his card on the desk between them. 'But do me a favor. You get out there, you let me know what's up. And you start taking care of yourself.'

'For what?' Almighty said.

Rocco walked him out of the office. It was raining, and the potholed strip that ran from the skyway to I-9 was almost purple with gloom. He was supposed to offer Almighty a ride home but all he said was, 'You hear anything, you give me a call, OK?'

Almighty pulled down his Orlando Magic cap and loped off into the evening without saying anything. Rocco watched him blend into the wrecked landscape, and suddenly he remembered the guy's scavenge in the back of the Nova. He opened his mouth to call out Almighty's name, but then let it go, thinking, The hell with it.

Rocco wandered back into the interrogation room, began to clean it up and noticed that Almighty had left the calling card on the table. Rocco swept a little pile of potato chip crumbs into his cupped palm. The hell with it.

13

Strike stood in the center of the small overstuffed living room looking down at Rodney, who was sitting on the couch in his underwear, a low-voltage pain-reducing kit attached to his trick knee. Ten years before, Rodney had injured himself falling off the roof of a federal prison while doing a storm gutter repair job, dropping kneecap first onto an acetylene tank, and since then, whenever it rained Rodney had to put his knee on a wire so that the throbbing didn't drive him insane.

'Lookit.' Rodney extended an American Express gift catalogue to Strike. 'What you think of that?'

Strike looked at the picture of a male model wearing a three-hundred-dollar pair of suede pants.

'The way *you* eat sometimes? Shit, I'd get me suh-some *oil*cloth pants.' Strike scanned the other offerings: hooded cashmere bathrobes, terra-cotta planters, diamond rings. Who the hell would order a diamond ring from a catalogue?

'Naw, I like them.' Rodney adjusted the voltage on his leg.

Two of the three stacked TVs were on, one showing 'The Jeffersons,' the other playing a videocassette of *The Good, the Bad and the Ugly.*

'So what's up?' Strike said. He took a seat across from Rodney on the other couch. Rodney started to fall asleep. The electrical vibrations always put him out.

Strike leaned over and raised the volume on the TV, blasting Rodney upright into a blinky alertness.

'What's up, Rodney?' Strike lowered the TV again.

'Yeah . . . ol' Erroll got locked up.' Rodney's head started lolling back again.

'What for?'

'He shot this guy in the leg. You know that nigger Chickadee? Yeah . . . Erroll asked him for some money and Chickadee wouldn't give it

up, so he shot him. But he'll be out tomorrow on bail, and then Chickadee
best withdraw the complaint.'

'I thought you said Erroll ain't shooting people?'

'It was only in the leg. But like Erroll was supposed to pick up a package
tonight from Papi? So now I need you to do it. I would go but . . .' He
pointed down to his knee with the index fingers of both hands.

'*I'm* gonna pick it up?' Strike felt himself getting sucked into Rodney's
game again: half-truths, quarter-truths, out-and-out lies.

'Yeah, uh-huh. Unless you got other plans.'

'Where at?'

'You know the methadone trailer some blocks off Cooper? Near the
scrap-metal yard? He gonna meet you at – ' Rodney hit the time button
on his remote control; 6:15 showed up on some actor's forehead. 'In
a hour.'

Rodney pulled a taped-down grocery bag filled with money from under
the couch. 'Just drive up, leave this under your seat. Get on out, make
talk with the man, watch for police. When Papi say goodbye, just get
back in the car. The package gonna be in there. Go take it over to your
cutting house, whack it in fours, spread the three out to some other safes,
come on back here. Tomorrow we'll start workin' it out of the store.
Get to meet some faces, like we talked about.' Rodney said all this to the
TVs, fighting off drooping eyelids, sliding both palms under his knee
and slowly kneading it, looking as if he was on a heroin nod.

'I'm going myself?' Strike tried to make it sound like a question instead
of a whine.

Rodney started to snore. Strike hit the volume knob and Rodney
boomed upright again, looking around the room.

'What if they take me off?'

'They ain't gonna take you off,' Rodney said, closing his eyes.

'Yeah, but I ain't no Erroll Barnes.'

Rodney perked up at that. 'See? Hear what you said? You ain't no
Erroll Barnes. And you ain't *me* either. But you *from* me, you understand?'
Rodney leaned forward, going almost nose-to-nose, smirking. 'Still think
you doin' all the work?'

Strike massaged his neck. He hated it when Rodney crowed like this.

'Yeah, heads you win, tails I lose,' Strike muttered to himself.

Rodney cocked his head and spoke with a dangerous lightness in his
tone: 'What you say?'

As Strike drove along I-9, the road rain-slick and empty, he continued to talk back to Rodney. 'I said, "Heads you win, tails I lose." You fuckin' deaf? You want me to do it in *sign* language? Watch my lips, motherfucker.'

But there was no getting around it: after all the bullshit 'my son Strike' declarations, he was nothing more than Rodney's A-1 coolie boy and would never be more. Whether Rodney was asking him to run out for a sandwich or for a kilo, he was not to be denied.

Strike turned off I-9 at the Cooper Street exit and stopped for a traffic light. Lost in a sulk, he idled there through several changes, watching the colors bleed into the wet asphalt stretching before him.

Rolling forward again, he drove down three lifeless blocks, then turned into a narrow and desolate lane bordered by tattered warehouses and weedy lots, at last coming to a stop alongside the fence surrounding Kelso's scrap-metal yard.

Across the street was the methadone trailer, and behind that was a junkie encampment in a debris-strewn field. But with his engine shut down and the rain obliterating his view, Strike could barely make out the bright orange siding of the trailer, and the junkie camp was lost in a boiling mist. Nervous about being taken by surprise, his imagination calling up a vision of half-dead noddies trudging in the direction of his car, Strike turned on his wipers and saw that in fact the street was virtually deserted. The rain had washed away the usual shopping cart traffic between the field and the scrap-metal yard, and now there was only one staggering drunk about fifty feet away on the trailer side of the street, the guy reeling and lurching in aimless circles alongside a car with New York plates.

Both tense and bored, Strike decided to wait for Papi under an overhang. He put up the hood of his sweatshirt, kicked the money deep under his seat and opened the door, but as soon as he stepped out of the car he heard tinny Latino music, the same kind of music that Papi's crew had been playing that first time they met, by the cemetery wall. Strike took a step toward the New York car and saw a boom box sitting by its front tire. He squinted through the rain at the stumblebum: it was Papi.

Maybe he isn't drunk, Strike thought. Maybe he's dancing, dancing in the rain by himself. Strike felt his stomach go light as he took a few tentative steps forward.

'Papi,' Strike croaked. He cleared his throat. 'Papi!'

The guy didn't answer, just continued to stutter-step in a distracted circle, Strike thinking, The motherfucker *is* drunk. And where were his gun boys, the black-eyed skinny kid in the watch cap and the other vulture?

'Papi!'

Papi finally heard him and stood his ground, legs planted wide, shoulders jerking back and forth to keep his balance, belly peeking out of the same orange Milwaukee Brewers T-shirt he'd worn three days before.

'What's happenin'?' Strike stepped closer, feeling the rain on his face, ready to bolt at a second's notice.

Papi's hair was a mess, the nap standing up in forky clumps here and there. And now Strike saw that he was covered with something. It looked as if someone had winged a half-dozen fistfuls of food at him, peppering his shirt and pants.

Papi stared at him stupidly, silently, and Strike was about to go back to the car when he realized that it wasn't food – it was blood.

'Papi,' Strike whispered, hands out, floating, not knowing what to do, wondering how the radio could play in the rain without shorting out. Papi turned in a dazed circle as if looking for something. The song ended on the boom box and the disc jockey began talking in rapid Spanish, indecipherable to Strike save for the words 'Tidy Bowl.'

Strike's eye was drawn to what appeared to be a red pulsing light just to the left of Papi's crotch, on the inside of his beefy thigh, a glistening beat in the rain. Strike, unable to run away now, in shock himself, was taking the time to stare at the blinking light, as if it had nothing to do with the man, the pulsations making Strike think of Rodney's electroshock machine, of stoplights on deserted streets. Papi grunted with annoyance and kicked off a cracked tan woven loafer. Strike saw that it was filled with blood and abruptly recognized the bright red pulse for what it really was: a gunshot wound, the life blood pumping in a weak fountain from Papi's inner thigh with the slow and steady throbbings of his heart.

Hunching his shoulders, shivering, Strike looked into Papi's eyes. 'Yo, suh-sorry, man.'

Papi came alert, as if seeing Strike for the first time, glaring at him with those yellow cat's eyes, Strike numbly thinking that Papi was reacting to the stammer, watching Papi reach around, go for something stuck in the small of his back. 'I'll kill *your* nigger ass too,' Papi said hoarsely.

Kneecaps locked, Strike stood stock-still, wanting to apologize for something – but what? – hearing high-pitched notes inside his head.

Papi pulled out his beeper, muttering, '*Kill* your nigger ass.' He picked up his radio from the street, tossed it into the car, then drove away in a drunken swerve, sailing right past Strike.

His knees starting to vibrate a little, Strike chanted the words 'Ho shit, ho shit, ho shit' ten, twenty, thirty times, like a prayer.

'I didn't *do* nothin'!' Stunned, talking out loud to himself, Strike drove blindly along JFK.

'I swear to *God!*' He was talking to Champ, really, because Champ had to be behind what he'd just seen, shooting up Papi for selling weight in Champ country. Which meant that the next one going down would be Rodney, and after that Strike himself.

'But I didn't *do* nothin'!' Strike shouted as he sideswiped a double-parked car, drawing some startled frowns from a clot of people standing under an awning. Strike's vision went blurry, his world suddenly a killing floor, Strike hoping to keep his chin above the bloodline, seeing Darryl again, Papi, both of them sprouting deadly blooms.

Unable to drive, Strike pulled over to a bus stop and tried to collect himself, palming his temples and breathing through his mouth. Darryl, he thought, how long ago was Darryl shot? Then: Maybe it wasn't Champ tonight. Maybe it was Victor again – not Victor, but Victor's man. Maybe the guy is some kind of wind-up monster that can't turn off once he's set in motion. No, it had to be Champ.

Strike's stomach came at him then, announcing itself with a raw stabbing sensation. He blindly opened the glove compartment and grabbed a half-full Yoo-Hoo. As he twisted off the cap, the bottle slipped from his fingers, splashing the drink on his chest and leaving a chalky stain on his sweatshirt.

Strike sat there gasping for air, his shoulders heaving, this last small disaster leaving him trembling: Everything happening to *me*, just look at this shit. There was no way he could go out in public now, not with the stain on him. *Look at this shit*, and then he was butting the steering wheel with his forehead, punching the horn and making noises behind his teeth that sounded like the high whine of grinding gears. As the fit receded, he noticed that several people were circling the car, peering in at him. Strike peeled away from the bus stop, almost mowing a man down in his rage and shame.

He had to find Rodney. Forcing himself to drive slowly, to regain some semblance of self-control, Strike slipped into the nighttime car parade along JFK. At the intersection of JFK and Krumm, right in front of a candy store with at least six clockers working the sidewalk, Strike saw a uniformed cop writing a parking ticket. Eight o'clock Saturday night on JFK, the street knee-deep in bottles, and some bugged-out uniform is spending his evening writing up violations. Strike was so riveted by this absurdity that he almost didn't see Rodney's car coming toward him through the traffic. He pulled over to make a U-turn and go after Rodney, then saw the battered Cadillac screech to a halt, jamming the flow of traffic.

Rodney stuck his head out the window and yelled to the cop writing up the ticket. 'Yo Bones! What the fuck you doing!' The guy looked up, grinned at Rodney, and Strike recognized him as that crazy cop who remembered everything and everybody: Bobby Bones. Strike had heard that the guy was so into his job that on his days off he volunteered to fill in for anyone, no matter what the shift or detail was.

'Go *home*, motherfucker,' Rodney shouted. 'Watch some television, memorize the damn *phone* book or something. Jesus Christ, it's Saturday night, man.'

'The city never sleeps,' Bones shouted back.

'Well, catch some criminals then, gah-*damn*.'

Strike honked his horn and waved to catch Rodney's eye, but Rodney rolled off, oblivious, and only Bobby Bones looked at Strike, squinting and then smiling in recognition.

Strike eventually caught up to Rodney in a small Italian neighborhood at the tail end of the boulevard. Rodney was standing in front of a glass-bricked corner bar, talking to an old bony white man whose cheeks and temples were covered with quarter-size liver spots.

Anxious about walking around in this neighborhood, Strike double-parked across the street and waited for Rodney to finish his business. The two men were out of earshot but Strike saw that whatever they were talking about was making them both chokefaced crazy: Rodney was standing coiled and knotted, his lips clamped tight; the white guy's eyes glittered, giving off a watery shine of anger.

Strike's stomach was on fire again. He looked down at his hands, lying palms up in his lap, and thought about New York, about haircuts and hot dogs, about how long ago that all seemed. He thought about Tyrone, his vague plans for the kid – or was that going to be a bad move too? Absorbed in his own misery, Strike didn't notice the bronze Reliant creeping up behind him until the car came to a stop abreast of his window, startling him, the adrenaline squealing in his gut. The driver and the passenger, two plainclothes knockos, eyed him impassively, then made a lazy U-turn so that they were alongside Rodney's Cadillac.

Belching away the jolt of terror, Strike watched the driver get out and stand on tiptoes, then stretch like a yawning cat right in the middle of the street. Ignored by Rodney and the old guy standing just a few feet away, the knocko leaned into the open window of Rodney's car and came out with an envelope, which he jammed sloppily into the back pocket of his dungarees. A moment later the two cops were gone, their car receding into the combat zone at the heart of JFK.

The bony white man finally waved Rodney off, as if to make him vanish. When the man walked back inside the bar, Rodney seemed to contemplate going in after him, then limped across the street to Strike.

'I don't believe this shit,' Rodney said, leaning down, forearms crossed over the bottom of the window. 'I say replace the motherfuckin' Super Mario or I'm gonna throw the piece of shit out into the street, throw *all* the goddamn machines out into the street, fuck *all* you Dempsy Guineas, I go over to goddamn New York City, buy my own damn games. He say, "You do that, you ain't gettin' no *milk* deliveries, no *bread* deliveries, no *candy*." I say, "Hey, you do what you got to, 'cause I don't give a fuck. I don't give a fuck be you Mafia, Colombian, black, white. Just so long you ain't a cop, it's me and you, 'cause I just don't *give* a fuck." You know what I'm sayin'?' Rodney stood up straight, arched his back, then dropped back down to the window. 'The delivery man come up so much as one quart of milk shy on me? Shit, I'll come back up here, snap that ol'-time motherfucker like a kitchen match.'

'They shot up Pa-Papi.' Strike closed his eyes, concentrating on the effort to control his tongue.

'I'll take out that whole motherfuckin' bar. I'll get me Erroll, I'll get me – '

'You *hear* me?'

'Yeah, I heard you,' Rodney said. 'Who did?'

'I don't know. Champ?'

'So . . .' Rodney shrugged, then pushed off from the window, looking tense and defiant. 'They kill him?'

'He drove off buh–but he all shot up.' Strike let loose with another burning belch.

'You still got the money?'

Strike hunched down and brought the bag up to his lap.

'How you know it's Champ?'

'Well, who else?'

'What happened to his boys? They get shot up too?'

'Th–they weren't there.'

'See? Maybe *they* did it. Took him off. See what I'm sayin'? Maybe he got problems with his own people in New York.'

Strike nodded, only half listening.

'Maybe Papi, maybe . . .' Rodney faltered, frowning at the street. He reached in and took the money off Strike's lap, then added vaguely, 'You don't know it's Champ.' He palmed his midsection, turning in a gimpy half circle, the money bag held between his elbow and ribs.

'You think we next?' Strike asked it lightly, lucidly, as if he didn't really care.

'I ain't got no beef with Champ.' Rodney's voice went singsong. 'I don't know what the fuck you talkin' about. I ain't the one that come in here from New York try to sell shit. I *work* for the man. He got a beef with me I'm right here, 'cause I don't *give* a fuck.'

Strike stared at Rodney, watching him swell up with his own words.

'In fact, I got some business with the nigger to*night*.'

Strike looked down at his upturned hands again, telling himself that it was every man for himself – like it always was, always would be. But then Rodney hunched back down into the car window, his voice holding a teasing confidentiality.

'You want to come? Or you want to *run*?'

Strike sat in Rodney's Cadillac. He had left his own car back in Guineatown. They were parked in a shut-down gas station in Dempsy, and Strike waited while Rodney talked on a pay phone. Strike thought about Tyrone again, thinking, Watch it, don't buy anything else for the kid because he'll just get spoiled, get into expecting shit for nothing, and then he'll be no use at all. Wind up just like everybody else, blank-faced and treacherous.

Rodney came back to the car and drove off in silence. When he reached Jersey City he pulled into the lot of an all-night diner and sat there, fanning his knees and saying nothing.

Finally he spoke: 'Where Papi get shot?'

'Right where we was supposed to meet, right outside – '

'Naw, I mean on his body.'

'Aw-all over. Up and down . . .'

'His face?'

'Unh-uh, his legs and chest. He had this shoe? It was like fuh-filled up with blood from his leg.'

Rodney sucked his teeth and shook his head. The car returned to silence.

A minute later the rear door opened and someone slid into the back. Strike jumped in surprise but Rodney didn't even turn his head, just extended his arm back over his shoulder for an upside-down handshake.

The guy was young, black, maybe a few years older than Strike. He wore gold, but a nice quarter-inch herringbone chain. He was dressed clean too: acid-washed jeans, a pullover shirt in a matching shade of gray, red and white Air Jordans. Strike first thought he was a hit man – he could sense that the guy was carrying a gun somewhere on his body.

'Who the fuck is this?'

Strike turned to see the guy nodding at him but looking at Rodney, as if Strike was there but not there.

'He's with me,' Rodney said.

'Yeah, I *see* that. Who the fuck is he?'

'That's Strike. He's OK.'

The guy lurched forward off the back seat. 'What the fuck you think you doing, Rodney?'

'Hey, hey. I *know* the man, see, and I'm tellin' you, it's better we go over there in a group – all casual, you understand? We go in a group, it takes the eyeball weight off you. See what I'm sayin'?'

'You don't spring somebody on me without some beforehand say-so.' The guy poked Strike in the back of the head with a fingertip and Strike instinctively snatched at the air where the offending finger had been. He had had enough, more than enough.

'Hey, I tried to call you, man,' Rodney said, palms up. 'You just don't answer your damn beeper. What can I do about that?'

The guy snorted and Strike looked out the window. Hit man: Was Rodney going after Champ before Champ could come after him?

'Strike.' The guy said his name as if it had just come to him. 'Yeah, I know you. Yeah, yeah, I *know* you, you understand?' He leaned forward and put his hand on Strike's arm, waiting until Strike turned around and met his threat eye-to-eye. 'You fuck with me, my man, you into a *world* of darkness. You want to get verification on that, you check with my man over here.'

Strike almost squawked with revelation. Only a cop could deliver a proprietary speech like that one, talking as if he owned Rodney, as if he owned Strike too, Strike and all the once and future jailbirds out on the street.

Rodney clucked his tongue and laid his fingers on the cop's arm. 'Yo, lighten up, man. Strike's right. I wouldn't have asked him if he wasn't right.'

The cop sat back, still boring into Strike with his eyes. 'Yeah, well, he's right *now*.'

Strike figured the guy was probably an undercover who Rodney hoped
to introduce into Champ's machine, although Strike had no idea why
Rodney would want to take such a risk to help out the cops. But having
anything to do with a knocko bring-down on Champ was almost too crazy
to think about, and Strike intuitively understood that the way to survive
the night was to go loose, just glide until the sun came up. And despite
Rodney's snaky ways, staying close to him right now was probably the
best plan. Stick tight with the survivors: the man was thirty-seven and
still around.

'Gerbers.' The cop frowned down at some cartons of strained fruit from
the store that sat next to him on the back seat. 'Goddamn, Rodney, how
many kids you got?'

'I got me a tribe.' Rodney turned on the ignition.

'Hold up, hold up.' The guy leaned forward again, extended a staying
hand. 'Don't go nowhere. Let's just . . .'

Rodney sighed, rubbing his eyes under his sunglasses.

'Newark, Delaware,' Rodney said, the name a tired announcement.

'New *Ark*, New *Ark*.' The guy was very tense now, Strike seeing a
shiny film appear across his forehead.

'New Ark, Delaware.'

'And?'

'You my cousin Lonnie.'

'Nephew. I'm your motherfuckin' *nephew*.'

'What's the difference?' Rodney said.

'The difference is, that's what you already told the man, so stay
with it.'

'My nephew Lonnie, my sister's boy.'

'And?' The cop nodded for more, knees pumping as if ready to race.

'Your connect's doing thirty in.'

'Thirty in, that's right. Let's go.' He smacked Rodney on the arm with
the back of his hand and threw himself against the rear seat, chewing on
his thumbnail as Rodney pulled out of the lot.

The O'Brien Houses, Champ's base of operations, were six high rises
aligned in a crescent just inside the Dempsy city line. The long driveway
in front of the houses served as a drive-by dope market for neighboring
all-white Rydell, and in the evenings, especially on weekends, the gently
curved one-way strip was often bumper-to-bumper with white-boy
muscle cars, sports cars, jeeps and vans, the servers working the line like
carhops. About a third of the dope was beat, but a customer had to be high

out of his mind to come back and complain. The Rydell dopers knew the odds of getting burned, knew the odds of getting robbed if they came over in the hours after midnight when the traffic was slower. They also knew that the Rydell cops were often staked out on the Rydell side, scoping out the dope line with binoculars so they would know who to pop the minute a customer came back into town. But O'Brien was so convenient, and the drive-up crescent so fast and simple, that the customers took their chances. Besides, the same coke or heroin automatically doubled in price if they bought it a hundred yards east, over the line, so it all evened out in the end.

Rodney parked the car on a small rise overlooking the projects, and the three of them watched the O'Brien run, the procession of stop-and-go headlights steaming in the drizzle, the six towers looming behind the clockers like giant dominoes.

'White, white, white.' Rodney clucked his tongue. 'Oh please, Officer, it's my first time. My father gonna kill me.' He laughed but the knocko was too tense, not listening, and just then Strike spotted Champ standing in front of one of the buildings. Champ was hard to miss even in the nighttime mist: jumbo-size in a white T-shirt, white knee-length shorts and a fat pair of Reebok Pumps, each sneaker looking big enough to house a puppy. He lumbered back and forth like a caged bear, divorced from the action, ignoring the servers out in the rain, wading through a cloud of aimless teenagers who seemed to follow him wherever he moved. Strike noticed that if Champ waddled fifty feet to the west, the human cloud would somehow re-form around him a few moments later. When he waddled fifty feet to the east, the same slow re-formation took place.

'Look at that boy,' Rodney said affectionately, as if he'd forgotten about Papi altogether.

Champ stepped back to the sidewalk and yelled something up into the nearest building. Seconds later a bucket was lowered out a third-floor window into his waiting hands. Rodney said, 'Snack time.' Champ shuffled back under the overhang, plunked himself down on an overturned shopping cart and pulled out a crab with each hand, alternating his bites from fist to fist, the cloud of kids forming a loose circle around the shopping cart now.

'Look at that boy eat,' Rodney said. 'Y'all don't have to bust him, he gonna bust hisself. Shit, he's gonna explode.'

None of the kids around Champ talked to him or even acted as though they were aware of him; they simply moved with him, unthinkingly. Strike knew what it was – it was the Power. He had met Champ only two times, but each time he felt it. When you stood next to him, you just didn't want to leave. The Power. Rodney had it too.

The knocko barked 'Go!' then made the sign of the cross.

Strike was amazed by the gesture, but Rodney laughed. 'You like my goddamn wife with that,' he said.

'Just go, motherfucker. *Go, go.*'

Strike shut his eyes, feeling the downward roll of the car in his belly. The thing was, he really didn't have any need for Tyrone now that Papi was gone. He guessed that meant he was out of the ounce business. Out before he even got in.

Rodney coasted into the drive and parked next to a new black Mustang. The car was all tricked out, from fully dropped skirts to leather grille covers to overhead stun lights, just the thing for some nighttime hunting in the bush.

'New *Ark*,' the knocko snapped. 'Say it.'

'Wilmington,' Rodney said.

Champ had seen Rodney's Cadillac come in. Now he kicked up and rose off the shopping cart and walked toward them through the mist like a baby dinosaur, the cloud of kids hanging back for a few seconds before starting to follow him. Strike was worried by Champ's aggressive lope, not knowing if they had stepped into the shit now or what, then deciding it was probably OK because of all the customers. It amazed Strike that Champ always looked so bummy – pigpen bummy, with yellowy slices under the arms of his T-shirt, belly hanging over the wrinkled jumbo shorts, filthy laces on his sneakers, Mets hat hanging sideways over his ear. He was six foot two, three hundred fifty pounds, and his tiny, bearded head sat on a long and thick curved stalk of a neck like a petal-less sunflower. At twenty years old Champ directed the whole show: he ran Rodney and six others besides, raking in a hundred thousand dollars a week.

'Yo, pimp!' Champ bellowed as he skipped sideways between the customers' cars, moving fast toward Rodney. He wore a paper bag upside down on his hand like a wrist cuff, his fingers thrust through the bottom and clutching a quart bottle of malt liquor.

The three of them were out of Rodney's car now, Strike tensing for an explosion.

'What's up, pimp!' Champ beamed through his beard, looking at Rodney as though he might taste good.

'Watch your fuckin' mouth,' Rodney snapped back, wading into Champ, pummeling his midsection, hulling him backwards. Champ crossed his arms, yelling 'Help! Help!' and laughing, dropping his, bottle, the crash making all the servers straighten up and turn their heads for a second.

'Look what you did.' Champ flicked a hand at the puddle and the broken glass. 'That was my goddamn dinner, pimp!'

The cloud had completed its drift out to Champ, and Strike saw that two of the older teenage girls were still sucking their thumbs, and one of the boys had the hung-open mouth and dull eye of an idiot.

Champ turned to one of the kids and gestured limply to the broken bottle. 'Kick that away, gonna slice up my damn tires.'

The kid played soccer with the glass shards as Champ handed two dollars to another kid and jerked his hand lazily in the direction of a mini-mart.

'This your new short?' Rodney nodded to the Mustang.

'Yeah,' said Champ. 'I don't go in for no broke-down pimp-mobile.'

'What it do?'

'One forty, one fifty?'

Rodney grimaced at Champ's belly. 'One fifty with *you* in there? Shit, then it *got* to do one eighty with me, I'll bet.'

'Who's this?' Champ eyed the undercover cop.

'Yeah, this my cousin Lonnie, I told you about him?'

The knocko nodded, stone-faced.

'I thought you say he was your nephew.' Champ smiled slowly, looking at Rodney through narrowed eyes.

'Yeah, well he my sister's boy. I call 'em *all* cousins.'

Champ grinned at Rodney a little longer, the knocko dancing in place as if he was freezing.

A short skinny guy in a floppy camouflage hat ambled over to the group, hands in his pockets, eyes down. Strike recognized him from the last time he had been to O'Brien: it was Buddha Hat, Champ's enforcer. Champ was smart that way, picking the small, heartless ones who shoot without blinking instead of the big muscle boys, knowing that enforcement isn't a bodybuilding contest and that besides quality, the other thing needed to keep it together and stay on top was fear. Buddha Hat was a walking ice cube, and Strike knew that if anyone here shot Papi it was him.

Strike found himself inching back to the car. The night, the colors of things, the feel of the misty air on his face, all became vivid and strangely precious, and he imagined moving quickly from safe house to safe house, picking up his money and hitting the turnpike. He had about twenty-two

thousand dollars. Scoop it and go: all he had to do is survive this thing
here. His mother had people in Henderson, South Carolina. Or was it
North Carolina? His father had people in Columbus, Ohio. That might
be better; at least people wore shoes there.

Champ was still smiling at Rodney, chewing over the cousin story.
Finally he let it slide and turned to the knocko. 'You know you uncle a
famous pimp?'

The knocko grunted noncommittally. Strike stood behind Rodney
now, hiding behind Rodney's age, Rodney's knowledge.

'And who's that?' Champ stood on tiptoe to look at Strike over
Rodney's shoulder. He laughed. 'That your muscle?'

Strike casually strolled back into sight, trying to show that staying
behind Rodney was no big thing, but he was unable to look Champ in
the face. He noticed that Buddha Hat was staring at him – no, not at him,
at his sweatshirt. Looking down, Strike saw the dried Yoo-Hoo splatter
and felt a rush of disgust and shame.

Rodney hooked his arm around Strike's head. 'That's my man Strike,'
he said playfully. 'You know Strike.'

Champ didn't answer, turning back to the knocko. 'Yeah, so you his
nephew, huh? I'm sorry about that.'

The knocko shrugged, then looked around like time was tight.

'Yeah,' Champ said, 'so Rodney say you in a jam.'

'My connect's doing thirty in.' The cop's voice cracked on the last
word; he sounded scared. Strike spun in a little circle.

'Where at?' Champ was all big white teeth and concentration.

'Florida.' The knocko's voice was stronger but he still didn't meet
Champ's eyes, Strike thinking, This motherfucker stinks. Scoop and go.

'Florida. What he do for thirty in?'

The knocko shrugged, dancing from foot to foot. 'You know, nothin'.'

Champ laughed, but Strike saw that he was still thinking things over.

'Motherfucker's got the *hot seat* down there,' Rodney said, starting into
a nervous little rain-gimped jig of his own. Strike thought the three of
them must look like a goddamn bunch of break dancers or something.

Champ and Buddha Hat didn't move, their eyes patiently reading
the show.

'Motherfucker's got a sign in the execution chamber?' Rodney made a
frame with his hands. 'Justice – Regular or Extra Crispy.'

Champ ignored Rodney. 'What you paying now?'

'Twelve,' the knocko said.

'A what?'

'A pound.'

Champ winced, sucking air as if that was way too much. 'Where's
that?'

'New Ark.'

'Newark?' Champ hunched his shoulders in astonishment.

'New *Ark*, Delaware,' Rodney said, sounding proud.

'New Ark, Delaware,' Champ announced. 'I don't know nobody
down there.'

'It's there,' the knocko said to the sky.

'Delaware,' Champ murmured to himself, then looked down at Buddha
Hat. 'Get Aisa over.'

Buddha Hat turned to the servers and the line of cars. 'Yo Aisa,' he
called, his voice tinny and small to Strike's ears. A tall, lightskinned kid
walked over with the easy stride of a hurdler.

Champ put an arm around the kid's shoulders and tilted his head toward
the knocko. 'Tell Aisa here where you from.'

The knocko took a heavy breath as if losing patience. 'New Ark.'

Champ looked at Aisa. 'Where you people from?'

'Wilmington, but I know New Ark too. Where in New Ark you
from?'

'You know, like near the *down*town?'

Strike saw Buddha Hat watching him and read a message in his
eyes: everybody's just running a game here. Then Buddha Hat nodded
imperceptibly, as if to add, But I'll see you later.

Strike strolled behind Rodney again. Rodney casually reached behind
his back and crushed Strike's elbow, this message clear too: Stop hiding.

'Near the college?' Aisa looked back at the cars, hungry for dope.

'Yeah, near there.'

Champ studied the knocko, reading his hands, his eyes, Strike thinking,
Just like a cop.

'You know Tito?' Aisa asked, his tone challenging.

The knocko reared back in disdain. 'Shit, I know like *three* Titos.'

'Tito Clark.'

'I don't know nobody's last names. Is that the fat one?'

Aisa hesitated. 'Yeah, well, he's chunky, but . . .'

'Yeah, I know him. Hey look.' The knocko turned to Champ. 'I got to
book – can we *do* something? 'Cause like, my time is money, you know?
I mean, I got me a problem.'

The kid came back with Champ's quart of malt liquor and started to
walk away.

'Hey yo! Yo!' Champ snapped his fingers at the kid's back. The kid turned. 'You slick or something?' The kid did a bad act of coming on surprised, then handed over the thirty cents change.

Cracking the top of the quart, Champ turned back to the knocko. 'Yeah, well, I don't have nothing now. How long you gonna be around?'

Strike saw both Rodney and the knocko relax with secret relief. He looked to Buddha Hat, wondering whether he'd seen it too. Buddha Hat caught Strike's glance and again tilted his head in some kind of acknowledgment.

'Two days,' the knocko said. 'But like I got to set something up. You know I got a contact in Queens, but Rodney said to see you first, but I only got but two days.'

'That's OK,' Champ said.

'So like when you *have* something, how do I get in touch?'

'Through Rodney.'

'Aw man.' The knocko waved Champ off. 'Don't put me on Rodney. The nigger never answers his beeper. Let me check in with you direct. Just give me your number.'

Champ's eyes suddenly went big and he strode over to Strike, hunched down and bellowed right in his face, 'This nigger's gonna set me up! *Oh!*' He howled and threw a wet, heavy arm over Strike's shoulder as if they were drunk together, Strike staggering under the weight, a strand of bile burning in the back of his throat. Champ laughed wide-mouthed, talking right into Strike's face again. 'Haw! Gimme your *num*ber! Motherfucker's settin' me *up!*'

Rodney went into a manic boxer's shuffle, laughing and yelling out loud. 'Tha's right! Put your ass in jail! Take over the show!'

Rodney and Champ were shouting now, Champ still holding Strike in a near headlock, Strike reeling under the loudness, the weight and the smell of Champ, terrified that the play was over and that Buddha Hat was going to pull out some kind of weapon and finish the Papi business right here, take out Rodney, Strike himself, maybe even the knocko, just because he was here, a witness.

Disgusted, the knocko grabbed Rodney's arm. 'C'mon mother-fucker. Let's jet, let's jet.'

As the knocko threw open the car door, Champ let Strike free. Strike clambered into the back seat.

'Hold on, hold on.' Champ grabbed the door. 'Gimme *your* number. Maybe I'll call you, see what I can do.'

The knocko hesitated, playing hard to get, then wrote a number in pencil on a dollar bill. 'Yeah, this my beeper. When you punch in, put like a twelve on the end of it so I know it's you. But like, you know, I'm gone in two days, so . . .'

'Yeah, I'm gone too,' Champ said.

'Where you going?' Rodney asked as he slid into the driver's seat.

'Disney World.' Champ grinned.

Buddha Hat came up behind Champ and stared at Strike through the open window. Strike thought maybe all this eyeballing was instinctual, maybe Buddha Hat was just automatically zeroing in on the weakest player. But then Buddha Hat said in a small voice, 'You Victor's brother,' said it not as a question or as a conversation starter, just as a registration of fact, talking more to himself than to Strike. Then he stepped back into the shadows as if he'd got what he wanted. Speechless, tilting, Strike unthinkingly covered his stained sweatshirt with crossed arms like a woman hiding her breasts.

'Yeah, I'm gonna take us to Disney World,' Champ said. He finished his malt liquor and flung the bottle into some weeds.

'In *that*?' Rodney's voice went high as he frowned at the Mustang.

'Hell no.' Champ massaged his wet chest. 'Take us a *plane*.'

As Rodney started the car, Champ reached through the rear window and grabbed Strike by the sweatshirt.

'Don't you be bullshittin' me now.' He smiled, licking his chops in good cheer. 'Is this motherfucker settin' me up?'

Strike tried to say no, but the word came down like a steel trap on his tongue. All he could do was moo like a cow.

Strike and Rodney sat in the Cadillac on a side street in Jersey City, watching the knocko piss in some bushes and then disappear down the street.

'See, I *told* you don't worry about no Champ.' Rodney turned to Strike in the rear seat. 'Didn't I say that?'

'Uh-huh,' Strike said, but he was hearing Buddha Hat again: 'You Victor's brother.' The words were setting up house in Strike's head.

'See, what happened was, the state knockos? They got me on this wiretap talking to this guy? We wasn't talking about nothin' *too* bad, but bad enough for it to be a conspiracy on me. And like now I got to work that off. So I said, Shit, I'll help you get inside on Champ, take down Champ, 'cause for me that's like killin' two birds with one stone, you know? Work off the charge and clear the road for business.'

Rodney started to drive back to Dempsy. 'Champ ain't stupid, but he's greedy. I told him this guy's product is so raggedy he could step three times on his package, the guy'd *still* be happy. Yeah, Champ is goin' *down*.'

But Rodney's revelations barely registered. Strike was still communing with Buddha Hat, lost in his eyes, trying to translate his words: 'You Victor's brother.' And then it came to him: My Man. Buddha Hat was My Man.

Rodney blathered on. 'See, the only thing, it might take some time. This shit always takes some time, because now they want this guy tonight to introduce like another guy, let that second guy get in good, make the big buys, and *then* take him down. You know, so Champ won't know it's *me* behind shit. I told them, though, I don't give a fuck. Take him down fast. I ain't afraid a no Champ. Fuck him and take him down *now*.'

Strike pictured Buddha Hat giving him that knowing head bob, then remembered Victor's secret smile in that bar two nights before. My Man: Had to be.

'Champ,' Rodney muttered through his teeth. 'I used to bounce that nigger on my knee. I gave that fat boy his start – he used to be my spy boy. Paid him twenty dollars a day? He'd run out and spend it all on candy. *Champ* . . . shit. Buddha Hat too. I used to go out with his mother before he was even born. He might even be mine if I think on it. I used to catch him playing hooky? I scooped his ass up by the ear, dragged him off to the school my damn self. Bunch a damn ungrateful kids.'

Strike smelled Champ on him still, saw Buddha Hat's mope-faced stare, felt the rude poke of the knocko's finger on the back of his head – this city closing in on him again like a bloody-knuckled fist.

'And that fat boy's comin' after *me*? Who the fuck does he think he's playin' with?'

'Champ killed Papi, man,' Strike said, his own voice sounding far off and mournful.

'Hey, fuck the Papi thing, *fuck* that shit. You don't know nothin' about that. And even if you do? Hey, that best end right there between him and him, 'cause someone comin' after *me* is gonna die his own self – 24, 7, 365, because that's the way I am. Shit, I ain't afraid a no Champ.'

Strike looked at Rodney's bulging eyes: Rodney was a fool. 'Yeah, well then you should drop a *dime* here, man, 'cause they don't wait to set up on a shooting. They just go in an' snatch him up.'

'Yeah? What kind of proof you got? That's just like *hearsay*. That's just word on the street. Besides, Champ didn't do Papi, man. He had it *done*.'

Strike looked out the window, thinking, Yeah, just like you did on Darryl. Then: And just like *I* did on Darryl.

But how did Victor come to know Buddha Hat? Victor never did anything but work his whole life, never even hung out on the street. And then Strike began sweating out another question: Did Buddha Hat know the real reason why Victor had asked him to cap Darryl? Did he know that Strike and Rodney were dealing behind Champ's back? Strike stared out the side window and fought down a wave of burning belches.

'Fuck that nigger's fat ass.' Rodney stomped the accelerator as if the speed of the car was directly connected to the pressure behind his eyes. 'And he's comin' after *me*? Well, come on then, motherfucker. Come on and *come*.'

Flying down I-9, Rodney swerved tight around a car that was already doing seventy. When the driver honked, Rodney pulled over one lane, slowed down until the car came abreast of him, went eyeball-to-eyeball with four white teenagers for a long minute and then veered sharply back into their lane, making them drive off onto the shoulder.

Strike hid his eyes, trying to be casual about it, gripping his temples with the thumb and index finger as if he had a headache. He had to get away from Rodney, think this through.

'Yeah, I left my car by that bar in Guineatown? Wuh-Where you was before?'

'Goin' down to Guineatown,' Rodney said in a clenched-teeth singsong. He hit JFK and plowed through the red lights, ignoring people, making for the white gangster section of town.

A new thought crashed into Strike as he imagined telling Rodney how he had fucked up and somehow got Champ's hit man to shoot Darryl Adams: he might as well have gone directly to Champ and announced that they were dealing behind his back. Strike glanced quickly at Rodney, saw all that fury and fear, and suddenly he was more scared of Rodney than of a dozen Buddha Hats. What if Rodney found out that Strike had exposed his play? But if Strike didn't tell him, they'd both be killed the minute Buddha Hat and Champ decided to stop playing with them. Either way . . .

Strike rolled open his window, belched deep and froglike, spitting out something reddish-brown. 'Let me out, man,' he said in a whisper. 'I'm gonna be sick.'

Rodney looked at him intently, then pulled the car over to the curb in front of a beauty parlor about six blocks from Guineatown.

'Yeah, I'm gonna go back to the benches.' Strike reached for the door handle, avoiding Rodney's eyes. 'You know, take care of business.'

'Don't you want your car?'

'I get it later.' Strike spit up more red bile.

'Yeah, you do that,' Rodney said. Then he grabbed Strike's wrist. 'I wanna tell you something. I know *everything* you thinking right now. You thinking Champ killed Papi, Buddha Hat killed Papi. You going, Ho shit, I'm next, I'm next, ho shit.'

Strike nodded, staring at his knees, thinking, You don't know the half of it.

'But you gotta be like *me*. See, I don't give a fuck, 'cause coming after me and coming after Papi is two different things. I ain't no Papi. I'll kill you right back, so I just don't give a fuck and I know those niggers know that, and if you was any kind of *man*, any kind of *player*, you'd be thinking like me too.'

'Yeah, I hear that.' Strike eased his wrist free, desperate to be out of the car.

'Fear got a odor, like sex. You know what I'm sayin'?' Rodney ducked down, looking over his nighttime sunglasses into Strike's eyes.

'Yeah, OK.' Strike stepped out on the street and began to toddle backwards, giving Rodney a little salute, hoping that when Buddha Hat finally decided to come after them, he'd hit Rodney first and at least give Strike a chance to run.

14

Rocco stood behind the lottery machine on the bottle side of Shaft Deli-Liquors, looking across the narrow aisle at Mazilli, who was manning the counter on the grocery and sandwich side. A thin but steady stream of customers bobbed between them on a wood floor so old and beaten down it looked more like tamped earth than anything man-made.

Mazilli had asked Rocco to help out because the wife of one of his black clerks had had a baby that afternoon and the Puerto Rican kid who worked for him had lost a grandmother the night before. Rocco and Mazilli were both on duty, but as long as they could hear their beepers nobody cared how they spent their shift. Besides, Mazilli was still the acting head of Homicide for another nine days, so there wasn't even anybody to duck.

It was slow for a Saturday night. The bank of pay phones on the corner made the street a natural dope market; on a normal evening there was always an army of clockers and baseheads marching in and out of Shaft for cigarettes, beer, pork rinds and sweets. But a few days before, the block association had made a stink, so tonight two uniformed rookies wandered in bored half circles in front of the phones, moving the action a block down the street. The cops would knock off at eleven, and the crowd would return to the corner by eleven-fifteen, but Shaft closed up at eleven-thirty, so Mazilli's impulse sales were way down. Still, it could have been worse: at least half of the customers lived off the mailbox, and since it was just two weeks into the month, many of them were still somewhat flush. Rocco could have guessed the date by how the store's customers held themselves when they walked in; as the end of the month neared, the postures would start slumping, but for now most everybody was carrying a little pride, a little spirit.

Rocco still felt shaky from his encounter with Almighty earlier in the evening. He had spent the last few hours trying to get the guy out of his head by keeping busy, fetching pints and half pints of Seagram's Gin –

a k a Knottyhead – Captain Morgan Spice Rum and various sweet wines
– all of it stoop booze – from the shelves behind him. He also ran Pik-6,
Pik-4 and Pik-3 numbers through the lottery machine, a procession of
wishful thinkers singing out birth dates, death dates, dream signs, street
addresses and, in one case, a six-digit FBI confidential informant ID code,
everyone hoping to score anywhere from fifty bucks for a Pik-3 box to
$2.1 million for a Pik-6 straight. The winning numbers would be drawn
on TV at eleven o'clock sharp, and as the hour crept toward the statewide
shutdown, the lottery line grew longer. Rocco was so busy between the
numbers and the bottles that the vodka and ice he had stashed behind the
counter for himself had turned into an alcoholic soup.

A ten-year-old boy with large sober eyes and a shaved head passed to
Rocco a scrawled list of ten three-digit numbers and a ten-dollar bill. 'She
say all straight.'

'Sorry kiddo, you got to be eighteen.' Rocco smiled apologetically.

The boy turned to Mazilli across the way, who was busy selling loose
cigarettes for fifteen cents a pop. Mazilli met the boy's patient gaze,
shrugged and waved a go-ahead. Rocco punched in the combinations,
took the money and handed the boy ten Pik-3 tickets.

Rocco then rang up a can of Budweiser, the guy buying it having already
bought three cans on three separate trips during the last hour. A lot of the
same people had been in and out several times, moving between the street
and the store all night, making repeat purchases of a single item. It drove
Rocco nuts: guys would buy ten loose cigarettes on ten trips for a dollar
fifty when they could have bought a pack – twice as many butts for the
same price.

A tall pregnant woman wearing a flimsy shift and a pair of rubber
flip-flops handed Rocco a neat list of twenty six-digit combinations, two
ten-dollar bills peeking out of her fist.

'Straight or box?'

'Straight.' Going for the $2.1 million: Rocco wondered what her
life would be like with that much money, what it would change
for her.

Rocco looked up from the lottery machine and saw Rodney Little
limp in, walking backward, talking loud to someone out in the street.
He wheeled around in the store and pointed his finger like a gun at
Mazilli, then took a garlic pickle out of a glass jar over the cold cuts
display window.

'How come I can't get these?' Rodney said to Mazilli. He leaked pickle
juice down his chin. 'Every time that motherfucker come by my store, I

say bring me some garlic pickles. He say he can't get them no more. I think the motherfucker's prejudiced.'

'He ain't prejudiced.' Mazilli ditched his cigarette. 'He just hates black people.'

Rodney reared up on tiptoe, his ass in the air, to keep the juice from dripping on his shoes.

Rocco hadn't seen Rodney in about six years, and he instantly resented the fact that he looked as if he hadn't aged at all. Rodney did a double take on seeing Rocco behind the lottery machine, reading 'cop' but not placing the face.

Rocco nodded in greeting, then answered the question in Rodney's eyes. 'I arrested you eight years ago for shooting Chewy Bishop.'

Rodney smiled. 'Yeah, how you been?'

'You want a napkin for that?' Rocco smirked at the sheen on Rodney's chin.

Rodney didn't respond. He turned his back on Rocco and pulled a fat wad of money out of the front pocket of his tight bicycle shorts. He limped over to Mazilli.

'What the fuck happened to you?' Mazilli tilted his head to Rodney's bad leg.

'Rain.'

'Yeah? I thought maybe Erroll Barnes winged one at you, too.'

Rodney grunted a laugh, moving his lips as he counted his roll.

'You best put a leash on that fuckin' psycho,' Mazilli said.

'It's a free country – so they tell me,' Rodney said while whisper-counting his money.

'Not if you're in County it ain't,' Rocco mumbled as the computer screen announced that night's shutdown.

Mazilli rang up a box of Pampers. 'Yeah, about three hours ago, I go to pick up Chickadee Willis to talk about that Ahab's thing? He got the best alibi in the world. Laying up in Christ the King with a slug in his thigh. Your buddy Erroll missed his femoral artery by a half inch.'

'That must hurt.' Rodney bared his teeth and wrinkled his nose in mock pain, recounting the wad now. 'How you fixed on Similac?'

'What do you need?' Mazilli asked.

'A case – two if you could spare it.'

Rodney's store was two blocks away, and he had a reciprocal deal with Mazilli: if either of them ran out of something, he could buy it in volume from the other at wholesale.

'I could spring for one.'

'How about Chore Boys?'

'They pipin' up heavy by you?' Mazilli winked to Rocco.

'Saturday night.' Rodney shrugged. 'Don't tell me *you* ain't sellin' any.'

'Let me check.' Mazilli walked back to his supply room, leaving Rodney with Rocco.

The ten-year-old came back in, out of breath from running, with a list of ten more three-digit combos.

'Too late, kiddo.'

The boy gave a little gasp of fear before he sprinted out of the store.

The guy who had already bought four cans of Bud came up to the counter for a fifth. Rocco shook his head, his mood turning sour with Rodney standing there. 'You ever hear of a six-pack?' The guy just looked at him. 'One trip, about ten cents cheaper a can. You should think about it, you know?'

The guy walked out of the store muttering something under his breath.

Rodney wheeled around to Rocco on his good leg. 'Let me ask you something. You go into a bar, you sit down, you say to the bartender, "Give me *six* beers"? Or you say, "Give me *one* beer"?'

Rocco didn't answer, his face growing hot.

'The man got no money to sit in a bar, pay bar prices, leave a tip an' shit. See that street out there? *That's* his bar. Sit on a nice stoop, watch the girls go by. An' *you* the bartender. See what I'm sayin'?'

'Fuck you.' Rocco was barely able to get the words out: A lecture about 'the people' from this freaking parasite?

'Gah-damn, don't you know nothin' about these niggers out here? How long you been a cop?' Rodney shook his head in disbelief as Mazilli returned from the supply room with two cases of baby formula and a carton of Chore Boy pads.

Rodney dropped some cash on the counter.

'Hey listen, before I forget,' Mazilli said. 'You know that new flying squad going around popping people?'

'Yeah, that cop Jo-Jo?' Rodney tucked his chin into his chest and looked at Mazilli over the rims of his nighttime sunglasses, hands resting on the cartons but not picking anything up yet.

'Yeah, Jo-Jo,' Mazilli said. 'He came in here about two days ago. He was asking about you – what you're up to, who you're running with. You best watch your ass.'

'Hey.' Rodney stepped back, snapping his hands down in disgust. 'I'm a motherfuckin' hard-workin' businessman. Fuck Jo-Jo and them.'

'I'm a *bith*nith mayn,' Rocco said.

Rodney didn't seem to hear this, and Mazilli threw Rocco a look to knock it off.

'Hey, you got to admit, Rodney, you got some fucking rep out there,' Mazilli said. 'You know, anytime anybody talks to anybody about anything, your name pops up.'

With the lottery shut down, the store had begun to empty out. Rocco took a quick sip of his drink, came out from behind his counter and sauntered over to Mazilli's side. He leaned on the front of the cold cuts case, positioning himself at the edge of Rodney's vision.

'All I'm saying, Rodney, is watch your ass.' Mazilli sounded sincere. 'I think they're looking to fuck you good. Don't use your phone for talking, you know what I mean?'

'My *phone*!' Rodney squawked. Then he said to the wall, 'Ain't this some shit?'

'Let me ask you something.' Mazilli's voice went low and confidential. 'What do *you* hear about Ahab's?'

'What Ahab's?' Rodney's voice went flat, his eyes darting between Mazilli's and Rocco's. 'What, you mean that boy that got shot up?'

'He used to work for you, no?' Mazilli lit a cigarette and squinted through his own smoke.

'Yeah, Darryl. He was OK.'

Rodney looked at Rocco, expecting him to start something. But Rocco knew he had to keep his mouth shut now: he'd had words with the man, established himself as not his friend.

'He was OK, hah?' Mazilli made a bologna sandwich for a street dealer without losing eye contact.

'Yeah,' Rodney said, looking antsy now.

'Yeah?' Mazilli stared, waiting, until Rodney started playing bongo riffs on the Chore Boy carton. 'We found like twenty-five hundred dollars on him.'

'Maybe they was wanting to take him off with the store receipts,' Rodney said, 'then they panicked.'

'You think so?' Mazilli said.

'You got me.'

'I got you?' Mazilli gave him a long, slow smile. Rodney made a full revolution, a distracted, limpy pirouette.

The store was quiet and still. For a moment they listened to the hum of the display cases.

'Can you work on it for me?' Mazilli asked gently.

Rodney looked away. 'Sure.'

''Cause I can talk to Jo-Jo for you.'

'That's cool.'

'Yeah?' Mazilli said.

'Yeah, awright. I'll get my people on it.'

'And I'll tell Jo-Jo you're doing a thing for me, get him to lay off.'

'Yeah, gimme a day or two. I got my people out there.' Rodney grabbed the boxes, backing away.

'Good,' Mazilli said. 'I'll see you in a day or two.'

'Uh-huh.'

'You need a hand with that?' Rocco threw Rodney a warm smile but made no effort to move as Rodney pushed through the door.

'Bye, now,' Rocco said under his breath.

A customer came up to the liquor side of the store, and Rocco returned to his register to sell him a bottle of Cold Duck.

Mazilli watched the customer leave, then looked over at Rocco. 'So what do you think?'

'I think he's a motherfucking dope-dealing shit-skin cocksucker.' Rocco grinned, still seething over Rodney's lecture.

Mazilli yawned. 'C'mon, what do you think?'

'You *know* he knows something. He was doing fucking Buddy Rich on that carton there, you know, when you asked if he knew that kid?'

'Fucking Rodney,' Mazilli snorted, coming from behind the counter and aping Rodney's gimpy pirouette.

'You wanna bring him in?' Rocco asked.

'Nah, it's easier to work on him out here.'

'Who the fuck is Jo-Jo?'

'Kronic. The guy used to be in motorcycles?'

'The guy's a thief, right?' Rocco knew Jo-Jo Kronic mainly from the papers. He had been acquitted on charges of extorting money from dope dealers five years before.

Mazilli shrugged. 'Yeah, but he was McGoorty's bodyguard for the campaign. The guy worked around the clock for free, plus he threw five large into the war chest. When McGoorty got in, he says, "What can I do for you, Jo-Jo?" The guy asks for his own flying squad. They go out, they don't answer to nobody but McGoorty. Do whatever the fuck they want – you know, street pops, raids, whatever.'

'Jesus Christ.'

'You know how many Narcotics squads they got out there?' Mazilli counted on his fingers. 'City, State, FBI, DEA, County, Housing –

nobody telling anybody nothing, everybody banging into each other, arresting each other's undercovers every time there's a raid. And now here comes Jo-Jo fucking Kronic into the soup, and you *know* what he's doing, right?'

'Going around making everybody pay up to stay in business.' Rocco drained his drink and poured another, this time without ice, past needing any.

'Jo-Jo's got a boat? If it had numbers on the side it could've won the battle of Midway. And his new house? He's half a mile down the road from Richard Nixon. And nobody can say shit, because he's McGoorty's man.'

'But he's going after Rodney?' Rocco said.

Mazilli made a face. 'Nah. I just made that up on the hoof. Rodney's gonna come in here three days from now and I'm gonna say, "Hear anything?" He's gonna say, "I'm working on it, I'm working on it." I'm gonna say, "Yeah? Me too." Fuck him. I'll just start dropping by his craps garage later in the week, throw his action off a little. He'll tell me something good.'

'Fucking prick. When you were in back? This guy buys his fifth can of Bud, I tell him to spring for a six-pack, you know, get with the program? Fucking Rodney starts giving me this speech about the people's street bar, how *I'm* the fucking bartender. Can you believe the balls on him?'

'Yeah, well, he's kind of right.'

'Fuck you too,' Rocco said, anger coming into his face again. 'That's the problem with these people, they don't plan ahead.'

'Is that the problem?' Mazilli hiked an eyebrow.

'"He's kind of right,"' Rocco muttered, feeling as if he'd just flunked a wisdom test.

The ten-year-old came into the store for the third time, walking slowly now, heading for Mazilli's counter.

'Kools,' he said, spilling a dollar and change on the counter. The boy's lip was swollen and bloody. Rocco assumed that someone had cracked him good for coming home without the lottery tickets.

Rocco felt a sharp twinge of sympathy, imagined walking the boy home and tuning up whatever prick did the deed, but when their eyes met, he saw in the boy a look of pure hatred, as if it was Rocco's fault that he'd been smacked. Suddenly Rocco was glad to live in New York, glad to be married and have his own kid, his own family way out of town. It was time to chuck this life, with its Jo-Jos and Rodneys, its bloody burning children and walking-dead parents, just kick dirt over the whole show, like a cat burying its shit. Retirement. It was just a word, not a medical condition. But where the fuck was Sean Touhey?

The Bud man came up to buy his sixth can, glaring at Rocco too, daring him to say something, but Rocco pointedly avoided his eyes until he rang up the sale.

'You have a nice night now,' Rocco said.

The guy stood there wanting to say something, looking hot, but he made it all the way to the screen door before he turned back and started barking.

'I buy a motherfuckin' six-pack, sit out there, how many goddamn beers you think *I'm* gonna have, and how many beers you think I'm gonna get *mooched* on, stupid.' The guy stalked out under the streetlights.

'When you're right, you're right,' Rocco said to the screen door. He gulped down his drink and tossed the cup, then cracked the register and paid himself forty-three dollars, one for each year of his life.

'I'm out of here,' he announced to Mazilli.

'C'mon, another half hour,' Mazilli whined, glancing at his wrist-watch.

'Hey, get your pal *Rod*ney to cover.'

'I don't believe this.' Mazilli looked both amused and annoyed as Rocco walked out into the night, bumping into one of the displaced dealers, all of whom were strolling back to where the cops had stood until ten minutes before.

Rocco fully intended to make it straight home to Patty from Mazilli's store, but at the approach to the Holland Tunnel he pulled over and stopped at a bar in a gentrified section of Jersey City, telling himself that he was waiting for the toll-booth lines to thin out.

The bar had a brand-new antique look, oak and brass and hanging plants, with nineteenth-century advertisements for foot powders and neuralgia cures framed on the walls.

Rocco weaved his way through a flush-faced gaggle of young stock-broker types hoisting oversize cans of Foster Lager and booing Darryl Strawberry on the wall-mounted television. He took a seat at the bar and ordered a Cape Codder, deciding that since he was paying for it, this was his first real drink of the night. Next to him sat a woman who looked about Patty's age, and Rocco furtively studied her reflection in the bar mirror as he took the first tart sip of his drink.

She was tall and thin, nice-looking, and she wore a derby, dungarees and a satin-backed brocade vest. Reflexively Rocco felt obliged to imagine

picking her up, but he had never in the last twenty-five years figured out
how to start up a conversation with a woman at a bar that didn't sound
moronic. She abruptly solved that one for him by simply catching his eye
in the mirror, smiling and saying 'Hi,' something he had never thought
of trying in a quarter century of racking his brains in the semidarkness.

Unnerved, Rocco talked directly into the mirror. 'Good, and you?'

'I've been better.' She turned to him now, some kind of invitation in
the casual candidness of her remark.

'Oh yeah?' Rocco forced himself to face her.

'Rough night in Jericho,' she said, and Rocco was drawn to the offbeat
tone of her line. He stole a peek at her hand on the bar, the graceful arches
of her bent fingers, the nibbled edges of her nails. He hadn't so much as
kissed another woman since that day he had forced his way into Patty's
apartment looking for a dead baby.

She followed his eyes to her hand, watched it with him for a moment,
then let it slide an inch or two in his direction.

'Yup.' Rocco hissed at his drink through bared teeth. Feeling the need
to slow this down, he rose from the bar. 'Excuse me a second.'

Weaving his way through the rowdy young brokers, who were now
bellowing the 'Jetsons' theme song in each other's faces, Rocco made his
way to a phone and dialed home. He hung up as soon as he heard Patty
say hello.

What would he say to her? That he was coming home? She knew that.
Stop me before I fuck somebody? That really wasn't a possibility; he could
barely work up the inspiration to flirt.

Rocco stood before the phone, his hand on the hung receiver, trying
to get his bearings, figure out how to get fed right now without hurting
himself. Looking back through the drunken brokers to the bar, he saw
that the girl was watching him through the mirror. Blindly he started to
dial again.

Since the Ahab's shooting the previous night, the urge to call Sean
Touhey had become a nearly chemical impulse. It was just like a craving
for alcohol or sugar: whenever he had felt anxious or depressed in the
last few days, he would unthinkingly reach for the phone. And it didn't
seem to make a difference whether anyone picked up or not. He was
more addicted to the gesture, to the ritual, than to anything involving
true contact.

The actor answered on the first ring, and Rocco was so startled to get
a voice on the line that he barked, 'Who's this.' Touhey said 'Sean!' as if
he had been caught at something.

'Sean! Hi, sorry, this is Rocco, man.' Rocco looked at his watch: almost midnight.

'Rocco.' Touhey's voice was flat and queasy.

'Yeah, hi – how you doing? You coming in?' Rocco said impulsively, deciding to play it as if he was still sitting at his desk in the Homicide office. He cupped the mouthpiece to muffle the singing by the bar.

'Coming in?' the actor repeated weakly.

'Yeah.' Rocco's face was radiant with shame. 'I got a murderer for you. He's right in the next room. The kid who did the job you saw. Remember? He's right here.' Rocco could hear the actor breathing, sense his feeling of being cornered, but he plowed ahead. 'Sean, listen. I'll come pick you up. I could be there in half an hour, OK? You'll be ready for me? 'Cause the guy's right here, you know?' Rocco put a hand to his forehead and it came away damp. He saw the girl at the bar talking to another guy about half Rocco's age, giving him the same inviting smile.

'Rocco . . .' Touhey spoke his name as if something significant would follow, but then he exhaled heavily and said, 'Hang on.'

Rocco listened to the muffled rustling of a smothered receiver before a husky-voiced woman came on the line.

'Hi, Rocco. This is Jackie, remember me?'

'Hey Jackie, how are you? So, what do you guys got there, like a combination apartment-office?' Rocco heard himself babbling. 'I mean, I was like amazed anybody answered the phone, you know? I didn't realize how late it was.'

'Yeah, it's an apartment,' she answered patiently.

'I mean, no offense, it's none of my business. I was just surprised because – '

'Listen, Rocco,' she cut him off, 'I have to tell you something. Sean's decided to shelve the police movie for now.'

Rocco experienced a sizzling buzz of disappointment.

'How come?' He scanned the bar – the girl was gone.

'Well, something came up.'

'Is it something I did?' He tried for a jokey, self-mocking tone but felt disgusted by his own question.

'No, no,' Jackie said, 'you're great, you're great. It's just that the financing came through for another project that's been very close to Sean's heart for six years, and out of the blue it came together and, you know, when the light turns green, you go.'

'Six years.' Rocco took a pen out of the inside of his sport jacket and drew a six on the side of the phone enclosure, then a line of sixes. He felt dead calm now.

'It's about the earth.'

'The earth. What do you mean, the planet?'

'You know, about pollution.'

'Great.'

'It's Sean's passion.'

A recorded voice asked for a quarter. Rocco fed in all his change without counting it.

'Rocco, could you wait a minute? Wait.' There was more muzzled rustling, and when Jackie came back on, her voice was quieter, more personal. 'Sean just left the room, so let me be up front with you while I can, OK?'

'Shoot,' Rocco said.

'Rocco, Sean's A.A. He's been sober for five years.'

'Yeah?' He waited for the punch line.

'What the hell did you get him so wasted for?'

Rocco palmed his forehead. 'Oh, Christ.'

'Rocco, he's spent the last two days going to meetings – and I'm talking five a *day*. He's scared to death. You go on a bender after all those years, it's like all that sober time never was. Do you know what I'm saying?'

'Why didn't he say something?'

'Well, I guess you showed him some heavy stuff and, I dunno, he didn't want – he wanted you to think – you understand, you're a guy.'

'Listen, let me talk to him.'

'He left.'

'He *left*? I was just talking to him. He just gave you the phone and left in the middle of a conversation?'

'Rocco, he can't do you, he can't be *around* you.'

'This is not right.'

'I know, I know.'

'This is not . . . A guy should open his mouth and say stuff at the *time*, you know? Say, "Hey, I'm in A.A.," something . . . this is not my fault. This is *bullshit*.' Rocco didn't care about the movie right now. He was momentarily overwhelmed by the feeling that he had fallen into a trap laid by the actor's weakness of character.

'I know, I know.' She sighed.

Rocco held the receiver to his chest for a moment, feeling a mixture of panic and relief, telling himself this was all for the better, that he somehow deserved this for betraying his own integrity and becoming a celebrity kiss-ass.

'I know, Rocco,' Jackie said again.

'So it's blown, right? And the guy can't even tell me face-to-face on the phone.' Rocco rubbed his eye sockets: Let it go, let it go.

'I'm really sorry.'

Rocco searched his brain for a farewell witticism, something to show her that he was bigger than this minor disappointment, but then out of his mouth it came: 'How about the earth movie?'

'What about it?'

Rocco touched his forehead to the phone, studied his nails. 'You think maybe there's something for me there? I don't know, I don't mean necessarily an *actor* thing, but you know, maybe you need somebody to work security or something?'

'Rocco . . .'

He felt his cheeks rise into his eyes.

'I'm kidding there, Jackie.' He voice was hollow with mortification. 'I'm kidding, I'm kidding.'

15

Strike woke up at noon, shaking off the last fragments of a dream about Papi – Papi's car sprouting wings and taking off like an airplane across the Hudson River – and although he almost never picked up a newspaper, on his way to the benches Strike bought the fat Sunday edition of the *Dempsy Advocate* to see if there was a story about what he had seen the night before.

He didn't have to look far. Even from across the candy store he could read the headline off the stack: TUNNEL OF DEATH. Picking up the paper, he saw the grainy black-and-white photo that dominated the front page. Papi in his car, slumped down, chin into chest, eyes glazed, wearing a skirt of blood from the nicked artery that had finally drained him. He had died inside the Holland Tunnel, slamming into the wall right at the state line and shutting down the whole New York-bound tube for hours.

The paper also reported that there was a big debate about whose investigation it was, New York's or Hudson County's, but Papi had driven far enough away that Dempsy wasn't even mentioned in the article.

At least two people were dead now, but a few minutes later Strike crouched on his customary perch, the front section of the paper folded and quartered on his knees. Papi's frosted and melancholy gaze seemed to be assessing his own jittery eyes and mouth, watching him jump and twist every time a car alarm went off or someone shouted or laughed too abruptly. Strike heard in all the charged noises around him the coming of Buddha Hat.

The afternoon passed uneventfully, but with the beginning of the dinner hour, business around the benches became more intense. The crew picked up on Strike's paranoia, everybody acting more edgy than usual, as if anticipating that something bad was about to happen. And then Horace began arguing with a white guy on the sidewalk, both of them shooting out their arms and yelling. Horace's face became choked with rage. He cut the guy off and walked over to Strike, the veins dancing in his temples.

'This motherfucker say he gave a hundred dollars to a guy around the corner for a clip, says the guy say to come around get the dope from *me*. *What* motherfuckin' guy? They ain't no guy. He running a *game*.' Although school was out for the summer, Horace held a book bag loosely by the straps, the bulk of it trailing over his shoes, Strike thinking, The kid doesn't even show up for class during the school year, what the fuck's he doing with books today?

Strike leaned sideways to see past Horace. The white guy stood on the sidewalk, pacing nervously, not willing to walk inside the projects and risk getting beat.

Strike held Horace by the arm to keep him in place and turned to Futon, who was holding his trick Gummi Bear jar again. 'Go over ask him what guy, what he looks like.'

Futon strolled out to the street as Strike turned to Horace and said, 'You best relax, my man, or somebody's gonna get hurt.'

Looking over Horace's shoulder, Strike saw Tyrone come slowly down the path from 8 Weehawken. Tyrone took his seat on a slump of chain between two metal poles bordering the grass. Strike felt a little kick in his chest but refused to acknowledge the boy. It was too soon.

Futon came back from the sidewalk. 'He say it was a tall skinny guy with a red shirt and scars coming up on his neck.'

'Stitch,' Strike said, more irritated than angry.

Horace snapped his hand out of Strike's grip and stalked off to hunt Stitch down, holding his book bag like a weapon. Strike wanted to call Horace back but his nerves had drained him of all resolve, leaving only an exhausted disgust for himself and all the people around him. He stole a peek at Tyrone and almost barked with surprise when he saw the kid rolling a bottle of vanilla Yoo-Hoo between his palms.

'What do I tell this guy?' Futon popped a Gummi Bear in his mouth.

'What guy?' Strike was momentarily lost. 'Tell him he got beat.'

Futon shifted his focus to someone approaching behind Strike, his mouth opening a little. Strike read Buddha Hat in Futon's eyes, wondering with a dazed lucidity if Rodney was dead too now, or if Champ had said, 'Do Strike first.' The white guy on the sidewalk saw whoever was coming too, and bolted.

Futon saluted and a voice boomed, 'You raisin' up on me?'

'Yo Andre, man, no *way*.' Futon shook his head.

Overwhelmed with relief, Strike couldn't turn to look. He felt a hand on his head and tasted his own adrenaline, like licked metal.

'You OK?' Andre asked.

'Uh-huh.' Strike ran the heel of his hand across his brow, then forced himself to twist around and make fleeting eye contact with Andre the Giant. Bald and goateed, almost as tall as Big Chief, Andre sported a gold tooth, an earring and the expansive gut of a man who liked his desserts.

'Yeah? How's business?' Andre smirked down at Strike and then casually took the Gummi Bear jar from Futon.

'Business is good,' Strike said distantly, reading Andre's T-shirt. The outline of a police shield framed the words 'Centurion Society,' and a black man and a black woman, both in uniform, stood on either side of the emblem.

Andre unscrewed the false bottom of Futon's jar. It was empty, and Futon leaped into the air with glee, haw-hawing and pointing at him. Andre gave Futon a long look, appearing to take inventory from head to toe: nice smile, clear eye, good presence, what a waste.

'Get over here,' he snapped at Futon, sounding more like a tough uncle than a cop. Leaning across the back of the bench, Andre searched through Futon's clothes.

'You know that boy Tariq Wilkins?' Andre said to Futon and Strike. 'He just got a scholarship offer from Saint Peter's for basketball.'

'A scholarship?' Futon squawked. 'That nigger can't play no ball.'

'Yeah, and Daviel Cross? He just got his GED.'

'Daviel's a dummy.' Futon unzipped his jacket for Andre to take a peek.

'Yeah? Compared to *who*? You got *your* GED?'

'I'm still in school.'

'Yeah, I see that.' Andre ran his hands up Futon's socks. 'An' how 'bout *you*, mastermind?'

'I'm working on it,' Strike said stiffly.

Horace came stomping back around the corner with his book bag, got uh-oh eyes when he saw Andre, did an about-face and disappeared behind a building. Strike saw Andre read it, then stow it away for later.

He also saw Andre spot Tyrone sitting on the chain, saw him take note of the vanilla Yoo-Hoo. 'What's up, little man?' Andre called out, but his greeting was flat and distracted, no humor in it at all. Tyrone shrugged, eyes on the ground, and Strike realized that the rumors about Tyrone's mother being tight with Andre were true, and that there would be hell to pay for that bottle of Yoo-Hoo.

Just then the Fury rolled up, a weekend overtime special, a surprise party rocking to a stop opposite the benches. Big Chief rose from the car and growled in his gravel-bottom bass, 'Fucking up my timing there, Andre.'

'Come back in half a hour.' Andre flashed teeth through his goatee. 'These knuckleheads ain't gonna remember.'

Thumper and Smurf zipped up behind Andre, closing the pincers, and soon the bench was a milling traffic jam of Housing and city knockos, clockers and residents, backpedaling customers and scooting children. Strike ignored the commotion. He was busy making a mental list of all the people in his life who were causing him grief right now.

Thumper put his hand down the back of Strike's pants, making him jump. 'You do Kingpin here, Andre?'

'Naw, I got to check him out yet.'

Thumper wrapped a forearm almost affectionately around Strike's throat. 'You mind if I do it? I *loves* doing Strike.'

Strike saw Andre's eyes go back to Tyrone. 'Yeah,' Andre muttered, 'I'll do him next time.'

As Thumper ran his hands up Strike's legs, Andre started in the direction of his surveillance roost, then wheeled around. 'Little man,' he called, holding out his hand for Tyrone to join him.

Tyrone shot Strike a fleeting look of embarrassed apology as he groaned upright and walked off under Andre's arm.

'Dicky check,' Thumper sang out, and when Strike, lost in fretful thought, didn't respond quickly enough, Thumper took the liberty of unbuttoning Strike's pants himself.

Strike squatted in front of the safe hidden under the sink and counted his money. He was in the suffocatingly greasy kitchen of an old shotgun flat, a safe house, this one owned by an elderly couple with a retarded middle-aged son, the last white people in an all-black neighborhood. Almost invisible even when they were here, the owners were out now, and Strike had the entire place to himself.

Still feeling jumpy and unhinged, Strike had walked away from the benches as soon as the crowd of knockos had cleared out. He had driven aimlessly through the deserted Sunday streets of downtown Dempsy for a while before deciding to make the rounds of his safes. He didn't need to visit his money – he knew to within a hundred dollars how much he had stashed across town – but he wanted to reassure himself that he had the means if not the resolve to make a new life for himself.

Now Strike flicked a roach off his jeans with a fistful of twenties, thinking, Seven thousand here, fifteen thousand in the other two safes, equals a lot of miles and a lot of time away from all this business.

But the numbers gave him small pleasure: that kid was tugging at him again. He never should have gotten him a haircut, and he could just imagine the grilling Tyrone's mother must have given him, could see her running to Andre, saying, 'Somebody out there gave your son a *hair*cut.' When talking to Andre, a lot of the women in Roosevelt referred to their kids as 'your son' or 'your daughter,' half joking, half trying to get him to take a proprietary interest. But Iris already had Andre's attention, and the Yoo-Hoo told Andre all he needed to know.

Strike knew Andre's style with young kids and figured Tyrone was probably up in the surveillance apartment right now, Andre letting him scope out the benches with his binoculars or fool with the cement-filled barbells, just roam around free-form for a few minutes, and then *wham*, Andre would suddenly pull the kid close and say, 'See, now he's not talking to you. He got you all messed up wondering how come he don't like you no more. But I'm gonna tell you something, Tyrone. Maybe not today, maybe not tomorrow, but someday soon he's gonna come up to you and say, "Take this package over to this man's house" or "Follow that nasty-looking guy over there" or "Take this bag upstairs and keep it for me," and you're gonna jump like a puppy and do anything he wants just so he keeps talking to you, treat you nice again.' The kid would stare at his feet for a long minute and then Andre would say, 'Just watch yourself, 'cause I'd hate for you to be wearing my bracelets someday.' He'd put the finishing touch on it by wrapping the boy in a bear hug and saying, ''Cause you my special man. You know that, right?'

Strike knew all about that speech. It was exactly the one Andre had given to him, complete with hug, when Strike's mother had gone to Andre four years ago, after some long-gone local crew chief had taken Strike out for *his* haircut. That was two years before he'd ever heard of Rodney Little, and Strike would never forget that day – the visit to Andre's old basement office, the mixed feelings of hunger and contempt he'd felt for Andre and his transparent play, the whole thing collapsing into almost unbearable jealousy when Andre had walked him out of his office and they had passed another kid standing at the door, waiting for *his* man-to-man talk.

The heat in the kitchen and the smell of garbage became intolerable and Strike rose to his feet. He turned and was frozen in his tracks by the sight of the retarded son, a rubber-faced man with a wet lower lip who stood in the kitchen doorway, rocking a little, smiling tentatively, his fingertips playing delicately in front of his chest. Strike had no idea how to handle this – he had never been alone with him, had never seen him without his parents. Looking skittish about being alone with Strike too, the retarded man abruptly announced, 'My daddy was a train driver. He once took me on it.'

Spooked by the mystery of this kind of affliction, Strike experienced a welling sensation in his chest. Impulsively he took out his money roll, peeled off a five, handed it to the man and said, 'Here.' Gently pushing him back into the living room, Strike moved past him quickly, walked through the apartment and cut out for the benches.

There was nowhere else to go.

Later, just as Strike expected, Andre came back. Wearing his game face now, Andre walked slowly and kept his eyes on Strike's crew. He was trying to make somebody nervous enough to bolt.

Strike sat quietly on his perch, watching the play develop. Peanut pointed at Andre and chanted 'Five-oh! Five-oh! Five-oh!' as if it was OK to be obvious, since Andre was being obvious too. Grinning, Futon held out his phony jar, and Horace danced from foot to foot, his book bag swinging low, brushing his sneaker laces. Then Strike saw Andre give Horace the thousand-yard stare, and Horace began to lose it as the giant knocko came straight at him. When Andre was ten feet from a reach-out, Horace raced into the street, leaving his book bag on the ground.

Andre sat down on the bench next to Strike's sneakers, put the book bag in his lap and sighed. 'Now where you think he's running to?'

Strike shrugged.

Andre palmed his face as if he hadn't slept for days, which was possible, since he worked city Narcotics five nights a week in addition to his full-time one-man Roosevelt tour.

A guy in a fatigue jacket and red sneakers walked up to the bench, looked from Andre to Peanut to Andre to Futon, sensing something was wrong but not getting it yet. 'Where the bottles at?'

Andre blinked at him, amazed. 'You stupid or something?'

The guy nodded as if in agreement and then trotted off.

'Gah-*damn*.' Andre shook his head, then opened the book bag on his lap. 'What we got here?' He took out an English book, a math book, a steak knife and a loose-leaf binder. Andre flipped open the binder and Strike saw Horace's childish writing from the just-finished school term: homework assignments, spelling tests, compositions. Nothing looked completed.

And then from the bottom of the bag came two clips – two ten-bottle rounds of powder coke wrapped with rubber bands.

Strike blew air, more angry that Horace was holding than that he got caught. Futon and Peanut started to walk.

Andre looked around, bouncing the clips in his hand. Strike saw Horace standing on the street corner a block away, trying to see what was happening.

'OK.' Andre faced forward but Strike knew the words were meant for him. 'I'm gonna write up a warrant on him tonight. You tell him I want for him to turn hisself in. If he don't – '

'Aw, c'mon Andre.' Strike tried for a reasonable tone. 'Just th'ow the shit down the sewer.'

'If he *don't* turn hisself in come two o'clock next Friday, I'm coming to lock him up. You know why two o'clock Friday? 'Cause that's when the Juvenile Court shuts down for the weekend. That means the boy goes to the Youth House until Monday morning. And he's gonna be a young first-time boy in that place with a weekend's worth of some bad kids. Can you remember all that?'

Strike snorted dryly. 'Everybody likes Andre 'cause Andre for the *people.*'

Strike knew immediately that he had stepped over the line. Andre rose. He seemed to be resisting an impulse to backhand Strike off the bench. When he spoke there was no play in his voice.

'Get up.'

Strike sighed, stood away from the bench and raised his arms elbows high, like bat wings.

But Andre wasn't interested in a frisk. 'How's about I lock *you* up instead? And *you* ain't going to no Youth House. You old enough for County.'

'It ain't *my* book bag.' Strike wasn't too alarmed. Andre had never really come down on him before.

'Yeah? Alls I know is, when I got to this bench you sittin' here with this bag by your feet. I got enough here for possession with intent. That's three sixty-four mandatory, and even if they make it simple possession, you *still* gettin' ninety days in, and I'm gonna make some calls to the inside, make sure that's gonna be ninety days the *hard* way. Are you ready for that?'

Strike looked away. 'I ain't doin' no ninety days. That ain't my dope.'

'It is if I say it is.'

'It ain't mine.'

Looking off at a brick wall, Strike could feel Andre's hot stare. After a long thirty seconds Strike broke the silence. 'It ain't mine,' he said again with mournful insistence.

Andre muttered 'Shit,' and suddenly Strike's wrists were behind him, steel cuffs biting into his skin. Futon and Peanut strolled out of sight, but several people on the sidewalk meandered over. A lady said 'Good!' real loud, and a man said 'About time.' Another lady let loose with a singsong 'Oooo.'

Andre grabbed a fistful of shirt between Strike's shoulder blades and marched him through the projects, hissing in his ear, 'How's that taste? That taste good?'

Strike walked with a light tripping tread, shocked and embarrassed, his face filling with blood as if the cuffs were on his neck instead of his wrists.

'That ain't my dope,' he repeated, but he said it numbly now.

Andre walked him back to the building that housed the surveillance apartment, a small crowd following. Strike heard his name over and over, heard laughter, and again that hateful 'Oooo.' Andre pushed him into the lobby, then into the stairwell, but instead of heading up to the apartment, Andre took him down to the basement.

Strike tried to concentrate over the pain of the cuffs. 'Where you goin'?'

Andre didn't speak, pushing Strike ahead into the dank windowless underground, just the two of them now, walking right past Andre's old office. He steered Strike over to a steel door, then looked for a key on the ring hanging off his hip.

'What you doin', Andre?'

Andre opened the door and shoved Strike into a long, narrow, low-ceilinged space, a cement corridor lined with storage cubicles and littered with broken bikes, discarded stoves, fifty-pound bags of rock salt. The hot stench of urine made Strike's eyelids flutter.

'Hey, what you *doin'*, Andre?' He wasn't really scared yet – people had seen them go down here together, there were witnesses. But Strike flashed on that lady who said 'Good,' and a wave of self-pity washed over him. He didn't deserve that kind of disrespect. He had never pushed dope on anybody in his life, had never gone door-to-door with it. They all came to him.

'You see this room?' An overhead pipe grazed Andre's head as he circled Strike. 'What you think of this room?'

Strike didn't believe Andre would hit him, but just in case he tried to back up against a storage fence. Andre put a hand on his shoulder to keep him planted.

'What you think of this room?' Andre said again, his taunting voice echoing off the cement walls.

'I don't like it.'

'Yeah, *I* do, though.'

'Can you loosen the cuffs?' Strike bared his teeth, unable to mask his discomfort.

'Yeah, I like this room fine.' Andre walked behind him. 'You know what I want to do? I want to clear all this out, all this garbage, then I'm gonna line this corridor with mattresses. What do you think of that?'

'These cuffs are *tight*, Andre. They the wrong size.'

'You know why? 'Cause I see the kids outside, they always jumping on throwed-out mattresses, or they always rolling down the hill – you know, doing flips an' leaps an' shit? And there's all that *glass* out there, rusty shit, but they just, they don't care. Because you know when you a kid that age, you don't have no *fear* in you.' Andre put a big hand on the back of Strike's neck. 'But what I wanna do is line this with mattresses in here where it's safe, and like maybe get free weights set up in one of these storage bins, start like a *gym* club down here. Teach some tumbling, maybe get somebody who knows his shit come in here, you know, get 'em really *young* and do something *pos*itive with them.' Andre started squeezing Strike's shoulder muscles as if loosening him up before a prize-fight. 'Don't that sound good?'

'Yeah, it does.' Strike coughed, not listening to any of it, brooding again on the way people treated him like a criminal. Shit, at least he *earned* his money.

'You know, 'cause like I say, kids, when they're young? They don't know enough to be afraid, and that could be like a good thing or a bad thing depending on what you're doing with them. You agree with that?' Andre moved in front of him, his breath smelling like mint, Strike reflexively jackknifing a little to guard against a punch.

'Uh-huh.'

'But I got me a problem.' Andre smoothed the top of Strike's head, Strike staring at the two black police officers on Andre's T-shirt. 'Housing don't have no money for my gym club.'

'Uh-huh.' Strike's face felt like it was starting to swell, as if from an allergic reaction to the piss stink.

'So I got to raise the money on my own, you know what I'm sayin'?'

'Uh-huh.'

'I need me a sponsor.'

'Uh-huh.' Strike kept his voice low, Andre beginning to scare him a little more now.

'I need me a *ben*efactor.'

'I hear you.'

'You hear me?' Andre strolled behind Strike again. 'That's good, 'cause I could lock you up. Shit, I could even mess you up first, say you tried to fight me, you know what I'm sayin'? But I know Rodney'd just put someone in your place out there and the goddamn beat would just go on and on.'

'Uh-huh.'

''Cause you ain't nothin'. You just holding down a spot out there. You know that, right?'

'Right.'

'You just one in a long line of parasites out there, right?'

'Right.'

'So maybe instead I should just try to get some of that money recirculating – you know, like coming back into the community. You know what I'm sayin'?'

'I hear that.'

'So maybe instead of me and you going off to County, we could maybe go off shopping. How's that sound?'

'Good.'

''Cause the kids'll be real grateful.'

'Yeah, OK.'

For a long and close minute Andre stood silently, his chest in Strike's face, Strike tense and alert, looking at the ground, realizing that he'd heard little of what Andre had been saying – something about 'community' and 'positive.'

'Yeah, an' one thing.' Andre reached behind Strike as if to unlock the cuffs, but instead jerked Strike's arms straight up behind him, the pain so sharp and unyielding that Strike made a bleating noise, saw zips of light behind his eyelids.

'One last thing.' Andre embraced Strike in a loose bear hug, his big cracked lips right in Strike's ear. 'I ever see you so much as make *eye* contact with that boy Tyrone? I'm gonna personally fuck you up so bad you gonna *wish* I just throwed you in jail.'

Strike trembled from his legs to his lips, barely able to whisper, 'Please . . .'

16

Rocco sat in the windowless Homicide office, staring at the picture of Papi on the front page of the *Dempsy Advocate.*

'Do you realize what this guy had to do to die in the tunnel?' he said to Mazilli. 'He went *in* there all shot up, right? That means he had to pay his toll. He had to wait on line, hand over three dollars, get the green light. Unbelievable.'

'Maybe he went through the exact-change lane.' Mazilli was watching an old Richard Widmark movie on television.

'No, I mean there he is covered with blood, handing a five-dollar bill to some fucking boingo in a booth, waiting for his two dollars change, right?'

'The guy was in shock.' Mazilli yawned and tilted his chair back at a 45-degree angle.

'Yeah? Another thing, they found two kilos of coke in the car. Who the fuck brings coke *from* New Jersey *to* New York, right? It's like bringing clap to Saigon.' Rocco watched as Richard Widmark put on a bulletproof vest.

'How do you know the guy was starting out from New Jersey?' Mazilli said. 'Maybe he was making a run from down south. Flew right up the corridor from Georgia or Florida, right onto the turnpike and into the tunnel.'

'Well, he stopped somewheres.' Rocco flopped the paper on his desk. 'It's like a math problem. Juan got whacked at point X, he drove away losing blood at the rate of a pint every ninety seconds. He was driving forty-five miles an hour and he bought the farm two miles inside the tunnel.' Rocco's phone rang and he scooped up the receiver. 'So for ten points, what shit-skin in what New Jersey town did Juan? Piece of cake . . . Hello, Homicide.'

'It's not *my* problem.' Mazilli strolled out of the room. 'Not my table, not my problem.'

'Yeah, hi there, my name's Bill Walker.' The voice sounded black to Rocco's ear. 'I'm a retired detective out of Newark P.D.? And ah, I got a bit of a situation here.'

'Shoot.' Rocco yawned into the side of his fist.

'I'm at the First Baptist Church on Lexington and Royce? And ah, I got a young man here, he says he shot somebody last week.'

Rocco turned down the volume on the TV. 'Oh yeah? Where at?' Rocco figured the shooter was listening, because the detective was picking his words carefully.

'At that restaurant.' The detective put his hand over the receiver for a second and asked, on his end, 'Ahab's?' Then, to Rocco: 'Ahab's. On Friday night.'

'Does he know the name of the victim?'

He heard the detective say to the shooter, 'You know the boy's name?' There was a silence, then back on line: 'No, he don't know.'

Rocco pulled over a pad. 'OK. You know where we are?'

'Well, I'll tell you, the boy is here with the reverend. He gave up the gun to the reverend, and the reverend would prefer you come by here.'

'Hey, no problem. I'll be there in a half hour.'

'Half hour?' The detective sounded unhappy.

'No later, I promise.'

Rocco hung up. Lexington and Royce: he was surprised, because that section of town, known as Bellevue, was overwhelmingly white, and he didn't think there was enough of a black presence to support its own church, unless it drew its congregation from other neighborhoods or even other towns, some of the well-to-do blacks from Newark, Jersey City and the Oranges going to church in Bellevue for the change of scenery. Which probably explained the retired detective who made the call: Rocco assumed that the cop was a member of the congregation, and the reverend must have asked him in to handle the situation. And now, Rocco thought, the poor guy's Sunday afternoon was blown to hell.

'You want to pick up the Ahab's shooter?' Rocco called across the desks to Mazilli. As he got to his feet he was overwhelmed by a full-blown flashback of his conversation with Touhey and Jackie the night before. Experiencing a momentary fatigue – half hangover, half shame – he plopped back down at his desk and didn't get up again until he had found the actor's business card and tossed it in the trash.

The church was an enormous peaked chalet with white stucco walls, blond wood pews and a whitewashed wooden cross thrust out above the congregation like a figurehead on a ship's prow. High over the pulpit, twenty feet up on the pristine front wall, 'Christ Is the Answer' was scripted with such delicate luminosity that the words seemed to hover there, weightless and free.

The sanctuary was empty save for the detective, the reverend and the shooter, who were clumped together in the front row, waiting. Rocco hadn't been in a black church since an elderly woman had died of a heart attack during a storefront service fifteen years before, and that place had been cramped, sweaty and hysterical. This time he felt as if he had walked into the center of a cloud.

The reverend and the detective were both overweight and middle-aged. Between them sat a kid in his late teens or early twenties, bony and sad, scrunched up and staring at the floor, his shoulders pulled forward as if he was being crushed by the bodies on either side of him.

'Hiya. Rocco Klein, prosecutor's office.' Rocco held his hand out to the detective. Mazilli trailed behind, hands in his pockets, looking around the place.

'Bill Walker.' The detective, looking a little dressy for church, wore a three-piece cream suit, cream tie and cream chest hankie, and his iron-gray mustache and sideburns were clipped with topiary precision. 'And this is the Reverend George Posse.'

The reverend, a dumpy, dark-skinned man, rose from the bench in a cautious crouch, a clipped bow tie hanging off one side of his open shirt collar. He remained in his crouch throughout the introductions, then settled back down, his arm protectively behind the shooter's head, his mouth twisting with unspoken anxieties.

Rocco turned to the shooter, who sat slouched in the pew, the side of his face pushed up into his eye by the heel of his hand. He wore a blue crewneck sweater, the collar bulging slightly over the knot of his tie, and a cheap but pressed pair of gray slacks.

'How ya doin'?' Rocco said cheerfully.

The kid looked at him with one eye but otherwise remained immobile on the bench, his legs crossed, a shiny patch of shin visible above a collapsed sock.

'This is Victor Dunham.' The reverend squeezed the kid's shoulder. 'He's in my congregation.'

'Good.' Rocco nodded, dancing on tiptoes, beaming down at the kid as if he had just won first prize but was too shy to accept.

Ready to start things rolling, Rocco opened his mouth to speak but then stopped, distracted by Victor's thick eyebrows. He looked over at Mazilli, then gave the kid a closer look. 'Don't I know you?'

'Victor's a good individual.' The reverend's voice was husky and pained, but Rocco noticed that the detective's face stayed neutral.

'Great.' Rocco came back to himself, flashed a smile and extended his hand for Victor to rise, eager to get him out of there and away from the reverend before the guy started talking about civil rights and lawyers and screwing up what should be a quick, simple confession.

As Victor got to his feet, the detective handed over a wedge of tinfoil. At first Rocco thought the guy was passing him a slice of leftover cake for some reason, but the package was too heavy, its heft that of a handgun.

The reverend moved between Rocco and Victor, as if to shield him from arrest. 'What happens now?'

Rocco took a breath. 'Well, if he *did* do this, he's gonna have to, you know, I'm sure he had a reason and, ah, that's what I'd like to talk to him about.'

Victor dropped down to the edge of the pew, then slid back into a comma of despair, his thick eyebrows arched over barely open lids.

'*Then* what?' said the reverend, sounding more concerned than hostile.

Mazilli muttered something and did a little stroll.

Rocco looked to the detective for help but he just nodded for Rocco to keep stroking the reverend. At least the guy was on Rocco's side; he hadn't mentioned lawyers either.

'Can I talk to you in private?' Rocco put a hand on the reverend's arm and led him in a slow walk around the church.

'Look, I'll tell you anything you want to know, but I don't want the kid to panic,' Rocco said quietly. 'He's got to be charged with unlawful possession for the gun, that's for starters, but what *my* hunch is, just from talking a little to Detective Walker on the phone, is that he's probably who we're looking for on the homicide and, ah, I don't want to go into all of this in front of *him* because he probably doesn't realize that in a few hours he's got to go to County, you know, the jail, and if it's a murder charge the bail's gonna be high, so he's probably gonna be in there for a while, and I don't want him thinking about that right now and all of a sudden jumping up and trying to run out of here.'

Rocco took a fast breath, wanting to keep talking, keep the reverend off balance and prevent him from asking questions. 'Look, obviously he's been raised to know right from wrong, his conscience is bothering him, he must have been going through *hell* these last few days, so if you don't mind, let me take him to my office and get to the bottom of this, because from what I see, here's a kid who should *not* be in this predicament, so he must have a damn good reason for what happened, and the sooner I can *get* to that damn good reason, the better prepared I can be to speak out for him at the arraignment, OK?'

The reverend stopped walking and absently picked up a paper fan from a pew. He sighed heavily and shook his head. 'But this don't make any sense . . .'

Rocco let the silence hang for a few seconds, gathering his strength. 'Look, I'm gonna take him down to the office, charge him with the gun. I'm gonna send it out to be tested. If it comes back the murder weapon, we'll charge him with the homicide. If it's not the murder weapon, the kid's obviously in need of professional counseling, so I promise that he'll walk on the gun charge, I'll turn him back over to you so you can get him some help and . . .' Enough. Rocco was tired of blowing smoke, and there was really nothing more to say. He turned the reverend around and began walking him toward Victor Dunham. 'So let me get it rolling, OK?'

'I don't know.' The reverend sounded anguished.

'You don't know *what*?' Rocco felt his face getting hot.

'It just don't make no sense at all, none of it.'

Rocco was tempted to say, 'It doesn't have to make sense, it's the law,' but he saw that the reverend was ready to give it up and knew that the best thing to do now was remain silent, just *be* the law in all its unstoppable officiousness.

'Ready to go?' Mazilli smiled tightly at the reverend.

'Let's go, Victor.' Rocco gently hooked his elbow, and as the kid rose from the bench, Rocco was struck by his floppy passivity, a lack of resistance so absolute it seemed that he had been taken away days ago and what Rocco now had at the end of his arm was an after-image. Compared to the rude heft of the foil-wrapped gun, this kid Victor seemed weightless.

With Mazilli walking ahead of him, Rocco began the promenade down the aisle to the door, supporting Victor like the father to a groom but feeling knotted inside, bracing for the reverend to open his mouth, say the word 'lawyer' and scotch everything.

'Are you gonna tell his wife?' the reverend called out.

'How old are you?' Rocco asked Victor.

'Twenty, twenty-one,' Victor whispered hoarsely.

Rocco wheeled around and walked backwards toward the door without breaking stride. 'Why don't *you* do that,' he replied. 'I'm not supposed to make notifications, the guy's over eighteen. But I think that could be the best thing for *you* to do right now.'

The reverend nodded, looking heartsick. The black detective stood next to him, watching Rocco go, hurrying him along with furtive waves of his hand.

Rocco got in the back seat with Victor, Mazilli the silent chauffeur. Arching up to slide his gun off his hipbone, Rocco launched into his usual rap.

'Normally I'm supposed to cuff you, there, brother, but you look like the type of guy I can trust.'

Victor leaned his temple against the window and stared with mournful eyes at the front seat headrest.

'Listen, when we get to the office, what do you feel like eating? Pizza, burgers, we can send out for anything. Sandwiches, there's a great deli that delivers, you want a sandwich?'

Victor dug a finger into the corner of his eye, and Rocco heard him breathe through his nose. Mazilli pulled out onto I-9.

'That reverend, he throw a good sermon?'

Victor grunted softly but Rocco couldn't tell whether he meant yes or no. Shrugging it off, Rocco launched into an inane patter, as if trying to entertain a dull guest of honor. He had to engage the kid, keep his mind off what he was about to do, which was send himself off to jail. And Rocco needed the kid to think of him, the expeditor of his doom, as his friend.

'Let me ask you something,' Rocco said, keeping his voice light. 'When was the last time you were arrested?'

'It was thrown out,' Victor said, talking into his wrist.

'What was?' Rocco was relieved to hear him finally say something.

'My case.'

'Oh yeah? What was the original charge?'

'*Eye* contact.' The kid twisted his mouth into a private smirk.

'Eye contact. Hah, that's a new one.' Rocco caught Mazilli's glance in the rearview.

'It's an *old* one. Happen all the time.'

'What do you mean?' Rocco tried to draw him out but the kid wouldn't say any more about it and Rocco didn't push.

'So Victor, what do you do for a living?'

'I work.'

'Doing what?'

'I'm a manager of a restaurant.'

'Oh yeah? No shit. In Dempsy? Maybe I ate there. Which one?'

'Hambone's.'

Rocco snapped his fingers. '*That's* where I know you. I polygraphed you about nine months ago. You remember me? Somebody was stealing meat – or bread, that's right – and they called me in, you know, I used to do that back then. Make a little extra money. Yeah, I was the one who polygraphed everybody. I remember you. You were the guy that was pissed because you had just gotten some kind of achievement plaque and now there you were being polygraphed. Yeah, yeah.' Rocco recalled setting up his portable kit in a clamorous nook of the kitchen, conducting the tests in all that noise and humidity.

'I was the one who sug*ges*ted that they call the police,' Victor said.

'Yeah, well, I didn't go in as police. I was moonlighting doing security, but yeah, I really felt bad for you. I remember thinking that. They ever catch that guy?'

'Unh-uh.' Victor smiled, his eyes almost shut.

Ever since being introduced, Victor had barely opened his eyes, peeking out at the world from under his lids like a child pretending he was asleep. Rocco had seen this before; murderers often adopted the attitudes of sleepwalkers in order to cope with the ordeal of confession and incarceration, although Rocco thought that for some, this shut-eye routine also had a lot to do with feelings of shame.

'So, they still working you sixty hours?'

'Fifty, but I got another job too.'

'Yeah? Doing what?'

'I'd rather not say.'

'OK.' Rocco shrugged cheerfully. 'You married?'

'Uh-huh.'

'Kids?'

'Two.'

'*Two* . . . Good.'

Rocco trailed off, thinking, Jesus, two jobs, two kids, a wife, surrenders to his minister instead of his lawyer. Rocco realized that he had completely misunderstood what the reverend meant when he said, 'This don't make sense.' The comment wasn't about the arrest procedure; it was about the improbability that Victor had killed someone in the first place. But the kid *did* confess, so he probably did shoot Darryl Adams. Rocco recalled the reverend's dismay, figured that this kid must have had one hell of a good reason for capping the other guy. And then Rocco started thinking about the victim as if *he* was the perpetrator: What the hell did Darryl Adams do to this poor mope to push him over the edge like that? Maybe the guy was banging Victor's wife, or his girlfriend. The cash on the body, the loose word of mouth about drugs – was he selling dope to Victor's kids?

'Victor, how old are your kids?'

'Three, one.'

Something else, then. Rocco began consolidating his attack plan for the interview to come: blame the victim, probe for the outrage, isolate the flashpoint. He was pretty confident they'd get down to the motive without too much trouble, because all his instincts and experience told him that this Darryl Adams kid must have had it coming.

'You sure you're not hungry now?' Chin to chest, Rocco stared at the kid as if this was the toughest question he would ask in here.

Victor tightened his mouth and shook his head, his gaze roaming the bare walls of the interrogation room, settling on the only distraction, last year's calendar, sporting a picture of two kittens playing with a ball of yarn above the month of October.

Mazilli coughed from the hallway where he was standing out of sight, listening in on the preliminary interview, a corroborating witness in case the kid confessed but then balked when it came time for the formal taping. He was also there to swear in court, if need be, that he had heard Rocco read the interviewee his rights, including his right to counsel – which Rocco always put off doing for as long as possible at this stage of the game.

'OK, anytime you want to stop and get a pizza, cup of coffee, you got it, OK?'

Victor didn't answer, his gaze now on the yellow pad on Rocco's thigh.

'First I'm gonna ask you some boring stuff, you know, just for the records, so bear with me.'

Rocco ran through the background questions, the kid answering each in a resigned monotone, never offering two words where one would do. Victor Dunham was two months shy of his twenty-first birthday, had lived all his life in the Roosevelt Houses, worked at the same place since he was sixteen, had not married the mother of his children but lived with her and their two kids like man and wife, had a social security number, a car and a NOW account. Rocco shook his head as he took it all down. He hadn't had a shooter as upright as this since the time a bus driver killed a priest who had made sexual overtures to his son.

'And what's your phone number, Victor?'

'Four two one, three three oh nine.'

Rocco jumped right in.

'Tell me what happened.'

Victor raised his ankle to his opposite knee, hunched over and started pulling lint balls off his sock, frowning down at the task as if it was delicate and demanding work. Watching him, Rocco knew the kid would lie even before he opened his mouth.

'I had a few drinks, you know, at the bar,' he said softly to his ankle, 'and I was like walking home, shortcutting through the Ahab's lot, and the guy like – ' Victor shut his eyes, pulled his upper lip into his mouth and took a deep breath. 'He like *jumped* at me and I got scared and I shot him. He just, jumped *out*, like – ' The kid cut himself off, crossed his arms tightly around his chest and stared at a wall.

Rocco blew air through his front teeth: Shit. He had hoped this one would be a walk-through.

'Look, Victor, let me explain something.'

Still looking away, Victor sighed deeply as if he knew all along that Rocco wasn't going to buy it.

'You got to understand, we've done a lot of work on this. We have eyewitnesses' – Rocco thought of Carmela Wilson, stoned to her eyebrows on gin – 'and I know you think that just because you're telling me you *did* it, that's all there is to it – you go to court and it's over.'

Victor scowled open-mouthed at the ceiling tiles.

'Look,' Rocco said, 'you tell me something I know couldn't have happened, that means I got a blatant falsehood. I just can't sit here and accept that. It's not gonna do you any good to put down a falsehood.'

Well, anyway, it won't do me any good, Rocco thought. If the kid told one story now and another one at the trial, the county prosecutor might wind up getting screwed, wind up standing flat-footed in the courtroom, having to run down and refute a year-old situation that his office had no previous awareness of. Rocco's boss went to trial only with cases he felt were absolute locks, and the best way Rocco could protect himself here was by getting at the bare-bones truth now.

'Do you understand what I'm saying to you, Victor?'

Victor shook his head, smiling, as if Rocco was the one who just didn't get it.

'What's so funny?' Rocco leaned back and raised his chin, hoping the kid's blatant pantomime was meant as an invitation.

Victor said something to his own chest that Rocco couldn't pick up.

'Excuse me?' Rocco slid forward in his chair.

'I said, Nothing's funny.' Victor glanced up at Rocco. Wanting to hold those eyes, Rocco hunched forward even farther, but Victor went away again.

'All I want, Victor, all I want you to do, is to ex*plain* to me, what can make a man who routinely works eighty hours a week to support his wife and children, what can make a man like that *shoot* another person?' Rocco paused, head cocked, the silence broken by the distant ringing of a telephone and by the TV down the hall.

Victor appeared to be deep in thought, his lips pursed, his thick eyebrows almost touching, but all the gestures were internally oriented, nothing inviting further questions.

Rocco had no choice but to continue hammering away. 'What could a person have done that was so evil that it would make a guy like you shoot him? Because I know a guy like you has been in tough situations before – on the streets, on the job – and I *know* you never resorted to killing anybody, and I just can't believe that you were walking through a parking lot after knocking back a few beers and some guy comes jumping out at you so you take out a nine-millimeter pistol and *shoot* him?' Rocco gave that a second to sink in. 'I just don't buy it, Victor. It doesn't make any sense to me.' The minister's exact words, Rocco thought. Definitely what the guy had meant. 'Does it make sense to you?'

Victor looked up, about to answer but then catching himself and clamming up.

'Does it?' Rocco, getting frustrated, insisted on a reply.

'Don't make any sense to me either,' Victor muttered, sounding like a cornered child.

In the hallway Mazilli cleared his throat. Rocco relaxed, settling in for a long go-around, realizing the only way he'd get anywhere with this kid was to pull it out of him piece by piece.

'Awright, so . . . Where'd you have the drinks?'

'At Rudy's.'

'Where's that?'

'On De Groot, like across the street.'

'How long were you there?'

'An hour.'

'From when to when?'

'Eight-thirty to ten.'

'That's an hour and a half.'

Victor shrugged. 'Could be longer than that. I don't remember exactly.'

Rocco noted that straightforward questions seemed to loosen him up. 'Longer than ten?' he asked, knowing the shooting happened at about ten-fifteen.

'Nah, I was gone by ten. Longer than eight-thirty, earlier maybe. Because see, I'm supposed to – my shift don't end till ten usually, but I wasn't feeling good so I left early that night.'

'You weren't feeling good, so you went to a bar?'

'Well, it wasn't like a going-home type of not feeling good.'

'What kind was it? What happened?'

Victor became distant again. 'I just didn't feel like working, I guess. That kind.'

'OK.' Rocco nodded amiably. 'Rudy's, are you a regular there?'

'Sometimes like after work.'

'You talk to anybody that night?'

Victor was silent a moment. 'I was to myself.'

'Why'd you hesitate?'

'I was thinking.'

'How about the bartender?'

'What?'

'You talk to him?'

'To order.'

'What's his name? You know his name?'

'No. He's just bald, that's all I know.'

'Does he have a mustache?'

'I don't remember.'

'You don't remember? When was the last time you saw a bald black man without a mustache?'

Victor shrugged, Rocco's levity falling flat.

'So you didn't talk to anybody except the bartender, to order.'

Again he paused. 'Unh-uh.'

'You hesitated again.'

'I was thinking again.'

'You sure, now?'

'Uh-huh.'

'What did you drink?'

'Scotch.'

'How much?'

'Three, maybe four, maybe two.'

'Were you drunk?'

'I was high but not like, you know . . .'

'So you had a few shnorts.'

'What's that?'

'Drinks.'

'Yeah, uh-huh.'

'What then?'

'I got up, left, cut across the lot.'

'Did you talk to anybody outside the bar?'

'Unh-unh, just walked.'

'Walked to . . .'

'Across the street to the lot.'

'Then what?'

'The guy, like as I was coming up on the building? The guy came out at me.'

'From where?'

'From the shadows.'

'Shadows where?'

'By the dumpster. The lights was out and there was shadows all over but it was from the dumpster.'

'Did he say anything to you?'

'Unh-unh.'

'Did he have anything? Was he holding anything?'

'In his hand?'

'In his hand, in his teeth, anywhere.'

'He was in shadows, so I don't . . . He just *came* at me and I got scared. I wasn't even thinking. Just, you know, *bam*. Then I got scared and ran.'

'You mean *bam bam bam bam*.'

'Huh?'

'There were four bullets recovered.'

Victor didn't react to that, and Rocco didn't know how to read it.

'When the guy jumped at you, before you shot him – you say you were scared. Did you try to run?'

'Before? Unh-unh, I was like . . . startled.'

'Startled. But you stood your ground. It wasn't like you ran and he was chasing you.'

'Well, if I did run, I guess he maybe would have.'

'But you didn't run.'

'Unh-unh, not till after.'

'And when you shot him, where were you?'

'There.'

'I mean, were you facing the building or the parking lot?'

Victor squinted as if he was trying to remember, but the gesture seemed heavy-handed, and again Rocco was certain of the huge lie behind all of this. 'I was facing the building.'

'So your back was to the lot.'

'I guess.'

'So like you *could* have turned and run if you wanted to, without banging into any walls.'

'I guess.'

'So it wasn't like you were trapped in any way.'

'Like what?'

'You know,' Rocco said. 'Boxed in, your back against a wall or something so that you just *had* to stand your ground.'

He didn't answer. Rocco saw him withdraw, not liking where this was going.

'OK, OK . . . You OK?' Rocco broke the pace. It was time to cool him down. 'Let's go backwards for a minute. Where were you before you were at the bar?'

'At work.'

'At Hambone's, right?'

'Yeah, uh-huh. I said that.'

'And you left, what time?'

'I don't know, exact.'

'Take a guess.'

'Eight.'

'Because you weren't feeling good, right? What was it, a headache, an argument?'

Victor seemed to retreat further. 'Just, you know, tired,' he said quietly.

'You talk to anybody there?'

'Yeah, I talked to *ev*erybody. I'm the manager.'

'I mean, did you get into any conversations other than "Do this, do that"?'

'Same ol', same ol' . . .' Victor shrugged.

'Are you close to anybody there?'

'Close?'

'Anybody you talk to more than the others?'

'Hector.'

'Hector?'

'Yeah, he's the other manager, Hector Morales.'

Rocco made a note of the name.

'So it was the usual day – ballbreaker?'

Victor shrugged again, fending off Rocco's sympathy.

'And where were you before work?'

'At the other one.'

'Other one?'

'Job.'

'What's the other job?'

'I'd rather not say.'

'Why not?'

Victor gave him a fast look of discomfort.

'Is it illegal?' Rocco asked, thinking drugs, working in somebody's crew. 'You can tell me.'

Victor was silent.

'Look, I'm gonna find out anyhow.'

He put his hand over his mouth and mumbled, 'Security.'

'For who?'

'This store in New York.'

'What store?'

'To Bind an Egg. It's a Japanese store.'

'What's the address?'

'Four Seventy-three Columbus Avenue. It's got like kimonos, tea pots . . .'

'So what's the big secret? It sounds like a good job.'

Victor murmured something into his shoulder.

'What?'

'It's off the books.'

Rocco resisted rolling his eyes. 'Who's your boss?'

'This lady Kiki.'

'Kiki . . .' Rocco waited, pen poised.

'Kiki . . .' Victor squinted, trying to remember a last name, then gave up, embarrassed. 'Kiki, that's all.'

'You wear a gun there?'

'Unh-unh. I got like a nightstick.'
'So where'd you get the gun?'
'Found it.'
Rocco felt a headache coming on. He stifled a yawn. 'Where?'
'Under a chair at the restaurant when we was cleaning up one time.'
'When was that?'
'Month ago? Five weeks?'
'Was it loaded?'
'I guess so,' he said, fighting down a twisted grin.
'Before you shot that guy, how many other times you fire the gun?'
'I didn't even know it was loaded.'
'So you just picked it up, pointed it, pulled the trigger.'
'I guess so.'
'Did you always carry it?'
'Yeah, uh-huh. It made me feel safe.'
'Where'd you carry it?'
'In my bag, like a gym bag.'
'So the guy jumped at you, you stepped back, fished around in your gym bag . . . What else was in your gym bag?'
'My uniform.'
'Fished around in your gym bag, found the gun, aimed it and shot him four times. Is that right?'
Victor didn't answer and Rocco felt a surge of impatience.
'What you do after that?'
'Went home, *ran*.'
'Which way you run?'
'To the boulevard.'
'Jersey City direction or Newark direction?'
'Jersey City direction. I just ran home, got sick in the toilet.'
'Ran home to . . .' Rocco checked the first page of his notes.
'Forty-one Dumont Place, apartment Eleven G?'
'Uh-huh.'
'Who was home?'
'My wife, my kids, my mother . . . everybody.'
'What did you tell your wife?'
'Nothing. I just got sick, washed up my face and went to sleep.'
'So who *did* you tell?'
'Nobody. Just the reverend.'
Rocco took a breath, ready for a new tack. 'When was the last time you were up in Ahab's?'

Victor gave a dry snort.

Rocco smiled as if they shared the joke. 'Before that time.'

'Like . . . never.' Victor frowned and shook his head at his cuff.

'Not once? You live so close, you never walked by on a hot day with your kids and just stopped in there for a soda or something?'

Victor looked up, his eyes igniting now, burning right into Rocco's. 'With my kids? I never *see* my damn kids. I'm always *working*. Then I get home, I'm so damn tired I'm always *sleeping*.'

Rocco was silent for a moment, wondering how to open the door here even wider, but Victor plowed on without any prompting. 'My *kids*. Hell, I'm gonna take my kids to a restaurant for a soda, I'll take 'em to my *own* damn restaurant. I say to my wife, "Bring the kids to the restaurant," she says to me, "How'm I gonna do that? *You* got the car, your mother got the other car." I say, "Take a damn cab," she says, "What's the big deal about eatin' for free if you got to pay for a cab gettin' there, pay for a cab goin' back." I say, "That's not the damn point," she says, "You can see your kids at home for free anytime you want, that's why they *yours*." I say, "I come home, I'm like exhausted to death."' Victor was talking right at Rocco now, his words coming so fast he had to wipe his lips. 'You know that feeling you get sometimes? You come home, you so tired it's like the sound of your own kids is like some *hor*ror sound?'

Rocco nodded sympathetically and kept his mouth shut, deciding to stand back and let Victor take off, see where he landed.

'That's a terrible feeling, man, when you can't stand the sound of your own damn kids? I try to tell her that, she says, "So quit a job, you *got* two." See, she don't understand. You know, like . . . I'm tryin' to get out of the projects, and where you gonna go if you don't got it saved up? I mean, you got to make it while you *can*, you know? Make it while you *able*, because you never know what's gonna happen tomorrow, like, I got us on this waiting list for these co-op apartments over in Bayonne? There's this complex, Evergreen Village, and it's *nice*, man, and they're taking black families now because there's this big rent strike going on, so like for re*venge* or something on the whites, I don't know, alls I know is that it's nice, but you got to have eight thousand dollars down, and like the maintenance for a two bedroom is eight hundred and fifty a month, and it's hard to get a loan because I can only put down but one job because the other's under the table, and that makes me a twenty-thousand-dollar-a-year black man walking into a bank asking for money, you know what I'm sayin'?'

Victor paused, his eyes hungry for Rocco's commiseration. Rocco made a sympathetic noise but withheld any comment.

'So like I got to make it myself right now 'cause I don't *know* when my name's coming up in the list, and like what happens if I get shot by some crackhead while I'm coming home from work? Or I get sick or something? Then I got *no* income, *no* job. I mean, right now it's like, you know what I make? I bring home three hundred ninety-five dollars twenty-seven cents after taxes from the Hambone's and a clean two eighty from the security in New York, but then you take away fifty a week in gas out-of-pocket and PATH fare, OK? But still, I'm bringing home six hundred twenty-five dollars a week right now, so why she rattling my cage about it? I'm doing it for *her*. For the *kids*. I mean, I don't know, maybe she *likes* living in, in Roosevelt with all the crime and shit. I don't. My *mother* don't. You know, when I was a kid there? It wasn't *like* that, Roosevelt. There wasn't dope like that. There wasn't – you know, people was working. I mean, it wasn't rich or nothing but it was *proud*, or proud*er*.' Victor paused, winded. He rubbed his knees anxiously. 'I don't know, man, I don't know.'

Rocco had to think hard to recall the question or comment that had triggered all this – something about if he ever took his kids to Ahab's for a soda. Rocco felt sorry for the guy: the poor bastard had ranted and raved like he still had all those jobs, as if confessing to a murder was just a temporary time-loss thing, a tangle he'd be out of soon.

Rocco wondered where to take it. The wife: it didn't sound like he had the happiest of marriages. 'What's your wife's name again? ShaRon? How you get along with her?'

'When I see her, it's OK. She always running off to her church, though. At night, you know, and on the weekend.'

'What church?'

'Some lady's house. I don't know the name of it.'

'Some lady's house? You ever go with her?'

'Yeah, I went once. I dint like it. They were all speakin' in *tongues*. That ain't, you know . . .'

'You got a girlfriend?'

'Nope.' Victor fought down a smile, looking embarrassed.

'You're not dating any girls from Hambone's? All those girls working under you?'

'They just young kids.'

Victor blushed and Rocco felt another twinge of sympathy.

'How about anybody else? You seeing anybody else?'

The smile left Victor's face and he looked Rocco in the eye again. 'Hey, I don't even have time to make love with the woman I'm *supposed* to make love with. How'm I gonna make love with somebody else?'

Touched by his innocence, Rocco couldn't help smiling. 'Hey, you know how guys are. Where there's a will – '

'I don't even have time to see my damn kids, play with my damn kids.'

'OK, OK, Victor. Calm down, calm down. Look, it's just . . . Look.' Rocco slid in close, resting his fingers on Victor's crossed knee, thinking that the kid was as open as he'd ever be in here. 'Victor. Put yourself in my place. You get a guy comes in tells you he murdered somebody. This guy, he was born and raised in this town, knows the streets, the people, he's holding down two jobs, killing himself to improve his family's situation, a guy who's got his income organized down to the penny, who's proud, self-sacrificing, hard-working, and for *my* money, about as close to an unsung hero as you can get around here.'

Victor was sitting hunched over, elbows on knees, eyes on the floor, but Rocco could tell that he was listening. 'OK, so this guy tells you he's walking home one night through the parking lot of a popular restaurant and he's probably walked this route every night on his way home for *years*. He's approached by the assistant manager of that restaurant in that parking lot, who jumps at him with *no* weapon, and all of a sudden this guy panics, steps back, fishes around in a gym bag he uses for carrying around a nine-millimeter gun – which he *found* under a chair – shoots the manager *four times* and runs off.'

Rocco gave it a long silence, his face inches from Victor's. 'Now, you tell me . . . What would *you* think after *you* heard that story? Wouldn't *you* think there was something else to it?'

Victor exhaled heavily, then spoke in a dejected murmur. 'I don't know what you would think.'

'Ex*cuse* me?' Rocco put his ear near the kid's mouth, wincing in showy concentration.

Victor didn't repeat himself.

Rocco leaned back, giving him some air. 'OK, look, I know you're frightened and I know you're thinking all you got to do is come in here, say what you say, and that's the end of it. But that's just not the way it works, so now listen to me, Victor. You're a good, decent, hard-working guy, and if you did it you must have had a damn good reason other than that man jumping out at you unexpectedly, because I have to ask myself *why* – *why* did that man jump out at you like that? It wasn't to rob you –

why would the manager of a restaurant try to rob someone in his own parking lot? So I have to think that it was something *personal* that went down. I have to think that you guys had a *problem* with each other. I have to think – '

Victor cut him off. 'I never seen the guy before in my life.' His eyes were burning a hole in the floor, but his voice rose to a shout. 'He just *jumped* me.'

Rocco returned the heat, hoping the kid's anger would make him slip. 'He just *jumped* you. And you *shot* him. He didn't threaten you, he didn't talk to you, and I *know* he didn't wave no weapon at you. He just – '

'I don't want to talk to you no more.' Victor's voice went flat and sullen, a slight shakiness there too. He glanced quickly at Rocco and then went back to studying the carpet. 'I dint *know* the guy. I said that. I told you what happened.'

Rocco smiled and shook his head. 'Victor . . .'

'I gave you the gun. Now I don't want to talk to you no more. So like just, do with me what I got coming. I don't want to talk to you no more.'

Rocco held his hands up. 'Wait a minute, wait a minute, don't, let's not . . . Don't get all angry now. I'm not calling you a liar or anything. It's just I think there's something deeper here, and for some reason, you're not telling me.'

The kid breathed through his mouth. 'Ah!' he gasped.

Rocco spoke softly. 'Hey look, I'm on *your* side. I'm not trying to screw you here. Believe it or not, I'm doing what I'm not supposed to be doing. I'm helping you organize your defense, I'm allowing you to put your justifications on record in your recorded confession.' Rocco boxed Victor's knees with his own, put a hand on his bony shoulder, talking to him as if *he* was the victim. 'If this man *did* something to you, to your *fam*ily, if he threatened you, if he in any way made your life miserable, this all helps *you*.' Rocco put both hands on the kid's shoulders. 'You could have been beside yourself with rage, you could have been unable to sleep, to eat. This all helps you. In *court*. C'mon, Victor, I can't do it alone. Help me help you. What did that fucker do to you?'

For a long, agonized moment Victor looked like a fish flopping on a deck. Rocco thought he finally had him, but then gradually the kid seemed to calm down and refocus. He was still avoiding Rocco's eyes, but Rocco could sense there was something new working in him. Thinking it could go either way now, Rocco waited, his hands still draped on Victor's slumped shoulders.

'It was self-defense.'

'Nah.' Rocco sat up, disappointed. 'Nah nah nah, that's not gonna hold water. The guy didn't have a weapon – *you* did. You didn't even perceive him as having a weapon. You just told me that. You didn't make any attempt to run, which you also just told me. In fact, to tell you the truth' – Rocco tried to drop this little bomb delicately – 'we have a witness who says that they saw you waiting for the guy, who says that they saw the guy back away from *you*. I mean, if you ran, if he had you cornered, which you also just told me he didn't – I mean, Victor, they have legal definitions of things like self-defense. There's requirements. We got *no* gun on the victim, *no* physical entrapment of the shooter, *no* effort to flee on the part of the shooter, *no* forensic signs of a struggle, *no* bruises, *no* skin or hair under the fingernails, *no* powder burns, it was a distant shot, so . . . Nah, I'm sorry, I'm sorry.'

Rocco waited for a sign, hoping he had overwhelmed the kid with logic, but Victor was gone, off somewhere, shut down. Rocco was amazed at how still he could become, so totally withdrawn as to appear weightless.

Then Victor seemed to rise within himself, vacating his own mind and body, leapfrogging over Rocco's little logic boxes, sailing past hard reasoning and bald truth to a safer place.

'Yeah.' Victor nodded, as if settling an argument that Rocco was not privy to. 'It was self-defense.'

'Victor, look,' Rocco said, almost pleading. 'Put yourself in my place . . .'

But Rocco saw the faraway look in Victor's eyes and stopped: This kid was gone.

Rocco hammered away at Victor for another forty-five minutes, but the kid placidly held to his line, becoming more and more distant as time went on. Musing on how someone could be so vaporous and unmovable at the same time, Rocco eventually tired of hearing himself talk. He flipped through his notes and, yawning, stretched his arms in a seated crucifixion.

'All right,' he said regretfully. 'I don't think you're being fair to yourself, but I'm gonna go out, get a tape recorder, my partner's gonna come back in with me, I'm gonna tell you what you're charged with, give you your Mirandas and then, you know, basically I'm just gonna ask you, once again, in your own words, what happened that night. Anything I ask you you don't want to answer, just say

so, OK?' Rocco rose. 'So I'll be right back. Can I get you something?'

'I'd like to go to the bathroom.' The kid was looking right at
him now.

'Hey, no problem.' Rocco extended an arm.

When Victor got up, he lost his balance and fell back into his seat,
looking slightly surprised.

'You OK?' Rocco had seen that before, after long sessions like this one,
guys going dizzy and light-headed, spooking themselves when they first
tried to use their legs.

'I'm good.' Victor tried it again, this time holding on to both the table
and his chair.

'There you go.' Rocco held out his arm, the kid blinking and smiling
with disorientation.

He walked Victor through the Homicide office to the bathrooms in
the rear. Mazilli was the only detective in the room now, talking into
the phone in a low voice to his wife or his bookie.

'Maz, you want to set up the tape in there?'

Mazilli held up his hand and signaled that he needed two more minutes.
Continuing his murmured conversation, he blindly fished around in his
drawer and came up with a six-pack of blank cassettes.

Rocco stood right outside the open bathroom door, fiddling with a file
cabinet, trying not to be too obvious about keeping an eye on Victor but
needing to make sure he didn't dive through the window or something.
He felt a stab of depression: he had just spent an entire Sunday afternoon
in a windowless office extracting a confession that would read like the
bullshit it was, giving the prosecutor absolutely no way to assess how
hard to push the charges or how much egg on his face he'd be risking by
taking this kid to trial, where the truth of what happened could finally
come out.

Brooding about the ass-chewing he'd probably get from his boss the
minute the guy read the transcripts, Rocco looked into the bathroom
and saw Victor move to the sink to wash his hands. Rocco was mildly
taken aback: usually murderers, like detectives, just went in there, pissed,
whacked their Johnson against the shower stall partition a few times and
marched out, still zipping up.

He felt a mixture of sympathy and resentment toward Victor, with his
sad-sack face, his neat cheap clothes, his common-law wife and two kids,
probably up to his neck in grease and heat six days a week at that ptomaine
palace – walking around town carrying a pistol in a gym bag.

17

Yesterday's newspaper had carried such startling news that on Monday morning Strike bought the paper again, and there it was on page three, right below the headline, in the second sentence: Victor Dunham. Strike stared at his brother's name, twelve letters that held a face, a voice and a twenty-year patchwork of moments, the newspaper talking to him directly two days in a row now, sending him bloody valentines.

Victor. Strike's stomach got humpy on him: No way. Strike saw his brother in that stupid brown and orange polyester uniform standing in the rain two days before, water dripping off the bill of his Hambone's hat as if an open faucet hung out over the crown. No way Victor did this.

Helpless, afraid to turn and look behind him to Victor's window, his mother's window, Strike drifted off in his dismay and confusion, waded through his memory in search of images of his brother that would jibe with the newspaper's story. But he couldn't remember Victor ever throwing a punch or even raising his voice – he had always been the complete master of himself. Strike recalled the time that he and Victor were riding on a crowded PATH train to Jersey City maybe two years before. They were sitting across from a big, yellow-eyed drunk in construction boots and chinos, and the guy was singing, 'My girl, my girl, my girl, talkin' 'bout . . . my gir-r-rl,' sounding a little like their father, making all the white people laugh, some of them even applauding and hooting sarcastically. Victor left his seat, walked across the car and got down in front of that bigfoot motherfucker, gripped the guy's kneecap as if to keep his balance in the rocketing train, dug in his thumbnail to get some undivided attention, then said, 'Why don't you shut yourself up. You're being a fool.' He spoke this so low and calm that most people probably thought Victor had been putting in a song request. And later, when they got off the train, the drunk was still sitting there strained and quiet, and Victor patted his shoulder, as if both to apologize and forgive.

His brother had always been that way: screwy and private, with a hard and hypnotic dignity, an ability to rope you in, speak to you down low with this look in his eyes that made you shut up because suddenly you felt it was important to hear what he was saying. But he was no killer – this didn't make no sense at all.

Which left My Man, and Strike still felt sure that My Man was Buddha Hat. And then it came to him, making him feel better and worse at the same time: Of course Victor didn't do it – he was taking the weight for Buddha Hat. Had to be. Except why would Victor cover for an ice-head psycho like the Hat?

Strike heard a honk and saw Rodney's Cadillac roll up to the benches with a bunch of teenage boys in the back, everybody looking out the street-side windows at Strike. Rodney honked again, reached over and opened the front passenger door, waiting while the engine gargled.

Strike couldn't read Rodney's face, couldn't tell if he'd heard the news about Victor. For a moment Strike entertained the idea of telling Rodney everything he knew, explaining that none of it was his fault, but then he looked at Rodney sitting there fanning his knees, staring at him expectantly, and he knew he'd never risk telling Rodney any of it. And as he walked to the car, stormed up with his own helplessness, it hit Strike why Victor had confessed, had taken the weight for the shooter: he was told to.

Rodney took Strike and the teenagers to the Red Rooster for lunch. On the way to the restaurant Strike checked out the guys in back, five young clockers wearing gold chains over college shirts and baseball jackets, a new crew of Rodney's from somewhere in the Eisenhower projects. One kid was on his knees because there wasn't enough room on the seat, and the other four were practically on top of each other.

Rodney could have put one of them up front, but Strike knew that Rodney wanted the clockers to think of Strike as minor royalty. That was the idea: several times over the past couple of months, Rodney had taken Strike with him to one of these lunches, and while Rodney lectured the kids about having the proper mentality on the street, about the importance of long-term goals, he would point to Strike as a man who was doing things right. At first Strike had enjoyed these sit-downs, but lately this street-corner-prince business had become a little old.

Rodney pulled up to the restaurant, and a minute later the seven of them stood huddled together near the bar, waiting for the maitre d' next to a wall covered with blowups of Dempsy in its all-white, World War II glory days. Hanging tight, unsmiling, the clockers whispered as if this was a museum or a private home. Even Strike was tensed up, not just because they looked like a pack of dope dealers but also because the clientele in the place were all old people, in their forties and fifties, the crowd looking like a convention of goddamn speech therapists and parole officers.

Rodney ushered the boys into the dining room, and the maitre d' seated them at a large round table, its starched blood-red cloth anchored by silver platters. A smiling waitress came by, wearing a straw boater and a red-and-white-striped shirt with arm garters.

'Would you fellas like something to drink?'

A kid named Charles looked to Rodney, who gave him a raised eyebrow to go ahead, then said solemnly, 'I'll have a magerita.' The waitress wrote this down as a kid named Roy coughed into his fist and said, 'I'll have a coneyak,' which caused Charles to clear his throat and say, 'Yo wait up, make mine a coneyak too.'

Strike looked at Rodney, surprised he wasn't saying anything, not even shaking his head.

All the other kids ordered cognacs. Rodney got a Coke, Strike water. For a moment, watching the waitress write up the order, Strike was embarrassed, but then he thought, They're kids, they'll learn. Or they won't – whichever.

Rodney made a toast when the drinks came, a toast to family, to helping each other. He played it deadpan, watching them try not to make faces when they tasted the cognacs. Then everybody ordered food, and as they waited for it to come Strike noticed that the Eisenhower boys were tense and silent. They were trying so hard to be there, to make a stand, frowning with self-consciousness, touching their clothes, furtively eyeing the other tables.

When the food came – ribs for Rodney, hamburgers for everybody else – the boys hunched over their plates, eating hard but still glancing around the room.

Rodney finally started in. 'Look at you motherfuckers,' he murmured to the tablecloth as he chewed on a rib. 'Look at you motherfuckers looking at them look at you, unh-unh-unh.' Rodney licked his fingers, shaking his head.

'There's more motherfuckin' money made at this goddamn table than in the whole goddamn restaurant. They ain't a nigger sittin' here ain't makin' five hundred a week.'

But that's *this* week, Strike thought. No saying who'd be sitting here *next* week, turnover being high with greed, jail, stupidity, falling off into product and simple bad luck.

'Rich, street-smart young men. But look at you all sittin' scrunchy in the chair.' Rodney made a clucking noise, then threw Strike a quick wink.

'Well, damn, Rodney,' the kid named Roy hissed, his eyes big and burning. 'What you got to do to get over with these people?'

Rodney sighed deeply and put down his rib as if he was too sad to eat, his hands dropping to his lap in despair, Strike thinking, Here it comes.

'Yo Roy, that the wrong question. The question is, what you got to do to get over with your*self*. It ain't them. It's *you*. You got to say, Hey' – he counted off on his fingers – 'I'm a businessman, I make sales, I handle product, I deal in inventory, I take risks, I work long hours, I deal with the public and I do it all *well*. That's why I'm holding such a big roll, that's why I'm eating in this nice restaurant, because I earned it. I deserve to be here. And if those motherfuckers out there at those tables don't know it, fuck them, man, *I* know it.'

'Yeah, but none of those motherfuckers get arrested for what they do,' Charles said.

'Don't you believe *that* shit. This whole country run by criminals – Wall Street, the govament, the po-lice. How you think the dope gets in town to begin with? Don't you get me started.'

No chance of that, Strike thought. He saw that the kids weren't really following Rodney's words, but their faces were softening with pleasure, Strike thinking, They love him just for talking to them.

'Besides, ain't no criminals here.' Rodney's voice went high and singsong. 'Shit, you all ain't even *done* nothin'. No stickup mens, no muggers, killers. I don't truck with that. I don't take on nobody with violence on they jacket. You motherfuckers are making it the only way they let poor niggers make it. On the street. Hustlin'. It ain't even criminal, man, it just sur*vival*. But you clean, strong young men, and if you play your cards right, someday you be working on the *in*side, you be sittin' at them other tables. Shit, you might even own this damn restaurant.' Rodney shrugged, working on a rib, as if the picture he was starting to paint for them was no big deal.

Strike silently mouthed, But what do I mean by 'playin' your cards right'?

Rodney said, 'But what do I mean by playin' your cards right? How you gonna buy this restaurant if every time you make ten dollar you go out and buy a ten-dollar ring. Every time you make a hundred dollar, you buy a hundred-dollar chain. A nigger does that, always broke. Gets busted, ain't got the money to make bail. Buy a new car, ain't got the money for gas. Charles, how many sneakers you got?'

Charles looked off, lips moving, frowning, then announcing, 'Twelve.'

Rodney sat up straight, taken aback. 'You got twelve pair?'

'*Six* pair, twelve sneakers.'

Everybody but Strike laughed.

'Yeah, OK, you got six pair. How many *feet* you got? See what I'm sayin'? You all just throwin' it away.' Rodney reached over and grabbed the chains on Charles's chest. 'Look at this.'

'Hey, don't yank it, man!' Charles flashed up, grabbing Rodney's wrist for a second before remembering who it was.

Rodney let it slide. 'You look like motherfuckin' Mr T.'

Everybody laughed again, high and jerky. 'Charles, check this out, man.' Rodney paused so the kid could get ready. 'How motherfuckin' invisible do you think you are, that you got to have *all* this goddamn gold hangin' around your neck just so you could feel like you're bein' *seen*, man.'

Charles blinked at him, and Strike knew that the kid was totally missing it. If Rodney repeated himself five or six times, Charles might get it, but that instant of anger – grabbing Rodney's hand like that – behind it was a whole lifetime of impulses that ran too deep for words and cocktails. Strike knew it; Rodney knew it too, but he was still trying to get through, still holding that fistful of chains, waiting for comprehension. Rodney tried it again. 'I take these motherfucking chains away, are you less of a man?'

'Yeah, well, he a *punk* then,' said a kid named Down.

'Why?' Rodney scowled.

'He let you take them away from him.' Down sounded scared, as if he had just been called on in a hated classroom.

'My God,' Rodney said in disbelief, letting go of Charles's chains.

Strike guessed that he was probably the only kid who had ever received Rodney's restaurant lecture and understood right away what he was saying. During that first lunch, a year ago, Rodney's eyes had lit up with gratitude and pride when he saw Strike stay right with him – finally he'd saved one. Rodney's other clockers always went down: they were too poor, too immature, a lifetime of One Way going up against two months of Other Way. Other Way didn't stand a chance.

'You got to start respecting yourself.' Rodney was still hammering away, not ready to give up. 'The nigger that spend it fast as he make it don't believe it's real. Don't believe in his*self*. He's thinking with like a two-minute clock, thinking like a poor man, like his life is like day-to-day, minute-to-minute. He *got* no future 'cause he don't *think* of no future.'

Strike watched them tune out, dipping fries in ketchup, one by one turning to wave down the waitress and order orange sodas or Cokes, the cognacs left unfinished.

'You got to *believe* in yourself, you got to start thinking about your future, and that means you got to start saving your damn money. Shit, *they* do.' Rodney pointed out to the room. 'There ain't a motherfucker in this restaurant right now can't go home and show me a *bank*book, and you niggers making more day by day, week by week, than them all. But I'll bet, come the end of the month, they got more'n you do.' Rodney whirled his hands around each other, cocking his head. 'D'y'all get what I'm sayin'?'

'I hear that,' Charles said automatically.

Rodney sagged with frustration, looking like the old man of thirty-seven he was, then said, 'Well, fuck it, I tried,' and got back to his ribs.

Strike was relieved that the lecture seemed to be over, glad that Rodney didn't do his self-image exercise, making everybody come up with a positive word that started with the same letter as their first name, going around the table, people saying shit like Terrific Tyrone, Sexy Strike, Rockin' Rodney. Six months ago one kid had called himself Brightful Booker and then almost put his fork in someone's chest when everybody laughed.

But Rodney wasn't done. He lit up again, tried one last approach. 'I mean, look at Strike here.' The kids did as they were told, Strike looking away as if he had seen something out at the bar. 'Look how my man dress. No flash, color coordinated, nice pair of dark Reeboks – none of them paratrooper sneakers you all like to wear. Jump out a window, you bounce right back.'

No one laughed.

'I mean, check this out. The knockos roll up on my man at a red light. What do they see, 'cause you *know* they gonna be profiling. They see a nigger in a two-year-old Accord, no gold on, nice hair, not no high-rise billboard up top his head, nice dark sweater. Nigger probably driving like my grandma. You think the knockos gonna be thinkin' clocker? Hell no, they thinkin' a nine-to-five nigger working at First Jersey or some damn thing. Strike's doing it *right*, Strike's getting *over*, 'cause Strike's Quiet Storm.'

Strike fumed, thinking, Lose the Accord, a table of strangers now knowing it's a dope car.

'And Strike got hisself a *safe* house.'

Abruptly Strike rose from his chair. Now they all knew he saves it, which means he's got it – Rodney getting him killed.

Strike stood over Rodney, trying to hold in his anger, keep himself stone-faced. 'I got to book. I got to see muh-my PO.'

As Strike walked from the table he heard Rodney say, 'Strike's got like four safe houses, so come knock night? They can't confiscate his money. See what I'm sayin'? I mean, Strike's here to *stay*.'

Strike palmed his gut. Lose the safe houses, lose the Accord. Lose Rodney too.

Strike parked in the lot behind the Municipal Building, where the probation offices were housed. For a minute or two he sat in the car, taking in the sight of the tall, soot-streaked County Jail, which was joined to the courtroom-and-office complex by means of an underground tunnel.

He had spent one night in that building, coiled in the bullpen waiting for a morning arraignment. In the two hours it had taken for Rodney to get the word in to lay off him, he'd had his sneakers stolen and his elbow burned with a lighter. Since then, he had often told people that he'd blow his own head off before he'd ever go back in here. But instead of going straight, he'd become super-cautious – as if the point of jail was to teach him the importance of not getting caught.

And now Victor was somewhere inside that seven-story sinkhole, and he didn't have Rodney's name to protect him, and there was nothing Strike could do to help.

But Victor could be a tough little motherfucker sometimes, stubborn and one way – he had used that steel-eyed dignity of his to control an entire roiling fast-food kitchen without ever having to raise his voice, as far as Strike knew, for three years now. Strike had seen his brother on the job at Hambone's, seen him striding from griddle to ice chest to deep fryer to dishwasher, barking out orders with a crisp Please and Thank You in every command. And it wasn't just Victor who talked that way. He had made it a commandment in the Hambone's kitchen that nobody could ask anybody for anything, no matter how frantic it got, without

putting Please and Thank You on each end of the sentence. So maybe he
was doing OK in jail after all. And maybe, Strike thought, I should go
visit him, see him face-to-face and try to find out what happened with
Buddha Hat and Darryl.

But not today, he decided, getting out of his car. The hamburger started
to repeat on him as he walked up the hill and then around to the front of
the Municipal Building. He pushed through the revolving doors, getting
hit with the toxic smell of brass polish, the aroma of authority in his life.
He worked his way through the security check, dropping his keys in a
plastic bowl and standing for a metal detector frisk. He walked through
the marble lobby and headed for the stairwell, recalling Victor that night
in the bar, thinking about how all that dignity had turned goofy after
a few drinks. When Strike had last lived at home, sleeping on the sofa,
Victor was starting to become a private nipper – his cocktail lounge
usually a midnight kitchen or a parked car. But Strike had never held
it against him: self-control was important, but a man's got to have *some*
kind of release valve. It was just that he'd never considered his brother
a bar drinker before.

Strike trotted down the two flights of stairs to the sub-basement of the
building, then walked along an echoey hallway filled with cops, victims,
caseworkers, secretaries, defendants out on bail. He was moving fast
now, imagining Victor in the bullpen last night, all those hard-time
motherfuckers in there smacking him around, taking his food, his clothes,
his pallet, his dignity, but saying Please and Thank You each and every
time. Strike felt something gritty rise in his craw, then realized that it
couldn't be the hamburger coming back on him: in all that time at the
Red Rooster he hadn't taken a single bite of food.

Strike sat in the tiny waiting area of the probation office, choosing one
of the two molded plastic chairs over the cotton plaid couch because
the fabric could take in stink and crawling things off people's hair and
clothes. Besides, the couch was occupied by a light-skinned man with
dried blood on his T-shirt and a face so swollen Strike couldn't tell if
he was black or Puerto Rican or white. He wasn't wearing shoes, just
bedroom slippers that didn't hide his scabby and swollen ankles. Strike
believed in going to see your PO looking a little bummy, so no one
would think you were still clocking, but this was going the whole
other way around. It was best to dress down – down, but clean.
A nice fresh sweatshirt, pressed stone-washed jeans, shoes instead of
sneakers in order to suggest that he wasn't the type who ever needed

to *run* anywhere – everything in Strike's PO wardrobe was clean, cheap, respectful.

The waiting area was cut off from the huge room of interview cubicles by frosted glass partitions and a bulletproof reception window. Half a dozen fruity-smelling deodorizing strips were glued to the walls, and Strike didn't know whether to be insulted or grateful. He was required to visit his PO for just fifteen minutes a month, but it felt like going to the dentist or the Roosevelt rental office, the visits filling him with an unfocused dread that he hadn't felt since childhood.

Strike sat holding his passport-size probation book out in front of him. He wished he had a Yoo-Hoo to calm his empty stomach, but he was afraid that sitting with a bottle of anything, even Yoo-Hoo, would be enough to trigger his PO, make him think 'attitude,' and that's when shit could happen. Even if they didn't throw you in County, they still found some way to make you pay.

The door to the outside hallway opened and a guy whose face Strike recalled but couldn't place entered the waiting area and took the other plastic chair.

'Wha's up?' the guy said to Strike, not knowing exactly who Strike was either. Strike thought the guy looked like an advertisement for clocking: snow-white high-top BKs, a royal-blue Fila warm-up suit that must have set him back two hundred dollars, a gold nameplate hanging off his neck, two gold rings and an ID bracelet. Strike imagined the guy telling his PO, 'Yeah, I'm still making deliveries for Shop-Rite, just like last month.' Maybe he had the blind PO, the lady whose bruised-looking eyelids opened only a tiny bit, who had no lamp on her desk, no posters on her walls, the one whose cubicle looked as if a shitstorm hit it. Strike's stomach jumped just thinking about her. God*damn*, they make you pay.

Finally Strike's name was called, and as he walked up the center aisle to his PO's desk, he passed ten probation meets on either side of him. He nodded in recognition to three of the guys and one of the girls.

He took a chair across the desk from Mr Lynch. A heavy-jowled Irishman with wavy white hair that was starting to yellow, Lynch had his head down over some paperwork. Strike scanned the walls. His eyes stopped at a poster of a skeleton on a pitcher's mound winding up to fire off a hypodermic, with 'AIDS' on his baseball cap and 'Don't Let Him Strike You Out' in red along the bottom. The only other poster was a poem called 'Invictus' written over a picture of a sunrise. Strike had been coming into this cubicle for six months now, had always stared

at that poem but had never read it through. He just liked the name.
Invictus.

Lynch cleared his throat, opened a huge green ledger with MALES
written on the front and started right in, not even looking at Strike.

'You still live with your mother?'

'Yeah, uh-huh.' He had moved out of his mother's house after his first
PO meet, the next day in fact, but he didn't want Lynch to know he had
enough money for his own place.

'Same address?' Lynch's voice was preoccupied and automatic.

'Uh-huh.'

'Same employment?'

'Rah-Rodney's Place.' Although he could have controlled it, he tended
to let his stammer ride in here, wanting to come across as slightly
pitiful.

'Still' – Lynch squinted at his book – 'night manager?'

'Uh-huh. Yeah.'

'So how's it going?' Lynch didn't look up.

'O-OK.'

'No other arrests, pending charges, drug use, problems?'

'Ah-I'm good.' Strike never used dope in his life, just said he did when
he got busted so he could hook up with Second Wind, the drug treatment
sentencing alternative, and avoid spending ninety days in County, the
mandatory time on a 364 for selling drugs in Dempsy. In retrospect he
wondered if that was so smart, because he had to do three months as an
outpatient in a drug treatment program – all those 'tough love' sessions,
two hours of everybody screaming at each other – and he still had to see
Ron, his Second Wind counselor, every month for a year. But anything
was better than County. They had two to three Virus deaths a week in
there. In there: Victor. Shit.

'You got some money for me?' Lynch hawked into his fist, a phlegmy
cough that made Strike turn away.

Strike dug in his pocket for some crumbly bills, pulled out a twenty,
two tens, a five and a single, flattening them out on the desk as if they
were all he had in the world.

'I got like forty-six. I'm ha-having trouble this month. Can I, you
know, like bring in fifty-four next month, to even up? It a ha-hard
month right now.'

Strike always felt it was a good policy to be shy a few bucks, maybe
even show up flat broke every now and then – a working man with bills.
He had a $1,080 mandatory fine to pay off in $50-a-month installments

from the drug charge, including the $30 Victim Compensation Board tab and a $50 lab fee for spot urine testing. He could have paid it off in one lump sum, but it was smarter to drag it out, play it straight.

Strike opened his probation book for a receipt stamp, laid the bills on top and slid it a few inches toward the PO. 'Suh-so, Mr Lynch, it OK if I slide the four dollar till next month?'

Lynch looked at him for the first time since he'd come into the cubicle, his face all eye slits, boils and wattles. Strike felt a horrible sliding sensation, a sweaty panic, as if he was a little kid whose mother had taken him in for a routine checkup only to have the doctor pull out a harpoon-size hypodermic.

'What do you mean, a *hard* month? How was it hard?' Lynch's eyelids were so red they looked skinned.

Strike's throat constricted, the stammer uncontrollable now, the truth coming to him in one big picture: Victor had given him up, and this whole visit to the PO was a trap. They knew all about him, about his slick caution, about how he'd never miss a PO appointment. A trap, and he had walked right into it.

Lynch kept staring. 'How was it hard?'

'You know, wuh-with bills and all.'

'What bills?'

'House bills, whatnot. My muh-mother's not working this month.'

'*House* bills . . . What other kind of bills?'

'Hey.' Strike felt lubricated, his T-shirt swimming across his ribs. 'It only four dollars. You want me to get it now? I probably ga-got it at home, you know.'

The more Lynch stared, the more Strike wanted to talk, tell him he didn't have anything to do with the Darryl Adams murder, that Buddha Hat was the hit man. Strike's fear of County was greater than his fear of any one psycho out there.

'What else you spending money on?'

'F-f-f-fuh-h . . .' He couldn't get the word 'food' out of his mouth. Goddamn POs, they were just like cops – kill you with a look, tear out your heart with a mumble.

Lynch watched Strike sputter for a minute, then stared down at the open probation book and crumpled money. He reached for his phone.

'Larry, Dan Lynch.'

Strike was almost in tears now, all his carefully planned lies in shambles, sitting there nerveless and floppy, saying in a small voice, 'It was Buddha Hat . . .' But Lynch didn't hear him, and before Strike could repeat himself, another county worker came by, a soft hairy man in glasses with curvature of the spine and a low-slung potbelly under his belt like his ass was on backwards.

Lynch slid back from his desk and pulled out a glass beaker about twice the size of a ten-dollar bottle of coke.

Strike went cold with comprehension: The motherfucker wants a urine sample. Relieved, insulted, disgusted with himself for panicking, Strike stood up, leaving the money and the book on the desk.

'It best not come back dirty.' Lynch was already heads down in his big green MALES book, looking up something else, somebody else.

The Dempsy probation office was across the hall from the Municipal Building's cafeteria, and as Strike and the urine-test supervisor walked to the john, Thumper, Crunch and Smurf appeared with coffee and candy bars, Strike guessing that they were on their way upstairs for some overtime-paying court testimony. The three of them saw Strike and the supervisor walking toward the john, the supervisor holding a clipboard in one hand and the beaker in the other. The cops started howling like dogs.

'You got a piss test, Strike?' Thumper said.

'Don't you worry 'bout Strike,' Crunch bellowed. 'Strike be *clean*. He be clean as a *Strike!*'

Crunch squeezed his crotch and all three started hissing, '*Pss pss pss.*' Strike tried to ignore them. The supervisor was oblivious behind his glasses as he led Strike into the men's room. Even with the bathroom door shut, Strike heard Thumper bawling, 'Dicky check! Dicky check!' somewhere down the hall.

Strike took the beaker and headed for a stall, but the supervisor touched his elbow again and extended a hand to the open urinals. 'Got to do it in front of me.'

'What?' Strike was outraged, but the clipboard and the glasses took away all recognizable contact points, cut off all hope of arguing for some privacy.

Strike turned slightly toward the wall, took himself out of his fly. The supervisor shifted his stance, tilted his head to get an unobstructed view, then waited in the silence of the four-stall, three-urinal, two-sink municipal bathroom for Strike to pee.

'Guys go into the stalls, they like to fill the bottle with water from the toilet.'

Strike closed his eyes to concentrate.

'I get the bottle back, first thing I do is feel if it's cold or hot. Cold means toilet water.'

The silence stretched out. Strike was furious at Lynch: a piss test after all this time. Six goddamn months and Lynch still didn't trust him, didn't *know* him.

'You want me to turn on the water faucet? That helps some guys.'

Strike tuned this little four-eyed rat out of his head, trying to will a trickle down from his belly.

The bathroom door opened in a burst and six lawyers came in, moving to the urinals, the stalls, the sinks, talking basketball, all of them taking in Strike with his bottle and the supervisor pushing his glasses up his nose, all milling around him in a busy, distracted swirl. They were tall, white, wearing wash-and-wear suits and taking jump shots with their paper towels into the wastebaskets, announcing 'Dr J!,' 'Bird!,' squinting into the mirrors, combing their hair. Strike stood frozen, his dick dead in his hand, not feeling, not thinking, everything coming at him in colors right now.

Goddamn, they do make you pay.

When Strike returned to the projects an hour later, a crowd was circling something or someone by the benches. A crowd usually meant a spectacle of misery – an arrest, a fight, someone having a seizure. But when he waded through the shoulders, he was surprised to see a source of joy: Wayne Dobie, The Word's big brother, home on leave from Wiesbaden in a crisp, clean Green Beret uniform, looking tight and right, girls reaching out to touch his epaulet braids, guys giving him the 'god*damn*' treatment, backing up to get a better look at the double chevrons, the insignias and sharp-shooter bars.

Strike, who was about the same age as Wayne, had never really known him, but he remembered that two years ago Wayne was bad news, a street fighter and a clocker who ran with a crew under a guy named Shavawn Deeds, who was now in Rahway for murder. Wayne himself had stabbed someone from another project, put him in intensive care. He would have gone straight to jail too except that his lawyer was able to argue self-defense. Then Andre the Giant interceded, and Wayne was given the choice of prison time or enlistment.

Reluctantly joining the crowd, Strike studied Wayne, who was nervously pulling on his jacket, stepping in place with those high black paratrooper boots like a show horse, then standing still, chesty, glowing and heroic, happy to be home. Strike was entranced, but he resented

Wayne too, for breaking free of the game and coming up winners. As if
picking up on his thoughts, Wayne jerked his head in Strike's direction,
bellowed 'Hey!' and plowed through the crowd. Strike was about to
duck but Wayne bulled right past him and into Andre the Giant's arms.
Andre smiled and hugged him, whooping like a siren, then stepped back
and checked out the new Wayne, wringing his wrist as if trying to bring
down a thermometer.

'Gah-*damn*! You see your grandmother yet?'

'I just got here!' Wayne yelled.

'Well, what you doin' hangin' out down *here* for, man? Git up there!'

Wayne yanked his duffel bag to his shoulder and headed for his
building, with half the crowd following him.

Strike took his seat on the top slat and watched Andre, who stood hands
on hips, gazing after Wayne, his pride obvious. Andre made a high noise
of pleasure, as if to sign off on the subject, and then turned his attention
to the bench just as Horace came out of his building. Horace froze in his
tracks, ready to run.

'I told you I ain't gonna chase you,' Andre said. 'You surrender
yourself yet?'

Horace gave him a bewildered look.

'You got till two o'clock on Friday.' Andre turned to Strike. 'You tell
him what I told you to?'

Strike shrugged in a way that could have meant 'of course' or 'I don't
remember.'

'You a boy with a outstanding warrant on your ass, Horace,' Andre
said. 'You best get your mother and go over to Juvie Hall to*day*, you
hear me?'

Horace hunched his shoulders and backed into the building.

Andre waved him off and beamed at Strike. 'You ready?'

Strike froze, then tried to calm himself. 'I didn't do nothin'.'

'I *told* you we were goin' shoppin'. I said it and I meant it.'

'What?' Strike felt a little tremble of relief.

'You got money on you?' Andre leaned over him, throwing shadow.

'Unh-uh.'

'Well, you best get some because we goin' right now.'

'I got to get it.'

Andre shrugged. 'Well get it, then – I give you fifteen minutes. Bring
about this much.' Andre held his fingers apart a half inch, then pointed
at Strike. 'Fifteen minutes.'

Strike made a slow trip to one of his safe houses and got back to the benches in half an hour. He had hoped that Andre would be gone, counseling the broken of spirit or off on some just-say-no mission, but there he was, sprawled out on the bench with some of the crew, shooting the breeze and shutting down the action.

Strike held his arms high as Andre patted him down.

'How about I give you the money,' Strike said. 'You can do whatever you want – you know, judge ha–how best to spend it.'

'Naw, I ain't taking no money from you. That don't look too *kosher*, me taking cash from you. You gonna do it all. I ain't gonna touch it.'

'What you think, I got drugs on me?' Strike put some scorn into it. At least Andre didn't humiliate you with Johnson checks or look in your mouth like a slave trader.

'Just makin' sure.' Andre ran a fast hand around Strike's waist and palmed the arc of his crotch. 'Let's go.'

Andre used his own car, a Jeep Cherokee, bright red, the kind of ride a player would drive. They cruised JFK, Strike sitting in the shotgun seat.

'Check it out.' Andre nodded to a row of shut-down storefronts, their riot gates framed by chipped wood. Slowing down, he pointed out a forest-green storefront flanked by the Mount Pisgah Church and the Slo Cooked Gizzards Restaurant. 'The one in the middle? I just took a lease on that. I'm gonna open a gym for cops in there, get it cleaned up, get some mirrors, lights. I'm gonna charge ten dollars a month for membership, put like a police hangout right in the middle of all this. What you think of that?'

'Where you get the money to open a gym?'

'Hey, I got houses. I got six houses, I got two jobs.' Andre raised an eye. 'What you think, you the only hustler around here? You ever see me *not* working?'

Strike shrugged.

'Look here.' Andre pointed out the faded white hand-painted sign over his gym-to-be. 'Mr and Mrs Little Grocery Store. What you think of that?'

'What about it?'

'This place used to be Rodney's. This was his first store. I'm gonna put a cop club right in your boss's old place. You think he'd appreciate that?'

Strike didn't answer, although he thought Rodney wouldn't have any problem with it at all, since he got along with the police pretty well.

A block farther down the boulevard, Andre parked in front of a store called Operation Takeback, which sold books and T-shirts.

'You got your money with you?' Andre leaned against the driver's window.

Strike frowned. 'We going in there?'

'Let me see what you got.' Andre tilted his chin to Strike's front pocket.

Strike produced a two-inch-thick roll of twenties wrapped in a rubber band, pulling it half out of his pocket, then jamming it back in. Andre motioned for Strike to get out.

The store had been around for years, but Strike had never been inside, never been curious about it. The owners were big on the Jamaican-African connection – every surface was painted red, black and green, and reggae music blasted continuously – but there were as many posters of Malcolm X and Martin Luther King as there were of Bob Marley and Nelson Mandela.

Andre steered Strike by the shoulder and planted him in front of a rotating rack. All the books on display were biographies of black Americans.

'Pick me out about ten,' Andre said.

'You said mattresses, man.'

'Yeah, we get there too. Just do it, awright? Ten.'

The books belonged to a series, each volume costing eight dollars and forty-five cents, Strike thinking, Times ten equals a lot of money for books.

He scanned the titles and started plucking: Malcolm X, Martin Luther King, Muhammad Ali. Those names he knew, but most of the rest were unfamiliar. He pulled out a book about Sojourner Truth, liking the sound of that name. He took a Jack Johnson book after he saw the face on the cover. The boxer looked to Strike like a guy Rodney used to run with, Soupy Davis, such a hard-core psycho that not even Erroll Barnes could look him in the eye.

Strike regarded the books in his hands, liking their clean smell, the slick smoothness of their spines. He looked across the store to the cash register, where Andre was waiting for him. The self-satisfied smirk on his face sent Strike back to the shelf, and he picked out an extra biography – Chester Himes – for spite.

Walking outside, Strike's first impulse was to dump the books in Andre's hands, divorce himself from this bullied purchase. But he couldn't get over the heftiness of his own acquisition, the way all the books matched each other in their glistening black covers, and when they got in the car he put them in his lap instead.

As they headed down the boulevard, Strike could tell who was hanging out working and who was hanging out for nothing – it was in the eyes and the posture. Some of the clockers he knew recognized him but quickly looked away.

'Shit, they aw-all think I'm turning *state's* or something.'

Andre laughed. 'Yeah.'

'You gonna get me killed driving around like this. Any a them get locked up tonight? They gonna say, "Yeah, Strike was with that cop today. The nigger put the fuh-finger on me."'

'Yeah.' Andre laughed again.

Every time Andre saw a police car he slowed down and leaned out the window, waving and tossing banter. He even joked with some off-duty sheriffs who were drinking beer in front of a grocery. Strike felt a strange dizziness come over him: this was just like driving around with Rodney, but Rodney for the other side.

The Furniture Shack was a big concrete hangar off I-9 and Horton Avenue, right across from a combination driving range and batting cage park, and just up the road from the prosecutor's office, where the Homicides hung their hats.

Pulling up alongside the store, Andre pointed to the batting cages across the road, which were empty in the gray afternoon. 'I used to take Wallace Mooney there when he was a kid. He had them quick wrists even then. Twelve years old and he got around on a fastball like a major leaguer.'

Mooney, now a minor leaguer in the San Diego Padres farm system, was a Roosevelt success story, another trophy on Andre's wall. Strike had been in a few classes with him in high school; he was a nice guy who always dressed clean and sensible, and never gave Strike a funny look when he had trouble talking.

'Wallace Mooney,' Andre announced, 'now there was a boy with destiny in his genes. His grandfather played on the Birmingham Barons with Willie Mays. You know that?'

'Huh,' Strike said. He was looking down the road at the prosecutor's office, hulking under the skyway.

'Quick wrists, good family.' Andre stared at the empty cages. 'So how you feeling about your brother?'

The question caught Strike off guard and he fought down his stammer to answer. 'I don't know nothin' about that.'

'I didn't ask you what you *know*, I asked you how you *feel*.'

'It's beat, what can I say? I don't know, you know, it's . . . He

must've had his reasons.' Strike exhaled, running options through his
head, wondering if there was anything he could say that would help
Victor out. But he couldn't, not without implicating himself. Andre was
smart, and even if Strike had said something about 'word on the street,'
Andre would be on him in a heartbeat.

'How's your mother holding up?'

Strike shrugged. 'She don't taw-talk to me, so I couldn't tell you.'

Andre gave Strike a weary smirk. 'Can you blame her?'

'Naw, Andre, I guess not. You know, it's not like I had quick
wrists or nothin'.' Strike got out of the car, thinking, Get this bullshit
over with.

The Furniture Shack was a vast and gloomy space, a hot airless sea
of cheap goods in plastic sheathing. Both side walls were covered with
propped-up rolls of carpeting, and the far rear wall was a filmy nimbus of
wrapped and stacked mattresses. The entire floor area was an imploded
living room hosting dozens of couches and recliners jammed shin to shin.
Gooseneck lamps arced over the velour and naugahyde like lone reeds in
a pond.

Strike made a face at the choking smell of plastic, but his eye feasted on
the rolling walls of color, the endless styles and finishes of the couches, the
newness of things. He walked through a lane of carpet sample displays, his
hand running from one rainbow hump to another, then down a staggered
waterfall of shaggy squares. His eye was drawn to an imitation-leather
recliner with a bronze finish, a rust-colored velour love seat and couch
in the middle of the room and a Chinese-red Formica bedroom set with
brass trim. He returned his attention to the bronze recliner, experienced
a chewy desire even though he couldn't imagine owning it, coming into
his house and just sitting in it. Sit and do what?

'Yes, fellas?' A wiry salesclerk with a mustache and a flickering eye
tic sidled up to Strike, his movements quick and ratlike.

Strike looked back at Andre, who nodded primly for him to proceed.

'I want some mattresses,' Strike said, the craving still in his guts: Who'd
steal wall-to-wall carpeting from you?

'Mattresses.' The salesman bobbed his head, snapped his fingers in the
air for them to follow and brought them to the rear wall.

'Size?'

Strike looked to Andre, who spread his hands wide.

'Full. And just ma-mattresses, no box springs or nothin.'

'Mattresses. More than one?'

Andre held up ten fingers.

'Like nine.'

'Nine. What's this, for a school?'

'Yeah, it's for kids.' Strike felt good when he said that; he was starting to enjoy this. Something bright orange caught his eye over by the couches and he wanted it, whatever it was.

'Well, if it's for kids, let me see what I can do for you.' The salesclerk pulled a wafer-thin calculator out of his shirt pocket and started poking. 'What are you, City?'

'Unh-uh.' Strike's attention strayed to a twin mattress, outer-space blue with exploding rocket ships and asteroids. He thought of Tyrone: maybe he needed a mattress too.

'Are you tax-exempt?'

Strike hesitated, not sure what that meant.

Andre laughed. 'Yeah, he's kind of tax-exempt.'

'Normally it's sixty for a full, but for nine? For what you're doing for the kids? Forty-five, how's that sound?'

'Yeah, OK.' Strike wondered what the salesman thought they were doing for the kids, but obviously the guy assumed it was something positive. Strike liked that. If he thought about it, he had always liked kids. He was good with kids. Like José – getting José to bed in Crystal's house. Rodney had once said that Whitney Houston was dead-on when she sang, 'The children are the future.'

'I say forty-five, I'm assuming you're talking cash, because credit cards, checks' – the salesman made a clicking noise – 'you know what I mean?'

'Yeah, cash, cash,' Strike said, thinking someday he'd work with kids, help kids, thinking of Victor's boys, turning that image off real quick, thinking of Tyrone – Tyrone looking up to him, *all* kids looking up to him, the way they looked up to Wayne today. But Wayne was about War; Strike would be about Peace.

The salesman asked for a fifty percent deposit, but Andre jumped in to say they'd pay for it all now, giving Strike a look that made it clear he didn't want to hunt him down the next week in order to get the rest of the money. Strike didn't care; surrounded by all this fresh merchandise, he was lost in an image of Whitney Houston singing 'The Children Are the Future,' imagining himself being mobbed by adoring kids. He felt loose and generous. Even the overheated plastic lost its stench. It was now the scent of newness, of variety, of options.

Andre pulled up to the benches, threw the Jeep into park and sat slouched in the driver's seat, smiling through his goatee.

'You know what we gonna do next week?'

'Aw c'mon, Ah-Andre. That's it, man.'

'We gonna clean out that space down there. Get rid of that piss stink.'

'Oh yeah?' Strike turned his head away, smiling, thinking that he had never run from cops in his life, but if Andre came after him for *that* . . .

Strike took the books from his lap and gave them a last sniff for that smell of newness before jamming them between the dashboard and the window.

'OK, Andre.' He moved to open the door.

'What are you doin'?' Andre's voice went high.

'What?' Strike had one foot on the ground.

'Those books are for *you*. They a thank-you present *from* yourself *to* yourself.'

Andre palmed all eleven and dropped them back on Strike's lap. He put out his hand. 'You did good today.'

Strike turned away, fighting down another smile. 'Everybody likes Ah-Andre, 'cause Andre for the *people*.' He tried to put a sarcastic spin on it, tried not to admit to himself that this was about as happy and hopeful as it ever got for him.

18

Walking into the office on Monday afternoon, Rocco saw an article on the arrest in the Darryl Adams job pinned to the bulletin board. Rocco's name was mentioned twice. Usually that gave him a little kick, but this time the article served to remind him of how unnerving and frustrating the interrogation had been.

The night before, when he had handed Victor Dunham over to County, Rocco had reached out to one of the ranking correction officers, a sergeant named Frank Lopez, and asked him to keep an eye on the kid. Over the years, Rocco would occasionally call Lopez or some other buddy on the inside and request that an incoming mutt be put in a cell with a certain informer, or that a particularly nasty scumbag be assigned a nightmare roommate, but last night was the first time Rocco had ever asked a CO to do some babysitting for him and watch a confessed murderer's back. Given Victor's background, it had seemed like the decent thing to do.

On the way to dinner with Mazilli, Rocco parked for a minute outside the Municipal Court and went downstairs to the Bureau of Criminal Identification to get a copy of Dunham's pedigree for the homicide folder. BCI was in the basement of the court building, below the ground-level police garage. It was a gloomy antique of an office, with mint-green walls, oily wainscoting and an ancient scale that had once taken the height and weight of young punks like Carmine Galante, Frank Costello and Longy Zwillman in the days when 'consorting with known Italians' was a criminal offense on the Dempsy books.

Rocco walked up to the waist-high counter that divided the holding cells and fingerprinting station from a cluster of battered desks and filing cabinets. He gave a short salute to Bobby Bones. The ID King was holding down the fort solo, sitting behind a typewriter and eating a sandwich.

Bones met Rocco belly-to-belly across the divider and braced himself like a goalie. 'Hit me.'

'Victor Dunham.'

The crow's feet at the corners of Bones's eyes turned to starbursts. 'Who?' His mouth hung open, a crescent of yellow cheese plastered along his jaw.

'Victor Dunham.'

Bones reared back and smoothed his hair. 'He got a moniker?'

Rocco shrugged.

'Dunham, Dunham . . . Victor Dunham . . . You sure he's Dempsy?'

'Yup.'

Bones looked lost. 'You sure that's his name?'

Rocco scratched his jaw. 'Do me two favors, OK?'

'Sure.'

'Number one, look it up in the files, OK?'

'Yeah, well of course,' Bones said unhappily.

'Number two, take that fucking piece of cheese off your face.'

Bones moved toward a six-foot-high cabinet, fingers twitching at his hips like a gunslinger. 'Dunham . . .'

'Look under D.' Rocco leaned forward on the counter. 'Please.'

'How about a *Ronald* Dunham?' Bones offered, sounding like a desperate salesman. 'I got a Ronald Dunham.'

'Please.'

Hissing in defeat, Bones finally went into a drawer and pulled out a file card. 'Son of a bitch.' He glared at it, committing it to memory. 'Victor Dunham . . . who the fuck is *this* prick?'

Rocco and Mazilli sat over screwdrivers and a pizza, Rocco reading a printout of Victor Dunham's sheet. It contained only one charge, assault on a police officer, which was downgraded to a disorderly person and dismissed a month later in Municipal Court. The arrest report consisted of a perfunctory paragraph about the kid assaulting Thumper, referred to here as P.O. Michael Carney, and hindering him in the performance of his duties. Rocco read into what was there and not there – nothing about possession of drugs, no language like 'in the commission of a crime' or 'in the company of,' meaning Victor wasn't in a fight or part of a gang. Whatever went down was between Thumper and the kid, and since it was downgraded to a disorderly person and ultimately thrown out, Victor had probably filed a countercharge, claiming that it was Thumper who was out of line, the two charges then canceling each other out.

Rocco remembered the kid's comment in the car about the incident

– 'arrested for eye contact,' he'd said – and made a mental note to ask what had happened next time he ran into Thumper.

Rocco pulled another wedge off the pie and said, 'When do we get the ballistics back on that gun yesterday, in like two weeks?'

'Ten days, two weeks, like that,' Mazilli said.

'You know what I want to do? Let's go over to the kid's house, talk to his old lady, make sure he's not some whack job who confesses to everything like a hobby.'

Mazilli waved Rocco away. 'He did it. Don't get crazy on me here.'

'Yeah, I know. It's just, you know, that confession reads like such horseshit. If the gun comes back clean, plus we find out he once confessed for snatching Judge Crater, I'm gonna feel like a fucking horse's ass.' Rocco put a little pleading in his voice. He always had to song-and-dance Mazilli into doing any kind of work on a case once they had the perp locked up.

Looking sour, Mazilli waved again. 'It's on you.'

Rocco did the driving, and thirty minutes later they pulled up alongside the benches of the Roosevelt Houses. It was a balmy, starry night and nearly a hundred people were hanging out, every one of them taking note of the two Homicides in the Chevy, some pointedly looking away, others muttering or making side-mouthed comments.

'They're gonna trash the fucking car,' Rocco said. 'Maybe we should go in with Housing.'

'C'mon.' Mazilli got out and walked directly to the bench, picking out a kid he knew from his liquor store. 'What's your name again?'

'Futon.' The kid wore aqua headphones and was eating Gummi Bears out of a jar. He looked to his friends on the bench, all of whom had suddenly become stony and distant. One kid eased off the slats and casually strolled away. Probably holding, thought Rocco, coming up behind Mazilli.

'Where you live, Futon?' Mazilli squinted, half smiling.

'Here.' He raised a limp hand at 6 Weehawken.

'What floor?'

'Three.'

Mazilli scanned the third-floor windows, then looked back at the car.

'Who's your mother, Futon?'

'Doreen Owens.'

'Doreen Owens.' Mazilli nodded as if he knew who she was. 'You know me, right?'

'You the Homicide from the store.'

'Watch the car for me.'

'I might have to go.' He stole a peek at his friends again. Rocco could hear the insect tinniness of the music leaking out of the headphones.

'Just watch the car for me,' Mazilli said softly, then walked away before the kid could protest.

Making his way across the esplanade from the benches, Rocco saw that the news of their arrival preceded them by about a hundred yards; everybody seemed to be looking in their direction even before they came into view. A dust cloud of children followed them. It began with two or three kids from the benches and picked up new members along the way, and by the time the men arrived at Victor Dunham's building, enough kids skipped and chattered in their wake to make Rocco feel like the Pied Piper.

One of the kids from the parade entered the building with Rocco and Mazilli and stood by the elevators. He was a boy of about twelve, handsome and serious-looking, and when he stepped into the elevator with them but didn't press for a floor, Rocco figured that someone had sent him to find out where they were going. As the car began its slow, clanky ride to eleven, Rocco studied the boy, who in turn studied the warped floor.

'Where *you* going?' Rocco asked.

'My friend's house.' His voice was shy and far away.

'You didn't push his floor.'

The boy hesitated, then pushed ten.

'You almost took an extra ride for nothing, see?'

When the elevator opened at ten, Rocco barked, 'Hey!'

Poised for flight, the boy turned to Rocco with one hand holding the elevator door.

'Who's Mister Big?' Rocco growled, playing the hard guy in a B movie. To Rocco's surprise the boy got the joke, his face flattening in pleasure for a second before running off down the hallway.

'Nice kid.' Rocco held the elevator door open until he heard a heavy steel door slam down the hall. The boy was taking the stairway back to the street, to report to whoever sent him.

Rocco and Mazilli walked down the musky, graffiti-scorched hallway to apartment 11G. Rocco hit the bell a few times before hearing a husky voice say 'Who . . .' above the TV noise from within.

'How ya doing. It's Rocco Klein, prosecutor's office,' he shouted, standing on tiptoes and fingering his shield in its billfold.

An overweight, soft-faced girl of about nineteen opened the door and looked at Rocco heavily, ignoring his shield.

'Are you ShaRon?'

She didn't answer, just walked back into the living room and left the door open for them. After sitting down on the edge of an easy chair, she glued her eyes to the screen of a console television.

Mazilli came in behind Rocco and closed the door. A baby and a little boy slept on an open convertible sofa next to the television, and at the far end of the living room, in the doorless archway to the tiny kitchen, an older woman stood with her back to them, working briskly over an ironing board.

Rocco moved between the girl and the television. 'You're ShaRon, right?'

She nodded blindly, delicately scratching the rim of her nostrils with a pinkie nail.

Rocco moved a step toward the woman ironing shirts and raised his voice. 'Are you Mrs. Dunham?'

The woman nodded but didn't turn to face them.

Rocco spoke to the girl again. 'Can we sit down for a minute? Tell you what we're here for?'

'Uh-huh,' ShaRon grunted without suggesting where. They side-stepped the sofa and slid into two chairs at a small dining table set flush against a living room wall, right behind the older woman and her ironing board.

Rocco was impressed with the apartment; it was cramped but clean. The open convertible took up the heart of the living room, and the sofa pillows stacked alongside the wall were sheathed in clear vinyl, as were three lampshades, ShaRon's easy chair and the VCR on top of the TV. The dining table was already laid out for tomorrow's breakfast – cereal bowls and silverware on plastic placemats – and the kitchen beyond the ironing board had an air of scoured spotlessness.

'Have you spoken to Victor yet?' Rocco addressed the house at large, squinting across the room at a wall unit covered with framed family photographs.

'Yeah.' ShaRon's gaze shifted from the TV to the baby and the boy spread-eagled on the sofa bed.

'What's his bail?'

'Fifty thousand.'

'No ten percent, hah?' Rocco tried to sound sympathetic.

'All cash,' said the older woman, snapping out a wet shirt.

Hearing a wheezy sound coming from the kitchen, Rocco wondered if something was boiling over on the stove.

'It'll come down in about two weeks,' he said to the older woman's back. 'Who's his lawyer?'

'Mister Newton,' she answered, and gave the shirt another snap. Her back was still turned, and now Rocco realized that the sound he heard came from the woman herself: it was her labored breathing.

'Jimmy Newton? Good man, good man, I went to high school with him.' Rocco locked eyes with Mazilli, then spoke to the room again. 'Victor – did he say anything to you when you talked to him?'

No one answered.

'Did you know he had a gun?'

No answer again. Rocco watched ShaRon staring at the TV and thought, Fuck this, the kid is locked up, why am I even bothering? So fucking typical: the family of the do-er treating him like shit the day after the lockup, as if it was *his* fault their kid was a goddamn murderer.

'ShaRon, listen. I'm trying to help here. You got to understand, as far as the prosecutor's office is concerned the case is closed. Victor came in, told us he did it, gave up the gun. But he didn't tell us *why* he did it. He didn't give us any reason. I'm sitting here and I see he's got a nice home, nice kids, a wife. I know he works like a dog. Why would he throw that away? It doesn't make any sense, a guy like that just . . . He had to have a good reason, and if I *knew* that good reason, it would help him. *I* would help him.'

Rocco looked from woman to woman, both of them treating this like a visit from the army of the occupation, which wasn't too far wrong. The truth was, they were better off keeping their mouths shut, since Rocco was really asking them to help nail down the case on behalf of the prosecution.

The little boy sat up, rolled off the convertible, blinked a couple of times at Rocco and sat down on the floor between his mother's feet.

Rocco turned to the older woman one last time. 'Can you help me help him here?'

'He has a stomach condition,' she said.

'Yeah?' Rocco waited.

'They gonna give him his medication in there? He's got to have his medication.'

'If he told them about it, I'm sure they'll attend to it,' Rocco said reassuringly, thinking, They always bitch about the service.

Mazilli jerked his head toward the door but Rocco gave it another shot.

He turned to ShaRon again. 'Did he have a drinking problem?'

She hissed at her son before answering, 'He only drank at night.'

'Yeah? Me too. How about drugs, did he have a problem with drugs?'

'Unh-unh, he dint have nothing to do with that.'

'Did he seem different to you this last week? Did he behave differently, act any way unusual? Tense, agitated, different?'

ShaRon shrugged. The older woman seemed as if she was trying to iron a shirt right through the board and into the floor.

'Did he have any new friends recently – you know, hang out with new people?'

'He dint hang out. He just worked.' ShaRon plucked at her son's hair.

Mazilli nodded to go again. Rocco held up a finger.

'Look, Victor's claiming self-defense, and it's not gonna wash the way he's got it laid out. If I don't get some help, if *he* don't get some help, he's looking at thirty years with no parole. That's the law. Please, if there's anything, any way you can help me help him, tell me now. Because we can fight the *truth* with the *truth*, but we can't fight the truth with a *lie*. So is there anything you can help me help him with? Now's the time.'

It was silent save for the TV. Fed up, Rocco groaned to his feet.

'He got to have his stomach medicine,' Victor's mother said again.

She turned, finally, and Rocco was startled by her face, the flesh carved lean with exhaustion, the eyes bulging slightly.

'He got to have it or he's gonna get sick.' Her mouth hung open and her chest gently heaved with her breathing.

'I'll make a call tonight, check up on it,' Rocco lied, staring at her taut and lined face, those haunted protruding eyes.

As Rocco inched past the open sofa, he scanned the photos on the wall unit. His eye caught a color shot of a skinny teenager in a tuxedo.

'Can I ask you a favor? Can I borrow this picture? I got to go around to people where he hung out, the places he worked. I don't want them looking at a mug shot of him. I'd rather show a nice picture if I can, you know what I mean? Keep people's minds open.'

'Why you want *that* picture?' ShaRon cocked her head, a kind of half-dead amusement in her face.

'Because he looks good in it. He looks like the nice guy I know he is.'

'*Who* is? That ain't Victor. That's his brother.'

'His brother.' Rocco looked closer: it really wasn't the kid after all. 'Gee, looks a lot like him, don't it? What's this guy's name?'

'Ronald.'

'Ronald Dunham?'

'Yeah,' ShaRon said. 'They brothers.'

'Ronald Dunham.' Where had he heard that name?

'They call him Strike.'

'Strike. Is he around?' Rocco remembered now, from Bones at BCI.

'He don't live here no more.'

'No? Strike Dunham, what's he do?'

'He's around,' ShaRon said.

'You know where I can find him?'

'Just around.'

Mazilli leaned across Rocco to take a close look at the picture, then stepped back and gave Rocco's arm a short tug toward the door.

Rocco took out two calling cards and dropped them on the top of the console TV.

'ShaRon, what do *you* think happened?'

She nodded slowly at the television. 'He's to himself. I don't know.'

Rocco ignored a second tug from Mazilli. 'Mrs Dunham?'

'*Ta*gamet. The doctor says he's got to have that *Ta*gamet.' She stared intently at Rocco, her terrible dried-out eyes pushing him out the door.

'*Ta*gamet,' Rocco growled, still spooked by the older woman's face, the pain in it. 'I think she knows something. She's got them uh-oh eyes.'

'Strike,' Mazilli said softly as he banged the back of his head against the elevator wall in time to the rhythmic knocking of the creaky gears and pulleys.

'What about him?'

'Strike.'

'You know the kid?'

'He's a no-good arrogant dope-dealing piece of shit comes into my store all the time like he craps beige. He used to work in Rodney's grocery, like a year ago? But he got promoted. Now he's running that crew by where we left the car. He's probably down there right now.'

'So he must have known this Darryl Adams kid, right? Wasn't he working in the grocery too, back then?'

'Absolutely. I used to see the two of them in there all the time last year.'

'So if these guys are brothers – Victor, Strike – and one's tied in with Rodney that we *know* of, used to work *with* the victim at Rodney's . . .' Rocco whirled his hands. 'So what do you think? Maybe this is a drug thing after all?'

'Yeah,' Mazilli said, 'maybe this Victor kid's a hit man. A quiet-storm hit man.'

'Double-oh-seven,' Rocco said.

They walked out into the night and headed back to the car.

'So, Maz, if you see this brother, what's his name, Strike, you want to take him to the office? Talk to him?'

'Nah, not right now. Let me take another pass at Rodney first.'

When Rocco and Mazilli came up on the benches again, they saw a full-blown street scene. Big Chief was putting Futon in handcuffs, Slick and Crunch were on their knees shaking out discarded paper bags, looking for bottle stashes, and Thumper was in a red-faced shouting match with a fat lady in a housedress, both of them waving their arms and bellowing as a crowd surged around them.

Rocco and Mazilli stood off to one side, watching the show.

'That boy do nothin' to nobody. He just a *boy*.' The woman was heaving with outrage.

'Who the hell asked you?' Thumper squawked, leaning into her.

'*Nobody* ask me, I'm *tellin'* you!' The woman stabbed the air in front of his face, a tissue in her hammy fist.

'That's *right*,' Thumper said, giving her his back.

'That's *right*,' she said, following him.

Thumper turned back to her again. 'You best get the fuck out of my face or I'll fucking throw you in there with him.'

'You gonna ar*rest* me? You gonna ar*rest* me?'

'If I can find cuffs big enough.' Thumper began to walk away again, agitated and scowling, Rocco reading in his face a disgust both for the woman and for himself.

'What you say?' The woman started to go after him, but Big Chief blocked her charge and her friends stepped in, talking to her, walking her into one of the buildings as she bellowed back, 'Who the fuck he think he is? What you gonna ar*rest* me for, for having a mind?'

'For having a *mouth*,' Thumper shouted back.

Big Chief took Thumper's arm and said, 'Cool out there.' He waved the crowd back, looked to Rocco and Mazilli and made a face.

'Fat fucking whale,' Thumper muttered, walking in small circles.

Mazilli went over to Futon, who was handcuffed and leaning against the fence. 'What the hell you do?' he said, sounding amused.

'Check it out.' Big Chief held out the Gummi Bear jar, twisting off the false bottom to reveal four purple-stoppered bottles.

'Aah,' Mazilli grumbled in mock disappointment.

'I didn't know about that,' Futon said. 'Somebody just gave it to me like if I wanted some candy.'

'Shut the fuck up,' Thumper tossed in, still walking off the shouting match.

'Futonnn,' Big Chief growled mildly. He turned to Mazilli. 'He says he was working for you.'

'Oh yeah?' Mazilli said. 'Sure, he's my undercover man.'

'I would've been gone,' Futon said, 'but he said to stay here and watch his car. Then this guy come up, he says, "You want this jar of candy?"'

Rocco grinned. 'See what you did, Mazilli?'

'It just baking soda,' Futon said halfheartedly. 'It ain't even mine.'

Big Chief pulled his troops and walked off with an arm around Futon's neck like a paternal camp counselor.

'Call my aunt,' Futon said to his friends around the bench.

'Mikey,' Rocco said, walking alongside Thumper. 'I want to ask you about something. Where you headed, BCI or Juvie?'

Big Chief appraised Futon, then said, 'Juvie.'

'Where you going after, like late, the Pavonia?'

'Most likely,' Thumper said, steering Futon into the back of the Fury. 'I'll catch you later.'

As the Fury rolled, Rocco looked up and caught the eye of a heavyset middle-aged woman leaning on her meaty forearms out her third-floor window.

The woman smiled at Rocco, furtively mimed applauding the arrest, her palms not meeting. Rocco was struck by the secretiveness of the gesture: You come in, take away a dope dealer and one person *almost* claps. Locking up murderers, locking up dope dealers . . . well, that's the thanks you get when you're in the army of the occupation.

Unlocking the Chevy, Rocco noticed the boy who had spied on them in the elevator. He was perched on a low-slung garden chain and nursing a vanilla Yoo-Hoo. Rocco narrowed his eyes and pointed an accusatory finger. 'Who's Mister Big?'

The boy grinned and turned away in shy delight, Rocco thinking, Well, maybe not everybody hates us.

Back in the office, Rocco saw that someone had left a *Daily News* on his desk, the paper open to the People page, which featured a grainy photo of Sean Touhey and some woman all decked out for a benefit. Next to the picture was a drawing of Aquaman, standing spread-legged and arms akimbo in his fish-scale costume. Under the caption 'Glub, Glub,' an accompanying squib reported that the actor had just gotten the go-ahead on *Aquaman* and quoted Touhey on how this movie wasn't going to be just another superhero spinoff: 'Think of all the ecological issues around the sea. Oil spills, whale hunting, toxic dumping, dolphin deaths. This will be no comic book.'

'Fucking asshole,' Rocco muttered, eyeing the bulletin board across the office and thinking, Well, I'm in the paper too.

He slowly turned to face Mazilli. 'Aquaman . . . Did you put that on my desk?'

'Don't look at me.' Mazilli stuck a cigarette in his mouth to mask a smile and reached for the phone.

Rocco studied the picture of Touhey again. He carefully scissored out the drawing of Aquaman, then taped it to his desk light as a reminder to himself that at forty-three you don't make plans to dabble in different lives. At forty-three, what you are, what you know, is about as far as you're going to go in this life; about the most you can hope for is a little fine tuning and a pay hike or two.

Rocco sat with his hands clasped in his lap now, staring at Touhey and rocking in his chair. Behind him, Mazilli whistled tunelessly through his teeth as he began writing up the report of their visit to Victor Dunham's house. Mazilli was the better writer and usually took care of the reports. He was the better hunter too. Rocco was the glad-hander, the interrogation artist, the confession king. They had come to this honest division of labor a long time ago, and as Rocco gazed down at the waving, grinning movie star, he understood for the first time that whatever was jamming him up in his life right now would never be healed by any kind of glory or fame or recognition from others, that the healing would come from the life around him – his work, his partner, his family. It was just a matter of finding a few small gifts of connection. He had to have something to take home with him, something to bring into work, just get a little wheel of gifts going.

As Rocco was trying to decide whether this curative scenario had even a glimmer of tangibility, Rodney Little walked into the office from the deserted reception area. Looking tentative, Rodney stood slightly hunched forward, his Jheri curls gleaming under the fluorescents. His opaque sunglasses caught the bars of overhead light in a double image.

'What's up?' He stood in front of Mazilli's desk, ignoring Rocco, unconsciously touching the beeper on his hip. 'You called me, right?'

Mazilli leaned back, lit a cigarette and clasped his hands over his stomach. 'So, you got anything for me?'

'I'm workin' on it,' Rodney said. 'I got my people. How about you? You talk to Jo-Jo yet?'

'I'm working on it,' Mazilli said.

Rocco sat silently two desks back from the play: Rodney was Mazilli's action.

'Is that it?' Rodney seemed to unwind a little, and Rocco decided that the arrogant prick kind of liked strutting around a squad room without cuffs on.

'So, what do you hear from Victor Dunham?' Mazilli flicked his cigarette and missed the ashtray.

'Who?' Rodney hunched his neck. Rocco wished he wasn't wearing shades. He wouldn't have put it past Rodney to have slipped them on right before entering the office.

'Victor Dunham,' said Mazilli, staring at his reflection in Rodney's glasses.

'What's his name?' Rodney asked neutrally.

'Just that.'

Rodney made a face, shrugged.

'C'mon Rodney, Victor Dunham.'

'Show me a picture.'

Rocco pulled a glossy Polaroid from the homicide report and skimmed it to Mazilli's desk.

Rodney pushed up his shades and held the photo a few inches from his nose, scrutinizing the face with myopic concentration before dropping it back on Mazilli's desk. Rocco thought his blank reaction was genuine.

'You don't know him?' Mazilli cocked his head and smiled as if he was being teased. 'That's Strike's brother.'

'Well, I know *Strike*. You want to know something about Strike?'

Mazilli jerked his shoulders indifferently.

'What this guy do?' Rodney ran a shiny gray fingernail across Victor's face.

'We got him on the Ahab's job.'

'Yeah?' Rodney's voice went high. 'Huh,' he said, picking up the picture again and shoving his glasses back up to his hairline. He looked directly at Mazilli. 'Yeah, I wondered who did that, you know? 'Cause nobody that I know *knew*, you know?' His eyes went back to the picture. 'Wait a minute, I know this guy. What's his name?'

'Victor Dunham.'

'I seen him at Hambone's.'

'Not anymore.'

'Man, they got some nasty-tasting chicken there, you know, like they fry their shit in *hair* oil. Somebody once told me that they don't even slaughter their chickens, they just wait for them to get sick and die their *own* selves.' Grinning, he dropped the picture back on Mazilli's desk.

'You ever hear of anybody selling dope there?'

'Where.' Rodney blinked. 'Hambone's?'

'Ahab's.'

'Shit. I wouldn't misdoubt it. Goddamn, this city? You can't go like two blocks without scoring something if you got a mind to.'

Mazilli smiled. 'You should know, right?'

'Hey, Mazilli. Be nice now.'

Mazilli bobbed lazily in his chair, then sighed and skimmed the photo back to Rocco. 'So what's cooking out there, Rodney? What's shakin'?'

Rodney pouted, pulled on his crotch. 'Yeah, I got to talk to you about something.' He said this out the side of his mouth, implying it was for Mazilli's ears only.

Rocco got up to leave, reasonably certain that Rodney had never had any dealings with Victor Dunham, or at least nothing involving a conspiracy to commit murder.

'Maz, I'm going over to BCI on something. Where you gonna be?'

Mazilli swirled his finger in a little circle. 'Around.'

'I'm gonna want to go to that bar later, Rudy's. You up for that?'

'Beep me. I'll meet you there.'

Taking one last look at Rodney strolling around the office like he owned the place, Rocco slipped the Polaroid of Victor Dunham into the pocket of his sport jacket and headed for the door.

Outside in the parking lot Rocco pulled up short, the night so soft he lingered a moment before getting into his car. Above the coke-smelting plant and the arc of the skyway, stars hung crisp in a deep purple sky like a promise that all grief is temporary, and Rocco experienced a transcendent flush of well-being. Patty, Erin, Homicide – he had it all. It would be so easy to get that wheel of small gifts going, so easy to heal himself if he wanted to. The hell with Sean Touhey, the hell with any life that wasn't truly connected to his own.

Rocco continued across the lot, then saw a battered Cadillac with Garfields suckered to the windows parked next to his car. A thirtyish but matronly black woman was half dozing in the front passenger seat. Rocco assumed she was Rodney's wife.

He walked over to her side of the car. She rolled down her window, blinking and half smiling.

'How are you?' Rocco kicked at some loose gravel.

'With the Lord.' She gave a firm bob. 'And yourself?'

'Holding my own. How about Rodney, he with the Lord too?'

'I'm trying, you best believe that.'

'Yeah?' Rocco grinned.

'I'm gonna *get* 'im, too,' she said.

'Yeah? Me too.' He rocked his head from shoulder to shoulder, then said, 'Good night now,' and strolled off, thinking, One way or another no one gets away with anything in this life.

19

It had been two hours since the Homicides had left the projects, and Strike was still hiding in the lobby of 6 Weehawken, still brooding over the image of the heavyset detective who passed Tyrone on his chain perch, saying something that had made the kid smile, had made him turn his head and laugh. Two hours now and Strike was still pacing, thinking, What the hell is going on here?

Earlier in the evening, coming downstairs from the stash apartment, the books from his shopping trip with Andre under his arm, Strike had spotted the two Homicides just as they walked up to the benches. He recognized them both: one was the ballbreaker from Shaft Deli-Liquors, the other the heavyset cop from the night of the Ahab's. Certain they had come to pick him up, Strike hunkered down by the mailboxes with the books at his feet and peeked out the door until he caught Tyrone's eye. He beckoned the kid to the lobby, and when the Homicides began walking into the interior of the projects, Strike held Tyrone by his unmuscled arm and hissed, 'See where they go,' the first words he had uttered to the boy since their return from New York on Saturday. Big-eyed with mission, the kid flew off after the cops, then jogged back to Strike ten minutes later and breathlessly whispered, 'Forty-one Dumont, eleventh floor.' Strike had sent Tyrone back to his chain, and just as the kid took his seat, the benches exploded again – the Fury rolling up and grabbing Futon, Thumper and Futon's aunt going in each other's face, the Homicides returning to the scene just as it was cooling down.

Now, prowling the lobby like a tiger in a tight cage, Strike tried to think it through. The Homicides had gone to his mother's house, Victor's house, probably to ask his mother and ShaRon if they had any idea what happened at Ahab's. But maybe they were looking for *him*, asking where they could find him.

He stared out at the benches. They were empty now, the crew

temporarily scattered, Tyrone upstairs for the dinner hour. For a few minutes longer Strike watched the cars going by, hesitating, looking for clockers, the drivers put out, strung out, reluctantly moving off. When Tyrone finally came out of the building and resumed his position on the chain, Strike left his hideout and walked slowly toward him. They exchanged glances, then Strike turned and headed back to the lobby of 6 Weehawken.

After a minute or two Tyrone appeared in the doorway.

'What that cop say to you before?'

'Nothin',' Tyrone said hoarsely.

Strike studied his profile, trying to decipher the tension he saw there. 'Hey, don't disrespect me by *lyin'* to me. I saw him sayin' somethin' to you and I saw you *laugh*in'.'

Speechless, Tyrone gave a little shrug.

Strike sensed the kid's fear and remembered Andre, his warning about dealing with Tyrone, Strike thinking, But I'm not asking the kid to *do* anything.

'C'mon, man.' Strike spoke more softly now, as if Andre was eavesdropping. 'After all we done together? What's up with you?'

Tyrone fought down a smile on the word 'we,' and Strike knew he had him.

'He ast me, "Who's Mister Big."'

'He dint ask about me?'

'Unh-uh.'

'How about Ronald Dunham. Did he say, "Where's Ronald Dunham?"'

'He just say, "Who's Mister Big."'

Mister Big? What the hell did that mean? 'How come you ain't wearing those sneakers?'

Tyrone shrugged, looking ashamed.

Strike read the story in the shrug and let it slide; the kid's mother was supposed to be a third-degree artist, and new sneakers in the house probably wouldn't have gone unchallenged.

'C'mere,' he said. Seeing Tyrone hesitate, he impatiently gestured for the kid to come close. 'I ain't gonna *bite* you. C'mere.'

Strike picked up the stack of books from under the mailboxes and pressed them to Tyrone's midsection, moving the kid's arms for him so that he had a firm two-handed grip on all eleven volumes.

'Here,' Strike said, trying to come off positive and strong. 'You should learn about yourself, where you're coming from.'

Tyrone stared at him, mute and solemn.

Strike stared back, then turned his head away in exasperation. 'God-damn, don't you *ever* say thank you?'

About a half hour later, soon after Strike got up the nerve to resettle on the benches, Rodney drove by and honked his horn. He had his wife with him, dozing in the front passenger seat, her temple pressed flat against the window. She awoke with a start when Strike slid in the back and slammed the door after him. For the duration of the ride from the benches to her home, she hummed a gospel tune in a faint, high-pitched trill.

Rodney parked across the street from his house and watched in silence as Clover got out and then fumbled with her keys at the front door. When she disappeared inside, he turned to face Strike, who was still sitting in the back seat. 'How come you didn't tell me it was your brother did it?'

Strike stopped himself: he'd been about to say that Victor didn't do it. But then Rodney would say, 'Well, who did?' and the thought of telling Rodney about Buddha Hat filled Strike with terror.

Strike tried to keep his voice even. 'You said you dint want to know nothin'.'

'Your brother best not say nothin'.'

'He-he don't *know* nothin'.'

'Then what he do it for?'

Not knowing how to answer, Strike kept his mouth shut.

'You pay him?'

'Unh-uh.'

'What do you mean, he don't know nothin'?'

'I told him some story.'

Rodney gave him a steady look, then turned around and drove off. After a few minutes of silence, he caught Strike's eye in the rearview mirror. 'How come he gave hisself up? He religious?'

'I don't know. I don't think so. I mean, he go to-to church sometime, but he don't talk about Je-Jesus or nothin'.'

Rodney chewed on that, then said, 'I thought you told someone in a bar who was supposed to reach out, get somebody else.'

'I did. I told *him*. I don't know what happened.' Strike leaned forward, feeling awkward riding alone in the back seat. 'The Homicides come by to see my mother.'

'They just doing a follow-up. That's their job.'

Strike was surprised that Rodney didn't seem especially worried about any of this news; it was as if the murder was old business, not his concern. 'You think they'll come and talk to me?'

Rodney shrugged. 'They might. I was them? *I* would. But Mazilli? The guy with the store? Once they got somebody, he don't care too much on post-arrest follow-ups. He likes to move on, so I wouldn't worry about it. By the time they get around to you? Shit, there's gonna be another murder anyhow.'

'Who?'

'I don't know who. I'm just sayin', it's over with, they got their arrest, that's all I'm sayin'.'

Rodney waved a hand as if to declare the subject dead, and Strike felt overwhelmed with the urge to confess, the impulse stronger than any fear of what Rodney might do. This time he didn't hold back: 'I don't think he did it, my brother.'

'What's that?' Rodney glanced into the rearview again and the car slowed.

'I think my brother's taking the weight for-for someone.' Strike floated off somewhere, watching himself speak as if in a trance. He distantly wondered if he could take it all the way and utter Buddha Hat's name.

'Who's he takin' the weight for?' Rodney asked, that dangerous mildness creeping into his tone.

Strike hesitated, daring himself to give it up, but then said only, 'I don't know.'

'You sure?'

Strike said nothing.

'Well shit, you don't know? Then that's good, that's good. Like I always say, what you don't know don't hurt you. Don't I always say that?' Rodney studied Strike in the mirror, then eased to a dead stop in the middle of the street. 'What you sittin' back there for? I ain't no fuckin' chauffeur.'

Rodney patted Clover's seat, and as Strike got out of the car, he was swamped by the return of that sweaty assessment of himself he had experienced skulking around Ahab's – no plan, no heart. And then it occurred to him that Buddha Hat was getting away with a triple murder here: Papi, Darryl and his brother.

With Strike next to him, Rodney turned onto the boulevard and started waving at people again, all the clockers out in force now. Three blocks farther on, Rodney pulled up alongside an older, crook-backed pipehead, jerking the Caddy toward the sidewalk as if about to mow the guy down, making him scuttle for safety. Strike recognized Popeye from the benches.

Popeye shuffled up to Strike's open window. Rodney laughed. 'What the fuck you jumpin' for?'

'Rodney,' Popeye mumbled, scouring the car interior with hungry eyes. 'Rodney the *man*. Strike the man too.'

'Where you gonna be later?' Rodney reached over and tapped Popeye's hand, which rested on the edge of the window. 'Look at him,' Rodney said to Strike, 'he's tryin' to sniff out the dope.' Then, to Popeye: 'Where you gonna be, man? I need a taster.'

'I be wherever you want me to be,' Popeye said, giving them a tiny smile, a paydirt smile.

'Come to the store about twelve.'

'Yeap, yeap.' Popeye straightened up. 'You got anything for me you want sampled now?'

Rodney smirked and rolled off.

'What you need a taster for?' Strike asked.

Rodney reached under his seat and pulled up a Ziploc bag of blond-tinted coke. 'This from some Colombians in Jersey City. They wanted to give it to me free, you know, like a free sample? But I said, "Fuck that, you *take* my goddamn money, motherfuckers, 'cause gifts have a habit of coming back on you." You know what I mean?'

Rodney tossed the bag into Strike's lap. It was about a quarter ounce, the trial-size offering of a kilo supplier to a prospective customer. Strike let it lie there, his anxiety over Buddha Hat, over Victor, replaced now with an exhausted resignation.

'Yeah, some people you never take gifts from. You always keep it on a strict business level. I mean, other guys, like the guy that owns the building for my store? He's Egyptian or Israeli or some damn thing, yesterday he says to me, "You ain't foolin' me, I know what you up to," and I'm thinkin', "Damn, he's gonna kick me out I just moved in, or he's goin' to the *cops*." But he says, "You ought to try *my* shit sometime, I'll give you a good price." So, him . . .' Rodney reached over and opened his glove compartment, revealing another Ziploc bag. 'Him I'll take a free sample off. He's OK, but the other guys? Business is business.'

Strike tried to tune out the fact that they were driving around with felony-weight cocaine.

'Israeli,' Strike said, just to say something.

'Well, I just got to wait till Popeye comes by the store, see who wins the *taste* test.'

'So you going back into weight, huh?' Strike said it more as a sorrowful announcement than a question.

'Yeah, well, I figure they got their lockup on the Ahab's, and I'm just about coming to the end of my grief period over Papi, you know? So, yeah, the good news is we're going into business in a few days. Just like we planned.'

We: Shit.

'So ha-how's it going with Champ?' Strike tried to sound casual. 'The knocko make his buys yet?'

'Hell yeah, he's in like Flynn. Champ's goin' down, goin' down, goin' . . . mother*fuck*er!'

Rodney floored the Caddy, banked the steering wheel hard to the left, spun in a shrieking about-face and took off.

'You got anything?' Rodney said angrily, taking the dope from Strike's lap and tossing it under his seat.

'Anything what?'

'Anything to go to *jail* with.'

Rodney didn't wait for an answer. He roared up behind a bright red van, honked as if to pass, then pulled abreast and shook a fist at the driver. Strike looked up: it was that white-bearded knocko named Jo-Jo. Sitting above them, his elbow cocked high, Jo-Jo had a hand deep in his shirt as if ready to draw a gun on whoever had been chasing him.

He broke into a big cheery grin and waved when he saw Rodney. But Rodney was having none of it. He leaned across Strike's lap in order to look up into Jo-Jo's face and waved for him to pull off the road, acting as if he was the highway patrol and Jo-Jo was some speeder.

Jo-Jo laughed and gunned the engine in little spurts. 'Rodney, you wanna drag?'

'Pull the fuck over!' His face livid, Rodney waved wildly for the van to stop.

'What's up, Rodney?'

'Just pull the fuck over!' Rodney shouted again, misting Strike with spittle.

With an amused, mock-fearful look on his face, Jo-Jo did as he was told, gliding into the parking lane and stopping under the flashing orange chase lights that framed the storefront of an all-night video and smoke shop.

Rodney jerked to a rocking halt parallel to the van, blocking traffic, both cars winking metallically in the lurid gleam.

'What's up, chief?' Jo-Jo looked down from his roost into Strike's window.

Rodney, stretched out across the length of the front seat, planted his elbow on Strike's thigh and bellowed up at the cop. 'We finished, motherfucker. Me and you. We *through.*'

'What's the problem?' Jo-Jo said mildly.

'*You* know what the problem is.' Rodney dug deeper into Strike's thigh.

'Hey Rodney, I'm not a fucking mind reader.'

'You hung my motherfuckin' phone.'

'*Me?*' Jo-Jo pressed his fingers to his chest, smiled through his beard.

'Yeah, *you.*'

Jo-Jo retreated from his window, apparently in conference with whoever else was in the van, then popped his head out again.

'Who told you this, Rodney?'

Rodney glared at him.

'Hey, you might have a tapped phone or not, but we didn't hang it.'

'I ain't payin' you one red dime *no* more!'

Not following any of this, worried about the sample under the driver's seat and the other quarter ounce in the glove compartment, Strike casually turned his head into Rodney's ribs, which were almost crushing his nose. There was something so physically overpowering about the way Rodney was ignoring him now, something so willful and unstoppable in the way he had reduced Strike to the status of furniture, that Strike experienced a moment of pure clarity: he would never make it out of here, would never rise above his current position as Rodney's lieutenant, because all the intelligence and prudence and vision came to nothing if it wasn't tempered and supported by a certain blindness, an oblivious animal will that Rodney had, that Champ probably had and that he, Strike, did not have. Rodney would survive all this – Champ, Buddha Hat, Darryl Adams, Jo-Jo, the Homicides, the Latinos, the Mafia, the Virus, maybe even old age – not because of his guts or his brains, but because he understood that there was no real life out here on the street, no real lives other than his own, and that what really mattered was coming first in all things, in all ways and at all costs.

Jo-Jo's face had lost a little of its humor. 'Hey Rodney, you're paranoid enough to be a cop.'

'Not one red *dime!*'

'Hey, what can I say?' Jo-Jo scratched his beard. 'It's a free country, right?'

'And you *know* I got a mouth, so you best not be thinkin' payback on this, 'cause I swear before God – '

'Hey Rodney, did I not just say it was a free country?'

Rodney gave him a long stare, Strike's thigh going pins and needles from the pressure.

'We finished!'

Jo-Jo sighed, gazed dreamily down JFK, shook his head with theatrical regret. 'Paranoid, very paranoid, Rodney.'

'And stop calling me *Rod*ney.'

'Very paranoid.'

'Yeah, I'm paranoid. I'm stupid too.'

Rodney straightened up off Strike, gestured 'finished' to Jo-Jo with the flat of his hand and sped off down JFK. 'Paranoid,' he muttered. 'That's why I'm rich and alive, you short fat ugly potato-teeth motherfucker. Paranoid . . . I'm payin' off that motherfucker every fuckin' week and now Mazilli tells me he's settin' me up *any*how, tappin' my phone. "Buy me a Cadillac" – I'll buy you a fuckin' Cadillac, you pink-eyed piece of shit, you motherfuckin' *ham*ster . . .'

Rodney retreated into mumbles for a while, then turned to Strike. 'So your brother, he's gonna keep his mouth shut?'

Strike didn't know how to answer; he'd said all he could say. 'Victor ain't no killer,' he said finally. 'That's all I know.'

'He got family?'

'Yeah.'

'Maybe you should help them out, you know, financially. You should always take care of your family, because a man's family is the most important thing in his life. Besides, next week?' Rodney winked, then waved expansively toward the boulevard as if the city was an unlocked, unguarded treasure chest. 'You gonna start makin' some *serious* money.'

20

Rocco shared the stairs down to BCI with Thumper and Smurf, who were leading a herd of chained white weightlifters, a few with cuts and bruises, the one bringing up the rear dripping blood from his nose in rich steady splashes on the back of the kid in front of him.

Rocco nodded to Smurf. 'They look like a volleyball team.'

'From Rydell. A guy got beat on some bad coke over in O'Brien. Came back with his friends.' Smurf rolled his eyes. 'A whole fucking Brannigan went down.'

'Serves them right, right?'

'Lucky they weren't killed.'

Bobby Bones saw Rocco coming down the stairs and stood at the BCI counter looking tense, almost hateful.

'Ready?' Rocco grinned.

'Who . . .'

'The guy you mentioned before, Ronald Dunham.'

'*Now* you're talkin' business,' Bones said, his face lighting up with relief.

'Please.' Rocco bowed a little for Bones to proceed.

'OK, ah, OK, you got a Possession with Intent about six months back, plea'd to Possession, drew a fine, probation and I think some rehab. You got an Aggravated Assault Second Degree three months ago, plea'd out to Third, drew probation concurrent with the previous beef. Ah, the guy runs with Rodney Little, something like a crew chief, medium-high mojombo, or whatever the fuck they're calling themselves these days and, ah, that's Ronald Dunham a k a Strike.'

'Can you cut a picture for me?'

'Absolutely. No problem.'

'You happy now, you fucking whacko?'

'Victor Dunham,' Bones growled. 'Fucking guy comes in asks for Victor Dunham.'

'Cut me Rodney Little too, while you're at it.'

'Rodney Little,' Bones announced, 'a k a Hot Rod, a k a Mister, a k a Scorpio, Armed Robbery Third Degree, June 4, 1973 – '

'Just a picture, Bobby.'

Waiting for his mug shots, Rocco went over to the holding cells, where Thumper was talking to one of the white weightlifters through the bars, the kid holding a paper towel to his face to stanch the flow of blood.

Thumper looked stunned. 'Forty-one fifty an hour?'

'Yup.' The kid delicately refolded the paper to find an unbloodied section.

'So what do you take home, seven fifty a week?'

'More, plus overtime.'

'Overtime . . .'

'Yup.'

Two more of the prisoners joined their bloody friend at the bars.

'Are you kidding me? You know what *we* pull down on forty hours?' Thumper dropped his voice. 'Six *hun*dred, Jack, and we're fucking *out* there, you know?'

'You go time-and-a-half after forty?' asked one of the kids. 'We go after thirty-five.'

'Jesus fucking Christ.' Thumper stepped in place, gripping the bars. 'Thirty-five hours. You got any openings?'

'It's pretty tight.'

'What's the local?'

'Electrical Workers Seventeen.' All the kids hung around the bars now, Thumper's envy picking up their spirits.

'Are you kidding me? Ten years, I'm locking assholes with every fucking shithead in town? I mean hey, you just came from O'Brien so you *know*, right? Ten years, I got shot at, stabbed at, broke my nose, my ankle, my finger, ten years in, I *now* got a base pay of forty-two, three ninety-seven. How old are you guys?'

They sang out a chorus of twenties and twenty-ones.

'The only thing keeps my head above water is court time. Collars for dollars. I get called in for an appearance, you know, to testify? Sometimes I'm there seven hours, reading the newspaper, waiting for my name, or sometimes I'm in and out in like a half hour. But the minute I step in the courtroom? I'm on the clock and they got to pay me four hours overtime minimum, no matter what. Collars for dollars.'

They all nodded in faint admiration.

'But seven fifty for thirty-five hours . . . Jesus, Jesus.'

'Yeah, but you're out there, we're in *here*.'

'Well, that's just tonight. Plus, it's your own fucking fault. What the hell you copping in O'Brien for?'

'It's cheaper,' someone said.

'Cheaper!' Thumper squawked. 'I had your paycheck I'd hop a fucking Avianca flight, buy it at the source.'

Laughter came from the shadows of the cell, and Rocco could see that everybody thought Thumper was a great guy. But Rocco felt unmoved by the talk about paychecks: it was never about money with him.

'Mikey.'

'Roc, you want to join the Electricians with me?'

Rocco sauntered over to the bars. 'Maybe you guys could do some rewiring when they ship you over to County.'

No one in the cell had thought that far ahead.

'Yeah, watch your back in there tonight.' Thumper sounded mournful and ominous. 'Don't go to sleep or nothin'.'

The electricians got very quiet.

'Mikey.' Rocco tilted his head and touched Thumper's arm.

'Fuckin' idiots,' Thumper mumbled as Rocco led him up the stairs and into the night.

Out on the street, they leaned against the brass handrails that led up to the courthouse entrance and watched two kids in handcuffs being ushered through the police garage to the stairs that led down to BCI.

Rocco took a roll of mints from his pocket, popped one in his mouth and offered one to Thumper. 'Victor Dunham, you remember him? You arrested him about a year ago in the Roosevelt Houses. Assaulting an officer?'

Thumper passed on the mints and lit a cigarette. 'Dunham, yeah. What about him?'

'We got him on the Ahab's shooting.'

'*That* was the guy?' Thumper frowned in disbelief. 'No shit.'

'Why "no shit"?' Rocco wished he could take notes, but he wanted Thumper just to talk and not think about what he said.

'That guy, I though he was pretty solid – he worked, you know. *He* did the Ahab's? Huh, you never know, right?'

'What went down on that thing with you? I'm just trying to put this kid together.'

'Ah, yeah, that was fucked up. Between me and you? That was fucked up. We were doing a roll-up on the Dumont side of the projects, and there's this kid, Dunham, and at first I thought he was on his own because he's got this Hambone's monkey suit on, like he's going to work. But I see this other kid raise up right next to him, then *he* raises up, you know, a real big healthy sky hook, says "Five-oh" clear as a bell, and he's looking right at me like "Fuck . . . you." It's like if they raise up on the sly, there's some kind of respect in it at least – fear, something – but this kid, "Five-oh" right in my face, plus, plus, I thought I saw him throw something, you know, *drop* something, so I'm out of the car like a shot, I get excited sometimes you know, upset? So I grab this arrogant disrespectful shit-skin sneak, I throw him against the fence and the kid goes all like, startled on me. I say, "You raisin' up on me?" He says, "*What*?" like I'm crazy, and then he says, "I was *goofin*'," like I'm supposed to believe he was just making fun of the real raisers, right? I get him up against the fence, I say, "What you drop?" He says, 'I didn't drop nothin'. What you doin' to me?" I go, "Shut the fuck up." Then I go through his pockets. He's got a set of car keys but that's it. I make him drop his pants, check up under his Johnson, go into his socks, nothing, I say, "Stay the fuck there." You know, SOP?'

Thumper looked to Rocco as if for verification and Rocco nodded. 'OK, so, meanwhile the peoples be starting to come around saying, "Yo Thumper, this a workin' man, this a workin' man. This *Vic*tor, Thumper, he a *wor*kin' man," you know, the usual bompie bullshit? Big Chief and them are down a ways doing some other scumbags, I'm alone, I got this kid against the fence and' – Thumper narrowed his eyes – 'I wanted to nail him *bad*. I mean Rocco, "Five-oh," he said it right in my fuckin' face. So like now we got a crowd. I tell this kid, "Don't fuckin' move," and I'm on my knees, looking in the garbage for the bottles he threw. He's standing there, acting all fucking outraged, the people are gassing up his head, gassing up *my* head, "Yo Thumper, this boy be OK," "Thumper, this boy a father," "Yo Thumper, this ain't right, that ain't right." And I *hate* being called Thumper by them, and it's hot and I'm on my knees in the grass, in the garbage, and this kid's starting to *talk* to himself now, sayin', "I'm gonna be late, damn, shit, damn, shit." I tell him, "Shut the fuck up," I tell the herd the same thing, but like it's a party now. And all of a sudden this fuckin' kid starts *walk*ing, just walking away. I couldn't believe it. I got a fucking audience on my hands and this nigger's walking. I get up, he's mumbling, "I got to get to work, I got to get to work," not even to me, like to himself. I throw him back on the fence, I say, "Don't fucking move or I'll flatten your ass right here and now." People start going "Whoo" and "Oh! Oh!" like they do, right? I go back into the grass and the kid starts *walk*in' again, I don't fuckin' believe it, and the crowd's yellin', "Fight the power! Fight the power! Fight the power!" like I'm some kind of fucking symbol or something. So I grab him. Not *grab* him, just . . . All I did was I just flicked his hat, you know, a fingertip, like a little fucking head slap to flip that stupid Hambone's hat off his head, get his attention. Next thing I know the kid *wigs*, he turns and he shoves me, *boom*, right in the chest. The herd goes nuts, right? Right? I gave him a shot like – '

Thumper flicked his cigarette into the street, then put the heel of his hand under Rocco's jaw and slightly pushed upwards. 'I almost snapped his fuckin' neck. So Big Chief and them come running, I got this yomo down, knee in the back, cuffin' him up, the kid's crying, 'I got to get to work,' like *cry*ing, like tears. Everybody's going "Fight the power, fight the power," and I'm thinking we gots to go, every old-time nigger in the projects is like inching up, saying "Officer, Officer," you know, like trying to get me to cool out? But, hey, like this little prick shoves me in front of a fuckin' herd and I'm all alone? *I'll* show you fuckin' cool out. So we get him up, all of a sudden his *mother* comes running, she's all bug-eyed an' shit. She's screaming, "Where's my boy?" putting her hands on me, and I'm yelling at her friends, "Get her the fuck away from me" and I'm draggin' this kid to the car and she's shrieking, "Don't worry baby, don't worry baby," bugging her eyes, and now she's doing this *wheez*ing number.'

Thumper put his hand on his chest, opening his eyes wide and breathing deeply but strained, as if the air was coming through a pinched straw. 'So now I'm thinking, she's fuckin' puttin' it on, let's *jet*, but then, but then, she tries to snatch the fucking car keys from me like, *snatching* at them, and I start screaming, "Keep your fuckin' hands to yourself!" She's screeching, "That's *my* car keys, that's *my* car keys," but like, hey, I took them off the kid, I'm not giving them up. But she's coming off like she's gonna have a heart attack or something. "They *mine*, they *mine*, I'm gonna follow you!" Everybody's yelling, "Give her the keys, fight the power," and Roc' – Thumper gripped Rocco's wrist – 'you know, if that lady had asked me for the keys like a human being you know, *maybe*. But she fuckin' snatched at them, I mean, fuck her, I got a hundred niggers watching me like a *hawk*, so I say, "Keep your fucking hands to yourself," fuck the keys, because like if I backed down? I don't care *who* it is . . . they're watching me like a hawk. So anyways she's yellin', "Don't worry baby, don't worry baby," the other niggers are yellin', "Yo Thumper, that ain't right, that ain't right," and now the kid is crying but like *angry*, you know? Not like a crybaby, like angry because, you know, I'm like tellin' his mother to fuck off and all, and she's buggin' out all over him with this heart attack routine.

'Anyways, we get him in the car, and his mother's banging on the window, "I'm comin' baby, I'm comin' baby, don't you worry." The crowd's all raw, any second they're gonna start throwin' shit, believe me, I *been* there. So we pull out, we're going to the Western Precinct, right? The kid's in back with me, crying. The minute we're offstage, I'm cool. Offstage I'm always cool, I say to the kid, "See what you started? See what you did? Get your mother all upset?" Kid don't say nothin'. Anyways, we take him over to the Western Precinct, he's in the cell, I'm typing up the arrest report – *boom*, the door blows in, here comes that fucking lady again. She's got a whole bunch of friends, bunch of old-timers, she's wheezing and doing that ol' Fred Sanford bullshit like when he talks to his wife in heaven? She's saying, "Where's my boy!" Then she like, sees him in the cage, she goes *nuts*, her friends are like restraining her, she's wheezing and gasping and popping them bug eyes, and I'm getting really fucking pissed, but you know alls I say is, "Lady, you should give up cigarettes," like a joke to break the tension? And she gets all fucking blinky on me. "What you say! What you say!" I say, "You heard me." Meanwhile, I'm just heads down typing, I got my glasses on, tap-tap, she says, "I got emphysema! How *dare* you make comments like that! My doctor says I got a *year*! I got to go into the hospital next week. He says I got a year! How dare you say that to me."'

Thumper took a breather as two cops escorted a middle-aged barefoot man through the garage to the BCI stairs, the guy laughing to himself and talking a line of gibberish.

'Like . . . anyways, maybe I shouldn't have mouthed off, but Rocco, this fucking lady, I don't know if she was telling the truth about this emphysema thing, I mean, I've seen her around and all since then, she's walking an' shit, but anyways, so like to change the subject, I just tossed her the car keys like, "Here, take a ride." I didn't *throw* them at her, I just, you know, like underhand. She starts screaming again. "Don't you throw things at me!" Meanwhile, the kid starts going nuts in there like a fucking rabid ape, I don't think he knew his mother had emphysema or whatever, because he went *nuts* when she said that, I mean, who knows, she could've just said that for effect, and then when I tossed her the car keys, like ho shit, they start yelling to each other, mother and son, everybody's crying, she starts running around the fucking room, he's punching the *bars* now, hurting himself a lot fucking more than I did, right? And who do you think got blamed for *those* goddamned bruises? She's yelling, "I want to file a complaint!" I say, "Hey, do your worst," I give her my name, my number. Then all of a sudden this fuckin' minister waltzes in, some fucking Donovan-looking motherfucker's got big blond curls, sandals, these Banana Republic shorts on with the thigh hairs sticking out, all of a sudden it's, "Hi, I'm Reverend Bob Gould from Most Holy?" He's got his arm around this lady, she's wheezing, "Look a my boy, look a my boy." The kid's sobbing, fucking cursing me out, "You leave my mother alone." This *folk* priest says, "Can I help in any way? I know the family. Can I help?"

'The prick *helped* OK. The cocksucker helped the lady file a Six Twenty on me for abusiveness. He helped the kid file a Six Twenty on me for excessive use of force. "Can I help?" So like I file *my* charges, they file theirs, you know, and with all the filing, counterfiling, all that bullshit, everybody wound up dropping everything. It was just a whole big bunch a bullshit. The kid told his lawyer he just saw everybody raising up and he just did it as a goof, he didn't run with any of that crowd, he was on his way to work, who knows, he said he just . . . did it. Like, who knows?'

Thumper shrugged, looked off unhappily down the quiet side street, then turned back to Rocco. 'You know, I'll tell you what the whole shouting match came down to. *Dis.* It was all about dis. The kid disrespected me by raising up in my face. I dissed him by throwing him up against the fence and doing the Johnson check. He dissed me by walking off. I dissed him by flicking his hat in front of his people. He dissed me by giving me a shove. The mother comes along, she disses me by snatching the keys. I dis her by making fun of her wheeze. Everything's *dis.* Because, you know, out there all you got to your name is your heart. You got a crowd around you, you got to show heart. Not just them but us too. We go in, we don't show *heart*, we let ourselves get dissed, Jesus Christ, they'll be all over us, we might as well disband the unit, you know what I'm trying to say? I mean, I *know* you know what I'm trying to say. The whole thing's a trap. You got a crowd on you, you best got to act the part or you're *nothing*. It's unfortunate, but them's the rules. I don't know, I see the kid around, I see the mother. I don't say we're friends now, but like everything's cool more or less. We all understand everybody did what they had to do and . . . you know, life goes on.'

Thumper lit another cigarette, walked off a few steps, walked back, flicked the cigarette in the street. He flung a leg up on the steps leading to the courthouse and retied his sneaker.

Rocco sighed and jammed his hands into his pants pockets. Thumper's story made him think again of that lady in the window almost applauding the drug collar earlier that night, made him think of all the cops who went into the projects as if it was enemy territory and treated everybody like criminals, made him wonder if the class-action insult was really worth the handful of ineffectual arrests. On the other hand, Thumper was a brother officer and no matter what had gone down, Rocco would defend him and his actions without blinking; he would no more criticize or in any way turn on him than he would his own flesh and blood.

But he hated hearing about this kid getting treated that way. At least it explained something: why Victor's mother and his wife hadn't given him the time of day.

This kid Victor . . . he was starting to get under Rocco's skin a little, but the feeling was not altogether unpleasant. In fact, for Rocco this wasn't turning out to be a bad day at all: his concentration was good, he felt alert and genuinely curious about the stories he'd heard, intrigued by the small discoveries of character and attitude, how names and circumstances were starting to click and connect in some vague but tantalizing way. He felt engaged, *present.*

'Mikey, you think this kid Victor's any kind of dirty?'

'Like how?' Thumper arched his spine, flung alternating elbows behind his back to stretch his ribs.

'Like drugs.'

'Nah. I tell you, I almost wish he was. I'd feel a lot better about what went down.'

'His brother's this kid Strike?'

'Strike.' Thumper whacked his knuckles into an open palm. 'Now *there's* another story altogether. That kid drives me nuts. Nice-looking, clean, bright, you know, all things considered, so what's he do with himself? He sits out there running a crew like clocking's all the world has to offer him, you know what I mean? It's like, "What's your *problem?*" He *irks* me.'

'Yeah, so this kid's brother is Strike, and now I'm thinking maybe this shooting was a drug thing.'

'To tell you the truth, I see Strike all the time, I see the other Dunham kid now and then, but I tell you I never seen them together. I mean, you got what, how many thousand people in Roosevelt? Somebody keeps his nose clean – you know, runs a tight ship – I'm not gonna know them, how would I ever get to know them?' Thumper hunched his shoulders, covering his chest with his hands. 'What am I gonna do, arrest somebody for going to work?'

Rocco smiled, did a little spin himself, breathing in the cool night air. 'So you don't think this kid runs with Rodney at all?'

'Rodney Little?' Thumper made a face. 'I doubt it, Roc. The kid's pretty well legit. I mean, Strike, if you think this was drug-related, yeah, Strike and Rodney, if they were involved I'd say look into *that*. But shit, even Strike, he's not a shooter, he's just a snake. How do you know this kid did it?'

'He came in and gave it up. Don't you read the papers?'

'Really,' Thumper said. 'What he say?'

'Nothin'. Some bullshit about self-defense. I really don't know what happened. What would *you* think?'

'Hey, that's why you's be the Homicide and me's be the Housing. Fucked if I know. Could be . . . maybe he's telling the truth?' Thumper winced, the word 'truth' halfhearted and faint, as if it wasn't worth the breath it took to say.

Rudy's was beer-damp, dark, long and narrow. A radio station blared music over the speaker system, drowning out the TV. To Rocco it seemed a peaceful enough place, most of the customers looking to be either on the other side of thirty-five or prematurely aged by a hard life. Taped to the mirror behind the liquor stock was a sign-up sheet for a charter bus trip to Virginia Beach; next to it was a hand-drawn announcement for a special night honoring the women cooks of Rudy's, featuring a spaghetti and crab dinner.

Mazilli wouldn't go much past the front door. Leaning against the unplugged juke box, he folded his arms across his chest and stared out across the street to Ahab's. Rocco left him there and walked up to the bar, sliding between a heavyset woman talking to an old man in a Count Basie skipper hat, and a red-eyed security guard, his cap and nightstick lying next to his drink.

The bartender, a tall bald man with a mustache and a gold earring, came up and nodded hello. Rocco immediately sensed the guy would be straight with him. There was no attitude in the air, no stiffness, the bartender reading 'police' and patiently waiting for the questions to begin.

'What you got cold?' Rocco shouted over the music.

'Miller, Bud . . .'

'Miller sounds good.' Rocco turned and called out to Mazilli. 'How about you, Cheech?'

Mazilli shook his head and looked back out to the street. Rocco caught a few sidelong glances from the regulars, but the vibrations were more of curiosity than hostility. Rocco found it a little strange to think of Victor Dunham drinking in here: he would have been the youngest by about ten years. Rocco imagined the kid coming in, hanging out by himself, getting a little buzz on, start talking to his shots after a while, everybody just leaving him be.

The bartender came back with the Miller but no glass. Rocco flapped out his badge and offered his hand. 'I'm Rocco Klein from the prosecutor's office. You Rudy?'

The bartender's answer was lost in the music.

Rocco squinted as if in pain. 'Could you turn the music down a little? My hearing's for shit.'

The bartender shrugged and clicked off the radio, the sudden silence making everybody sit up straight.

'Come again?' Rocco said.

'Rudy's my father. I'm Lamar.'

'Lamar . . .' Rocco waited.

'Lamar McCoy.'

'Lamar, I wonder if you can help me out.' Rocco pulled a photo out of his jacket and handed it over. 'Did you ever see this kid around?'

The bartender took a long time to study the picture, and the security guard leaned forward on his elbows to catch a peek. During the post-arrest interview, Victor had said he was a regular here; why was it taking this long for these people to ID him?

Finally the bartender nodded. 'Yeah, he was in here once. I don't know him, though – you know, his name.'

'Once? Do you happen to remember when that was?'

'Yeah. He was in here like, last week.'

'You wouldn't know what day last week, would you?'

'Thursday, Friday, something like that.'

'Both nights?'

'One or the other, I forget which. Now wait, it had to be Friday because I wasn't working Thursday. Yeah, it was Friday.'

'Can I ask you something?' Rocco leaned forward on his elbows. 'I used to tend bar over in Jersey City, and after a while? Unless the guy's a regular I would never in a million years remember a one-time customer. It was just bodies and beers, bodies and beers, unless the guy had something memorable about him, acted some way unusual. I assume you got to be like that too, so how come you remember him?'

'He asked for something, some drink, and I had to go down to the cellar to see if we had it.'

'No kidding.' Rocco thought Victor had said he drank scotch. 'What the hell was it, Ovaltine?'

'Nope. Coco Lopez, straight out of the can, no alcohol.'

'Like a Shirley Temple piña colada?'

'Yeah. That was like a first for me. Plus he was a young guy, and like we don't get young people in here that much.'

'So he wasn't drunk?'

'Nope. He just had that one Coco Lopez, straight out of the can.'

'Was he with anybody?'

'I think he came in by himself. He might have held conversation, but I can't tell you that for sure.'

Rocco looked away for a moment, thinking back on all that time in the interrogation room. He believed the bartender's version of Victor's evening in here – why would the bartender lie? which meant that the kid had been sober, come in for the one time only. Which meant that Victor must have bullshitted him about everything, right down to his choice of drink. Rocco gestured for Mazilli to come over and listen in.

'You know that shooting last Friday across the street?' Rocco asked.

'Yeah, the detectives came around. I was the one who called the police.'

'Would you remember what *time* the kid was here? You know, was it before or after that incident over there?'

The bartender got a look of slow fascination on his face. '*That's* who you looking for?' He studied the picture again, and the security guard and some other customers leaned closer too. 'I would have to say he was in here before, because after, all hell broke loose with the situation over there, people runnin' in and out, and I doubt I would have remembered him in all that. But it was pretty quiet before, so I would have to say before.' He tapped the picture with a long finger, nodding. 'Yeah, he was in here before.'

'Before. OK, good, before. And how about when he *left*. Was that before or after the thing across the street?'

'I couldn't say.' The bartender sucked his teeth. 'Like I said, all hell broke loose.'

'Yeah, he was in here,' the security guard joined in. 'He was all *jumpy* like. He wasn't sitting down or nothing.'

Rocco was only mildly intrigued by the guard's comment. Now that the cat was out of the bag, the guy might be giving it some extra color.

'So *this* the guy?' The bartender shook his head and dropped the picture on the bar. 'Huh.'

Rocco absently looked down at the photo lying next to his beer, then reared back and muttered, 'Jesus Christ.' He had handed over the wrong one. The mug shot of Victor Dunham was still in his pocket; on the bar was the photograph of his brother, Strike.

Rocco swallowed his shock and calmly switched pictures, Strike going back in his pocket, Victor going down in front of the bartender. 'What about this guy?'

'Oh yeah,' the bartender said. 'This guy's in here all the time. What *he* do?'

'When was the last time he was in here?' Rocco could feel his heart flapping in his shirt: Strike was in here the night of the murder too.

'Well, I don't think he was in here Saturday.' The bartender flashed the picture to a few regulars on either side of Rocco, the people grunting negatively.

'Friday, I would say. That's like the last time I saw him,' the bartender added.

'Yeah, he was in here Friday,' the red-eyed security guard piped up, looking a little self-conscious about talking to real police.

Rocco tried to calm down. 'Is he usually in here on Saturdays too?'

'I'd say so, yeah. Saturdays, Sundays,' the bartender said. 'He's here like most every night of the week, has like two, three drinks and goes out.'

'What's he drink?'

'Scotch, scotch and soda.'

'Does he get drunk?'

'Nah, he gets up shaky sometimes but nah, he's like internal – you know, quiet style.'

Rocco turned to the security guard. 'How come you remember him Friday night?'

The guard gathered himself up to answer. ''Cause he come in in this brown and orange uniform from Hambone's? Then sometime later he goes into the bathroom and comes out dressed in normal clothes.'

'So he doesn't usually do that?'

'Well, sometimes he do, sometimes he don't.' The guard was sounding a little more confident, warming up to the job.

'But he doesn't change into his street clothes every night in here?'

'Just some of the time. But he definitely did *that* night because I'll tell you, anytime somebody sit down next to me in one set a clothes go in there, come out in another? It's gonna make an impression on me.'

'So you caught that, huh?' Rocco smiled admiringly.

'Also, when he does change clothes? He never goes right in there to change. He always has a drink or two first.'

'Do you remember what he came out wearing Friday night?'

The guard hesitated, then looked a little depressed, his streak over. 'Not really.'

'What did he carry his clothes in?' Mazilli asked, speaking up for the first time since joining Rocco.

'He always carrying this little bag,' the bartender said.

'What kind of bag?' Mazilli took a sip of Rocco's near-empty beer.

'Like a little valise, like a gym bag.' The bartender held his hands apart about twelve inches.

'You think he was involved too?' the guard said. He signaled for another drink, gestured toward Rocco's empty beer and the bare space in front of Mazilli's crossed arms.

Rocco shrugged evasively and took over the questioning again. 'Do you remember if he was with anybody Friday night?'

'He always by himself.' The bartender slid two fresh ones in front of Rocco and Mazilli, and they both nodded thanks to the security guard.

'Did he talk to anybody that night?' Rocco said.

The guard narrowed his eyes. 'I think he was talking to that other young guy, the jumpy one.'

Rocco kept his voice neutral. 'You hear anything of what they said?'

'Naw,' the guard said. 'I'm not even sure if they were together. I think they were for a time.'

'So they didn't come in together?'

'Naw, I don't think so.'

'Did they leave together?'

'I don't think so.'

'Do you remember who left first?'

The guard squinted into the distance, then shook his head. 'Unh-uh.'

Rocco was disappointed, but it sounded honest at least. He wanted to buy the next round but he thought the guard was too excited, would drink too fast and get fucked up on him.

'Now wait a minute, wait a minute.' The bartender repeatedly snapped his fingers. 'It was definitely the other guy, the one-time guy, that left first. You know how I know?'

'Hit me.'

'Because Friday night? There was this movie on the TV that I wanted to watch, and before I turn off the music in here, I like to ask everybody if it's OK, and I remember I had to wait for him to come from the back.'

Mazilli and Rocco turned their heads toward the back: a skittles game, a phone booth and the bathroom.

'Wait for who? Which one?' Rocco asked.

'The guy that comes here regular, this one,' the bartender said, tapping Victor's picture.

'What was he doing back there?'

'I don't know.'

'Was he on the pay phone?'

'I didn't notice. He might've just gone to the bathroom. But I do remember asking him if it was OK if I turned up the TV and turn down the music and like, the other guy must have been gone by then because I would've asked him too, because, you know, my philosophy is this bar belong to the customers, as long as everybody acts right.'

'What was the movie?'

'*Thunderbolt and Lightfoot.*'

'With Clint Eastwood?'

'Yeah, uh-huh, and Jeff Bridges. I must've seen that like five times.'

'That's the one where the bank money's stashed in the black-board?'

'Yeah, uh-huh, the blackboard.'

'So what time did the movie go on?'

'Nine o'clock.'

'So the other guy, the one-time guy, was gone by nine o'clock?'

'I guess so.'

'And how about the regular guy, this guy, did he stay for the whole movie?' Rocco asked, thinking that would take him to eleven, roughly forty-five minutes past the murder.

'I couldn't say. I tell you though, nobody was watching the movie after that *thing* happened. I can tell you that much.'

'Well, let's put it this way – do you remember if the regular guy was still here when the shooting happened?'

'I tell you, I really couldn't say. He might've or might've not.'

'OK, let me put it another way. Would you remember what was going on in the movie when the guy tabbed out for the night?'

The bartender shrugged.

'OK. This guy.' Rocco held up Victor's picture, opening his questions to the bar. 'Do you remember anything else about him Friday night? Did he seem different in any way? Did he say anything unusual? *Do* anything unusual?'

The security guard nodded. 'Yeah. He had two more drinks than normal.'

'Really, you remembered that? How the hell did you remember that?' Rocco tried to sound awed.

'I always watch him to see if he's gonna change his clothes, go in the bathroom after one drink, two drinks . . .'

'Yeah, and . . .'

'He had two drinks.'

'So?'

'But when he came out? He had three more. Most times, he just has one more, for the road.'

Mazilli grunted but made no comment.

'So he *never* has that much?' Rocco looked back at the bartender.

'Sometimes he do, most times not, though. He's right on that.' The bartender slid a bottle in front of Rocco, ice chips clinging to the side. Rocco didn't even remember drinking the last one.

'Did he seem upset? Angry?' Rocco scanned the half-dozen faces turned his way. One or two people shrugged. 'Did he seem different to you'– he spoke directly to the guard again – 'after he talked to this other guy?'

'I just don't remember. I *think* they were talking but I can't swear to it.'

'And when he went to the back, before the bartender here asked him about the TV, what was he doing back there, changing out of his uniform?'

'Naw, he was changed out of that already.' The guard waved to the wall. 'I think he was on the phone back there.'

'So he *was* on the phone?'

'I can't say for sure. I *think* . . .'

'Do you have any idea who he might've called?'

'Unh-unh, I don't know. He might've just been in the bathroom. I might of mis-*seen* him on the phone.'

Rocco nodded, thinking he'd have to remember to request a log of the bar's phone calls. 'Well, let me ask you this. Was he in the habit of making phone calls from here?'

'Not really,' the guard said. 'That's why I say I might have mis-seen that. He might've just been passing the phone coming out of the bathroom. Because I really can't say I ever truly saw him talking to nobody on that phone *ever*. Don't talk to nobody at the bar either, for that matter.'

'He just don't talk to nobody,' the deep-chested fat woman said as she lit a cigarette.

'OK,' Rocco said. 'Is there anything else you could tell me about this guy, you know, in general?'

'He writes on his cocktail napkins.' The bartender wiped down the bar in front of Rocco's beer.

'Oh yeah?'

'After his first drink? He always starts writing on the napkin.'

'You ever see what he writes?'

'Yeah. Teams.'

'Basketball, baseball?' Rocco said, thinking, Gambling?

'No, like made-up teams. Like one time I saw he had writ down New York Destroyers, Texas Tornados, Cleveland something, a whole list. I didn't recognize any a them. I asked him what it was, he said it was Aroundball teams. I said what the hell is *that*? He said it was a game he was inventing and he was just fooling around with team names for when he got it all organized. I asked him how do you play, he said he wasn't at liberty to talk about it, like he was still ironing out some rules. But yeah, a lot of times after he had a drink or two? He'd be writin' down team names on his napkin.' The bartender shrugged apologetically. 'Aroundball.'

'Aroundball,' the security guard repeated, sounding frustrated at having no more to add.

The fat woman grunted three times as if to say, Ain't that a shame.

Mazilli arched his back, restless to go.

'He ever write anything else down?' Rocco asked the bartender.

'Just team names. All the time different team names.'

'No real names? People's names?'

The bartender shrugged.

'And you can't remember when he left that night – even a rough guess?'

'Unh-uh.'

Rocco turned to the security guard, who shrugged helplessly.

'So like, you don't know if it was before or after the incident over there?'

The bartender shook his head. 'Man, he's in and out of here like a whisper. Shit, he's comin' in here six months maybe? I don't even know his name.'

They drove away from the bar in silence, Rocco still buzzing a little from the photo switch, savoring that jolt, how it felt in his chest, his head.

Victor: Rocco pictured the kid coming into the bar every night from Hambone's, still wearing his uniform, having to throw down a few shooters before he could feel human enough to change back into street clothes. Once he got a buzz, he'd start daydreaming about himself as an inventor, or a sports tycoon. And then he'd go home with his load on, dreaming his dreams, pass out, get up the next day, slog through the bullshit all over again, land on that wet cocktail napkin the next night – same time, same station.

'This kid sounds like a fucking nut-boy.' Mazilli chewed his thumb joint. 'Aroundball.'

'I don't know.' Rocco felt a little defensive. Aroundball didn't sound any loonier than being an actor, or whatever it was that Rocco had been so pumped about over the weekend. 'It's probably like an escape valve. So what do you think of the brother being there?'

'What of it?' Mazilli said.

'The kid's a known shithead, goes in there only one time, leaves be*fore* the shooting, leaves sober.' Rocco felt that rush again, that shock of discovery. 'Meanwhile, nobody can even say this Victor kid wasn't sitting there watching TV when it all went down.'

'Hey,' Mazilli said, 'who came to us with the gun?'

'Well, what was this Strike doing there, then?'

'How the fuck do I know? They're brothers, right? One guy sees the other. Hey, how you doin'? Goes into the bar. They're brothers, they're seen together, big fuckin' deal.'

Mazilli pulled in at the drive-in window of a Burger King. 'You want anything?' Rocco shook his head, and Mazilli ordered himself a strawberry shake.

'Thumper told me these two never hang out together,' Rocco said.

'Well, all the more reason to have a drink. Long time no see. How's tricks? How's Ma?' Mazilli pulled back into traffic, driving slow and slurping through his straw.

'I dunno. I just think he's dirty on this, this other kid.'

'Because he had a drink with his brother? *Maybe* had a drink? The square-badge wasn't even sure they were together. And even if he is involved, it's like, we're gonna bust our ass for a conspiracy charge? Hey, it's locked. We got a gun, we got a confession.'

'I dunno, I dunno,' Rocco said. 'Maybe this Victor kid's taking the weight for something he didn't do.'

Mazilli raised an eyebrow. 'What do you mean, out of brotherly love?'

'I don't know, maybe. Maybe the shit brother's got something on him. Or yeah, maybe the kid's trying to keep his brother out of jail. I mean, he's got no record to speak of, he's a solid citizen, he's claiming self-defense. Maybe he thinks he's got a better chance of beating us on this than his brother. Maybe he thinks he can even *walk* on this. Hard-working guy comes in, confesses, claims he was attacked. Self-defense. Who are we to say no? Meanwhile, his brother's off the hook. I dunno, maybe his brother promised him money if he confessed. Maybe the guy threatened him. What do *you* think?'

Mazilli pulled over at a garbage can and tossed in his empty milk shake container. 'Hey, the security guard said the kid was two or three drinks over his usual. So what *I'm* inclined to believe is that he just walked out of there with a red brain, you know, doin' figure eights without skates, the Adams guy startles him and, ah, he did something like he said he did. You know, like the capper on a bad fuckin' day.'

'Wait a minute, wait a minute,' Rocco said. 'My witness says the do-er was waiting for the vic to come out. Leaning against the car and *wait*ing. Don't sound like no startlement shooting to me.'

'I thought you said your witness was all stupefied on gin.' Mazilli lit a cigarette.

'Oh yeah? And I thought *you* said you thought this Victor kid was a hit man.'

'I was goofing.' Mazilli shrugged and waved lazily to a double-parked cruiser. 'Besides, after tonight? I'd say he sounds more like a hapless putz with a gun and a red nose.'

'I don't know, Mazilli, this shit brother's like a pebble in my shoe. What did Rodney say to you after I left?'

'I'm off Rodney on this,' Mazilli said. 'He don't know this kid. Besides, if anybody'd be running dope out of there it would most likely be Champ.'

'Well, what did Rodney want to talk to you about?'

Mazilli laughed. 'He got into a beef with some old goombah down at Benny's Lounge over his video games. He lost his temper and smacked the guy upside the head. Now he's nervous. He wants me to talk to them.' Mazilli played cards with the old-timers and their soldiers almost every day.

'So he's gonna give us nothin' on this?'

Mazilli shook his head. 'I dunno. Every time somebody gets whacked in this town Rodney's name comes up. You remember that dog-poisoning epidemic about eight years ago? I had two guys tell me it was Rodney. Meanwhile, where's Rodney then? He's in federal prison out in Wisconsin.'

'Well, that was then, this is now.'

'Nah, nah, I'm just not smelling this on him,' Mazilli said. 'At first, when he got all jumpy in my store Saturday, I thought, Well, maybe. But after he came in tonight? I mean, I *know* him, and I was watching his face like a hawk, so . . . And now with the bartender and that square-badge? We're talking five schnorts and a gun. I'm not wasting my time on it.'

'I want to tell you something, Maz. No offense, but sometimes I think you're a little naive about your street connections, like you think there's no way they can put one over on you.'

'Oh yeah?' Mazilli glared at Rocco, flooring it a little in his anger. 'Well actually, I think *you're* the one who's a little fucking naive. You think just because a guy's got a family, a job, minds his own business in the bar of his choice, he can't be a shooter? Who's naive here, Rocco, me or you?'

Looking out at the passing boulevard, Rocco sighed: Mazilli had it all wrong. Rocco was sure he wasn't being sentimental about the kid. In fact, his interest in the case had hardly anything to do with Victor at all. It was just that he felt something powerful click in him when he asked the right questions about the wrong picture, something that had been building in him all day since the mother's house, BCI, Thumper's story . . .

'Will you please slow the fuck down?' Rocco smiled at Mazilli, feeling good.

'You gonna tell me how to drive now?' Mazilli raised an eyebrow, then eased off the gas pedal. 'Listen to me, Rocco. This kid got his load on, staggered out of there with his piece like he's in Tombstone Arizona and now he's in the hoosegow. And whether Rodney's selling dope over there or not, or Champ, or anybody else, it's got nothing to do with what went down. And even if this kid *was* selling us a line of shit on the tape, which is what they all do anyhow, even if they're giving it up, this is still a good, solid "Closed by Arrest." And if I'm wrong? If Rodney's conspired on this? Or Strike? Or the fucking Medellín cartel? I don't give a fuck, 'cause *we got the shooter.*'

'And *I* think we locked up the wrong brother.' Rocco felt both steely and serene.

Mazilli laughed, tilting his ear to his shoulder as he drove. 'De wrong brother.'

21

Strike finally got loose of Rodney about ten o'clock, and now he walked from Weehawken toward the benches, thinking about Victor, realizing that his brother was about to spend his second night in County. County: the word, the memories, came down on him in a rush, and Strike experienced a wave of powerless misery that made him stop in his tracks and hold his stomach with both hands. When the pain passed he walked on, swearing to himself that he was going to do something about this. Something . . .

About a block away from Roosevelt, Strike saw most of his boys loping off, hands in pockets, the way they always did when there was a Fury roll. But as the benches came into view, he saw that it wasn't the Fury, it was Buddha Hat. He sat alone, his arms flung out along the top slat of Strike's bench, his knees spread. With his floppy-brimmed camouflage hat, a khaki T-shirt and baggy fatigue pants, Buddha Hat looked as if he'd just finished mopping up some little military operation all by himself.

Strike would have kept walking, but Buddha Hat got him in an eyelock and waved him over. Feeling a breeze at the back of his head, Strike stood before him, nodding and grimacing. 'What's up?'

Buddha Hat sat up straighter. 'Waitin' for you.'

Strike pressed the flat of his hand against his solar plexus, then glanced at Buddha Hat's waist, looking for the bulk of a weapon.

'You want to go across the river?' Buddha Hat said.

Strike didn't know what that meant, but he was sure he didn't want to go anywhere with the Hat, now or at any other time. 'Yeah, well, for what?'

'I want to show you something.'

'I'm kind of aw-on the *job*, so like . . .' Strike went silent as Buddha Hat rose from the bench, his head looking like a skull wrapped in skin, all eye sockets and cheekbones. Strike's resolve to help Victor evaporated.

Buddha Hat said 'C'mon' and walked away, disappearing around the side of 8 Weehawken. Feeling he had no alternative, Strike followed and found Buddha Hat standing next to a forest-green Volvo, holding open the passenger door.

The car was free of extraneous flash and relatively clean. Strike noticed that the radio and tape deck had been pulled out.

'I got to change first,' Buddha Hat said, pulling away from the projects.

'What kind of music you like?' Even as the words left his mouth, the question made no sense to Strike.

'I got me a Benzi Box?' Buddha Hat responded, his tone faraway and dreamy. 'I forgot to take it home with me one night. Made it real easy for the thief who took it, you know?'

'I hear that.'

'You know anyone trying to sell a Benzi on the street?'

'Unh-uh.'

'Let me know if you do, 'cause I'm gonna have a conversation with him.'

As they drove toward O'Brien, Strike tried to imagine asking Buddha Hat about how he knew Victor, but he couldn't even work up the courage to choose the words he'd use. And he could feel his stutter waiting to ambush him; it had been there all day, fading in and out, and by now he'd almost become used to it again. But he wanted the words, when he was ready to speak them, to come out easy and natural. Fear got a odor, Rodney had said.

Buddha Hat pulled up in front of the O'Brien projects and parked. It was a hot, muggy night, and a number of kids had lit strips of newspaper, making a game of swirling them in loops, trying to smoke away the mosquitoes and no-see-ums. Strike had grown up in the Roosevelt Houses, and even on the best of days all the other projects had a vaguely alien and hostile color to him. Now, trailing Buddha Hat through the swirls of burning paper, past the conga line of dope cars and toward the six looming domino-shaped towers that made up O'Brien, he felt like a prisoner dragged into an enemy camp, felt himself in an agony of helplessness at being so effortlessly abducted, paralyzed between running for his life and staying cool, between mortal terror and fear of embarrassment. But even if he ran or struck first, Dempsy was a small city and there was no place to hide. You had to flee, go live someplace else, and no one Strike knew had ever had the imagination or the courage to do that.

'Yo, Hat.' Both of them turned to see Champ under the breezeway, sitting on his overturned shopping cart and surrounded by his cloud of children, some of them burning paper too. Champ lurched upright and waved them over, hitching up the waist of his baggy white shorts, a melon slice of flesh peeking high over each hip.

Champ squinted at Strike as if trying to place him. Strike looked away, and then Champ took Buddha Hat under his arm, giving Strike his back, and the two of them went for a walk around the building. Strike breathed through his mouth, thinking, What the fuck is going on? As he waited he watched the clockers serve the cars, everybody racing down the line and trying to beat each other to the open windows, thrusting bottles on the drivers, barking, 'Yo Ry*dell*, Ry*dell*,' breaking their ass. Strike wondered why Champ would let his own people compete against each other like this, what the point of it was.

Buddha Hat and Champ reappeared from around the building and walked toward Strike. Champ stopped a few yards away, rocking lightly from leg to leg. Then Champ beamed. 'You a *un*dercover man!' Laughing huskily, he massaged his own chest.

Strike turned right, then left, then forced himself to stand his ground and keep his mouth shut.

Champ closed one eye and pointed an accusing finger, his gestures exaggerated and playful, then gave Strike his back again.

Buddha Hat had gone on past Strike, and now he waited for him to catch up. 'Come on,' Buddha Hat said, standing in front of a breezeway. And once again Strike found himself with no option but to do as he was told.

The lobby of Buddha Hat's building was filled with the whine of mosquitoes and the acrid stench of burning paper. The kids playing by the elevator bank ignored the bugs, lighting the strips just for the fun of it.

Strike and Buddha Hat shared the buckle-floored elevator car with a disheveled white woman wearing thick glasses and hauling a shopping cart filled with unfolded laundry. All three of them stared straight ahead as they rode up to seven, where Buddha Hat held the elevator door for the woman, and then to twelve. As he walked behind Buddha Hat down the hot and close corridor, Strike passed a stairway entrance and fantasized about bolting down twelve flights of stairs. He didn't think Buddha Hat would chase him, but somehow the image of the Hat just standing there listening to his fleeing footsteps stopped Strike from making a move.

Buddha Hat shared a tight four-room apartment with his grandmother, the walls in the living room and kitchen painted brown and yellow, shining and greasy with the heat. The grandmother – heavyset, bespectacled, an elderly fifty-five, one leg swollen to twice the size of the other – sat in a red vinyl recliner, her bad leg propped on a matching ottoman. As they walked in, she was leaning forward, poking the buttons on a nineteen-inch television set with a broomstick from across the small room.

'Where's the remote at?' Buddha Hat sounded annoyed. Strike stood right behind him, staring at three velvet paintings on the living room walls: Isaac Hayes, topless save for heavy gold chains; Levar Burton, topless save for slave shackles; and Jesus Christ looking up at something.

'Lost.' She winced with the effort of speaking.

Buddha Hat got down on all fours, slid his hand under the set and retrieved the dusty remote control.

Strike rocked sideways and glanced into the kitchen. The air was faintly smoky, although there was no sign of recent cooking. A brand-new microwave oven, the energy-saver decal still in place on the glass front panel, sat balanced on a stove-top burner like a huge pot. Two pieces of masking tape on the refrigerator door formed a crucifix, and Strike had a dim childhood memory of his grandmother making the same sign on her refrigerator as a way of assuring that the house would never be without food.

Buddha Hat motioned for Strike to follow him, and they walked down a short hallway to the Hat's bedroom. The room was austere but not really clean, and Strike stood in the doorway taking inventory: bare walls, a cold overhead light illuminating the need for a fresh coat of paint, a pink portable fan on a folding chair aimed at a narrow bed, a twenty-five-inch TV topped with a VCR, and on the floor, two foot-high speakers flanking a CD player. There was no chest of drawers, no desk, no rug, no personal doodads, no pictures, photos or phone, and nowhere to sit except Buddha Hat's unmade bed, the bedsheet half off revealing the same deep blue Star Wars mattress that Strike had seen in the Furniture Shack with Andre. Strike tried to draw some reassurance from the humanity of the details but it didn't work – most everybody he knew lived this way, and having a little fan in his room or a masking tape crucifix on his refrigerator didn't make the Hat any less a killer.

Buddha Hat stood in front of his open closet door, his back to Strike, and stripped down to a pair of oversize boxer shorts. With his tight skull-head, his bony legs, his shoulder blades flaring out like twin shark fins, Buddha Hat looked like either a little boy or an old man. Looking

from the Star Wars mattress to the Hat, Strike remembered something
else Rodney had once said: It ain't the body, it's the heart.

Buddha Hat tossed his fatigues into the closet, on a pile of clothes
almost two feet high, then plucked a pair of razor-sliced jeans from
deep in the same tangle.

'How you like Rodney?' he said as he draped a thin gold chain over
his collarbone.

'He's OK,' Strike said warily, wondering how to play this, thinking Buddha Hat wouldn't do anything with his grandmother in the
next room.

'I don't like him.' Buddha Hat stooped to retrieve an orange perforated
Syracuse football jersey. 'He thinks nobody knows nothing, you know?'

Strike didn't answer.

'He thinks he's the only one who got the *know*ledge.' Buddha Hat
turned to Strike finally, palmed down his tight cap of hair, then replaced
his jungle-fighter hat. 'You ever been in jail?'

'Aw-aw-on a overnight, that's all.'

Buddha Hat gave him a curious look when he stammered, then seemed
to shrug it off. 'I *never* been in jail, not even for a hour. How many times
Rodney been in jail? If he's got the knowledge, how come he always in
and out of jail? See what I'm saying?'

Strike bobbed his head, pressed a finger to his eye.

'I ain't disrespecting him. I'm just saying, If you gonna *act* superior,
you got to *be* superior to back it up.'

Buddha Hat drove out onto I–9, and Strike watched the New York
skyline appear as they shot past Jersey City into North Bergen and then
followed the Hudson River.

'You like to get high?' Buddha Hat drove with his wrist, his hand
riding limp over the top of the steering wheel.

'Unh-uh. Not really.'

'I used to do reefer a little, like when I was twelve? But I dint like
what it made me *think* about.'

'Yeah, I do–don't like it.'

Buddha Hat gave him another frowning puzzled look, which after a
moment turned into that icy evaluating stare of his. He scanned Strike
from head to toe. 'How tall are you?'

'Five seven? I don't know.'

'I'm five six and a half,' Buddha Hat announced, adjusting his hat as
he studied his reflection in the rearview mirror.

'Ha-how you know Victor?' Strike startled himself with his own question.

'Victor?' Buddha Hat gave him a slow glance. 'He go to the same church with my grandmother. One time I come to pick her up, but when I got there my damn car was all fucked up an' he gave us a ride home. Then like that same night he gave her a ride to her sister's house in East Orange. He dint even charge her. He just did it for free because I couldn't take her, you know, with my car all like it was.'

'Yeah, Victor, he in jail now.' The words drifted out of Strike in a gentle exhalation, as if he was making small talk.

Buddha Hat didn't respond, and Strike wasn't sure if he hadn't heard or was simply shutting down the conversation.

Strike opened his mouth and again the words seemed to float out: 'How you know *me*?'

Buddha Hat didn't answer for a moment, just watched the road. Then, without turning his head to Strike, he said, 'How you know *me*?'

Buddha Hat veered off the river road and followed a descending curve into the cavernous mouth of the Lincoln Tunnel. As they approached the state boundary marker midway through, he passed a hand across his mouth, then his crotch.

'You hear about that Dominican guy got all shot up an' died in the Holland Tunnel last Saturday?'

Strike said nothing. Buddha Hat sniffed and quickly pinched his nostrils.

'Shut down the whole damn New York tunnel for like four hours. Anybody in New Jersey wanting to go through to New York? No way, not for like four hours.' His voice dropped, becoming both musical and solemn. 'Four fucking hours, the whole of anybody wanting to go through to New York – '

'I don't' – Strike shook his head to prompt the rest of the sentence – 'know nothing about that.'

'No?' Buddha Hat turned to look at him, a dreamy half-smile on his face. 'You should read the papers more.'

Strike and Buddha Hat stood in the glass arcade of a martial arts store on Forty-second Street, the display windows on either side of them bristling with a huge collection of stabbing and hacking implements, from ten-foot silver-plated pikes to four-finger butterfly knives, from samurai swords to brass knuckles crowned with steel studs. There were Rambo knives, switchblades, throwing stars, the entire armory interspersed with aikido and judo pamphlets, illegal police patches, Green Beret T-shirts with ironic death slogans, and a rainbow of child-size Chinese pajamas.

'Man, this shit is clown show.' Buddha Hat pointed to a gold-plated sword, the blade the size and approximate shape of an adult dolphin. 'What the fuck you gonna do with that? The nigger starts running away? You gonna have to chase him in a station wagon, hope he don't hop a fence or run upstairs on you. I tell you one thing, though, with knives? I can't negotiate knives. It take a lot of anger to stick somebody, you know? That's like real *personal*.'

'I hear that.' Strike bobbed his head automatically, distracted by the weapons. He kept an eye on the street, which was somehow brighter at night than during the day. Everybody who passed looked like some kind of prey fish, some kind of hunter.

'How much you weigh?' Buddha Hat gave him another of his head-to-toe looks.

'One th-th – '

'One thirty?'

'Two.' Strike wiped his mouth.

'One thirty-two?' Buddha Hat compressed his lips. 'Yeah, I weigh one twenty-eight.'

Buddha Hat walked into the store. Strike followed, moving to a glass counter filled with security IDs, dog tags, more knives and several varieties of counterattack sprays. He watched as Buddha Hat tried on different fatigue jackets and soft khaki headgear, buying two more hats identical to the one he had on.

As they waited for the Asian salesman to ring up the purchase, Buddha Hat cocked his head at a photo nook set up in a corner of the store. A tripod-mounted Polaroid camera pointed toward a high-backed wicker chair set in front of a red velour curtain. Next to the chair, a gold and white fake antique phone rested on a small wicker side table.

'You want to get your picture took?'

Strike shook his head.

Buddha Hat sat stiffly on the wicker throne, legs crossed. The Asian salesman appeared, squinted through the viewfinder and chirped, 'Ring! Ring!'

Buddha Hat shot Strike a quick, nervous look.

'Ring! Ring!' The salesman gestured with an upturned palm.

'What . . .' Buddha Hat looked tense, on the verge of anger.

'Hallo? Who dere? Ring! Ring!' The salesman gestured again and finally

Buddha Hat got it. Blushing a little, he picked up the gaudy receiver and the camera flashed.

Back outside, his purchase stuffed into his back pocket, Buddha Hat led Strike to a hot dog stand next to a peep-show parlor. Buddha Hat was soon finishing the first of two hot dogs, but the chlorinated reek of disinfectant wafting through to the street from the porno store made Strike nauseous; it was all he could do to sip at a coconut drink in a conical paper cup.

Buddha Hat nodded toward two Muslims down the block who were manning an incense and pamphlet stand. He eyed their combat boots, ankle-length white robes and knit white skullcaps. 'They good, you know, for like the community? They keep theirselves clean and all and that's good, but like, if they keep marching into places they don't belong? They asking for something, and pretty soon, you know, like, they gonna get it. But they good for the community. How come you not eating?'

'I ain't hungry.'

'What's wrong with your stomach, then?'

'Nothin'. I ate before.'

'Goddamn, my cousin? One time he was holding his stomach all the time? Just holding it, bitchin' like for about a week? He went to the hospital, they opened him up, he had like a cancer in there, like all over in there. My uncle, he said everybody thought he was bullshitting or like ate something, you know, but that ol' boy had a cancer all up in there. You have a girlfriend?'

'Yeah.'

'What she look like, your girlfriend?'

'She's nice, she's got like greeny eyes, you know up in the Bronx?'

'That's nice.' Buddha Hat sounded far away.

'Yeah.' Strike nodded, the stomach cancer in him as tangible as undigested food.

'I had a girlfriend but I just cut her loose, man. I like to keep myself free most times. You want this?' He offered Strike the cardboard-framed photo of himself on the phone. 'I don't like it no more.'

'Thanks.' Strike took the picture, not knowing where to put it, making a show of admiring the portrait. And then, as if completely undone by the gift and with a sudden hope that Buddha Hat wasn't going to cut him down after all, Strike opened his mouth and let it run, talking about Victor.

'Yeah, my brother, man, huh-he . . . he crazy. He got this game he invented? He call it *Around*ball. He woke up one night from a dream, he say he dreamed a *game* and he got to write it down, he say there's all the people in a circle an' you in the middle an' they got to get this ball past you. An' if they get it past you on a fly? It's one point. On a bounce? It's two points. Aw-on a roll it's three. An' it's like you got to block too, an' every time you block *you* get a point, but like it the *opposite*, so you block a fly you get three, you block a roll it's one, an' after ten balls you-you see who got more points, you or the people surrounding you. He think he can get rich off that.' Strike looked at Buddha Hat directly for the first time since he started babbling. 'He-he *crazy*.'

Buddha Hat stared distantly at Strike, expressionless save for a pulsing tautness along the line of his jaw.

'Ha-how much time you think he's gonna *get* in there?'

Buddha Hat was silent, a last bite of hot dog still in his hand, giving Strike that lifeless gaze. Strike found it impossible to read – it could be anything from boredom to dreamy distraction to mounting fury – and he was on the verge of begging him to speak his mind, just get it over with, when Buddha Hat dropped his hot dog and grabbed Strike by the elbow, a rush of tense resolve breaking through the stony wall of his expression, as if he'd just made a momentous decision.

'I want you to see something,' Buddha Hat said, the words far off and flat. He pulled Strike into the fluorescent glare of the peep show next door.

Strike had never been inside one of these places, and he hated it instantly. It stank of that disinfectant, and the long corridors of private booths with men slipping in and out, heads down, sneaky and silent, made him both disgusted and nervous.

Buddha Hat gave a dollar to an Arab behind a raised platform. The guy pumped once on the bottom of what Strike thought was a microscope and dropped four tokens into Buddha Hat's palm.

Still holding Strike by the elbow, Buddha Hat dragged him down a red-lit lane of doors until he came to a stretch of three unoccupied booths. He dropped the four tokens into Strike's hand, looked both ways down the aisle, then shoved Strike inside the middle booth. 'Channel eight,' he said, 'push channel eight.'

As the door shut behind him, Strike stood in the sickly light with his back flush to the side wall. The booth smelled of spunk and he knew now that in a second or two Buddha Hat was going to shoot him through the door and go back to Dempsy alone. A girl wailed in ecstasy on somebody else's video. He put his hand to his mouth, wanting to block out the smell. Suddenly the door jerked open. Strike slid to his knees in fear.

'What the fuck you *doin'*, man?' Buddha Hat leaned in, snatched back the four tokens from Strike's limp paw, pumped them into a slot and stabbed a red channel selector above what looked like a digital clock. Strike, ashamed of being seen on his knees, scrambled to his feet as the booth abruptly went dark. A rapid series of sexual tangles popped on the screen, the personnel changing every time the channel selector beeped.

'Yeah, here.' Buddha Hat's voice shook as the selector stopped on eight. 'Watch that.' He slipped out of the booth and shut the door.

Strike remained glued to the wall, ignoring the video, ignoring the moaning under the wah-wah-pedal sound track, bracing for the bang, making himself as thin as possible, thinking Buddha Hat wanted the ecstasy and the music to smother the noise, trying to remember if he'd checked Buddha Hat for a gun since they left O'Brien, straining up on tiptoe, eyes shut, sucking in his belly, silently chanting, 'Do it, do it, do it.'

The lights came up, the moaning cut out and the screen went blank, a red zero beaming at him from the electronic counter. At first the booth seemed utterly silent, and then Strike heard canned grunts and wails coming at him through both side walls. Woozy, Strike looked down and saw a token rolling to a stop by his foot, followed by a white hand groping blindly under the raised partition.

'So what you think?'

They strolled down Eighth Avenue, Strike still feeling giddy and light. 'About what?'

'About channel eight. What you think?'

'It's good.' Strike nodded vigorously. 'It ga-got me *hot*.'

'Yeah? I tell you what happened. I was over my cousin's house when I was fifteen? He says he knows this guy, he'll pay us a hundred dollars to fuck this lady while he shoots the whole thing. So we went over to this motel in Queens. Man, I was scared. That lady had to like play with me for an *hour* before I got my dick hard. But when I did, man, we had us a *time*.' Buddha Hat stopped dead in the street, hunched over and lit a cigarette, his first of the night. Strike saw that his hands were shaking.

'I never showed that movie to *nobody*, but you know you can't do that shit and not show it to nobody. I don't know why I showed it to you, but I guess the other night? With Champ and Rodney? You so quiet-style, I figure you ain't the type that's gonna say nothin'. But I'm tellin' you, man, you best keep it to yourself, you know, like take it to your *grave*, 'cause if I start hearin' about it, I'm gonna know from who it started, you understand?'

Strike held up his hand as if being sworn in.

'Yeah, that was fun when we did that.' Buddha Hat glanced furtively at Strike. 'So like that got you all turned on?'

'Yeah well, you know.' Strike passed his hand over his mouth, dropped his ear to his shoulder. 'That lady was aw-all right, you know?'

'Yeah,' Buddha Hat said, smiling a little. 'She took my damn virginity too.' They walked a few blocks before he added in a self-conscious murmur, 'What you think of *me* in there?'

As they headed for the car, Buddha Hat telling and retelling the story of the porno movie, Strike floated in a buoyant bubble of relief, certain that for at least tonight he was out of danger. Did Victor get Buddha Hat to kill Darryl Adams? Strike just didn't know, because every time he said anything about Victor, the Hat went all blank. Did he kill Papi? That seemed like a good bet, given the way he'd said, 'You should read the papers more' with that dreamy look in his eye.

But Strike wasn't worried about that now, his mind focusing instead on a simpler thought. Once again Rodney had it right: The only real life out here was your own.

For the moment it seemed like a liberating lesson, something worth celebrating, but Strike's elation didn't last. As they drove out of the city, taking the sharp bend that led from Eleventh Avenue into the Lincoln Tunnel, Buddha Hat flew right past a Port Authority blue-and-white, parked in the nook of the curve. The cops had chosen a perfect spot for profiling the Jersey-bound traffic, and although neither Buddha Hat nor Strike so much as blinked, the cruiser rolled out as soon as the Volvo had passed.

'Now they gonna fuck with us,' Buddha Hat said. The police car hung back half a car length in the parallel lane. 'You got anything on you? Throw it out now.'

'I'm clean.' Strike reflexively patted himself down, then sunk back against the headrest.

When they broke clear of the tunnel, Buddha Hat was careful to use his turn signal to shift lanes, careful to avoid driving over the painted boundaries of the breakdown zones. But the blue-and-white still trailed them by half a car length, and Buddha Hat said, 'Fuck this,' and took the first turnoff, the Hoboken ramp. 'Let's get this over with.'

The cruiser followed suit, hitting its misery lights as soon as both cars were clear of the mainstream traffic. 'Park it there, brother,' a voice blared hollowly over the police loudspeaker. Buddha Hat pulled alongside a car wash and the cruiser stopped twenty feet behind them, turning on its take-down brights and training a spotlight on the Volvo's rearview mirror, leaving them so cocooned in whiteness that it hurt to look up.

Buddha Hat spoke in a calm murmur. 'One's coming up your side, so don't get jumpy.'

'Hands on the dash, fellas?' The voice in Strike's window seemed disembodied.

'Where's the papers at, Home?' Another voice floated in through the driver's window.

Buddha Hat nodded to the glove compartment, both his and Strike's hands splayed on the dash.

'Look at me.'

Strike turned to the voice in his window, and the cop drilled the beam of his flashlight into his eyes, lights on top of lights on top of lights, Strike instinctively curling his chin into his shoulder.

'C'mon, don't be shy, look at me, look at me. Whoa, this one's fucked up there, Fred. C'mon out, son.' The cop held the door for him, palming Strike's chest to gauge the pound, a heart test.

The other cop trained his light on Buddha Hat's outraged sockets. 'This one too, Bobby. Whoo!'

'Where you been, brother?' Strike's cop sported a flaring wax-tipped handlebar mustache and longish blond hair, and he loosely held a cigarette in his free hand, as if this roust was on his own time. 'Where you been?'

'New York.' Strike tried not to look at the cars coming off the Hoboken ramp, their drivers rubbernecking.

'I *know* New York. *Where* in New York – and don't look at him, look at me.'

'Times Square, around.' Strike tried to sound neutral, as if this whole thing was reasonable.

'Score some good shit?'

'N–nuh-no.' Shit, Strike thought. Here we go.

'You nervous? I'd be nervous too. Lying always makes me nervous. What you do, pick up a package?'

'Cuc-clothes.'

'Oh yeah? No package? No smack? No blow?'

Strike reared back in disdain. The cop hit his eyes with the light again and began going through his pockets, patting him down. 'No smack, huh? Step back a few feet please? But stay out of the car wash, it'll shrink your clothes.'

The cop ducked into the car, feeling around and under Strike's seat, then fingering the change caddy, the visor and the glove compartment. Finally he turned on the air conditioner, palming the air streams for blocked vents.

The side of the car wash was quivering with purple and gold Mylar disks in the shape of a whale, and Strike stood framed in the light-dappled glitter, furtively watching Buddha Hat and his cop, a muscular Hispanic with a small ponytail under his cap, probably a plain-clothes working the odd night in uniform. Strike saw the cop's frisk come up empty. No gun.

'Who's Yvonne Carter?' Buddha Hat's cop frowned down at the registration.

'M'grandmother.' Buddha Hat was tight-lipped, distant.

'She know you got her car?'

'Yeah, uh-huh.'

'Let me ask you. Your grandmother, she's a working woman?'

'She's retired.'

'Yeah? You help her on the car payments?'

'Some.'

'You good to your grandmother?'

Buddha Hat didn't answer.

'When was the last time you were arrested? Don't look at him, look at me.'

'I never . . .' Buddha Hat stared intently at the Hispanic cop's throat.

'No?'

'Nope.'

'Good. Let me ask you. Why do you think I stopped you?'

'I don't know.'

'You don't know? I'll tell you. You were driving too cautious. Isn't that a pisser? You were driving like you wouldn't fart without putting out your hand to make a fart signal. Damned if you do, damned if you don't, ain't that a bitch? So what did you score on the Deuce?'

'Two hats.'

'Two hats, huh?'

'They in the car.' Buddha Hat pointed with his chin.

'Two hats,' the Hispanic cop said. 'Is that what they're calling
it now?'

'Two hats of *smack*.' Strike's cop straightened up from his search
grunting and wincing, then threw a thumb at Strike. 'This one's *all*
fucked up, Fred.'

'No I ain't,' Strike said, fighting to keep his voice mild.

'Hey, you can't hide your lying eyes, Home. They're like fucking pin
dots, and your heart's pumping Kool-Aid. *You* know that, *I* know that,
so why don't we cut the shit, just tell me where it is.'

'They *ain't* none.'

'Look, you two bozos are under arrest anyway for driving under the
influence, for *being* under the influence. You know what that means?'

They both stood silent, letting the game run its course.

'That means this fine car is mine, right Fred?'

The other cop nodded. 'Mine too.'

'You say you don't got no drugs, so now I got to impound this bitch
and tear it apart. But let me tell you something. You make me do that,
go to all that work, and we find some? Against your lying? *Holy* shit,
what happens to you.'

For a moment no one spoke, all four of them standing there as if waiting
for a bus. Strike's cop lit another cigarette, took a languorous drag,
stretching his throat for maximum inhale. 'Are you a gambling man?'

'No.' Strike shook his head.

'What are we gonna find in your urine right now?'

Strike shrugged. 'Piss, mostly.'

Buddha Hat turned away quickly, hiding a smile, and Strike felt a
sudden glow of friendship.

The cop belly-bumped him slightly, his voice going quiet. 'You giving
me shit?'

'No sir.'

'You want to fucking dance with me?' He tilted his head to one side
to peer up into Strike's eyes.

'No sir.'

"Cause I *like* to fucking dance, Home.'

'No sir.'

'You don't have *no* drugs in here?'

'No sir.'

'You don't have no drugs in *you*?'

'No sir.'

The cop retreated, then walked in a slow circle around Strike, all three of them watching him, waiting. 'Are you queer?' he asked with theatrical sincerity.

'No.' Strike stepped back a foot.

''Cause you yanking my chain.' The cop shrugged as if the evidence was obvious to everyone.

'No I ain't.'

'Sure you are.' The cop walked back to his cruiser, retrieved a nightstick and ambled back. He reached behind himself and slipped the nightstick between his legs so that it stood out like an eighteen-inch hard-on from under his gut.

'You know what this is? This is called a visual aid.'

Strike stared at the car wash wall. The cop was standing with his back to the exit ramp so none of the drivers could see what he was doing.

'Grab it. G'head, it's OK, grab it.'

Strike stared off, sighing.

'I said *grab* it.'

Strike delicately fingered the tip as the cop started sliding the stick back and forth. Staring off at the glittering disks of whale, Strike blew air through his cheeks and tried to hold it together.

'That's it, yeah, OK, just keep it up, 'cause that's what you were doing to me before anyhow, jerking me off. So just keep it up, and while you're doing it? Think about where the dope is. Take your time, though, take your time.'

The cop was sliding the stick and moving Strike's arm for him. Strike felt his scalp creep, his head becoming lighter than air as it began to fill with visions of taking the cop's stick and rapping his balls, smashing his skull.

The Hispanic cop put his arm around Buddha Hat's shoulders, spoke intimately by his ear. 'That's really embarrassing innit? Makes you want to blow a gasket, seeing that, don't it? Phew. Maybe you should tell us where the dope is.'

'Ain't no dope,' Buddha Hat said.

'No, huh?' The cop stared at Buddha Hat's license. 'Where you work at? What you do?'

'In Dempsy for my uncle's truck. Help on the truck.' Buddha Hat stared at the ground, and Strike saw his eyes go wide and icy.

'A trucker's helper? How the fuck can you afford this car?'

'My grand – '

'*Fuck* your grandmother. Don't give me this grandmother bullshit.

This is a fucking dope-bought car and I don't wanna hear about anything else.'

'I never sold dope in my life.' Buddha Hat's eyes showed whites all around but his voice remained small.

'You know what I drive? I drive a five-year-old Honda Civic and I got two years of college, so who the *fuck* are you, tell me that.'

Buddha Hat said nothing.

'Trucker's helper,' the cop hissed. 'And don't give me them King Kong eyes 'cause I'll put you through the fucking ground right here and now, Yo.'

'That's it, man, I'm starting to get hard for *real*.' Strike's cop leaned back, his hand sliding obscenely between the cheeks of his own ass. 'Anytime you feel like you wanna stop, alls you got to do is tell me where it is, brother.'

The cop started whistling, 'I've Been Working on the Railroad' to accompany the strokes, lit another cigarette with his free hand, and then Strike was gone, lost in a fantasy of violence, gripping the nightstick white-knuckled now, his neck aching from the way his chin was turned almost clear behind his shoulder so that he didn't have to look at the cop. He started to make a noise no one could hear but himself.

'Whoa, there horsey!' the cop squawked. 'Fred, check out *this* action.'

Strike snapped into focus. Looking down, he was shocked to see that while he was lost in his bloody visions he had started jerking on the nightstick so vigorously that the cop didn't even have to hold it for him. Horrified, he let the stick go and watched it clatter to the ground.

'Did I tell you to stop?' The cop blew a cloud of smoke.

'I ay-ain't do-doin' it no more.' Strike stared intently at the cop's shoes.

'Are you telling me to go fuck myself?'

'N-n-n-no. I ju-juh-juh . . .'

The cop hesitated, appraising the stammer. 'Just tell me where the package is,' he said quietly, his voice suddenly sober.

'N-n-n-n . . .' Strike began thrashing his head, trying to physically whip out words that just wouldn't shake loose. 'N-n-n-n . . .' Something danced in his eyes as he clenched his teeth. 'N-n-n-n . . .'

The cops exchanged a quick embarrassed look.

'Just take the *car*, man,' Buddha Hat almost shouted, sounding angry and pained. 'You gonna take it, then just take it.'

Strike could see a spray of diamond chips hanging from his own eyelashes. 'Gerr-gerr . . .' His nostrils filled with mucus, a wet '*hoop*' sound escaping his throat. 'Guh-rrr . . .' Rooted to the ground, lost and blind with a dewy rage, he didn't even try to shape words anymore, surrendering to the sounds as they came, pure fury, pure music.

'Easy, easy.' Strike's cop put out a placating hand but kept his distance. 'Easy there, Home.'

'Im*pound* the motherfucker,' Buddha Hat snapped, making a gun with his thumb and forefinger. '*Please.*'

An hour after the cops had beat a wordless retreat, piling into their cruiser without threat or apology, Strike and Buddha Hat sat in silence, parked on the Jersey side of the river right on the water's edge, staring out at the shut-down New York skyline.

Buddha Hat lit a cigarette and Strike rolled down his window for air. It was three o'clock in the morning. The only other life around them was a gray-haired white man in a soft gray sweater. Baby-faced, smiling, he paced rapidly back and forth along the river railing, talking to himself.

Buddha Hat squinted at the white man, then slowly turned to Strike. 'When do you think you're gonna die?'

Strike pressed a forearm across his gut, the pain like a vicious intelligence announcing a response to the question.

'I don't know, I got some years. Twenty maybe? Yeah, I'd like twenty more if I can get it.' Strike nodded, completely exhausted from the night.

Buddha Hat tapped his ashes into the gap where an ashtray should have been. 'Yeah, well, I don't think I got much more to go myself.' He shook his head. 'When it happens? I hope they put it right here.' He touched a hollow behind Strike's left ear, his fingertip like iced wax. ''Cause right there? You don't feel *nothin'*. You go like . . . *crack*.'

'Um.' A soft sucking noise escaped Strike's lips as he pressed his forearm so deep into his stomach that the bone of his arm locked in behind his lower ribs. He could feel a bit of something climb up his throat and into his mouth.

Buddha Hat sat quietly, as if taking his measure in the darkness. 'You got your high school diploma?'

'Unh-uh,' Strike said, trying to unclench.

'Can I say something to you without disrespect?'

Strike waited.

'You should go back to school or something.'

Strike looked up at Buddha Hat in surprise. Buddha Hat winced apologetically, then gently added, ''Cause you in the wrong line of work.'

Part Four

THIRTY IN

22

Tuesday was Rocco's night off. He sat at the dinner table not listening to anybody, the liquor in his eye giving each glass rim, fork tine, and candle flame a slightly haloed gleam. He slouched at the head of the table, feeling like the Father; before him sat Patty and six friends of hers. They were all so young and bright, and in his slightly sullen stupor Rocco decided to label them the Quick and the Weak.

Patty had arranged the dinner in honor of their third wedding anniversary, and the guest list was all hers. He had thought about inviting Mazilli, but she was put off by his partner – she said he spooked her. In fact, Patty didn't like cops as a rule. She thought of them as nerve-racking presences, heavy-handed charmers who addressed women that they had just been introduced to by half their first names – Lil, Vy, Jude, Deb – and who, at best, treated women like lovable baby animals in a petting zoo. By now, after three years of marriage, Rocco felt so self-conscious and defeated by Patty's take on cops that he no longer wanted to invite anyone from the Job to the loft, imagining her polite smile when they would moo over the view, exclaim 'Holy shit' or make some comment about how he had it 'made in the shade.'

Rocco stared down at the remains of his wife's offerings: softshell crab on a bed of Boston lettuce, baby shrimp, slices of avocado and yellow pepper. An old friend of Patty's named Gerry, seated at the opposite end of the table and facing Rocco across the candles – overweight, bearded and bespectacled – laughed at something Patty said, the laugh a deep, stuttering jackhammer. Rocco heard Erin rustle in her crib behind the sliding rice-paper partition. Then someone held up a skimpy crab and launched into a droll lecture regarding the difference between good cholesterol and bad.

Rocco sipped his vodka, then cleared his throat. 'In Dempsy?' he said loudly. 'If we were eating in Dempsy, it would be crabs and spaghetti tonight.'

All other conversation came to an end, seven faces turned his way, attentive smiles all around.

'They fish the crabs out of the creeks,' Rocco continued. 'I know what it sounds like, but it's better than you think. I mean, not as good as *this* but . . .'

'Where do they get the spaghetti?' asked a slender young man dressed in black and white like a waiter, an ex-boyfriend of Patty's from college.

'Well, you know, they have orchards outside Bayonne.' Rocco tossed off the rest of his drink.

'Oh God,' Patty said. 'Did you ever see that old BBC clip where they did the thing on spaghetti harvesting in Italy? With the spaghetti hanging off the trees?'

A chorus of 'yeahs' followed as Rocco withdrew into a paranoid sulk. Why did she want to shut him down? He wasn't being unsociable or anything.

'Hey, Rocco?'

Rocco didn't hear his name. He was debating with himself whether to simply stand up and start clearing the dishes or first signal Patty for permission.

'Rocco.'

It was Gerry, who tilted his head slightly to catch his eye out of the line of candles.

'Rocco . . . Is that your real name?'

'Why wouldn't it be my real name?'

'Rocco *Klein*?' Gerry took out a pipe and sucked air through the empty bowl.

'What are you, an anti-Semite?' Rocco said too quickly. He glanced at Patty as the words left his mouth. 'I'm only kidding.' The table went quiet again. 'Actually Rocco's a nickname. My real name is Dave, David.'

The vodka bottle was on the sideboard, just out of his reach, and he didn't want to get up and pour a refill in front of this crowd. In a burst of anxiety he began to talk.

'See, when my parents split up? I went to live with my mother's parents. My father went back to live with *his* parents, and my mother took off, just took off.' Rocco shot a hand toward the window like an arrow.

The guests were all listening now, leaning over their empty plates. Patty began to peel tears of wax off a candle, Rocco thinking, Hey, I listen to *your* stories over and over.

'My grandfather, he was a teamster – you know, a truck driver – and the reason I became a cop was because he once beat a guy half to death, his *boss* in fact, and this cop, this detective, had fixed it with the judge so that when he was arraigned he wouldn't go to jail. This cop told him that when he went before the judge he should plead guilty, that the judge would just pass some sentence for show, and then he should leave by this door, this particular door to the left of the bench. And that's what he did. Went up before the judge, the judge mumbled some bogus sentence, and then my grandfather went out the door next to the bench. The door led to an alley, and right behind that door was the detective, who then booted him right in the ass, told him never to fuck up like that again. So my grandfather always talked about this detective Rocco Aiello that fixed it for him, kicked him in the ass. The guy was his hero, and when *I* came to live with him, well, he gave me the nickname Rocco. In fact, that was why I went into the police academy, hearing all my life about this guy, who I never actually met.'

Patty got up and started clearing dishes. Rocco still couldn't read her face.

'Why'd he beat up his boss?' It was Gerry again. What was *with* this guy? But Rocco had a second wind now.

'Yeah, well it's funny. I always heard that his boss had blacklisted him in the poultry business – my grandfather delivered poultry – and there had been a hijacking and this boss thought my grandfather was in on it. My mother, who was a little kid at this time, had pleurisy or something and my grandfather, he was so pissed off at being fired for no reason like that, that he just marched in on the guy at this poultry clearinghouse on Fourteenth Street, just marched in with blood in his eye because his daughter's sick and he can't even put food on the table. And then he beat this guy, his boss, half to death in front of everybody. And the colored guys, these guys that drove with him before he got shitcanned? He always got along with colored guys, and we're talking 1935 now, and . . .'

Rocco saw Gerry wink at Patty, who stood at the dishwasher. What the hell did *that* mean? 'And anyways these colored guys, they got him out of there, told him to go home, but the boss filed charges from the hospital so . . . I used to love to hear the stories of his life, you know? It was always him walking in somewheres and kicking ass because enough is enough . . .'

Rocco remembered his last visit with his grandfather: he'd stood over the comatose old man in a hospital bed, one hand on his chest as if to keep him from floating away, just stood there watching 'Kojak' on the ceiling-mounted television. Lost in his thoughts, Rocco whistled absently through clenched teeth, then looked up to see Patty standing over him. With a reassuring nod she handed him a fresh vodka and he felt flushed with gratitude. Looking around the table, he sensed that his audience was still with him.

'Anyways, that's the story I always heard, but one of the last times I talked to him? About four years ago, before he died? He was in the hospital already, going pretty fast, and I guess he was feeling sorry for himself dying and all, and he told me about the beating again, but this time he told me the truth of it, which was, well, his job was delivering chickens and ducks and sometimes eggs to restaurants, and this one day the eggs got mixed up and they hatched, you know, *peep peep* in the back of the truck, and he figured, what the hell, and put a couple in his pocket to take home to my mother, like a treat for a kid, baby chicks. The boss heard somehow that Sonny Marx had stole some chickens, so he – Moskowitz was his name – he'd had it with stealing, so he fired my grandfather and spread the word that Sonny Marx was a thief. It was a closed business and my grandfather just couldn't get work anywhere and I guess he was really in a bad spot over these chicks, these two chicks for his daughter, and finally after two weeks when he couldn't get hired he went to talk to this Moskowitz, to ask why, but to *ask*, to go hat in hand, Why are you taking the food out of my family's mouth? What did I ever do to you? It was two chicks, baby chicks for my daughter, I'll pay for them, *please* Mr Moskowitz . . . And Moskowitz wouldn't even look at him, he just, Get out of here, Marx. You're a thief, a *gonif*, you're finished, and my grandfather started to beg . . . He begged in this giant chicken hall surrounded by all these guys he worked with, Please Mr Moskowitz, I swear, please, I never, and then he started to cry in front of . . . And then I guess he lost it and did what he did, fractured the guy's skull, stove in half his ribs, and then the colored guys got him out of there. And I think this was the true story – I mean, I'm a detective, right? I should know the truth from the lie when I hear it, right? But with your family you get, you know, the truth is a while in the coming.'

Rocco nodded to himself, feeling vaguely humiliated now, trying to bail himself out. 'One thing, though, that he was always proud of? He always said, No matter what, I always put food on the table – good times, bad times, there was food on the table.'

Rocco looked up and saw everyone watching him, heads bobbing in polite acknowledgment.

Patty brought the dessert – sliced papaya dipped in chocolate and frozen to the consistency of hard ice cream. The guests were all smiling and exclaiming, and then one of the women at the table began to talk about being a waitress, how bad she was at it, tripping over things, screwing up orders, but laughing about it. She was twenty-two and was really a painter, and this is what she happened to find herself doing to make ends meet. There was no despair in her voice, no sense of identification with the job. Listening to her, Rocco felt a stab of resentment at the open-endedness of her life, at her blissful assumption that she could play an infinite number of roles through the coming years.

Rocco withdrew again, thinking about that last long wrenching talk with his grandfather and about how when he was a kid his grandfather had withheld the true angle on things. Rocco had grown up with his grandfather's stories, and they'd always centered on the defiant declarations, the successful showdowns – Sonny Marx don't take no crap here, Sonny Marx don't take no crap there. But Rocco had left the hospital that day thinking about the man pocketing baby chickens, begging Moskowitz for his job back, getting kicked in the ass by the detective, had left the hospital with the sickening intuition that all the stories were slanted halfway to pure bullshit, and that more than likely, the watermarks of this man's life, this man that he had revered, had all been humiliations.

Erin started to cry behind her partition – a hesitant, barely conscious croak – and Rocco shot up as if she was shrieking in pain. 'I'll get her.' He held a hand out to Patty, snatched the vodka off the sideboard and disappeared behind the partition.

Erin was sitting up, blinking and frowning, on her way back down to sleep. Rocco lifted her out of the crib anyhow and carried her into the small guest room so they could lie down together. On his back, he closed his eyes and drifted, taking a nip now and then, some of the liquor trickling into his ear. He heard the conversation at the dinner table take on a reassuring rhythm of a good time had by all. Good food, good conversation. Good. Happy anniversary.

To celebrate, Rocco had bought Patty a three-hundred-dollar leather shoulder pouch that he had seen in the window of Crouch and Fitzgerald. It was similar to the one Sean Touhey carried around, and it cost Rocco half his paycheck. But Patty hadn't gotten him a damn thing. She didn't know you were supposed to exchange gifts on a wedding anniversary. Well, maybe you weren't, what did he know? He lay there feeling sorry for himself, musing on how being around a bunch of twenty-five-year-olds made him act like a twelve-year-old, whereas when he was working across the river, truly *working*, he felt centered and unselfconscious, his deepest talents sometimes emerging quick and true.

He had felt that way the night before at that bar, Rudy's, and now Rocco began running the Darryl Adams job through his head, thinking again about that truculent and eerily weightless kid Victor Dunham, about his hunch that the brothers were running a confession game on them. The case was definitely beginning to get inside him, which made Rocco feel both leery and primed. He had always believed that a major occupational hazard for a homicide investigator was catching a job that somehow got you by the balls, because when that happened a job could turn into a mission, and you could wind up humping on it, grinding your teeth about it for years, past the point of anybody's caring, sometimes including the family of the victim.

Mazilli had a mission like that: four years before, he had caught the murder of a twelve-year-old black kid by three equally young white kids, a meaningless impulsive stabbing. He knew who the perps were, and they knew he knew, but he couldn't prove it so he had them monitored throughout the city. Whenever one of them was picked up for petty theft or drug possession, there wasn't a cop in Dempsy who didn't know to call Mazilli immediately so that he could come down to threaten, cajole and bargain with the kid to turn state's evidence against the others. The perps were all sixteen now, a bad lot, each of them arrested at least three times since then. But so far none of them would rat out the others. Mazilli didn't know how long it would take, how many arrests, how many bully sessions, but there was no doubt in his mind that someday one of these kids would get nailed for something bad enough to trade on, and when that happened – a year, two, five years from now – he'd be right there.

Rocco had always felt sorry for guys who got sucked into missions like that, thought of them as modern-day Ancient Mariners, but now he wasn't so sure. Maybe a mission was just the thing he needed to clean himself out – salvation through obsession, get that small wheel of gifts rolling, discover a way to live beyond the time clock.

This Darryl Adams job: maybe what interested him here was less about getting justice for Darryl Adams than getting it for Victor Dunham, and Rocco envisioned the day, a few weeks or months from now, when the brothers would switch places, when this kid Strike would be in County instead. Lying there, Rocco began spinning out strategies, angles of approach, game plans, thinking maybe Patty didn't have to give him an anniversary present after all. Maybe he had just given one to himself.

Wednesday brought a new job, Mazilli's catch, a white eighteen-year-old girl found nude in the St Andrew's Cemetery, her face punched in and a pocketknife rammed to the hilt in her chest. When Rocco walked into the office a little after four P.M., Mazilli was already off in Jersey City, where the girl had lived, making the rounds with local detectives, trying to track down the boyfriend, the boyfriend's best friend, the mother's boyfriend and the uncle. A discarded gift box for a bottle of Boggs cranberry liqueur was found near the body, and the day tour had made the rounds of liquor stores in a five-block radius of the cemetery in the hopes that some salesclerk would ID the victim, but so far nothing doing. The liqueur was probably purchased the night before, which meant at least half the stores canvassed had different people working in them when the day tour came through, which meant that Rocco was supposed to do the canvass all over again tonight.

Rocco looked down at two photographs on his desk, the first a head shot of the girl. Her cheek rested on the clipped grass of the cemetery, eyes raccooned in blood, broken jaw ballooning blue. It had been hot the previous night, and maggot larvae, looking like a small cotton ball, were already nesting in the shell of her ear. The other picture, coaxed from the mother by local detectives, showed the girl sitting on her boyfriend's lap on a steel-framed chair against a backdrop of cheap wood paneling. She was lean and bright-eyed, with dazzling teeth and black bangs, a little kohl around the eyes – a nice-looking girl. She sat with her arm behind the neck of the boyfriend, a thick-faced, ruddy blond with heavy lips and brow. The camera flash had given him red irises, making him look possessed, and Rocco found himself looking forward to meeting him, having a little chat.

The Ahab's killing was already threatening to become yesterday's news. Mazilli was completely off it now, and if Rocco intended to keep after it with any conviction, he'd have to make something happen fast. It was now five o'clock; according to the medical examiner, the girl was killed at about ten the night before. Rocco decided to start his canvass at seven, guessing the killer probably bought the booze around eight or nine and headed right for the cemetery.

Rocco grabbed a set of keys and headed out the door, figuring he had a couple of hours to kill, enough time to check out this kid Strike, get the smell of him and then decide whether to keep pushing his hunch or let it go. As he drove toward the projects, he recalled fragments of his humiliating ramble at the dinner table. The baby chickens story, Jesus Christ. He tried to remember if he had apologized to Patty or not, and then thought, Apologize for what?

He double-parked a half block from the Roosevelt benches. Even before he got out of the car, Rocco saw an unquiet stillness come over some of the people milling around, a side-mouthed irritation, and he knew that if he sat where he was for the next six hours, he would not see a single drug transaction, although his guess was that at least four or five kids were either holding or waiting for customers in order to scoop and serve from a central stash.

At first he thought the kid perched on the top slat of the center bench was Victor Dunham. Startled, Rocco wondered how the hell he had made bail. Rocco leaned forward a little, looked more closely and saw that it was actually Ronald Dunham. It was amazing how much the brothers resembled each other, not so much in actual looks as in carriage and aura – the same small, bird-boned frame, the same fretfully responsible expression, alert and sorrowful, as if they were in charge of overseeing some obscure but endless crisis.

He pulled the car right up to the benches, all eyes on him now, and got out with a little hop and a skip. But instead of walking directly to the dope crew, he made a detour to the looped chain surrounding the grass. That sharp eleven- or twelve-year-old boy was still sitting there, hunched over and rocking just like last time.

'I thought I told you to get out of town,' Rocco growled, giving him a beady stare. The boy turned his head, hiding his brights again, and then Rocco got down to business, hitching up his pants, straightening his tie and strolling to the bench. He didn't feel entirely comfortable about going into this by himself to begin with, and when Ronald Dunham made a quick move to his waistband, Rocco had a real oh-shit moment. But then the kid pulled a key ring with a ridiculous number of keys from his front pocket and Rocco relaxed.

'How ya doin', fellas?' Rocco stood in front of the center bench, bouncing on the balls of his feet, jangling the change in his pocket. Half a dozen teenagers stared at him, but no one answered.

Rocco turned to Victor's brother. He refused to call him Strike: he hated using any of their street names, it was too much like kissing their ass.

'Are you Ronnie Dunham? I'm Rocco Klein from the Homicide squad. You got a minute for me?'

Arm high and curled in a slight crook, Rocco gestured for Strike to come down off the top slat, then walked him to the sidewalk, still in full view of his friends on the benches. It was a good spot for a casual grilling. By standing here, he would shut down all business, plus the kid would be off balance with everybody watching. Having an audience would be dangerous if the kid felt obliged to mouth off, put on a show, but Rocco didn't think that would be a problem because this first time he'd play it in his nicest-guy-in-the-world mode, just two guys shooting the shit.

Now that both of them were standing more or less face-to-face, Strike looked even smaller, his eyes level with Rocco's tie knot. His clothes were immaculate and modest, giving Rocco the impression of tight-assed tidiness.

Strike went up on tiptoe to jam his key ring back in his pants, and Rocco smiled at him.

'Jesus Christ, you're about one key shy of a hardware store, there.'

The kid shrugged, waiting for real talk. He didn't seem particularly nervous, more like distracted and vaguely irritated.

'Ronnie.' Rocco stepped toward him a few inches and spoke in a confidential murmur. 'I'm working the Darryl Adams homicide and, ah, how's your brother doing? He holding up in there?'

'I haven't suh-seen him yet.'

'No? That's a rough joint, County. You ever see that place?'

'No. I mean, ju-just like overnight aw-on a confusion.'

A confusion: Rocco thinking, I love it. 'Yeah, well, so you *know*, right?'

Strike didn't answer. He looked over Rocco's shoulder, into the distance. Rocco liked the stammer. He hoped it was a sign of distress and easy breakdown.

'How's your mother doing?'

'Sh-she's, you know.' The kid stopped, giving it just a quick huff of breath and a shrug, his feet shifting as if he had to pee, Rocco thinking, Guilty.

'Listen, I got to tell you, I'm not too happy with how things went down with your brother.' Rocco tried to sound apologetic, as if the whole thing was his fault. 'I mean, he gave it up, he's gonna swing for it, there's nothing to do for that, but I dunno . . . I just don't think it went down the way he said it did. Do you know what he said about it?'

Strike looked away. 'How would I know? I wasn't there.'

'Wasn't where?'

The gaze swung back. Strike looked at him with barely concealed contempt for his heavy-handed ways. 'Where he *talked* to you,' he said, speaking slowly in case Rocco didn't get the message.

'Well, he's claiming the guy jumped him out of the blue and it was self-defense.' Rocco sighed. 'Between me and you, he sticks with that? He's adding twenty years to his jail time. No fucking jury on earth's gonna buy that, and it's bugging the hell out of me because I know it's just not what happened, and Jesus, your brother's such a hard-working guy, you know?'

The kid's mouth tightened and he studied the traffic.

'I mean *you* know, what the hell do I gotta tell *you* for? But let me ask you. What do *you* think happened? How the fuck did he get into this mess? You got any ideas?'

'I don't know. He don't lie, Victor, so like, maybe he–he's sayin' the truth.'

Rocco instantly regretted his strategy. He had told Strike too much, had given him Victor's story to agree with and then clam up on. This kid's no dope, he thought, and the stammer's probably chronic, nothing to get excited about. Shit.

The kid's eyes focused on something along the row of parked cars. Rocco turned to see the famous Erroll Barnes leaning against an old pea-green Le Baron, a brown bag pressed between his elbow and ribs.

'Hey-y, how ya doin'?' Rocco held up a hand in a half-salute. 'Long time no see.'

The two of them had never met, but Erroll smirked and nodded at Rocco in dismissive greeting. Rocco just wanted to neutralize the guy, hoping he'd figure Rocco was one of the dozens of detectives who had arrested him over the years. The guy looked bad, sick. Rocco wondered what was in the bag.

'He waiting for you?' Rocco asked Strike.

'No,' the kid said too quickly. 'I dunno.'

''Cause I'll be outa here in a minute.'

'Yeah, OK.'

The crew at the benches walked off two and three at a time, glancing at Erroll Barnes as they left, and soon there was no one around but the boy sitting on the chain.

'So you think your brother's telling the truth, huh?'

'Yeah, he don't lie.'

'So you don't think there was maybe something between him and Darryl Adams going down?'

'I couldn't say.'

'Did you know this guy Darryl?'

'Unh-uh.'

Bingo: Lie number one. Mazilli had said that Strike and Darryl had been co-workers in Rodney's store for close to a year.

Rocco spun in a slow and casual circle, watching the kid try to find a sight line that didn't take in Rocco or Erroll. 'You didn't know Darryl Adams at all, huh?'

Strike hesitated. 'Unh-uh.'

Rocco could see the wincing regret in the kid's face, the kid *knowing* he had just fucked up. Rocco sighed, forcing himself to be cool, pace himself. 'When was the last time you saw your brother?'

The kid lightly touched his stomach and burped silently. 'Not, like, you know, na-not for a while.'

'You mean not for a few weeks, a month, two months?'

'Yeah, about two months.'

Lie number two. Rocco took another slow spin around himself, letting the adrenaline subside, not saying anything for a moment. Rocco winked at the boy on the chain before turning back to Strike.

'Ronnie, let me ask your opinion on something. Let's say, like you say, that your brother's telling the truth, OK? Why do you think this guy Darryl would come out of the blue like that, attack him, *knowing* he had a gun?' Rocco held his breath, hoping the kid would answer in a way that would tie him into prior knowledge of the gun, the players. But the kid just shook his head, his expression blank.

A beeper went off and Rocco almost laughed, debating with himself whether to use this right now, swing the dope dealer hammer at him. He decided to back off: it was way too soon to be a hard-on.

'You got to get that?'

The kid jerked back, smiling. 'It ain't me.'

'No?'

The beeper sounded again and Rocco checked his hip, saw his home number blinking up at him.

The kid shot him a fast smirk and Rocco laughed. 'How 'bout that,' he said, then held up his hand. 'Awright, look. I was just hoping, talking to you, maybe you could've helped me figure out a reason for that guy attacking your brother like that. Otherwise, shit, man, thirty years . . . He's got those little kids. It's fucking rough, you know? I don't think he understands what he's doing, sticking to this out-of-the-blue bullshit. He's just hurting himself, and if he had *one* justifiable reason, he could halve his time in.' Rocco exhaled, shook his head. 'Thirty fucking years.'

Strike's face took on a congested color, as if he wanted to say something. But whatever it was, he swallowed it.

'Is there anything on this you can help me help him with? *Anything?*' Rocco tried to sound concerned without going all sobby about it.

Strike crossed his arms over his chest. 'Well, like maybe the guy dissed him sometime aw-or, you know, they had words aw-or something.'

'What do you mean?'

'Well, maybe this guy had like, a, *a at*titude.'

'An attitude . . .' Rocco waited.

'Like, I ha-had *heard* that he wasn't like . . .' The kid coughed into his fist. 'Like he was disrespectful of the people.'

'What people?'

Strike floundered. 'You know, in the store, the customers, the workers.'

'Yeah? You heard this? Who'd you hear this from?'

'Just, you know, around.' Strike danced with his palm on his gut, an anxiety samba. 'No people that cuc-come to mind, just, but maybe he ah-and my brother had words. Maybe he, I don't know, maybe he-he disrespected my brother wuh-one day, you know in the store, and held it like a *grudge*.'

'Your brother held it like a grudge?'

'No, no, the other – Darryl. Maybe he had it in for him, you know.' Strike exhaled heavily as if disgusted with his own performance.

Rocco was sure the kid was lying out of his ass, making it up as he went along. But that was OK. Each lie opened the door wider for future talks.

Rocco reached into his wallet and extracted his card. 'Listen, one last thing. I hear rumors that that Ahab's was a drug spot, selling drugs. You ever hear anything like that?'

'No.' The kid caressed his torso and looked away. 'I don't know about that.'

'All right, whatever. Just do me a favor, OK? Here's my card. If you hear anything, help your brother and give me a call.'

Strike ignored the card. Rocco slipped it into his sweatshirt muff for him.

'I'm just curious. Where do you work?'

'In a grocery store aw-on Jackson.'

Lie number three, at least. An embarrassment of riches.

'On Jackson. What, Rodney Little's?'

'Naw.'

'That's the only grocery store I know on Jackson.'

'Naw, I mean yeah, Ra-Rodney's. Uh-huh, I guess it's Rodney's.' The kid bared his teeth and shot Rocco a fleeting murderous glance.

'OK.' Rocco quickly retreated, not wanting his line snapped. He slipped his hands in his pants pockets and slowly wheeled around. 'I'll be seeing you.'

Walking to his car, he nodded to Erroll Barnes, who was still leaning on the Le Baron. 'How ya been?'

Erroll nodded minutely and Rocco wondered if the package was drugs: not his department. And as he drove off to canvass liquor stores on the cemetery job, he had the fleeting thought that Erroll Barnes was the actor on this Ahab's shooting. But then he dismissed it out of hand. It's the brother, he thought. It's this lying little shit right here.

Rocco hit a half-dozen liquor stores within walking distance of the cemetery, automatically flashing the photo of the girl and her boyfriend to a dozen clerks and cashiers. None of the people could identify either one of them, and given that the neighborhood was predominantly Puerto Rican and Filipino, Rocco tended to believe the shrugs and head shakes. Young white customers would have stood out.

Rocco worked slowly, distractedly, his mind still back by those benches in Roosevelt. He drove at a crawl from store to store, mulling over his options, wondering how to work Ronald Dunham. His instincts told him that if he came down too hard or too fast, the kid would simply disappear or, worse, go to a lawyer. So how should he play it?

Visiting the neighborhood's last liquor store, Rocco finally came up with the beginnings of a plan. As he walked in, some clocker was buying a wine cooler. The kid had his roll out, exposing what looked like a few hundred dollars to pay for a two-dollar drink. When he saw Rocco standing there, he got so spooked that he jammed his roll back in his pocket as if the money itself was illegal. It took a few seconds for the kid to figure out that Rocco wasn't Narcotics, and then he took his money out again, almost defiantly. But by that time Rocco was already leaving.

He found Jo-Jo Kronic in the Narcotics squad room of the Eastern District station house fifteen minutes later. Jo-Jo's crew must have just come in from a bounty run, because there were four mutts in the holding cell and four narcs typing at their desks under the bare overhead lights.

Jo-Jo and one of his boys stood just outside the cell. Arms across their chests, they watched a young muscular guy pull off his pants and boxer shorts for a body check. The guy grinned and held out his shorts for their consideration. Even from a distance, Rocco could see the bright brown stain.

'I got *scared*, man,' the prisoner said. 'I dint know *what* was happenin'.'

'Put them the fuck down, will you?' Jo-Jo shielded his face with his palm, but the guy held them up a little longer. The three other grabs behind bars paced like nervous cats, waiting their turn, as iridescent green moths flitted around a bare overhead bulb.

Jo-Jo shook his head and then noticed Rocco in the doorway. He fixed Rocco with eyes that appeared bleached and electric. His white beard was luminous under the harsh lighting.

Rocco introduced himself and shook Jo-Jo's hand, instinctively looking for telltale signs of secret wealth – a Rolex, some neck gold – but all he saw was a Santa's helper in a pair of dungarees and a Hawaiian shirt.

'I'm working a job now, it involves this bottle crew, and I can't get anybody to talk to me.' Rocco took a seat opposite Jo-Jo's desk. 'I tell them, Hey, I don't give a fuck about your business out here. I'm into the *dead*, not the living. But they think they're hot shit, you know?'

'So who do you need help with?' Jo-Jo swiveled in his chair, struggling to lift an ankle up and across his knee.

'You know that guy Rodney Little?'

'Rodney?' Jo-Jo stared off at the mint-green walls. 'Yeah, I know Rodney.'

'Well, there's this kid who works for him in the Roosevelt Houses named – '

Rocco was interrupted by one of the guys behind bars, a tall, thin kid with huge hands. 'You motherfuckers got some motherfucking *quota* thing here, because I dint serve nobody. I'm a *man*, motherfuckers, and you all faggots, sucker-punching blind-side faggots that got to keep a man behind bars because you can't *deal* with that.'

Jo-Jo glanced at Rocco. 'Excuse me,' he said, then walked over and unlocked the cell. He slipped inside and locked himself in. The kid growled a little and Jo-Jo backed him into a corner.

'Hey, Alfred, listen to me.' Jo-Jo touched the kid between the eyes with a fingertip, his face right under the kid's chin. 'Listen to me. You were leaning up against the dumpster like *this*, yes? Your arm was up like *this*, yes?' Jo-Jo raised an arm, forking the fingers of his other hand back and forth under his armpit like somebody working something sneaky.

'We saw you serve five people, three of which we popped right after, so for once in your fucking life be fucking smart and shut the fuck up, yes?' He crowded the kid, jamming him up, and then after a long moment let himself out of the cell, winking at Rocco as he tossed the keys on an empty desk.

'Give me re*spect*, man,' the kid muttered to Jo-Jo's back.

Jo-Jo wheeled around and spoke in a placid, firm tone. 'Hey, you want respect? Then act like you fucking deserve it. You want to be treated like a man? Then *be* a fucking man and stop your fucking crying. You're dirty and you're grabbed, so shut the fuck up.'

Jo-Jo returned to the desk. 'Sorry,' he said, then added in a low voice, 'We got this apartment overlooking Pavonia and JFK?' He mimed looking through binoculars. 'It's like a turkey shoot, a sniper's dream.'

Rocco decided that perhaps Jo-Jo was on the up-and-up after all – he was doing an awful lot of garbage-level grabs here. But maybe all this was just for appearances. Maybe Rocco was too naive, not ever having liked the odds of being dirty on this job.

'Anyways, Rodney Little, he's got this kid, Strike? In Roosevelt. You know this Strike kid?'

Jo-Jo squinted. 'Skinny little prick? Looks like he hasn't shit in a week?'

Rocco laughed. 'He's the kid I need to talk to. You think you guys could give him one of these for me?' Rocco took out a few business cards, laid them on Jo-Jo's desk. 'I just need him a little stressed out right now.'

Hands clasped over his belly, Jo-Jo regarded the cards on his desk and shrugged. 'What are you gonna do for me?'

The question was so blunt that for a moment Rocco didn't know how to respond. 'Hey,' he finally said, 'summer's almost here. It's getting all hotted up out there on the streets. You guys never know when you might need a friend on the shooting team, right?'

Jo-Jo thought about that, then bobbed his head. 'Fair enough.'

Rocco drove back to the office, his head buzzing, wondering if there was anything more he could do on the Darryl Adams job tonight. Strike: this kid was in the crosshairs.

Mazilli was interviewing the boyfriend of the murdered girl in the interrogation room, and Rocco stood for a moment outside the door, eavesdropping.

'C'mon, hey. Look at me. Do I sound pissed? You're no killer. It was a crime of passion, she just got to your head. It happens. Listen, this is how I see it. She rolls you into the van, drives you all the way out to the cemetery, rolls you out of the van, helps you onto the grass, gets you down there all damp in the dew and shit, you're helpless, you're horny, you got a hard-on to play fucking jump rope with, she gets down next to you, rubbing up all against you and shit, you go to do the deed, she says . . . What, what did she say? You tell me.'

Thrown by the details of that scenario, Rocco sneaked a peek through the window. 'Huh.'

The boyfriend was sitting in a wheelchair.

'Huh,' Rocco said again, then lost interest and began pacing the hallway, his mind already busy roughing out his next encounter with Strike. Arms outstretched, he slapped cadence on the glazed walls and muttered like a mantra, 'What next, what next, what next.'

23

Forehead to knees, his stomach on fire, Strike sat on the lower part of the bench, in too much pain to perch on top. He could feel Tyrone staring at him from his chain, but he couldn't even muster the strength to wave the boy off.

Are you Ronnie Dunham . . .

At first, between the smooth and dangerous talk of the Homicide and the squinty-faced silence of Erroll Barnes, he was scared, but then he felt anxious and down. The Homicide had made him think about things he didn't know how to handle – his brother in County, the kids with no father now – and there was no way to pull the Homicide's coat about his brother taking the rap for Buddha Hat without implicating himself. Hoping to take the weight off Victor, he had sputtered out some spontaneous badmouthing on Darryl, but even that was a mistake, because the minute you imply other knowledge, you're involved, and they never let you go until the truth comes out. And that held for talking to any of them: Rodney, Andre, the Homicide.

Are you Ronnie Dunham . . .

The slick Homicide had come on all concerned, as if he was queer for Victor – what have you heard from him, how's he holding up in there? How the fuck does he *think* he's holding up in there? Strike told himself he had to go see Victor. He'd get it up for a visit, go see if his brother needed anything. But not right now, not with this gut ache here.

Erroll finally came forward and stood over him, looking off through his eye slits. He still had the brown bag under his arm.

'What he want?' Erroll said, talking softly out of the side of his mouth.

'He was asking about the Ahab's thing, muh-my brother'n shit.'

Strike tried to take a deep breath in order to straighten up, but he didn't think he could. Erroll sat next to him on the bench, slightly tipped

forward like he was noddy, but his cheeks and forehead glistened with
sweat. Strike realized that Erroll, too, was bricked up with pain.

'Where's your car?' Erroll's words were like a rustling in his head.
'Bring it round.'

Strike did as he was told, walking off bent over as if carrying a huge
stone. A few minutes later Erroll leaned on the open passenger-side
window of the Accord, supporting himself on his forearms, his craggy
face inside the car. He dropped the package on the empty seat.

'This from Rodney.'

'OK.'

Erroll zoned out for a second, his eyes going dim, a tiny high moan
escaping his cracked lips. Strike chilled with horror, then noticed that
Tyrone was still watching from his perch on the chain.

'Rodney say whack it up, he'll bang you on it tonight.'

Strike kept bobbing his head for a good thirty seconds while Erroll
struggled with the intimacies of his pain and marshaled the strength to
push off from the window.

Strike looked down at the brown bag on the shotgun seat, thinking,
Now we're dealing weight; thinking, This is no way to live anymore,
but you are where you find yourself, so what can you do?

Are you Ronnie Dunham . . . He wished the answer was no.

As Strike drove, he weighed the package in his hands. Half a kilo, Jesus
Christ. Rodney was acting like there was no one in the world but him,
nothing to worry about but what's in the fridge.

Strike took the package to one of his houses, a sixth-floor walk-up
not far from his own apartment, in an old but well-kept building, the
hallways always clean and odor-free, the lobby freshly painted a glossy
beige. The mailboxes were bordered by notices of community board
meetings, petitions for more police patrols and exterminator sign-up
lists. Poor but proud – Strike admired the spirit, hated the climb.

Herman Brown was ninety years old and the cleanest dresser Strike
had ever known. He always wore crisp white shirts, and if his suit
was gray, his socks and tie were always maroon. He owned a dozen
beautiful old-time hats, the colors soft and rich – pearl gray, chocolate
brown, charcoal, camel. But it took him twenty minutes to rise from
his easy chair overlooking the street, and whenever Strike stopped by
his railroad flat, old Herman would insist on standing up to shake his
hand, which was no good if Strike was trying to make some time.
Strike told Herman he was a college student, and as far as the old man

knew, Strike actually lived in the small padlocked room at the end of the apartment.

Strike liked Herman. He had dignity, he had books, and he had framed portraits of famous black leaders every three feet in his hallway, like a private Afro-American hall of fame. The only thing that worried Strike about using Herman's place was that everybody thought the old man was secretly rich, because of his clothes and because three times a week he paid two kids from the neighborhood five bucks each to carry him down to the street for air. But he knew Herman didn't have any money except for what came in the mailbox. His clothes were thirty years out of style, and the five-dollar bills came from Strike, who sometimes overpaid his rent, depending on his mood.

When Strike entered the long narrow flat, Herman was asleep in his window chair, his head back, his lipless mouth gaping open as if food was about to drop from the ceiling. Strike tiptoed down the creaky corridor. Leaning against his locked door was a yellowed paperback book, *Cane*, the cover showing the silhouette of a young black man in front of a cotton field that rose mysteriously into an urban skyline. Herman had left other books on his doorstep, apparently his idea of helping out a young man in college. Strike slipped the book under his arm, next to the package, and quietly opened the lock on his door. He wouldn't have bothered with a lock except that he didn't trust Herman's lady friend, a fifty-year-old Oriental who cleaned up and made the old guy's meals. All Strike knew about Oriental people was that they worked hard and didn't laugh, but he figured they were greedy and sneaky just like everybody else.

Strike's room consisted of a narrow bed, a card table and a beat-up maple dresser. Under the bed was a safe, and the only things in the dresser were a soup spoon, a brown bottle of Italian baby laxative, a box of pint-size Ziploc bags and a triple-beam scale, all in the bottom drawer.

He put the book and the dope on the card table and rested for a second on the edge of the pillowless bed. A pulled-down manila window shade threw the silent and bald room into golden shadow. Strike absorbed the barrenness and thought that being in this room was like being in solitary. Thirty years in. For what?

As he took out the half ki, Strike remembered a day when he and Victor were kids, maybe six or seven years old. They were in the schoolyard, and a bunch of boys had circled Victor and were taking turns punching him in the back. Strike saw the crowd, saw his brother getting pummeled, and then suddenly he was joining in – not for any reason he could understand, just knowing he wanted to, and feeling love for Victor while he did it. Love wasn't a word Strike thought about a lot, but remembering the startled look on Victor's face when he'd seen Strike join in, he also recalled the indescribably sweet feeling he'd had for his brother right before hooking him in the ribs, and then the pleasurable remorse he had felt afterward, while walking home with him, both of them acting as if nothing unusual had happened.

Strike felt a headache coming on. He looked at the half ki in his hand; heat-sealed in plastic, it looked like a flat, see-through brick made of white crumble. Strike imagined razoring off a pebble or two, cooking it up, seeing what all the fuss was about. He closed his eyes and felt scared again, but not of the Homicide, not of Erroll or Rodney or Andre or Buddha Hat, or of his own torn guts. He was scared of this room, the silence of it. He felt sure that if he didn't get out quick it would crush him flat, and no one would hear him scream.

As Strike was locking up, Herman sensed company and began his struggle to rise, blinking at the ceiling, moving his arms and legs like an overturned beetle. Strike dashed over and shook the old man's hand before he could get a grip on the armrests for leverage. 'Yo Herman, thank you for the buh-*book*, man.' Avoiding the watery, confused eyes, Strike scanned the silver platter of prescription bottles and this day's wardrobe. 'That's a nice tie,' he added, then bolted for the door just as the old man was about to find his voice.

Strike was the only male in a loose and snaky line of a dozen women standing outside an aluminum-sided trailer in the parking lot of the Dempsy County Jail. The trailer looked like the contractor's shack on a construction site, but for anyone attempting a visit to the inside, it was Checkpoint Charlie. The jail stood fifty yards away, its seven stories of sooty brick seeming to lean forward, tilting toward Strike under the scudding clouds.

Some of the women around him held envelopes that Strike assumed contained ten or twenty dollars for deposit in a son's or boyfriend's prison account. Others held shopping bags filled with pajamas, sneakers, underwear, maybe cigarettes if the jail wasn't enforcing the regulation that you buy the packs from the inside concession. Strike hadn't brought anything, not even a comic book or some T-shirts. Just getting here was about all he could manage.

The line moved slowly toward the door of the trailer. Strike saw the woman next to him slip a deflated balloon into the side of her mouth like a wad of chewing tobacco – a dangerous play. He looked up at the jail, wondering if something bad, something uncontrollable, would happen once he got inside and saw Victor.

The interior of the trailer was surprisingly roomy. Two correction officers sat behind a collapsible table covered with long plastic cases filled with index cards. A half-dozen visitors, already cleared, sat on a bench bracketed into the rear end of the room; in another corner, a male and female CO stood by, ready for pat-downs and bag checks.

'Who you for?' A young black CO in a crisp uniform gave Strike a quick up-and-down.

'Viv–Victor Dunham.' Strike leaned forward on his fists as the officer finger-walked through his box and pulled out a long yellow card. Strike recognized Victor's handwriting.

'What's your name?'

'Victor Dunham.'

The CO looked at him patiently.

'Ronald Dunham.'

The CO scanned the card. On it was a list of allowable visitors, all approved by Victor. Trying desperately to read upside down, Strike saw their mother's name first, then his own, then ShaRon's, then two other names that he couldn't catch. Victor had put him ahead of his wife, which made Strike feel both moved and miserable. They hadn't been close in over a year, yet there it was in Victor's own handwriting – Strike's name, number two on the list. Did this mean his brother forgave him? Or maybe he just wanted Strike in there with him.

'You got some ID?'

Strike offered the CO his old high school photo ID and his New Jersey driver's license.

'Over there.' The officer flicked a finger toward the pat-down corner, then called Victor's name into a hand-held radio to someone on the inside.

Strike gave up his pockets to a plastic dish, then raised his arms. The pat-down was light compared to a Thumper Special, but the hands made him tense, made him feel there was no going back.

Looking out a small louvered window as he was being frisked, Strike saw a group of visitors being escorted out of the prison. Trailing just behind a knot of six women was Buddha Hat, and Strike unthinkingly moved to the window in the middle of his pat-down, the CO saying, 'Easy, easy,' grabbing Strike by the hip to keep him in place.

What were the two other names on that yellow card? Strike debated asking the CO at the desk if he could take a look, but he already knew how the CO would answer. He craned his neck to watch Buddha Hat walk to his Volvo, wondering if the Hat had visited Victor, but then reasoning that there were eight hundred prisoners inside, and somebody like Buddha Hat probably had at least a nodding acquaintance with a hundred of them.

When enough visitors had been cleared to make up a decent herd, a CO sent them single file out the rear of the trailer, into a fenced-in walkway topped with razor wire. The woman who had slipped the balloon in her mouth kept sliding it from cheek to cheek, a flash of bright blue showing between her lips now and then, and Strike imagined that he might get busted too, just for being near her. He looked up at the steel foliage overhead, feeling the wire in his belly, wanting to tell the CO leading them that this was a mistake, that he was sick, that he'd come back later.

The visitors were ushered through a side door. Walking the half-dozen steps to a waiting elevator, Strike picked up a sensory memory of school: glazed and stinky cafeterias, the misery of a frozen clock.

The elevator was huge and grindingly slow, the walls lined with the same greasy metallic sheeting that was used in Ahab's, and they had that same fried-food smell. A baby at the rear was yowling, the noise making Strike's temples bulge.

The doors opened onto a narrow vestibule. Beyond it was the visitors' room, a harshly lit rectangle dominated by a long banquet-length table. The table was bisected from floor to chest height by a slat of pegboard. Once seated, visitors had to stretch their spines to get a good look at whoever they were visiting. Two COs sat on high chairs at either end of the table, overseeing the conversations. A red hand-lettered sign in English and Spanish warned that any physical contact would result in ejection for the visitor and suspension of visitation privileges for the inmate, although Strike couldn't see how anybody could touch at that table, except for a quick and obvious high-five. He wondered what the hell the girl with the balloon in her mouth had in mind.

The visitors from his elevator group had to form a line again, and the CO at the door called out the name of the inmate to a CO across the room, who held off a corresponding line of prisoners. Standing there waiting his turn, Strike thought about what he would say to Victor. All his energy had gone into working up the nerve to get here, and now his mind was all feelings and no words.

'Who you for?' The CO held Strike by the elbow.

'Victor Dunham.'

'Dunham?' The officer frowned, cocked his head and then yelled across the room. 'Dunham. He's *in* already, right?'

The other CO pointed to the long table. 'He's got someone. What the fuck are they doing downstairs, playin' with themselves?'

Strike looked to where the CO had gestured and saw Victor's head above the pegboard. Sitting across from him was their mother – Strike recognized the labored rise of her shoulders. Neither of them were looking up. Victor's eyes were riveted and wild, cut off from the rest of his face by the divider. His mother, with her back to Strike, talked rapidly and passionately to her other son.

The guard took Strike's elbow again. 'They shouldn't've let you up. He's got someone. C'mere.' The guard steered Strike to a small bare room alongside the elevator, a waiting room with bone-colored walls and a scattering of orange plastic chairs. The air was dense with old cigarette smoke; a chrome torpedo-shaped sand urn sprouted a stubby crop of butts, some with lipstick stains, and the sight turned Strike's stomach.

'I'll bring you out when he's free.' The CO paused, amused at his unintentional pun. He raised an eyebrow and said, 'Who *is* this kid, the ex-mayor?' Then he closed the door behind him, leaving Strike alone.

The walls of the waiting room were hung with black-and-white cautionary posters, encircling Strike with admonitions, the subjects ranging from AIDS to pregnancy to crack to alcohol, each one a little masterpiece of dread. Strike hated posters. If you were poor, posters followed you everywhere – health clinics, probation offices, housing offices, day care centers, welfare offices – and they were always blasting away at you with warnings to do this, don't do that, be like this, don't be like that, smarten up, control this, stop that.

Strike wondered if the door to this room was locked. He thought about being here at the same time as his mother, and he panicked a little. Would they bump into each other by the doorway? What would they say to each other? Did she know what had happened, how he was behind all this misery? Strike was afraid that if she fixed him with those eyes of hers, he might just spin out completely, blurt a spontaneous confession, bring down the whole house of cards, everybody, all the players, coming after him in this jail where anything could happen.

Pacing, trying not to look at any of the posters, feeling as if he might throw up from the heavy pall of cigarette smoke, Strike suddenly had to get out of this room right away. But he didn't trust himself to go to

a CO and ask to leave, explain why he had to, because he was afraid that
the words would shatter in his mouth, that his guilt was so transparent
that he'd never make it to the elevator, never see daylight again.

The door opened and the woman with the yowling baby entered.
Then the CO leaned in. 'We told him you're out here. It shouldn't be
long.' He gave Strike a long look. 'You OK?'

'Yeah, uh-huh,' Strike said, turning away so his face couldn't be
read.

The baby was quiet now, lying belly up in its mother's lap. The woman
was Latino, her head shaved close along the temples in a military cut but
sprouting a spiky hennaed crop up top and a thin long tail of hair from
the otherwise bare nape of her neck.

Sitting in one of the orange chairs, the woman opened the baby's
diaper, slipped it out from under the baby and curled it into a ball.
She dropped it on top of the cigarette butts in the urn. Its adhesive
tabs covered with sand, the diaper began to open up, and Strike was
riveted by the sight of it, slowly unfurling like a dead man's fist. But
it wasn't the brush strokes of shit that revolted him – it was the plastic,
the gleaming white plastic squirming on sand.

Strike moved for the door, which wasn't locked after all. He tiptoed
back out into the vestibule and tried to get the guard's attention without
causing alarm.

'Yo, excuse me. I ga-got to go.'

'Go where?'

'Out. I can't visit right now,' he whispered, and furtively glanced
at the back of his mother's head. Victor's loopy eyes danced over the
pegboard, and Strike experienced a sudden and sensuous fantasy of both
Victor and his mother locked in here until they died.

'He'll be free in two minutes.'

'I'm *sick*.' Strike gripped his stomach, a hot swirl of filthy sand whipped
up in there.

The elevator opened to disgorge another group of women.

The CO reared back and gave him the up-and-down. 'You came all
the way up here, now you don't want to visit the guy?'

Strike eyed the empty elevator, turned back to the CO and pleaded
silently.

The CO grabbed the elbow of the first woman on line, then shot Strike
a disgruntled look. 'What are you sick with, a guilty conscience?'

As Strike drove through the Holland Tunnel, heading for the Bronx, for

Crystal, his mind was at a boil, jumping from acting out what he would have said to Victor if he had stayed, to replaying everything he had said to the Homicide this afternoon; from marveling over what a beautiful name Crystal was, to thinking about getting his GED, maybe moving to the Bronx; from worrying about whether the Homicide would check out everything he had said today, to deciding that he was too sick to be in the game anymore. Maybe he should just stop; maybe he should let Crystal just take care of him for a while, help him start over in his new life.

The minute he left the Accord in the garage two blocks from Crystal's house, Strike sensed that something was not right. Walking down the street, he felt off balance, out of touch with his surroundings. It wasn't until he passed a handful of police entering a seemingly abandoned building that he realized what was wrong: he had left his .25 in the car. In Dempsy it wouldn't matter, but he never walked these streets without the gun.

As he entered the exterior courtyard of Crystal's building, he remembered what had happened during his last visit here almost a week ago – the run-in with that cop Malfie, his fear that Malfie would see his piece. Well, this time he had nothing to hide. This time he wouldn't have to stare at the motherfucker's shoes or be a prisoner to his bullshit for even one damn second. When Strike entered the lobby he was primed, almost wishing that Malfie would be there hanging out in front of the elevator again, ready to block his path. But the cop was nowhere to be seen.

Strike rode the elevator to Crystal's floor, the car smelling like laundry soap, Strike watching the falling moons of glass, thinking about Crystal, surprised to feel a sexual thickness come on him, a backup of spunk. He hoped José would be away somewhere.

He took out his key but decided to ring the bell like a gentleman, remembering how Crystal had gotten spooked last week when he walked in with no warning. The bell had no body to it, just a tinny *ching* sound. He didn't know if anyone could hear it inside, so he hit the bell again, then rapped his knuckles on the metal door.

He stood in the hallway trying out smiles, wanting desperately for her to be bowled over by his charm and offer him a home away from home, an option for a new life. He knocked again and then heard a rustling of fabric, a soft and quick step, the turning lock. The door opened a crack, revealing a two-inch slice of Crystal's face and a startled eye.

'Oh,' she said in a small voice, then added, almost as an afterthought, 'You got to call.' She sounded the way she always did when displeased with him: like an adult gently correcting a small child.

'Well, that's why I rang the bell.' He cocked his head, trying to come on playful and charming. He saw that she was wearing her quilted pink bathrobe. 'You not glad to see me?'

'I'm cleaning the house.' The door stayed where it was.

'Oh yeah? It's a-about time.' He meant it as a joke, but her face went instantly dark.

'*What*?' She glared at him with that one burning eye.

'I'm goofin', you know me.' Strike's words sounded false even to his own ears. He exhaled long and slow, telling himself he was trying too hard.

Unappeased, she clutched the collar of her robe and stared at him. After hesitating a second, he reached through the open slit of the door to slide his hand inside the folds of her robe. But she wasn't having any of it. She backed away, inadvertently opening the door wider.

Strike stepped inside. There was no sign of José.

'You can't stay here now.' Her voice lightened with a touch of anxiety.

But Strike was already in the kitchen, crouched before the open refrigerator, looking for Yoo-Hoos.

He didn't see any, which gave him a bad feeling. Until now, she'd always had at least one stashed in the back for him.

When Strike straightened up and turned around he saw Malfie standing behind Crystal in the kitchen doorway. He was smiling as if his teeth hurt, staring at Strike with those flashlight eyes of his.

'How are you?' the cop said.

'He's fixing the bathroom,' Crystal said. Hugging herself, chin tucked into her chest, she looked up at Strike with a mixture of reproach and apology.

Malfie was dressed and wore a service revolver on his hip, but his feet were bare. His eyes followed Strike's down to his rippling toes.

'So how are you?' he said again. He moved a step into the kitchen, dropped one hand to a nearby cutting board.

Strike turned to Crystal. 'Woo-where's your son?'

'He's at his grandma's house.' Her voice was tight, a little hoarse.

'His grandma's house.' He repeated her words meaninglessly, talking from inside a dream, trapped in this cramped room in a crossfire of eyes. More than anything else he felt embarrassed by the attention, but when he stole a glance at the cop, he saw right through the guy's slick bully-boy routine – the wolfish grin on his face had a frozen quality to it, and the defiantly casual slouch against the kitchen counter masked a tense rigidity. Strike studied his own hands, thinking, This cool-hand moonlighting motherfucker is scared, scared and armed, a bad combination.

'His grandma's house,' Strike said again, not knowing where to rest his eyes, remembering Crystal smelling like lamb chops the last time he was here, how he didn't like that smell, didn't really like *her* anymore.

They stared at him, waiting, and Strike settled on making a disgusted hissing sound, wearily shaking his head, acting as if he was punishing them by giving them his back. Slowly, proudly, he limped his way to the front door.

Standing in the hallway waiting for the elevator, not trusting his legs to make it down six flights of stairs, Strike muttered, 'You best watch you don't cut up your *feet* like that.'

Crystal's worried voice drifted through the apartment door: 'He's got his own key.' A moment later, Malfie opened the door and faced Strike with an empty holster and one hand out of sight behind his leg. Before the cop could open his mouth, Crystal's key bounced off his chest. Malfie regarded the piece of dull brass lying between his feet and gave Strike a whole new look.

He stooped to retrieve the key, then slipped his piece back in his holster. 'They get like that, you know? Don't worry, it happens to *me* plenty.'

Driving through the Bronx on his way back to Dempsy, Strike finally got angry at Crystal, at how she disrespected him, made him a fool in front of that white cop. His beeper went off – Rodney – and he pulled up hard next to a pay phone on a barren street. He put his gun into his waistband, more or less for protection but feeling as if he just might shoot Rodney through the mouthpiece with it too. Somehow everything, even this falling out with Crystal, seemed to be Rodney's fault, although he couldn't explain why.

Rodney scared him, though. He told Strike he was about to send Erroll out to find him, thinking maybe Strike had skipped with the dope, saying, 'You best get your ass back and bag those motherfucking ounces *now*.'

There was nothing left for Strike in the Bronx, or anywhere else on the New York side of the tunnel, but the drive back into New Jersey hurt even more. He had no desire to go back up to his cutting room again, get all buggy with his thoughts. At a red light two blocks from the benches he saw Tyrone walking with his mother. They were holding hands, but when Tyrone saw the Accord he quickly disengaged himself from Iris's grip. He was too embarrassed to meet Strike's eyes, so he studied the sidewalk as if tracking game.

Strike found himself grinning, something he never did, and he drove at a crawl behind mother and son. Iris seemed unaware of his presence. He followed them to the benches and watched Tyrone take his perch on the chain. The boy's mother disappeared into their building. Strike waited another minute or two, then got out of his car, yawning and stretching. He caught Tyrone's eye and gave him a furtive, beckoning wave: Get himself some company.

'What's wrong with your hand?' Strike frowned down at the Velcro-backed blue and orange glove on Tyrone's left hand. He was driving lazily toward Herman's apartment, not really wanting to go there at all, even with company.

'Nothin',' Tyrone said, looking scared but pumped. He had gotten in the car without a word, his usual breathless and deadpan style, as if he had been waiting for this pickup for days.

'Well, what you got that *glove* on it for?'

'It's a batting glove.'

'Batting glove. You mean like a baseball glove? That's some skinny-looking baseball glove.' Strike never liked baseball, wasn't even exactly sure what all the rules were.

Tyrone turned away, his eyes flat with swallowed laughter.

'What's so funny?'

'It's a *bat*ting glove.' Tyrone mimed choking up on a bat.

'Oh yeah? You like baseball?'

Tyrone nodded mutely.

'You got quick wrists? 'Cause if you don't got quick wrists, you might as well forget about it.'

The kid blinked uncomprehendingly.

'Let me see how quick you got your wrists. Put you to the *test*.'

Thinking, Fuck the package, Fuck Rodney too, Strike drove to the batting cages across the road from the Furniture Shack. He and Tyrone wandered past the miniature golf and the driving range, then waited for the batting cage attendant, who was harvesting rubber baseballs from the littered field beyond the cages.

As the attendant wandered back in from the field, a full basket in each hand, he stared at Strike for a long moment. It made Strike nervous, but then he put it together: the guy was a customer from the benches.

'How you doin', fellas?' the attendant said, talking slow, his eyes filled with that familiar foxy yearning.

Strike pretended he didn't recognize him. 'How do we do this?'

'It's sixteen pitches for a token. Token's a buck.'

Strike looked to Tyrone. 'How many you want?'

The kid shrugged, looking away.

'Yeah, give us six.'

The attendant's eyes never left Strike's face as he blindly felt around in a coin apron and passed over ten tokens.

'Is that your little brother?' The question was insincere, fawning, but the words made Strike feel strange

'Yeah,' he said, then looked down in his hand. 'I just want but six.'

'That's OK, it's on me,' the attendant said. 'You don't know me?' His voice was dreamy, creepy, and Strike didn't answer, even to say thanks.

The cages ranged from slow-lob softball to Gooden Fast. Tyrone chose El Sid Medium, and Strike watched from a bench as the kid coiled over the plate, the balls coming in with a buzzing sound, Tyrone smacking each one squarely with a smooth swing. Strike was awed to stillness by the secret grace in him, the balance and the power, knowing in his heart right then that he should leave this kid alone, let him have his life, because he could be anything he wanted to be if Strike and everybody else just backed off and gave him some room.

Strike sat on the bench and went off into his thoughts, not watching anymore, only vaguely aware of the buzz-and-whack rhythm from the batting cage, musing on the fine line between Promise and Too Late. He felt sorry for himself, because at nineteen and a half years old, he was way over into Too Late. But when he finally looked up, Tyrone was standing over him, holding out a batting helmet and an aluminum bat, smiling as if he could read his thoughts and was here with a reprieve. 'Now you.'

Strike dug in. He could see the prosecutor's office about three hundred yards past the big deserted field, and as he waited for the first pitch he imagined the balls as hand grenades. He would belt the first one clear through a window down there, blow the fat Homicide to chunks, the second one right on top of Rodney's car, the third one all the way across the river to the Bronx. But when the first pitch came, it sizzled right past his hands, scaring him a little, making him wobble with surprise.

'This ain't no medium,' he said out loud to himself, too embarrassed to face Tyrone.

He missed the first eight pitches altogether, nicked the ninth by accident and let the last seven go by without swinging, too humiliated to whiff anymore. He stared out at the sun going down behind the prosecutor's office and felt himself drifting deeper and deeper into the land of Too Late.

By the time he tossed the bat into the dirt, disgusted, he had just about decided to drive Tyrone home, let him get on with his life. But on the way to the car, the attendant caught up with them, walking slightly behind with a limpy little trot, murmured, 'You got any bottles?' and Strike changed his mind right there, thinking, Fuck it, nobody goes home tonight.

Sliding behind the wheel, Strike let loose with an angry, squawking laugh. 'No wonder I couldn't hit the goddamn ball! Lookit!' He turned to Tyrone and pulled up his shirt to display the gun stuffed into his waistband. 'The motherfucker was cutting right into my damn guts. How you like that?'

Back in Herman's apartment, Tyrone sat on the edge of the bed in Strike's room, watching Strike measure out two ounces of laxative, then ladle it with the soup spoon onto the wax-paper-covered circular platform of the triple-beam scale.

'The profit's in the brown bottle,' Strike said, talking low and steady with concentration. 'Always remember that.'

Strike lifted the wax paper and carefully dumped the cut into a mixing bowl with eight ounces of coke.

'I ever see you do this?' Strike glanced over at Tyrone, then started chopping at the bigger rocks with a single-edge razor and stirring the mixture with the spoon. 'I ever see you put this shit in your nose or in a pipe or in your arm? Shit, I'll come and kill you my *damn* self.'

Strike kept chopping, stirring, pouring powder over powder. 'You probably asking yourself, how come I sell it, then?'

Strike really had no idea what this kid was asking himself. Tyrone sat silently, so Strike answered his own question. ''Cause if *I* don't, somebody else *will*. Me not selling it ain't gonna stop nothing out there but my money flow.'

Strike transferred the stepped-on coke back to the scale, a spoonful at a time, weighing out ounces. 'See, my boss buys him a ki for twenty-two, and that bottles up into thirty-five hundred ten-dollar bottles. That's seventeen thousand profit on a ki takes us like a week to sell.'

Strike emptied an ounce off the wax paper into a Ziploc bag, noting to himself that here it was, his first ounce in his new weight business. 'Now my boss, he takes sixty percent of that ki profit, but that leaves us seven thousand dollars, and I take like fifty percent of that, divide up the rest with my boys. So how much does my cut come to? Let me see how smart you are.'

Bagging up ounce number two, Strike cocked his head and frowned. Something ticked at the edge of his awareness, something *off* right now, and then it came to him: he was speaking without stammering. He didn't stammer when he was around this kid.

'How much is fifty percent of seven thousand?'

'Three thousand five hundred,' Tyrone said quietly.

'Yeah, that's right. I make me three thousand five hundred dollars a week out there.' He hesitated for a moment, wondering why, if that was the case, he never took home more than two thousand. 'I got me a nice apartment, stereo, *women.*' An image of Crystal came into his head and he shook it off. 'Yeah, and I got me another house on a mountaintop? Nobody even knows about it. It's like hidden in the rocks. You got to press this button, the rocks slide up, there's the house. And *that* house, that house it's like a *palace.* It got a indoor swimming pool, everything.'

Feeling foolish, he sneaked a peek at Tyrone, but the kid wasn't even there. Hungry to get him back, Strike shifted gears. 'You see that ugly man I was talking to before? The guy that came up to me on the benches?'

'The white man?'

'What white man?' Strike said. 'No, the *black* man give me this package. You see that man?'

Tyrone nodded, getting a spooked look, and Strike decided that the kid was either scared by Erroll or off somewhere again, maybe wondering how he would explain to his mother where he'd been this evening. Strike momentarily worried about that himself, imagined the news of this little adventure filtering all the way back to Andre, and his anxiety made him paint Erroll with ghoulish strokes.

'That man's a *killer.* That man'd kill you soon as look at you. That man got more bodies on him than a army. But he's still walking free. You know why? They can't find the damn bodies. They just find like a *blood* stain.' Strike nodded in agreement with himself.

'You know why I carry this?' Strike held up the gun. 'Because if that man ever come up my wrong side? It's gonna be me or him, and it's gonna be over like *that.*' Strike snapped his fingers, listened to himself as if he was on television. 'That man ever come up to you, you better shoot first, ask questions later, because he *never* got any good news on him. Shoot first, ask questions later, even if he just wants to know what time it is, just say it's *dyin'* time, Erroll, and shoot him right in his ugly face.'

Tyrone sat as still as a monk, watching the line of ounces grow.

Strike held up a finger. 'And don't think he wouldn't shoot you just 'cause you little. Shit, I think he killed himself a eleven-year-old boy just last year.'

Strike wasn't exactly sure how all this would make the kid feel tight with him. He looked at Tyrone, saw a boy who was all eyes and coiled secrets. Why wouldn't he just *say* something?

'You ever shoot a twenty-five before?'

Tyrone shook his head, and Strike placed the gun in his hand.

'It don't feel like nothing, right?'

Tyrone stared down at his palm, his fingers splayed as if he was too shy to close his fist, to hold the thing like a weapon. The kid looked unnerved, but Strike saw something else coming off him too: there was a secret giddiness in the widening of his eyes, in the way he held his lips between his teeth.

Eight bags were full now, about two ounces left in the bowl. Strike was tempted to give the soup spoon to Tyrone and let him measure out an ounce, but something about that made him queasy, so he bagged up the rest himself and put them in the bureau.

'See, now this here, this ain't bottles. With this here, I'm getting into a higher bracket thing right here. Make me a millionaire. What you think of that?'

Tyrone didn't answer.

'What's up with you?'

Tyrone made a noise that approximated 'nothing.' He was still looking at the gun, gazing at it as if it were a tiny but vicious animal sleeping in his upturned hand.

Strike took the gun out of Tyrone's palm and placed it in a nest of unused plastic bags in the bottom drawer of the bureau. Wanting to break the kid's trance, he had Tyrone help him gather up all the mixing paraphernalia and transport it to the kitchen. At the sink, he stood behind Tyrone and watched him rinse off the mixing bowl and the soup spoon. He could tell by the way the kid held the bowl under the faucet that he was trying not to come into contact with the chalky veil of cocaine residue.

'You want a Yoo-Hoo?' Strike pointed to the refrigerator with his chin.

Herman materialized at the doorway, uttering half-words to himself and badly scaring Tyrone, who dropped the bowl into the sink with a hollow *bonk*. Herman's neck was as corded and thin as a broccoli stalk, the collar of his starched white shirt two sizes too big.

'Hey *Her*man,' Strike said in a shout. He shook the old man's hand.

Herman nodded, then turned stiffly to Tyrone with a sweet feeble smile. His chin was patched with white stubble.

'That's my brother,' Strike blared, winking at Tyrone.

'College boy?' Herman tried to pat his head, but Tyrone jerked backwards and bumped into the counter. For the first time since he got into the car, Tyrone sought out Strike's eyes, and Strike was startled to see that the kid was on the verge of tears.

It was almost eleven o'clock, an hour past Fury time. Strike sat on his perch overlooking the bottle traffic. It was moving briskly but there was nothing much to do, just wait on Rodney to beep him and tell him what next with the ounces. Rodney had screamed at him on the phone to get his ass bagging, and now here it was four hours later and nothing was happening. Hurry up and wait. Always hurry up and wait.

When he got back to the projects, Tyrone had flown out of the car and into his building, and Strike cursed himself for telling the kid all those lies about secret houses and Erroll Barnes killing eleven-year-old boys. But he felt worst about making Tyrone wash out the mixing bowl, as if it was some kind of initiation rite. Well, shit, at least he didn't make him bag ounces.

Out on the sidewalk, one of the lookouts tentatively raised up. Strike saw a five-year-old Delta 88, a rusty warhorse filled with bulky silhouettes at every window. It wasn't a Fury car but it smelled like knocko anyhow, and Strike braced for trouble. Both of the front doors flew open and two Hawaiian shirts stepped out. The raiser barked 'Five-oh' and split.

The two knockos moved to the bench at a fast clip, ignoring the bolting clockers, making a beeline for the bench, for Strike.

It was too late for Strike to move, but running wasn't his style anyhow. His beeper went off, and then he saw that one of the knockos looming out of the darkness was Jo-Jo.

Strike didn't get a chance to open his mouth. Jo-Jo and the other guy grabbed his arms and lifted him off the bench, walked him over to 8 Weehawken and slammed him into the outside wall. With his cheek mashed up against the brick and Jo-Jo's hand jammed into his back, Strike listened to the other knocko tell people to move the fuck on. Strike willed himself to go slack and passive; he was clean.

'I'm gonna take my hand off your back now, but if you move your face from that wall, I'm gonna cave in your ribs, OK?' Jo-Jo spoke in a low, reasonable voice but there was a quiver of adrenaline in it.

'Yeah, OK,' Strike whispered, closing his eyes.

Strike's beeper went off again. Jo-Jo grabbed it and read the phone number coming up. 'Hey, my friend Rodney,' he said, then put the beeper back in Strike's pocket and started a frisk, working from the calves up.

'So what's up, Strike? What's happenin'?'

Jo-Jo's pat-down felt a little strange to Strike, the touch too quick and light. 'Nothing, Officer.'

'Jo-Jo. Call me Jo-Jo.'

'Nothing Jo-Jo, just sitting.'

'Look, Strike,' Jo-Jo said, his whiskers in Strike's ear. 'The reason I come by, I just wanted to tell you that tomorrow night's knock night. We're coming down on Roosevelt like a fucking broom, OK?' His fingers played Strike's clothes like piano keys. 'So if you can remember that, and I was you, I'd take all my boys out for Blimpies about nine, nine-thirty, come back around eleven, OK?'

'OK.' Strike inhaled brick dust, his cheek starting to sting. 'Tha-*thank* you.'

'From now on, I'll tell you when shit's coming down, OK? Week in, week out.'

'Yeah, OK.'

'I'm your friend.'

'Yeah, I hear that.'

'Are you *my* friend?'

Strike hesitated. 'Uh-huh.'

'What are you gonna do for me?'

Jo-Jo's beard was tickling Strike's ear, and Strike sighed out loud, thinking fast, an involuntary ripple running through his upper body. 'Fuh-five hundred?'

Jo-Jo paused in his phony frisk. 'That's beautiful, Strike, that's perfect.' He rubbed Strike's neck, giving him a massage now. 'I'll send someone around in an hour, corner of Krumm and Loyola, in front of the candy store, OK?'

'Yeah, OK.'

'That's great, that's great.' Jo-Jo made a clicking sound of approval, patting him on the back in such a way that Strike knew it was all right to come off the wall.

Jo-Jo and his partner started walking back to the Olds, Jo-Jo getting as far as the benches before turning back to Strike. 'You OK?'

'Yeah, I'm OK.' Strike looked off, breathing through his mouth.

'Good.' Jo-Jo nodded once. 'Me too.'

When Strike's beeper went off fifteen minutes later, he was alone, pacing in front of the benches like a crazy man. None of the clockers were back at work yet – a knocko visit was worth at least an hour's step-back. He reached into his pocket for the beeper and found a business card. Turning it to the light, he read the name: Rocco Klein. Strike stood still, confused, not knowing if this was the card the Homicide gave him yesterday or one just laid on him by Jo-Jo. After a moment he resumed patrol, tallying in his head all the cash he had hidden in various safe houses around the Heights. Six thousand plus seven thousand plus nine thousand equals twenty-two thousand. Scoop scoop scoop and out.

24

When Rocco awoke Thursday morning, Patty had already left to take Erin to her Gymboree session and the apartment was empty. He lay on his back in the silence with a pillow over his head and began automatically running some faces and places behind his eyelids: Strike, by the benches, aggrieved and jittery; the Dunham apartment, spotless, the air charged with stifled emotion; Victor, sitting across from Rocco in the interrogation room like a stony shell, the heart of him, the truth of him, vanishing like sucked smoke right before Rocco's eyes. Victor: Rocco wished he could get another crack at the kid, especially given what he had learned since the lockup. But there was no chance of that now; a lawyer would have to be out of his mind to allow the arresting officer to have any contact with his client.

Rocco tried to drift back to sleep but couldn't. The mother had told him that Victor had drawn Jimmy Newton as a public defender. Rocco and Jimmy had known each other for twenty-five years: Rocco thought that ought to count for something, and he allowed himself to imagine that Jimmy might let him reinterview his client. But that would mean exposing Victor to the possibility of self-incrimination, *further* self-incrimination, which could set Jimmy up for an incompetency hearing. No way in hell Jimmy would do it.

But the idea stayed with him, and Rocco began working out his pitch in his head. It's not like I'd be going in there to *fuck* the kid, he thought. Hey, I'd be trying to cut the kid loose.

Rocco pressed the pillow into his eyes, tried to untrack his thoughts, but after a long moment of enforced stillness he rolled out of bed and jumped into the shower.

Rocco hounded the courtrooms and cafeterias of the Municipal Building for close to an hour. He finally found Jimmy Newton emerging from a conference with a client in the men's room, coming out of a toilet stall followed by a middle-aged fat man dressed in a blood-spattered raincoat and a cracked pair of bedroom slippers.

The fat man headed for the hallway as Jimmy bent over the sink and washed his hands. 'And lose the raincoat, Octavio,' he said, looking over the top of his bifocals.

The guy raised his arms and snapped his head to get the hair out of his face. 'This all I got.'

'Don't worry, I'll take care of it.' Jimmy threw the guy a reassuring squint, then saw Rocco. 'Heyyy, how you doing?'

'I thought you were over that,' Rocco said, nodding to the open stall. 'I thought you went back to women.'

Jimmy laughed gamely. 'What's up, there, Rocco? Long time no see.'

Rocco leaned against a sink as if this was his usual hangout. 'Can I buy you lunch?' He yawned his way through a sudden gust of anxiety.

'We can go Dutch.'

The mild note of caution in Jimmy's voice turned Rocco's yawn into a small groan.

As they walked out of the Municipal Building to the row of bars and restaurants across the street, they made meaningless small talk. Rocco saw that Jimmy was on his guard, which wasn't surprising given the adversarial nature of their respective jobs. But Rocco was pretty sure he could break through that instinctive wariness, because Jimmy was basically a good man. In fact, Rocco considered Jimmy Newton just about the most decent person he knew.

Most Dempsy public defenders worked for the county for three to five years, got their combat ribbons and moved on to private practice so they could start raking it in. But Jimmy was pushing forty-five and still grabbing manila folders out of the arraignment basket every morning, interviewing an anonymous and endless stream of indigent mutts through the grills of the processing pen, haggling over bail reductions, jail time, accepting collect calls from the coinless phones up on the tiers – all this for forty-five thousand dollars a year, with no outside legal work allowed. But where was the satisfaction? Even the skells in the cells treated Jimmy like shit, not even regarding him as a real lawyer because he was free.

Rocco was convinced that the reason Jimmy had never moved on from the public defender's office was that he genuinely felt bad for his clients. Jimmy wasn't politicized, wasn't by any means an activist or even a Democrat. He was just a sweet guy who happened to believe that most of his clients were hapless hard-luck bozos who had the misfortune to be born when and where they were, who at this point in their lives needed a friend on the Inside, needed Jimmy Newton.

Nothing symbolized Jimmy's approach to his job more than the half-dozen sport jackets he always carried in the trunk of his car – polyester thrift-shop horrors in bizarre color combinations like blue and cream, raspberry and tan. The jackets were for his clients. Jimmy believed it was in their best interest to go before the judge dressed respectfully, and there wasn't a judge, court officer, district attorney or geriatric courtroom buff in all of Dempsy County who couldn't pick one of Jimmy Newton's clients out of a sea of bench-warming felons on the day of sentencing. In legal circles, the jackets were known as Newt Suits.

Rocco put his palm to the small of Jimmy's back and steered him into the Old Town, the most expensive restaurant on the strip. The hostess ushered them to a booth in the nearly deserted room, and a few minutes later Rocco watched Jimmy toss back an 11:55 A.M. Gibson like he was trying to wash down a Ring Ding.

'You want another one of those?' Rocco asked.

'Nah.' Jimmy smacked his lips and made a growling sound. 'I got to keep my wits about me. What's up?'

'OK, OK.' Feeling nervous again, Rocco scanned the sea of unoccupied tables. 'I want to throw something at you. Just sit and listen to me, and if it bothers you ethically, just forget I said anything.'

Jimmy stared at him through lowered eyes, waiting.

'Your client, Victor Dunham. He's in the can for homicide, right?'

Jimmy went very still.

'Look, I took that confession and I *know* it's horseshit. You know it's horseshit too, right? So what am I saying, that I think this kid's dirtier than he says? No. Me to you, off the record? We're not even here? Yes?'

After a long moment Jimmy reluctantly grunted, 'Off the record,' one half-open fist curling inside the other on the tablecloth.

'Jimmy, what I'm saying is, the kid didn't do it. Well why not, and who did, you ask. OK, well, the word on the street is that the vic, this Darryl Adams, was selling dope in there, in that Ahab's. Word on the street – but the fact is, we *did* find a lot of cash on his body, none of it from the store receipts as far as we know, so I mean it could have been a holdup, a fucked-up holdup, the shooter could have panicked and run off without the money. But I doubt it. I think it was an execution.'

Jimmy puffed his cheeks and rubbed the back of his head.

'You hangin' in?' Rocco tapped Jimmy's wrist, worried that he was losing him when he wasn't even halfway through his warm-up.

'G'head, g'head,' Jimmy said brusquely, looking off to the bar.

'OK, just stay with me. Now, this kid Darryl used to work for Rodney Little, the dope guy, in his grocery. Victor has a brother, a kid called Strike, who used to work with Darryl in that same grocery. This kid Strike is now out there on the streets clocking for Rodney, like his lieutenant or something, OK? So, what do we have here so far? This kid Strike's selling dope, this kid Darryl's selling dope, they both used to work for Rodney. Now, here's the thing. Are you ready for the thing?' Rocco tried to catch Jimmy's eye, make him smile.

'Just talk, Rocco.'

'OK. This Strike, Victor's brother? Well, the bartender of that Rudy's, the bar that Victor came out of, he also ID'd Strike in there the night of the shooting, said he never saw the kid in there before. So then I go to interview this Strike kid and he fucking lies about everything. He says he hasn't seen Victor in two months. He says he didn't know the vic, this Darryl Adams, when *I* know they worked together in Rodney Little's hole-in-the-wall grocery store for a whole fucking year. Then, on top of that, he tells me some bullshit story about Darryl having an attitude problem as being the reason his brother shot him – like this kid Victor is into killing people because they wear their smile buttons upside down, you know?'

Rocco leaned back for a breather. Jimmy's eyes were focused on the tablecloth.

'But to be in that bar for the first time on *that* night? Not ever having been there before? Plus, he left *before* the shooting, stone sober, so give me a break. Plus, plus, the kid's got some violence on his jacket, an Aggravated Assault. I mean, I don't know yet what this kid Darryl did to piss somebody off – that somebody probably being Rodney Little, is my guess – but who knows, maybe he was skimming profits or stealing the product or hey, maybe it wasn't Rodney. Maybe it was Champ, that guy Champ. Maybe it was territorial, because I understand Champ controls the dope around here and maybe this kid was freelancing on his turf. I don't know, maybe *Champ* got this kid Strike to go in and jap his old buddy from Rodney's store. But all I can say for now is that, Jimmy, given all this shit I'm telling you, circumstantial as it may sound, I wind up arresting a clean-cut kid who tries to sell me this cock-and-bull self-defense scenario. I mean, what's going on?'

Jimmy threw Rocco a furtive glance, then looked away, as if desperate to be gone.

'Yo Jimmy!' Rocco mock-shouted through cupped hands.

Jimmy laughed, baring his teeth. 'I'm not hearing this, Rocco,' he said almost shyly. 'You're setting me up for something here.'

Rocco ignored the comment. 'But so, OK, so how did it come to pass that this wrong kid, this Victor, came in on it, gave it up? Well, I don't know. Maybe he's protecting his brother. He's got no jacket more or less, he's a church kid, hard-working. Maybe he thinks he's got a better chance of beating the rap or serving less time. I mean, when I interviewed the kid he came off like one of these heavy scrimper and saver types. He sounded to me like he hated a nickel because it wasn't a dime, so I don't know, maybe his brother promised him a shitload of money to take care of his family, build a nest egg for when he gets out. Or maybe this *bad* brother's got something on him, maybe he threatened him, you know, threatened his family, *made* him do it . . . I don't know, but I *do* know that what we got here is the wrong brother walking in with the right gun. I mean, given all I'm telling you, what would *you* believe?'

'What would *I* believe?' Jimmy waved for another Gibson, cracked a bread stick. 'I believe that in my profession it's very dangerous to believe or not believe – that's what I believe.'

'OK, well put, but look, here I am, you know?' Rocco turned to the waitress. 'Can I have a white wine spritzer? No, make it a white wine with ice.'

Jimmy brushed away his bread crumbs with an extended pinkie. 'You know, Rocco, you're not supposed to even *talk* to me about this. I can use everything you just said to me in court to fuck up your case, right?'

'Hey, don't you think I know that?' Rocco raised his chin as if to offer his throat for slitting. 'Look, here it is, OK? Let me ask you. You know me like twenty-five years, right? Have I *ever* come to you like this? The reason I'm here is because I know what I'm saying is the truth. Twenty years of dealing with these jamokes says to me it's the *truth*. Do you think I would be sitting here like an asshole if it wasn't? What the fuck do I care if this goes in as a solve or a beat – I got more good confessions in this county than any fucking investigator alive. I don't need this win, who gives a fuck. It's just that it *bothers* me what's happening here. I mean, when do I ever encounter a truly innocent man? It's like a pebble in my shoe.'

Not sure who he was trying to convince now, Rocco had to force himself to keep up direct eye contact with Jimmy. The truth of it was, he had been so worried about Jimmy not hearing him out that he hadn't really thought about his own jeopardy.

The waitress came by and they both ordered blindly, some pasta special. Rocco's wine tasted like flat, sour soda, not a real drink at all.

Jimmy looked at Rocco over the top of his bifocals. 'You know, I already talked to your boss. He's offering me a good deal – Aggravated Manslaughter, twenty years with a third in. That's pretty good.'

'Of course he's offering you a good deal, I gave him a bullshit confession. What do you expect?' Rocco's spirits sagged as he realized that the prosecutor would never allow him to talk to Victor and afford a confessed murderer the chance to recant his own testimony. He would have to do it on the sneak, keep everything under wraps until he could walk into his boss's office with enough on Strike to justify this dangerous breach of procedure. Shit: a good way to lose his job, too. 'Of *course* he's offering a good deal,' he repeated hollowly.

Jimmy hesitated. 'Yeah, well, there's only one problem. I go to this kid, I say, "What happened?" and I think, *he* thinks, like many of them do, that I'm an extension of *you* cocksuckers, a white man in a tie, you know? I say, "Talk to me, I'm on your side." He says, "Self-defense." I say, "Hey, I can have you out in six and a half years, just tell me something else, anything but that." He says, "It was self-defense, that's all I wanna say to you." I say, "Hey, you say that, we'll have to go to trial, because the PA ain't gonna negotiate that, and we go to trial with a self-defense defense, we're probably gonna lose." Then I explain to him all the shit about unarmed vic, distant shot, no retreat, et cetera, tell him that if we go in like that, we got a seriously handicapped roll of the dice there, and I tell him, "If I was you I'd plea out, I'd take the Aggravated Manslaughter. Get out of jail, my kids are still in elementary school." And then he says, "It was self-defense."'

Jimmy flapped his hands in exasperation. 'So once again, I'm trying to explain to him that on this one, self-defense is an insult to the good will and the intelligence of the prosecuting attorney, and how they get very pissed off if you make them go to the expense and time of a trial, and how if you *lose*, you're gonna get it put up your brown but good. I say, "You're flirting with thirty fucking years, here, Victor. I don't have enough fingers and toes to illustrate that number." So what does he say to all this? "Self-defense." I tell him, "Victor, Victor, listen to me. You can bullshit me, that's why I'm here, to be abused, but you can't bullshit your*self*. I am your lawyer . . . *Help* me."'

'Help me help you,' Rocco said, surprised by Jimmy's sudden candor.

'Exactly.' Jimmy reared back from a steaming bowl of ziti, wincing at the sudden humidity. '"Help me help you." I like that. Anyway, like I say, I don't believe or *not* believe, but if I did, I'd believe this kid is holding back something. But they all do.'

'I hear that,' Rocco said automatically.

Jimmy drained his Gibson and leaned forward on his forearms. 'So what do you want, Rocco?'

Rocco slid his ziti to the side and took a deep breath. 'OK, here we go. I want one crack at your client. You be there, sit in my lap, sit in *his* lap, anything, any way you want, any conditions, just so long as I get a shot at the truth. And if he tells me what I *think* he's gonna tell me, and it's the truth, I can go back to my boss and I'm pretty sure he'll drop the charges. Then I go after this other brother, nail his dong to the wall.'

'What makes you think you can do what *I* couldn't do?' Jimmy said, his expression predictably unhappy.

'Hey,' Rocco said, smiling, 'I make all these bozos think I love them. That's how I fuck them.'

He thought Jimmy would laugh at that, but the worried look stayed.

'Does your boss know you're doing this with me here?'

'Nah,' Rocco said, feeling charged now, 'this is between me and you. He'd go fucking nuts if he knew what I'm doing. I'll go to him when I got it wrapped. This is just me for now.'

Jimmy sighed and twisted sideways in his chair. 'Rocco, think this through. Right now we're off the record. But the minute I agree to this it becomes official. What if he doesn't tell you shit? What if he sticks to his story and we go to trial? You're doing this on the sly, but I get you up on the stand and you *know* I'm gonna ask you, "Was there ever a time when you ceased to believe that Victor Dunham did this and thought someone else did?" And how are you gonna answer that? Are you gonna *lie*? Or are you gonna jeopardize the state's case?'

Rocco felt a rush of cool air in his belly. He hadn't thought through this angle of things either, but the bravado of his own proposal carried him forward. 'Hey, I'll deal with it, you know me. Worse comes to worse, they'll pack my ass up, make me walk a beat in O'Brien. Fuck it. I'll be a detective again in six months. Nobody ever gets hurt in this town for fucking up a case. I'll buy a few hundred-dollar-a-plate dinner tickets and get my ass back in a sport jacket just like that.'

Jimmy gazed at him woefully. 'OK Rocco, look. Let me think about this, OK? I mean, I think you're a prick, you think I'm a sucker, but other than that we go back a long time and, ah, we're kind of like the *glue* . . .' Jimmy pressed his splayed hands together. 'We're the *spine* of things, you know what I mean? We're . . . if things are gonna work around here, you know, society, it's important that you do what you do and I do what I do, you know?'

'Jimmy.' Rocco put a hand on his arm. 'You're boring the shit out of me.'

Jimmy laughed, a blush coming into his cheeks. 'OK. Alls I'm trying to say is, let me think about this, because if I say OK and you fuck up, it's your ass. And then I have no choice but to go after you, and that would make me feel like shit.'

Rocco faltered. The fact that Jimmy seemed to be more concerned about Rocco's skin than his own, or even his client's, made Rocco wonder if he might be stepping off a cliff here. And now that the deal seemed to be just about closed, Rocco wasn't at all sure he wanted to go through with it.

As if reading Rocco's mind, Jimmy said, 'You ever hear that expression, "If God hates your guts, he grants you your deepest wish"?'

Rocco stuck his fork in the ziti, leaving it there like a naked flagpole. 'Jimmy, I tell you what. Give me a few days, let me do some digging on this Victor kid. If I come up with anything negative I'll back out of this, but if I still feel like I feel about him now? You let me in there with him, plus you can have all my character witnesses, all the Citizen Victor stuff I dig up, everything. It's like I'm working for you, and you *know* I'm fucking six times better an investigator than any of those clowns in the defender's office.'

He thought about the deal he had just offered. Right off the top of his head – not bad at all.

'Jimmy.' Rocco held out his hands, palms up, and raised his shoulders. 'Alls I'm asking you to do is give me a chance to throw out my own arrest.'

Eager to resolve his own doubts about Victor's innocence, Rocco had called in sick from the restaurant, and now, two hours after breaking bread with Jimmy Newton in Dempsy, he sat under a Cinzano umbrella on Columbus Avenue in New York, a vodka collins in front of his clasped hands, directly across the street from To Bind an Egg, the store where Victor had worked as a security guard.

A marathon must have just finished over in Central Park, because it seemed that every third person on the street was bare-legged and wore waffle-tread sneakers. The runners staggered past him looking pained but happy, huddled inside plastic silver blankets that were covered in a checkerboard pattern of alternating Big Apples and Lemon Pledge bottles. Watching them, Rocco felt angry and defensive. Sometimes he hated New York.

Self-conscious about his own corrupted dimensions, he pushed himself away from the table and trotted across the traffic to the store. He almost sprained his wrist pushing on the locked door, then jumped a little at the delayed buzz of electronic permission.

To Bind an Egg was about the size of a bedroom, a claustrophobic explosion of Japanese knickknacks, everything appearing to be lacquered, burnished, varnished, petite. It was like walking inside an Oriental hope chest: there was hardly room to move; even the walls were plastered with T-shaped kimonos pinned helter-skelter like a flock of kites frozen in midflight. The store had a subtle scent – not unpleasant, just there – somewhere between tea leaves and potpourri, which gave Rocco a chalky catch in the back of his throat.

Two people worked in the store, a blonde woman sorting cook-books in the back and a short Puerto Rican kid in a blazer, striped tie and charcoal slacks. The collar of his shirt was frayed, and he stood uneasily against a rack of kimonos. Rocco assumed he was Victor's replacement.

'Hi!' The blonde woman greeted Rocco so cheerfully that for a second he wondered if they used to go out. She was tiny, the perfect size for the store.

'How you doing?' Rocco's eyes fell on a wicker basket filled with smooth greenish-black pebbles.

'Good! What can I help you with?'

Rocco took out his badge and eyed a child-size kimono on the wall, priced at sixty dollars. 'I'm Rocco Klein, with the Dempsy County – '

'Shit, that poor kid. Tell me about it. He was such a doll. I still can't believe it.'

Rocco hesitated, wondering if she was referring to Victor or Darryl Adams.

'Are you the owner?'

'Yeah, Kiki Cord.' She gave Rocco her hand.

'Did you know him well? Victor?'

'Hey, you see how small this place is? It was me and him, thirty hours a week in here.'

'So you know him well?'

'Look, I don't know how well you can say you know *any* of these kids, but Victor – a doll, a gentleman and a doll.'

'Well, let me just ask you. I'm doing some background, we're trying to put something together here. How often was he late for work? Was he ever late for work?'

'Late for work?' She made a face. 'Swiss movement, that kid.'

'Did you ever suspect him of stealing?'

She reared back in disdain at the question.

'Did the other employees ever see him steal?'

'What others?' She laughed. 'I can't even afford *me*.'

Rocco smiled sympathetically. 'Did he ever catch anybody stealing, then let them go?'

'Do you mean, was he in cahoots with anybody? *That* would break my heart.'

A half-dozen miniature trees stood near the cash register. Rocco was momentarily distracted by their gnarled yet delicate wholeness.

'Bonsai,' she said, reading his eyes.

'Yeah, that's what they said when they crashed their planes into the battleships, right?'

'That's bon*zai*.'

Rocco smiled tightly at her, then looked out at the endless stream of half-dead runners. He was sweating profusely.

'Victor – he ever have any visitors?'

'Nope.'

'Anybody ever come to pick him up?'

'Nope.'

'Did he ever make friends with anybody, like a customer?'

'Nope.'

Rocco pulled a few mug shots from his pocket. Strike first. 'Have you ever seen this guy around here?'

'Nope.'

Then Rodney. 'Him?'

'Nope, and I hope I never do.'

Then Darryl Adams's employment ID from Ahab's. 'How about him?'

'Nope.'

'Awright.' Rocco packed away the photos, looking at the Puerto

Rican kid. He was so quiet and still that Rocco had forgotten all about him.

'He just started yesterday,' Kiki whispered.

'Yeah? Let me ask you. How'd you find Victor? You didn't get him through an agency, did you?'

She gave Rocco a hesitant look.

'Hey, I'm not with the IRS.'

'Is this going into any official report?'

'If it does, I'll leave this part out. I don't want to make trouble for you. You're talking to me here, and I appreciate it.'

'I'm . . . I don't care about the IRS.' Her voice dropped. 'I live in Newport City – you know, that development in Jersey City?'

'Oh yeah, that's nice there.'

'But no.' Her voice dropped even lower, now becoming a murmur. 'I was jogging one afternoon last year in Liberty State Park? This kid comes out, knocks me down, starts . . . you know. There were two men, at least, who saw it, and both of them just kept walking. Meanwhile, this kid's trying to get me in the bushes, and I'm screaming. And for a couple of minutes nothing, no help from anybody. But finally, Victor was coming by with one of his kids. He hears me, he starts walking toward us, and the kid who was trying to, to *get* me, runs away. He was the only one who helped, Victor, and he was the smallest of the three men. All I got was a little scratched up, but I was shaking like a leaf.'

Kiki raised her arms as if to hold something at eye level; with fingers extended, her hands started to tremble. 'Anyway, he starts following this other kid, but then he sees me, how I'm shaking, and he stays with me. I see he's with his little boy, I feel like he's on the up-and-up, and then he offers me a ride to a police station. So we began talking – *me* mainly, ninety miles an hour, but the truth was, I didn't want to go to the police station with this thing. Anyway, I offered him money, some kind of thank you, but he wouldn't take it. It's like, who was that masked man? And the next day I go in to work – here – and I'm all alone and I start thinking about that *kid*, the one who dragged me, and I start shaking again. I had to close the store. I couldn't be in here alone – I was *sure* someone would come in and . . . Maybe you think I'm crazy because this is Columbus Avenue, but you don't know what goes on here. With the kids? It's everywhere now. And the store owners, we're like victims to them. You wouldn't believe these last two years. It's horrible, nobody's safe, they hunt you, like in packs. I always dealt with it before, but all of a sudden I'm so scared with this image, this memory, that I can't, I can't be alone. Three days in a row I had to close up in the middle of the afternoon, and pretty soon I'm on the verge of a nervous breakdown. I figure I've got to hire a security guard, I've got to get somebody in here with me, otherwise I'll never open again. So first I get somebody from an agency, but the guy frightened me more than that kid. Big, sullen, a beard – all day he's looking at me with that *beard*, I can't stand it.' She shuddered. 'So I get rid of him and I start thinking, How about that kid who helped me? A gentleman, a family man, clean-cut. I remember he told me that he works at this godawful Hambone's, so I go down there, Hi, remember me? I offer him ten dollars an hour free and clear, all he's got to do is stand there and keep me company, but he says no, he can't, he's got this job here, this responsibility. Then, the next day, who should come in the store but Victor, all dressed up. He says he's been thinking, he can shift to nights, work nights, do me days. He's trying to save up, he wants to move his family into some co-op apartment, he needs the money.'

Rocco was getting pumped again. Kiki's story was starting to purge him of his fears, make him believe again in his hunches. What a great story for Jimmy Newton, for the jury: the kid's a fucking hero.

'And I got to tell you something,' Kiki said. 'It turned out not to be such an easy job, working for me. Not because of *me*, but we have a high school about two blocks from here and the kids got sticky fingers. They're, well, they have a lot of anger. It's not their fault. It's their environment, society, whatever, but you know, at lunch hour or three o'clock they walk by, they see it's Oriental, and immediately they start thinking Times Square, Kung Fu, weapons, they want to come in. So before, it was all me, following them around, watching the hands, the eyes, but now I have Victor. He's my doorman, he's my screener. They buzz, he's right there, says, "What do you want?" And if they say they're looking for a tea set for their mother or a certain book I happen to have in stock, that's one thing, but if they're looking for a throwing star or nunchaks, he stands in the door and tells them that's not us and saves them a trip around the store, saves me the worry. But some of these kids, they see he's a kid, standing there, and some of them see him, *saw* him, as like, his job is to keep black people out of the store. Which is not true, but when *that* happens, sometimes he had to take a lot of anger coming at him, a lot of verbal abuse.'

Rocco unbuttoned his collar, pulled down his tie knot. He ran a finger along his forehead and it came back damp. 'Did he ever get into any fights? Anybody ever threaten him?'

'Yeah, well, a few times kids challenged him to step out or said stuff like, "I'll be waiting for you." But the worst thing that ever happened was one time, this kid's trying to get inside, Victor's at the door, you know, "What do you want," and the kid says, "I'm just looking." Victor says something like, "You gotta know what you want 'cause maybe we don't have it." And this kid, he gets all, he thinks that Victor's, you know, insulting him. What do they call it? *Dissing* him. So he starts calling' – her voice dropped to a whisper – 'he starts calling Victor a nigger, a security nigger.'

Rocco grunted in encouraging disapproval, and then Kiki startled him by taking one of the pebbles from the wicker basket and popping it into her mouth like a sucking candy.

'Anyway, Victor's about to close the door, because I told him, don't ever get down on their level.' She spit the pebble into her palm. 'And then this kid reaches into his pocket and I almost had a heart attack. I thought he had a gun because he had this *look*. But you know what he comes up with? A hundred-dollar bill. He holds it up and says, "This is what I think of *you*, motherfucker," then crumbles it up and throws it right in Victor's face, says, "Here's your salary, nigger. But next time I see you, I put a *hole* in your chest. And my word is *bond*."'

Rocco raised his eyebrows and Kiki nodded, confirming the truth of her story.

'Anyway, the guy walks off and Victor closes the door like nothing happened. The hundred dollars, it's lying out on the sidewalk. He won't even *look* at it. He's just standing by the kimono rack like a cigar-store Indian. The kid who came by must've been a drug dealer or something, throwing away that kind of money. What was that, allowance? Anyway, I felt so bad for him, for Victor. The money lay out there for two hours before somebody picked it up. Both of us were like holding our breath for two hours. And when somebody picked it up I saw Victor, his whole body goes – ' She slumped forward in a deep exhalation of relief.

Rocco absently eyed the new guard. 'You ever see that kid again? With the money?'

'Nope. But sometimes they'll be a group of women. Not kids, *people*. Women who work – you know, outer-borough types.'

Rocco nodded, assuming 'outer borough' meant nonwhite.

'I don't know what they do, work for the city or something, but sometimes there'd be five or six at a time out there trying to come in. I told Victor to only let them in two at a time, and, you know, they read into it, get offended. But hey, my markup's not so big that I can absorb a hell of a lot of shoplifting, so if I have to take some verbal abuse for defending my stock, so be it. You can't be thin-skinned and run a retail business. But of course *he's* the one that's got the arm across the door, not me, so . . .' She shrugged, looking around. 'Shit, this city – you know what I mean?'

'Hey, that's why I live in Dempsy,' Rocco said. When he realized that for a moment he'd forgotten where he lived, he became a little rattled. Suddenly he was anxious to wrap it up. 'So Victor never lost his cool in here?'

'He was the best. You know, we had a lot of dead time in here, me and him. We used to have these long talks. Well, mostly oneway, he wasn't much of a talker, but he was . . . I never picked up any anger, any attitude. He was a real doll, a sweetheart.' In a lower voice, nodding toward her new guard, she said, 'This kid, I don't know about yet.'

'OK.' Rocco stuck his hands in his pockets and slowly wheeled around for the door. 'Last thing. What did you think when you first heard about him getting arrested? First thought that popped into your head.'

'Look,' she said slowly, 'let me tell you. Victor was unprovocable, absolutely unprovocable. I don't know how he pulled it off. What he put up with, the, the *women* out there. Those goddamn *kids*. Just unprovocable.' She cocked her head at Rocco. 'Are you sure it was him who did it?'

As Rocco left the store, he had to squeeze around the security guard, passing so close that he picked up the sour tang of the kid's perspiration.

Kids. He had never thought of that word as a racial epithet before.

25

'Erroll told me you talked to that Homicide cop,' Rodney said mildly as he palmed two nickels off the counter glass, then adjusted the vertical hold on the tiny TV perched on top of his cash register.

'How'd that go?'

'OK.' Strike jiggled a Yoo-Hoo bottle cap and leaned against a cracked bar stool behind the counter.

'OK?'

'Yeah. He just wanted to know about my buh-brother'n shit, but like what could I say about it? You know?' Strike slid away from the subject. 'Meanwhile, that muh-motherfucker Jo-Jo? He put his hand in my pocket for five hundred dollars last night.' He left out the part about the Homicide's business card, which was definitely from Jo-Jo, since this morning Strike had found the first card, the one the Homicide himself had given him, in the muff of a sweatshirt he'd worn yesterday.

Rodney took some grape gum from the candy display and came around the counter. He gave a stick to his eighteen-month-old son, who was sitting in a stroller by the pool table.

'So now he's takin' it from you, huh?' Rodney laughed. 'Flexible motherfucker, ain't he?'

'So now, like, I got to pay it?' Strike smelled the gum; it was like a cloud of purple chemicals.

'Well *I* ain't payin' it,' Rodney said.

'That's every woo-week, man.'

'Well hey, tell him to go fuck himself. *I* did.'

Rodney tilted his head to peer out the doorway, and Strike's eyes followed. A car with Delaware plates pulled up across the street.

'Yeah, here we go.' Rodney touched Strike's arm and spoke quickly. 'These niggers getting two ounces with a half-ounce cut.' Then he barked out, 'Uh-oh! Uh-oh! *Hold* up!' He laughed loudly as three grinning teenagers wearing enough gold to snap a skinny man's neck walked into the store, hands raised for a pound.

Rodney made the introductions, and Strike, torn between excitement and a vague paranoid gloom, committed the faces and the cut ratio to memory for future business.

After a few minutes of small talk, Strike slipped out of the store, made his way to Herman's and weighed out the dope. A half hour later he returned with the two stepped-on ounces in a paper bag and tossed it under the rear wheel of the teenagers' car. He walked into the store empty-handed.

When the country boys left they were eighteen hundred dollars lighter, and Rodney was holding a clear profit of one thousand fifty dollars.

'The further south you go, the weaker the blow,' Rodney recited. 'Except if you go *too* far south, then you in Miami.'

'So Delaware's like perfect, right?'

'More like Virginia.' Rodney counted the money with his back to the street. 'So tell me more about this Homicide cop.'

'Nothing *to* tell.' Strike hoped he sounded casual.

'Nothing, huh?'

Strike hoped that was the end of it, but then Rodney glanced up from the money and gave him a long penetrating look before asking, 'Did I ever tell you the first time I killed somebody?'

Strike shook his head, then went still.

'It was me and Erroll like in seventy-two, seventy-three, something like that. We was over in New York and we got beat on some dope. Erroll says to me, "Let's kill them motherfuckers." I says yeah, you know, so we go to where we copped. It was this tenement uptown. There was a shooting gallery on the top floor, so we go up there, *nasty*-looking place. Erroll had like a sawed-off, I got like a thirty-eight. I used to carry this thirty-eight . . .' Rodney was talking with his eyes drifting between Strike and the TV, and now he paused to adjust the vertical hold again. 'We get up there, go in waving the guns, we see the three guys that beat us sitting on the floor with their works, tying up and shit, everybody else going like, "Whoa, whoa." Erroll yells for everybody to get the fuck out. He's holdin' down the three guys with the sawed-off, people running out of there, an' these three motherfuckers on their knees, they start blubberin', you know like, "Yo please, please, it ain't personal man, it's the *sickness*, it's the *sickness* man." And then one motherfucker tries to make a run for it. Erroll just take that sawed-off . . .' Rodney hunched down in a slight crouch, aiming, shouting '*Boom*!' so loud that Strike let out a yelp.

Rodney screwed up his face in distaste. 'The motherfucker like *splat*tered all over the wall, come right up off his feet like a pulled puppet just . . . oh shit it was like, you know, and like *me*, I jumped twice as high as the guy that got shot because when Erroll said let's *kill* them, I thought he meant like, just fuck them up because I used to pistol whip an' shit, baseball bats an' shit, but I never, I mean, I was a damn *kid*. So I'm lookin' at this guy all over the wall and I'm *scared* and I'm sayin', "Erroll, let's go, man, let's go," and Erroll just . . . you know, *boom*! That *second* guy's all over the wall.'

Rodney's son started to cry, the gum all sticky in his fist. Rodney gave his kid a sour look, then turned back to Strike. 'His head just *fly* off. I ain't never seen nothing like that. I'm sayin', "Oh Erroll, c'mon man," and this third guy, he's sobbing, begging, *snot* coming out, and Erroll says to me, "Shoot him." I says, "*What*?" Erroll says, "Shoot him." I says, "You crazy? I ain't shooting nobody." Erroll puts that sawed-off right in my goddamn face, he says, "You shoot him or I'm gonna shoot you." And I ain't believing this now but Erroll's crazy, you know? And this third guy, he's begging, "Please mister, please mister, I ain't gonna tell. I'm sorry man, I'm sorry I get your money back, it's the *sick*ness." And Erroll's aiming that thing at me, so I just take out my piece. I can't even *look* at the guy, I just hide my eyes, go *boom boom boom*.'

Rodney's son started crying again. Strike fought down twitches, hoping Rodney wasn't going to do any more sound effects.

'We get back to Dempsy? Man, I was never so scared in my life. See, I didn't *know* you could get away with murder. I was so scared, I wouldn't come out my house for like two weeks. Every time a police car come by? A siren? I *never* been so scared. But then Erroll starts comin' around, like coaxing me out and then, like little by little I start hangin' out again, doin' other shit and then, one time, like about a month later? When I'm getting all calmed down? I finally ask Erroll, I say, "Erroll, would you have really shot me up in that place?" Erroll says, "Shit yeah." An' I says, "Why, man? *Why*? It's *me*."'

Rodney leaned forward and his voice went low. 'He says, "Because you were so motherfuckin' scared up there, if I had to do all of them myself and the cops got hold of you with nothing hanging over you from that? Like in Dempsy, New York, Newark or like anywhere for anything? You would've given me up in a motherfuckin' minute. An' I ain't goin' down like that if there's something I can *do* about it. So yeah, I would've shot you dead 'cause you *knew* too much and you was too scared to be trusted."'

Rodney paused to look Strike in the eye, leaning forward some more. 'In a motherfuckin' minute. My best friend too.'

Strike grunted and shook his head appreciatively. He was amazed at how calm he felt while listening to this story.

Rodney continued to stare at him for a minute, then added, 'See, I guess that's why I had been hoping that you had got yourself a little *bloody* on that Darryl thing, you know what I mean? Give me some peace of mind.'

'I'm involved,' Strike said, avoiding Rodney's eyes, looking out to the street.

Rodney regarded him for another long minute. He sighed, opened the Delaware envelope and took out three hundred dollars, folding the money over forked fingers and passing it to Strike. 'Awright, why don't you go see what's happenin' on the benches.'

Strike counted the bills, all twenties and smaller. 'This ain't no fuh-fifty-fifty, Rodney,' he said.

Rodney shrugged. 'Yeah, well, we ain't set up yet. We working out of *here* this week. The risk's on me now, so . . .'

Strike knew right then that he would never get fifty percent no matter what. But now was not the time to pursue it. He took the three hundred, stuffed it in his pocket and stared blindly out to the street.

'You OK?' Rodney cocked his head, still in his intense eyeballing mood.

Strike shrugged.

'I tell you one last thing about that story. After that first time? Killing that guy? Man, after that there was nothing to it. Shit, for a while there it even got to be like *fun* – you know, back when I was young.'

Strike walked from his car to the benches in a heads-down funk. He was sick of everybody asking him, You OK? You OK? Rodney, Jo-Jo, everybody out to fuck him and always ending by asking if he was OK. Strike thought about Rodney's story, wondered if he should start carrying his gun. But how could he, with Andre, Thumper and every other damn cop patting him down every time he turned around? Are you OK? Yeah, I'm great, doing great, just fucking great. Strike stared at the rolling sidewalk as he marched full steam ahead – and then crashed into somebody's chest. He fell back on his ass, sneakers high.

'Holy Christ, just the man I want to see.' The heavyset Homicide, beaming and red-faced, went into a crouch and extended a hand to help him to his feet. 'You OK?'

Dusting off his pants, Strike got to his feet on his own.

'I mean, I was hoping to run into you but . . .' The Homicide laughed. Strike smelled alcohol and wrinkled his nose.

They were standing on the sidewalk in front of the benches, the same place they had talked the last time. The crew sat there silently, watching them again.

'No, I was just asking the fellas here where I could find you. They said to hang around, I'd probably run into you sooner or later.' He laughed again. 'So how you been? You OK?'

Strike didn't answer. He frowned down at himself and brushed at his sweatshirt, the red glow coming into his stomach like a familiar enemy.

'Listen, can I talk to you?'

'I got to *book*.' Strike started to move off.

The Homicide extended an arm to block his escape. 'Hey Ronnie, your brother's looking at thirty years, you think you could spare me five minutes?'

Strike saw no way out. 'Yeah, what's up?'

'Nothin'.' The Homicide shrugged as if he was killing time. 'You know, just, well, remember when we were talking? You said that Darryl Adams, that kid, had like an attitude. You know, maybe he dissed your brother, maybe he was *nasty* to people, like the customers or the other workers. You remember that?'

Strike regarded the Homicide's curious and expectant expression, the bastard coming on to him like some TV detective, being nice, setting him up. The glow in his belly got redder, but he also felt a new pain, a stabbing sensation, as if someone was in there with a knife.

'Yeah, well, I said like I didn't know. I was just thinkin' that, you know, like to be helpful.'

'Hey, any help I can get.' The Homicide held out his hands, palms up. 'It's just that I did some heavy checking on that, trying to back that up? See if there was anything to it? I must've asked twenty people about him, the vic, what's he like. Everybody, I mean *every*body, said, "No, man, Darryl was a great guy. Darryl's the best. Darryl give you the shirt off his back."' The cop gave the lines a mild street spin. 'Right down the line, "Darryl was *solid*, Darryl was my man."'

Strike thought the Homicide was lying. Darryl wasn't one way or the other, just quiet.

'So, now.' The Homicide turned to the bench for a second, fingertips on his chest. 'Now I'm really fucking confused because *you* said, in so many words, the guy was a fucking prick, but it turns out you're the only one to have that opinion.'

'I said I didn't know. I was juh-just imagining.' Strike puffed his cheeks, the knife in his guts jabbing harder. 'It's my brother, man. I was just trying to help my buh-brother.'

'But you had to know *some*thing to say it, right? I don't understand. Are you sure you didn't know him?'

'Well, I might have seen him in the street or in the Ahab's, just like, you know, you *see* people.'

'But you called him a *prick*.'

'I-I didn't say that,' Strike said, his stammer making the words float away from him. 'Unh-uh.'

'OK, you said he had an attitude, same thing. How can you say that if you didn't . . . Look, tell me the truth, just between me and you, no big deal. Did you ever have a confrontation with this guy?'

'Unh-uh.' Strike was grateful for a question he could answer straight.

'You never had any dealings with him?'

'Unh-uh.' Strike looked over at the bench, the crew sitting there without business, restless and frowning, Strike thinking, Who's ready to spy on this to Rodney?

'You never had so much as a conversation with this guy?'

'I told you . . .' Strike watched the traffic, feeling too naked and off balance out here with all the eyes on him and this new stabbing pain, as distracting as loud music.

'You told me what?' The Homicide leaned forward as if he was hard of hearing.

'No.' Strike couldn't remember the question.

'No.' The Homicide went upright again. 'OK, so like in other words, there's no reason that the victim would have attacked your brother walking across the lot because he thought it was *you*, that he was jumping on *you*.'

'What?' Strike wasn't following, his concentration torn to pieces by the pain.

'There's no way that guy would have seen your brother and think, There's that motherfucker Strike and – '

'Huh-*hell* no,' Strike said.

'Because in the dark, you and your brother, you got the same build and all. You probably come off like two peas in a pod, you *know* that, right?'

Strike felt clammy now, trying to stay alert, keep Victor out of his mind.

'Are you guys close?'

'Not really.'

'Yeah, I forgot, you haven't seen each other in a long time, right?'

'Yeah.'

'How long has it been?'

'A month.' Strike looked down at the cop's pebble-grain cordovans: Ugly, ugly kicks.

'Jesus, I thought you said like *two* months last time we talked.'

'Yeah? I said that? If you *know* I suh-said that, then ha-how come you asked me like you didn't know?' Strike spoke in small gulps, the anger finally breaking through, helping him to deal here.

The cop laughed. 'You know what Alzheimer's is?'

'Some kind of *beer*?' Strike twisted his mouth in disdain but winced inside, cursing himself for mouthing off. You *never* dis a cop, any kind of cop – they were worse than street people about getting dissed.

The Homicide flashed teeth and got a little redder, but Strike couldn't tell if it was anger or blush. 'Yeah, well, some people into dope, some into booze. Pick your poison, you know?'

Strike nodded, tired of swapping lies. The knife in his stomach made him desperate to sit down.

'Awright.' The Homicide shrugged, took a little spin on his heel. 'So anyways, is there anything else you can think of to tell me? Any new thoughts?'

Strike envisioned Buddha Hat coming out of the jail again, heading for his Volvo.

'Not really.'

'You get to see him yet?'

'Not really.' Strike felt slightly spooked. It was as if the guy had just read his mind.

'Can I tell you something? Like unofficial?'

Strike waited.

'This lawyer he's got? A real fucking bonehead. A real snowball in hell. They go to trial?' The Homicide looked off, shaking his head.

'You ever think may-maybe he didn't do it?' The words came out of him in an unthinking rush, and Strike was instantly horrified.

'What do you mean?' The Homicide turned back toward him.

'May-maybe somebody *else* did it.'

'Like who?'

Like Buddha Hat. Say it. Say it. Strike dropped onto one knee on the sidewalk and bowed his head. 'I'm just sayin' . . . buh-but I don't know.'

'You OK?'

'Yeah, gimme like a second.' Strike made himself rise, hissing through clamped teeth.

'You all right?'

'Yeah, buh-but like I got to *go* now.'

The Homicide stared at him, and Strike could feel him thinking. What the hell was this guy thinking?

'OK, OK.' The cop reached into his pocket. 'Here, take my card.'

'Yeah, I aw-already got *two*.'

'Two? Jesus, it's that Alzheimer's beer, I guess.'

'Naw, it's from Jo-Jo.'

'Jo-Jo!' The Homicide looked surprised – sheepish but not unhappy.

'You know what it is? My friends, I run into them, everybody, you know, a homicide's the heaviest crime, so it's, "Hey Rocco what's happening." I tell them, they get all excited, they want to help out, so they, you know . . .' He shrugged. 'Anyways, well look, just take this one, you know, in case you lose the others and you need to give me a call or something, OK?'

Strike nodded, the new card in his hand now.

'OK, so, take care of yourself there, Ronnie. I'll be seeing you around.'

Strike dropped back down on one knee like a batter in the on-deck circle. He looked away, watching the Homicide out of the corner of his eye as he drove off in an ugly tan county car, made a U-turn in front of the benches and waved to him as if he knew Strike was watching no matter where his head was turned.

The stabbing man inside hacked away even fiercer, the pain so bad that Strike felt a rush of fear. What the fuck was happening? He wanted to scream out how sick he was, tell the world to leave him alone.

Everybody on the bench stared at him, but no one stepped up to help, Strike hating all of them, hating this life. He forced himself to rise. The crew watched him stagger toward the bench, Tyrone on his chain the only one looking at him with concern. Strike knew the kid couldn't come forward to give an arm, but he was sure Tyrone would help if he could. Tyrone was his only friend in the world now, everybody else out for themselves, Strike staring at them, thinking up horrible deaths for them. Hanging them up on a hook, peeling off their skin in long strips, rubbing pepper on the raw flesh: How's *that* feel?

Strike burped up a little blood, then caught Peanut making a face. 'The fuck *you* lookin' at?' Strike wiped the red off his lips. 'Get on out to the corners. What you suh-sittin' for.'

Somebody screamed from inside the hallway of 6 Weehawken and Stitch came loping out onto the street. A big heavy girl was holding on to the back of his collar, bellowing, 'Give me my money back! Give me my money!'

Bug-eyed, choked by his own shirt, the girl holding on, Stitch lurched forward, struggling to run away, going up and down like a boat bucking waves.

Everybody on the bench rose, but only Horace went forward. Stitch finally swung around and punched the girl on her ear to break free, the girl losing her grip and falling on the sidewalk. Horace yelled something, hopped over the girl to get to Stitch, tripped and fell on top of her. Strike grabbed an empty soda bottle from a garbage can and stepped into Stitch's path, Stitch running as if to leap past him, but Strike caught him flush in the face. The bottle didn't break, but Stitch went down, hands over his eyes, moaning, 'God, God.'

Strike dropped to his knees on Stitch's chest and pounded away, screaming, 'Leave me alone!' as if it was Stitch who was doing the beating. As Horace clambered all over the big girl, trying to regain his footing and get to Stitch, Strike punched down at the fingers masking Stitch's face, all his hate and panic going into it. He saw Andre come on the run but far away still, and then Stitch stabbed him in the stomach, *must* have stabbed him in the stomach because Strike was lying there curled on his side like a shrimp, clutching his guts, walleyed with agony, thinking, Stitch even left the knife in, tasting the blood on his tongue, all alone, whispering his hurt, seeing sneakers, shifting sneakers, hearing someone say, 'Leave me alone, please, please,' but in a vicious, mocking tone, then hearing himself say the very same words, realizing that they were mimicking *him*. Then someone yelled into his ear, 'What's a matter with you? What's a matter with you?' sounding pissed off, like Strike was some kind of fuck-up. 'What's a matter with you?' but he couldn't talk, could barely comprehend the voice shouting, 'Why you holding your stomach? Why you holding your stomach?' too shut up in a shell with his pain to answer. 'You crack up today? Huh? You crack up today?' Strike heard some kid yell for his friend, somebody else laughing, then again, 'You crack up today? You hit the peace pipe?'

Strike felt himself being lifted. He screamed, then heard his scream imitated beyond his eyelids, over and over, then the outside voices shut out save for one: 'What's your date of birth, huh?' He felt himself being set down somewhere indoors, mouthed 'Leave me alone,' mouthed 'Please.' 'Where do you live,' the hacking in his gut steady like rain. 'Where do you live,' feeling something being wrapped around his arm, something pinching like a too-tight cuff. 'Why you holding your stomach, huh? Momma *told* you not to do those drugs, right? *Now* look where you at. Where do you live?' Then Strike heard Andre's voice down by his feet: 'I'll give you all that.' Strike wanted Andre to arrest everybody. He whispered, 'Andre,' but the name was drowned out by the pain.

'This ever happen to you before? Huh? This ever happen to you before?' His interrogator was coming back at him despite Andre, talking in a flat blare as if Strike was ninety years old. Strike just wanted to be left lying here, curled tight, his mind picturing a sea-shell, a snail, an electric spiral. 'You cough up anything? Answer me, Home. You cough up anything?'

And as if it was easier to illustrate than describe, Strike hawked up something almost solid through his teeth. The voice winced in disgust: 'Coffee grounds.'

He felt the cuff ripped from his arm.

'Eighty palp.'

Strike finally opened his eyes and saw a tall, red-haired man in a yellow jacket flap out a pair of rubber pants fringed with tubes. 'C'mon Yo, straighten out for a sec.' Gloved hands pulled on Strike's kneecaps, prying them from under his chin, Strike seeing the electric spiral in his head go from pink to neon green to pale blue, all on a field of black.

'Let me see my face.'

'What's your name?'

'I ain't *got* no name. I was *hatched*, man.'

Strike woke up to this exchange, finding himself in a hallway lit the color of heavy urine. He was flat on his back. Ten feet away, three cops were arguing with a five-foot-tall Latino whose face was a mask of blood.

'You want to see your face? Tell us your name.'

'Angel.'

'Angel what?'

'Let me see my face an' I tell you my name.'

Too exhausted to move, Strike watched as a cop held up a small mirror. Liking what he saw, the little guy smirked through all that blood.

'Rodriguez. Who hit me? Who's the faggot who hit me?'

'You hit yourself.'

Strike looked at his arm and saw a tube going into a drip bag. He didn't feel the knife in his gut anymore: Good, that's good.

'What am I supposed to do? It's my *kids*, man. You saying the niggers are better than my kids? I defend my family and the faggot bust my head. I ain't even seen it coming. Like a *fag*got man, not like a man.'

Strike's throat hurt and there was something in his nose. He put his hand to his nostrils and touched rubber tubing.

'I fuck faggots in the ass. Where's the faggot who hit me? This fucking city, man. We got a faggot mayor and faggot cops who hit you in the fucking head and hide.' The Latino was enjoying himself, pacing in a tight trench, dwarfed by the cops. 'I'm a *man*, motherfuckers. I'm a *man*. So what you gonna do now, slit my throat? Finish me off?'

Strike closed his eyes and imagined Victor saying that. He was too sick to help his brother, but then behind his shut eyes he received a vision of Victor, motionless and blank-faced, like a paper doll, hovering in front of a solid background, hanging in an objectless vacuum. But *he* was alone too – alone in this hospital, with not even his mother knowing, maybe not even caring.

Something was tickling Strike's thigh, something lying along his leg. Opening his eyes again, he saw Rodney walking down the hall, curling his lips in disgust at the moans and odors. Rodney spotted him and bellowed his name, laughing, as if he was glad to see him. But Strike wasn't fooled. The frozen vision of Victor said it all: every man for himself.

Strike weakly pulled off the thin blanket covering his legs to see what was tickling him. He saw a tube trailing off between his feet, followed it to its source, then gasped in disbelief, the world flying up into his eyelids and out.

26

Rocco kept the engine running in the Hambone's parking lot, watching three kids down the block standing under a bus shelter, quietly clocking. He had been sitting here for twenty minutes, collecting his thoughts, and had seen four or five sales – not much, but still, fifty bucks in twenty minutes came to a hundred and fifty dollars an hour.

Rocco had intended to stay in New York and go home after the interview at To Bind an Egg, but he had left the store craving another bite of Strike. And the second go-round with the kid had him straining at the leash. He could've sworn Strike was about to give it up, saying, 'Maybe somebody else did it,' and then going down on one knee like that. This kid would definitely break. All Rocco had to do was keep coming back at him, keep up the 'Gee, I thought you said, so then how come' bullshit. He didn't for one minute think that Strike wasn't wise to his routine. Even so, he could tell that this bad brother was in hell over this – a shithead with a conscience.

After working over Strike, Rocco, forgetting that he had called in sick, dropped by his office, anxious to keep it going, praying that no other jobs had come in. Fortunately there was nothing new on the blackboard, and lying on his desk was the call log from the pay phone at Rudy's that he had subpoenaed. Noting that eight calls had been made from that phone between seven-thirty and eleven on the night of the murder, Rocco guessed that Victor probably made at least two of them, one to his home and one to Hambone's. Somebody else could have made either call – his brother, for instance – but Rocco didn't think so. The other six calls were made to numbers in Newark, Dempsy and Beaufort, South Carolina, and Rocco, eager to keep moving, had decided to track down those parties later.

Out of his car now, striding across the lot, Rocco opened the door to the restaurant. He surveyed the brown and orange room, and felt like a fireman coming back the day after a six-alarmer. The exhaust fans over the grills must have died, and a grease mist hung so heavy in the air he could lick it. Hambone's was in chaos: the tables full up and rowdy, long lines at the cash registers, ketchup slopped over the stainless steel rim of the condiment bar, a puddle of orange soda on the floor in the bathroom alcove, a garbage can with decal eyes on the side of its mouth gagging on cups and wrappers. Rocco's first response was to wonder, Where the hell's the manager? But then he remembered.

He waded through the clatter and bubble of the steel-on-steel kitchen area and reached the manager's office. He opened the door and heard Hector Morales, Victor's partner, chanting at someone on the phone.

'No fuckin' way, no fuckin' way, no fuckin' *way*!' He screamed on the last beat, punching wood.

Rocco rapped lightly on the open door and stepped inside the tiny room, his badge flapped out. The office was two beat-up desks, two chairs, a phone and a hand-drawn work schedule.

'She's my kid too, bitch!'

'Hector.' Rocco waited, holding his ID before him like a cross. Hector turned and Rocco took a step back. Hector's face was striped with long bloody scratches from eyebrow to chin, and another jagged gouge ran the length of his forearm. Half the wounds were covered with yellow ointment. Hector held a jar in one hand and was applying salve with the other, the phone in the crook of his neck.

He held up a finger for Rocco to hang on. 'You're fucking dead. That's right . . . that's right . . . that's right.' He hung up.

'Bad fucking day, bro.' Hector was brisk, manic, fingerpainting his face with salve, going into a grotesque imitation of a Latino woman: '"You na' fokin' seein' huh today, she got a *flu*, she see you *nes*' week."'

Rocco sucked his teeth in sympathy. 'Women – can't live with 'em, can't kill 'em.'

Hector gave the one-liner a quick straight face as if to say, 'Oh yeah?'

'I'm Rocco Klein.'

'You got to give me like *ten* minutes.' Hector held up both hands, then moved past Rocco to the door. Rocco decided not to push it, just walk in Hector's shadow and look out at the world through Victor's eyes.

Back in the kitchen, a young kid was nibbling french fries off the fry scoop as if he was at home. Hector scowled at the cockeyed heat lamps over the frying racks: one was trained on the floor, the other focused on the boiling shortening. The grease smell was even thicker back here, the air just getting whipped around by big stand-up fans not connected to any exterior exhaust vent.

Hector refocused the overhead lamps on the fries and grabbed the kid by the upper arm.

'Eric. Why don't you please go out and empty up the Garbage Monster, my man. Thank you.'

'That's Derrick's job.'

'That's your job for right now, please. *Thank* you.'

The kid stood still and sullen, not wanting to go. 'Where the garbage bags at?'

Hector didn't answer. He grabbed a stumpy girl working the tomato slicer and stuck a mop in her hand, pushing her through the door into the dining room with a please and thank you. He snatched a spatula out of the hands of a kid trying to clean the surface of the meat patty grill and gave him a little lesson, putting some steel wool under the edge of the spatula, getting up on his toes and scouring the surface with two hands on the handle, then giving the spatula back. Moving on, he dropped six rectangular blocks of frozen pollock into a fryer basket, dropped the basket in the shortening and picked up a handful of burger patties, dealing them out on the grill like playing cards. Right next to the french fry baskets, Hector spotted an unmarked cup filled with liquid. He sniffed it, looked up to Rocco with alarm, then shrugged it off and dumped the contents into the sink, the air suddenly clogged with the pungent reek of bleach.

Then Hector was on the move again, Rocco dogging behind, trying to appear casual about this burning ship, but the frying smells were making him nauseous. He imagined his insides all crusted up, the grease lying in his veins, circling his heart. Watching Hector from behind, assessing the spare tire around his middle, Rocco remembered Victor's mother saying, 'Tagamet, he's got to have his Tagamet,' and then he tried to imagine Victor working in here, with an ulcer on top of everything else.

'Clarence!' Hector yelled while scooping a pile of fries. 'Where's Clarence at, please?'

'He ain't come in today,' the girl at the drive-through window answered as she turned to him with a ten-dollar bill. 'This man say he gave me a *twenty*.'

Rocco looked out the window and saw three crew-cut Latinos in an Audi, the bass of their sound system cutting through the noise of the kitchen, thumping like a big heart.

Hector and the cashier stared at each other, the girl deadpan, holding out the ten, elbow cocked into her hip. Hector stared at her until she shook her head. 'Unh-uh. They give me this *ten*.'

'Tell 'em to come back at midnight. If we over ten dollars, it's theirs.'

Hector moved off, obviously not wanting to deal with the problem now, Rocco thinking about that three-thousand-dollar thump, thinking, Making money hand over fist, but still trying to hustle an extra ten dollars off Hambone's.

Hector scanned the hissing kitchen, probably looking for someone to shanghai for bussing tables, but everyone seemed to be locked into their own locomotion. Rocco followed him out front, stepping back as Hector pulled the head off the Garbage Monster and, using the flat of his hand, swept fries, wrappers and soggy napkins off the orange trays.

'Hey, yo, please, thank you.'

Both Rocco and Hector turned to face a kid of about fifteen in a red, white and blue Nike running suit and a gold chain with a six-inch gold anchor pendant. His name was shaved into the hair over his left ear: SHAY.

'My man Hector,' Shay said, warily taking in the stripes on Hector's face.

After slapping his palms free of ketchup and salt grains, Hector shook hands. 'What's up?'

'Please, thank you. Please, thank you.' Shay smirked, checking out the room from the corner of his eye to see if he was being noticed, admired, envied, anything. 'I just came back, you know, to see how you doin'.'

'Hangin' in.'

Rocco could see that Hector was fuming, antsy to get back to work, but the kid was still shaking his hand.

'You still sayin' please and thank you all the time?'

'I try.' Hector started to move away.

'Yeah, I'm doin' OK now, myself.'

Hector took his hand back. 'That's good. I'll see you around.'

'Yo whoa. Wait up, wait up,' Shay said, stopping him. 'This my man De Wayne.' He nodded down to a hulking baby-faced teenager wearing orange sweats, top and bottom, 'Syracuse' in white letters running down the thigh, as if being muscle for a fifteen-year-old dope dealer was some kind of collegiate sport.

De Wayne sat hunched over a giant orange soda. He twisted his head sideways to look up at Hector and shook hands without straightening up or taking the straw from his mouth.

'This my boss Hector, from when I worked here,' Shay said.

Hector gestured to Rocco. 'Yeah, and this is my friend Chuck Norris from Dempsy County Narcotics.'

Shay and De Wayne got a little woody in the face but toughed it out.

Rocco had a flash of premonition: De Wayne would be dead within a month, maybe Shay too. Dead boys – he was fairly sure of it.

'I'll see you around. You all have a good meal now.' Hector moved off and Rocco followed.

Hector shook his head as they stepped behind the counter again. 'Fucking kid works for me three weeks, comes back here wanting to reminisce like we was in Vietnam together or something. I fired his ass too, he was stealing buns, can you believe that?' Hector thrust his hand into the ice chest and popped a cube in his mouth to crunch. 'I mean, if you're gonna steal, *steal*, don't boost no buns . . . Well, now he's king of the world, right?' Winking at Rocco, Hector returned to his office, made a sweeping gesture of welcome. 'King of the world.'

Rocco took a seat while Hector leaned a thigh against the edge of the desk, his wrists curled over each other. He kept one eye on his watch.

'It's bughouse now because I got no partner up here, as you well know.'

'Yup.' Rocco felt the sweat begin to cool inside his shirt.

'So how can I help you?'

'I don't know, but let me ask you. What did *you* think when you heard about it?'

'What I think?' Hector shook his head, blew out some air. 'I feel for the guy because . . . let me ask *you*. You hear me out there – Please Thank You Please Thank You – that little shithead out there dissin' me on that? You know where I got that from? Victor, man. Victor said everybody got to say Please and Thank You, because courtesy brings down the temperature, courtesy breeds teamwork. And he's right. Like I said, things is shit right now because you can't do this with one guy, but when Victor was here, like last week? This place . . . I mean, the owner's bringing in somebody to help me from over in Jersey City 'cause no one can deal like this, but you see them antique *car* prints on the walls out there? And the nice overhead fans? The old-time fans and the plants? Real plants? That was all Victor's idea.'

Rocco didn't recall seeing any of it, but he hadn't lingered on the decor.

'Victor said you got to make it like a home, make it like people are coming into a person's house, like they're guests. So you ask me what I *make* of it? I don't know, and I wish I had the time to sit down and figure this shit out, but I don't. Alls I can say is that it beats the hell out of me. You sure it was him?'

'So he was into the job, hah?' Rocco said reflectively, trying to get Hector to slow down.

'Let me tell you, Victor treated everybody with decency, and on both sides of the counter, you know? Like the kids we get workin' here? This is a shitty kind of job if you're a kid, but Victor gave them some *air* in here, like he told them what the job was, told them how to relate to the people and to each other, and as long as they doin' what they supposed to be doin' he let them alone, because the kids? Alls they want is respect, freedom and some cash to buy some clothes, go take a girl out, an' he had that thing here like, You got a job to do, just do it and everything's gonna be OK – like controlled freedom. See, he taught *me* that, because me, I'm like a throwback. When I started here, it was like don't even look me in the *eye*, I'm the boss, you know? Like I'm going down with the *ship*. But Victor, man, he's like – '

'How was he with the customers?'

'The customers?' Hector made a face and waved off any suggestion of a problem. 'I'll tell you *one* thing, man. Victor, he knew how to weigh a dollar. Somebody come in here all bummy, they say, "Yo, I'm hungry, man," Victor give 'em a hamburger just like that, no money. He said to me, "Hey look, you give 'em one so they don't steal two, protect yourself, protect your investment." And the first time he told me that, I'm thinking, Somebody ask for something free, hey, I'm a Puerto Rican, you stealing *my* sweat, I'm coming *out* with something. But he was right, he was right . . . And even with the drug dealers. You know they come in here, start selling shit? Victor's going over to their table with a Coca-Cola in each hand, sits down, "Yo brother, you ain't *clock*in' in here, are you? 'Cause this like a family place." Then he passes out sodas, says, "I would appreciate if you would do that stuff off the property." And nine out of ten they leave, you know, because basically no matter who you are – dope dealer, welfare, working man – people respond to re*spect*, getting respect.' He leaned back on the edge of his desk, folded his arms across his chest and nodded in agreement with himself.

'Huh,' Rocco grunted, envisioning Victor coming out of the kitchen with his game face on, his hands full of sodas, heading for a table of clockers. 'But you said nine out of ten.'

'Tenth time? He gets his crazy Puerto Rican partner coming out of the back with a baseball bat.' Hector laughed hard and short. 'Nah. Nah. Tenth time you call the cops, 'cause you bend but you don't break, you don't retreat, you know what I'm sayin'? And we got some hard boys comin' in, they got guns and shit, everything.' Hector stole a look at the time.

The office door puffed open a crack and Hector's head jerked up at the clattery sounds that leaked into the room. Rocco stuck his leg out and shut the door again.

'Let me ask you something. You say guns. Did *he* have a gun?'

'Victor? Not that I know of.'

'He told me he found a gun here, cleaning up once.'

'Well, I don't doubt it. You wouldn't believe what we find here sometimes. I found a goddamn human pinkie in the bathroom once, a flesh-and-blood pinkie under the sink. I thought it was a piece of bacon or something. But you say guns. Man, we got guns, gold, big fat wads of cash, the people coming in here? Yeah, OK, like for example, the other night? We got two kids outside the store hangin' on the kiddie climbers, two teenagers selling bottles. Victor goes out there to do his "yo, yo, brother" routine. He comes back in all rattled and I say, "What's up?" He says he told them they got to go, but one kid pulls out his cash, looks like four rolled up socks it was so much, the kid says, "My boss says he'll pay you five hundred cash every week you let us work out here. We got the cops paid off, nothing's ever gonna come down, just say the word."' Hector shrugged and threw Rocco an apologetic smile. 'I mean, no offense to you.'

'So what'd he say?'

'Well, I wasn't there, but my guess is he said, "No please, thank you."' Hector laughed and gently touched his glistening stripes. 'That's some rough shit to pass up, hard as *we're* working? But you got to pass it up regardless, 'cause when the shit comes down you're losing it *all*, salary and, so . . . But you know, they offer you that, it's like a mockery on you. You know what I'm saying?'

Rocco gave him a sympathetic nod, but his mind was focused on details, implications.

'When was this again?'

'Friday? Yeah, Friday.'

'You sure?'

'Yeah, most definitely Friday.'

'Do you know these kids that were out there? Who they were?'

'Just some kids.'

'He left early that night, right?'

'Yeah. Jammed me up too.'

'Why'd he leave?'

Hector shrugged. 'It might've been because of those kids. He didn't say as much, but sometimes that shit can *get* to you. That shit can cut your heart out.'

'Did he call here after he left?'

'Call here?' Hector squinted, then laughed again. 'Yeah, yeah, he called to say he quit and for me to tell Wally.'

'Who's Wally?'

'The owner. This a franchise.'

'Why did he quit?'

'He didn't say. He just said, "Tell Wally I quit." He was high, you know, drunk a little, so I didn't tell Wally. The next day, Saturday? Victor came into work like he didn't remember quitting. He does that sometimes, leaves work early, all fed up, gets a few drinks, calls up and quits, comes in the next day like nothing happened.' Hector tilted his chin toward Victor's desk. 'Open that there by your foot.'

Rocco pulled out a drawer and a bottle of store brand scotch rolled into view.

Hector shook his head. 'He shouldn't drink, Victor.'

Rocco spied a photograph lying flat under the rolling bottle, a glossy black-and-white eight-by-ten of two black kids and a woman, their mother maybe, all three of them smiling at the camera.

'Who's this?'

Hector shrugged. 'It ain't his family, I know that. He found it out in the restaurant one night.'

'It looks like models.'

'I don't know. He found it and he kept it. He used to have it hanging over the desk.'

A guy with a wife and kids hangs a picture of someone else's wife and kids over his work desk . . . Something about that chilled Rocco's bones, made him feel for Victor more than anything else he'd heard.

'Yeah, he didn't get on with his wife too much. They were always yellin' about money, about his kids, how she never brought the kids by the restaurant for him to see them. He liked his kids at least, I know that.'

Rocco took out a few photos of his own, starting with Darryl's ID. 'Did you ever see this guy with Victor?'

'Nope. That's the guy that got killed, right? I never seen him in here. They got some nasty shit at that Ahab's, though. Maybe he died of eating it.'

Rocco laughed by reflex.

'That's terrible I said that.' Hector put the heels of his palms in his eyes, touched his stripes, checked the time again.

'How 'bout him?' Rocco offered up Strike.

'No . . . Well, one time, that's his brother, right? Yeah, he came in here to say hello one time.' Hector laughed. 'He looked like he was gonna puke.'

'Victor ever say anything about him?'

'No. I know he's dealing, but Victor never said nothing.' Hector pushed off from the side of his desk. 'Yo I'd like to help you more, but I'm like scared to death to open this *door* here, see what's been happening behind my back.'

Rocco rose to his feet, about to express his thanks, but before he could get the words out Hector was past him, out of the office, head up, hands out, plunging once again into the roiling stream of his job.

Controlled freedom. Rocco lay in bed flicking a stack of prosecutor's office business cards, wondering if that expression was something Hector had come up with spontaneously tonight or a catch phrase that Victor had created as a tag for his managerial philosophy. Whichever, the idea tickled at him.

The bathroom door was ajar and Rocco could hear Patty undressing, the rustle of falling clothes turning him on a little, stirring up a dreamlike vision of rocking her soft and steady, her fingers playing at the back of his neck. But he didn't know whether they'd wind up making it tonight. Patty sometimes liked a full day's worth of compliments, unexpected hugs and kisses, random outbursts of affection, and he'd been pretty distracted since coming home a couple of hours earlier, the Strike-Victor thing still filling his head.

Rocco silently mouthed 'I love you,' practicing for when she came into the bedroom, hoping that the words would allow him to make a quick end run around all that emotional foreplay.

As the shower hissed to life, Rocco drifted back into the Darryl Adams case, scanning tomorrow's moves. He was about ready to come up on Strike again, pay another visit to the benches, and maybe this time he'd drop the hammer a little harder. He planned to visit the mother again too; the phone log told him the call to Victor's house from Rudy's on the night of the murder lasted thirty-five minutes, and Rocco wanted to get another read on her, what she knew. And a talk with that reverend in Bellevue might not be a bad idea either – find out exactly what Victor had said to him when he gave up the gun.

Rocco was getting dopey with sleep. Through the partially open bathroom door he could see Patty's silhouette on the shower curtain. Rocco put the prosecutor cards on the night table to have his hands free for when she came in. He was filled with the presexual rush of affection that felt like love: he lived here, with her and the baby, and it was good to be home. Turning his head, Rocco looked out the bedroom window at their nighttime view of the bridges leading into the southern tip of Manhattan. Underlit by the city, the sky was an eerie muddy purple. He remembered his visit with Kiki in To Bind an Egg, the moment he'd startled himself by announcing he lived in Dempsy.

The bathroom door opened and then Patty stood at the foot of the bed, wrapped in a thick kelly-green towel, her skin heat-mottled and vibrant from the shower.

Rocco felt his eyes brimming with fatigue, and he heard himself speaking in a druggy garble. 'I love you, you know that?'

Patty's voice floated back at him. 'Good. I love you too.'

Rocco closed his eyes and smiled. 'Good . . . good.'

He rolled on his side and crashed.

A few hours later, Rocco opened his eyes and saw a living, fully animated bust of Darryl Adams. In the gray-green stillness of the bedroom, the kid's head and shoulders sat on his night table. One of Darryl's eyelids was the shiny purple-black of a mussel shell, and a curl of bright pink flesh dangled like an inverted question mark from the entry wound on his chin.

Rocco couldn't move but he wasn't panicked. Darryl looked at him, shook his head and said, 'Controlled freedom.'

27

Early Friday morning, Strike opened his eyes and saw a black man in a white coat standing over him. The cops and the Latino with the bloody face were gone.

'You know how much blood we took out of your stomach?' The doctor sounded pissed at him.

Strike looked around for Rodney, remembered the tube in his dick and touched himself.

'It's out,' the doctor said. 'I asked you, do you know how much blood we took out of your stomach?'

Strike felt his face: no tubes in his nose either, although his throat still hurt. And he still had one tube in his arm.

'Two liters,' the doctor snapped, answering his own question.

'What's a liter?'

'How long has your stomach been hurting you?'

'Did they arrest him?'

'Arrest who?'

The doctor looked confused, and Strike shut up about it: this knifing situation was between him and Stitch.

The doctor leaned down. 'What the hell are you talking about? Do you know what a perforated ulcer is? Do you have the *slightest* idea what's been going on inside you?'

'Ulcer.' Strike looked blankly at the doctor, saw him glaring down with obvious disgust, and finally understood. He felt swallowed up in shame.

The doctor told Strike that he had almost died and should stay in the hospital for a few more days, for observation. But when Strike heard that his blood pressure was back to normal, he said he wanted to leave right away, so the doctor settled for giving him a brisk lecture on the consequences of not getting some follow-up treatment.

An hour later, carrying a referral slip to a gastrointestinal clinic and a bag full of assorted medicines, Strike walked into the sunlight. He felt rubber-legged, but at least the stabbing pain in his stomach was gone.

As he approached a line of gypsy cabs, he saw Rodney's Cadillac swing out from the curb. Rodney flung the passenger door open before he came to a full stop.

'What you do, wait out here aw-all night?' Strike wasn't comforted by the thought.

'Hey, you my man.'

'Yeah, thanks.'

'Dint I tell you to see my doctor? You see what happened?'

Rodney rummaged through Strike's bag as he drove, dumping out antacid tablets, a small bottle of Mylanta, some Tagamet, a stapled packet of Valiums.

'You get yourself all boiled up on that bench top, all crabbed over, sucking on that Yoo-Hoo shit, worried about this, worried about that.' Rodney threw the Valiums into his glove compartment. 'You smart, but you stupid too.'

Strike tuned him out, then tensed when Rodney pulled up in front of his apartment building. Strike had never told Rodney exactly where he lived.

'Why don't you just, like, lay out for a few hours, watch some TV, get your strength up. Come down to the store this afternoon, we can run a few ounces. Maybe get that boy Tyrone to do the legwork for you today.'

Rodney gave Strike a small shrug, as if to say that knowing about Tyrone was no big deal. But his message was clear: I am everywhere and into all things.

'From now on, I want you to re*lax*, you hear me?'

'Yeah.'

'Nobody lives forever, so you got to learn not to *give* a fuck. You understand what I'm saying?'

'Yeah.'

'So get on up and relax.'

'OK.' Strike reached for the door but Rodney put a hand on his arm.

'Yeah, I heard that Homicide came back on you again yesterday.'

Strike didn't answer.

'What's he, like your *boy*friend now?'

Strike sat curled up on Rodney's stool behind the counter, haunted by the previous night's hammering and braced for its full-blown return. But he had been out of the hospital for several hours now, and so far he seemed to be holding up pretty well. He had chugged down about half of the Mylanta. It had given him the shits but it didn't taste bad, and he thought maybe he would start drinking it instead of the Yoo-Hoo.

Rodney's beeper went off, and Strike tried to read Rodney's lips as he decoded the numbers.

Rodney looked over to the twelve-year-old mule playing pool by himself. 'Get ten for the benches,' he said, and the kid skipped on out to a safe house somewhere, disappearing through the doorway like a glint of light.

In his watery state, Strike imagined himself having to fly down the street on a bicycle like Rodney's go-boy. Just the thought of it made Strike sick again, made him feel like an old man.

Over the past two hours, Strike had met three more sets of customers: two white boys from a high school in Short Hills, who got an ounce that was cut to almost nothing; a black gym teacher from his own high school, who copped a half ounce while pretending he didn't recognize Strike; and a white corrections officer from County, who got an uncut ounce for half price – Rodney's way of getting a little insurance for when he had to go in next time. Strike took it nice and easy, walking over to Herman's apartment for every order, cataloguing all the faces and cuts for future reference, thinking that this was definitely better than the benches. But he missed the benches too; it made him feel off balance and unprotected to work or even hang out anywhere else. Besides, he couldn't let himself get too comfortable here. Next week he would be moving over to Ahab's, he and his perforated ulcer in all that sizzle and clamor, and that might be another story altogether.

'Yeah, here he comes,' Rodney said to Strike, gesturing to the street and laughing affectionately as Bernard, sad-faced and slump-shouldered, walked down the block toward the store. 'He up to a ounce now, but we'll see what happens *next* week.'

Bernard came in as Strike left to get the ounce.

'Oh Rodney, man, that bitch is fucked up, man. I'm gonna leave her for *good*, man.'

Rodney haw-hawed, bawling, 'Yeah? She told me she was leavin' *you*.'

Hearing the same conversation as last time, Strike felt comforted by the predictability of some people.

He walked three blocks to Herman's building, pondering the notion of a hole in his stomach. He tried to envision what it might look like. A slit, a tiny circle? As he unlocked the outside door, he heard someone tapping 'Shave and a Haircut' on a car horn. He spun around and saw Jo-Jo and his crew in their beat-up Delta 88. Jo-Jo urged him over with a toothy grin.

'This where you live, Strike?'

'No, not really.' Strike forced himself to maintain eye contact.

'So then what's with the keys?'

'I was just helping a friend.'

'Yeah? How so?'

'You know, he faw-forgot his car keys, so I was getting them for him 'cause he's at work.'

'No shit. Took the bus, huh?'

'I guess so.'

'Well, were you goin' in or comin' out?'

Strike hesitated. 'Comin' out.'

'Good.' Jo-Jo reached outside the window to open the rear door. 'We'll drive you back to Roosevelt.'

'That's OK.'

'C'mon, it's free.'

Strike slid in back. There were three other cops from the flying squad in the car. All ignored him except Jo-Jo, who leaned over the seat back.

'Yeah, we come down on Roosevelt last night? We grabbed some shitheads on the Dumont side but we came up empty by the benches.' Jo-Jo nodded. 'But I think we're gonna take another crack, like next Monday.'

Strike paused before answering, wondering how best to say it. 'Yeah, well, you know, I'm not working there anymore, so . . .'

'No? That's good, I guess, but you know what? We should probably stay friends anyhow.'

'Well, you know, that might not be necessary and all.'

The Delta 88 pulled up a block from the benches, as if out of respect for the delicacy of Strike's situation.

'Hey Strike.' Jo-Jo reached over the seat and put a hand on his kneecap. 'You could get popped just as easy coming out of your friend's *house* back there as anywhere else, you know what I mean?'

Strike felt the faint vibrations of another ulcer attack coming on.

Jo-Jo eyeballed him for a long minute, then extended a hand. 'Friends?'

Strike surveyed the lunchtime bench scene: the mothers, the babies,

Peanut absently spitting between his sneakers, Tyrone sitting on his chain perch, still wearing his batting glove. At least six other kids, including Horace, were wearing batting gloves now; Strike decided that Tyrone had started something, and that by next week every kid in Dempsy would be wearing one.

Strike saw Andre two buildings away, slowly making for the benches. He turned back to the street. Jo-Jo was still idling there, seemingly ignoring him, Strike thinking, Cops in front of me, cops behind me. He thought of Bernard waiting on his ounce, wondered how safe Herman's place was right now, whether he should go back to the store empty-handed or take a chance. He looked at Tyrone looking at him. Shit. Rodney had said it himself: Get that boy to run for you today.

Strike moved closer to the benches as Andre put his wristwatch in Horace's face.

'You got like ninety minutes left, my man,' Andre said. 'I said Friday two o'clock and I meant it. So you get your ass walking now over to the Western. I'll tell your mother where you going, but don't make me *find* you 'cause I will, and then it's gonna be a long weekend in that Youth House for you.'

Horace writhed under Andre's hovering gaze, his eyes scouring the ground until Andre turned and spotted Strike.

'How you feeling today?'

'Yeah, I'm OK.' Strike made a conscious effort to keep his eyes from straying toward Tyrone.

'You see how nothin's for free out here? You always looking over your shoulder, eating yourself up, then something goes *bang* on the inside.'

Strike nodded, scowling at the clouds. 'Yeah, well, I ain't even doing nothing ah-*out* here no more.'

'No?'

'Unh-uh. I'm not gaw-gonna be around here no more.'

Andre chewed his lower lip. 'How come I don't hear that as anything *posi*tive?'

'I don't know,' Strike said. ''Cause you don't. That's the way you are.'

Andre stared at him as if lost in thought, then let out a heavy hiss of surrender. He headed off in the general direction of his surveillance apartment.

Strike stood still for another minute or so, eyes skyward, playing it safe. He turned to check the street: Jo-Jo was gone. With a quick nod to Tyrone, Strike walked toward the Accord.

A few minutes later, Tyrone walked up the old lady's driveway, and
Strike noticed that he was wearing his new sneakers. When the kid
climbed into the car without a word, Strike swallowed an impulse to
compliment him on his footwear.

He drove by Roosevelt on the way over to Herman's. The benches
were empty now except for Horace, who was pacing, waving a sharp
stick and talking to himself. As they flew past, Tyrone ducked out of
sight, cracking a small smile as he did it. Strike barked out a dry laugh,
feeling a twinge of affection.

Outside Herman's house, Strike made a show of handing all his keys
to Tyrone, gesturing for the kid to lead the way and then following him
up the six flights to the apartment. At the sixth-floor landing Tyrone
balked, standing motionless outside the door until Strike had to say,
'C'mon, man, open up.' Tyrone cracked the lock as if the wrong twist
would blow up the building.

Herman sat in his easy chair by the sunlit window at the far end of
the apartment. His head was tipped back, his mouth gaping open like a
baby bird waiting on its mother.

Tyrone stood frozen in the vestibule, staring until Strike gave him
another nudge to proceed. He tipped down the hall, opened the padlock
and slipped inside Strike's room. At Strike's urging, Tyrone pulled open
the deep bottom drawer and came upon the nest of packed bags, the
brown bottle of cut and the triple-beam scale. He looked up at Strike,
his eyes dizzy with adventure.

'Don't lose them keys now,' Strike said. 'Them are the keys to the
kingdom.'

Speaking in a whisper in deference to the kid's fear of Herman, Strike
laid out the plan – how Tyrone would be his official runner, shuttling
between this room and the Accord, which would serve as their secret
checkpoint. Nervous about Tyrone's mother finding out about all this,
Strike asked him what he would say to explain the afternoon when he
got home tonight. But Tyrone shrugged the question off, saying that
his mother would be in Newark all day and into the evening doing
braid extension work for somebody, and that he was staying with his
half-blind grandmother.

Satisfied, Strike hustled back to Rodney's store and at last dropped off
Bernard's ounce. Over the course of the afternoon and into the early
evening, Strike went to the car eight times to dispatch Tyrone on runs,
even trusting him to put varying cuts on some ounces. Strike would
always find Tyrone sitting in the passenger seat of the car, stiff as a

mannequin, all the windows up despite the heat. Tyrone never let the key ring out of his hand, and Strike imagined him making a solemn ceremony of locking and unlocking everything in sight – the car, the building, the apartment, the room. He could see that the kid was having himself a ball despite his impassive demeanor; Tyrone would bust out of the Accord each time and race toward Herman's as if he had a little girlfriend waiting on him. Strike tried telling him to slow down, but the boy, trembling with freshness, simply could not be made to walk.

At seven o'clock, Strike came out of Rodney's Place for the last time. He was holding a two-thousand-dollar roll, less than a third of what was cleared on the package he'd picked up the day before. That was bad enough, but what really frustrated him was the news that it would be a while before they re-upped. As Strike was counting his cut, Rodney had mentioned that the Colombians he had decided to go with had disappeared, and his Egyptian or Israeli landlord was having supply problems of his own. So now it looked as if they were back to hunting down a good connection again, which meant Strike was back on the benches after all.

He strode up to the Accord and rapped on the driver's window. Tyrone jerked with surprise, his eyes a little wild. Recovering, he slid over to the passenger side, but Strike had to rap on the window again to get him to unlock the door.

On his way back to the old lady's driveway, Strike was in such a funk that at first he didn't notice how scared and straight-ahead silent Tyrone was. The kid looked as jumpy as he had on their first day together; he even held a hand over his gut as if he'd caught Strike's ulcer. Strike reminded himself that Tyrone was only a little kid, and wondered whether he was suffering a fear and remorse attack after the high of the day's work.

Strike tried to rally past Tyrone's silence. 'How *was* that?'

'What?'

'What you did.'

'OK.'

'It wasn't too much?'

'No.'

'Because you did good.'

Tyrone didn't answer, and Strike pulled into the driveway. He shut the engine and waited for a minute, watching Tyrone sit rigidly and hold his stomach. Strike reached into the glove compartment for the Mylanta, took a pull and screwed the cap back on slowly.

'What's wrong with your stomach?'

The kid gave a minute jerk of his shoulders.

'Then how come you're holding it?'

Another shrug.

Strike thought about offering him some Mylanta. 'You did *good*, you know that?'

Tyrone nodded.

'You were like real responsible.'

Feeling strangely guilty, Strike reached into his pocket for his roll and peeled off five twenties. 'This for you.'

Tyrone took the money blind, holding it in his hand, still silent.

Strike could tell that Tyrone was dying to get out of the car, but he didn't want to let him go just yet. Why was the kid so frozen?

'Ain't you gonna put that in your pocket? Somebody's gonna take you off if you walking with it out in your *hand* like that.'

Strike was suddenly seized by a dark thought. 'You dint put none of that shit in your *nose*, did you?'

Tyrone didn't turn, but his lips twisted in disdain.

'Good,' Strike muttered.

After another minute of staring at the kid's profile he gave up. 'Awright,' he said, hearing the pissy tone in his voice. 'Go on out.'

Strike watched Tyrone walk off stiffly and carefully toward the projects, his hand still pressed to his belt buckle. What the fuck was his problem? Strike didn't know, but he'd seen a sneaky flash of elation cross Tyrone's face as he got out of the car, and he could swear that the kid had fought down a quivering fit of nervous giggles when he got far enough away to think that Strike was no longer watching him.

As Strike walked from the driveway to the benches, he came up behind the big girl who'd been punched and robbed by Stitch the day before. Beside her was a tall guy wearing a fatigue jacket, both of them also headed toward the benches, tense and firm-faced. The guy held his coat together in a way that made Strike walk slower, put more distance between him and them, and finally Strike stopped, stood in the middle of the street and watched them steam ahead like warships.

There was nothing he could do. He didn't want to see what would happen, didn't want to get dragged into this as any kind of witness. But then he thought of Tyrone, pictured him sitting on his perch, and suddenly Strike found himself walking again, out in the street, hugging a line of parked cars, moving parallel to the couple but out of sight, hoping that Tyrone was on his way up to his grandmother's house. But as the benches came into view, Strike saw the kid rocking on his chain, still holding his gut, a stupid and strange grin on his face as he watched the clockers and their absentminded horseplay.

Horace still had the stick that Strike had seen him waving around earlier. Andre's deadline was gone by almost half a day now. Horace looked knotted and crazy: he was pacing, laughing shrilly, poking people with the stick.

The fat girl and the guy in the fatigue jacket turned in off the street and walked slowly toward the benches, both of them frowning, their heads swiveling as they scanned the clockers, looking for Stitch. Strike saw the frightened awareness come into Tyrone's face and body, nobody else sensing the danger, and he prayed that Tyrone wouldn't panic, wouldn't bolt or do anything to catch their eye.

The couple came to a dead stop ten feet in front of the benches, the guy putting a hand deep in his jacket. Now the crew took notice, some of them recognizing the girl, everybody getting quiet and nervous, not sure what to do. The girl looked from face to face, then zeroed in on Horace, hesitating as if she knew this one from the other day, but wasn't sure just how. The guy said, 'That him?' Horace had a trapped, guilty scowl on his face, and the guy took one step forward and said, 'You remember her?' Then he pulled out a handgun and fired, the puff and crack jerking Horace back on one side like a punch in the shoulder, making him retreat two steps and drop onto the bench in a perfectly normal position, his face still showing that perplexed scowl, just sitting there as if deep in thought. Everybody but Tyrone screamed and ran, the shooter standing quietly for a second, the girl touching his gun hand almost tenderly, and then both of them turned around and stalked off, the shooter looking back over his shoulder only once.

Strike was so entranced by the shooting that when the couple walked past him he didn't even have the presence of mind to duck behind a car. He saw that Tyrone still hadn't moved. The kid seemed calm, interested, as he looked across from his perch to Horace on the bench, the two of them the only souls in sight.

Not until he heard the sirens coming did Strike become unglued, finally deciding to make himself scarce. He glanced at the benches one last time and saw Horace muttering away, his shoulder blooming red. Tyrone seemed to be jarred loose from his chain by the sirens too, gingerly rising to his feet, still palming his gut as if holding something, looking impassive, almost bored. But as he watched Tyrone head off toward 6 Weehawken, Strike saw the cloudy stain on the kid's jeans, and even from this distance he could swear he smelled urine.

28

On Friday morning, Rocco sat across the desk from Reverend Posse in a wood-paneled office in the musty basement of the First Baptist Church. The reverend was sprawled in his vinyl-covered recliner, swiveling back and forth, looking far off and unhappy as he reflected on Victor Dunham.

The long room was lined with bracketed shelves filled with various Bibles, biblical encyclopedias and almanacs. Sprinkled among the books were National Youth Congress trophies and appreciation plaques from various civic associations. On the wall were framed photographs of the reverend embracing a number of clerics of various faiths, clipping a ribbon on a new bus for the gospel choir, accepting and handing over checks, clasping hands with Jimmy Carter and standing behind Jesse Jackson at a microphone somewhere. In the pictures the reverend appeared confident and spiritually flush, but to Rocco the man sitting across from him looked distant and aggrieved. The can of root beer and the dish of peach cobbler that his secretary had silently placed on his desk five minutes before remained untouched.

The reverend finally opened his mouth with a deep and weighted inhalation, as if the words were costing him dearly. 'See, my particular pain here, now, is that I can't tell you much about him, if you want to know the truth.'

'No, well, anything would help.' Somewhat intimidated by his surroundings, Rocco sat up straight in his hard wooden chair.

'See, a young man comes into this church, nineteen, twenty years old, I'm just glad to *see* him out there, and I don't want to scare him off.' The reverend leaned forward, elbows on his desk, his dry fingers sliding into one another.

'I don't want to push unless I am sure a person is ready to jump, but now my particular pain is that I didn't have enough faith in God, in regards to that kid, didn't have enough trust in what I was being told by God to *do*, which was reach out, come off the pulpit specifically to go over to that boy and say, "Hey, how are you, you enjoying the services?" I kept feeling, Wait for him to make the first move, this one looks like a bolter, he'll come to you. But I waited too long on him, didn't I?'

'I'm sure you got your hands full,' Rocco said.

'See, lots of people come in here for the first time, they don't have no concept of God, they're unchurched. So me up there, *I* become God because I'm tangible. Now, for a lot of these people that are burdened, they want to be helped. But how do you approach God? So I have to come down and break the ice, put my hand on them, say, "How are you? You look a little heavy in the face, sister, brother. You know, anytime you want to talk I'm always available." And I do *do* that, don't get me wrong, but with this Dunham kid, I just blew it, man. I just . . . I wanted him too. I remember noticing him first time he came in about four months ago. He came into church by himself, wearing a red sweater and a white tie. Yeah, and he sat near the back on the aisle, like in case he needed to make a quick getaway.'

Rocco returned the reverend's grin with one of his own.

'I guess I noticed him because of that red and white combination, but how many young black men do you think I get in here like that? I got women over men in here seven for every three, sometimes eight for every two, and a lot of the men are older, in their forties and up, so I *want* a young man like that, I *need* him. But that first service he just sat there real quiet. I don't think he looked at me even one time that morning. I don't know if you're at all familiar with the services in a church like this . . .'

'Me?' Rocco palmed his chest. 'No, not really.'

'Well, there's a point in the service, many points actually, when I'll say in so many words, "If you believe that Jesus has been good to you, if you think Jesus is on your side, shake your neighbor's hand and let him know." That's where I want the congregation to make a physical connection to each other, and most everybody does too, because there's that contact high you get in sharing the spirit. But Dunham, he was . . .'

The reverend drew his shoulders close, put his chin on his chest, shrinking himself. 'Well, he wasn't about that, and I tell you I was a little amazed to see him come back the next week, the week after that, and *every* week. He'd be all shelled up but every week there he was, and at the end of the service here I always do what is called opening the church, you know, invite people to come up and accept Jesus. I got my deacons up there like a welcoming committee, and I'm looking for people who want to take the next step, commit to the spirit inside them. I usually know who's gonna come up too, who's struggling to make that commitment. I'm real good at reading faces out there, and if I see someone struggling? I'll hang in until they feel me feeling them, until they feel God using me like a mirror catching the sun, you see?'

The reverend pointed up to the ceiling, his other hand thrust straight out from his chest to illustrate the angle of spiritual beaming. 'And I'll look right out at them eye-to-eye, say, "Jesus, there's someone out there who wants *so* bad to come into your arms. Lord, I'm just a mailman delivering your letter, and there's somebody *out* there who wants to come up here and read it, read the good news, someone who knows that next week might be too late, someone who wants to get sentenced to *life*, Jesus."'

He lowered his voice, talking to Rocco as if he was giving away secrets, but he winked as he did so, his look gently self-parodying. 'So then I tell them, "Come on up, come on up, and if you can't make it all the way, I'll come down, meet you halfway." And I come down to the aisles, stand right there in the pews . . .'

The reverend spread his arms and smiled. Rocco smiled back, enjoying the man, feeling the sweetness in him, the bigheartedness.

'And every week I get two, three new people to commit, and every week I looked out to that kid. I wanted him, he was definitely in my thoughts, but I guess I just wanted that *eye* contact first, I wanted to see an invitation there.' The reverend ran a hand across his mouth and his face became clouded again.

'Did he ever bring anybody with him to a service?'

'No, always by himself.'

'Never came in with his kids? His wife? His mother?'

'I thought he was all alone in this world until he came to me that day.'

'Did he make any friends here?'

'Not really, but I'll tell you, every week he always sat behind this one particular family, nice people, a young couple with two kids and a grandfather. They usually sit in the same pew every week and he always sat behind them. At first I thought nothing of it, but one week they came late and their customary spot was taken up, so they had to sit somewhere else. And then I saw Dunham get up and change his seat too, so he could *still* sit behind them. See what I'm sayin'?' The reverend smiled and opened his hands, and Rocco thought of the family photo under the scotch bottle at Hambone's.

'See, this is what I'm thinking right now.' The reverend hesitated, picking his words. 'This church, it's a middle-class church. We got parishioners here, not that they don't have their troubles, not that they don't have their memories of poverty, of drugs, of any and every kind of human misery out there – and not just memories either, OK? But most people are doing pretty good out there now. I got policemen, educators, businessmen, social workers. We have us a large body of accomplishment in here, and I know Victor Dunham, he's a working man, he was doing everything he could for himself, for his family, but I'm thinking now, maybe what this church, what the church experience was about for him was just *being* in here on a Sunday morning, coming in nice and early, everybody looking fresh, feeling glad to be here, dressed nice. There's always this rush of something when people come here for services, especially right before we start – excitement, hopefulness, people saying hello to each other, everybody all powdered and sharp. I got to tell you, that's *my* favorite time of the day maybe because I haven't done no work yet, but right then the spirit is like pure oxygen.'

The reverend's secretary ducked in to see if he was finished with his snack, made a face at Rocco as if he was keeping the man from his nourishment. 'I'm good, I'm good,' said the reverend. His hand hovered over the dish and soda can, waiting for her to close the door.

Rocco realigned himself in his chair and raised his chin to signify a shift in focus. 'So, what happened that day he came to you?'

The reverend shook his head. 'Well, the ironic thing is, I opened up the service talking about that boy, that Adams boy that got killed.'

'Yeah? What you say, you remember?'

'Well, he had just got killed at the beginning of that weekend, so I asked people, "Do you think that that boy *knew* when he woke up Friday morning that this was his day to die? He was probably fit as a fiddle – young, strong, healthy. But you never know when it's going to be too late to get in on God's lifetime guarantee. You never know, so you best be ready, because night is coming, night is coming for us all."'

He caught himself getting into a pulpit rhythm and smiled at Rocco. 'See, maybe you don't have a condition, but you *might* have a situation.'

'How did he react to that?'

'I didn't notice, but later on, well, the sermon I gave that day was on Caleb, Caleb and the mountain.'

Rocco caught an appraising look from the reverend and nodded encouragingly, hoping his ignorance wasn't too obvious.

'See, Caleb was one of Moses' spies that went into Canaan to check out the Promised Land. The first year in the desert, the children of Israel came upon Canaan and Moses sent in twelve spies, and ten of them came out saying forget it, we can't go in there, we can't conquer the land. They had brought out giant grapes, grapes so big they had to carry them between two men on a staff, and they said the people are too strong, the cities are walled, you got' – the reverend counted off on his fingers – 'Amalekites, Hittites, Jebusites, Canaanites, Amorites, *and* you got the Anakites, and the Anakites were giants, physical giants eleven to thirteen feet tall. And ten out of the twelve spies came out saying' – the reverend drew himself up for the quotation – '"We were in our own sight as grasshoppers, and so we were in their sight."'

Rocco shifted his weight, nervous about Bible stories.

'Ten out of twelve came out saying, "We be not able to go up against the people," came out saying, "It is a land that eateth up the inhabitants thereof." But the two *other* spies, Joshua and Caleb, they waved that nonsense off, and Caleb said, "Let's go up at once and possess it, for we are well able to overcome it," because Caleb kept faith in God's promise not just to deliver them from Egypt but to deliver them to the Promised Land. See, it's pick up *and* deliver.'

The reverend winked at Rocco again, then continued. 'Well, the children of Israel turned their backs on Canaan. They ignored Caleb, they despaired of God. They even wanted to return to Egypt, and God became so angry at them, and at these ten other spies that thought Canaan could not be taken, that he sent them back out into the desert for thirty-nine more years, until every one of them over the age of twenty had died. God said, "Your carcasses shall fall in the wilderness." But he spared Caleb, saying, "Because he had followed me fully, him I shall bring into the land and his seed possess it." And when Joshua conquered the land like God had promised, Caleb was eighty-five years old, the spy who kept his faith, and when Joshua's warriors were dividing up the conquered territory, they turned to Caleb and asked him, "Old man, what do you want, some nice rich bottomland?" Caleb said, "Give me that mountain there, Hebron." And all the young bloods turned to him and said, "Why do you want that mountain? There's nothing but trouble on that mountain. There's Amalekites still fighting, and Anakites, *giants* in there. Why don't you take some nice rich easy parcel, old man? You earned it." But Caleb turned to these young men and said, "I want that mountain because it would please God for me to tame it." See, Caleb, as old as he was, was still ready to fight, to roll up his sleeves and do God's work, just as he was thirty-nine years before. "We were in our own sight as grasshoppers, and so we were in their sight."'

He paused, savoring the passage. 'And then I tell my congregation of Caleb's commitment, his ever-readiness to do battle with the giants, an eighty-five-year-old senior citizen, and I ask them how about us, how many of *us* are willing to roll up our sleeves and do battle with the giants right outside our own church, the giants of drugs, alcoholism, poverty – how many of *us* have the commitment to bring peace to the mountain that is this city, because it would please God, because it is doing battle *for* God.'

He looked at Rocco expectantly. Rocco nodded, surprised to find himself moved by the story. 'Yeah,' he said awkwardly, 'it's like I guess people sometimes feel like grasshoppers against the drug problem out there, right?'

The reverend aimed a finger at Rocco's face. 'Exactly! Hey man, you got some preacher in you!'

Rocco blushed. This guy was good.

'See, with my congregation, it would be easy to turn this church into some fortress of gratitude, but it ain't just about coming together and giving Him thanks. No, it's going out and doing His work because, man, if this city ain't Caleb's mountain, I don't know what is, and those giants out there are just stomping people into the ground.'

The reverend took a long breath. 'But anyways, after the service I came down here to this office, and I always got a million people wantin' to see me, a million projects going, but I saw, out in the hall' – he squinted as if looking through a narrow crack in the door – I saw Dunham out there and I thought, I got him, thank you Jesus, I got him, and I was so worried about him changing his mind and leaving before he had his chance to come see me – you know, to have second thoughts. But so I got all the people out of my office and I went to that door myself and I said, "Hey, c'mon in," and he came in, quiet, took your seat there, and I asked him, "How'd you like the service today?" He said, "Not too much," and I said, "How come?" He said, "Hey, I live in the Roosevelt Houses. I got two kids and a wife, I manage a Hambone's. Man, you talking about going out and taking on the giants, that's all I do is take on the giants, six days a week and half a day on Sunday take on giants." And then he said, "I thought church is supposed to be a sanctuary. I come in here, it's like you telling me to go back out there," and he gave me this little laugh. But I could see the beating in his face, the weight, so I said, "Well, how are you doing out there with them giants?" He said, "Sometimes I'm winning, sometimes they're winning," and I didn't exactly know what he was talking about. I thought maybe he was struggling with a drug problem. But as soon as he said that, he reached into his pocket and came out with something wrapped in foil, and at first I thought it was food and I was confused, but then I heard that *thunk* it made, and I know that *thunk* sound because I had heard it once before, right on this desk about five years ago, and as soon as I heard it I knew I had waited too long.'

The reverend paused, chewing his lips. 'So then he said to me, "You know that guy you was talking about that got killed on Friday?" And I just thought, My God, why did I wait? Why did I wait? I said, "What happened?" and he told me how that boy had startled him walking across the lot and he shot him and . . . You know when something like this happens, I got to be like you, I got to be a cop. I want the truth because I don't want no kid using me like a patsy, using me like for self-protection, making me part of his surrender package like for publicity. I don't want to be manipulated because of my collar, you know what I'm saying? Somebody tells me they did something, I want the whys of it, I want *all* of it, I want corroboration on it, 'cause if I get that, I'll go the distance. But so when he told me what happened, *how* it happened, I knew right away he was lying, and as much as I wanted that kid in my church, I had no choice but to say, "Man, you are lying out your ass." But the funny thing was, I wasn't sure which way the lying went – much worse than what he said or, well, not less than what he said, but . . . ' The reverend squinted at Rocco. 'You remember when you came in that day, I told you this don't make no sense?'

'Yup.'

'That boy's supportin' a wife, two kids, comin' to church, working hard as he was, then he goes and commits a crime like that and lays some see-through story on my lap. And when I told him I thought he was lyin', he just walls up, won't say another word about it. So I don't know, I just don't know. But there he was, giving it up, so I told him to pray for God's forgiveness. I told him I would pray for him, and I did, too, right then and there, and I told him to try and forgive himself, because even if God forgives you, you ain't getting no inner peace unless *you* forgive you.' He stopped, then pointed at Rocco. 'I had a woman who came in to me once, she had stabbed her husband to death in his sleep. He'd been beating her for years, a bad guy, bad guy.'

'Otis Randall?'

'Yeah, Otis, his wife, Janelle Randall.'

'Yeah, I remember that. She beat it, though. I tell you the truth, I was glad she did.'

'The law forgave her, I believe that God forgave her, but her *dreams* – for years she had some horrible dreams, you see? So I told him, "You got to forgive yourself," and I felt uncomfortable about that because I knew he was lying to me about the circumstances, but you know you can't lie to yourself. And then, well, finally I said to him, "And you got to make it right with the law."'

'"Render unto Caesar what is Caesar's."' Rocco had no idea where that came from, but the reverend snapped his fingers, gave him a heartsick but game smile.

'See, I *told* you you got some preacher in you.'

Rocco felt another blush rising. 'Well, so, what did he say then? Anything?'

The reverend looked at Rocco and shrugged. 'He says to me, "Do with me what I got coming, Reverend. That's why I'm here."'

Back in the office a good four hours before his shift was due to begin, Rocco found the ballistics report on the gun that Victor had surrendered. The ejection markings on the cartridges recovered from the scene matched the markings on cartridges ejected in a test firing from the same Browning 9 mm automatic – which meant the gun was the gun. Rocco felt relieved: at least he hadn't locked up the kid with the wrong weapon. But now he had to figure out how and when the real shooter had passed the gun to Victor. Maybe in a day or so he'd be ready to pay another visit to Strike.

Rocco took up the subpoenaed phone log from Rudy's and began calling the numbers, hoping that one of them would somehow tie Strike in tighter. The first number on the list was in the O'Brien Houses – no one home. The second was to a pay phone on JFK. Rocco talked to a drunk who kept calling him Chucky. The third was to Newark, a little kid answering, then dropping the receiver, letting it hang and swing against a wall. And the fourth was that thirty-five minute call to Victor's home.

Putting down the phone log, Rocco fought off a baffling surge of anger and tried to collect his thoughts. He had been so focused on Strike lately, so pumped to nail him, that he hadn't thought much about Victor's role in all this. He had no trouble believing that the kid was innocent, but he was also a liar. Rocco still wasn't sure what was behind Victor's surrender. He didn't think it was a promise of cash, so it had to be either a threat from his brother that was worse than possible jail time or some demented vision of self-sacrifice. But whatever the motives, Victor Dunham had used both Rocco and the reverend as unwitting co-conspirators in the obstruction of justice, and Rocco deeply resented being played for a jerk.

For a hot minute Rocco considered dropping the entire investigation. No one in the squad was even asking about it anymore, while he could think of little else – the classic mission syndrome. But then he thought of all the goggle-eyed nights he usually spent in here, all the spacy dinners, and then thought of how much this job had brought him back to himself during the past week. He picked up the log, found the kid's home number and reached for the phone, thinking, Victor Dunham might have used him, but to be honest, he was using the kid right back.

Rocco rode up in the elevator of 41 Dumont with a dying woman. She was thirty or thirty-five, emaciated and with glazed eyes, wearing a Bart Simpson T-shirt and hugging a carton of cigarettes. Her little daughter, beside her, stared at the boxed cake Rocco held out from his hip like a helmet. He debated with himself about whether to crack the seal and give this orphan-to-be a treat. But he didn't think walking in on Victor's mother with a used gift would go unnoticed. She had been both wary and incurious when he called her from the office and attempted to seduce her into letting him come by. He had promised 'good news and no questions,' but she put him off, telling him she was busy and that he could just give her the news over the phone. In the end he had bluffed her out, telling her it was official business, as if she had no say about whom she admitted into her home.

When she opened the door, Victor's mother gazed at him as if he was a bill collector. Rocco was again stunned by her buggy eyes. Struggling to recover his beefeater smile, he held out the box of chocolate cake. She ignored the gift, and Rocco was stuck standing there, waiting for her to step back so he could come in.

'Where's the kids?' He put some disappointment into his voice, showed her the cake again. 'I hope you're not on a diet or nothing.'

Rocco was a firm believer in chocolate cake. Sponge cake, crumb cake and various pastries all had their fans and detractors, but he had never met a resident of the projects who could resist chocolate cake, and there was nothing like sitting down at someone's table over food to get them relaxed and talking. But Victor's mother seemed unmoved by the offering, barely glancing at it. She headed for the kitchen, leaving him standing in the middle of the living room alone.

The apartment was spotless and silent, the late afternoon sun giving the walls a glow, the air redolent with the chemical fruitiness of some kind of room spray, the only sign of disarray a big sprawl of coins on the dining room table, maybe fifty dollars' worth of silver and pennies.

'So how's Victor doing?' Rocco called as he went to the photo cabinet and picked up a framed studio portrait of a heavyset thirtyish man. He was dressed in soul style from the late sixties or early seventies, with a high Afro, mustache and sideburns, and a floral print shirt with long collar points lying over a solid brown vest. Rocco assumed he was Strike and Victor's father.

He returned the photo to its niche as Victor's mother came back into the living room with one dessert plate, one fork and one napkin, no coffee, and set them down on the small dining table. Taking a seat in front of the mountain of coins, she nodded for Rocco to sit and started sliding quarters into a red ten-dollar coin sleeve, making up change rolls for the bank.

Rocco felt like a horse's ass, eating his own cake in this lady's house, but he had no choice. In fact, he had to admire the move, her ability to throw him off guard with his own props.

'Tips?' He nodded to the mountain of money.

'Uh-huh.' She refused to look at him, her nimble fingers flashing, her upper body rising and falling with the effort to draw breath. She had a scooped-out look to her that Rocco hadn't noticed before, a slight coat-hook curve from her shoulder blades to the nape of her neck.

'Where do you work?'

'Restaurant.'

Rocco sighed and put down the fork. 'Look, here's my problem. I'm the guy who took Victor's confession. And I got everything cold except the motive. I can't figure out *why* Victor would do this, *why* he'd throw his life away. I spoke to everybody I could about him – the reverend from First Baptist, the Hambone's people, the people he worked for in New York, you name it. Everybody said the same thing. He's the finest kid they ever knew, the absolute finest.'

'So what's this *good* news?' She spoke to her furious fingers, asking the question quick and low as if it might earn her a blow.

'Welp, I've been thinking, and you know what?' He paused, trying to get her to look at him for this. 'I don't think he killed this guy. I just don't think he did it.'

He got no reaction. Nothing, just the fingers flashing silver, that tortured look of concentration. Rocco hesitated, completely thrown. He had thought that at least she would make eye contact, if not jump right out of her seat, give it a few hallelujahs.

'And, ah, I think that the person who *did* kill this guy is still out there, running around free, and . . .' Rocco faltered, confused. 'Is there anything you could tell me, any way you could help me on this?' He waited: still nothing. 'I mean, tell me what *you* think. Because I know he didn't do it, just like *you* know he didn't do it.'

She gave him a fast, fuming shrug, then went back to the coins.

'See, my problem is, it's easy to take credit for the solve right now, but I'm not interested in arresting the wrong man. I clear a hell of a lot of cases, and I don't need this. What I want to do is arrest the *real* killer, and if I can do that, Victor is a free man. *That's* the good news.'

She rose from the table, a half-dozen coin rolls standing open-ended in a tiny skyline. Rocco watched her as she walked across the room, opened a drawer and took out an inhaler. Turning her back, she took two quick pulls, hunching her shoulders each time.

'Can I ask you something?' Rocco waited for her to turn around so he could read her face. 'When he called here Friday night, what did you talk about?'

'He didn't call here Friday night.' She gave him her back again, puttering around in the open drawer.

'Well, I just happened to go over some phone records from a bar across the street from the incident, and *some*body called up this house from there at about nine-thirty, talked for like a half hour, and I just assumed it was Victor.'

'Nope.' She made busy movements with her hands in the drawer as if folding a pile of napkins.

'OK,' Rocco said, reading the lie. 'So who *did* call, if you don't mind me asking.'

'I don't know. I was working.'

'So who would've – '

'I don't know. I was out.'

'Would ShaRon – '

'Maybe.'

She said it quickly, the word bitten off, and again Rocco knew she was lying. ShaRon hadn't talked to Victor that night. Remembering her mute immobility during his first visit here, Rocco doubted that ShaRon and Victor talked much at all anymore. No, Victor had spent thirty-five minutes talking to this lady right here. But what the hell had they talked about? What does she know?

Rocco tried to think on his feet, recalling how Thumper described going toe-to-toe with her a year ago. Maybe she's protecting Strike, the prodigal son, protecting him the same as Victor was protecting him.

'Did your son ever see a psychiatrist?' Rocco asked gently.

'No.' She returned to the table, to her coin work.

'Is there any reason why your son would take the blame for anybody else? Someone he was close to? Someone he felt responsible for?'

She said nothing. Exasperated, Rocco drew her a picture with giant crayons. 'Maybe there was someone he let down, someone he was supposed to be a role model for, and maybe this person didn't turn out so good, and maybe Victor felt like it was *his* fault that this other person turned out this way. And then by making this incredible sacrifice, he'd be giving this other kid one more chance to straighten out his life, you know?'

Rocco looked at her expectantly, waiting for her to punch in the name. Finally she met his eyes. 'I know he told you that boy attacked him. I don't see why you don't believe him.'

Running out of guile, feeling he had nothing to lose now, Rocco decided to drop it right in her lap. 'Well, look . . . I thought I was coming over here with some good news but, ah, do you know what the word on the street is about this?'

'I'm not *about* the street,' she said, fast and angry.

'Yeah, well, the word on the street is that Victor is taking the weight on this for his brother. For Ronnie.'

The woman smiled, the first smile Rocco had ever seen from her.

'Why are you smiling?'

Her voice became almost conversational. 'Well, now wait a minute. I'm not gonna pretend like I don't know what he's *doing* out there, but' – she gave him a dry laugh – 'Ronald has his limitations.'

'And what does *he* have to say about what happened? Did you talk to him?'

Her hands stopped moving, her eyes flew up, and then her words came in such a rush that Rocco imagined that someone else had just inhabited her body. 'Let me tell you, about a year ago? Ronald, he started getting into that business down there. I called him out on it, he says to me, "But Mommy, I'm making it the only way they *let* a black man make it," and

I said, "I don't wanna *hear* that garbage. Who do you think you're talking to with that? Your brother ain't doin' that, your father didn't do that." He says to me, "Well, that was their prerogative. Besides, Victor ain't making it, he just working himself down, he ain't goin' nowhere, that ain't *making* it," and I said, "Well, do you really consider selling that poison making it?" And I remember he couldn't even look me in the eye. He just said, "I just want to make enough money to get out of here, then I'm out of it," and I said to him, "Oh yeah? How much money is *enough*? What do you mean by enough . . . How long do you think Rodney Little been at it, how many years, how much money do you think Rodney Little has made, and *he* can't get out of it, he never seen enough, and I bet you he always talks about getting out, always talks about enough, huh?" See, I said that to him because I know Rodney last year got to be like a father to him because their real father died when they were little, and I should have never let him go to work in that candy store, but my boys always worked, both of them, ever since they were fifteen, sixteen. But Rodney takes advantage of these – some of these kids without fathers. Rodney gets into their heads, so I stayed on him that time because I know all that "I'm making it the only way a black man can make it" nonsense, that's just Rodney inside his head, and I told him, "I don't want you living in this house if you're out there doing that," and he says to me, "Mommy, let me tell you something. Victor's always talking about moving out. Victor's got six thousand dollars saved up to move, it took him two years and two jobs. I got me six thousand dollars in a *month*." I say to him, "But someone come up to Victor, ask him, 'What did you do for that money?' Victor says, 'I manage a restaurant, I do security work.' Victor can answer with his head high because he didn't hurt nobody to make it." Ronald says to me, "I never forced nothing on nobody." I say, "Ronald, look me in the eye and tell me what you do. What's its *name*. Say it. Say it out loud. What do you do? Give me its *name*." He couldn't do it. He couldn't look me in the eye and he couldn't say it. He just got up, said, "Mommy, next time I come into this house, I'm gonna be rich and I'm gonna be out of it. I'm gonna be flush and legitimate. I'm gonna come up and take you away from here, take *all* a you, and Victor's still gonna be counting his pennies." And I just said to him, "You ain't takin' me *nowhere* on drug-bought money," and that was that.'

She paused, exhaling slowly and passing the heel of her hand under a dry eye. 'That was the last time I talked to him, and I won't even walk out that end of the projects, because I know he's out there doin' his business, and I don't ever want to *see* that. He's a young man and maybe he's got to do his young man things, make his young man mistakes, and I hope one of those mistakes don't kill him. But he's also a young man on his own now, and I can't take responsibility for his decisions anymore. I pray he'll come back to himself one day, but . . .'

Gesturing, she accidentally backhanded a few open-ended coin rolls, spilling the money back on the table. She took in the damage and, without blinking, began to restack the pennies and dimes. Rocco watched her, confounded: Not two words in defense of Victor, but this other little scumbag rates a whole speech.

She took another deep breath. 'What I'm trying to say to you is, I know Ronald's out there doing bad things. *He* knows he's doin' bad things, because he was brought up in this house, and that is causing him no end of pain out there. But one thing . . . Ronald, he might be an angry kid, he *is* an angry kid, but he ain't no killer. This I would lay my life on.'

'Do you think Victor's a killer?'

'Let me ask you something,' she said, nodding to Rocco's sport jacket. 'You carry that gun. Someone's coming up on you in a alley or out of the dark. You go to defend yourself and you shoot that person. *You.*' She pointed at Rocco. 'Does that make you a killer?'

Rocco was so baffled by this woman that for a moment he stared at her as if taking her question seriously. 'Can I ask you something? And I hope I'm not out of line here, but . . . I asked you if you talked to Ronald, to Strike, about this, and you come back at me with this, this long, heartfelt candidness, telling me all about him, how he's a good kid in a bad head and all, defending him – well, not defending, ex*plaining* him. And I also know that last year when Victor got into that stupid shoving match with the Housing cop? I know how you went to bat for him, how you literally took your life in your hands in the street, in the police station. I mean, I know you're a fighter, a striver, I can tell, and that thing last year came to nothing, it was a glorified shoving match, but there you were, like a tiger for your son. But that was nothing, this is *homicide*, and I'm the arresting officer, I'm not Thumper. This is *me*, and I'm coming to you. I'm saying I think your son Victor is innocent. I'm on *your* side . . .'

Rocco paused, his arms spread in bewilderment. 'Mrs Dunham, the stakes are so high. He could go to jail for thirty years on this. Where *are* you . . .'

She was staring at Rocco's shirt, her mind miles away, and each word came out chiseled and heavy. 'Victor is a beautiful, hardworking boy.

He don't lie. If he *said* he did it, then he *did* it. If he *said* it came about the way it came about, then that's what happened. He told you it was self-defense . . .' Her eyes came up at him with a burning dryness much more terrible than tears. 'Why don't you just believe him?'

In the long silence that followed, Rocco heard the echoing steps of her grandchildren walking to the apartment from the elevator. The idea of continuing this conversation with the apartment filled with children struck him as unbearable, and Rocco rose, frowning with frustration. He dropped his calling card on the table, thanked her for the cake and her time, and left her to her stacking, her fingers flying with the intimate precision of a lifelong weaver working her loom.

Standing near Big Chief, who was studying an apartment layout for the 'H' line in the O'Brien Houses, Rocco slipped on a borrowed bulletproof vest, a white one, with a drawing of a samurai across the chest. He was surprised at how light it felt. Either the vests had been improved since the last time he needed to wear one or he had gotten that much more padded himself.

'Get us the *Hat*,' Thumper drawled as he stuck two light bulbs in a nine-by-twelve manila envelope and jammed the flat half deep into the back of his pants. Some people would sit in the dark for six months before they'd replace a bulb, and the last thing a cop wanted to do after plowing through an apartment door was search a bedroom by flashlight.

The Fury office was in the midst of a feeding frenzy. The four Housing cops, Mazilli and two Jersey City detectives – everybody was dribbling Drake's cakes over their vests, drinking cold coffee or flat soda, grabbing petrified slices of Swiss cheese, eating anything, Rocco the only one whose anticipation-pump blocked his appetite.

One of the Jersey City detectives flipped through a magazine from the milk crate of porn, then ran off to the john down the hall. Crunch followed after him to piss for the third time in an hour as Big Chief folded up and packed the Rabbit, a ten-pound pneumatic crowbar that could pop a door off a frame, make it fly straight back five feet before it even fell.

'Get us the *Hat*!' Smurf readjusted the Velcro cinches on his vest, which was white like Rocco's, this one adorned with a grinning skull pierced by a hypodermic needle from crown to jawbone. Rocco knew they'd all get to the heart medicine a little early tonight; that was part of the ritual anytime they had to serve paper, go through a door. So he went to the refrigerator and chugged down a pint of half-and-half to coat his stomach for the celebration to come.

It was eight o'clock, about four hours since his visit with Victor's mother. Bugged all afternoon by the mystery of the Dunham brothers, Rocco had felt grateful for the call to action when it came through. These days, he rarely did any physical or even remotely dangerous police work, and tonight's job seemed just the thing to cleanse his blood of too many dinners, too many drinks and not enough fear. For ten years, first as a uniform and then as an anticrime cop, Rocco got a daily jolt of adrenaline; now, he had almost forgotten what that rush was like.

The Jersey City detectives had come to Dempsy with an arrest warrant for one Moses Worthy. Worthy had murdered Daniel Burgos, a k a Papi, and wounded José Obregon – the survivor giving up the shooter from his Bronx hospital bed in exchange for downgrading an attempted homicide charge that he was facing himself. Jersey City had caught the homicide even though Burgos had died three feet over the state line on the New York side of the Holland Tunnel; since the victim was traveling from New Jersey, where the crime had obviously been committed, New York had thrown the case back across the river. When the Jersey City cops got to work, they found two sets of blood stains in the dead man's car, suggesting that the victim had not been alone when he was shot. Within forty-eight hours, the detectives had traced Burgos, a Dominican kilo dealer, back to his Bronx neighborhood and found his bodyguard, Obregon, recovering in a nearby hospital from what he'd claimed were self-inflicted gunshot wounds in the lower back. After a little bargaining, Obregon gave up a street name for the shooter – Buddha Hat – and a crime scene location, off Cooper Street by Kelso Salvage, city of Dempsy.

Armed with only a moniker, the Jersey City detectives then went to Dempsy BCI, where they were the beneficiaries of the compulsive work habits of Bobby Bones, the ID King. Never having spent any time in County, even on an overnight, Buddha Hat shouldn't have had a mug shot on file. In fact, there was only one charge on his sheet: a motorcycle cop had stopped him one night six months before on suspicion of being a nineteen-year-old black kid driving a brand-new Volvo. The cop ran a radio check right on the street, which yielded a contempt of court warrant for a failure to pay thirteen hundred dollars in parking tickets. The cop took him down to BCI for processing, and when bail was set at the cost of the parking tickets, Buddha Hat produced the money after making a phone call. But then Bobby Bones happened to look up from his typewriter as Buddha Hat was heading for the door. Knowing all about the Hat and his reputation as a drug enforcer for Champ, Bones detained him for prints and a mug shot anyhow, the ID King's dream being to create a jacket for every adult male in the city.

Earlier today, the Jersey City detectives had offered up their moniker and made Bobby Bones's week. They walked out of BCI with Moses Worthy's picture and the mug shots of five other locals who looked vaguely like him, got Obregon to pick Buddha Hat out of the photo array, then traveled back to Dempsy BCI to get an arrest warrant. And two hours ago they had walked into Dempsy Homicide, looking for some help on the arrest, and found Mazilli and Rocco. Mazilli, who also knew all about the Hat, came up with the idea of going in with the Fury, since O'Brien was their domain and the herd hanging around outside the building would be fooled into thinking it was just another Fury roll.

The preparations for the raid complete, Rocco and the others left the office. They took two cars, both Fury bombs, with the Housing cops divided up and fronting the four sport jackets to mask the mission. The plan was to drive up on either side of the breezeway of Buddha Hat's building, enter front and rear, and take separate stairways to make everybody in the lobby think it was just a vertical pincers patrol. They would then rendezvous at the third-floor elevator bank and ride up to twelve, where the Hat lived with his grandmother.

Rocco rode with Big Chief, Thumper and Mazilli, their car leading the war party to the crest of the hill overlooking the projects. Everybody looked down on a stuttering line of cars being served bottles and bags around the curved driveway of Buddha Hat's building, and Rocco felt like an Indian in a western, pausing on a butte above a small wagon train before swooping in – except that there were only two cars here and a whole nation of enemies down below.

'There's the fucking guy *I* want.' Big Chief pointed out Champ waddling around the breezeway, dressed all in white. 'He's got a pit bull named after me.'

'Me too.' Thumper turned to the back seat. 'Arouff.'

Rocco threw a gum wrapper out the window. 'I hate to bring this up, but did anybody call to see if this yomo's even *home* now?'

Big Chief and Mazilli exchanged glances, gave a quick shake of their heads. Rocco rolled down his window and asked the cops in the other car, drawing only shrugs.

Rocco got the phone number from the warrant and wrote it down on the back of his hand. 'Anybody got a quarter?'

Big Chief handed over five nickels. 'I hope he paid his phone bill.'

'He paid it.' Mazilli lit a cigarette. 'It's in his grandmother's name. The kid's always coming into the store buying her groceries. Buddha Hat be good to his grandmother.'

Rocco retreated half a block to a pay phone and dialed while reading his knuckles.

The grandmother picked up on the third ring. 'Who.'

'Nyeah . . .' Rocco put a yammery drawl on it. 'Hat be dere?'

'Hat sleepin'. Who this?'

'This Tyrone.' Rocco threw a thumbs-up sign to the cars.

'He sleepin'.'

'I'll call back when he awake.' He hung up the phone, feeling a little skippy in the gut, savoring the realness of what he was about to do, glad that everything else in his mind had been put on hold.

As the Fury junkers descended into the crescent, the line of customer cars peeled out, a few scraping bumpers, one of them almost tearing in half a server who was leaning into its open window. Most of the clockers flew into the heart of the projects. Getting out of the car, Big Chief and Thumper stood to their full heights, Big Chief carrying the Rabbit in a vinyl gym bag and pulling his jacket close to hide his vest. Champ bellowed at them good-naturedly through cupped hands: 'Five-oh! Five-oh!'

Big Chief nodded to Champ as he walked swiftly to the breezeway. 'How's my *dog*, there, fat boy?'

'He's shittin' up my new wall-to-wall carpet.'

'That's too bad, that's too bad.' Big Chief and Thumper broke into a run pretending to chase the clockers. Rocco and Mazilli were right behind them.

'I'm gonna trade him in for a *pussy*cat,' Champ yelled after them as they hit the stairs. Looking back at Champ, Rocco saw a hesitant curl coming into his brow and sensed that the guy knew something was up other than the usual nickel-and-dime bullshit.

The climb to the third floor was clogged with little kids and teenagers. Rocco held his breath against the piss stink and saw the big eye come into the faces of the older kids coming down the stairs, who flattened against the bannister to make way for the Fury and the sport jackets. Rocco was a little worried that one of these kids would figure it out and somehow warn Buddha Hat, but they mostly looked relieved at being bypassed.

On the third floor, they had to wait for the elevator for five minutes, everybody nervous about being seen now, congregating here and losing time, the adrenaline having no outlet. Rocco suddenly had to pee so bad he was doing a jig. When the elevator finally opened, it was full of little kids and women. Big Chief took over, making everybody get out. The people crabbed and groaned, one woman saying, 'How you like I come to *your* building tell *you* to get out of the elevator,' to which Thumper replied, 'He lives in the basement, Mommy.'

The ride up was as slow as an old judge. Rocco, rolling his eyes, tasting his bladder, unsnapped his hip holster, the sharp sound getting everybody's attention.

'Who's the point man?' Big Chief asked.

One of the Jersey City cops, who was tall and muscular with a misaligned toupee, said, 'I got it,' but Rocco surprised himself by saying, '*I'm* point.' He looked at the Jersey City cop with an apologetic shrug: 'It's my town.' He didn't believe what he'd just said – it sounded like a line from a Sinatra tune or a bad movie – but he wanted to ride this flashback for all it was worth, earn his hangover.

The elevator stopped on eight and a thin, pock-marked girl took a step in, looked up and voluntarily retreated to the stairs without anything coming into her face. But when it stopped on ten, the teenager waiting there backed away with a little too much light in his eyes, and Thumper reached out and pulled him in.

'Take a ride, Skeeter.'

The kid became wild-eyed. 'Yo Thumper. I ain't telling nobody nothing.'

'Nothing about what?' Thumper handcuffed him to the handrail.

'Aw man, now Hat gonna think I'm *in* on this.' The kid looked as if he was going to cry.

'Relax. I'll cut you loose before we take him out.'

'Aw man.'

'Ssh.' Thumper held a finger to his lips.

When the elevator opened on twelve, Big Chief led the way down the hall, and everybody took out his gun. Rocco was amazed that he was holding it in his hand for anything but a cleaning, then began feeling nostalgic for the arrest of Buddha Hat even before it had gone down.

Big Chief dropped into a squat in front of 12H and unzipped the gym bag. Rocco stood behind Big Chief, the other cops forming a sloppy V in back of him. Rocco stared at the door, feeling the high whine of his nerves, worried most of all about getting shot from behind during the chaos of the rush inside. None of the cops here were very experienced in what they were about to do, but no one had even considered bringing along a SWAT or Emergency Services crew.

Big Chief got a grip on the Rabbit and started feeling the seams of the door, looking for the best point of insertion. Rocco whispered, 'Try turning the fucking doorknob,' and just then the door opened inward as if on its own. His back to the cops, Buddha Hat stepped across the threshold and put a foot right in the empty gym bag. He was talking to someone inside, unaware of what he just walked into.

The kid turned and Rocco flew right at him, accidentally kicking Big Chief in the head, belly-flopping on Buddha Hat, slamming his back to the floor, lying on top of him in the doorway, breathing out loud, each exhalation like a word, his gun pressed into the kid's right eye. All the other cops clambered over them, racing to secure the apartment, someone stepping on the back of Rocco's inner thigh and breaking skin.

Rocco heard the grandmother's croaky and cracked bellow. 'Hat don't do drugs! Hat don't *do* drugs!' At the sound of her voice the kid wriggled a little. Rocco felt the bony, crablike scuttle of Buddha Hat's frail body, then gasped, 'Say "Dempsy burnin'."' The kid didn't say it, but he settled down and stared up at him steadily with his one uncovered eye.

Rocco got up on his haunches, the grandmother still bellowing, 'Hat don't *do* drugs!' He put his free hand on Buddha Hat's chest for leverage, then realized he could feel the kid's heart beating under his palm, feel it beating slow as a dirge, the kid staring at Rocco with his unobscured eye, breathing evenly through his nostrils, Rocco thinking, This is one cold-blooded little fuck. Buddha Hat's one-eyed gaze promised him something in the future, but Rocco was too high right now to give a rat's ass. He flipped the kid over on his stomach, straddled his hips and snapped on handcuffs.

'Hat don't *do* drugs!' Rocco looked up to see the grandmother, her eyes bewildered behind her thick glasses, her slippers scuffling across the linoleum, Thumper yelling at her, 'Who's here! Who's here!' Vaguely aware of the slamming doors, the shouted coordinations, Rocco patted down his prisoner and took a few deep breaths to begin slowing down his own heart, years of lethargy exorcized for at least a moment, the surging of his blood like music, Rocco crooning to himself, 'The best, the best. This is the best.'

Erin staggered briskly through the toys on the living room floor, the child half crazy with the hour. It was two o'clock in the morning. When Rocco had come in walleyed with vodka, she had awakened in her crib, but instead of easing her back to sleep, Rocco lifted her out, dropped her on the rug and scattered a bunch of toys around her like rose petals. Still high from the night, he just wanted to *be* with her, but as he lay on the rug studying her, being with her, absorbing the solemn jerkiness of her movements, he was swept by a wave of anxiety at the wrongness of what he had just done, the havoc he was playing with her metabolism. And gradually his anxiety retreated into an absolute conviction that whatever was taking daily precedence over being with his daughter – work, alcohol, preoccupation with future plans – would, in five years, become a painful memory of pathetically blown priorities.

Rocco congratulated himself for having such a profound thought by getting up and taking a Breyer's Pledge, licking his lips and coming back to the rug. His elation at the arrest and the camaraderie of the Pavonia Tavern had completely evaporated now, the only artifacts of tonight's escape into the past being the faded phone number on the back of his hand and the purple, blood-rimmed halfmoon on the back of his left thigh.

'I almost got *killed* tonight,' he said out loud to Erin, hearing the hollowness in it. His child was pop-eyed with exhaustion. Ignoring him, she was playing with two plastic shoehorns, slowly rolling them up the side of a chair leg and making a high, soft noise. Rocco shook his head, watching her, feeling desperate and lost, and then Victor Dunham came back on him like a sharp pain, like an almost forgotten prayer.

29

After the shooting at the benches, Strike walked back to his car, pulled out of the driveway and headed for the New Jersey Turnpike. He didn't have a destination; it was more that he wanted to be able to drive fast without negotiation, as if unmitigated speed would clear his head and steady his hand.

He wasn't too worried about Horace. It looked like just a meat shot – it wasn't as if he was dead or anything. In fact, it was all for the good in a way, since Strike had been trying to figure out how to lose him for days. Horace should have listened to Andre; he'd be safe in a nice cozy Youth House bunk right now.

Somewhere north of Newark, Strike found himself reexperiencing the shooting so vividly that he flinched at the sharp crack of the recalled gunshot. He flipped up the step well for his .25, the memory making him want to check, and when his hand came out empty he began fishtailing across three lanes of highway. His mind jammed with paranoid scenarios, Strike pulled into a service area parking lot and chugged his Mylanta. It took a good half hour of sitting there before he remembered that he had taken the gun with him to his room at Herman's two days earlier with Tyrone, and that he had left it in the drawer with the ounces.

Heading back to town now, Strike wondered where to go. There was no real need to get the gun, and it would probably be a good idea to stay away from the benches. There wouldn't be any business tonight until later, what with all the detectives canvassing the crowd, and Strike didn't want to be around to give out any information.

Coming off the turnpike and driving over to JFK, Strike headed for Rodney's store, reflex making the choice for him. But after turning onto Jackson Street, he barely slowed down – when he thought about it, the idea of seeing Rodney had less and less appeal these days. Feeling rudderless, Strike cruised the streets of Dempsy trying to think of where he could go. He wandered the city for the better part of an hour before announcing to himself both the obvious and the unthinkable answer: Home.

Hours later, Strike lay in his underwear in the moonlit stillness. Two of the whores who worked his corner chattered a line of coke-fueled blather under his window, the sound of their high heels on the pavement like the tired clomping of an old horse. The air of his bedroom was tinged with silver, and Strike knew that if he lifted his head he could see the three calling cards from the Homicide lying in a row on his dresser top.

Despite the two noisy whores, the apartment seemed quiet. Strike stared at the splintered posts at the foot of the bed and thought of the red Doberman he'd bought six months ago to guard this place. He had never bothered to train it and the thing had chewed the shit out of his bedroom ensemble, reducing all the bamboo posts and sidings to giant shredded teething sticks. The dog, like most things, sounded better than it was, and he'd gotten rid of it after only a few weeks.

Sitting up in bed, Strike was overwhelmed by the thought of how it always turned out that any hustler's ultimate and true victim was himself. He recalled telling both Andre and Jo–Jo earlier in the day that he was away from the benches for good, but now, only eight hours later, here he was, ready to return as if he was nothing but mouth all along. Looking across the room to the three Homicide cards, thinking about how stinky and small his world was, Strike sighed through his teeth: Rodney had best get himself a reliable supplier quick. Ounces, bottles, benches, hole-in-the-wall candy stores, greasy lies, greedy people, everybody fucking everybody – he was sick to death of it. Then he remembered Tyrone at the end of the day, sitting in the car, holding his stomach, tense, dying to bolt. And no wonder. Strike had pushed him into this game – as if ruining Victor's life for no good reason wasn't enough.

It was close to midnight, and Strike envisioned the last squad car, the last tan Plymouth, just now rolling away from the benches. He slid his legs over the side of the bed and began to pull on his clothes, his movements slow, his head thick. And as he reached for his mound of keys on the night table, he swore to himself that he'd never talk to Tyrone again.

Back at the benches, Strike's customers had just started coming by for bottles again, some making small talk about the shooting but most just copping and splitting as usual. Futon told Strike that right after the cops left, Horace's mother's boyfriend had come by, a big, heavy-chested man in a bus driver's jacket. He'd been asking about the shooting, trying to get a name, but everybody shrugged and mumbled as if the guy was a cop. Nobody wanted it to get back to the shooter who it was that had set this big-foot motherfucker on his tail. It just wasn't worth it.

Around one A.M., with business nearly back to normal, Rodney dropped by. He sat for a few minutes in his car while three or four girls flocked around the windows like pigeons on bread. When he emerged he walked backwards toward Strike, still talking to one of the girls. 'What apartment you in?'

'Twelve A,' she said, chewing on a comb and looking serious.

'I'm coming right up.'

'My mother up there.' The girl spun on one heel.

'I don't care. She cute too?'

'She already *got* a boyfriend.'

'Hell, I'll fuck him too.' Rodney started to shadowbox. 'I'm a *con*vict.'

That broke the girls up, Rodney laughing too, his tongue hanging out as he rubbed his belly. He turned to Strike. 'So what you gonna *do* about this?'

'Nothin',' Strike said, shrugging. 'It ain't about business.'

'Yeah, well, if it was *my* boy, that nigger'd be layin' in a pool of blood right this minute.' Rodney looked away, furtively pulling up his shirt and showing Strike the fat wood-grain grip of a .38. 'I just shot me a pit bull,' Rodney said, palming his mouth, the information coming out in a confidential mutter. 'I'm standing on Krumm and JFK? That Cuban motherfucker who runs the video store? He come out the store with a damn pit bull, like to run everybody off from in front? Those Cuban motherfuckers think they superior to everybody, I *hate* them, especially that little motherfucker. He sells his share of shit too. So he come out, tell us to walk. I tell him, "You best get back in the store like now or I'm gonna shoot your *wife* down there, then I'm gonna shoot you." And he's looking at me like I'm made of shit, you know, so *Boom!* The dog's like all over his shoes, man. But I got to hand it to him. The motherfucker didn't blink. He was just standing there looking at me, you know, like trying to decide if it was worth it, me and him. But then he just walk back in, leaves the dog right where it's shot, cold-blooded bastard leaving his dog right on the street like that. I shoulda shot him too . . . So you takin' your medicine?'

'I'm all out.' Strike looked off, wanting Rodney to split.

'Yeah? You best re-up your prescription. You got your appointment at that clinic yet?'

'I'm gettin' it.'

'Yeah, good. So look, I got me another package for tomorrow, so be by the store in the afternoon.'

'What you get?'

'Not much, but it might be a good connection. And it's right on time too, because I got them three geechee boys from Delaware coming back. They beeped me, say they run out already. Must be some good business down there. So you come around about two, OK? I got a few more people comin' by too, we make a little money.' Rodney honked his crotch. 'Buy us some *real* estate.'

A Toyota Corolla pulled up behind Rodney's Cadillac. Thumper emerged from the driver's side, and the clockers faded fast.

'Now what *this* crazy motherfucker doing here?' Rodney said in a high mutter. 'This the craziest motherfucker in town.' Then he gave it a cackly laugh and boomed out, 'Uh-oh! Uh-oh! Five-oh! Five-oh!'

Thumper trudged to the benches as if he was walking uphill. Strike backed away a little. Thumper must be pure bughouse: he was taking his life in his hands by showing up at this hour, alone, off duty and drunk.

'Ho shit!' Thumper said in a wobbly squawk. 'It Mister Big!' He fell on Rodney, starting to wrestle and box, Rodney playing with him but playing light.

'Reviewin' the troops?' Thumper's eyes were at half mast.

'Troops!' Rodney reared back. 'This motherfucker thinks he's in Vietnam.'

'Hey Rodney,' Thumper said, talking loud, 'let me ask you something. Who makes more money off the drug war, me or you? I make forty-three six, plus court appearance overtime, comes to last year sixty-two three, and I don't have to worry about gettin' caught.'

'Yeah, well, I don't have to worry about no *in*come tax.' They both laughed, Rodney dropping a hand on Thumper's shoulder, Thumper swatting it away, both of them red-eyed and showing teeth. Strike started to walk off, thinking, Two angry motherfuckers, both with guns, what's that spell?

'Hey you!' Thumper called out. 'Don't you go nowhere.'

Strike flapped his hands: Shit.

'Just sit down, sit down, I got to *talk* to you.'

'What you got to talk to him about?' Rodney said. 'He ain't got nothing on him.'

'Would you excuse us?' Thumper hunched over in a half-crouch and swung both arms in the direction of the Cadillac, signaling for Rodney to get lost.

Rodney glanced at Strike, Strike sensing that Rodney knew it was best to leave but that he hated being dissed and dismissed this way.

'Please?' Thumper added in a mocking tone.

Rodney started walking backwards to the car, eyeing Strike, eyeing Thumper, then getting in the last shot: 'Yo Thumper. There ain't no drug war save for who gets the best corners. *You* know that.'

'Yeah, good night, motherfucker.' Thumper hung his hands at his sides like a gunslinger, only a little play left in his voice now.

Rodney drove off, Thumper staring after him, moving his lips, then turning to Strike on the bench. 'That fucking dogshit nigger. How the fuck can you stand being around him?'

Thumper flopped down next to Strike, head straight back to the stars, tapping his high-top Ponys on the bricks, giving off a mixed reek of scotch and lime cologne. 'Oh Strike, Strike, Strike. I'm fucked. I'm fucked. I go home now, I'm on the couch. So fucked . . .'

He lunged forward, elbows on knees, grinding the heels of his palms into his eyes. 'Grabbed this shooter tonight over in O'Brien? It went like fucking silk.' Thumper blinked his crushed eyes. 'So how you been?'

'Yo Thumper, I ain't got nothin' aw-*on* me,' Strike said, feeling fluttery, as if all of Roosevelt was watching.

'Relax, relax, it's Miller time.' Thumper yawned into his fist. 'What a fuckin' day. I heard one of your crew got binged here.'

'Hey, I don't know nothin', man.' Strike craved some Mylanta, thought maybe he should start taking the other stuff the doctor gave him too.

'Hey, I don't give a fuck. You guys do each other in all you want. I'm just, you know . . . So how's it been?'

'OK.' Strike looked around, imagined seeing people in windows. Then he actually saw a few.

Thumper draped his arms out along the top bench slat and crossed his ankles. Strike sat under the shadow of one arm like a nervous date in a movie theater.

'You know, when I first came out of the bag? Like, plainclothes? I had Roosevelt on the midnight tour, anticrime squad. We had this prick captain who made us go all the way to eight A.M., no going home at six, six-thirty. You had to check in, punch out, the whole nine yards, so for like the last hour, hour and a half, we just used to sit in our car right over there, watch the sun come up over the buildings. You know, lay back, have a few beers.'

Thumper belched, then lightly punched himself in the chest. 'You ever see the sun come up around here? It's nice. It makes everything all peaceful, soft. You'd never *know*, you know? Man, you'd be surprised how many people get up early and go off to work in this project, getting up, getting out, women going to work, men going to work. There's a lot of hard-working people in these houses. Me, being police, I don't have dealings with them, so like I tend to forget about them. But I feel for them, what they have to put up with living here. I mean, who's got the money to move? *I* don't, but you know what the problem is with a lot of the others? The parasites? And I'm wasted now, so I'm saying the truth . . . You know what the problem is? They're angry, and they feel sorry for themselves. It's like, nothing is their fault, it's society, it's, you know, I'm not talking about some little kid – no father, the mother's all fucked up, drunk, high, violent – I mean, that kid's going down in *flames*. I mean, he don't have a chance. That's not his fault, but I mean . . . I mean *you* . . . Look at you. What the fuck you doin' out here selling drugs? I mean, what is your *problem*?'

'I ain't got no problem,' Strike said, deciding to let Thumper say anything he wanted.

'I mean, your family's not fucked up. Your mother works fuckin' hard, I know that. And your brother, your brother did the right thing all his life. I don't know what happened last week, but he was one hard-working cocksucker, right?'

Strike didn't answer.

'Right?' Thumper backhanded his arm.

'I work hard too,' Strike said, speaking as softly as he could.

'Don't give me that.' Thumper sprayed as he spoke. 'Where the fuck do you get off comparing yourself to your mother and your brother. You're fuckin' out here pumping bottles, I mean, what's your problem, you got a *speech* defect? That's just an anger thing. Shit, my brother? He's got scoliosis and a clubfoot but the guy's an engineer, he pulls down seventy-five thousand a year, and that four-eyed fuck never cracked a schoolbook in his life. So what is it? You're black? So fucking what. You think the Irish had it easy? We were hated. *Hated*. We were the *white* niggers.'

Strike stared at his sneakers, his guts grinding in rage now, Thumper's rap so gallingly familiar.

'So what is it – you got no father? He's dead? Fuck it, you're probably better off. The guy was probably a prick. I used to *wish* my father was dead. That bastard used to gargle down a fifth of scotch a night. Beat the fuckin' piss out of me every night for sixteen years. Are you kidding me? There wasn't a day gone by I didn't wish the cocksucker dead. So I don't want to *hear* about your problems, OK?'

'I dint say nothin'.'

'I mean, you're sitting here, I'm sitting here, you might even be smarter than me. You probably are, but you feel *sorry* for yourself and you're angry, that's what this is all about.'

A little crowd was shaping up at a safe distance. Thumper stood, his legs shaky, then began pacing with his Glock and his long black leather-covered sap, rumbling like a caged bear. Strike watched the crowd out of the corner of his eye, hoping someone would call a cop.

'Hey, and I know angry.' Thumper poked Strike in the arm. 'Do you know I had extreme unction said over me three separate times before I was twenty-five?'

Strike didn't know what that meant, but he raised an eyebrow as if impressed.

'Do you know why? Because I always thought I was *right*. Do you follow what I'm saying? I *know* angry.' He began pacing again, then hunched down close to Strike's face, his breath strong enough to make Strike feel hung over. 'And I'll tell you something else. I used to sell dope, you know, in high school. I cleaned up on it too, so I know what *that* feels like.'

He collapsed back on the bench, his voice in Strike's ear now. 'But what I'm saying is, look at me now. I'm a cop. Next month I'm taking the sergeant's test. Angry, bad fucking childhood, whatever – I *made* something out of myself. I'm thirty-three, and I'm proud of who I am. Where the fuck are you gonna be at thirty-three?'

'Not here.' Strike murmured.

'You'll be dead.' Thumper stared at him from two inches away. '*Dead*.'

Strike said nothing.

Thumper's voice dropped to a hiss, his lips brushing Strike's ear. 'New York? Newark? Jersey City? They scrape you off the sidewalk every fucking day and night of the week.' Thumper leaned back, then came in close again. '*Dead*.'

'Yeah, I got to go home now,' Strike said, staring straight ahead, afraid to get up and get tackled.

'Wait a minute. You want to go home? OK, I want to ask you

something. OK? I got a proposition for you. I'm gonna save your life, OK?'

Strike nodded.

'My uncle, he's a dock foreman at UPS in Secaucus. I'll get him to put you on the line. I think you start at like eight an hour, but then it goes up after a year or two? You start making some good money. Good pension, good medical. You tell me yes, I'll go call him at his house right now, get you set up in a New York minute.'

'Yeah, lul-let me think about that.' Strike tried to sound sincere.

'Yeah, lul-let me think about that,' Thumper mocked him in a disgusted nasal drawl. 'Nah, you'd rather be out here fucking the world because the world fucked you. You'd rather sell dope than take home a paycheck like a real human being, like your brother or some other poor fuck.'

'Oh yeah?' Strike said, his voice rising. 'Last time *you* saw my brother you beat him up, so I don't know what you tuh-talking about.'

Braced for some kind of payback, Strike was surprised when Thumper rose slowly from the bench and then replied in a mild tone. 'Yeah, I know, I know, I fucked up. You're right, you're right.'

Thumper walked in a lazy circle, then went for his wallet, Strike seeing a glint of credit card in there, making himself focus on that, wondering what that would be like, having a credit card, drifting off a little, then hearing Thumper say 'Ah' and watching him pluck out a business card. 'Here you go. This is for you.' Thumper yawned, going up on tiptoe, arms high.

Strike glanced down. Another goddamn card from that goddamn Homicide.

'Anyways, it's always nice to chill out, have a talk now and then, right? But I better go home, face the music.' Thumper rubbed his temples, began walking toward his car. He turned back to Strike.

'Yo Strike, you best *talk* to that cocksucker. Tell him what he wants to know, 'cause between me and you, he wants us to start coming down on you like the *rent*, OK?' Thumper crouched as if waiting for a pitch, pretended to take little warm-up swings with a bat.

Strike stared down at his sneakers, shook his head in sorrow. 'I don't *know* nothing, so what he want from me?'

'Yeah, well, anyways, tonight?' Thumper took a few short swings, then swung as if belting one out of the park. 'This was halftime, motherfucker. Third quarter starts tomorrow.'

30

Rocco, a little wobbly on his feet, wearing sunglasses despite the promise of rain on this overcast Saturday afternoon, popped two more Tylenols and headed toward Strike. A few yards from the benches he stopped short: a heavy, jet-black woman was approaching the same target from the breezeway of 6 Weehawken, chugging right at the kid, a red cigarette case in her hand. Strike looked at her with only mild interest, and Rocco saw that the kid was misreading her mood, saw him standing there off balance as the woman came right up in his face, swinging wild, her claws just missing his eyes, the cigarette case soaring into some bushes.

Stunned, Strike bounced on his toes, screaming, 'What the fuck's your problem, bitch!'

'You stay away from my son!' The woman swung again, another near miss, Strike having to dance backward to avoid getting hit, everybody around the benches watching the scene with frowny fascination.

'Don't you eh-*ever* put your hands near my face!'

'I'll put my goddamn hands anywhere I want. You stay away from him!'

Rocco leaned against a parked car, deciding to let this play out, watching the kid trying to think, to find a way of neutralizing all those staring eyes and open mouths.

'You just keep your hands from my damn *face*!' Strike waved his arms as if trying to fend off a swarm of bees.

'You just best stay away from Tyrone.' Her voice went deep. 'Or my hand's gonna wind up someplace worse than *that*.'

'I don't even know who the fuh-fuck you are.'

'The *hell* you don't.'

She took two steps forward and he wheeled away from her. 'Get out muh-my fuckin' face.'

'Yeah, I'm gonna get out. I'm gonna call the police, get *you* out, you stutter-mouthed piece of shit.'

'Call whoever the fuck you wuh-want, woman!'

'Yeah, OK, I'm gonna call me *Andre*, and Andre gonna stomp your fucking ass, you dope-dealing faggot.'

Strike's head jerked back, his expression more confused than insulted. The crowd closed in tighter around the two of them.

'Well go on then, bitch. What you standing here for? Go get Andre then, go do it. Maybe I'll go get the po-po-lice too, get you locked up for assault.'

As Rocco watched, he saw the boy from the chain perch come out of 6 Weehawken, take one look at Strike and the heavyset woman going at each other, and stop dead in his tracks. This woman was obviously his mother.

'Yeah, you call the police on *me*. You do that.' The woman laughed hard and mean, not seeing her son standing there.

'Hey, you do wuh-what *you* got to do, 'cause I got to do what *I* got to do.'

The boy ran back into the building.

'Yeah, we'll *see* on that.'

The woman turned and headed across the projects, toward Andre's surveillance apartment, the circle of people breaking into a horseshoe to let her go.

Rocco hung back by the car for a few minutes, watching Strike pace, listening to him mumble curses to himself. Strike looked livid, but self-conscious too, as if hoping that when he finally looked up, everybody would be gone.

Rocco took off his sunglasses. He hoped the kid was still thinking about calling the police, because when Strike at last looked over to the sidewalk, Rocco glared at him, arms folded across his chest, trying hard to come off like a pissed-off and just-summoned genie.

Strike began walking in circles, clutching his gut and heading nowhere with a brisk limpy strut.

Rocco sauntered over to the benches. 'Hey, Ronnie, have I been a hard-on to you out here?' he said quietly.

'What?' The kid looked stricken.

'Have I not treated you like a man out here? Talked to you with respect? With courtesy?'

Strike didn't answer.

'So why are you trying to make a fucking boob out of me?'

'What are you taw-talking about?'

'What am I talking about? You told me you didn't know Darryl Adams.

I'm running around like a horse's ass on that, and now I find out not only
did you *know* the guy but you worked with him in Rodney Little's store
for like a year. Why the fuck didn't you tell me that?'

The kid's eyebrows rose. 'Yeah, no, see, I got confused. After you
left last time? I realized I *did* know him buh-but only not by that name.
I know him by Spook. I didn't realize who you was talking about. You
was talking about Suh-Spook.'

Rocco had trouble keeping a straight face. 'Oh yeah?'

'Suh-Spook,' Strike declared, bobbing his head.

'Spook.' Rocco bobbed back.

'Yeah, he was so quiet he was like a go-ghost, so – '

'Is that right?'

'Yeah. I thought it was someone else.'

'OK.' Rocco shrugged as if it didn't mean anything either way. 'OK,
but explain something else to me. You said you didn't see your brother
for two months now, right?'

The kid went still.

'But I was just in this bar, Rudy's? Where your brother was drinking
before the shooting? Guess what. The bartender ID'd *you* in there
that night.'

'He said *what?*'

'No, he didn't say "*what.*" He said "that guy," looking at *your* mug
shot, he said, "That guy was in my bar that night." He even described
the drink he made for you. Coco Lopez, straight out of the can. Does
this all ring a bell?'

Strike seemed about ready to bolt, twisting his head right and left,
Rocco trying to keep this going without having it explode.

'Why did you lie to me, Ronnie?'

'It's my buh-brother.'

'What's your brother? Your brother made you lie?'

'No, I'm just, you know, I'm trying to help him . . . you know.'

'I don't get it. Explain to me how lying to me helps him. I mean,
he's locked up, so who are you helping? I don't get it.'

Strike turned to the benches. Three or four of his buddies stood
watching the show. He waved them away, but no one moved.

'Talk to me, Ronnie.'

'Woo-what are you saying, *I* did it?'

'I didn't say that. *You* said that. I just asked why you were throwing
me a line of shit.' Rocco felt his temples pulsing. 'Why did you just
say that?'

'I dint say that. I just suh-said . . .' Strike was breathing out of his mouth, almost panting. 'You got me saying shit in a *knot*, man. You twisting me up.'

'Me?' Rocco hunched forward, laughing. 'Who's twisting who here, Ronnie? Alls I'm asking is why did you play me like such a jerk on this. What's in it for you?'

Strike looked at the ground sadly, as if to suggest that he couldn't possibly explain.

'I mean, what gives here?'

Strike shook his head.

'And another thing. You tell me you're working in that grocery, so I go off there asking about it, people start laughing at me like I'm fucking Elmer Fudd and you're the Tricky Rabbit. They start telling me, "Hey asshole, you're out there talking to this kid all polite, man to man, meanwhile, he's selling shit right in your face, behind your back, in between your legs "'

'*Hey.*' Strike leaned back, his hand out, his cheeks puffed. 'Look, why don't you just stop playing with me, OK? Don't buh-be running this Columbo game on me no more, OK? I know you know what I'm doing here, OK? 'Cause you got all kind a dogs barking up my tree here day and night, nuh-night and day, so . . .' Strike moved his face close to Rocco's, going up on his toes to be eye to eye. 'You know, I know, everybody in *town* knows what's goin' on here. So like i-if you want to arrest me for *that*' – he held his wrists out to Rocco – 'just go ahead, 'cause I ain't gonna stand out here no more with you like this.'

'Ronnie, listen to me . . .'

Strike waved him quiet. 'If you don't want to arrest me, then get out muh-my face so I can *work*.' His eyelids fluttered with the effort of his words, his tongue making strange clicks and squeaks. 'You want to give me another cuc-*card* before you go, so I can have a whole set? Fine. I got like one pocket left that got no card yet. Just do what you guh-got to do and let me deal with the reality from there. So am I under arrest or what?'

'Hey Ronnie, can you at least understand why I'm upset?'

'Ah-am I under arrest or *what!*'

Rocco flinched. The crowd was growing, the street no place to talk, no place to go toe-to-toe. He had to get this kid over to his office, but it had to be voluntary – arrest meant jail, which meant no access to the prisoner. Besides, arrest for what?

'Ronnie, ease up, ease up. Alls I'm saying here is I need your help, that's all. Look, let's me and you take a ride, talk calm about this.'

'Am I under arrest?'

'Fuck no, just come back with me. I'll get you a sandwich, we'll put our heads down on this – '

'Then I ain't goin' nowhere with you.'

'Fine.' Rocco shrugged. 'You don't have to do shit. But if you want to continue business out here without Jo-Jo, without Thumper, without anybody else I can think of climbing up your ass and throwing you in County every two minutes, I would really think about taking a ride right fucking *now*.'

Strike gave Rocco a breathy '*Huh*,' then shook his head. Everybody that had been sitting on the bench was standing up and milling around silently.

Rocco felt the growing heat and decided that with or without Strike he had to leave.

'You coming or what?'

Looking past Rocco's shoulder, Strike suddenly gave out a little squawk of alarm, then said clear and fast, 'Yeah, OK, let's go.'

Rocco turned toward what had spooked the kid and saw Andre striding to the benches. Rocco headed across the street to his car, satisfied to see that Strike was already there, waiting for him to unlock the door.

'Can I stop by my house, get something?' Strike twisted and twitched in the shotgun seat, looking out the rear window to check on what was happening by the benches.

'What you need?' As Rocco pulled out into traffic, he saw Andre in the rearview mirror, the big cop standing with hands on his hips, staring after the car.

'My stomach medicine.'

'What you got, an ulcer?'

'An ulcer, yeah.'

'We got stuff in the office.'

'But this is like from the ha-hospital.'

'What's it, Mylanta? Maalox?'

'Yeah.'

'You're covered.'

A few minutes later, Rocco stopped alongside a dumpster and threw the car into park. 'Hey Ronnie, do me a favor, before we get down there, I don't want to walk into the office, all of a sudden find out you got a ton of dope on you or a gun or something, OK? I don't want to search you, pat you down, nothing like that. But if you got anything on you it would be best for me not to find . . .' Rocco nodded to the dumpster. He knew the kid was clean, but he wanted to get back in his good graces. 'Now's the time, OK? I can't be any more decent with you than that.'

'I'm cool.'

'You sure? Because I don't know if you were ever down by my office, but we're right across the hall from county Narcotics and sometimes they get these man-eating dope dogs padding around and I don't want to wind up pulling some humongous rottweiler off your dick, next thing I got to explain to everybody how I let you walk in the building holding like that. I mean, this here is between me and you.'

'I'm good, I'm good.' Strike waved the subject dead.

'Good.' Rocco pulled out into traffic again. 'Can I ask you something? Unofficial? How long do you stand out there by the benches every day?'

Strike shrugged. 'Law-long as it takes.'

They drove in silence the rest of the way. When they got to the office, Rocco dug out some Mylanta and a plastic soup spoon and then stood in the doorway of the coffee machine nook, watching Strike shake up the bottle. But instead of pouring himself a tablespoon or two, the kid chugged it straight down, Rocco watching his Adam's apple contract once, twice, three times before he replaced the cap.

'That's gonna give you shits there, Ronnie.'

'Nah, it's good.' Strike wiped his lips, then surprised Rocco by taking a paper napkin and wiping away a trickle of chalky liquid that was creeping down the side of the label. Rocco flashed on Victor: like Victor washing his hands after taking a leak.

Rocco led Strike into the interrogation room and sat him down at the table. 'OK, let's start from the beginning. I don't want any lies, because whatever you been saying to me I've been taking in good faith up to now. And all I got for my good faith so far is a lot of bullshit, a lot of running around knocking myself out and feeling like a total moke, OK? So I don't want to hear any more "Oh *that* Darryl Adams" or "Oh *that* bar" or "Oh *that* brother" – you understand?'

Strike nodded.

'Now, let me tell you something else. I don't give a fuck about drugs. You can stand out there by those benches, sell bottles till your dick falls off and you'd never have any problems with me. The thing with Thumper and Jo-Jo? That's just me asking you for help. Help me and those guys vanish, OK? Alls I care about is dead people. The living, that's somebody else's problem. So if I'm asking you questions and you're afraid to tell me the truth because you're afraid it's going to affect *your* drug operation or *Rod*ney's drug operation or *Champ's* drug operation, don't worry about it. I never share anything with Narcotics, because if I did nobody'd ever talk to me. Do we understand each other?'

Rocco gave the kid a long, steady look. Strike seemed impassive but not shut down.

'Because now I'm gonna ask you some sixty-four-thousand-dollar questions and I want the truth, because if I go running around out there and wind up looking stupid again, you're gonna have to find a new city to work out of, and wherever you go, I *know* you're gonna sell drugs, because there's too much money to be made for you not to. And that means that eventually, wherever you are, you're gonna get popped, and if there's a little mark on your statewide file that says "cocksucker," no DA is ever gonna cut you a deal. But if there's a mark that says "call Rocco Klein"? It's like a credit card, OK? Do we understand each other?'

'Uh-huh.' The kid clasped his hands across his chest.

'Good.' Hoping against hope, Rocco swung for the bleachers. 'OK. Right from the gitty-up – did you kill Darryl Adams?'

Strike made a face, shook his head. 'No way.'

'Good.' Something broke inside Rocco's chest but he pressed on, knowing it never comes that easy. 'That's fine. So now I don't have to advise you of your rights. Anything you tell me now, about people, about drugs, can*not* be held against you in a court of law. So far so good, right?'

Strike waited.

'So when was the last time you spoke to your brother?'

Strike sighed. 'Saturday.'

'OK.' Rocco nodded as if he knew it all along. But the answer threw him for a loop: he'd thought Friday was the last time, at the bar before the killing. 'OK, where?'

'In the projects.'

'What you talk about?'

'Nothin'.'

'Nothing?'

'That's about aw-all we usually talk about. We're not that close.'

'OK, when was the time before?'

'That night in the bar.'

'What night was that?'

'Like, Friday – you know, that night that thing happened.'

'Well, why didn't you tell me that when I asked you on the street?'

'Because I didn't want nothing to *do* with that. I figured if I told you that, then you'd be bringing me down for a statement. Next thing I know I'm helping to ha-*hang* him, you know?'

Rocco found it hard to tell if the kid was lying: he was avoiding eye contact on everything, but his demeanor was distant, preoccupied, as if his troubles were all over the place. 'Yeah, but Ronnie, he already confessed, remember?'

'I don't care.'

'Ronnie, if you told me the truth the first time, I would've handled the interview so fast you'd've been back on the bench in an hour. I mean, I wouldn't've had to shut you down three times, your ulcer wouldn't've acted up, I wouldn't have had to waste all those goddamn man-hours. The shortest distance between two points is the truth. For *every*body.'

The kid still wouldn't come out of his moody distance, and Rocco drifted off for a moment, thinking of the best way to Mirandize him if he should be so lucky as to hit pay dirt here, already beginning to imagine himself in court, flatly recounting the circumstances that led to the unexpected confession.

Strike began to fidget and Rocco continued.

'Why'd you meet him at Rudy's?'

'It was just a bump-in, like a accident.'

'OK. Who got there first?'

'Him I guess. He was there when I got there, like sitting down.'

'Was he glad to see you?'

Strike shrugged. 'Not *un*glad, I don't know.'

'What you talk about?'

'You know, my mother, ha-how she doin', his kids, I don't know, nothing. It wasn't but ten minutes. I didn't even sit down.'

Rocco smelled a lie in that but didn't push. 'Who bought?'

'Nobody.'

'Who left the bar first?'

'Me.'

'Before you left, did your brother say where he was going afterwards?'

'Nope.'

'Did you *ask* him where he was going?'

'Nope.'

'How did he seem to you?'

'Dopey.' Strike gave Rocco a little smile. 'He was drinking, so, you know, dopey.'

Rocco let the interview hang for a minute, wondering how and when Strike got Victor the gun. Saturday: he said it himself. In the projects. And that's why Victor didn't confess until Sunday.

'Ronnie, let me ask you something. The bartender says that was the first time you were ever in that bar. Is that true?'

'I guess. I ain't a bar person.'

'Well, why *that* night? I mean . . .'

'I dunno. My stomach was hurting and I just wuh-went in to get something sweet and heavy for it.'

Strike was looking a little more alert, working harder now, and Rocco wanted to turn it up, but carefully, not wanting him to think that he was a suspect.

'Yeah, but if you just wanted something sweet and heavy like, what was it, Coco Lopez? Why didn't you just go into a candy store or a mini-mart?'

''Cause I didn't see none open right there.'

'Gee, I could swear there's a candy store and a bodega on either side of Rudy's that's that's open till like midnight.'

'Well, I must not've *noticed* them.'

Easy, easy: but Rocco wanted to give him one more nudge. 'And like just for my own edification, why *that* bar? You never go into a bar, but you pick this one out of a million bars in town, and hey, there's your brother. That's like one in a million, and next thing, bing bang boom, there's a shooting right across the street, your brother's the do-er, holy shit. So why that bar, Ronnie? That's like hitting the bad-luck lottery.'

''Cause that's the bar I found myself in front of wuh-when my goddamn perforated ulcer started *hurtin'* me.' The kid was spraying a little, getting too hot now. 'You want to check with the hospital? I got like a perforated ulcer!'

'Hey, hey, relax, relax. I believe you, Ronnie. I believe you.' Rocco decided to retreat, calm the kid down. 'Let me ask you. What did *you* think when you heard Darryl Adams got killed?'

'I didn't think nothin'. People get killed like all the time out there. Hey, *you* should know, you a Ha-Homicide.'

Rocco laughed. 'Yeah but Ronnie, you worked with the guy, right? I mean, you knew him pretty good, right?'

'Hey, I know like four, no five people that got killed so far since high school. He just number six.'

'OK, I buy that.' Rocco paused. 'But did it ever cross your mind that your brother did it?'

Strike looked straight at him. 'No way, unh-uh.'

'Well, who did *you* think did it?'

Strike's mouth started working itself into tortured shapes, his eyes suddenly seeming to burn with secrets. Rocco felt as if he was watching some kind of internal wrestling match, but then the kid dropped his eyes and swallowed whatever had been trying to break through.

'I really don't know. I know like lots of bad people out there, buh-but . . . I really don't know.'

Rocco was momentarily confused, thinking he'd heard sincerity in the kid's voice. He shook it off and went on. 'What's the talk on the street?'

Strike shrugged. 'I didn't . . .'

'Didn't what?'

'I was sorry to hear about it . . . It's my buh-brother, you know?'

'OK.' Rocco nodded, ready to shift gears again. 'OK, let's go back to Saturday. The last time you saw Victor, what happened, you saw him, said hello, how's tricks . . .'

'Yeah, uh-huh.'

'OK. Were you coming from a store or something when you saw him?'

'Naw, I was like, coming from the benches.'

'And where was he?'

'He was coming from out his house to his car on Dumont.'

'So what happened? You saw him come out of his building and . . .'

'I walked over, like, across the projects and talked to him by his car.'

'You walked from Weehawken to Dumont, then, right?'

'Yeah, I guess.'

'Did you have a package? Any kind of package on you?'

'I don't think so, no.'

'OK. Did Victor have a package?'

'I don't remember. I don't think so.'

'OK, now think carefully about this. Did you shake hands with him, hug him, pat him on the back?'

'Nope.' Strike made a face.

'You sure, right?'

'Naw, we just yo, yo, and out, you know.'

'You remember what I told you about lying to me? That whole fucking riot act I read you before?'

'Yeah, so?'

'Well, then explain to me this. You say you guys didn't touch, no one had a package. Yet we got a lady, a witness in the projects who told us she looked out her window, *saw* you guys come together, talk for a few minutes, then, she's not sure who was who, but she knows the both of you from around the houses, and she told us *one* of you had a package, and before you split, the package changed hands.'

Rocco held his breath, waiting to see if his bluff was going to pay off, but Strike looked steadily at him, calm as grass. 'I don't know what the fuck you talking about.'

Rocco felt frustration begin to pull on him and he gave himself a moment to calm down. 'You remember the weather that day, Ronnie?'

Strike tilted forward, blinking. 'Rain.'

'Yeah, rain. You get drenched?'

'I don't know.'

'You must've, right? I mean, you walked all the way across the projects, stood there talking, then walked all the way back, no?'

'Yeah.' Strike's shoulders tightened.

'So let me ask you. What did you talk about that was so urgent you had to get soaked like that? You don't carry an umbrella, do you?'

'No.'

'So what was so important?'

'I was walking that way anyhow.'

'Then why'd you walk back?'

'I faw-forgot something.'

'Huh, OK, OK,' Rocco said, hearing a lie. 'So you didn't talk to him about the shooting?'

'I don't think so,' Strike said, a ripple running through him. 'It wasn't no big deal. It was across the street, you know? It wasn't like, in the bar or anything. La-lots of shit happens across the street from things.'

The kid was too tense, too alert, and Rocco could feel that time was running out. 'Look, I'm supposed to go back to speak to your brother again,' Rocco said, as if he was wrapping it up. 'His lawyer is doing me a favor, getting me in there to see him. Anything you want me to tell him?'

Strike didn't answer, his eyes wary.

'I got some friends in there. I told them your brother's good people, you know, to take care of him, because shit, I don't want to go in there next week, he's wearing a *dress* already, you know?'

Strike looked instantly alarmed. 'Victor ain't no *punk*. Anybody fuh-fuck with him got to deal with *me*.' He blinked furiously, as if amazed by his own outburst.

'Look, there's a lot of guys in there, they don't give a rat's ass about you, Rodney, Erroll Barnes, Champ, *any* of you. All they know is there's this young guy, like a helpless virgin.' Rocco winced apologetically. 'And even if they *were* scared of you, which I doubt, what's the old saying? When the dick stands up, the brains get buried in the ground? You ever hear that?'

Strike appeared fascinated, horrified, Rocco thinking, Bombs away, then continuing. 'All of which is why I'd like to go in there, talk to people, at least get his *bail* reduced, you know? Get him back out on the street with his family where he belongs, give him at least a year to take care of them before the trial, let him bust his ass out here, make them some money. Because when it's trial time, he is *gone* – thirty years, maybe twenty if he pleas out. But that's it, and it *kills* me because to tell you the truth I've come completely around to *your* way of thinking on this, you know that?'

'What's my way of thinking?'

'Hey, this is the third time we talked like this, right? And now we're here, in this room with no outside bullshit, just me and you, and I'm looking right into your eyes and down into your soul and I *know* that all this talk about your brother is tearing your heart out, because I know that *you* know that somebody else killed Darryl Adams and that your brother is taking the fall for it. And I swear to God, I'm with you all the way on that. I *know* your brother is an innocent man, just like you do. And if he was my brother? And I knew what you know? Every day of my life would be a living hell.'

Strike said nothing, his mouth hanging open. Rocco felt as if he was talking to a man made of baked clay.

'And your brother is such a fucking decent sonofabitch that he'd rather get degraded, beaten and raped every day of his life for the next three decades than tell anybody the truth of what happened.'

Rocco let it float, the kid looking riveted, as if desperately wanting Rocco to say a name.

'Do you think there's anything we could *do* about that, Ronnie?'

'What . . .'

Jesus Christ: the kid seemed to be truly asking, his face filled with a
crazy hopefulness. 'Hey . . . me, you, your brother – we all know who
shot Darryl Adams.'

'Who . . .'

'Who? Who do you *think*, Ronnie?'

The kid's mouth started working again, the wrestling with angels or
demons lighting up his eyes like the windows of a burning house. But
then the fire went out and his face fell as if in shame. 'I don't know.'

Rocco sat back, his hands trembling, wondering if he had anything
left inside him to start a new round of cat-and-mouse, then thinking,
Fuck this, no more verbal chess, no more head games. His words came
out edgy and dry: 'Who do you *think*, Ronnie?'

Strike looked up again, his lips pursed like a keyhole. '*Who* . . .'

The sincerity in the kid's eyes made Rocco lose it completely. '*You.*
You did it, you little fuck,' Rocco shouted, his voice shaking. 'You. *I*
know it, *you* know it, and your *brother* knows it. What was the theory
behind this, he'd get off on self-defense because he's got no record,
while if you got popped on this you'd go away for good? Well, *he's*
going away, motherfucker – not ever having *done* it before is no excuse
on a homicide charge. His life is *over*, and I know it's rough out there,
but you're the fucking king snake, you're a cold-blooded evil junkyard
nigger like I never seen in twenty years in this town.'

Strike was half standing in horror but Rocco couldn't stop, his own
despair driving him on. 'What was the deal? You'd take care of his
family while he was away? You're gonna take care of those kids for
ten, twenty years? Who the fuck are *you* kidding? You're not the Mafia.
You're not even Rodney Little. You're a skinny-ass snake motherfucker
nobody-to-nothing piece of street shit.'

Strike almost lunged across the table. 'You don't know nothin'! You
don't know nothin' *about* it! You just a puh-pig-faced motherfucker
po-lice who don't know nothin' about what's out there, nothin' about
me, an' nothin' about what ha-*happened*.'

Rocco resisted smacking him, hoping for one last chance to get
something. 'So *tell* me.'

Strike's eyes lit up again. He seemed to be teetering, but then held
firm. 'I don't know, you fa-fat muh-motherfuckin' piece of shit! I
don't know.'

'Welp,' Rocco said, his voice fluttery with rage, 'I might be a fat
motherfucking piece of shit, I might be nobody to nothing, but I tell
you, when I wake up in the morning? And *you* wake up? I see what I see

and you see what you see. I don't *have* no brother in jail for something *I* did. How about you?'

Strike pressed his palms into his eyes, and for a wrenching second Rocco thought the kid was going to give it up after all, give it up and save them both, save all of them.

But then Strike spoke from behind his hands. 'You want to talk to me, you get me a lawyer.'

'Get your *own* damn lawyer.'

Looking battered, Strike rose. 'That's what I meant.'

Rocco pulled out a Homicide card and spun it across the table, hitting the kid's thigh. 'I'll be talking to you, Ronnie. Now take a fucking hike.'

Rocco stood on the steps in front of the prosecutor's office, watching Strike walk off in the direction of the batting cages and the Furniture Shack.

Thinking about how badly he'd blown it, Rocco was filled with a belated energy, a dizzy astonishment. He had handled the interview as if he'd never gotten a confession in that room before and had no idea how to go about it. And calling the kid a nigger: Jesus. Rocco wondered if he should have just arrested him, borrowed a little package from Narcotics across the hall and then busted the kid. But then he *really* couldn't talk to him, so what would that accomplish? Besides, he'd never done anything like that in his life, and he was potentially in enough trouble already.

Strike walked past a parked Cadillac, and Rocco saw Rodney Little pop out on the driver's side and call something across the roof. The kid almost jumped out of his skin, but after a few moments of conversation, Rodney and Strike got in the car and drove off.

Rodney. Rocco watched the car make its way to I-9 and vanish. Fuck Mazilli: Rodney was the guy behind the death of Darryl Adams. Rocco just knew it. But he also knew that Rodney would get away with it, because you can't convict on hearsay. Maybe if Strike testified about how things had really come about, they could nail Rodney on conspiracy, but . . .

'Shit,' Rocco said aloud, smacking his head. The Rodney angle – why hadn't he pushed that? He should've told Strike that he knew he'd had no choice, that Rodney must have threatened him, *made* him do it, and was he gonna let that lowlife scumbag ruin his life, his brother's life? He should've given the kid the old tag about how if you were coerced into the commission of a crime, you were really a victim yourself; should've

convinced him that his real target was Rodney, that he had no interest
in locking up Strike as long as Strike helped him land the bigger fish.
But of course that wasn't true. Knowing he'd never get anything solid
on Rodney, Rocco just wanted the bad brother. He had wanted him ever
since that night in Rudy's – maybe even before that, when something
made him ask for the photograph in the mother's house. There was
a rightness to the exchange, a symmetry in brother for brother that
was irresistible, and Rocco saw no reason to mess with the clarity of
that vision.

Rocco trudged back into the prosecutor's office. Brother for brother:
now that he'd blown his chance at tripping up Strike, his last hope was
getting a jailhouse confession out of Victor. But Jimmy Newton was
right. If he interviewed Victor in jail and couldn't get him to change his
story, it would be pure humiliation for Rocco up on the stand. Jimmy
would get him to admit that he didn't think the kid he arrested was
guilty, force him to completely sabotage the prosecutor's case, condemn
him to the seedy grind of midnight shifts in a squad car.

Rocco recalled his bullshit bluster to Jimmy that day in the restaurant,
how he'd shrugged off the prospect of getting kicked out of Homicide.
He tried to envision himself as a middle-aged uniform like Harris or
Dolan, grunting with the effort every time he had to get out of the
cruiser to hassle some two-bit clocker, who would then take off on
him like a gazelle. The picture was humiliating, unacceptable – he could
never retire from the Job at the bottom after eight years at the top.

Rocco stood by his desk trolling his nails across the blotter. It was
time to admit that the idea of getting Victor to tell the truth about the
night of the Ahab's murder was pure fantasy. Rocco flipped through his
Rolodex, stopping on Jimmy Newton's office number. He decided to
blow off the whole scheme.

After the sixth ring Rocco remembered it was Saturday. He pulled up
the card to get Jimmy's home number off the bottom – do it now rather
than Monday – but instead he found himself ringing up the County Jail
and asking for Frank Lopez, Victor Dunham's designated babysitter.

'So how's he hangin' there, Frank?' Rocco asked halfheartedly when
Lopez came on the line.

'Not so good, my man. He was in Gen Pop for like two days? They
stole his sneakers, his food, his cigarettes. He got beat up both days. He
just couldn't stand up so I shipped him to Protective, but that turned
out not so good either.'

'Yeah? Why's that?'

'Well, like at first it was OK. You know, usually there's nothing up there but snitches, baby bumpers, but then there was this other guy? Orel Carmichael? This guy Orel's like a real antisocial. He knows karate an' shit, he beat up like six guys already, gashed 'em all up, every ten minutes with him it was a war. So they had to put this motherfucker up in Protective too, but now he's like a shark in a goldfish bowl, plus, he's got a crush on your boy. So I know you're looking out for him so I had him shipped back down to Gen Pop.'

'Who, Carmichael?'

'No, Dunham.'

'Why the fuck didn't you ship Carmichael instead?'

'To where?'

As Rocco hung up, all his hunger for breaking the brothers came clawing back. Now would be the time to hit on Victor, now when he's all trembly and exhausted, terrorized, willing to say anything to get out. In a few days he'd probably get a bail reduction hearing, get the ten percent option and be out on the street, where he wouldn't be as vulnerable. Now was the time to help a kid who had been fucked all his life – by his brother, by Thumper, by alcohol, by the water torture of seeing the world through Hambone's service windows. Victor Dunham was guilty of nothing more than sitting on the truth, and by breaking him down, Rocco could help this kid help himself. It was Rocco's oldest line, but this time it wouldn't be bullshit.

Rocco looked at the Rolodex card in his hand and picked up the phone. 'Jimmy, it's Rocco . . . Listen man, you got to let me in there with him. I swear this poor fucking kid is as pure as the driven snow. You got to let me in.'

31

Strike sat in the car next to Rodney, his hands fluttering on his thighs, a noise like a tuning fork or a dog whistle in his head. He was thinking that he had just decided to quit this work, this town, maybe as soon as he got out of Rodney's sight.

'You was supposed to be by my store like an hour ago.'

'Yeah, wuh-well, what was I supposed to do, tell this cop I had to go cut some ounces?'

'Did he arrest you?' Rodney stopped for a light by the batting cages, empty now in the late afternoon smog.

'Unh-uh.'

'Then why the fuck did you go down there? You shoulda told him to go fuck himself. He can't take you down there unless you let him. Don't you know nothing? Gah-damn, you a infant or something?'

Strike opened his eyes wide, as if to get air around the sockets. 'I had a situation on me with Andre.'

'Fuck Andre. He ain't nothing. What did that fat cop want?'

'Nothin'.'

Strike held his head, remembering the interview, recalling how Buddha Hat had floated above that table, daring him to speak his name.

'Nothin', huh? Don't give me that nothin' shit.' Rodney was sailing down I-9 now, looking at Strike as he drove. 'Did he ask you about me?'

'He didn't say nothing about you.'

''Cause I never said nothing to you about shootin' nobody. Alls I said to you is, if you want that slot you got to go get it for yourself, and shit, I didn't even say *that*.'

Strike let the challenge go, too beat up to protest, wondering if Victor could really be doing worse in jail than he was out here.

Rodney drove in silence for a few minutes, turning off the highway onto JFK. 'So what did he want? What was he asking about?'

'He say he thinks *I* did it. Caw-called me a nigger too.'

'Well, *did* you do it?'

'*Fuck* you.'

Strike said it fast and hot, the words liberated by his bleeding nerves. At first he thought Rodney was reaching out to pat his shoulder, but then Rodney's hand grabbed the top of his hair and yanked him down under the steering wheel. His head in Rodney's lap now, Strike looked up into Rodney's nostrils as he drove one-handed, Rodney's lips bunching mean and tight as he pulled over and threw it into park, Strike suddenly finding that big .38 in his face, the muzzle flattening his nose to one side, Rodney's elbow cocked high, his bug-eyed face shimmering behind the grip.

'Who you talkin' to like that? *Who?*' Rodney dug the muzzle into cartilage, Strike lying limp, one sneaker pressed against the passenger window.

'I ain't one of your little *crew* boys, motherfucker. You watch your fuckin' *mouth* or I'll blow your face off, you understand?' Rodney gripped Strike's hair as if he was holding a shrunken head, but Strike was off into static and colors, not resisting, not even there.

'And I'm gonna tell you something else. If I ever hear about you talking to that Homicide one more time, if I ever hear my name come up on this at *all*, I'm gonna know you said it an' I'll kill you before you can *blink*. I swear before God, any police come up on me on this? I'm gonna know it was you, and you are *killed*, you understand?'

Rodney waited, his stomach pressing into the side of Strike's face. Strike nodded, closing his eyes and pretending to go to sleep.

'Word is *word* on this, you got that?'

Strike nodded dreamily as someone came up alongside the car and rapped on Rodney's window, making Rodney drop the gun down under his seat.

'Hey, what's up?' Rodney said, his tone instantly casual.

'Nothing from nothin',' a voice said.

His head still down, Strike watched Rodney rummage in the glove compartment and peel off three white cards from a stack four inches thick, then leave the car without another word.

Strike sat up and saw Rodney stroll across the street with his arm around a white guy's shoulder. The Cadillac was parked alongside a children's clothing store; Strike glanced at the window and saw a cloud of pink and blue polyester hanging on a field of plaster balloons.

Strike took the stack of cards out of the glove compartment – they were New Jersey state auto insurance cards. He recalled Rodney saying that he had a friend who worked at the printing plant, that the friend had sold him a hundred blanks for ten dollars each. With Rodney probably selling them off for about seventy-five dollars apiece, anybody who could type could save a grand a year in premium payments.

Strike opened his door to get out, then remembered that Rodney needed him to cut and run some ounces. He sat back, exhausted, thinking, The last package, I swear to *God*. He stared dopily at the pastel playsuits in the store window: maybe after this he'd work with kids. The notion made him think of the Homicide asking him if he was going to take care of his brother's kids. Looking for distraction, Strike started to count the plaster balloons, and they triggered a memory from when he was eight years old, of a night when his father had come home from the dress factory in Secaucus with at least fifty balloons, all blown up. How, where and why he got them no one knew, but he had put Strike and Victor in the bathroom with all those balloons – the bathroom because it was the smallest room in the house and because it would make fifty balloons seem like a thousand, like a world of balloons. His father had let them go wild, he and his brother jumping and screaming and punching balloons, rolling on them, popping them. Strike remembered feeling hysterical with happiness until Victor slipped and cracked his chin on the edge of the bathtub, the game over then, his brother spilling a stream of blood over his lower lip, his father barging in and grabbing up the balloons, squeezing them out the small bathroom window one by one, yelling, 'You kids got to learn to play *right*!' And Strike remembered that despite his own sense of unfairness, despite Victor's bloody mouth, he had felt worst for his father when he saw him watching all those balloons floating free, sailing high over the projects on their way across the Hudson River.

Strike squinted in the general direction of the Roosevelt Houses, thought again of his failed attempt to give up Buddha Hat's name, and spoke aloud. 'I tried, man.'

Rodney came back to the car and threw himself into his seat. Sighing, he counted a thin roll of twenties, then reared back to slip the cash in his front pocket.

'I ever tell you about this insurance card thing I got going? Yeah, I should let you get in on it. How's about I sell you fifty cards for fifty dollars each? Shit, you can sell 'em out here for like a hundred. What you think of that? You up for something like that?'

As Rodney drove Strike to his car, hammering away at him on this new scam, Strike tuned him out, savoring his secret decision to bolt, wondering where he should move to. Jersey City? Elizabeth? New York? And do what? Sell drugs, most likely – the Homicide was right about that. Or maybe he'd move to Secaucus, work UPS. Work for Thumper's uncle. Haw.

'What's *this* now . . .' Rodney slowed down about a block from Strike's car, and Strike saw Errol Barnes hovering over Tyrone, the kid leaning backwards over the rear of the Accord, Erroll sandwiching him in. Tyrone looked terror-stricken. Strike figured the kid must've been hanging around waiting for him and then run into Erroll, who had come to the same place to deliver the new package.

Strike and Rodney watched as Tyrone tried to squeeze away. Erroll didn't move, just squinted down at the kid with those miserable slits. Tyrone did a sideways shuffle until he was free of the car, then casually jogged away up the street as if too embarrassed by his own smelly fear to race off. As Strike watched him go, he noticed that Tyrone was still holding a hand over his gut even as he ran.

Rodney turned into the old lady's driveway. Strike got out and sat behind the wheel of his own car, unrolling the passenger window and waiting for somebody to drop in the package. He looked in the rearview mirror: Rodney and Erroll stood with their backs to him, leaning against the rear end of the Accord, preventing him from leaving.

After a few minutes, Rodney came around the driver's side and hunched over the window.

'Yeah, so you OK?' he said lightly as if nothing had happened.

'I'm good.' Strike looked straight ahead. His nose was still tender from Rodney's gun.

Rodney flopped the dope on the seat. 'So you got a quarter there.'

Strike nodded slightly.

'Just whack it, put aside like two ounces with a half-ounce cut like before. And listen.' Rodney waited for Strike's eyes. 'You best lose that little boy Tyrone.'

'I don't even talk to him no more.'

'Yeah.' Rodney poked Strike's nose, his fingers miming a gun, his mood playful. 'Yeah, you best lose him before his Momma tear you a new asshole.'

Strike nodded, thinking, Unload this last quarter ki and then fly.

Three hours later, Strike sat behind the candy counter looking out at the sun, which began to dip behind a row of abandoned walkups. Rodney had been in a good mood all afternoon, almost affectionate, and it made Strike paranoid, made him think Rodney could read his mind and was trying to seduce him into staying on until the bitter end. But at least business was brisk. Rodney made some calls to tell a few of his local customers that he'd gotten a package and now there were only a few ounces left to unload.

Rodney stood over his eighteen-month-old son and plucked at his nappy hair. 'I'm gonna give him a haircut. His damn mother don't do shit.' He looked over at Strike. 'Yeah, I didn't tell you – you hear what happened in the Papi thing?'

'What . . .'

'They arrested Buddha Hat. How you like that?'

'*Who* did?'

'Jersey City detectives. They got them a witness. One of Papi's boys who was in the car that night? This boy got all shot up in the back, he must've run off before you got there. They got him in a Bronx hospital. The police told him if he ID'd the shooter they'd drop a homicide charge they had on him. So he went and put the hat on Buddha Hat.'

'How you know all this?' Strike was spellbound, everything rushing up into his head – the night in New York, the bullshit roust by the Port Authority cops, and then Victor, what this could mean for Victor.

'Yeah, I got somebody in the prosecutor's office out in Hudson County. You know, a friend.'

'So-so Champ – '

'Nah, it ain't Champ. It's Buddha Hat. Papi was selling kis to like me and three other people in town. Buddha Hat knew about it and he had Papi payin' him – for protection or, you know, permission to sell it like from behind Champ's back, you know, pay up or I'll get Champ to get me to kill you – and like I guess Papi didn't want to pay no more and it went down like that. But yeah, Buddha Hat was acting on his own.'

'Ha-how you know all this?'

'My Hudson County friend says it's all in the deposition. Pisses me off too, 'cause Papi never told me about no other business he had in town. I guess he must've not trusted me.' Rodney lifted his son by the armpits and dropped him on a stool. 'It's a damn sneaky business, ain't it?'

'So Boo-Buddha Hat *knows* about us?' Strike found himself grinning, though he had no idea why. There was nothing funny about this at all.

'Yeah, but I ain't worried about it,' Rodney said, opening the cash register and taking out a pair of barber scissors from under the change tray. 'They got him on a homicide in Hudson County. They ain't gonna trade that off for drug information in Dempsy. Maybe they trade it, but only to get somebody like Champ – you know, maybe like for some kingpin bring-down. But shit, that's good for us too.'

With Buddha Hat locked up, Strike wondered whether it was safe to tell Rodney that Buddha Hat killed Darryl Adams too. But he wasn't sure what would be gained by that. It wasn't like Rodney would go running to the cops with it, help him out with Victor. And he still might be enraged at the idea that Champ's hit man got involved in his secret business.

'Ha-how many bodies you think Buddha Hat got on him?'

'Not as much as people think.' Rodney gave his son's head a one-eyed squint, planning his angle of attack.

'I heard *lots*. Shit, I woo-wouldn't be surprised . . .' Strike didn't know where to take it.

'Surprised at what?' Rodney raised the scissors over his son's head, snipping air.

Strike shrugged.

'Surprised at what?' Rodney repeated, but before Strike could figure out how to slide away from the subject, Rodney put down the scissors. Following Rodney's eyes, Strike saw the Toyota from Delaware pulling up in front.

Rodney laughed and bellowed out, '*Gang*ster time, *gang*ster time,' making both Strike and his son jerk backward.

The Delaware boys ambled into the store wearing their gold, but Strike noticed that this time they weren't acting goofy and grinning – not even smiling, in fact. And one of the guys was new; he was a little older and wore less gold.

'Who's this?' Rodney tilted his chin to the new guy, finally commencing to cut his son's hair.

'This my cousin,' one of the kids said. 'Sneezy couldn't come, his father's in the hospital, so like this Carlton. He's my cousin.'

Carlton put his hand out to Rodney, who let it hang in the air for a few seconds as he worked on his son's head, finally shaking it after he'd gotten across who was on top.

Strike saw Carlton stiffen over Rodney's little power play but then quickly recover, shrugging it off and digging into his pocket to produce eighteen hundred dollars. And as he walked off toward Herman's, Strike thought about how swiftly this new guy had put Rodney's disrespect behind him. He tried to decide: should he feel impressed or worried?

*   *   *

Alone in his dope room, spooning the cut into the Delaware ounces, Strike thought about Buddha Hat in jail, remembered again that night in New York. He still couldn't figure out what the Hat had wanted from him. Some kind of friendship? Maybe, but neither of them had followed it up. Besides, as always, it was better to have enemies – at least with enemies, you knew what they were.

As Strike got ready to lock up, he realized that something else was bothering him. He stood in the doorway of the room running down an inventory of obsessions: Victor, Buddha Hat, Tyrone. Stomach medicine, Iris, Andre. Rodney sticking that .38 in his face. The Homicide and his accusations. His mother, his gun. His gun. It was supposed to be in the drawer with the dope, but it wasn't there.

Strike tried to think back to where he had seen it last. In the drawer? In the car? Or did he take it away from here and somehow lose it? Not that the gun couldn't be replaced, or even that he would want to replace it. It was just . . . What the fuck happened to it? Three hundred ninety-five dollars, too. Well, he'd have to figure out where he could have left it.

On his way back with the ounces, Strike realized how close he'd come to telling Rodney something he shouldn't have. But shit, he thought, the guy is locked up – somebody should tell *some*body about Darryl Adams, do *some*thing on that for Victor's sake. But here it was again, the old problem – how could he drop a dime on the Hat without getting himself in hot water?

And then it came to him, just like that: Do it anonymous. Just dial 911 like a citizen.

But maybe it would be best to call Homicide direct, 911 would probably fuck it up. Looking up and down the crowded Saturday night boulevard, Strike dug into his pocket for change, his temples pulsing. Just call Homicide direct, tell the secretary . . .

But what if one of the Homicides themselves answered the phone, especially that fat one who had been giving him such a hard time lately?

It would be better to call it in tomorrow, Sunday, when things were quieter. He couldn't imagine that Homicide working on a nice Sunday afternoon if the guy had any pull at all.

Standing by the phone, Strike did a little practice run, his words directed to his shoes in a self-conscious whisper. It would just take a couple of quick sentences, a few fast words, then hang up. Simple. Tomorrow.

32

On Sunday morning, Rocco surrendered his gun at the security gate and signed the visitors' log book. He'd brought cigarettes and a stack of magazines for Victor. A correction officer flipped through the magazines and dumped out the carton of Newports, looking for dope, weapons or whatever else Rocco might be trying to smuggle inside. Then the CO phoned Jimmy Newton in the conference room.

'He's here. You still want to see him?'

Rocco was escorted up to the third floor and down to the end of a narrow hallway decorated with prisoner art. The conference room was skinny and airless, with garish silvery wallpaper and no window save for the one set into the door. Jimmy and Victor sat at an old wooden library table. Victor was dressed in a T-shirt, sweatpants and rubber flip-flops. Rocco slid around to shake hands with both of them, Jimmy looking tense and Victor, his eyes smudged with exhaustion, looking as if he had just fallen off the earth. Victor's handshake was feathery and tremulous: Beautiful, thought Rocco, just perfect. On the table was Jimmy's tape recorder, a transcript of the confession and the arrest report. Dropping the magazines and cigarettes in front of Victor, Rocco took a chair.

'How you doing there, Victor, remember me?'

Victor nodded, his eyes focused on the table.

'I thought you could use something to read. I heard it gets pretty boring in here.'

Victor lifted a corner of his mouth but said nothing.

'Awright,' Jimmy said, and turned on the recorder. 'Victor? Investigator Klein is here to talk to you now, and ah, as I've said to you before, I strongly advise that you decline to talk to him at this point in time. As I previously warned you, if you say anything during this interview that deals directly with the circumstances surrounding the death of Darryl Adams, it can be used against you. So, once again, my advice is that you do *not* go through with this.

But if you want to waive your rights, you can speak to this man now.'

Rocco maintained a sober expression during Jimmy's disclaimer speech. He knew Jimmy was just covering his ass on tape as a hedge against any eventual charges of representational incompetence, but he also knew that Jimmy was intrigued by what might come out of this. Any mention of Strike, his drug dealing or his whereabouts on the night of the murder would open up an ocean of red herrings if the case went to trial. In fact, if Rocco even implied his doubts about Victor's guilt, Jimmy could lay down a serious charge of post-arrest negligence, since his client's lockup was based on a confession with no witnesses and no corroboration. So either way, mentioning either brother, Rocco could be hanging himself on tape for all the world to hear.

'Do you want to waive your rights and speak to this man?'

Victor nodded his head and pulled the red tab on the cellophane covering a pack of cigarettes. Jimmy had told Rocco on the phone that the kid had at first balked at the interview, then changed his mind even while insisting he didn't have anything to say that he hadn't said before. Which only confirmed Rocco's hunch: Why would Victor agree to the sit-down unless there was something he wanted to get off his chest?

'Investigator Klein, I'd like to establish some ground rules here. I'm not allowing any questions addressed to my client pertaining to the Darryl Adams homicide. Anything he may have said to you prior to this meeting in regards to that subject is off limits. Any references made by anyone else to his participation are also off limits. In other words, I want this to be a purely passive, nonincriminatory interview. If I feel you're asking him incriminating questions, or if I feel that you are trying to trick him or manipulate him in any way, shape or form, this interview is over.'

Rocco nodded, but he wasn't the least bit worried. He was smarter than Jimmy Newton. He would do Jimmy's job for him and peel this kid right down to his shorts.

'Fair enough, counselor.' Rocco hunched forward, elbows on the table. 'OK, Victor, before I get started, is there anything you want me to explain?'

Victor had stripped the last of the ten cigarette packs of its cellophane. 'Victor?'

'No. I told you what I told you.' Victor shrugged at the denuded packs, looking sulky and shut down. But there was a pulse in the corner of one eye, rapid as a heartbeat, and Rocco thought it could be more than just shot nerves.

'OK now, I tell you what I want you to do, just to keep this on the up-and-up? I ask you a question? I want you to count to five before you answer. This gives Mr Newton time to decide if it's inappropriate, and it gives you time to decide if you really want to answer for your own self. OK? Even if it's a simple yes or no response, count to five. Is that all right with you, counselor?'

Jimmy nodded in agreement.

'OK, good. Now, I want to tell you right up front. I am ninety-nine point nine percent sure you did *not* kill Darryl Adams.'

Rocco let that lie there, savoring the surprised look on Jimmy's face. First bang out of the box and he'd given Jimmy what he wanted for the cross-examination. It was his way of saying to Jimmy, It's my ass too, hoping Jimmy would now let him go over the edge a little with the questions to come.

Victor was shaking his head, smiling grimly, his eyes down.

'Do you want to know *why* I think you didn't do it?'

Victor palmed the side of his face as if bored.

'Because I don't think you have it *in* you to kill someone.' Rocco almost gagged on that, the dumbness of that kind of observation. 'I went back and talked to the reverend? Hey, *you* go to church, you believe in God, in heaven and hell, and I *know* that you know there's a price to pay for murder both in this world *and* the next, right?'

Surprised by the bizarreness of his own opening gambit, Rocco told himself to calm down, to focus. 'And I talked to your mother. Do you know what she told me? She says you're the gentlest man in the world. She says if you don't see your kids every day you completely fall apart, and *I* can't believe that a man as moral as you, as utterly devoted to his family as you, would do something *so* reckless, *so* stupid and out of character, something that he had to know from the git-go would deny him access to his wife and children for thirty *years* – '

'Investigator,' Jimmy warned.

'Or even for five years. Let's say you completely luck out on this, draw reckless manslaughter as opposed to aggravated manslaughter or purposeful homicide. Five years. Not see your kids for *five years*. Then you *still* got to worry about hell, and I don't think there's a deal element on that end of it, do you?'

Jimmy threw Rocco a begging look. 'Hey . . .'

Victor covered his face with his hands, and Rocco held his palms out to signal that he was backing off. 'Look, Victor. I'm just going to say something. It's not even a question, so just listen, OK? I think someone else killed Darryl Adams, and I think you know who that person is, and I think out of some misguided sense of love, loyalty, responsibility, hero worship or I don't know what, you're taking the heat for this other person, because I think somewheres you believed that since you've never been in trouble before and you're a family man and you hold down two jobs and you go to church and all that, that no jury would ever convict you of this crime.'

Rocco let his words hang for a minute. Still masking his eyes with his hands, Victor raised his chin so that his Adam's apple projected like a wedge.

'Would you like to know who *I* think did it? Hear me out. Darryl Adams, most likely, was a drug dealer and, I don't know, maybe he was selling on someone else's turf, maybe he was skimming. But whatever it was, he must have pissed off the wrong people and *I* think – '

'Excuse me, Investigator Klein.' Jimmy made a show of flipping through the arrest report. 'Where's all this? I don't have anything on this.'

'Well, this is just a theory right now.' Rocco gave him a dirty look, silently requesting that Jimmy wait until afterward to hang him on this.

Jimmy made a sour face but said nothing further.

'Like I was saying. I think Darryl Adams was screwing somebody, they found out about it and wanted him popped. And then . . . Well, your brother deals too, right? So they got your brother, they got Ronnie to kill him, and then Ronnie told you about it, and you knew that if he got convicted on it, with his jacket and his associations, he'd get thirty years or maybe even a lethal injection.'

Jimmy started to interrupt, jerking forward in his chair, but then let it go.

Victor dropped a pack of cigarettes on the floor and bent down under the table to retrieve it. Waiting for him to reappear, Rocco had the distinct impression that the kid was trying to hide.

'And I *know* you met with your brother in Rudy's the night of the shooting. And I *know* you met with him on Saturday, the day before you turned yourself in. And I think that that Saturday your brother gave you the gun and told you if he ever got caught you should come forward and say, "Hey, I'm the one, here's the gun." But you didn't wait. I don't know, maybe you just couldn't stand it, waiting around with a gun in your home. Maybe you were afraid of your brother getting killed by one of his higher-ups who was nervous about him talking. Maybe you were afraid that your brother would get shot by some young hot-dog cop during an arrest. Maybe you didn't want him taken in under any circumstances because you have such a great love and a sense of responsibility to your own flesh and blood. But whatever the reason, you couldn't stand waiting around, so you figured the sooner you got this over with, the safer everybody would be, and so last Sunday you walked up to Reverend Posse – '

'I told you before,' Victor said slowly, his hands over his face again. Jimmy jumped in. 'Victor . . .'

'It was self-defense.' Behind the mask of his hands Victor's voice had a little tremolo in it. Rocco felt like he would give anything for the kid to show his eyes.

'Victor,' Jimmy said again. Rocco looked at the lawyer and clasped his hands in prayer, begging him to hang in. Jimmy tilted back on his chair's hind legs, hissing his discomfort.

Rocco talked fast. 'Self-defense, OK, self-defense. But I don't know. I see how it is out there, all that blood money floating around, fifteen-year-old kids driving new cars, wearing gold – I mean, I don't know how *you* feel about it, working like you do, but I swear, sometimes *I see* that? I feel like I'm some kind of asshole for punching a time clock, you know?'

Victor put his hands down but spoke to his knuckles, anger edging into his voice. 'Me and you out there is two different things.'

'OK, you're right, you're right.' Rocco plowed through his own embarrassment. 'Alls I'm saying is, I talked to Kiki, I talked to Hector, I know all about the shit you had to put up with on both jobs to get those paychecks every week. But you did it, week after week. I mean, talk about self-defense, you must've felt like you were up to your chin in shit out there, you know, feeling like some kind of horse's ass for trying to do the decent thing. Not that I've ever thought you'd be the kind of guy to sell dope or anything like that, but' – Rocco put his hand in front of Jimmy's face to stop any protest – 'did your brother offer you money to come in on this? If he did, I would totally understand it.'

'Hey!' Jimmy snapped.

'No,' Victor said.

Rocco kept going. 'No, hah? OK, then let me ask you this. Your brother's out on the street. Is he doing the right thing by your wife and kids?'

'That's not his responsibility,' Victor said calmly.

Rocco paused, the kid's steadiness making him a little nervous. 'I understand you got another bail hearing coming up soon. There's a good chance with your background you'll get the cash option. Alls you got to put up is five thousand bucks. But according to your mother, that's like just about all you managed to save up for that co-op you wanted to move into. Unless, I mean, is your brother gonna at least help you out on the bail? I understand he's making good money out there. Is he gonna take care of your bail? Is he gonna do *anything* for you?'

'That's not his responsibility.'

Jimmy ran a thumb across his throat, then shook his head.

'Look, I got to tell you. I talked to him two, three times already, your brother, and you know what? He doesn't seem to be too concerned with this whole situation. I get such a feeling of nonchalance off him that, ah, it's like he's resigned himself to the fact that you're gonna serve thirty years and he's not. I don't know, maybe you think he's gonna come in like at the last second, tell the truth, or maybe *he* thinks you're gonna beat this thing. But I swear, whatever you guys got up your sleeve it ain't gonna work. It ain't gonna work.'

Victor shook his head, baring his teeth.

Jimmy hunched forward, the front legs of his chair hitting the floor with a bang. 'OK, Investigator.'

Rocco raced on. 'If you won't do it for yourself, do it for your kids. They're gonna be fatherless so long that by the time you come out of prison it's not even gonna make a difference to them anymore *who* you are.'

'Enough!' Jimmy put a hand in Rocco's face as a high-pitched noise escaped from Victor.

Sliding around Jimmy's hand, Rocco finally got a good look at the kid's face, saw those thick brows knotted in pain and the lashes starred with tears.

Rocco broke into a sweat: The kid is crying? Fuck the brother. What *gives* here?

Jimmy moved his hand away, fiddled aimlessly with his papers. 'I think this interview is over.'

'Naw, I want to say something,' Victor announced, rising to a half-crouch.

'Victor, I'm advising – '

'Naw, I want to talk. I wanna say something.'

Victor sat down again, seemed to gather himself for one burst of words. 'I understand what you're doing here, working this thing on me with my brother not caring an' setting me up. So OK, I'm just gonna tell you one more time. My brother was not there, *I* was. It was self-defense, OK? It was self-defense. I can *live* with that. I told *you* that.' He pointed at Rocco. 'And I told *you* that.' He pointed at Jimmy.

'Yeah?' Rocco leaned forward. 'Then why did you agree to talk to me like this? What did you want to say to me, Victor? Why am I here?'

'Hey, Rocco, that's it.'

Rocco ignored Jimmy and stared at Victor.

'This interview is over, Rocco.'

Victor's face vanished behind his hands again.

'It's over, Jimmy? Good. Turn the tape off. Turn it off.'

Rocco made no effort to rise. Jimmy hesitated, then did as he was told.

'It's over. Fine. I'm not even here now. But I got to ask you something, Victor, and I swear to both you and your lawyer that this is for myself and that I will *never* arrest your brother for anything that I hear the answer to right now. But if you don't come clean with me, I swear to God I'll hunt him down like a wild animal. Tell me the truth – and it's like I never fucking heard it. Just for myself. You want to protect your brother? Good. So seal it up with what I just promised you. Tell me the truth – did your brother kill Darryl Adams?'

'Jesus *Christ*, Rocco!'

Victor briefly met Rocco's eyes, shook his head sadly, stood up, collected all the individual cigarette packs and stashed them inside his T-shirt and down the legs of his sweatpants. Ignoring the magazines, he walked to the door and stood waiting as Jimmy phoned the guards to be let out of the conference room.

Rocco stared at the crystalline hill of cellophane, amazed at what had just come out of his mouth, at how he had just jumped off a cliff.

'OK, just tell me this,' he said softly, talking mostly to himself. 'When did he give you the gun. Saturday, right? Was it Saturday?'

'What did I *tell* you, you stupid bastard,' Jimmy yelled at Rocco, the two of them standing in front of the jail-courthouse complex, the only people for blocks around. 'Now look what you went and did. I got you by the *balls*. I got you on tape quacking like a duck, you dumb fuck. Tell me what I'm supposed to do now, Rocco.' Jimmy glared at him, his mouth open in a rectangle like a marionette.

'Hey, you gotta do what you gotta do.' Rocco felt there but not there, as unreal as the deserted downtown Sunday afternoon street. 'I came to you, right Jimmy? I'm a big boy. Every once in a while you got to go with your guts, you know? What's the point of doing something, developing all these instincts, and then when the time comes you don't go with your guts, like you never knew nothing but the rules. So . . . I went.'

'You went with your guts.'

'Exactly.'

'Nah, nah, come on, Rocco.'

'It wasn't just, I mean, in my heart, twenty years says to me this kid didn't do it. I fucked up today, but I *know* . . .'

Jimmy looked around, unzipped his pants and tucked in his shirt. 'Rocco, Rocco.'

'Jimmy, you should talk to this kid's people. I never – I mean, this kid's been hanging fire all his life . . .' Rocco trailed off, thinking about something Victor had said. 'Hey, Jimmy, "Self-defense. I can *live* with that" . . . "I can *live* with that." What's that supposed to mean?'

'Hey, Investigator, the interview's over.' Jimmy rebuckled his belt, hoisted his briefcase and gave Rocco his back.

Rummaging around in the Homicide supply closet looking for a notepad, Rocco came across a few vodka miniatures from Shaft Deli–Liquors nesting behind the quart of stoop wine that was reserved for witnesses. Half an hour later he sat alone in the office, playing with the empties, musing that they were the exact shape and size of the .50-caliber bullets displayed by the gun nut three desks back. Rocco twirled a bottle, fantasizing about how he should have overpowered Jimmy Newton on the deserted street, taken his briefcase and ripped out the tape. His word against mine. Cracking the seal on the last bottle, he heard himself offer to protect Strike from arrest if Victor would only tell him the truth. Was he completely nuts?

Still, what did the kid mean by 'Self-defense. I can live with that . . .' The words had sounded like the end result of a lot of internal juggling, but Rocco couldn't decode their significance.

Rocco looked down at the phone log. Except for the mother's house and Hambone's, none of the numbers checked out. Rocco rolled the print-out into a ball, hooked it into the wastebasket and considered jumping in after it, soggily thinking that maybe he should retire before the trial, which wouldn't be until next spring at the earliest. He'd be past his twenty by the fall, so he could retire from Homicide a few months from now and not worry about getting kicked off into a cruiser. He was planning on going out on his twenty anyhow, so what was the problem? And this way he would fuck up the state's case at the trial, save an innocent kid with no damage to himself. So what if Jimmy Newton made a horse's ass of him on the stand. Who cares?

Rocco scanned the calendar printed on his desk blotter, counting the weeks until September, October, and in a burst of warmhearted terror found himself dialing home.

'Patty, hey, listen, I don't think I ever really *tell* you how much I love you, you and the baby. You're the most important things in my life, people in my life, you know that?'

The words sounded tinny even to Rocco's ear. She took a few seconds to respond, Rocco guessing that the hesitation meant she was trying to decide whether to ask him if he was bombed.

'That's nice to know,' Patty said finally.

'Let me talk to Erin, let me talk to Erin.'

Erin came on the phone sounding distracted, as if in the middle of something complicated. 'Daddy . . .'

'Hi honey,' he said. 'What you doing?'

'The woof here. Hide Daddy. *Hide.*'

'The woof,' Rocco repeated, saying it himself to get a grip on the word. 'The wolf?'

'*Hide!*'

The other line started to ring on his phone. 'Hang on sweetie.' He punched in the call, praying it wasn't a job. 'Homicide.'

Rocco heard breathing, street traffic: someone on a pay phone. But the caller was silent.

'Homicide,' he said again, getting annoyed.

'Buh-buh-boo . . . Boo . . .'

A young black male doing baby talk.

'Buh-h . . .' There was a sigh of clammy exasperation, then a click. The caller had hung up.

Rocco frowned. Not baby talk: that was a stammer. Rising from his desk, forgetting his daughter on the other line, Rocco felt sure of it: A goddamn stammer.

Part Five

GIVE IT

33

The last of the package was taking forever to unload. At the time of Strike's butchered phone call on Sunday, there were only three ounces left, but now it was Monday afternoon and the three ounces remained. Strike had spent the past twenty-four hours sweating it out in Rodney's store, reduced to selling candy bars and sodas, dying a little every time a late-model American sedan drove by, sure it was the Homicide coming to snatch him up. All Sunday night Rodney had blathered on, telling Strike war stories about the seventies, explaining again how he had found out that Darryl was cheating him at Ahab's, even adding a new chapter about how he had taken care of Darryl's secret supplier too. The way Rodney told it, a white guy from Bayonne was now blind in one eye after getting whacked upside the head one night by some crazy unknown nigger flying out of a beat-up Cadillac with a softball bat.

Just before five, Strike sold two of the remaining ounces to a local kid. He was way past the point of caring what was Champ's territory and what was considered out of town – whatever moved the dope was fine by him.

One ounce to go. Strike stepped out of the store to ask the time from a passerby. Hearing that it was five o'clock, he signaled to Rodney that he had to leave.

Rodney strolled outside and leaned against the doorway. 'Where you going?' 'You know.' Strike started to walk backwards. 'My friend.' Rodney nodded. 'You come back right after.' Strike paced in front of the candy store at the corner of Krumm and Loyola for twenty minutes before Jo-Jo rolled up in his Delta 88. Leaning into the front passenger window, Strike dropped his payment on the seat.

'How you been, Strike?' Jo-Jo said, peeking into the envelope.

'Awright.'

'You want to buy some tickets to the Rappers 4 Life concert in Passaic?'

'Naw.'

'House seats, man.'

'That's OK.'

'How 'bout I sell them to you, and you can sell 'em for more on your own?'

Strike didn't bother to answer.

'Awright. So I'll see you next week, same time same station?'

Frowning, Strike abruptly pushed off from the side of the car.

'What's the problem, Strike?'

'No, you know, you got nothin' to tell me?'

'Nope.' Jo-Jo shrugged. 'Nothin' coming down.'

'Yeah, huh? Last time you said Monday night's gonna be *knock* night.' Strike sucked his teeth, a small wave of anger rising up.

'Hey kid, you know who you remind me of? My mother.' Jo-Jo leaned across the shotgun seat to speak more intimately. 'She's seventy-nine years old, goes to the doctor like you go to the corner store, has every medical test known to science, then she feels cheated because there's nothing wrong with her.' Jo-Jo came even closer. 'I said there's nothing coming down. What would you prefer, a brush with death?'

Buh-buh-boo.

The kid had sounded like Bing Crosby, but maybe Strike was trying to spit out somebody's name, tell Rocco something anonymously. Or maybe he was calling to work out a deal for himself and then changed his mind. Rocco was still trying to figure it out a day later as he sat in the Homicide office overseeing the haircut of a quadruple murderer.

The guy was handcuffed to a chair by Mazilli's desk, a Dominican who, along with another of his countrymen, had killed four Mafia-connected drug dealers over in Rydell. He had turned state's against his confederate and was now being groomed for tomorrow's trial by an effeminate Filipino barber. The murderer was six foot seven and thin, his shiny black hair hanging straight to his shoulder blades, his eyes baggy and deep from six months of looking over his shoulder in County.

Glancing at Rocco, the barber held out a fistful of greasy locks. 'I should shampoo this.'

Rocco didn't answer. He looked right through the barber, the murderer, his mind still playing with Strike's strangled phone call. The kid obviously had something more he wanted to say. Was there any point in going out to the benches again?

Mazilli walked into the office with a cup of coffee, and the murderer rattled his cuffs at him. 'Yo, can he shampoo me?'

'No. And don't get his fucking hair all over my desk.' Mazilli glanced at Rocco, then stopped and took a longer look. 'You OK?'

'What?'

'You have a fight with your wife?'

'Me? Not yet.'

Rocco turned on the five o'clock news, realizing that it had been days since he'd told Mazilli about his Strike and Victor action. Rocco imagined laying it all out for his partner, trying to justify his actions step by step, getting long looks and heavy silences in return. He blinked hard, trying to come back to the moment.

'Maz, when this guy's done, you want to get something to eat?'

Mazilli sipped his coffee. 'Nah, I got to go do something.'

'What?'

'I got to go arrest our friend.'

'Which friend is this?'

'I be arrestin' Rodney Little.'

'For what?'

Mazilli made a face. 'Jo-Jo Kronic called me. Couple of days ago they grabbed a car full of kids up from Delaware, they just bought two ounces off Rodney. These idiots had to stop and get some Hambone's before they went home, so they pull into the lot with Delaware plates and a car phone, right? Like a fucking neon sign. Anyways, the kids gave up Rodney, and Jo-Jo had them go back to the candy store with an undercover, make another buy, and now he wants me to pick the guy up. Figures with me, Rodney'll come in easy 'cause we're such good buddies.'

'Yo, could you turn that to channel seven?' the murderer asked, throwing Rocco a small polite smile.

'Let him make his own fucking arrests,' Rocco said, switching channels.

'You know what I think it is? Jo-Jo just don't want Rodney to know who's behind this. Rodney's probably got some dirt on him and he doesn't want to take a chance on the guy shooting off his mouth.'

Rocco swallowed a yawn. 'So why bust him at all?'

'Maybe Rodney dissed him, you know, cut off his extortion payments or something. So now he's getting back at him with a harassment bust, like a fuck-you bust. It's OK. I don't mind having a favor on that pink-eyed bastard.' Mazilli put down his coffee. 'You want to come?'

*   *   *

At six o'clock Monday evening, only minutes after Strike had returned
from paying off Jo-Jo, a huge white guy in a guayabera shirt waddled
into Rodney's store. He was a bartender from Greenwich Village, but
to Strike he was the last ounce, the end of the stash.

Strike walked out of the store like a rubber man, heading for Herman's
to retrieve the dope, tasting his freedom in the evening air. But after he
went a half-dozen steps, Rodney called out his name. When Strike turned,
Rodney flashed him two fingers – their signal for cutting an ounce halfway
to pure laxative – and Strike almost dropped to his knees in despair. If he
did it Rodney's way, they'd still have another half ounce to unload.

In his room at Herman's, Strike sat staring at the uncut ounce, at the
brown bottle, at the triple-beam scale, weighed his shot nerves against
the clock and thought, Fuck it. Putting the scale and the laxative back
in the dresser, he left the room with the uncut ounce.

Twenty minutes later, Strike and Rodney stood side by side behind the
candy counter, watching silently as the bartender, his right leg sticking
straight out behind him for balance, leaned over a garbage can directly
across the street from the store and fished out the package Strike had
dropped inside on his way back from Herman's.

As the bartender walked off for his car, Strike could feel his heart
beating in his face.

'Yeah, so, that's it,' he said.

Rodney scowled at his young son, who was toddling around the
deserted store licking one of the balls from the pool table.

Strike wasn't sure whether Rodney had heard him. He moved out
from behind the counter. 'That's it, OK?'

'What do you mean that's it,' Rodney said.

'We all *out*. No more left.' Strike fought to control his breathing.

'Yeah?' Rodney said. 'We don't got like a half ounce left?'

'Shit, inventory ain't your strong suit, you know?' The grin he was
trying to suppress spread from ear to ear.

Rodney gazed at him thoughtfully. 'We out, huh?'

'Yeah, so I'm gonna go now.' Strike rocked from foot to foot.
'Awright?'

Taking a Hershey bar from under the glass, Rodney eased himself out
from behind the counter and walked slowly toward Strike, the candy
bar between his teeth.

Strike shut his eyes and reflexively covered his stomach, but Rodney
moved right past him, picked up his son by the armpits and carried
him back to the stool. Strike exhaled heavily, feeling a dampness across

his middle as Rodney retrieved the scissors from the cash register and prepared for another go-around on his son's head.

Strike glided backward toward the door. 'Yeah, so I'll see you later.'

'Go by the benches,' Rodney said, talking through the chocolate.

'Nah, I got to stay clear of Andre, man.'

'Hey, *fuck* Andre. Don't be scared a no Andre.' Rodney clacked the scissors. 'When we was in high school together? We was both on the wrestling team? We had us a fight, and let me tell you, man . . .'

Rodney let it hang, and Strike waited.

'Yeah, well, he kicked my ass, but I got *his* ass suspended off the team. So fuck him. He just a fat-assed bully boy. Don't you be afraid a no Andre.'

'Yeah, uh-huh, awright. So, I see you later.'

Strike walked out the door and pulled up short. The heavyset Homicide and the one from Shaft Deli were just getting out of a tan Plymouth.

'Hey-y . . . look who's here.' The heavyset cop mimed holding a phone to his face and flashed teeth. 'Buh-buh-boo. Right?'

Milking the drawstrings of his sweatshirt hood, his face disappearing down to his nose, Strike took off up the street.

Rocco held Mazilli's arm for a moment, watching Strike scamper up toward JFK, Rocco thinking, On rat's feet. At the corner, Strike took a quick look backwards and Rocco threw him a wave.

Shrugging off an inquiring glance from Mazilli, Rocco followed him inside the store.

Rodney stood behind the counter, half a candy bar sticking out of his mouth like a stiff brown tongue, a pair of scissors poised over the head of a toddler. Trying to keep his balance on a vinyl bar stool, the boy looked miserable.

Hunching down, Mazilli looked the boy in the eye and made little twiddly finger waves. 'Love child, runnin' wild . . .'

'What's up, Mazilli? What you need?' Rodney gave Rocco a cool up-and-down look, then brushed a light layer of hair off the candy counter.

'I needs *you*, brother.'

'Yeah? What for?'

'I got me a warrant on you.'

'Say what? A search warrant?'

'Arrest.'

'What for?' Rodney said, sounding only mildly irritated.

Mazilli helped himself to a bag of chips. 'Draft dodging, what the hell you think?'

'Arrest for *what*, Mazilli?'

'You must've sold to an undercover, you dumb prick. What're you, so hungry you're selling shit yourself?'

Rodney's face went dark and dangerous. 'Who set me up?'

'Hey, what do I know? I'm Homicide.'

'What's that mean?'

'That means somebody says to me, Rodney's your buddy. He's not gonna break balls if you go in, so . . .'

'Gah-damn.' Rodney threw down the scissors in disgust. 'And you ain't gonna tell me shit about this, right?'

'You want to give somebody a call to come watch the store? Or you want to just lock up?'

'Yeah, an' what about my *son* here. What do I do with him, man?'

Mazilli nodded to the phone. 'Call his mother.'

Enjoying himself, Rocco watched Rodney dial, then listened as Rodney started to talk, hot and low, speaking to whatever woman answered the phone as if this whole thing was her fault.

'I said come on down and get him . . . Naw, not in no hour. I got to go in on something, I'm arrested . . . Yeah arrested . . . Never you mind on what. Get your ass down here *now*, just – ' Rodney pressed the phone to his gut and looked up at Mazilli. 'Jesus Lord Christ Almighty, this woman . . .'

Mazilli took the phone. 'Who's this, Deirdre?'

Rodney flinched at the name.

'Sorry, Carol? Carol, this is Mazilli. Listen, I got to take Rodney in, so either you come down here, get the kid in like ten minutes, or you come get him tomorrow morning from Youth and Family Services.' He winked at Rodney as the mother talked in his ear. 'We're going to the Western Precinct . . . OK, but you best get there before I finish the report or he's going into the shelter, OK? Yeah, bye.' Mazilli hung up. 'She says for you to take him with you. She'll pick him up at the station.'

Hoisting his son on his shoulders, Rodney hissed with exasperation. 'Who's behind this shit, man. Who served me up?'

The second stop on Strike's freedom run was Herman Brown's apartment. He carried seven thousand dollars in his pocket now, having already cleaned out the safe at the house with the crazy old people and the retarded man. He felt vaguely bad about not telling them that next month there wouldn't be any money from him to cover their rent, but if he told them, they might say something to somebody else, and pretty soon everybody would know that Strike was up to something. He drove slowly along the boulevard, thinking, Besides, they're getting money for just being the way they are, all stinky and crazy. It's not like they'd ever *done* anything for him.

Strike didn't think he had any money stashed up at Herman's, but he wanted to pick up the scale and throw away all the dope debris – he didn't like leaving traces that could come back on him. Plus, he wanted to look for that damn gun one more time. Maybe it was in a different drawer, or maybe in the safe under the bed. The safe: he'd pick that up too. Maybe he could sell it and the scale before he left town, add to his stake. And after he cleaned out Herman's, he planned to collect the rest of his money, another fifteen thousand at two other apartments, and then he would vanish.

But as he cruised JFK and tried to believe he'd never see the boulevard again, he began to question himself, wondering what the hell he was doing – if, in fact, he really did plan to go anywhere, live a different life. Dempsy was his world, and clocking his only experience with success – was he just making more trouble for himself, running away for no good reason?

Pulling up to Herman's apartment building, Strike saw a crowd and an ambulance. He rolled off slowly, the Accord in a creeping double-park, until he saw two medics come out the door carrying an orange body bag down the front steps. Following the stretcher was the fifty-year-old Chinese lady. Driving away, Strike wondered if it had been old age or some break-in mayhem, wondered what would happen to all those beautiful old hats, tried to remember if he had any money up there. Probably not, just the scale that cost him ninety-five dollars and maybe the gun that cost him three hundred ninety-five. Also the cheap Sears-bought safe. But everything was replaceable, and maybe this was a sign to leave well enough alone, time to just *go*. Strike thought again about classrooms, quick wrists, kids, some vague notion of working with kids, imagining Tyrone's mother coming up to him someday with tears in her eyes, saying, 'Goddamn, was I wrong about *you*.'

Rodney's girlfriend had never showed up at the precinct, and after a half-hour wait Mazilli had had no choice but to call for a social worker

from County, instructing her to pick up the child at BCI, the next stop
for Rodney on the road to jail.

At BCI, Mazilli had held the baby as Rodney, declining Rocco's offer
of assistance, fingerprinted himself. Mazilli had also carried the boy up the
two flights of stairs to the bail clerk's window so that Rodney wouldn't
get his son's clothes inked up. Leading the procession, Rodney had gotten
darker and tighter with every step, Rocco smelling the promise of violence
coming off him, wondering if the guy would blow and start a free-for-all
right there on the stairs.

And now Rodney stood in front of the barred window, cleaning the ink
off his hands with a Baby Wipe as the clerk scanned the arrest report and
the thick pedigree print-out. Finally the clerk cleared his throat, pushed
up his glasses and announced, 'Hot Rod Rodney Little. You nathty man,
five thousand dollars, that be your bail.'

'Hey, fuck you motherfucker. Call the damn judge like you supposed to.'

'Five large, chief.' The clerk gave the baby a hunched-up kootchy-koo,
impervious to Rodney's rage. The clerks were supposed to get the
numbers from the judge on call, but most judges didn't want to be
bothered until after the fact, especially since the clerks knew the bail
formulas as well as the judges did.

'Rodney, you want to give somebody a call?' Mazilli said, jiggling the
baby. 'Bring in the money?'

'Nah, fuck that. I ain't taking no five thousand dollars off the street.
I'll do the damn bullpen tonight. Tomorrow they gonna knock it down
to the ten percent anyhow. This a bullshit headache, man. Who the fuck
set me up, Mazilli? My damn kid's going into a fuckin' shelter? Who
the hell's behind this?'

Mazilli didn't answer, focusing instead on the baby, fussing over some
invisible problem.

'Yeah, you best *not* tell me.' Rodney looked directly at Rocco,
the first time he had acknowledged him all night. 'Save me from a
*homi*cide rap.'

Rocco laughed. 'Don't tell us be*fore*, man. It takes all the fun out of
the investigation.'

Heading down the stairs, Rodney carrying his son now, they bumped
into the social worker on her way up. A red-headed Italian woman, she
immediately complained about being called out of her house just as she
was sitting down to dinner with her family. When Rodney began staring
at her with hate-frosted eyes, Rocco again imagined the possibility of a

stairway brannigan. But a moment later, right behind the social worker, the baby's mother appeared. She was young and chunky, dressed in a silver jump suit, her hair braided and dripping amber beads.

'Where the fuck were *you*?' Rodney shouted over the social worker's head to the mother, ten steps below her.

'He say *Eastern* Precinct.' Her voice was sharp and loud, like an angry person talking over music.

'I said *Western*, Carol,' Mazilli said, smiling benignly.

Carol tromped up the stairs, roughly shouldered aside the social worker and snatched the kid away. 'Yeah, you *best* go to jail.' She wheeled around and marched down again.

'Yeah,' Rodney said, 'I'll go to jail. I'll go anywhere to get away from *you*.'

As Rodney led the two Homicides down to the street, Rocco shrugged to the social worker. 'Sorry about that.'

Driving over to the jail, Rocco thought about Rodney's reputation as the most feared man of his generation still out on the Dempsy streets. He probably deserved it: over the past hour Rodney had mostly confined himself to some dark mutterings, and he had even held his baby for a good part of the time, but Rocco sensed that just underneath the surface lived a blind bonehead fury that, once triggered, could be as nonnegotiable and deadly as any other force of nature. A lot of people on the street liked to bluff a homicidally dangerous side, but the real thing was fairly rare, and as Rocco looked in the rearview mirror at Rodney's rage-tightened face, he started working on a plan to harness what was building right before his eyes, to direct the inevitable firestorm so that it would come down on Strike, burn his house to the ground and send him running for shelter to his only friend in the world – Rocco Klein.

Strike couldn't say why, but instead of collecting the rest of his money and taking off, he found himself walking toward the benches. It was a stupid move, especially with seven thousand dollars in his pockets, but there he was. Maybe it was to take a last look, say goodbye to people, his boys. Maybe somewhere in his mind he even had the notion to go up and see his mother, drop off some cash for Victor's kids.

The sight of his crew lounging around the semicircle of benches filled him with great relief, the rightness of it tempered only by a peripheral tension about where Andre might be. But even that wasn't so bad: it was seven-thirty, and Andre was probably on the way to his knocko squad to start his eight-to-four tour.

'What you all sitting around for?' Strike tried to sound angry.

'They ain't no dope tonight.' Futon sat up on Strike's perch, acting cool, even a little distant. 'Rodney got locked up.'

Strike felt his gut clench. 'What he get locked up for?'

Peanut shrugged and Futon looked off, his aqua headphones replaced by a new pair, tomato red.

Everyone else stayed silent, avoiding Strike's eyes.

'Rodney in *jail*?' Strike saw Tyrone, not on the chain this time but pacing from his building entrance to the sidewalk, back and forth, furiously trying to catch Strike's eye. But Strike didn't want to have anything to do with him: that kid was bad, a bad idea.

'Goddamn, what . . .' Strike noticed Tyrone patting his belt buckle as if sending a signal. Irritated, Strike waved him off, and the kid threw up his hands in despair and vanished into his building.

'Hey, Ronnie!' The voice behind him made Strike want to drop to his knees. He didn't turn around, just sought out the eyes on the benches for sympathy, but the whole crew pretended they didn't see or hear either Strike or the Homicide.

'Ronnie!'

Strike turned to face him. The Homicide was all smiles, waving him over as if he had some great news, extending his hand for a shake, saying, 'Hey Ronnie, man.'

Momentarily seduced, Strike grasped the hand offered. He instantly regretted it.

'Your boss is in County, you hear that?' Rocco said. 'And, like, I just wanted to come by and say thank you for your help.'

Strike tried to extricate himself from the handshake but the cop wouldn't let go. 'Yeah, wuh-well, I don't know nothin' about that. Can I get my *hand* back?'

'Yeah, old Hot Rod. The guy's probably looking at three and a half in on this one, and ah, he don't know who set him up but he *does* know that me and you, we got to be like asshole buddies over this last week, and he *does* know that I was in on the lockup today, and you know, Rodney might be an ugly motherfucker but he ain't stupid. Plus, you see all these windows, empty windows with all those people up there *not* watching me and you shake hands?'

The Homicide kept squeezing Strike's hand and glancing around as if he'd never seen big buildings before. Strike high-stepped in place, thinking maybe he *should* punch this fat motherfucker – it might be worth it even if it did cost him the roll he was holding plus some jail time. But, as if he could read Strike's mind, the Homicide said quietly, 'Don't even think about it.'

Strike went still, his nostrils flaring.

'Yeah, all these windows, and your boys there, your posse. What do you call them, posse or crew?'

Strike looked away.

'Anyways, let me tell you. Rodney? He's gonna be pissed. He makes bail tomorrow, gets back out in the street? People start whispering, gassing up his head . . . Whew. He's gonna be one steamed-up brother.'

'I di-dint *do* nothin',' Strike said, trying to jerk his arm free. 'I dint *say* nothin'.'

The Homicide gripped tighter. 'I wouldn't know what the fuck I'd do if I was you come tomorrow. Probably the best thing? If I was you, I'd run down to the prosecutor's office to*night*, start banging on the door, "Let me in, let me in," work something out to get my ass protected.'

Strike flashed on the memory of looking up into Rodney's eyes, the gun in his face, the taste of metal in his mouth. He jerked his arm again and the Homicide hissed 'Easy, easy,' not letting him go, saying, 'Get yourself in a room with me, tell me what happened on that Ahab's thing, how Rodney pressured you into capping that guy. I mean, that's what you tried to tell me on the phone yesterday, right? Right?'

Strike palmed his face with his free hand, then briefly doubled over himself.

'Just get it off your chest, Ronnie. You'll feel like a million bucks. Just like you tried to do yesterday. C'mon in with me right now, we'll work something out. It'll be the best of all possible worlds, 'cause shit, this way Rodney's not gonna get out tomorrow or *ever*, and you just might beat the whole thing. I mean, nobody wants *you* on this. You had no choice, everybody knows that. Rodney had you scared to death, right? Right?'

The Homicide searched for his eyes, and Strike swiveled his head right left right to escape, to get air. 'But tomorrow? If you don't come in on this? It's just you, him and the foliage, you know what I mean? Hah?'

Right left right. Got to go.

'Hey Ronnie, you got a gun?'

'Naw, I-I ain't got no gun.'

'You want to borrow mine?'

'Man, what are you doing this to me for?'

'Because *you're* doin' it to him.'

'Who!' For a second, Strike forgot about his brother, and then his head filled with images of Victor – in Rudy's, in the rain, in the visitors' room at County. 'Gah-damn. Niggers say they dint do something, you don't believe them. Niggers suh-say they *did* do something, you *still* don't believe them. My brother said he-he did it. I didn't. Now *please* give me back my goddamn hand, 'cause right now you got me kuk-killed over nothing 'cause you don't even know what the fuck you're talking about.'

The Homicide's grip relaxed slightly, and at last Strike pulled free and held the squeezed hand in the cup of his other palm.

The cop eyed him coldly for a second, then reached into his sport jacket, came up with another card and dropped it into Strike's curled palm.

'Rodney gets out tomorrow, brother, you better *duck.*' He gave Strike a long look, then walked off.

Strike stared helplessly at the blank-faced boys on the bench, wanting and not wanting to leave, knowing the minute he walked out of sight the talk would start.

Rocco drove back to the office, exasperated by his inability to bluff the kid. Maybe he shouldn't have tried to scare him with Rodney. Maybe . . . No, Rodney was the right club. The kid said it himself: 'You got me killed.' So why hadn't he come in?

Maybe he'd come in tomorrow, when Rodney hit the street again. But what if Rodney didn't hear about the handshake play? Or what if he trusted Strike too much or trusted Strike's fear of him too much to ever fall for the rumors? Maybe he liked the kid too much to ever believe them or maybe Rodney was just too stupid to put it together or maybe . . . Getting more and more fretful about all the sputter-factors involved, Rocco decided as he drove that what he'd just done was no guarantee of anything. In order to bring this all the way home, he would have to walk right into the lion's den, throw the meat on the floor.

When the Fury rolled up an hour after the Homicide had left, all the boys on the bench chanted, 'Five-oh! Five-oh! Five-oh!' Completely clean of both money and drugs, they began laughing and stomping like fans at a basketball game.

Strike was the only one who walked off. He had never bolted in his life, but he was completely unstrung from standing in the same spot for so long, from trying to find something, anything, to say to the bench that would convince them that the handshake conversation with the Homicide was a setup and that he had nothing to do with Rodney going in. He didn't even realize he'd turned his back on Big Chief and Thumper until he was three steps gone. But by then it was too late: Thumper was instantly beside him, right in his face with that squawky voice – 'Whath up, Yo?' – his hand already in Strike's pocket, plucking out the fat roll like a bloody heart, holding it high and screeching to Big Chief in triumph, 'Mother's Day on Strike! *Ow!*'

'Hey . . .' Rocco stared blindly at the office TV, the phone alongside his jaw. 'I can't make it home tonight. I got a thing I got to do at the jail. I can't do it until like five in the morning.'

Patty sighed. 'Shit'

'Shit?' Rocco jerked his chin into his chest. 'What do you mean, "shit"?'

'No, I just . . . I got something on for tomorrow. I need you to stay with Erin.'

'What's wrong with the babysitter?'

'I gave her the day off. Her sister's coming in from Ecuador.'

'Ecuador, huh?' Rocco envisioned playing with Erin tomorrow morning without ever having gone to sleep.

'It's only the morning. I'll be back by one in the afternoon at the latest.'

'Good. I can sleep from one to three, then go right back to work.' The thought made Rocco feel as if his eyelids were caked with sand. 'Where you got to go?'

Patty hesitated. 'I got a job interview.'

'A what? *What* job? I thought you said you weren't going to work until she was older.'

'I know. I'm . . . I'm not gonna take it. I'm just going to see what it feels like.'

'You mean like a practice run?'

'Never mind,' she muttered. 'I just got a little bored this week. Forget it. I won't go.'

Feeling bad about being snide, Rocco tried to sound hearty. 'What kind of job?'

'Forget it,' Patty said, her voice sullen.

Rocco sat up straighter, a little angry. 'Let me ask you, though, you get some job now, OK?'

'I said I'm not going.'

'No, no. But what I'm saying is, if you *do* take some job, who's gonna be with Erin all day, Adis? The babysitter?'

'Well, you're home until midafternoon, you're free – '

'*Free?*' he snapped, starting to lose control, his mind roiling with images of Strike, Rodney, Patty.

'Well, then that's where Adis comes in. But don't you worry about it. You get your sleep.'

'You know, you say "free" like, I'm *free* all day like, sittin' on the dock of the bay, like, alls I do when I'm not here is fuck off or something.'

'Well, she's your daughter *too*, Rocco, and I would think that if I ever *did* go and get a goddamned job, you'd be hard pressed to find something you'd rather do than spend your days with her.'

Surrendering to the fight, Rocco suddenly became outraged. 'Well, she's your daughter too . . . *Mommy.*'

Rocco shocked himself with the ugliness of that line, but in the moment he took to collect himself to apologize, she said 'Fuck you' and hung up.

Strike was released from the Southern District station house at midnight, Thumper letting him go after keeping him caged up for a few hours while he ran some bullshit warrant checks. He returned Strike's money and walked him back to the street, saying, 'This the way it's gonna be, brother. You best *talk* to that man.'

Strike slipped into an alley to recount his roll – all there. Thumper might be a hothead but he wasn't a thief. A lot of knockos who caught you with a roll would back you up in a stairwell somewhere, the money already in their hand, and ask, 'How much you got here?' And you were supposed to answer half of what it was, the knocko giving you that much back and pocketing the rest. But Strike didn't even care about the money. He was just glad not to be sent over to County and wind up in the bullpen with Rodney.

Rodney. Heading home, Strike decided the best thing to do was be at the arraignment court in the morning, then go right in Rodney's face when he bailed himself out, tell him the situation before anybody else.

Rocco had a nightmare: Erin had vanished. He was running in some woods looking for her, came to a stream and there she was, on the opposite bank in the arms of her great-grandfather, Rocco's grandfather, who had been dead a good five years but was standing there, draped in a decay-splotched winding sheet holding Erin, the both of them smiling back across the stream at him, his grandfather saying, 'It's OK, Davey, she's with me now.' And Erin, with one arm around her great-grandfather's flaking and corrupted neck, waved goodbye to him forever and for all time.

The alarm went off at five A.M., the nightmare retreating into a trapped half-sob in his chest as he sat up on the holding-cell cot, tasting the hour behind his teeth. Rising, he pushed past the bars and staggered across the deserted squad room to the john.

A half hour later under a grubby white sky, Rocco drove down the ramp into the receiving bay of the County Jail. He gave up his gun at the door and walked past the two darkened bullpens to the processing desk. Behind a smoldering menorah of staked upright stogies, the sergeant was reading a fat paperback biography and didn't look up until Rocco said, 'Hey, how you doing? You got a Rodney Little here?'

Standing in front of the crowded bullpen, Rocco realized that he had hung in until this shitty hour for nothing. He had hoped to come upon Rodney dead asleep, but guys like Rodney tended to go for thirty-six hours before crashing, and now here he was, leaning against the back wall, his head right under the graffiti rainbow, holding court before three other prisoners, young men nearly half his age. Almost everyone else was asleep.

'See, the problem with you boys right from the gitty-up is you sell a clip, make your twenty dollars, *bam*, you go out buy a twenty-dollar ring. You hear what I'm sayin'? You *be* like that, no matter how much you make, you always wind up with nothin'. No matter how much you earn the night before, every day you start out with nothin', day after day. Don't *have* nothin', never *will* have nothin', gonna *die* with nothin'.'

Rocco leaned against the bars listening in, half interested.

'Now, you come to work for me, I don't want somebody who got that kind of mentality. 'Cause I ain't like no boss who says to you, What can you do for me? What *I* want to know is, what can you do for your*self*, 'cause a man who can't do nothin' for himself, shit, he can't do nothin' for anybody else either, see what I'm sayin'?'

The three prisoners nodded, two of them slapping palms.

Rocco looked around the bullpen, about forty deep tonight, half the prisoners sleeping on the bare floor while Rodney sat nice and comfy on two pallets. Between his sneakers were three half pints of milk and a pear, Rocco thinking, King of the jungle.

'Hey Rodney!' Rocco barked.

Rodney squinted through the gloom, then rose and stepped over people to see who it was.

'Rodney, how you doing?'

'Aw man, what the fuck *you* want?' Rodney clucked his tongue and turned his back, but he hung in by the bars.

'Nah, you know, it's just, I was thinking you got yourself in some fucked-up situation here. Maybe I could help you out on it. You know, if you help *me* on something.'

'I ain't in no fucked-up situation. This a bullshit CDS rap. I ain't never going in on this. This just a headache situation.'

'Gee, I don't know, I heard someone got you locked in real good on this. Someone that got themselves in a jam on something else served *you* up to get out from under the rock.'

Rodney turned back to Rocco, wanting a name. Rocco was a little surprised that he didn't get it right off the bat.

'I think you're looking at some years here – that is, you know, unless maybe you want to talk to me about something.'

'Like what?' Rodney's eyes were steady, faintly curious.

'You remember that Ahab's thing? I hear you know what happened.'

'Hey, *fuck* you man, this just a CDS. I ain't talking to you about no homicide. What you think, I'm stupid? How the fuck I talk about a homicide from on the inside without incriminating myself. Gah-damn, you a insult to my intelligence. I don't know a damn thing about that. Get the fuck on out of here.' Rodney started to walk away.

'I can get you immunity from prosecution.'

'Prosecution on what? Fuck you. I don't know nothin'.'

Someone on the floor woke up, grunted, 'Yo, shut up,' and Rodney kicked him in the back, the guy half rising to fight, seeing who it was, then going back down.

'The thing is, Rodney,' Rocco said, yawning, 'somebody deep on your *in*side got you in here tonight trying to save their own ass on the Ahab's thing, so alls I'*m* saying now is that this is a perfect opportunity to get back at them – but like in spades.'

Towering over all the bodies, Rodney stood in the middle of the bullpen. Slowly he turned his face back to Rocco, the name finally coming into his eyes, Rocco nodding, thinking, It's about time, asshole.

'So what do you say?' Rocco gave Rodney a hopeful smile.

'Fuck you.' Rodney walked back to sit under the rainbow, but silent now, big-eyed. And as Rocco left the jail, his back bowed with exhausted tension, he wondered which way Rodney would play it: make bail later this morning and go after Strike himself or hang in here, watch some

TV, play some cards, make a phone call from up on the tiers and then stay out of the line of fire.

The waiting room of the Central Judicial Processing Court smelled of sweat and potato chips, and Strike, his belly full of Mylanta, still thought he would vomit blood any second. At least fifty sad-sack-looking people, grown-ups and children, sat on the benches or leaned against the walls. Most of them had been in the room for a while now, since on Tuesday court always started at eleven instead of nine, but unless you'd been here before, to bail out a friend or relative on some other Tuesday morning, how the hell were you supposed to know?

After a sleepless night, Strike had arrived by eight-thirty, and like everybody else he did nothing for his boredom and misery but stare at the walls. There wasn't a newspaper or magazine in the room. Strike's gaze went back and forth from a hand-drawn sign over the courtroom doors – THIS WAITING ROOM IS A COURTESY. YOU ARE NOT IN THE STREET. ACT CIVIL – to a patch on the ankle of a little boy's sneaker, a red silhouette of a basketball player soaring spread-eagled to the hoop. Four years old and the kid is sitting around the waiting room of the arraignment court to bail out a father, a mother's boyfriend, a brother. Strike studied the boy's composed face, wondering how many years he had left before someone would be here to bail *him* out.

Still only nine-thirty: the clock was moving backward. Strike sat hand to forehead, immobile with exhaustion, thinking about Victor on the inside. What was he doing right now? Probably he felt a lot like Strike this morning, or maybe worse. Thirty in – what would that be like? Day in, day out, thirty goddamn years of feeling this way, nailed to the face of time.

At a quarter to ten, seventy-five minutes before the court was due to be in session, people began to drift toward the locked double doors, trying to peek through the center seam, squinting into the empty courtroom and making vague comments of frustration, until a court officer came out and yelled for everybody to sit down and behave or he would clear the house. And at a quarter to eleven, a woman came in with three kids, all eating burgers and fries. The smell of grease and fried meat, combined with the reek of his own exhausted body, had Strike running outside for air, had him standing on a strip of grass between the jail and the court building, amazed that he had ever seriously imagined himself selling dope inside a dump like Ahab's.

★ ★ ★

Driving down Broadway at ten in the morning, Rocco fought off
tremulous yawns as he rehearsed apologies for his behavior on the
phone.

Who cared if Patty got a job? If that's what she wanted to do, so be
it. Nobody had to explain to him how precious work could be. Besides,
she was right – what could be better than being with Erin?

As he pulled up in front of his building, Patty came flying out the
front door looking distracted, a little wild. Upon seeing him, she jumped
with relief, both feet actually leaving the ground.

Rocco was mystified, but he smiled anyway, eager to make peace.

Patty thrust her head in the car. 'Is she with you?'

Thinking she was asking him about some girlfriend, he beamed
stupidly, happy to be accused of something that he could honestly
deny. 'I left her in the motel.'

'What?'

Patty's face was raw with confusion, and Rocco finally read the panic.
'*Who* with me?'

'Erin.'

'I just got here. What do you mean?'

'She's gone.' Patty ran a claw of fingers through her hair. 'She's
gone.'

'What?' Rocco's hands started trembling on the steering wheel. 'Slow
down.'

'You didn't see her run out of the building?'

'What are you talking about?'

But Patty turned and ran, first up Broadway half a block, then around
the corner toward Lafayette. Rocco jumped out of the car. He caught up
with Patty and grabbed her arms. 'What are you talking about?'

'I was out in the hallway waiting for the elevator upstairs and I forgot
something in the house, so I turned to unlock the door and the elevator
must've come and she just stepped inside, and when I ran to catch the
elevator I pushed the button to keep it from closing but it closed anyway
with her in it. So I waited for it to come back up, I figured she'd stay
put but it came back up empty, so I just took it down now, thinking
she was in the lobby, but she's not there, so . . .' Patty's head twisted
past Rocco, scanning the clamor of Broadway – the traffic, the people,
the heart of ten A.M. New York. 'So she's *gone* somewhere.'

Rocco tried to collect himself. He stared at the endless stream of trucks
and taxis floating down Broadway like sailing ships and motorboats,
making their way downstream to the tip of the island, where the city

opened up wide, fanning out into the endless and irretrievable world at large.

'Hang on, hang on.' Rocco squeezed her arms but she twisted out of his grip and trotted blindly across the street, calling out Erin's name loudly but not quite shouting, as if her shock was cut with self-consciousness.

Rocco ran to the building and pulled on the locked front doors, his keys like glittery fish in his hands. He let himself inside and stood in the empty lobby trying to think. A package from the Book-of-the-Month Club was propped on the marble shelf below the mail-boxes, and in his dazed state he found himself checking the address to see if it was intended for him or Patty.

Rocco tried the door to the stairwell: locked. Then the elevator: all the buttons locked as well. Without a key for the floor you wanted, the elevator wouldn't go anywhere. It was the building's security – cheaper than a doorman, everybody said, the entire building a locked box.

Where was she? Rocco stood in the grounded elevator, uselessly pushing the dead buttons, the door finally closing but the elevator going nowhere, a monstrous joke.

Rocco ran outside again, hearing Patty somewhere down the street calling out Erin's name, hearing the hoarse panic in her voice. Running back into the vestibule, he started pushing all the buttons on the building's intercom, palming three, four floors at a time, the box coming to life, crackling with static and challenges, a number of people saying 'Who is it?' at the same time, then more voices coming in over the first inquiries, at least two foreign languages mixing in.

'Is my daughter on your landing?'

'Who is it?'

'This is eleven.' For some reason he couldn't bring himself to use his own name. 'Is there a child lost on your landing?'

'Who is it?'

Some people, in their confusion, buzzed him inside the already open door, but no one gave him any answers.

'Is there a *child* walking around on your *floor*?' Rocco bellowed, his lips brushing the speaker perforations.

Mumbling, feeling a damp line forming under the hair covering his neck, he went into the lobby and dumbly picked up the Book-of-the-Month Club package again. It was addressed to José Arenas. Who the fuck was José Arenas? He knew nobody in the building. He pushed for the elevator, thinking, So we'll have another kid; thinking, What cops do I know in New York? Do I know any good cops in New York?

He got in the elevator and unlocked the button for eleven, his only way in, and as the car began its ascent, he could hear Patty out on the street, her voice rising in the elevator shaft, getting progressively more broken and ragged, Rocco thinking, She'll get over it, she'll get over it.

The elevator stopped on eight and the door opened on a worried-looking Japanese woman.

'You lose a child?'

Rocco's knees sagged with relief. 'Thank God, you don't know – '

'She's not on *this* floor.'

His misery broke through, making him lose his balance inside the small space of the elevator car.

'Maybe you should call the police,' the woman said.

As the ride continued to eleven, Rocco felt more and more useless, and when the doors opened again he refused to step out, panicked at the thought of laying eyes on her empty stroller in the hallway, certain he would fall to pieces.

The doors closed, and as the elevator sank toward the street he ran down a list of New York cops he knew, inside connections who could help him out here. He began to hear Patty's voice again as the elevator got closer to the lobby, that frantic disembodied cawing of the baby's name over and over as his wife raced up and down the street. Rocco glided down to meet her anguish, his mind returning to that oceangoing fleet of vehicles sailing down Broadway, away from Manhattan, into eternity.

The elevator jerked to a stop on the second floor and the door slid back to reveal a group of people questioning each other about the crazy voice on the intercom.

Rocco stepped out onto the landing. When everybody turned, he asked the group, 'Somebody lose a kid?' as if he wasn't the one.

'Yeah.' A tall woman wearing a running suit stepped forward. 'Was that you?'

'Uh-huh, yeah.' Rocco bobbed his head. 'So nobody . . .'

Of all the people assembled on the landing, he was standing the farthest from the fire door that opened onto the stairway, so it astonished him that he was the only one who seemed to hear his daughter's drifty moans. They were obviously coming from right behind the goddamn door.

'Can't you *hear* her?' he snapped as he strode past the others. He pushed the door's heavy bar and didn't stop, running up seven flights to where Erin stood on the stairwell. She was holding her zebra and her bottle and softly banging her forehead on the locked fire door that led to the ninth-floor landing.

All Rocco could say upon seeing her was 'Oh,' as if she was nothing more than a misplaced set of car keys. His relief hammered at him but his manner was strangely casual, wildly out of line with the joy he felt. Erin, for her part, barely glanced at him, apparently too numb to understand that she'd been found.

Rocco and his daughter walked downstairs and saw Patty by the mailboxes, holding court before a half-dozen anxious neighbors, yammering away and hugging herself.

'I had my back turned and she got on the elevator, so I ran to the elevator and instead of holding the door open with my hand I pushed the button, because I thought if you push the button it keeps the door from closing . . .'

Rocco stepped across the lobby with Erin in his arms, Patty oblivious to their presence, Rocco savoring this moment, speaking in a high feathery voice, 'Mommy's here, Daddy's here, Mommy's here, Daddy's here.'

Patty was so dislocated that she couldn't stop babbling. She continued to chatter on about the elevator buttons as she absently reached out to take Erin from Rocco's arms, her eyes still on her audience, the neighbors all sighing with relief, Rocco bouncing on his toes but Patty still big-eyed and yakking, bringing Erin to her chest as if gently crushing a bolt of silk, the baby curling her forehead into the hollow beneath her mother's jaw, Rocco loving them both so much that he knew he'd never tell a soul about this moment, just take it to bed with him every night for years, like a miser's secret stash of gold.

'OK, listen.' Rocco put out his hand, let it hover over Erin's head, Patty's arm, without making contact. 'Let me move the car before I get towed.'

Strike sat in the fourth row of the arraignment courtroom, the closest they let visitors get to the defendants. He'd been sitting here for two hours, watching the previous night's bounty shuffle one by one from the holding cell to the defendant's table. It was a cavalcade of broken men, crazy men, mostly drug possessions and disorderlies, a few B&Es, a stickup man or two, some people barefoot, some bloody, one guy coming out in his underpants, everybody laughing at that. They paraded before the judge in cuffs, and Strike listened as a public defender or a pay lawyer automatically entered not-guilty pleas, the bail panel then giving its recommendations, the panel's supervisor talking in a monotone about income, family, property, criminal pedigree. Now and then mothers, fathers and grown children sprang up from the benches and waved their bail money to get the attention of some court officer, even though they had to pay the bail somewhere else.

Rodney finally emerged from the holding pen at five minutes to one and stood next to his assigned lawyer without even looking at him. Strike watched him closely, measuring the level of his anger, deciding he looked pretty relaxed, all things considered. The bail panel reviewed his sheet and the new charges, then read off their recommendations, talking about his roots in the community, his career as a small businessman. Rodney's PD entered a not-guilty plea. When the judge announced that the bail was being reduced from five thousand dollars with no cash option to the ten percent alternative, Rodney muttered in a stage whisper, 'Five hundred dollars. Gah-damn, I ain't even got me five hundred *cents*.' Alarmed, Strike stood up. He had assumed Rodney would just pay the bail and walk.

As Rodney was being led by a court officer back to the holding cell, Strike caught his eye and silently begged for understanding. Rodney stopped dead, his face grew icy, and he glared at Strike until he sank back down to the bench. Panicking, knowing Rodney must have already heard about the handshake with the Homicide, Strike held his hands up, mouthed 'Wait, wait,' tried to signal to Rodney that he had it all wrong. But Rodney just turned tightlipped to the holding pen and disappeared back into County.

Buzzed and helpless, Strike fled the courthouse and drove aimlessly around town. He was desperate for sleep but afraid to go to his apartment: Rodney might have sent somebody out for him, and whoever it was might get him while he was in bed. He couldn't go to any of his safe houses and pick up the rest of his money either. Rodney probably knew where the houses were, the same way he knew all about Tyrone and just about everything else.

Still ghost-driving, Strike rolled past the Roosevelt benches. Seeing only Peanut there, he had the thought that maybe the best plan would be to sit down with one guy, explain the whole situation and tell him how that Homicide was pressuring him, using every trick in the book, getting Jo-Jo in on it, Thumper in on it, but how he just wouldn't crack – never did, never will – how he was too much for all of them. Maybe he should tell all that to Peanut, one on one, let Peanut spread that around while Strike found someplace to lie low. Then he could come back in a few days, and maybe he'd even be a hero in people's eyes for everything he'd been through.

Strike drove to the old lady's driveway and parked. This would be good, this plan. He would stroll right into the projects like he had nothing to hide and no one to fear.

Strike walked to the benches and took a seat next to Peanut. The afternoon sunlight hurt his eyes, made his face feel pinched.

'Where's everybody at?'

Peanut shrugged. 'They not here.'

'You want to tell me something I *don't* know?'

'Erroll Barnes came by and everybody left,' Peanut said, looking away.

Strike went quiet, wondering what *that* could mean, then noticing that goddamn kid Tyrone come out of his building looking half crazy, starting to eyeball Strike again like he had to talk or he'd explode.

'What you mean, Erroll Barnes came by?' Strike said, turning back to Peanut.

'He was asking where you was.'

'What you talking about?'

'He was looking for *you*,' Peanut said, his voice turning malicious.

Strike turned in time to see Tyrone marching straight at him. The kid seemed determined to say what he had to say no matter what, but Strike exploded before he could get out a word. 'Will you get out my motherfuckin' face? *Please*?' Strike hunched over to be eye-to-eye, Tyrone looking stunned, Strike wheeling and walking, talking to himself about how Victor was lucky to be in there, away from all this, *all* of it.

He began to trot back to his car, thinking, Just get out of town now, take the money you got on you, fuck the other fifteen thousand, just leave. But half a block from the driveway, close enough to hear the gospel music raining down from the open window of the old lady's house, he saw Erroll Barnes leaning against the Accord's rear bumper, arms folded across his chest, just waiting, no package this time, and the grip of his .38 was sticking out of his pants like he didn't give a shit who saw it.

Strike walked quickly back the way he had first come, thinking about abandoning the car now, just taking a cab into New York. Then he saw Tyrone coming toward him, still with that determined look, probably heading for the car to catch up with him, the kid bug-eyed and muttering, his hand over his belt buckle again.

Strike ducked behind a parked car before Tyrone could spot him. As the kid chugged past, Strike overheard his private rantings.

' . . . if every time I try to earn some money I have to worry about you *lying*, lying to me, to your grandmother, to all the people that love you in this *world*, because if you don't know it I'm gonna tell you again – without your family you are *nothing*, you are alone out here, and I just want to know what kind of *boy* you are . . .'

Tyrone steamed out of earshot, heading for the Accord, Strike thinking, Goodbye, good riddance, hoping another accidental bump-in with Erroll Barnes might scare this kid out of his life for good.

Rocco was so electrified by the near tragedy of the morning that he didn't think he'd ever need sleep again.

Disoriented, giddy with exhaustion, he went in to work two hours early and began catching up on some reports. But after sitting at his desk for ten minutes, he decided to lie down on the cot in the cell again, try to stretch out some tension knots. He instantly fell down a dreamless hole.

He was awakened after an hour by one of the day-tour investigators, Bobby Colón, loudly singing a McDonald's jingle as he poured himself a cup of coffee. Rocco sat up, annoyed, thinking he'd say something to this inconsiderate asshole, but then he noticed that Colón had his sport jacket on and his death valise between his ankles.

Rocco pushed back his hair. 'What time is it?'

'Hey, it's alive,' Colón said, tilting his chin at Rocco.

'You coming or going? What time is it?'

'Three o'clock. Guess who's dead.'

'Who?'

'Guess.'

'Don't fuck with me, OK?'

'Erroll Barnes.'

'Yeah? Good. Who shot him? He got shot, right?' Rocco yawned. His shirt stank.

'He got capped by a little kid, can you believe that? Some ten-year-old from Roosevelt. Kids today, right?'

Mazilli came in for some tea, singing, 'Ding Dong, the Witch Is Dead.'

'Mazilli, what happened?' Rocco didn't trust Colón, who had once asked him how to clean a coffeepot.

'Erroll Barnes be dead.'

'And the actor's a kid?'

'Yeah, some eleven-year-old, twelve-year-old,' Mazilli said. 'They should give him a merit badge for it.'

Rocco sat on the cot trying to put his thoughts together. Erroll, Rodney, some kid, what kid?

'They catch him?'

'He's at Juvie. Gave himself up to Andre Gates.'

'Body on the scene?'

'Yeah, the day tour's going out there now.'

'Who's doing the kid?'

'Steinmetz. He's all pissed off because *his* kid's got a basketball game down in Old Bridge in like two hours.'

'He leave yet?' Rocco stood up, unzipped his pants and tucked his shirt into his underwear.

'He's on the phone in there, talking to his wife.'

Rocco walked into the squad room, caught Steinmetz's eye and signaled a time-out. The mopey-looking detective put the receiver to his chest.

'Billy,' Rocco said, winking, 'I'm gonna do you like a mongo-size favor here.'

A half hour later Rocco walked into the amber gloom of the old Juvie annex behind the Western District station house and found four kids cooling their heels, two in the cage and two with their mothers sitting on wooden benches across from the detectives' desks. Rocco figured the one lying sideways with his head in his mother's lap had to be the twelve-year-old shooter. The boy's eyes were moist and red, and he was shivering. His mother stroked his temples and was weeping herself. Taking a closer look, Rocco was surprised to recognize both of them: the mother was the chunky woman who had almost kicked Strike's ass, and the kid was her son, the sweet-faced boy who always sat quietly on the chain at the Roosevelt benches. Rocco winced and looked away for a moment, thinking about what a low-down scumbag Erroll Barnes was. Even in his dying he had to go and destroy one more life.

A tall black cop in dungarees and a sweatshirt rose from one of the desks. 'You from the prosecutor's office?'

Rocco extended a hand. 'Yeah, Rocco Klein. You Andre Gates?'

'Yeah.' Ignoring the offered hand, Andre opened a small brown bag to show Rocco the weapon, a .25 automatic. 'Can I talk to you for a minute?'

Andre took Rocco by the elbow and led him down a hallway. 'Yeah listen, I just want to tell you that that boy in there, Tyrone? I know him since he was a baby. I know his grandmother, his mother Iris there, they *all* decent people and like, whatever happened it must've been some serious mistake, because that boy never been in trouble *ever*. I mean, he's in something like the eighty-fifth percentile on this national education test that they give? And you know, whatever happens from now on in, that kid's life is ruined, but what *I'm* sayin' is, is that I would appreciate it if you help him on his *state*ment, you understand what I'm saying?'

'Hey.' Rocco held up his hand. 'The kid's never been in trouble, he was scared to death, and Erroll Barnes was a low-rent, lowlife scumbag who's off the streets forever. Right?'

Andre smiled tightly and nodded, saying, 'Yeah, that's good, that's good,' and then finally offering Rocco his hand.

Rocco slowly approached Iris and Tyrone. The boy was too much in shock to react to his presence, but the mother patted the wetness from her face and spoke through chattering teeth.

'He goin' to jail?'

Andre came up next to Rocco, and Rocco saw him give her a reassuring look, eyes half shut, hands out, as if everything was all right.

'Does he have to go to jail?' she said, ignoring Andre.

'Look.' Rocco squatted down on his haunches in front of her and put a hand on Tyrone's shoulder. 'Look, I have to find out what happened. Would you permit me to speak with him? I know whatever went down, he must've had a good reason for what he did. I just got to find out what that reason was. So can I talk to him now?'

'If he tells you what happened, can I take him home then?' Her voice was childlike, high with hopelessness.

Rocco looked at the shivering boy, figured a year in the Youth House, no more than that, maybe less if he was lucky.

'Well, he *did* kill somebody, OK? But what happens to him depends on the circumstances, see what I'm saying? I mean, I have to find out what happened. Was it cold-blooded murder? Was it because Erroll Barnes wouldn't buy *drugs* from him? Was it because Erroll Barnes robbed him of some money they were supposed to split on a holdup? Was it because Erroll Barnes was dating *you* and he didn't want him as a stepfather?'

Iris shook her head in outraged horror at all of Rocco's scenarios. Rocco adjusted his squat to take the burn out of his knee.

'Or did he kill him because Erroll Barnes threatened him with that thirty-eight he was carrying? Did he kill him because he was afraid that Erroll Barnes was in some way going to hurt *you*, his mother? I mean, was he so out-of-his-mind frightened by Erroll Barnes that he didn't even realize that he shot him? I don't know. Let me talk to him, then I can answer *your* question, OK?'

Iris nodded, her eyes desperate for some kind of comfort.

'Now listen, you'll be with him all the time. You have to be – it's the law, OK? You don't like any of the questions I'm asking, you just sing out, I'll retreat, OK?'

Wiping her cheeks, Iris nodded again and then gently helped the boy to his feet.

An hour after he had run away, Strike tried sneaking up on his own car again, hoping Erroll was too Virus-sick to be waiting for him still, hoping Tyrone was running blind to the goddamn North Pole by now. But as he rounded the corner and turned onto the old lady's block, Strike pulled up short again, this time seeing green and yellow cruisers, county Dodges and Plymouths – a death crowd. Two detectives squatted right by his car, dusting and photographing, the heavy aluminum cases open on the pavement. When Strike noticed that the window overhead was empty for the first time in memory, he figured the old lady must have fallen out somehow and landed right on his damn Accord. But then he saw the bloody sheet, saw that the hand sticking out belonged to a man, figured that Erroll had killed somebody, which was maybe a good thing here, because now Erroll would have to lie low.

Strike crouched behind a parked car and watched the detectives work, listening to the uniforms make jokes, wondering whether they were going to impound the Accord for fingerprints or something. One of the detectives abruptly turned his head in Strike's direction, and Strike deepened in his squat, knees to his chin, bitterly amazed at everything happening to him.

'Tyrone, you know what you did, don't you?' Rocco looked at him intently and the kid nodded slowly, his head back in his mother's lap, the three of them in a barren cubicle now.

'You know that it was wrong?'

The kid nodded again.

Rocco heard Andre pacing outside, eavesdropping on this pretape interview. Rocco was annoyed, insulted that Andre didn't trust him to do the right thing.

'OK. Now, you know what you did was wrong but you couldn't help it. You were scared, right?'

Another mute nod, the kid's eyes becoming a little wider.

'Look, Tyrone, I don't live around here but I can imagine how tough it is out there in your neck of the woods. You're a good kid, all you want to do is get an education, make something of yourself . . .' Rocco found himself thinking of Victor, feeling weird about the echoes, for a moment losing track of what he was saying. 'A good kid, hard-working, all you want to do is be with your family, do well in school, but you got all these people around you coming down on you, making you crazy. All you want to do is protect your family, and you're under so much pressure and they're coming down so hard on you for being the way you are that you go out and you get yourself a gun – but not to hurt anybody, just for protection.'

Again Rocco got a flash of Victor. 'I mean, not to protect your*self*. I know you're a tough kid, you don't need a gun to protect yourself, but your mother – you got to protect her too. Your brother, your whole family. It's like the Wild West out there.'

Iris nodded yes yes, but Tyrone looked at him as if he was crazy, not understanding that Rocco was handing him a script.

'OK, Tyrone, let me ask you. Did you know that man's name, that man you shot?'

The kid stared at him without signifying, the silence framed by Andre's heavy pacing.

'That was Erroll Barnes. That was the baddest guy in Dempsy. That man was a stone killer, did you know that?'

Tyrone stared at Rocco from his mother's lap.

'Well, you know that *now*, right?'

Rocco winked at Iris, hoping she understood and would help him coach her boy when the tape started to run. 'And I know you know Rodney Little and how bad *he* is, right?'

Tyrone seemed to be listening, but Rocco had no idea whether he knew Rodney Little from Little Stevie Wonder.

'Erroll Barnes was Rodney's gunman, and since you know how bad Rodney is, you gotta know that Erroll was even badder than him, right? Right? OK, so there you were, just walking down the street, minding your own business, you got a gun that you're not supposed to have, but you're not bothering anybody either. All of a sudden there's Erroll Barnes coming up right in your face, coming right at you, and he's got this horrible look in his eyes and you see him going for that thirty-eight in his waist and you *know* he's gonna hurt you, maybe even *kill* you, and who would protect your mother if you were in the hospital? Or in the grave? And you had never fired that gun before, right?'

Rocco paused, waiting to see if the kid would answer or in any way respond. Not yet.

'You never fired that gun before,' Rocco repeated, 'but Erroll had you so scared that you started seeing stars.'

Tyrone sat up, nodding, coming to life.

'You were so scared that you didn't even know where you were, but that *face*, it's coming at you, coming at you, you don't even know why, you don't even know what you *did*, just coming at you, coming at you, and the next thing you know . . . *Boom*!'

Iris and Tyrone jumped.

'And you don't even know how the damn thing got into your hand.'

The kid started to cry fresh tears, turning to his mother, nodding slowly, his face twisted with grief. 'Mommy, that's what happened,' he said, his voice climbing to a miserable squawk.

Iris held him, sobbing herself, whispering, 'Praise Jesus.'

Rocco slowly sat back, thinking, Goddamn, I'm good.

'That's what happened, OK? And when I ask you about it with the tape recorder going, that's what you're going to tell me, right?'

Iris and Tyrone nodded.

'And you're going to tell me that because it's the *truth*, right?' Iris hugged her son, both of them still avidly nodding.

'OK, now there's one last thing we should go over, and on this, Tyrone, I want you to answer me direct. Where did you get the gun?'

The boy stared at the floor and shuddered involuntarily, a residual sob escaping from him like a hiccup. 'I found it.'

Rocco kept staring at him. 'Where did you find it?'

'In the bushes.'

Just outside the cubicle, Andre hissed with irritation.

'What bushes?'

'By the front of my house.'

'When was this?'

'Yesterday.'

Rocco sat in silence for a second, debating whether to crack this open, then deciding to let it slide.

'And you didn't turn it in to the police because you wanted to protect your mother, right?'

The kid stared at Rocco's knees, gave a barely audible 'Uh-huh,' the lie obviously bothering him, bothering Rocco too.

'And you probably didn't even know how to take the magazine out, right?'

'Yeah.'

'So you didn't even know it was loaded, right?'

Tyrone nodded once.

'I mean, it's not like you ever fired it before.'

Looking dejected, the kid shook his head.

Rocco watched him in silence for a moment, then decided that he just couldn't let the gun-in-the-bush story stand after all.

He turned to Iris. 'OK, look, if what he's saying about finding the gun in the bushes is true, that's beautiful, it really is. But if he's saying that to protect someone, someone he stole it from, someone who gave it to him or who sold it to him?'

Iris looked at him strangely.

'What I'm saying is, if that gun belongs to someone else and it comes back from the lab and they find out it had been used in some other crime? That other crime, whatever it was – murder, robbery – that's gonna have to be charged to Tyrone too. I mean, I *know* he didn't ever use that gun before, but that's the law. So please, he has to be honest with me about where he got it. For his own sake.'

Iris pushed Tyrone away so she could look into his face. The kid curled his chin into his chest to avoid his mother's eyes.

'Give it,' Iris said flatly.

Tyrone spoke to his chest: 'I borrowed it by accident from Strike.'

'Mother*fuck*er!'

All three turned toward the hallway, then listened to Andre's retreating stomp.

'No kidding.' Rocco tried to keep calm. 'Strike from the benches? Yeah, I think I know him.'

'I was trying to give it back to him,' the kid murmured, 'but he won't talk to me no more. I tried *lots* of times.'

Toward the end of the afternoon, Strike finally got behind the wheel of his car again. He'd noticed some black powder on the front fender – fingerprint dust – and the police had most likely photographed the car as well, taken down the license plate, probably asked the old lady who owned it. More grief, and once again he hadn't even done anything to deserve it.

Unable to resist the benches, he drove past and saw the whole crew. Futon spotted him going by and pointed excitedly at the car, everybody turning and staring. Strike slammed on the brakes, threw it in reverse and rocked to a stop right out front, too strung out to be careful anymore.

He got out and headed for the benches, intent on telling people once and for all what had been happening, but they all began backing away from him, walking with little creepy steps as if he was contagious.

'What's up?' Strike asked.

'What's up?' Peanut mimicked, smirking.

'Hey,' Strike shouted, 'I dint say *nothin'* to that cop. That was like a *setup.*'

Everybody looked at him in disbelief.

'You know they was like brothers, Rodney and Erroll,' Futon drawled, sounding both mournful and threatening.

Strike pressed the heels of his palms to his eyes. 'What are you talkin' about?'

The entire bench turned as one to see Rodney's Cadillac come to a screeching stop right behind the Accord, Rodney rising out of the driver's side with something shiny in his hand, moving with a firm-faced skip around his car to the sidewalk, then coming up with an aluminum softball bat, everybody scattering, everybody but Strike, who stood there mesmerized, unable to move, thinking, Quick wrists, Rodney glaring at him, striding faster, giving the bat little warm-up shakes, then abruptly coming to a halt halfway to the benches and looking past Strike, cursing now, turning back around, the bat tucked under his armpit.

His body rigid with shock, Strike jerked forward, thinking, He made bail after all, that's good, that's good, saying, 'Rodney, man . . .,' then feeling someone clutch him between the legs from behind, another hand on his neck, the sky coming close, Strike going up, up, the buildings revolving, leaning over.

Strike croaked, 'Who . . .'

He came down in a rush, his nose exploding on the sidewalk, his kneecap on fire, his fingers scrabbling like crabs. Then someone lifted him by the back of his sweatshirt and threw him face first across a bench, his throat crushed into the top slat, into his own perch, a hand on the back of his head keeping up the pressure on his throat. Gagging, Strike saw a ring of people standing behind the bench, behind a red film, everybody wincing, frowning, silent, Strike thinking through the pain, Got to tell this hand on the back of my head about my throat, how it's being crushed, but his tongue was as fat as a fish and now everything was red going to brown.

A voice boomed from above: 'You are *gone* from here, gone from these houses, gone from these streets, gone from this *city*.'

Strike saw his mother in her window – no, it was a thought of his mother. There were lips by his ear now, a whisper: 'I ever see you again I'm gonna *kill* you. I'll kill you and put a gun in your hand, say you throwed down on me for this beating you just got. You understand that?'

'Ah-Andre,' Strike said, the name coming out like a squeaky cough.

'You murdered that boy's life and now you are *gone* from here.'

Someone in the crowd said, 'Yo Andre, ease up man, ease up.'

Strike was pulled to his feet like a child, bum-rushed from the benches across the sidewalk, arms flailing and helpless, then rammed chest first into the side of his own car, his knee cracking in his ears as he slid down to the concrete. He looked up: Rodney's Cadillac was still behind the Accord, waiting.

Strike made it into his car, his fingers fluttering among the keys hanging from the ignition. Eventually he managed to drive off, away from the mob of mute and fascinated faces. Rodney pulled out right behind him like an escort. If Strike ran a light, Rodney ran a light. If Strike stopped for a light, Rodney stopped too.

Strike watched Rodney in his rearview mirror. Rodney didn't shout threats out his window or use tricky car maneuvers to cut Strike off. Rodney conducted himself as if he was so focused and determined to do Strike harm in a serious and lasting way that he didn't want to waste any energy on preliminaries or empty gestures.

Strike caught a glimpse of his nose in the mirror; it was clownishly swollen and turning dark. Trapped in the Accord, he drove around Dempsy in ragged circles, wondering how long he could keep going on a half tank of gas.

Rocco sat at his desk and slipped a warrant into his typewriter, filling in the blanks: 'Ronald Dunham. Illegal possession of a firearm. Possession of a weapon without a permit. Possession of a weapon without a valid firearms ID card.' He knew that the thing had about as much chance of standing up in court as a charge of parading without a license – but what the hell, it was worth a shot. Rocco played out the whole encounter in his head: hauling Strike in on this, informing him of how the Graves Act mandates that anytime a gun is used in the commission of a crime it's an automatic three in, then laying Erroll Barnes at his feet, saying, 'Your gun, your crime,' the kid squawking, 'That boy *stole* my gun,'

Rocco shrugging, informing him that he was free to try that out on a jury, the go-around ending with Strike whining, 'Man, why you *doing* this to me?'

Rocco knew that Strike wasn't likely to react to this gambit any differently than he had reacted to all the others, but the Graves Act had a nice heavy ring to it, and maybe, just maybe, he could put enough fake heat on Strike to get him to start trading, to talk, and at last to tell the truth.

Tearing the completed warrant from the typewriter, Rocco rose and marched down the hallway to the glass doors, feeling for his car keys, thinking about how he'd play it after getting a judge's signature on this. He pushed out through the main doors of the building and crashed into Strike, who was limping up the stairs on his way in. Rocco, not missing a beat, smiled and said, 'Hey-y, happy birthday.' He flashed Strike the unsigned warrant. 'I was just coming to pick you up.'

Strike didn't look at the paper, didn't even look at Rocco, just stared over his shoulder, back to a gentle rise above the parking lot where Rodney Little stood, leaning against the passenger door of his Cadillac, arms folded across his chest, still as a hunting dog, eyes trained on Strike.

Rocco waved to Rodney but got not a flicker of reaction. At first Rocco thought Rodney had driven Strike to the office, but then Rocco looked at the kid's face and said, 'Jesus Christ, what happened to your nose?' Strike was transfixed by the sight of Rodney and didn't respond. Rocco made the connection, crumpled up the bullshit warrant and said with forced casualness, 'What's up there, Strike?' The kid still didn't answer. Pushing past Rocco, he moved deep into the safety of the building, limping, swollen-faced, ready to talk.

Strike sat by himself in the interrogation room, his mind fragmented by a riot of murderous faces and half-recalled threats, whatever alert-ness he still possessed drawn to the throbbing bloom in the center of his face, the jagged burn in his right kneecap. Massaging his knee, he stared stupidly at a calendar two months out of date on the wall in front of him. The door to the room was ajar, and he could hear the heavyset Homicide pacing in the hallway, breathing deeply.

Strike looked up and saw the cop from Shaft Deli-Liquors peering at him through the window, the other Homicide's face floating just behind the Shaft guy's shoulder. Feeling like an animal in a zoo, Strike averted

his eyes. The conversation between the two men came drifting through
the slightly open door.

'What's up?' the Shaft Homicide asked.

'Nothin'. Just some bullshit follow-up.'

'What the fuck happened to his nose? *Meep-meep*. That must fucking
hurt. You do that?'

The heavyset Homicide laughed. 'Not yet.'

'T and R, Tortured and Released,' the Shaft Homicide announced.
'When men were men . . .'

Staring at his knuckles, Strike heard the footsteps of one of the cops
retreat down the hall. When he looked up again, the heavyset Homicide
was entering the room.

'Do you want something for your nose? Some cotton balls? A cool
cloth?' Rocco nodded to the parking lot. 'Maybe we can file an assault
complaint.'

'Andre did this.'

'Andre the cop? Huh.' Rocco moved away from that quickly.

He wanted to stay with Rodney all the way, make an ally out of this
kid he had screamed at two days ago, called a nigger to his face.

'How come Ah-Andre beat on me like that?' Strike gently cupped his
nose with both hands.

'Hey, he was probably a little upset about what happened with
Tyrone.'

'With Tyrone? I don't hang out with him no more. What's he want
from me?'

'Welp, the kid did use your gun.'

'My gun for what?' Strike started, then added, 'I don't have no
gun.'

'Where you been, Strike? The boy shot Erroll Barnes.'

'He *what*! Shot how?'

'Dead.'

'Ahh, man.' His mouth wide open, Strike breathed heavily, cast a
sorrowful eye out to the street where Rodney was, then hunched forward
and clamped his hands to the sides of his head. 'What he do *that* for? I
don't know nuh-nothin' about that, nothin' about that.'

Surprised by the sadness in the kid's voice, Rocco withdrew for a
second, thinking about Rodney and Erroll, Rodney and Strike, that kid
Tyrone walking around with Strike's gun. The boy had said something
on tape about Erroll grabbing him by the elbow, asking, 'Where's he at,

where's he at,' scaring the piss out of him, Tyrone automatically going for the stolen .25 behind his belt buckle, everything flowing blind from that elbow grab. 'Well, I hope you don't have nothing coming down on you for that, because if it's your gun – '

'Why the hell he go do something like that for? What's gonna ha-happen to him?'

'Hey, right now I'd be a little more concerned with what's gonna happen to you.'

'He go to the Youth House?'

'Yup. That poor kid's fucked.' Rocco shook his head theatrically. 'But the thing of it is, you know *why* he shot Erroll Barnes?'

Strike looked at him blankly.

'Because he was protecting you. Because Erroll Barnes was hunting you down. He did it for *you*. Yeah, Rodney's not stupid, he's not gonna get blood on his hands. He sent Erroll after you, and this poor fuckin' kid just stepped into the breach like David and Goliath, and now he's a twelve-year-old murderer.'

Bullseye: The kid looked totally miserable.

'I tell you, Ronnie, you must be one hell of a guy, all these people going off to jail to protect you, you know? Your brother, this kid . . . But you know what? They all went down protecting you from the same guy, that prick out there, Rodney fuckin' Little.'

Strike turned in his chair, staring as if he could see Rodney through the wall.

'But now they're all in jail, and he's still out there, and he's still coming at you. All your protectors are gone, all the people that loved you. They're all fucked, he fucked them, and now it's just him and you, him and you.'

Rocco and Strike looked at each other for a long moment.

'Except you got one ally left.'

Rocco watched Strike's chin slowly drop to his chest.

'Now, I could lend you my piece, you could limp out that door, start shooting. Maybe you'll get lucky, nail him first.'

Strike grimaced with impatience.

'Or we could do this.' Rocco hunched forward, whispering as if Rodney might overhear. 'We put our heads together, right here and now. And after we talk? I make a call, get some goddamn SWAT team out there, he goes to blow his nose, he goes into his pocket, anything, they're going to wind up sponge-mopping the spot he was standing on last, OK? So what I want to happen here is, I get up out of this chair in a little while, me and you, we look out the window and see him being taken off in cuffs, dropped down some fucking federal hole somewheres, they have to airlift his meals to him for the rest of his life. That sound good to you?'

The kid nodded tentatively.

'Because let me tell you something, on that Ahab's situation? Regardless of who pulled the trigger – me and you, we know who the true shooter was, right?'

Strike let out a thin sigh.

'See, the way I see it, I think you got in way over your head on this Ahab's deal. I think maybe you owed Rodney big-time for something, and he just terrorized you into this thing. I mean, I just don't believe you had much choice one way or the other. And I *know* you didn't do it for cash.' Rocco gave Strike his out on the heaviest motive, murder for money, mandatory injection for that one.

'I mean basically, the way I see it, it was either you or Darryl Adams. One of you was gonna die, and I guess you figured, Hey, all I'm gonna do is get another lowlife drug dealer off the street. And you probably figured, If I do this, if *I* do *this* – which I have to do or Rodney is gonna *kill* me – then I don't owe Rodney shit anymore. I'm free. Now I can get away from the whole drug scene, just give it up, wipe the slate clean and start a new life.'

Strike still looked unhappy, but Rocco wasn't worried. A few more minutes and he'd have the kid believing that the murder was so understandable that it might even be technically legal or something.

'But what *I* think happened was that Rodney didn't keep up his end of the deal. He wouldn't let you go, plus, now he *really* had you by the short hairs, and he was gonna make you take the weight on this because that's just the kind of guy he is.'

Strike didn't move, didn't look up, Rocco thinking, Time for some amen bobs, what's the problem?

'And your brother, he hears what kind of jam you're in, he decides to save you. He decides that he's gonna come in on this because he's so clean he can beat the rap. Hey Ronnie, you know what it is? You're like a million guys out there. You got caught up in the streets, you got caught up in the survival game, you got your basic raw deal in life, and you thought that if you came in to tell us how it went down, who the hell would ever believe you?'

The kid shook his head, but Rocco couldn't tell what he meant by it. Rocco palmed his face and plunged ahead.

'And Rodney, he don't give a fuck either way. He don't give a damn *who* goes down on this – you, your brother, what's the difference, as long as it's not him, right? Fuck Victor, fuck Strike – hey, fuck Erroll and fuck Tyrone for that matter. But what I'm saying is' – Rocco leaned in – 'fuck Rodney. Nobody wants you on this, you're a victim. Man, we been after that prick for *years*. He's the brass ring. There's not a cop in this town who doesn't go to sleep every night dreaming about nailing his ass, OK? And don't take this in the wrong way, but you're nobody. You're small beer here.'

The kid had started to nod his head a little, but not enough.

'See, but you got to play your cards right. Because Rodney can still win and you can go down in flames, because I'll tell you something. I don't care that we got a confession from your brother – I'm not ever gonna let go of this. It's what we call having a mission. I know guys been on particular jobs *ten years*, they don't care, and this one's *mine*, I'm keeping it open because both me and you, we know Victor's innocent, we already discussed that, but here's the thing. On an active investigation like this? The person who's believed most is the first person who talks, because after that first person talks, we start hauling *everybody* in, and then all of a sudden everybody's talking. All of a sudden we got a real cluster fuck on our hands – information, alibis, bullshit – everybody saying, Yeah, I was there but I didn't *do* nothing. All of it horseshit at that point, because everybody's all jammed up, blaming everybody else, and nobody believes that second, third, fourth player like they do that first guy. And if that first guy comes in voluntarily like you are now? Ho shit, that guy's gold, that guy's in the catbird seat. See what I'm saying?'

Rocco paused, gathering himself for the final rush. 'But, say you sit here with me now, I ask you what happened, and you don't say shit. You walk out the door? Fine. What can I do? But Rodney? He's out on bail now but he's got this drug charge hanging over his head. They caught him' – Rocco winged it – 'with a kilo of coke. He goes to trial, shit, he's looking at some serious years. And what do you think he's gonna do about that? Just take it? Hell no, he knows how to play the game around here. He's gonna say, Hey let's make a deal, you cut me some slack here, I'll give you the *real* shooter on that Ahab's job. You got the wrong man in jail. And then he's gonna give *you* up in a snap. And when we come to get you, what are you gonna say? "It wasn't me, it was him"? Or "He *made* me do it"? Who the fuck's gonna believe you then? So Ronnie . . . now's the time. Get your brother out and Rodney in. Alls you got to do is tell me the truth. And don't tell me Rodney pulled the trigger if he really didn't. Because if I grab him wrong, it's not gonna play out the way we want, you understand? It doesn't make a difference who physically pulled the trigger here, I hope I made that clear to you. OK? So let's lock that motherfucker up. You ready?'

Strike nodded, rubbing his knee. Rocco's hands felt like ice, his breath coming in flutters.

'OK, so, let me just ask you, just to get it out of the way. Did you shoot Darryl Adams?'

Strike looked right at him. 'Unh-uh. No.'

Rocco curdled inside, suddenly feeling all the hours since he'd slept in his own bed. He took a slow breath. 'OK, who did?'

Strike began to tremble with a furious case of head-whip and lip-tremble, a riot of tics and squeaks. 'Buh-buh-boo . . .'

Rocco dug a thumbnail trench along his brow as Strike's voice floated off into clicks and a sigh.

The kid tried again, failed again. Then the name escaped: 'Buddha Hat.'

Strike nodded once, hard, then exhaled through pursed lips, exhausted as if he had just given birth. 'Buddha Hat,' he said again.

Rocco blinked. 'Who the *fuck* is Buddha Hat?'

'He-he that guy that got arrested last week for the other murder, in the tunnel.'

Rocco let his hands flop flat on the table, furious at being fed such predictable bullshit. It never failed: You grab a new murderer, and for about two weeks his name comes up a hundred times, on everything from overdue library books to infanticide.

'How do you *know* it was Buddha Hat?' Rocco said, the anger edging into his voice.

'He-he knows my brother, because my brother once drove his grandmother from church this one time.' Strike looked up expectantly. Realizing that this might not be enough, he added, 'He-he killed *lots* of people.'

'Like who?'

'Well, like one time he took me to New York? He says to me, "I got lots of buh-bodies and I ain't never been in jail."'

Rocco stared at Strike, waiting. The kid began to twist in his seat, the rest of his face turning as dark as his broken nose.

'He says he never did no time.'

Rocco settled deeper into his chair, watching the uncertainty creep into the kid's eyes as he absorbed the scantiness of his own evidence.

'Did you *see* him kill Darryl Adams?'

'Unh-uh,' Strike said, retreating, his body slumping as if it had sprung a leak.

'Did he *tell* you he killed Darryl Adams?'

'No.'

'Did anybody *else* see him kill Darryl Adams?'

'No . . . I don't know.'

'Did he *tell* anybody else he killed Darryl Adams?'

The kid said nothing, looking stunned by his own answers.

'And if he *did* shoot Darryl Adams, why did your brother confess?'

'Well, he knew my brother,' Strike said unsteadily. 'I told you that.'

'What are you trying to tell me? This guy Buddha Hat shoots somebody, then says to himself, "Hmm, who could I get to confess for me. Hey, I know! How about that guy that gave my grandmother a ride from church that one time." You mean like that? Is that what you're saying?'

Strike stared at the table.

'So I'll ask you again,' Rocco said. 'Who . . . killed . . . Darryl . . . Adams.'

His eyes blank, Strike took a short breath. 'I don't know.'

'You don't know.' Rocco nodded, biting his lip. 'You don't know,' he repeated, still nodding, his body rocking gently back and forth.

Rocco shot to his feet. 'Get the fuck up. C'mon, let's go.'

'What do you mean?' Strike grabbed his injured knee.

'I'm wasting my time with you. Just get the fuck out of here, OK? G'head, go on out to the lot and talk to your *pal* out there. I'm sure he's waiting for you.'

'Whoa, no wait, man, *wait*. I mean, I'll tell you everything I know. *Please*.'

Rocco stood above him, fuming, staring down at the kid's terrified face.

'I'll tuh-tell you everything I know, I *swear*.'

Rocco eased back down. 'You fuckin' better.'

'OK, we're gonna do this one last time.'

Relieved to see the cop drop back into his chair, Strike felt as if his life had been extended by a few minutes.

The Homicide seemed calmer now. 'Tell me everything you know. But I swear to God, the first time I hear you start giving me that shit about Buddha Hat or Mojo Nose or One Love or any of that "well I

guess if my brother said he did it then he did it" nonsense, or *anything*
. . . The first time I hear you blowing smoke at me in any way, shape
or form, I'll fucking hand feed you to Rodney out there myself. We
understand each other?'

Strike nodded, but he avoided the Homicide's eyes, his gaze drawn to
the cop's fingers thrumming the table. But what could he say? He'd been
so sure about Buddha Hat, and now all he had left to offer was himself
and Rodney. But he couldn't. Rodney would kill him, but if . . . Strike
touched his nose, his knee, itemizing the pain, weighing his options.

'Start at the beginning. What do you know?'

'Yeah, like . . .' Strike's words faded into a sigh. He felt almost
ashamed of himself now: the cop must think he was really stupid.
Maybe the Buddha Hat idea *was* stupid, but the Homicide just didn't
understand power. The power of a Rodney, a Champ, a Buddha Hat;
the grip that power had over his heart and imagination. Besides, just
because he couldn't *prove* it was Buddha Hat . . . But it had died in
him, the Buddha Hat idea. This cop had killed it with a few simple
questions. Well, this cop had power too – they all did.

'I don't *hear* nothing.' The Homicide made a big show of leaning
forward and cupping his ear.

'Yeah OK, OK.' Strike surrendered: Just do what the man says.

'OK, well, Ra-Rodney said to me – '

'When?'

'Like ten days ago. I'm not sure, but like maybe the day or two before
it happened.'

'G'head.'

'Ra-Rodney said that that guy – '

'What guy?'

'Darryl. Darryl, he-he was selling dope for Rodney, but he was also
selling dope for somebody else out of there.'

'Where?'

'Ahab's. Rodney come to me, he says, "You want to take over?"'

'Take over?'

'Take that guy's place.'

'In Ahab's, selling dope.'

'Yeah, uh-huh, selling ounces. But he says, "You got to get rid of
him. You-you want the spot, you got to *take* it."'

'Meaning what . . .'

'"You know, he-he says, "You got to do what you got to do."' The
cop stared at the ceiling.

'Get him ah-*out* of there.'

'Get him out of there,' the Homicide repeated. Strike saw that the man was getting red in the face.

'Yeah, you know.'

'No, I don't.'

'Well, he didn't say exact, buh-but I thought . . .' Strike realized he was rocking in his chair, massaging his kneecap, touching his nose. Rocking, practically begging for mercy.

'Thought *what?*'

'I thought he meant, well, Rodney was real mad about it, you know, this guy ripping him off, and he said, he said, "He guh-got to be got."'

'Look, you're fucking Morse-coding me to *death* here. And I'm –'

'*Shoot* him. I thought he meant shu-shoot him.'

The words startled Strike, and he instantly wanted to say them again. Shoot him.

'G'head,' the cop said.

And then Strike let it all go, the words flying out of him in clear flowing speech about that night at Rodney's house, bottling dope and getting the pitch, about Darryl's two-timing dealings, about casing out Ahab's the night of the murder and running into that baby-fat girl from Roosevelt, about casing out the parking lot of the Royal Motel and getting harassed by that gold-plated motel-squad cop. He talked about how he had felt torn between his relief at having bumped into too many potential witnesses to go through with it and his agony at discovering that he just didn't have the stomach, the heart, to kill anybody. He even confessed his worry that he'd wind up looking like a punk in Rodney's eyes.

And within the confines of relaying who did what, who said what, Strike tried to think of some way to describe how Rodney was propelling him, tried to find the words to describe Rodney's power, his effortless hold over him. If he could only capture Rodney with this tale, he thought, maybe the cop wouldn't think he was so stupid for having believed that the killer was Buddha Hat or that Buddha Hat could simply order Victor to take the weight. But the language eluded him. Maybe he just didn't understand that end of things himself.

Strike watched the Homicide lace his fingers across his belly, then realized that the cop was waiting for him to continue.

'So there you were for the second time that night in the Ahab's lot.'

Strike nodded. 'Yeah, so I figure, Shit, *now* what? So I go across the street to Rudy's, because my perforated ulcer is killing me. I figure I go in there, get something sweet for it. And you know it's nice and dark in there, maybe I can think. So I go in there . . .'

Strike hesitated, not wanting to take this cop into Rudy's with him, introduce him to Victor that night. But he really had no choice, so he talked on, told the cop about his surprise at seeing his brother there; how they had small-talked about their mother and Victor's kids; how Strike in his frustration had badmouthed Darryl, made up a story about him abusing some girl and then repeated Rodney's 'got to be got' line; how Victor had startled him by saying, 'Yeah, I hear he's a dope dealer too,' mocking his 'got to be got' and then bragging about some mysterious My Man character; how this My Man would do the job for nothing as a favor to Victor; how Strike had ultimately decided that his brother was just talking trash.

Strike paused, realizing that he was about to bury his brother, but then went ahead anyway, telling the cop about how when he got word of the murder only two or three hours later, he realized that this My Man was for real after all, then figured that Victor must have misunderstood something back in the bar and reached out for him, the guy then turning around and making Victor take the fall.

'I mean, talk about *me* being scared of Rodney? It must be like the same way with Victor and this other guy, you know?' Strike clucked his tongue, relieved to be at the end of his story. 'It's some sad shit, you know?'

The Homicide sat motionless, staring at him like a stuffed hawk. Strike had no idea what to do with his hands, where to train his eyes, how to keep his mouth shut. To cover the unbearable silence, he began to talk again.

'You know, I told you from the gitty-up I wanted to help if I could. But ha-how can I help? If I told you what I know, alls I know is that this guy name My Man did it. Or even if I said Buddha Hat did it, what you gonna do with that? You gonna spring Victor on that? No, the first thing you gonna do on that is throw me in there with Victor, be-because once I told you about *my* thing in this, that's like a, a, incrimination, right?'

The Homicide said nothing, his gaze both blank and penetrating, and Strike plowed on, word-dancing now, saying whatever came to mind.

'I mean, it was like this time when we was kids living on the second floor? I dared him to stand outside like on the windowsill, so he climbs out and he falls. You know what I did? I felt so buh-bad I jumped out after him. He broke his arm, and I like sprained my ankle, but sprainin' *my* ankle didn't make him break *his* arm any less, you see what I'm sayin'? Alls it did was make me fuck up my ankle for nothin'.'

Strike startled himself: he hadn't thought about that day in years. His brother's excited face came back to him now, Victor staring at him nervously through the panes, then vanishing, dropping straight down out of the window frame. Putting Victor up to it . . .

'I tried to call in on the Hat anonymous,' Strike said halfheartedly. But then Rodney came back into his mind and Strike put a stop to his own ramblings. 'Look, all I can tell you for real is what I'm saying now. And you *know* the man on top is ruh-right outside that door just like – '

The Homicide cut him off. '"Yeah, I hear he's a dope dealer too,"' he said, quoting Victor in a raw voice.

Strike said nothing.

'When your brother said that to you about Darryl, how'd he say it?' The Homicide regarded him through narrowed eyes, dragging him back to Rudy's, to Victor.

'I don't know.' Strike heard the whine in his own voice. 'He gave me this funny look.'

'What do you mean funny?'

Strike shrugged.

'You mean like, he crossed his eyes and stuck his thumbs in his ears?'

Strike looked away.

'Funny like how?'

'Like he knows something.'

'Like he sees through you?'

'I don't know.' Strike hesitated, recalling Victor's secret smile, his liquor-dimmed eyes. 'Yeah OK, that.'

'Don't *agree* with me.'

'Like he knows I'm bullshitting him on the girl thing.'

'And "got to be got."'

'What?'

'Then he said . . .'

'Naw, *I* said that.'

'But you said *he* said it.'

'Yeah, but like after me.'

'How'd he say it?'

'"Got to be got."' Strike shrugged.

The Homicide glared at him.

'He was goofin' on me. He was fucked up.'

'How?'

'Like high.'

'High. Roaring drunk? Semiconscious?'

'No, like . . .'

'Like what?'

'*Hunchy*.' Strike winced, unthinkingly imitating Victor by sinking his head between his shoulders, remembering the bloom of orange uniform peeking out under the footrail, the heavily inked cocktail napkins.

As if reading his mind, the cop said, 'Was he doodling?'

'I don't know.' Strike rubbed his mouth, not wanting this cop or anybody else to know about Aroundball. 'I was nervous. I wasn't, you know . . .'

'Was he angry when he said it?'

'Maybe, you know like, *under* things.'

'Under things?'

'On the inside.' Strike momentarily rested his forehead on the table, then lifted it up.

'"I know somebody'd do it, too,"' the Homicide quoted again. 'What did he look like when he said that?'

'He didn't look like nothin'. He was just writin' on that napkin, you – ' Strike froze, having just given his brother's doodling away, the Homicide catching it but looking as if it was no big deal, as if he knew it anyway.

'"My Man, he'd do it for nothing. He'd do it for me."' The Homicide squinted, cocked his head. 'For *you*?'

'No, for Victor. You know, like they were tight.'

'Tight,' the Homicide muttered, and then he was silent.

Strike stared at the calendar over the cop's head, the march of days, the long-gone month. He thought of Victor in jail.

'My Man,' the cop announced lightly, no question in his tone, no challenge at all.

Hating this, Strike spoke again. 'Yeah, I dint want to ask him like a name, so . . .'

'No, huh?' The cop sounded almost amused.

'Yeah. I mean, I said, "Do I know this guy?"'

'Yeah, and?'

Strike paused. 'He says, "I don't know *who* you know anymore. But you might, yeah, you might."'

'"You might . . ."' The cop aped him in a faint high voice.

Strike stared at the calendar again. The air felt heavy and muffled, as if this was a chamber at the bottom of the ocean.

'You gonna arrest Rodney now?'

The cop didn't answer.

'You gonna arrest me?'

Still no answer.

Strike greeted this possible good news with a wary nod. And then it just came out of him: 'You gonna arrest Victor?'

Rocco sat slumped in his chair, ignoring Strike's question, hearing himself pitching his case to Jimmy Newton in the restaurant: 'When do I ever encounter a truly innocent man?' Or better still, a few days later: 'This kid is as pure as the driven snow.'

It all seemed so obvious now. The only mystery was how he could have been so blind for so long.

Rocco heard the chorus of voices blaring in his head, the life-witnesses who had been hand feeding him the truth for the better part of a week. He imagined the day that had ended with Victor Dunham shooting Darryl Adams: the kid standing rigid and self-conscious for hours in a boutique on Columbus Avenue, then fending off a bunch of young clockers at Hambone's, then heading early to Rudy's, throwing back a few too many, listening to Strike's pernicious rantings, brooding about his day, his life, thinking about that dope dealer across the street, the gun in the gym bag at his feet . . .

There was no reason to doubt that Victor had found the 9 mm and had been walking around with it for weeks, like a stick of dynamite carrying its own detonator. Mazilli had just about had it right: the shooting was just the capper on a bad day.

Finally, after twenty years, a Mission.

Now *there's* an innocent man.

I know guilty and I know innocent.

Strike coughed nervously, nudging Rocco out of his sullen construc-tions. Rocco looked into the kid's anxious face, wondering what he could be thinking, him and his My Man theory, his Buddha Hat nonsense. The kid had been just as blind, both of them deluded by their own jaded innocence.

'It was Victor shot Darryl, right?' Strike said heavily, looking at Rocco open-mouthed, waiting for an explanation.

Rocco was surprised to discover that he couldn't meet the kid's eyes. Gazing off, he heard the mother's words coming back at him: 'If he said he did it, then he did it. Why don't you believe him?' Because, Rocco answered her now, he *needed* the other brother to be the do-er, he needed that fraternal symmetry in order to conjure up the spirit of Mission, in order to anchor himself in his job before he drowned in his own banal terrors. He just didn't *want* Victor to be dirty on this; it screwed up everything.

'Shit.' Strike whispered, shaking his head.

Still thinking of the mother, Rocco recalled her saying something else: 'He told you it was self-defense.' She had insisted on that bald lie; Victor too, coming on to him in the jail with a passionate dishonesty that didn't jibe with anything else in his character. Maybe it was just the two of them putting their heads together and coming up with a compromise between surrender and facing that mandatory thirty in, but . . .

'Woo-woo,' Strike stuttered softly, sounding like a mournful wind. 'Woo-what . . . Can I do something for him?'

Rocco watched the kid palm his gut, then looked him full in the face. It was amazing how much the two brothers resembled each other at certain moments.

'Nothing?' the kid asked dejectedly.

Rocco rose to his feet and extended a hand. 'You want to do something?'

Strike leaned back, looking both alarmed and hopeful.

Rocco escorted him out of the room and down the hall to the Homicide office, steered him to his desk, pulled out his chair and then pressed on Strike's shoulders until he sank into the seat, the kid's disoriented motions diminishing him, making him seem like a child.

Rocco sat on the corner of the desk facing Strike. He reached for the phone and placed it directly in front of the kid. Then he opened a drawer between his legs and took out a beat-up tape recorder and a suction-tipped induction wire, plugging one end into the machine and attaching the other end to the spine of the receiver.

'You want to do something? I want you to call your mother.'

The kid sat up in surprise. 'Whoa. We-We ain't talkin' to each other right now. We're goin' through – '

'I don't give a fuck!' Rocco exploded, startling both Strike and himself. 'What am I, your fucking social worker?' He took a slow breath and came back down. 'I want you to call your mother and I want you to ask her what Victor and her talked about over the phone the night Darryl Adams got shot. Just don't tell her where you're calling from. Can you handle that?'

As Strike dialed, the thin white induction wire dangling down his forearm to the desk, Rocco turned on the tape recorder and punched the loudspeaker button on the telephone. The amplified ringing on the other end sounded cheap and hollow.

Strike held the receiver pressed to his ear, his mouth open in a perfect loop of anxiety.

'Who . . .'

Rocco recognized ShaRon's voice. He took a position a few feet to the side of the desk, wanting to give the kid the illusion of privacy.

'My mother there?' Strike stared at his voice coming back at him from the speaker slats.

'Who . . .'

'This Ronald.'

Rocco didn't hear anyone come on the line, but after a few seconds Strike announced, 'Mommy . . .' His eyes briefly flicked toward Rocco in embarrassment.

'Ronald?'

Cupping the mouthpiece, Strike hunched over, 'Mommy '

'Are you hurt?' she said.

'Unh-uh. Why?' He touched his nose.

'What Andre did . . .'

Strike's face briefly buckled as he rubbed a bony finger along his brow.

'Mommy . . .'

Rocco heard the woman breathing, waiting.

'I ain't clockin' no more.'

The woman still waited.

'I know . . .' Strike sighed, as if not wanting to hear his own declarations, his eyes darting from the desk blotter to Rocco and back. 'I know you don't . . .'

Strike stopped again, and Rocco resisted making a speed-it-up gesture. The kid would have to get there his own way.

'Mommy . . .' A blind pause, and then he said it: 'Victor.'

A choked whooping sound rose up from the speaker, more pain in that one noise than anything Rocco had heard or seen in two interviews.

Strike glared at Rocco and put a splayed palm over the speaker slats as if blocking the lens of a camera.

'Oh Ronald,' she said, her voice cracking.

'I dint tell him to do that. I don't know what happened. Did he tell you I told him to do that?'

'Ronald . . .'

The kid punched his own forehead. 'I dint . . . I'm gonna *help*

him. I'm gonna *help* him.' He wiped a crescent of sweat from under
one eye.

Rocco could hear the voices of small children somewhere in the speaker,
fragmented and far away – voices heard while dozing at a beach.

Strike took a ragged breath. 'Mommy, what did he say to you on the
phone that night?'

'He didn't talk to me.' Her voice was suddenly sober and alert.

Confused, Strike looked to Rocco, who nodded, egging the kid on
to break down her lie.

'He said he called you.'

'He didn't call me.'

'Mommy, what did he say to you?'

More silence. Rocco slipped his hands in his pockets, waiting.

'Mommy, I'm gonna help him,' Strike said, looking to Rocco. Rocco
nodded reassuringly.

'He said . . .' Her voice died.

'What?'

'He called me from some bar, said to me, "I think I'm gonna do
something bad." I said to him, "What do you *mean*, you're gonna do
something bad?" He said, "I don't know, I don't know." I said "Victor,
what happened?" He said, "I'm gonna do something. I *got* to. I can't take
it no more." I said, "Come home," but he just keeps saying, "I can't take
it. I can't take it." I say, "Where *are* you? I'll come get you." He won't
tell me where he is, he just . . .' She took a chattery breath and started
weeping, her voice climbing to a light croon.

Strike's knees were bobbing like jackhammers. Embarrassed, Rocco
turned away.

'I can't take it no more,' she said.

'Mommy . . . I'm gonna *help* him.'

'He . . .' The woman's voice caught, pushed out a breath, then let
loose. 'He comes home like an hour later? He runs in the house, runs
right into the bathroom, gets sick for I don't know *how* long, comes out
and crawls into my bed, just like when you were kids. He got a fever,
I can see it in his face. I say, "What happened, Victor? What did you
do?" He says, "I shot somebody." He's so hot, he's so sick, he says,
"Mommy, I was gonna lose my mind. I couldn't take it no more."
He says, "It was me or him, me or him." "Who'd you shoot? What
he do to you?" He just runs out the room, starts throwing up again,
all night he's throwing up, him with his stomach. I can't even talk to
him, find out what happened. He's just rolling around the bed, running

in and out the bathroom. I don't know if that other boy is hurt, dead, alive, and come the morning he says he can't get out of bed, his legs are cramped, he can't walk. Then he says, "Mommy, it was like a dream. I just squeezed the trigger, he went down so *hard*." He says, "Mommy, tell me what I should do." I say, "Did you kill him?" He says, "I think so. What should I do?" Then he tells me to leave him alone for a while, close the door. I go outside to the living room, then I'm thinking, Wait a minute. I run back into the bedroom, Ronald . . . Your brother's sitting on my bed with a gun to his chest. He asks me again, "What should I do?" And you know what I said? I said, "You gonna be late for work." I didn't know what else to say. Can you imagine that? "You gonna be late for work."'

'I'm gonna *help* him,' Strike said, his eyes wild, his cheeks wet.

'Ronald, your brother was sittin' there with a gun to his chest. If I hadn't walked right back in . . .'

Strike turned to Rocco, jerking with surprise, as if he'd forgotten that Rocco was there. A little growl escaped from his throat, and he began punching at the telephone panel until the speaker shut off.

Rocco turned his back on their conversation, then took a walk around the room. He thought of Victor, saw him standing at the conference table in County, saying to him and Jimmy Newton, 'It was self-defense. I can live with that.' No wonder the mother had stonewalled him about getting the phone call. She had been afraid to say the wrong thing, knowing she might turn the investigation around and get her son truly and legally sunk. Victor had called her less than an hour before the murder, pretty much told her what he was going to do, then gone out and done it. Purposeful Homicide. Thirty in.

Behind him he heard Strike hang up the phone.

I can live with that. The prosecutor had offered Aggravated Manslaughter and was maybe even willing to downgrade it to Reckless. But given what he had just heard, Rocco's guess was that Victor had no interest in either of those deals, that the only thing he would permit himself to call it was self-defense.

I can't take it no more. Me or him. Self-defense meant different things to different people, and on this one, Rocco decided, he would accept the kid's definition. And if Victor wanted to take that to court, that was all right too. Rocco would let him roll the dice with a jury.

He turned back to his desk and saw Strike hunched over, the heels of his palms pressed into his eye sockets. Rocco leaned across him, said 'Excuse me' and popped the tape free of the machine.

Strike came up out of his curl, his eyes sticky-looking, the lashes matted by the pressure of his hands. 'You gonna lock me up?'

Rocco gave the question a moment, but answered before he had fully worked out his justification. 'No.'

Strike nodded into the distance. 'Yeah, OK. So you say you ain't locking me up, buh-but what do I do now?'

'What do you mean?'

'Well, I can't go out there, man.' Strike tilted his head toward the parking lot and Rodney.

'I'll walk you.' Rocco shrugged, still surprised at his decision to let this kid go free.

'What do you mean, you're gonna *walk* me. Where you gonna walk me *to?* Ha-how come you not arresting Rodney?'

'Well, that's gonna take some time,' Rocco said, knowing he would never even try to touch Rodney on this. Not Rodney, not Strike – nobody.

'Andre says he ever sees me again he's gonna shoot me.'

'Oh yeah?' Rocco ditched the cassette in a garbage can; it was illegally secured anyhow. 'Well then, maybe you should leave town.'

Strike looked up at him as if trying to read the setup behind the reprieve, but Rocco ignored him, still working out how he would make sure Victor was never connected to any of this. Rocco would lose some of the players for him – co-conspirators – and discreetly clear the boards as much as he could. If it went to trial, he'd keep his mouth shut, let Jimmy Newton throw up a parade of character witnesses, take whatever beating he had coming to him. It was the least – and the most – he could do.

Rocco walked Strike out of the office toward his car, one hand on the kid's neck, riding the bob and dip of his gimpy walk. Rodney was nowhere in sight.

'Listen, just because – '

'Jesus Christ,' Strike hissed.

Every window of the Accord was smashed, the ground littered with tiny cubes of glass, the crystal-fringed hole of the windshield gaping inward as if it had caught a meteorite.

'Gahd . . .' Strike said, his face twitching.

'Let me ask you.' Rocco massaged Strike's knotted shoulders. 'Do you think Rodney's thinking, "Now we're even"? Or do you think he's thinking, "This is just a taste"?'

Strike scowled at the glass on the ground.

'Where you heading, Ronnie? I'll drive you.'

Strike looked off, scanning all points of the compass. 'New York. No
. . . yeah, New York.'

'Follow me.' Rocco walked toward a sky-blue county-owned Aries,
but Strike, still gazing at his car, didn't move.

'Let's go,' Rocco said.

'I got my medicine in there.' Strike stepped closer to the car, moving
cautiously, as if he expected to find Rodney hiding behind the seat.

'Where's it at? The glove compartment?'

'Yeah.' Strike took a step back, raised a limp finger toward the car.
'The glove compartment.'

Rocco reached in the window and was instantly enveloped in the
hothouse reek of urine coming off the upholstery. 'C'mere, get it
yourself,' he said, wanting the kid to know what kind of animal he'd
be dealing with if he ever decided to come back to town.

Strike disappeared into the car, then quickly backed out, his face
twisted in disgust. A bottle of Mylanta dangled from his fingertips.

'So Strike,' Rocco said, squinting at the skyway, 'where do you want
to live?'

The Homicide's car entered the Holland Tunnel and Strike blinked in the
fluorescent glare. The long interrogation, the shock of his mother's words,
the violence that Rodney had done to his car – all combined in Strike to
make him feel so stunned and passive that he couldn't begin to understand
what had happened to him. He wasn't even sure how he'd ended up sitting
here, why this cop was speeding him away from the projects, away from
home. But he was so used to cops just *doing* things to him that the idea of
challenging this one right now was entirely beyond him. All he could grasp
at the moment was the fact that although he was carrying seven thousand
dollars in his pocket, he was leaving behind fifteen thousand in two safes.

He imagined asking the Homicide to turn around once they got out
on the New York side, to head back to New Jersey so he could scoop
up the rest of his drug earnings. He'd have to sneak back in town on his
own, steal his own money. But Rodney would probably be counting on
him to do something like that. Rodney and that bat . . .

Strike began to play back the phone conversation with his mother and
realized that not once had she accused him of getting Victor into this
mess. Maybe she didn't know about his participation, maybe Victor had
kept him out of it, for his sake and his mother's. His mother hadn't
even been angry on the phone; if anything, she had sounded glad for
the chance to unburden herself at last.

Victor. Strike couldn't shake the image of his brother sitting on their mother's bed, pressing the gun to his chest, asking her what to do. Every time Strike closed his eyes he envisioned the unnatural curl of Victor's wrist as he turned the gun on himself.

Strike remembered feeling stupid after telling the Homicide that My Man story. Well, Buddha Hat or not, on some things he didn't want to be any smarter than he was. Maybe he didn't *want* to know Victor that well, what his brother might be carrying around inside him.

Pressing that muzzle against his own skin, looking up to their mother . . .

Strike involuntarily winced, feeling that he had finally glimpsed a little of his brother's grinding rage and pain. He spoke without thinking: 'You know what he said to me once? Victor? We was in that bar that night? Rudy's? I'm just standing there, ready to leave, he says, "I miss my kids," juh-just like that.' Strike shook his head. 'I just thought, Gah-damn, then go *home*, man. What you doing here for, then? Go home.'

Out of the corner of his eye he saw the cop give him a quick frown, open his mouth as if to respond, then sink back, his focus returning to the driving.

Strike thought again of the fifteen thousand dollars. Maybe he should call his mother, give her the addresses, the combinations, tell her to get Victor a good pay lawyer like Champ or Rodney would have, or at least pay his bail. 'Mommy,' he'd said to her, 'I'm gonna help him.' What else could he do?

Strike imagined calling his mother again, the words he would use, telling her where the money was. But she would probably refuse to go get it because it was dope money, so maybe it would be better to tell Victor's wife. She probably wouldn't care where the money came from, but somehow, telling her about the money wouldn't be the same – there was no real audience for him in that call. Or how about Tyrone? Maybe he should call Tyrone's mother. The boy's face flashed at him, then Erroll Barnes's upturned palm sticking out from under the sheet. With *my* gun . . . But Strike pushed the thought away, focused on calling Tyrone's mother, telling her to get a good lawyer for Tyrone or save the money for his education. But she was like his mother; she probably wouldn't take it either.

Strike thought about how he had always told his mother that he was only in the business until he could get out of it. Well, he was out of it now. But then he started thinking about the future, what to do to get over, and the first thing that came to him was taking that seven thousand dollars in his pocket and buying a package, a quarter ki or something, put his money to work for him. Strike quickly changed tracks, got back to noble notions about making money to cover his obligations – getting Victor sprung, putting Victor's kids through college, Tyrone through college, getting his mother and the rest of them the hell out of Roosevelt and into private housing.

But what was he supposed to do, get a job? Well, why not? It's not against the law. He could do anything. He could work in a store again, maybe *buy* himself a store, a little store like Rodney's. Go down south, live in New York, go out west, anything. Strike started working on himself, trying to feel that the world was in his hands now – as if the urge to hustle, to make it the Rodney way, wasn't lying like a shadow on his mind. And despite all of his terrors about the past, the future, there was also a lightness rising in him, an airy disbelief: he had seven thousand dollars in his pocket and he was cutting out on *all* of it. He was shooting through a tunnel, out into a new life, and he had no idea what he had done to deserve it.

All he knew for sure was that someone – Victor, Tyrone, this cop, his mother, maybe God – someone was giving him a second chance, right now.

Strike had never really liked music. He had never cared about sports, even girls that much if he thought about it. But now he reached forward without thinking, reached for the car radio under the police receiver and turned it on, spun the dial until he found some music. The tunnel broke most of the tune into choppy static, but enough of the beat came through to make Strike bounce a little in his seat, make him think about all that music out there. All that *life*.

I miss my kids.

Rocco was still mulling over Strike's story about Victor's announcement in the bar that night. Rocco thought he knew that feeling, that anguished yet voluntary exile from your own child. Driving under the river, he thought about Erin, how just this morning he had thought she was gone forever; he thought about retirement, about everything and anything other than the fact that he was in the process of helping this kid to escape.

And then Strike had the balls to reach over and turn on the radio. Rocco was stunned by the self-centeredness, the arrogance of the move, and now the kid was sitting there bobbing to the beat, getting light in the face, shuckin' and jivin', just taking a ride . . .

Rocco stared at Strike in disbelief. Here he was, setting himself up, risking his career to give Strike the break of his life, and then the fucking kid reaches for the dial in a county car, plays music in *my* house . . . Rocco was too astonished to do anything but glare at him. He saw the bliss in Strike's eye as he tried to sing along with the tune without really knowing the words. The kid had an atrocious singing voice, but that didn't make it any less of an outrage. On the other hand, Rocco thought, he'd probably be singing along too if he was dancing out of some serious jail time.

Rocco's beeper went off and the office number came up on his hip. He hoped it was bullshit, but his instinct told him it was another job. It had been a while, after all. With the tunnel-dampened music crackling through the car, Rocco debated whether to return to Dempsy tonight. The hell with it; Mazilli could cover. Rather than hit the tunnel two more times in the next four hours, he would just go home and be with his family. Rocco thought of Erin again, savoring the terror he had felt this morning, the preciousness too.

But Erin wasn't eating at him right now. He was more concerned about the long-term fallout from the Darryl Adams murder. Maybe it would never go to trial. Maybe Victor would make his bail, get another taste of freedom, get to walk his kids through Liberty State Park again and wind up rethinking his self-defense. The kid should find some way to live with Reckless Manslaughter and take a deal – he'd be crazy if he didn't. Rocco drove almost blindly now, thinking, This *can't* go to trial; thinking, What about me?

He had always assumed that he would soon take his twenty, but what if he didn't *want* to retire? He was only forty-three. And the Victor Dunham job had recharged his life, had set that wheel of gifts in motion. Rocco began sweating it. Even as he realized how much he wanted to hang on to his job, he understood that he was at the mercy of whatever calibration set the final balance of pain in Victor's heart. Victor could plea out for minimal jail time or he could insist on calling it self-defense, and his decision between the two could come anytime from his first few days on the street to a year from now, when his trial would probably begin. Rocco imagined the kid waiting to plea out until a week, a day, an hour before his first appearance in court. A fucking year . . .

As the car shot up from under the Hudson River and broke into twilit Manhattan, the radio suddenly drew clarity and volume, making both of them jump. Rocco reached over and shut off the music.

'I ever see you in town, I ever even *hear* about you coming back to town or even crossing the river into New Jersey? I'll book you for criminal solicitation and conspiracy to commit murder. I'll pick up Rodney on the same charges, and I'll make sure you two go in together, draw the same tier, the same fucking *bed*, you understand me?'

Strike nodded mutely, and Rocco drove up the West Side until they reached the Port Authority Bus Terminal. He crashed a line of taxis at the main entrance, ignoring the pissed-off gestures of the dispatcher.

'You got enough on you for a bus somewheres?' Rocco asked, although up to this point nobody had said anything about further travel. He just wanted this kid gone as far as he could go right now.

Strike nodded noncommittally and cleared his throat. 'Can I ask you a question? One time I saw you with this other cop, he was like buh-*blond*, really handsome like a television announcer or something. You know who I'm talking about?'

Rocco said nothing.

'That cop, was he like a special cop? Like a expert or, you know a, a high-*up* cop?'

Rocco sat stone-faced.

'You know, like it's nuh-none of my business. I'm just curious.'

Rocco stared at the kid, thinking, It isn't too late to take him back; then thinking, Yes it is. Each step, each mile since walking out of the prosecutor's office, was impossible to explain in any salvageable way. And that tape was inadmissible, illegal – an embarrassment.

The beeper went off again. As if fearing that the number coming up would somehow put all his good luck in jeopardy, the kid quickly and wordlessly left the car.

Rocco watched Strike limp into the human slipstream of Eighth Avenue, watched him negotiate his way through lowlifes and taxpayers until he disappeared inside the terminal doors without a backward glance.

The kid didn't even say thank you. Typical, thought Rocco. So fucking typical.

Rocco sat in the idling car, still debating whether to go home early or call in and find out where the scene was. He drove over to Seventh Avenue and then headed south. But once downtown, instead of turning east for the loft, he kept going until the traffic slowed as it bottlenecked at the entrance to the Holland Tunnel. He'd be home soon enough.

Strike wandered the littered and seedy vastness of the terminal, the place so big that it seemed empty despite hundreds of people who were either race-walking or staggering everywhere he looked.

He wandered over to a pay phone, lifted the receiver and dialed his mother's number, his stomach gently palpitating as he listened to the hollow ringing.

One of Victor's kids picked up, filling Strike's ear with short, heavy breaths.

'My mother there?'

The kid kept breathing at him, sounding as if his nose was stuffed.

'Get my mother.'

More breathing.

'Get your grandma.'

'Daddy,' the kid said, 'Ivan fell down in the *bench*.'

Strike hung up, his stomach pounding him now. Daddy.

'Yo, yo.'

Strike turned to face a nervous-looking teenager talking to him out of the side of his mouth. The guy carried a small knapsack over his shoulder and some bills in his hand.

'Yo, buy me a ticket, man. *Charles*ton, one way.' His eyes averted, his head jerking like a bird, the guy shoved the money at Strike.

Strike read his play immediately. The kid was muling dope down south and was afraid to buy his own ticket, as if that was the only thing that would give him away. The idiot didn't even have enough sense to take some decoy luggage, look like everybody else traveling long distance. And with that stupid knapsack and those bug eyes, he might as well be wearing a sign.

Strike saw three white Port Authority knockos standing forty feet away by a newsstand. All three were dressed in dungarees and T-shirts, their heads buried in magazines.

'C'mon man, my boy dint show. Just buy me a ticket. I'll wait for you right here.' The kid finally made eye contact and did a double take upon seeing Strike's broken nose.

'Buy you *own* damn ticket,' Strike said, walking off to another bank of pay phones. Behind him, he heard the kid say only, '*Shoo.*'

Strike picked up a phone and watched the kid get on the ticket line himself. The cops still had their heads down in their *Times* and *Newsweek*s.

As Strike fished through his pockets for the change to call home again, his eyes wandered to the departure board above the Greyhound counter. Forgetting his coins for a moment, he whispered the name of every city up there, getting sucked into the list, the variety of places somebody could go, getting that greedy covetous feeling that sometimes came on him around things for sale. All those cities: Strike felt woozy with options, enraptured, and he stood there squinting up, moving his lips . . . Strike looked down from the board and saw that the dope mule had his ticket now. As the kid moved toward the escalators and the lower-level bus bays, one of the cops dropped his magazine and yawned, going up on tiptoes and running a hand over his bald head. A moment later, all three knockos ambled over to the escalators and glided silently down, out of sight.

Strike shook his head: Out of it for good, I swear to God.

He picked up the phone again, but instead of calling home he dialed Dempsy information and got the number for Tyrone's mother's house. He started to dial, hesitated, then hung up when he forgot the rest of the number. He wanted to help Tyrone out, but he was too scared of the mother's grief and anger. Maybe he could give his own mother the combination to one safe and mail Tyrone's mother the combination to the other . . . Strike tried to convince himself that in the long run this whole thing would turn out fine for Tyrone. He'd be scared straight by his time in the Youth House; then, with Strike's money, he could go to a good school when he got out. And the Youth House probably wouldn't even be that bad, since nobody would mess with him, Tyrone being a killer and all . . .

Strike's guts were rippling now, making him go for his medicine and take a long pull. He'd write Tyrone too, Strike thought, wiping his lips with the back of his hand. Tell him, *explain* to him . . . He couldn't feel the medicine coating the pain, so he drained the bottle. He burped wetly and then grabbed the phone again, pumping in silver.

'Hello?'

Strike was speechless – not scared, just unsure of what to say.

'Who's this, hello?'

'Mommy.' Strike blew air to slow down his heart.

'Ronald. Where are you?'

'Mommy, I'm in New *York*.'

A large hand snatched away the receiver and hung it up for him. Strike turned to face the three cops and the dope mule, the bald cop taking him by the wrist in a loose grip, carrying the mule's knapsack in his other hand.

'Take us a walk, Yo.'

Strike stood his ground. They'd have to kill him. 'I dint *do* nothin'.'

'What?' The bald cop handed off the knapsack and braced himself, rocking slightly from side to side.

The dope mule was in cuffs now, his head hanging, eyes still averted.

'Luh-look.' Strike blinked rapidly and palmed his own chest. 'I never seen this guy. He come up in my face, say, "Buy me a ticket to Char-Charleston." I don't even know what he's *talkin'* about, I swear. Ask him, man, ask *him*.'

Strike was addressing the cop but trying to meet the dope mule's downcast eyes.

'Ask him,' Strike said again, feeling a trembling in his jaw, a shimmery film building in his eyes, thinking about these cops finding his seven thousand dollars; thinking how, one way or the other, nobody ever really got away with anything in this world.

The cop took his arm. 'Come on.'

Strike felt his resistance drain, but then the kid spoke quietly to his shoes. 'I don't know this guy.'

Strike looked away, afraid to meet the kid's eyes now, afraid that the knockos would misinterpret the flush of gratitude in his face.

The cops went into a silent conference that culminated in a ring of shrugs; they had their grab for the night.

'Well, what are *you* doing here, then?' the bald cop said.

'I was just leavin' town.' Strike nodded fervently, figuring cops always liked that answer. 'On my way out.'

Backpedaling, watching the cops watch him, Strike moved toward the ticket counter. Once in line, he eyed the departure board directly overhead, reading the cities again.

'Washington, D.C.,' Strike announced, dropping a pinch of tens and twenties in front of a barred window.

'Washington, D.C.,' the clerk repeated, taking Strike's cash and moving to the keyboard of his computer.

'No, wait.' Still gaping up at the roll call of cities, Strike thrust a staying hand across the counter. 'Philadelphia . . . Yeah, Philadelphia.'

The clerk gave him a quick dry look and started to recount the money.

'Wait a minute, wait.' Strike waggled his hand, licked his lips, squinted upward again. 'Give me a second here. Just like one muh-more second . . .'

Thirty minutes later, Strike sat by the smoke-tinted window in the trembling bus, looking down at a scrawny line of passengers still toddling forward in the drafty bus bay. He held a dozen cities in his fist, the individual tickets in his See America booklet spread out in his grip like a fan. Strike gave himself a little breeze and thought about where to get off. Newark was coming up in about half an hour, but no *way* he'd be getting off there. The bus was scheduled to make stops in Philadelphia, Washington, Raleigh and Atlanta, but with the hand he was holding, he could get off just about anywhere and transfer to just about any other bus going somewhere else.

Strike thought of the hard-luck dope mule who had given him his reprieve from the Port Authority knockos. The kid didn't have to do that; earlier he had asked Strike for help and Strike had turned his back. Strike couldn't figure it. People were dropping out of the sky to cut him slack today, as if sending him a message, a blessing, a warning.

He thought of Victor's son calling him Daddy on the phone. For a moment he was pulled into Victor's world, Victor's loss, and the echo of that boy had Strike writhing in his seat, desperate for this bus to back out and roll.

Strike pondered Philadelphia coming up in about ninety minutes, wondering whether he should get off there, cash in all these tickets. Then he decided that he would probably stay on the bus, ride on to Washington, maybe even Atlanta. Maybe he'd try the South for a while, or maybe he'd use another ticket, go out west. He'd see when he got there. He'd just have to see how he felt, think about what he'd be thinking about when he got there.

Besides, there was hardly a place in America where you couldn't find a pay phone. Just walk right up to it, call anybody you damn want to.

Unannounced and unnoticed, Rocco took up his customary starting position at the back of the crowd. He watched Mazilli and Rockets work the body, Rockets slowly circling with the Nikon, ringing the corpse in a series of flashes while Mazilli logged the shots on a clipboard.

The victim looked to be about eighteen or nineteen. Tall and emaciated, he lay on his back in a puddle, his arms crooked like a cactus, his eyes staring up at the shattered marquee of a long-gone movie theater. Even from thirty feet away, craning past the heads of the onlookers, Rocco counted at least a dozen entry wounds from groin to collarbone. A scatter of ejected shells lay about two feet from the left arm, another grouping a yard south of the right foot. The victim had obviously been killed in a crossfire, and Rocco wondered what the kid might have done to provoke this kind of end for himself.

Rocco watched as Mazilli began to undress the body, initiate the official probe and tally of wounds. The kid wore two pairs of filthy sweatpants, a ripped orange Seton Hall T-shirt, no underwear, no socks, and there were holes on the bottom of his laceless shoes – a basehead chopped down in mid-mission, by the look of him. The mystery began growing in Rocco, taking up house: Who the hell would have bothered to set up an automatic weapons massacre just to take out this stinky and pathetic bag of bones?

Rocco winced as Rockets accidentally backed into his forensic case, knocking his camera to the ground, the flash going off on impact. A ripple of derisive laughter rose from the crowd.

Enough.

Rocco took a deep breath, held it, then let it out nice and slow. He began easing his way up to the yellow tape.

'He was a nice guy, right?' Rocco declared in a conversational tone, his eyes casually scanning the crowd. 'Who the hell would want to shoot him?'